ADVENTURES OF HUCKLEBERRY FINN

AN AUTHORITATIVE TEXT
BACKGROUNDS AND SOURCES
CRITICISM

SECOND EDITION

➤➤➤ A NORTON CRITICAL EDITION ⫷⫷

SAMUEL LANGHORNE CLEMENS

ADVENTURES OF HUCKLEBERRY FINN

AN AUTHORITATIVE TEXT
BACKGROUNDS AND SOURCES
CRITICISM

➤➤➤ ⫷⫷

SECOND EDITION

➤➤➤ ⫷⫷

Edited by

SCULLEY BRADLEY

PROFESSOR EMERITUS,
UNIVERSITY OF PENNSYLVANIA

RICHMOND CROOM BEATTY

LATE OF VANDERBILT UNIVERSITY

E. HUDSON LONG

PROFESSOR EMERITUS,
BAYLOR UNIVERSITY

THOMAS COOLEY

THE OHIO STATE UNIVERSITY

W · W · NORTON & COMPANY

New York · London

W. W. Norton & Company, Inc., 500 Fifth Avenue, New York, N.Y. 10110

Second Edition

Library of Congress Cataloging in Publication Data
Clemens, Samuel Langhorne, 1835–1910.
    Adventures of Huckleberry Finn.
    (A Norton critical edition)
    Bibliography: p.
    I. Bradley, Edward Sculley, 1897–   II. Beatty,
Richmond Croom, 1905–1961. III. Long, Eugene
Hudson, 1908–   IV. Cooley, Thomas, 1942–
V. Title.
PZ3.C59A86 [PS1305]   813'.4   76-30648

8 9 0

ISBN 0-393-04454-8 CL
ISBN 0-393-09146-5 PBK

Contents

79054

Criticism

EARLY VIEWS

FORM AND SYMBOL: THE RIVER AND THE SHORE

THE PROBLEM OF THE ENDING

HUCK, JIM, AND TOM

Contents · *vii*

Preface to the Second Edition

Mark Twain was a great writer who never wrote a great book. *Adventures of Huckleberry Finn*, so this argument runs, is Mark Twain's masterpiece; yet it is seriously flawed by a weak ending— the last ten or a dozen chapters, in which the author fails to sustain the tone and vitality of the long central section. If "great" is defined as "technically perfect," this argument is probably correct. Yet it is equally true, as Ernest Hemingway once said of the novel, that "all modern American literature comes from one book by Mark Twain called *Huckleberry Finn* . . . it's the best book we've had. All American writing comes from that."

Mark Twain began *Huckleberry Finn* as a sequel to *Tom Sawyer*, intending "to take a boy of twelve and run him on through life"; Huck's "autobiography" was to be a story of growing up. In the book Mark Twain actually wrote, however, Huck never reaches manhood. Though his age seems to waver between twelve (or ten or eight) and fourteen (or sixteen or thirty), it is not easy to say whether his knowledge of the world grows in any consistent way. Huck's narrative might properly be viewed as a sequence of assaults upon his innocence rather than a sure progress toward a healthy maturity. By brilliantly portraying the hazards of a journey that constantly forces Huck to alter his parentage, name and, therefore, his identity, Mark Twain helped guide American fiction toward its characteristic search for self. "Would you say that the search for identity is primarily an American theme?" novelist Ralph Ellison was once asked by an interviewer. "It is *the* American theme," he replied.

The geography of *Huckleberry Finn*, dominated by the great river, is another of the triumphs of the book, and it conveys a tension between the individual and society that has also been called typically American. In the nineteenth century, some British readers charged that American literature was basically antisocial. Its heroes lived only in remote regions— the dark forest, a whaling ship at sea, the distant Walden Pond of Henry David Thoreau's imagination; seldom did they thrive within the ordered society of town, city, or court. When the raft serves Huck as a free and easy refuge from the cruelty of the shore, it provides the solitude American literature has been said to require for the fullest expression of the self. When, however, the river delivers Huck upon its banks or makes him collide with such agents of "civilization" as the duke and the king or the steamboat in Chapter XVI, we should recall that the typical "hero" of American fiction makes his "separate peace" (the phrase is Hemingway's) in order to return whole to the challenge of living in groups. Mark Twain's satire of shore life, like all good satire, exposes to correct. Moreover, by using as the principal vehicle of his satire the mighty river (always eating away at the puny foundations of the St. Petersburgs and Bricksvilles lining its shore), Mark Twain paid homage to those unruly forces of nature which can overwhelm both self and society at almost any time in American literature.

It was largely because of Huck's colloquial language, most critics agree, however, that Hemingway credited Mark Twain with giving that literature a distinctive modern turn. Here, for example, is a passage describing Huck's separation from Jim in a dense fog:

> I throwed the paddle down. I heard the whoop again; it was behind me yet, but in a different place; it kept coming, and kept changing its place, and I kept answering, till by-and-by it was in front of me again and I knowed the current had swung the canoe's head down stream and I was all right, if that was Jim and not some other raftsman hollering. I couldn't tell nothing about voices in a fog, for nothing don't look natural nor sound natural in a fog.

This is the language of speech, and it is very different from the language in which most American literature was written before 1885. The language of Irving, Emerson, Thoreau, Hawthorne, and even Melville was a formal, "literary" language; at its worst, it was sometimes inflated into what Mark Twain called "the showiest kind of book-talk." Mark Twain's greatest achievement, perhaps, was to make a spoken language do everything a literary language alone could do before him. Nothing is lost when Huck describes his panic in the fog, or the coming of a storm, or Pap's malice, or Jim's kindness—all in the vocabulary and syntax of the uneducated son of the town drunk, whose special way of seeing beyond conventional prejudices required an unconventional way of speaking. Nothing was lost, and a great deal was gained for a literature which is so often *told* in the first person by narrators whose innocence is the highest knowledge.

This second Norton Critical Edition of *Huckleberry Finn* reflects the wealth of Mark Twain scholarship during the fifteen years since the publication of the first edition. Perhaps as many as 200 essays appeared in these years focusing upon *Huckleberry Finn* alone, not to mention chapters devoted to the novel in many books on Mark Twain and on American literature, plus new editions of Mark Twain's own writings. New selections in the Backgrounds and Sources section include five additional letters about the composition and publication of the novel, excerpts from the uproar in the press when the Concord Public library banned *Huckleberry Finn* from its

shelves, and Mark Twain's account of the Darnell-Watson feud in
Life on the Mississippi.

In the essays in criticism, Thomas Sergeant Perry's first American
review joins Brander Matthews's early review to give a fuller sense
of readers' response in 1885. The provocative essays by Trilling
and Eliot, along with Leo Marx's "answer," have been kept; but
new essays by James M. Cox and Roy Harvey Pearce on the ending
have been added. The Raftsmen's Passage is here given a separate
section, incorporating Peter G. Beidler's version of the argument
that the passage should be restored to the text. Other additions
include essays by Ralph Ellison, Edwin H. Cady, Judith Fetterley,
and Henry Nash Smith, whose important chapter on *Huckleberry
Finn* in *Mark Twain: The Development of a Writer* (Harvard,
1962) is reprinted in full. For the second edition, the text has been
newly collated with the American first edition, and the annotations
have been extensively reworked.

For their generous help and advice in preparing the manuscript, I
wish to thank Kenneth C. Burrows, Sheila P. Cooley, and Peter W.
Phelps. A special word of gratitude is due my colleague, Richard D.
Altick.

THOMAS COOLEY

The Text of

Adventures of
Huckleberry Finn

Adventures of Huckleberry Finn

(TOM SAWYER'S COMRADE)
SCENE: THE MISSISSIPPI
TIME: FORTY TO FIFTY YEARS AGO

NOTICE

Persons attempting to find a motive in this narrative will be prosecuted; persons attempting to find a moral in it will be banished; persons attempting to find a plot in it will be shot.

BY ORDER OF THE AUTHOR
PER G. G., CHIEF OF ORDNANCE.

EXPLANATORY

In this book a number of dialects are used, to wit: the Missouri negro dialect; the extremest form of the backwoods South-Western dialect; the ordinary "Pike-County" dialect; and four modified varieties of this last. The shadings have not been done in a hap-hazard fashion, or by guess-work; but pains-takingly, and with the trustworthy guidance and support of personal familiarity with these several forms of speech.

I make this explanation for the reason that without it many readers would suppose that all these characters were trying to talk alike and not succeeding.

THE AUTHOR

Contents of *Adventures of Huckleberry Finn* †

† The "contents" headings of the first edition were supplied by Charles L. Webster,
Mark Twain's publisher.

Chapter I

You don't know about me, without you have read a book by the name of "The Adventures of Tom Sawyer,"[1] but that ain't no matter. That book was made by Mr. Mark Twain, and he told the truth, mainly. There was things which he stretched, but mainly he told the truth. That is nothing. I never seen anybody but lied, one time or another, without it was Aunt Polly, or the widow, or maybe Mary. Aunt Polly—Tom's Aunt Polly, she is—and Mary, and the Widow Douglas, is all told about in that book—which is mostly a true book; with some stretchers, as I said before.

Now the way that the book winds up, is this: Tom and me found the money that the robbers hid in the cave, and it made us rich. We got six thousand dollars apiece—all gold. It was an awful sight of money when it was piled up. Well, Judge Thatcher, he took it and put it out at interest, and it fetched us a dollar a day apiece, all the year round—more than a body could tell what to do with. The Widow Douglas, she took me for her son, and allowed she would sivilize me; but it was rough living in the house all the time, considering how dismal regular and decent the widow was in all her ways; and so when I couldn't stand it no longer, I lit out. I got into my old rags, and my sugar-hogshead[2] again, and was free and satisfied. But Tom Sawyer, he hunted me up and said he was going to start a band of robbers, and I might join if I would go back to the widow and be respectable. So I went back.

The widow she cried over me, and called me a poor lost lamb, and she called me a lot of other names, too, but she never meant no harm by it. She put me in them new clothes again, and I couldn't do nothing but sweat and sweat, and feel all cramped up. Well, then, the old thing commenced again. The widow rung a bell for supper, and you had to come to time. When you got to the table you couldn't go right to eating, but you had to wait for the widow to tuck down her head and grumble a little over the victuals, though there warn't really anything the matter with them. That is, nothing only everything was cooked by itself. In a barrel of odds and ends it is different; things get mixed up, and the juice kind of swaps around, and the things go better.

After supper she got out her book and learned me about Moses

---

1. Published in 1876. When Clemens wrote the opening chapters of *Huckleberry Finn*, the stories of Tom and Huck were still closely linked in his mind. In 1876 Clemens thought he was halfway through "another boy's book," but it was to take eight more years of labor, by fits and starts, before Clemens finished "Huck Finn's Autobiography." Except, perhaps, for the controversial ending, the new book carried its hero and the American novel far beyond *Tom Sawyer* and the boy-book tradition.
2. A large barrel.

and the Bulrushers;[3] and I was in a sweat to find out all about him;
but by-and-by she let it out that Moses had been dead a considerable long time; so then I didn't care no more about him; because
I don't take no stock in dead people.

Pretty soon I wanted to smoke, and asked the widow to let me.
But she wouldn't. She said it was a mean practice and wasn't clean,
and I must try to not do it any more. That is just the way with
some people. They get down on a thing when they don't know
nothing about it. Here she was a bothering about Moses, which
was no kin to her, and no use to anybody, being gone, you see, yet
finding a power of fault with me for doing a thing that had some
good in it. And she took snuff too; of course that was all right, because she done it herself.

Her sister, Miss Watson, a tolerable slim old maid, with goggles
on, had just come to live with her, and took a set at me now, with
a spelling-book. She worked me middling hard for about an hour,
and then the widow made her ease up. I couldn't stood it much
longer. Then for an hour it was deadly dull, and I was fidgety. Miss
Watson would say, "Dont put your feet up there, Huckleberry;"
and "dont scrunch up like that, Huckleberry—set up straight;"
and pretty soon she would say, "Don't gap and stretch like that,
Huckleberry—why don't you try to behave?" Then she told me all
about the bad place, and I said I wished I was there. She got mad,
then, but I didn't mean no harm. All I wanted was to go somewheres; all I wanted was a change, I warn't particular. She said it
was wicked to say what I said; said she wouldn't say it for the whole
world; *she* was going to live so as to go to the good place. Well, I
couldn't see no advantage in going where she was going, so I made
up my mind I wouldn't try for it. But I never said so, because it
would only make trouble, and wouldn't do no good.

Now she had got a start, and she went on and told me all about
the good place. She said all a body would have to do there was
to go around all day long with a harp and sing, forever and ever.
So I didn't think much of it. But I never said so. I asked her if
she reckoned Tom Sawyer would go there, and, she said, not by a
considerable sight. I was glad about that, because I wanted him
and me to be together.

Miss Watson she kept pecking at me, and it got tiresome and
lonesome. By-and-by they fetched the niggers in and had prayers,
and then everybody was off to bed. I went up to my room with a

---

3. The widow wants to be compared
with Pharaoh's daughter, who discovered
the baby Moses floating on the Nile in a
basket made of bulrushes and adopted
him as the widow has adopted Huck
(Exodus 2:1–10). Having no piety to be
proud of, Huck claims no kinship with
the deliverer of the Hebrews and the
archetypal deliverer of Negro folklore; but
he soon leads a slave from bondage, escaping over water past a point of no return named Cairo and missing the promised land at journey's end.

piece of candle and put it on the table. Then I set down in a chair by the window and tried to think of something cheerful, but it warn't no use. I felt so lonesome I most wished I was dead.[4] The stars was shining, and the leaves rustled in the woods ever so mournful; and I heard an owl, away off, who-whooing about somebody that was dead, and a whippowill and a dog crying about somebody that was going to die; and the wind was trying to whisper something to me and I couldn't make out what it was, and so it made the cold shivers run over me. Then away out in the woods I heard that kind of a sound that a ghost makes when it wants to tell about something that's on its mind and can't make itself understood, and so can't rest easy in its grave and has to go about that way every night grieving. I got so down-hearted and scared, I did wish I had some company. Pretty soon a spider went crawling up my shoulder, and I flipped it off and it lit in the candle; and before I could budge it was all shriveled up. I didn't need anybody to tell me that that was an awful bad sign and would fetch me some bad luck, so I was scared and most shook the clothes off of me. I got up and turned around in my tracks three times and crossed my breast every time; and then I tied up a little lock of my hair with a thread to keep witches away. But I hadn't no confidence. You do that when you've lost a horse-shoe that you've found, instead of nailing it up over the door, but I hadn't ever heard anybody say it was any way to keep off bad luck when you'd killed a spider.

I set down again, a shaking all over, and got out my pipe for a smoke; for the house was all as still as death, now, and so the widow wouldn't know. Well, after a long time I heard the clock away off in the town go boom—boom—boom—twelve licks—and all still again—stiller than ever. Pretty soon I heard a twig snap, down in the dark amongst the trees—something was a stirring. I set still and listened. Directly I could just barely hear a *"me-yow! me-yow!"* down there. That was good! Says I, *"me-yow! me-yow!"* as soft as I could, and then I put out the light and scrambled out of the window onto the shed. Then I slipped down to the ground and crawled in amongst the trees, and sure enough there was Tom Sawyer waiting for me.

Chapter II

We went tip-toeing along a path amongst the trees back towards the end of the widow's garden, stooping down so as the branches wouldn't scrape our heads. When we was passing by the kitchen

---

4. Clemens's boyhood in Hannibal, Missouri, was almost as violent as Huck's, and his fiction depicts the world of boyhood as both idyll and a nightmare. This is the first hint of Huck's preoccupation with death throughout the novel.

I fell over a root and made a noise. We scrouched down and laid still. Miss Watson's big nigger, named Jim, was setting in the kitchen door; we could see him pretty clear, because there was a light behind him. He got up and stretched his neck out about a minute, listening. Then he says,

"Who dah?"

He listened some more; then he come tip-toeing down and stood right between us; we could a touched him, nearly. Well, likely it was minutes and minutes that there warn't a sound, and we all there so close together. There was a place on my ankle that got to itching; but I dasn't scratch it; and then my ear begun to itch; and next my back, right between my shoulders. Seemed like I'd die if I couldn't scratch. Well, I've noticed that thing plenty of times since. If you are with the quality, or at a funeral, or trying to go to sleep when you ain't sleepy—if you are anywheres where it won't do for you to scratch, why you will itch all over in upwards of a thousand places. Pretty soon Jim says:

"Say—who is you? Whar is you? Dog my cats ef I didn' hear sumf'n. Well, I knows what I's gwyne to do. I's gwyne to set down here and listen tell I hears it agin."

So he set down on the ground betwixt me and Tom. He leaned his back up against a tree, and stretched his legs out till one of them most touched one of mine. My nose begun to itch. It itched till the tears come into my eyes. But I dasn't scratch. Then it begun to itch on the inside. Next I got to itching underneath. I didn't know how I was going to set still. This miserableness went on as much as six or seven minutes; but it seemed a sight longer than that. I was itching in eleven different places now. I reckoned I couldn't stand it more'n a minute longer, but I set my teeth hard and got ready to try. Just then Jim begun to breathe heavy; next he begun to snore—and then I was pretty soon comfortable again.

Tom he made a sign to me—kind of a little noise with his mouth—and we went creeping away on our hands and knees. When we was ten foot off, Tom whispered to me and wanted to tie Jim to the tree for fun; but I said no; he might wake and make a disturbance, and then they'd find out I warn't in. Then Tom said he hadn't got candles enough, and he would slip in the kitchen and get some more. I didn't want him to try. I said Jim might wake up and come. But Tom wanted to resk it; so we slid in there and got three candles, and Tom laid five cents on the table for pay. Then we got out, and I was in a sweat to get away; but nothing would do Tom but he must crawl to where Jim was, on his hands and knees, and play something on him. I waited, and it seemed a good while, everything was so still and lonesome.

As soon as Tom was back, we cut along the path, around the

garden fence, and by-and-by fetched up on the steep top of the hill
the other side of the house. Tom said he slipped Jim's hat off of his
head and hung it on a limb right over him, and Jim stirred a little,
but he didn't wake. Afterwards Jim said the witches bewitched him
and put him in a trance, and rode him all over the State, and then
set him under the trees again and hung his hat on a limb to show
who done it. And next time Jim told it he said they rode him down
to New Orleans; and after that, every time he told it he spread it
more and more, till by-and-by he said they rode him all over the
world, and tired him most to death, and his back was all over
saddle-boils. Jim was monstrous proud about it, and he got so he
wouldn't hardly notice the other niggers. Niggers would come miles
to hear Jim tell about it, and he was more looked up to than any
nigger in that country. Strange niggers would stand with their
mouths open and look him all over, same as if he was a wonder.
Niggers is always talking about witches in the dark by the kitchen
fire; but whenever one was talking and letting on to know all about
such things, Jim would happen in and say, "Hm! What you know
'bout witches?" and that nigger was corked up and had to take a
back seat. Jim always kept that five-center piece around his neck
with a string and said it was a charm the devil give to him with his
own hands and told him he could cure anybody with it and fetch
witches whenever he wanted to, just by saying something to it; but
he never told what it was he said to it. Niggers would come from
all around there and give Jim anything they had, just for a sight of
that five-center piece; but they wouldn't touch it, because the
devil had had his hands on it. Jim was most ruined, for a servant,
because he got so stuck up on account of having seen the devil and
been rode by witches.

Well, when Tom and me got to the edge of the hill-top, we
looked away down into the village[5] and could see three or four
lights twinkling, where there was sick folks, may be; and the stars
over us was sparkling ever so fine; and down by the village was
the river, a whole mile broad, and awful still and grand. We went
down the hill and found Jo Harper, and Ben Rogers, and two or
three more of the boys, hid in the old tanyard. So we unhitched a
skiff[6] and pulled down the river two mile and a half, to the big scar
on the hillside, and went ashore.

We went to a clump of bushes, and Tom made everybody swear
to keep the secret, and then showed them a hole in the hill, right
in the thickest part of the bushes. Then we lit the candles and
crawled in on our hands and knees. We went about two hundred
yards, and then the cave opened up. Tom poked about amongst

5. St. Petersburg, a fictionalized version   6. A flat-bottomed open boat.
of Hannibal, Missouri.

the passages and pretty soon ducked under a wall where you wouldn't a noticed that there was a hole. We went along a narrow place and got into a kind of room, all damp and sweaty and cold, and there we stopped. Tom says:

"Now we'll start this band of robbers and call it Tom Sawyer's Gang. Everybody that wants to join has got to take an oath, and write his name in blood."

Everybody was willing. So Tom got out a sheet of paper that he had wrote the oath on, and read it. It swore every boy to stick to the band, and never tell any of the secrets; and if anybody done anything to any boy in the band, whichever boy was ordered to kill that person and his family must do it, and he mustn't eat and he mustn't sleep till he had killed them and hacked a cross in their breasts, which was the sign of the band. And nobody that didn't belong to the band could use that mark, and if he did he must be sued; and if he done it again he must be killed. And if anybody that belonged to the band told the secrets, he must have his throat cut, and then have his carcass burnt up and the ashes scattered all around, and his name blotted off of the list with blood and never mentioned again by the gang, but have a curse put on it and be forgot, forever.

Everybody said it was a real beautiful oath, and asked Tom if he got it out of his own head. He said, some of it, but the rest was out of pirate books, and robber books, and every gang that was high-toned had it.

Some thought it would be good to kill the *families* of boys that told the secrets. Tom said it was a good idea, so he took a pencil and wrote it in. Then Ben Rogers says:

"Here's Huck Finn, he hain't got no family—what you going to do 'bout him?"

"Well, hain't he got a father?" says Tom Sawyer.

"Yes, he's got a father, but you can't never find him, these days. He used to lay drunk with the hogs in the tanyard, but he hain't been seen in these parts for a year or more."

They talked it over, and they was going to rule me out, because they said every boy must have a family or somebody to kill, or else it wouldn't be fair and square for the others. Well, nobody could think of anything to do—everybody was stumped, and set still. I was most ready to cry; but all at once I thought of a way, and so I offered them Miss Watson—they could kill her. Everybody said:

"Oh, she'll do, she'll do. That's all right. Huck can come in."

Then they all stuck a pin in their fingers to get blood to sign with, and I made my mark on the paper.

"Now," says Ben Rogers, "what's the line of business of this Gang?"

"Nothing only robbery and murder," Tom said.

"But who are we going to rob? houses—or cattle—or—"

"Stuff! stealing cattle and such things ain't robbery, it's burglary," says Tom Sawyer. "We ain't burglars. That ain't no sort of style. We are highwaymen. We stop stages and carriages on the road, with masks on, and kill the people and take their watches and money."

"Must we always kill the people?"

"Oh, certainly. It's best. Some authorities think different, but mostly it's considered best to kill them. Except some that you bring to the cave here and keep them till they're ransomed."

"Ransomed? What's that?"

"I don't know. But that's what they do. I've seen it in books; and so of course that's what we've got to do."

"But how can we do it if we don't know what it is?"

"Why blame it all, we've *got* to do it. Don't I tell you it's in the books? Do you want to go to doing different from what's in the books, and get things all muddled up?"

"Oh, that's all very fine to *say*, Tom Sawyer, but how in the nation[7] are these fellows going to be ransomed if we don't know how to do it to them? that's the thing *I* want to get at. Now what do you *reckon* it is?"

"Well I don't know. But per'aps if we keep them till they're ransomed, it means that we keep them till they're dead."

"Now, that's something *like*. That'll answer. Why couldn't you said that before? We'll keep them till they're ransomed to death —and a bothersome lot they'll be, too, eating up everything and always trying to get loose."

"How you talk, Ben Rogers. How can they get loose when there's a guard over them, ready to shoot them down if they move a peg?"

"A guard. Well, that *is* good. So somebody's got to set up all night and never get any sleep, just so as to watch them. I think that's foolishness. Why can't a body take a club and ransom them as soon as they get here?"

"Because it ain't in the books so—that's why. Now Ben Rogers, do you want to do things regular, or don't you?—that's the idea. Don't you reckon that the people that made the books knows what's the correct thing to do? Do you reckon *you* can learn 'em anything? Not by a good deal. No, sir, we'll just go on and ransom them in the regular way."

"All right. I don't mind; but I say it's a fool way, anyhow. Say —do we kill the women, too?"

---

7. Euphemism for "damnation."

"Well, Ben Rogers, if I was as ignorant as you I wouldn't let on. Kill the women? No—nobody ever saw anything in the books like that. You fetch them to the cave, and you're always as polite as pie to them; and by-and-by they fall in love with you and never want to go home any more."

"Well, if that's the way, I'm agreed, but I don't take no stock in it. Mighty soon we'll have the cave so cluttered up with women, and fellows waiting to be ransomed, that there won't be no place for the robbers. But go ahead, I ain't got nothing to say."

Little Tommy Barnes was asleep, now, and when they waked him up he was scared, and cried, and said he wanted to go home to his ma, and didn't want to be a robber any more.

So they all made fun of him, and called him cry-baby, and that made him mad, and he said he would go straight and tell all the secrets. But Tom give him five cents to keep quiet, and said we would all go home and meet next week and rob somebody and kill some people.

Ben Rogers said he couldn't get out much, only Sundays, and so he wanted to begin next Sunday; but all the boys said it would be wicked to do it on Sunday, and that settled the thing. They agreed to get together and fix a day as soon as they could, and then we elected Tom Sawyer first captain and Jo Harper second captain of the Gang, and so started home.

I clumb up the shed and crept into my window just before day was breaking. My new clothes was all greased up and clayey, and I was dog-tired.

Chapter III

Well, I got a good going-over in the morning, from old Miss Watson, on account of my clothes; but the widow she didn't scold, but only cleaned off the grease and clay and looked so sorry that I thought I would behave a while if I could. Then Miss Watson she took me in the closet[8] and prayed, but nothing come of it. She told me to pray every day, and whatever I asked for I would get it. But it warn't so. I tried it. Once I got a fish-line, but no hooks. It warn't any good to me without hooks. I tried for the hooks three or four times, but somehow I couldn't make it work. By-and-by, one day, I asked Miss Watson to try for me, but she said I was a fool. She never told me why, and I couldn't make it out no way.

I set down, one time, back in the woods, and had a long think about it. I says to myself, if a body can get anything they pray for, why don't Deacon Winn get back the money he lost on pork?

8. Miss Watson has interpreted Matthew 6:6 literally: "But thou, when thou prayest, enter into thy closet. . . ."

Why can't the widow get back her silver snuff-box that was stole? Why can't Miss Watson fat up? No, says I to myself, there ain't nothing in it. I went and told the widow about it, and she said the thing a body could get by praying for it was "spiritual gifts." This was too many for me, but she told me what she meant—I must help other people, and do everything I could for other people, and look out for them all the time, and never think about myself. This was including Miss Watson, as I took it. I went out in the woods and turned it over in my mind a long time, but I couldn't see no advantage about it—except for the other people—so at last I reckoned I wouldn't worry about it any more, but just let it go. Sometimes the widow would take me one side and talk about Providence in a way to make a boy's mouth water; but maybe next day Miss Watson would take hold and knock it all down again. I judged I could see that there was two Providences, and a poor chap would stand considerable show with the widow's Providence, but if Miss Watson's got him there warn't no help for him any more. I thought it all out, and reckoned I would belong to the widow's, if he wanted me, though I couldn't make out how he was agoing to be any better off then than what he was before, seeing I was so ignorant and so kind of low-down and ornery.

Pap he hadn't been seen for more than a year, and that was comfortable for me; I didn't want to see him no more. He used to always whale me when he was sober and could get his hands on me; though I used to take to the woods most of the time when he was around. Well, about this time he was found in the river drowned, about twelve mile above town, so people said. They judged it was him, anyway; said this drowned man was just his size, and was ragged, and had uncommon long hair—which was all like pap—but they couldn't make nothing out of the face, because it had been in the water so long it warn't much like a face at all. They said he was floating on his back in the water. They took him and buried him on the bank. But I warn't comfortable long, because I happened to think of something. I knowed mighty well that a drownded man don't float on his back, but on his face. So I knowed, then, that this warn't pap, but a woman dressed up in a man's clothes. So I was uncomfortable again. I judged the old man would turn up again by-and-by, though I wished he wouldn't.

We played robber now and then about a month, and then I resigned. All the boys did. We hadn't robbed nobody, we hadn't killed any people, but only just pretended. We used to hop out of the woods and go charging down on hog-drovers and women in carts taking garden stuff to market, but we never hived any of them. Tom Sawyer called the hogs "ingots," and he called the turnips and stuff "julery" and we would go to the cave and pow-wow

over what we had done and how many people we had killed and
marked. But I couldn't see no profit in it. One time Tom sent
a boy to run about town with a blazing stick, which he called a
slogan (which was the sign for the Gang to get together), and
then he said he had got secret news by his spies that next day
a whole parcel of Spanish merchants and rich A-rabs was going to
camp in Cave Hollow with two hundred elephants, and six hundred camels, and over a thousand "sumter"[9] mules, all loaded with
di'monds, and they didn't have only a guard of four hundred soldiers, and so we would lay in ambuscade, as he called it, and kill the
lot and scoop the things. He said we must slick up our swords and
guns, and get ready. He never could go after even a turnip-cart but
he must have the swords and guns all scoured up for it; though
they was only lath and broom-sticks, and you might scour at them
till you rotted and then they warn't worth a mouthful of ashes more
than what they was before. I didn't believe we could lick such a
crowd of Spaniards and A-rabs, but I wanted to see the camels and
elephants, so I was on hand next day, Saturday, in the ambuscade;
and when we got the word, we rushed out of the woods and down
the hill. But there warn't no Spaniards and A-rabs, and there
warn't no camels nor no elephants. It warn't anything but a
Sunday-school picnic, and only a primer-class at that. We busted it
up, and chased the children up the hollow; but we never got anything but some doughnuts and jam, though Ben Rogers got a rag
doll, and Jo Harper got a hymn-book and a tract; and then the
teacher charged in and made us drop everything and cut. I didn't
see no di'monds, and I told Tom Sawyer so. He said there was
loads of them there, anyway; and he said there was A-rabs there,
too, and elephants and things. I said, why couldn't we see them,
then? He said if I warn't so ignorant, but had read a book called
"Don Quixote,"[1] I would know without asking. He said it was all
done by enchantment. He said there was hundreds of soldiers
there, and elephants and treasure, and so on, but we had enemies
which he called magicians, and they had turned the whole thing
into an infant Sunday school, just out of spite. I said, all right, then
the thing for us to do was to go for the magicians. Tom Sawyer said
I was a numskull.

"Why," says he, "a magician could call up a lot of genies, and
they would hash you up like nothing before you could say Jack
Robinson. They are as tall as a tree and as big around as a church."

"Well," I says, "s'pose we got some genies to help *us*—can't we

9. "Sumpter." fancy name for a pack
animal.
1. The ancient *Arabian Nights' Enter
tainments* (first English translation,
1838–41) and the "hero" of Cervantes's
picaresque narrative (1605) are the chief
romance authorities Tom garbles here.
The one most often satirized by Clemens
was Sir Walter Scott.

lick the other crowd then?"

"How you going to get them?"

"I don't know. How do *they* get them?"

"Why they rub an old tin lamp or an iron ring, and then the genies come tearing in, with the thunder and lightning a-ripping around and the smoke a-rolling, and everything they're told to do they up and do it. They don't think nothing of pulling a shot tower[2] up by the roots, and belting a Sunday-school superintendent over the head with it—or any other man."

"Who makes them tear around so?"

"Why, whoever rubs the lamp or the ring. They belong to whoever rubs the lamp or the ring, and they've got to do whatever he says. If he tells them to build a palace forty miles long, out of di'monds, and fill it full of chewing gum, or whatever you want, and fetch an emperor's daughter from China for you to marry, they've got to do it—and they've got to do it before sun-up next morning, too. And more—they've got to waltz that palace around over the country wherever you want it, you understand."

"Well," says I, "I think they are a pack of flatheads for not keeping the palace themselves 'stead of fooling them away like that. And what's more—if I was one of them I would see a man in Jericho before I would drop my business and come to him for the rubbing of an old tin lamp."

"How you talk, Huck Finn. Why, you'd *have* to come when he rubbed it, whether you wanted to or not."

"What, and I as high as a tree and as big as a church? All right, then; I *would* come; but I lay I'd make that man climb the highest tree there was in the country."

"Shucks, it ain't no use to talk to you, Huck Finn. You don't seem to know anything, somehow—perfect sap-head."

I thought all this over for two or three days, and then I reckoned I would see if there was anything in it. I got an old tin lamp and an iron ring and went out in the woods and rubbed and rubbed till I sweat like an Injun, calculating to build a palace and sell it; but it warn't no use, none of the genies come. So then I judged that all that stuff was only just one of Tom Sawyer's lies. I reckoned he believed in the A-rabs and the elephants, but as for me I think different. It had all the marks of a Sunday school.

Chapter IV

Well, three or four months run along, and it was well into the winter, now. I had been to school most all the time, and could

---

2. Where gunshot were made by dropping molten lead into water.

spell, and read, and write just a little, and could say the multiplication table up to six times seven is thirty-five, and I don't reckon I could ever get any further than that if I was to live forever. I don't take no stock in mathematics, anyway.

At first I hated the school, but by-and-by I got so I could stand it. Whenever I got uncommon tired I played hookey, and the hiding I got next day done me good and cheered me up. So the longer I went to school the easier it got to be. I was getting sort of used to the widow's ways, too, and they warn't so raspy on me. Living in a house, and sleeping in a bed, pulled on me pretty tight, mostly, but before the cold weather I used to slide out and sleep in the woods, sometimes, and so that was a rest to me. I liked the old ways best, but I was getting so I liked the new ones, too, a little bit. The widow said I was coming along slow but sure, and doing very satisfactory. She said she warn't ashamed of me.

One morning I happened to turn over the salt-cellar at breakfast. I reached for some of it as quick as I could, to throw over my left shoulder and keep off the bad luck, but Miss Watson was in ahead of me, and crossed me off. She says, "Take your hands away, Huckleberry—what a mess you are always making." The widow put in a good word for me, but that warn't going to keep off the bad luck, I knowed that well enough. I started out, after breakfast, feeling worried and shaky, and wondering where it was going to fall on me, and what it was going to be. There is ways to keep off some kinds of bad luck, but this wasn't one of them kind; so I never tried to do anything, but just poked along low-spirited and on the watch-out.

I went down the front garden and clumb over the stile,[3] where you go through the high board fence. There was an inch of new snow on the ground, and I seen somebody's tracks. They had come up from the quarry and stood around the stile a while, and then went on around the garden fence. It was funny they hadn't come in, after standing around so. I couldn't make it out. It was very curious, somehow. I was going to follow around, but I stooped down to look at the tracks first. I didn't notice anything at first, but next I did. There was a cross in the left boot-heel made with big nails, to keep off the devil.

I was up in a second and shinning down the hill. I looked over my shoulder every now and then, but I didn't see nobody. I was at Judge Thatcher's as quick as I could get there. He said:

"Why, my boy, you are all out of breath. Did you come for your interest?"

"No sir," I says; "is there some for me?"

---

3. Double sets of steps straddling a fence.

"Oh, yes, a half-yearly is in, last night. Over a hundred and fifty dollars. Quite a fortune for you. You better let me invest it along with your six thousand, because if you take it you'll spend it."

"No sir," I says, "I don't want to spend it. I don't want it at all —nor the six thousand, nuther. I want you to take it; I want to give it to you—the six thousand and all."

He looked surprised. He couldn't seem to make it out. He says: "Why, what can you mean, my boy?"

I says, "Don't you ask me no questions about it, please. You'll take it—won't you?"

He says:

"Well I'm puzzled. Is something the matter?"

"Please take it," says I, "and don't ask me nothing—then I won't have to tell no lies."

He studied a while, and then he says:

"Oho-o. I think I see. You want to *sell* all your property to me— not give it. That's the correct idea."

Then he wrote something on a paper and read it over, and says:

"There—you see it says 'for a consideration.' That means I have bought it of you and paid you for it. Here's a dollar for you. Now, you sign it."

So I signed it, and left.

Miss Watson's nigger, Jim, had a hair-ball as big as your fist, which had been took out of the fourth stomach of an ox, and he used to do magic with it.[4] He said there was a spirit inside of it, and it knowed everything. So I went to him that night and told him pap was here again, for I found his tracks in the snow. What I wanted to know, was, what he was going to do, and was he going to stay? Jim got out his hair-ball, and said something over it, and then he held it up and dropped it on the floor. It fell pretty solid, and only rolled about an inch. Jim tried it again, and then another time, and it acted just the same. Jim got down on his knees and put his ear against it and listened. But it warn't no use; he said it wouldn't talk. He said sometimes it wouldn't talk without money. I told him I had an old slick counterfeit quarter that warn't no good because the brass showed through the silver a little, and it wouldn't pass nohow, even if the brass didn't show, because it was so slick it felt greasy, and so that would tell on it every time. (I reckoned I wouldn't say nothing about the dollar I got from the judge.) I said it was pretty bad money, but maybe the hair-ball would take it, because maybe it wouldn't know the difference. Jim smelt it, and bit it, and rubbed it, and said he would manage so the

4. Most of Jim's superstitions have European origins, but the hair-ball is from African voodoo.

hair-ball would think it was good. He said he would split open a raw Irish potato and stick the quarter in between and keep it there all night, and next morning you couldn't see no brass, and it wouldn't feel greasy no more, and so anybody in town would take it in a minute, let alone a hair-ball. Well, I knowed a potato would do that, before, but I had forgot it.

Jim put the quarter under the hair-ball and got down and listened again. This time he said the hair-ball was all right. He said it would tell my whole fortune if I wanted it to. I says, go on. So the hair-ball talked to Jim, and Jim told it to me. He says:

"Yo' ole father doan' know, yit, what he's a-gwyne to do. Sometimes he spec he'll go 'way, en den agin he spec he'll stay. De bes' way is to res' easy en let de ole man take his own way. Dey's two angels hoverin' roun' 'bout him. One uv 'em is white en shiny, en 'tother one is black. De white one gits him to go right, a little while, den de black one sail in en bust it all up. A body can't tell, yit, which one gwyne to fetch him at de las'. But you is all right. You gwyne to have considable trouble in yo' life, en considable joy. Sometimes you gwyne to git hurt, en sometimes you gwyne to git sick; but every time you's gwyne to git well agin. Dey's two gals flyin' 'bout you in yo' life. One uv 'em's light en 'tother one is dark. One is rich en 'tother is po'. You's gwyne to marry de po' one fust en de rich one by-en-by. You wants to keep 'way fum de water as much as you kin, en don't run no resk, 'kase it's down in de bills dat you's gwyne to git hung."

When I lit my candle and went up to my room that night, there set pap, his own self!

Chapter V

I had shut the door to. Then I turned around, and there he was. I used to be scared of him all the time, he tanned me so much. I reckoned I was scared now, too; but in a minute I see I was mistaken. That is, after the first jolt, as you may say, when my breath sort of hitched—he being so unexpected; but right away after, I see I warn't scared of him worth bothering about.

He was most fifty, and he looked it. His hair was long and tangled and greasy, and hung down, and you could see his eyes shining through like he was behind vines. It was all black, no gray; so was his long, mixed-up whiskers. There warn't no color in his face, where his face showed; it was white; not like another man's white, but a white to make a body sick, a white to make a body's flesh crawl—a tree-toad white, a fish-belly white. As for his clothes—just rags, that was all. He had one ankle resting on 'tother knee; the boot on that foot was busted, and two of his toes stuck through, and he worked them now and then. His hat was laying on the floor; an old black slouch with the top caved in, like a lid.

I stood a-looking at him; he set there a-looking at me, with his chair tilted back a little. I set the candle down. I noticed the window was up; so he had clumb in by the shed. He kept a-looking me all over. By-and-by he says:

"Starchy clothes—very. You think you're a good deal of a big-bug, *don't* you?"

"Maybe I am, maybe I ain't," I says.

"Don't you give me none o' your lip," says he. "You've put on considerble many frills since I been away. I'll take you down a peg before I get done with you. You're educated, too, they say; can read and write. You think you're better'n your father, now, don't you, because he can't? *I'll* take it out of you. Who told you you might meddle with such hifalut'n foolishness, hey?—who told you you could?"

"The widow. She told me."

"The widow, hey?—and who told the widow she could put in her shovel about a thing that ain't none of her business?"

"Nobody never told her."

"Well, I'll learn her how to meddle. And looky here—you drop that school, you hear? I'll learn people to bring up a boy to put on airs over his own father and let on to be better'n what *he* is. You lemme catch you fooling around that school again, you hear? Your mother couldn't read, and she couldn't write, nuther, before she died. None of the family couldn't, before *they* died. *I* can't; and here you're a-swelling yourself up like this. I ain't the man to stand it—you hear? Say—lemme hear you read."

I took up a book and begun something about General Washington and the wars. When I'd read about a half a minute, he fetched the book a whack with his hand and knocked it across the house. He says:

"It's so. You can do it. I had my doubts when you told me. Now looky here; you stop that putting on frills. I won't have it. I'll lay for you, my smarty; and if I catch you about that school I'll tan you good. First you know you'll get religion, too. I never see such a son."

He took up a little blue and yaller picture of some cows and a boy, and says:

"What's this?"

"It's something they give me for learning my lessons good."

He tore it up, and says—

"I'll give you something better—I'll give you a cowhide."

He set there a-mumbling and a-growling a minute, and then he says—

"*Ain't* you a sweet-scented dandy, though? A bed; and bed-clothes; and a look'n-glass; and a piece of carpet on the floor—and your own father got to sleep with the hogs in the tanyard. I never see such a son. I bet I'll take some o' these frills out o' you before I'm done with you. Why there ain't no end to your airs—they say you're rich. Hey?—how's that?"

"They lie—that's how."

"Looky here—mind how you talk to me; I'm a-standing about all I can stand, now—so don't gimme no sass. I've been in town two days, and I hain't heard nothing but about you bein' rich. I heard about it away down the river, too. That's why I come. You git me that money to-morrow—I want it."

"I hain't got no money."

"It's a lie. Judge Thatcher's got it. You git it. I want it."

"I hain't got no money, I tell you. You ask Judge Thatcher; he'll tell you the same."

"All right. I'll ask him; and I'll make him pungle,[5] too, or I'll know the reason why. Say—how much you got in your pocket? I want it."

"I hain't got only a dollar, and I want that to—"

"It don't make no difference what you want it for—you just shell it out."

He took it and bit it to see if it was good, and then he said he was going down town to get some whisky; said he hadn't had a drink all day. When he had got out on the shed, he put his head in again, and cussed me for putting on frills and trying to be better than him; and when I reckoned he was gone, he come back and put his head in again, and told me to mind about that school, because he was going to lay for me and lick me if I didn't drop that.

Next day he was drunk, and he went to Judge Thatcher's and bullyragged him and tried to make him give up the money, but he couldn't, and then he swore he'd make the law force him.

The judge and the widow went to law to get the court to take me away from him and let one of them be my guardian; but it was a new judge that had just come, and he didn't know the old man; so he said courts mustn't interfere and separate families if they could help it; said he'd druther not take a child away from its father. So Judge Thatcher and the widow had to quit on the business.

That pleased the old man till he couldn't rest. He said he'd cowhide me till I was black and blue if I didn't raise some money for him. I borrowed three dollars from Judge Thatcher, and pap took it and got drunk and went a-blowing around and cussing and whooping and carrying on; and he kept it up all over town, with a tin pan, till most midnight; then they jailed him, and next day they had him before court, and jailed him again for a week. But he said *he*

5. Pay up, hand over.

was satisfied; said he was boss of his son, and he'd make it warm for *him*.

When he got out the new judge said he was agoing to make a man of him. So he took him to his own house, and dressed him up clean and nice, and had him to breakfast and dinner and supper with the family, and was just old pie to him, so to speak. And after supper he talked to him about temperance and such things till the old man cried, and said he'd been a fool, and fooled away his life; but now he was agoing to turn over a new leaf and be a man nobody wouldn't be ashamed of, and he hoped the judge would help him and not look down on him. The judge said he could hug him for them words; so *he* cried, and his wife she cried again; pap said he'd been a man that had always been misunderstood before, and the judge said he believed it. The old man said that what a man wanted that was down, was sympathy; and the judge said it was so; so they cried again. And when it was bedtime, the old man rose up and held out his hand, and says:

"Look at it gentlemen, and ladies all; take ahold of it; shake it. There's a hand that was the hand of a hog; but it ain't so no more; it's the hand of a man that's started in on a new life, and 'll die before he'll go back. You mark them words—don't forget I said them. It's a clean hand now; shake it—don't be afeard."

So they shook it, one after the other, all around, and cried. The judge's wife she kissed it. Then the old man he signed a pledge—made his mark. The judge said it was the holiest time on record, or something like that. Then they tucked the old man into a beautiful room, which was the spare room, and in the night sometime he got powerful thirsty and clumb out onto the porch-roof and slid down a stanchion and traded his new coat for a jug of forty-rod,[6] and clumb back again and had a good old time; and towards daylight he crawled out again, drunk as a fiddler, and rolled off the porch and broke his left arm in two places and was most froze to death when somebody found him after sun-up. And when they come to look at that spare room, they had to take soundings before they could navigate it.

The judge he felt kind of sore. He said he reckoned a body could reform the ole man with a shot-gun, maybe, but he didn't know no other way.

Chapter VI

Well, pretty soon the old man was up and around again, and then he went for Judge Thatcher in the courts to make him give up that money, and he went for me, too, for not stopping school. He

6. Whiskey strong enough to knock a man forty rods or kill him at that distance.

catched me a couple of times and thrashed me, but I went to school just the same, and dodged him or out-run him most of the time. I didn't want to go to school much, before, but I reckoned I'd go now to spite pap. That law trial was a slow business; appeared like they warn't ever going to get started on it; so every now and then I'd borrow two or three dollars off of the judge for him, to keep from getting a cowhiding. Every time he got money he got drunk; and every time he got drunk he raised Cain around town; and every time he raised Cain he got jailed. He was just suited—this kind of thing was right in his line.

He got to hanging around the widow's too much, and so she told him at last, that if he didn't quit using around there she would make trouble for him. Well, *wasn't* he mad? He said he would show who was Huck Finn's boss. So he watched out for me one day in the spring, and catched me, and took me up the river about three mile, in a skiff, and crossed over to the Illinois shore where it was woody and there warn't no houses but an old log hut in a place where the timber was so thick you couldn't find it if you didn't know where it was.

He kept me with him all the time, and I never got a chance to run off. We lived in that old cabin, and he always locked the door and put the key under his head, nights. He had a gun which he had stole, I reckon, and we fished and hunted, and that was what we lived on. Every little while he locked me in and went down to the store, three miles, to the ferry, and traded fish and game for whisky and fetched it home and got drunk and had a good time, and licked me. The widow she found out where I was, by-and-by, and she sent a man over to try to get hold of me, but pap drove him off with the gun, and it warn't long after that till I was used to being where I was, and liked it, all but the cowhide part.

It was kind of lazy and jolly, laying off comfortable all day, smoking and fishing, and no books nor study. Two months or more run along, and my clothes got to be all rags and dirt, and I didn't see how I'd ever got to like it so well at the widow's, where you had to wash, and eat on a plate, and comb up, and go to bed and get up regular, and be forever bothering over a book and have old Miss Watson pecking at you all the time. I didn't want to go back no more. I had stopped cussing, because the widow didn't like it; but now I took to it again because pap hadn't no objections. It was pretty good times up in the woods there, take it all around.

But by-and-by pap got too handy with his hick'ry, and I couldn't stand it. I was all over welts. He got to going away so much, too, and locking me in. Once he locked me in and was gone three days. It was dreadful lonesome. I judged he had got drowned and I wasn't ever going to get out any more. I was scared. I made up my mind I would fix up some way to leave there. I had tried to get out of that cabin many a time, but I couldn't find no way. There warn't a window to it big enought for a dog to get through I couldn't get up the chimbly, it was too narrow. The door was thick solid oak slabs. Pap was pretty careful not to leave a knife or anything in the cabin when he was away; I reckon I had hunted the place over as much as a hundred times; well, I was 'most all the time at it, because it was about the only way to put in the time. But this time I found something at last; I found an old rusty wood-saw without any handle; it was laid in between a rafter and the clapboards of the roof. I greased it up and went to work. There was an old horse-blanket nailed against the logs at the far end of the cabin behind the table, to keep the wind from blowing through the chinks and putting the candle out. I got under the table and raised the blanket and went to work to saw a section of the big bottom log out, big enough to let me through. Well, it was a good long job, but I was getting towards the end of it when I heard pap's gun in the woods. I got rid of the signs of my work, and dropped the blanket and hid my saw, and pretty soon pap come in.

Pap warn't in a good humor—so he was his natural self. He said he was down to town, and everything was going wrong. His lawyer said he reckoned he would win his lawsuit and get the money, if they ever got started on the trial; but then there was ways to put it off a long time, and Judge Thatcher knowed how to do it. And he said people allowed there'd be another trial to get me away from him and give me to the widow for my guardian, and they guessed it would win, this time. This shook me up considerable, because I didn't want to go back to the widow's any more and be so cramped up and sivilized, as they called it. Then the old man got to cussing, and cussed everything and everybody he could think of, and then cussed them all over again to make sure he hadn't skipped any, and after that he polished off with a kind of a general cuss all round, including a considerable parcel of people which he didn't know the names of, and so called them what's-his-name, when he got to them, and went right along with his cussing.

He said he would like to see the widow get me. He said he would watch out, and if they tried to come any such game on him he knowed of a place six or seven mile off, to stow me in, where they might hunt till they dropped and they couldn't find me. That made me pretty uneasy again, but only for a minute; I reckoned I wouldn't stay on hand till he got that chance.

The old man made me go to the skiff and fetch the things he had got. There was a fifty-pound sack of corn meal, and a side of bacon, ammunition, and a four-gallon jug of whisky, and an old book and two newspapers for wadding,[7] besides some tow.[8] I toted up a load, and went back and set down on the bow of the skiff to rest. I

7. To hold the powder in Pap's gun.   8. Flax or hemp fibers.

thought it all over, and I reckoned I would walk off with the gun and some lines, and take to the woods when I run away. I guessed I wouldn't stay in one place, but just tramp right across the country, mostly night times, and hunt and fish to keep alive, and so get so far away that the old man nor the widow couldn't ever find me any more. I judged I would saw out and leave that night if pap got drunk enough, and I reckoned he would. I got so full of it I didn't notice how long I was staying, till the old man hollered and asked me whether I was asleep or drownded.

I got the things all up to the cabin, and then it was about dark. While I was cooking supper the old man took a swig or two and got sort of warmed up, and went to ripping again. He had been drunk over in town, and laid in the gutter all night, and he was a sight to look at. A body would a thought he was Adam, he was just all mud.[9] Whenever his liquor begun to work, he most always went for the govment. This time he says:

"Call this a govment! why, just look at it and see what it's like. Here's the law a-standing ready to take a man's son away from him —a man's own son, which he has had all the trouble and all the anxiety and all the expense of raising. Yes, just as that man has got that son raised at last, and ready to go to work and begin to do suthin' for *him* and give him a rest, the law up and goes for him. And they call *that* govment! That ain't all, nuther. The law backs that old Judge Thatcher up and helps him to keep me out o' my property. Here's what the law does. The law takes a man worth six thousand dollars and upards, and jams him into an old trap of a cabin like this, and lets him go round in clothes that ain't fitten for a hog. They call that govment! A man can't get his rights in a govment like this. Sometimes I've a mighty notion to just leave the country for good and all. Yes, and I *told* 'em so; I told old Thatcher so to his face. Lots of 'em heard me, and can tell what I said. Says I, for two cents I'd leave the blamed country and never come anear it agin. Them's the very words. I says, look at my hat—if you call it a hat—but the lid raises up and the rest of it goes down till it's below my chin, and then it ain't rightly a hat at all, but more like my head was shoved up through a jint o' stove-pipe. Look at it, says I—such a hat for me to wear—one of the wealthiest men in this town, if I could git my rights.

"Oh, yes, this is a wonderful govment, wonderful. Why, looky here. There was a free nigger there, from Ohio; a mulatter, most as white as a white man. He had the whitest shirt on you ever see, too, and the shiniest hat; and there ain't a man in that town that's got as fine clothes as what he had; and he had a gold watch and chain and a silver-headed cane—the awfulest old gray-headed nabob in the State. And what do you think? they said he was a p'fessor in a

9. Adam is created from the wet earth in Genesis 2 : 7.

college, and could talk all kinds of languages, and knowed everything. And that ain't the wust. They said he could vote, when he
was at home. Well, that let me out. Thinks I, what is the country
a-coming to? It was 'lection day, and I was just about to go and
vote, myself, if I warn't too drunk to get there; but when they told
me there was a State in this country where they'd let that nigger
vote, I drawed out. I says I'll never vote agin. Them's the very
words I said; they all heard me; and the country may rot for all me
—I'll never vote agin as long as I live. And to see the cool way of
that nigger—why, he wouldn't a give me the road if I hadn't shoved
him out o' the way. I says to the people, why ain't this nigger put
up at auction and sold?—that's what I want to know. And what
do you reckon they said? Why, they said he couldn't be sold till
he'd been in the State six months, and he hadn't been there that
long yet. There, now—that's a specimen. They call that a govment
that can't sell a free nigger till he's been in the State six months.
Here's a govment that calls itself a govment, and lets on to be a
govment, and thinks it is a govment, and yet's got to set stock-still
for six whole months before it can take ahold of a prowling, thieving, infernal, white-shirted free nigger, and—"[1]

Pap was agoing on so, he never noticed where his old limber legs
was taking him to, so he went head over heels over the tub of salt
pork, and barked both shins, and the rest of his speech was all the
hottest kind of language—mostly hove at the nigger and the govment, though he give the tub some, too, all along, here and there.
He hopped around the cabin considerable, first on one leg and then
on the other, holding first one shin and then the other one, and at
last he let out with his left foot all of a sudden and fetched the tub
a rattling kick. But it warn't good judgment, because that was the
boot that had a couple of his toes leaking out of the front end of
it; so now he raised a howl that fairly made a body's hair raise, and
down he went in the dirt, and rolled there, and held his toes; and
the cussing he done then laid over anything he had ever done previous. He said so his own self, afterwards. He had heard old Sow-
berry Hagan in his best days, and he said it laid over him, too; but
I reckon that was sort of piling it on, maybe.

After supper pap took the jug, and said he had enough whisky
there for two drunks and one delirium tremens. That was always his
word. I judged he would be blind drunk in about an hour, and
then I would steal the key, or saw myself out, one or 'tother. He
drank, and drank, and tumbled down on his blankets, by-and-by;

1. The original constitution of Missouri
prohibited freed slaves and mulattoes
from entering the state. This provision
was stricken out in what is sometimes
called the "second Missouri compromise" of 1820; however, increasingly
strict laws were passed in the 1830s and
1840s. By 1850, a sworn statement by a
white "proved" ownership of a Negro
without freedom papers. Roxy's case in
Pudd'nhead Wilson shows how easily a
freed Negro could be sold down the
river.

but luck didn't run my way. He didn't go sound asleep, but was uneasy. He groaned, and moaned, and thrashed around this way and that, for a long time. At last I got so sleepy I couldn't keep my eyes open, all I could do, and so before I knowed what I was about I was sound asleep, and the candle burning.

I don't know how long I was asleep, but all of a sudden there was an awful scream and I was up. There was pap, looking wild and skipping around every which way and yelling about snakes. He said they was crawling up his legs; and then he would give a jump and scream, and say one had bit him on the cheek—but I couldn't see no snakes. He started and run round and round the cabin, hollering "take him off! take him off! he's biting me on the neck!" I never see a man look so wild in the eyes. Pretty soon he was all fagged out, and fell down panting; then he rolled over and over, wonderful fast, kicking things every which way, and striking and grabbing at the air with his hands, and screaming, and saying there was devils ahold of him. He wore out, by-and-by, and laid still a while, moaning. Then he laid stiller, and didn't make a sound. I could hear the owls and the wolves, away off in the woods, and it seemed terrible still. He was laying over by the corner. By-and-by he raised up, part way, and listened, with his head to one side. He says very low:

"Tramp—tramp—tramp; that's the dead; tramp—tramp—tramp; they're coming after me; but I won't go— Oh, they're here! don't touch me—don't! hands off—they're cold; let go— Oh, let a poor devil alone!"

Then he went down on all fours and crawled off begging them to let him alone, and he rolled himself up in his blanket and wallowed in under the old pine table, still a-begging; and then he went to crying. I could hear him through the blanket.

By-and-by he rolled out and jumped up on his feet looking wild, and he see me and went for me. He chased me round and round the place, with a clasp-knife, calling me the Angel of Death and saying he would kill me and then I couldn't come for him no more. I begged, and told him I was only Huck, but he laughed *such* a screechy laugh, and roared and cussed, and kept on chasing me up. Once when I turned short and dodged under his arm he made a grab and got me by the jacket between my shoulders, and I thought I was gone; but I slid out of the jacket quick as lightning, and saved myself. Pretty soon he was all tired out, and dropped down with his back against the door, and said he would rest a minute and then kill me. He put his knife under him, and said he would sleep and get strong, and then he would see who was who.

So he dozed off, pretty soon. By-and-by I got the old split-bottom[2] chair and clumb up, as easy as I could, not to make any noise, and

2. Splint-bottom.

got down the gun. I slipped the ramrod down it to make sure it was loaded, and then I laid it across the turnip barrel, pointing towards pap, and set down behind it to wait for him to stir. And how slow and still the time did drag along.

Chapter VII

"Git up! what you 'bout!"

I opened my eyes and looked around, trying to make out where I was. It was after sun-up, and I had been sound asleep. Pap was standing over me, looking sour—and sick, too. He says—

"What you doin' with this gun?"

I judged he didn't know nothing about what he had been doing, so I says:

"Somebody tried to get in, so I was laying for him."

"Why didn't you roust me out?"

"Well I tried to, but I couldn't; I couldn't budge you."

"Well, all right. Don't stand there palavering[3] all day, but out with you and see if there's a fish on the lines for breakfast. I'll be along in a minute."

He unlocked the door and I cleared out, up the river bank. I noticed some pieces of limbs and such things floating down, and a sprinkling of bark; so I knowed the river had begun to rise. I reckoned I would have great times, now, if I was over at the town. The June rise used to be always luck for me; because as soon as that rise begins, here comes cord-wood floating down, and pieces of log rafts —sometimes a dozen logs together; so all you have to do is to catch them and sell them to the wood yards and the sawmill.

I went along up the bank with one eye out for pap and 'tother one out for what the rise might fetch along. Well, all at once, here comes a canoe; just a beauty, too, about thirteen or fourteen foot long, riding high like a duck. I shot head first off of the bank, like a frog, clothes and all on, and struck out for the canoe. I just expected there'd be somebody laying down in it, because people often done that to fool folks, and when a chap had pulled a skiff out most to it they'd raise up and laugh at him. But it warn't so this time. It was a drift-canoe, sure enough, and I clumb in and paddled her ashore. Thinks I, the old man will be glad when he sees this—she's worth ten dollars. But when I got to shore pap wasn't in sight yet, and as I was running her into a little creek like a gully, all hung over with vines and willows, I struck another idea; I judged I'd hide her good, and then, stead of taking to the woods when I run off, I'd go down the river about fifty mile and camp in one place for good, and not have such a rough time tramping on foot.

---

3. Idly chattering.

It was pretty close to the shanty, and I thought I heard the old man coming, all the time; but I got her hid; and then I out and looked around a bunch of willows, and there was the old man down the path apiece just drawing a bead on a bird with his gun. So he hadn't seen anything.

When he got along, I was hard at it taking up a "trot" line.[4] He abused me a little for being so slow, but I told him I fell in the river and that was what made me so long. I knowed he would see I was wet, and then he would be asking questions. We got five cat-fish off of the lines and went home.

While we laid off, after breakfast, to sleep up, both of us being about wore out, I got to thinking that if I could fix up some way to keep pap and the widow from trying to follow me, it would be a certainer thing than trusting to luck to get far enough off before they missed me; you see, all kinds of things might happen. Well, I didn't see no way for a while, but by-and-by pap raised up a minute, to drink another barrel of water, and he says:

"Another time a man comes a-prowling round here, you roust me out, you hear? That man warn't here for no good. I'd a shot him. Next time, you roust me out, you hear?"

Then he dropped down and went to sleep again—but what he had been saying give me the very idea I wanted. I says to myself, I can fix it now so nobody won't think of following me.

About twelve o'clock we turned out and went along up the bank. The river was coming up pretty fast, and lots of drift-wood going by on the rise. By-and-by, along comes part of a log raft—nine logs fast together. We went out with the skiff and towed it ashore. Then we had dinner. Anybody but pap would a waited and seen the day through, so as to catch more stuff; but that warn't pap's style. Nine logs was enough for one time; he must shove right over to town and sell. So he locked me in and took the skiff and started off towing the raft about half-past three. I judged he wouldn't come back that night. I waited till I reckoned he had got a good start, then I out with my saw and went to work on that log again. Before he was 'tother side of the river I was out of the hole; him and his raft was just a speck on the water away off yonder.

I took the sack of corn meal and took it to where the canoe was hid, and shoved the vines and branches apart and put it in; then I done the same with the side of bacon; then the whisky jug; I took all the coffee and sugar there was, and all the ammunition; I took the wadding; I took the bucket and gourd, I took a dipper and a tin cup, and my old saw and two blankets, and the skillet and the coffee-pot. I took fish-lines and matches and other things—every-

4. Fishing line strung out over the water to hold shorter lines with baited hooks.

thing that was worth a cent. I cleaned out the place. I wanted an axe, but there wasn't any, only the one out at the wood pile, and I knowed why I was going to leave that. I fetched out the gun, and now I was done.

I had wore the ground a good deal, crawling out of the hole and dragging out so many things. So I fixed that as good as I could from the outside by scattering dust on the place, which covered up the smoothness and the sawdust. Then I fixed the piece of log back into its place, and put two rocks under it and one against it to hold it there,—for it was bent up at that place, and didn't quite touch ground. If you stood four or five foot away and didn't know it was sawed, you wouldn't ever notice it; and besides, this was the back of the cabin and it warn't likely anybody would go fooling around there.

It was all grass clear to the canoe; so I hadn't left a track. I followed around to see. I stood on the bank and looked out over the river. All safe. So I took the gun and went up a piece into the woods and was hunting around for some birds, when I see a wild pig; hogs soon went wild in them bottoms after they had got away from the prairie farms. I shot this fellow and took him into camp.

I took the axe and smashed in the door—I beat it and hacked it considerable, a-doing it. I fetched the pig in and took him back nearly to the table and hacked into his throat with the ax, and laid him down on the ground to bleed—I say ground, because it *was* ground—hard packed, and no boards. Well, next I took an old sack and put a lot of big rocks in it,—all I could drag—and I started it from the pig and dragged it to the door and through the woods down to the river and dumped it in, and down it sunk, out of sight. You could easy see that something had been dragged over the ground. I did wish Tom Sawyer was there, I knowed he would take an interest in this kind of business, and throw in the fancy touches. Nobody could spread himself like Tom Sawyer in such a thing as that.

Well, last I pulled out some of my hair, and bloodied the ax good, and stuck it on the back side, and slung the ax in the corner. Then I took up the pig and held him to my breast with my jacket (so he couldn't drip) till I got a good piece below the house and then dumped him into the river. Now I thought of something else. So I went and got the bag of meal and my old saw out of the canoe and fetched them to the house. I took the bag to where it used to stand, and ripped a hole in the bottom of it with the saw, for there warn't no knives and forks on the place—pap done everything with his clasp-knife, about the cooking. Then I carried the sack about a hundred yards across the grass and through the willows east of the house, to a shallow lake that was five mile wide and full of rushes—and ducks too, you might say, in the season. There was a slough or a creek leading out of it on the other side, that went miles away, I don't know where, but it didn't go to the river. The meal sifted out and made a little track all the way to the lake. I dropped pap's whetstone there too, so as to look like it had been done by accident. Then I tied up the rip in the meal sack with a string, so it wouldn't leak no more, and took it and my saw to the canoe again.

It was about dark, now; so I dropped the canoe down the river under some willows that hung over the bank, and waited for the moon to rise. I made fast to a willow; then I took a bite to eat, and by-and-by laid down in the canoe to smoke a pipe and lay out a plan. I says to myself, they'll follow the track of that sackful of rocks to the shore and then drag the river for me. And they'll follow that meal track to the lake and go browsing down the creek that leads out of it to find the robbers that killed me and took the things. They won't ever hunt the river for anything but my dead carcass. They'll soon get tired of that, and won't bother no more about me. All right; I can stop anywhere I want to. Jackson's Island[5] is good enough for me; I know that island pretty well, and nobody ever comes there. And then I can paddle over to town, nights, and slink around and pick up things I want. Jackson's Island's the place.

I was pretty tired, and the first thing I knowed, I was asleep. When I woke up I didn't know where I was, for a minute. I set up and looked around, a little scared. Then I remembered. The river looked miles and miles across. The moon was so bright I could a counted the drift logs that went a slipping along, black and still, hundred of yards out from shore. Everything was dead quiet, and it looked late, and *smelt* late. You know what I mean—I don't know the words to put it in.

I took a good gap and a stretch, and was just going to unhitch and start, when I heard a sound away over the water. I listened. Pretty soon I made it out. It was that dull kind of a regular sound that comes from oars working in rowlocks when it's a still night. I peeped out through the willow branches, and there it was—a skiff, away across the water. I couldn't tell how many was in it. It kept a-coming, and when it was abreast of me I see there warn't but one man in it. Thinks I, maybe it's pap, though I warn't expecting him. He dropped below me, with the current, and by-and-by he come a-swinging up shore in the easy water, and he went by so close I could a reached out the gun and touched him. Well, it *was* pap, sure enough—and sober, too, by the way he laid to his oars.

I didn't lose no time. The next minute I was a-spinning down stream soft but quick in the shade of the bank. I made two mile and a half, and then struck out a quarter of a mile or more towards

5. The island described in *Tom Sawyer;* actually Glasscock's Island, now eroded away by the Mississippi.

the middle of the river, because pretty soon I would be passing the ferry landing and people might see me and hail me. I got out amongst the drift-wood and then laid down in the bottom of the canoe and let her float. I laid there and had a good rest and a smoke out of my pipe, looking away into the sky, not a cloud in it. The sky looks ever so deep when you lay down on your back in the moonshine; I never knowed it before. And how far a body can hear on the water such nights! I heard people talking at the ferry landing. I heard what they said, too, every word of it. One man said it was getting towards the long days and the short nights, now. 'Tother one said *this* warn't one of the short ones, he reckoned—and then they laughed, and he said it over again and they laughed again; then they waked up another fellow and told him, and laughed, but he didn't laugh; he ripped out something brisk and said let him alone. The first fellow said he 'lowed to tell it to his old woman—she would think it was pretty good; but he said that warn't nothing to some things he had said in his time. I heard one man say it was nearly three o'clock, and he hoped daylight wouldn't wait more than about a week longer. After that, the talk got further and further away, and I couldn't make out the words any more, but I could hear the mumble; and now and then a laugh, too, but it seemed a long ways off.

I was away below the ferry now. I rose up and there was Jackson's Island, about two mile and a half down stream, heavy-timbered and standing up out of the middle of the river, big and dark and solid, like a steamboat without any lights. There warn't any signs of the bar at the head—it was all under water, now.

It didn't take me long to get there. I shot past the head at a ripping rate, the current was so swift, and then I got into the dead water and landed on the side towards the Illinois shore. I run the canoe into a deep dent in the bank that I knowed about; I had to part the willow branches to get in; and when I made fast nobody could a seen the canoe from the outside.

I went up and set down on a log at the head of the island and looked out on the big river and the black driftwood, and away over to the town, three mile away, where there was three or four lights twinkling. A monstrous big lumber raft was about a mile up stream, coming along down, with a lantern in the middle of it. I watched it come creeping down, and when it was most abreast of where I stood I heard a man say, "Stern oars, there! heave her head to stabboard!"[6] I heard that just as plain as if the man was by my side.

There was a little gray in the sky, now; so I stepped into the woods and laid down for a nap before breakfast.

---

6. Starboard, the right-hand side facing forward; "labbord" or "larboard" instead of "port" was Clemens's usual term for the left-hand side.

Chapter VIII

The sun was up so high when I waked, that I judged it was after eight o'clock. I laid there in the grass and the cool shade, thinking about things and feeling rested and ruther comfortable and satisfied. I could see the sun out at one or two holes, but mostly it was big trees all about, and gloomy in there amongst them. There was freckled places on the ground where the light sifted down through the leaves, and the freckled places swapped about a little, showing there was a little breeze up there. A couple of squirrels set on a limb and jabbered at me very friendly.

I was powerful lazy and comfortable—didn't want to get up and cook breakfast. Well, I was dozing off again, when I thinks I hears a deep sound of "boom!" away up the river. I rouses up and rests on my elbow and listens; pretty soon I hears it again. I hopped up and went and looked out at a hole in the leaves, and I see a bunch of smoke laying on the water a long ways up—about abreast the ferry. And there was the ferry-boat full of people, floating along down. I knowed what was the matter, now. "Boom!" I see the white smoke squirt out of the ferry-boat's side. You see, they was firing cannon over the water, trying to make my carcass come to the top.

I was pretty hungry, but it warn't going to do for me to start a fire, because they might see the smoke. So I set there and watched the cannon-smoke and listened to the boom. The river was a mile wide, there, and it always looks pretty on a summer morning—so I was having a good enough time seeing them hunt for my remainders, if I only had a bite to eat. Well, then I happened to think how they always put quicksilver in loaves of bread and float them off because they always go right to the drownded carcass and stop there. So says I, I'll keep a lookout, and if any of them's floating around after me, I'll give them a show. I changed to the Illinois edge of the island to see what luck I could have, and I warn't disappointed. A big double loaf come along, and I most got it, with a long stick, but my foot slipped and she floated out further. Of course I was where the current set in the closest to the shore—I knowed enough for that. But by-and-by along comes another one, and this time I won. I took out the plug and shook out the little dab of quicksilver, and set my teeth in. It was "baker's bread"—what the quality[7] eat—none of your low-down corn-pone.[8]

I got a good place amongst the leaves, and set there on a log, munching the bread and watching the ferry-boat, and very well satisfied. And then something struck me. I says, now I reckon the

---

7. People of high social status.
8. Cheaper because made with coarse corn meal and usually without milk or eggs.

widow or the parson or somebody prayed that this bread would find me, and here it has gone and done it So there ain't no doubt but there is something in that thing. That is, there's something in it when a body like the widow or the parson prays, but it don't work for me, and I reckon it don't work for only just the right kind.

I lit a pipe and had a good long smoke and went on watching. The ferry-boat was floating with the current, and I allowed I'd have a chance to see who was aboard when she come along, because she would come in close, where the bread did. When she'd got pretty well along down towards me, I put out my pipe and went to where I fished out the bread, and laid down behind a log on the bank in a little open place. Where the log forked I could peep through.

By-and-by she come along, and she drifted in so close that they could a run out a plank and walked ashore. Most everybody was on the boat. Pap, and Judge Thatcher, and Bessie Thatcher, and Jo Harper, and Tom Sawyer, and his old Aunt Polly, and Sid and Mary, and plenty more. Everybody was talking about the murder, but the captain broke in and says:

"Look sharp, now; the current sets in the closest here, and maybe he's washed ashore and got tangled amongst the brush at the water's edge. I hope so, anyway."

I didn't hope so. They all crowded up and leaned over the rails, nearly in my face, and kept still, watching with all their might. I could see them first-rate, but they couldn't see me. Then the captain sung out:

"Stand away!" and the cannon let off such a blast right before me that it made me deef with the noise and pretty near blind with the smoke, and I judged I was gone. If they'd a had some bullets in, I reckon they'd a got the corpse they was after. Well, I see I warn't hurt, thanks to goodness. The boat floated on and went out of sight around the shoulder of the island. I could hear the booming, now and then, further and further off, and by-and-by after an hour, I didn't hear it no more. The island was three mile long. I judged they had got to the foot, and was giving it up. But they didn't yet a while. They turned around the foot of the island and started up the channel on the Missouri side, under steam, and booming once in a while as they went. I crossed over to that side and watched them. When they got abreast the head of the island they quit shooting and dropped over to the Missouri shore and went home to the town.

I knowed I was all right now. Nobody else would come a-hunting after me. I got my traps out of the canoe and made me a nice camp in the thick woods. I made a kind of a tent out of my blankets to put my things under so the rain couldn't get at them. I catched a cat fish and haggled him open with my saw, and towards sundown I started my camp fire and had supper. Then I set out a line to catch some fish for breakfast.

When it was dark I set by my camp fire smoking, and feeling pretty satisfied; but by-and-by it got sort of lonesome, and so I went and set on the bank and listened to the currents washing along, and counted the stars and drift-logs and rafts that come down, and then went to bed; there ain't no better way to put in time when you are lonesome; you can't stay so, you soon get over it.

And so for three days and nights. No difference—just the same thing. But the next day I went exploring around down through the island. I was boss of it; it all belonged to me, so to say, and I wanted to know all about it; but mainly I wanted to put in the time. I found plenty strawberries, ripe and prime; and green summer-grapes, and green razberries; and the green blackberries was just beginning to show. They would all come handy by-and-by, I judged.

Well, I went fooling along in the deep woods till I judged I warn't far from the foot of the island. I had my gun along, but I hadn't shot nothing; it was for protection; thought I would kill some game nigh home. About this time I mighty near stepped on a good sized snake, and it went sliding off through the grass and flowers, and I after it, trying to get a shot at it. I clipped along, and all of a sudden I bounded right on to the ashes of a camp fire that was still smoking.

My heart jumped up amongst my lungs. I never waited for to look further, but uncocked my gun and went sneaking back on my tip-toes as fast as ever I could. Every now and then I stopped a second, amongst the thick leaves, and listened; but my breath come so hard I couldn't hear nothing else. I slunk along another piece further, then listened again; and so on, and so on; if I see a stump, I took it for a man; if I trod on a stick and broke it, it made me feel like a person had cut one of my breaths in two and I only got half, and the short half, too.

When I got to camp I warn't feeling very brash, there warn't much sand in my craw; but I says, this ain't no time to be fooling around. So I got all my traps into my canoe again so as to have them out of sight, and I put out the fire and scattered the ashes around to look like an old last year's camp, and then clumb a tree.

I reckon I was up in the tree two hours; but I didn't see nothing, I didn't hear nothing—I only *thought* I heard and seen as much as a thousand things. Well, I couldn't stay up there forever; so at last I got down, but I kept in the thick woods and on the lookout all the time. All I could get to eat was berries and what was left over from breakfast.

By the time it was night I was pretty hungry. So when it was good and dark, I slid out from shore before moonrise and paddled over to the Illinois bank—about a quarter of a mile. I went out in the woods and cooked a supper, and I had about made up my mind I would stay there all night, when I hear a *plunkety-plunk, plunkety-plunk*, and says to myself, horses coming; and next I hear people's voices. I got everything into the canoe as quick as I could, and then went creeping through the woods to see what I could find out. I hadn't got far when I hear a man say:

"We better camp here, if we can find a good place; the horses is about beat out. Let's look around."[9]

I didn't wait, but shoved out and paddled away easy. I tied up in the old place, and reckoned I would sleep in the canoe.

I didn't sleep much. I couldn't, somehow, for thinking. And every time I waked up I thought somebody had me by the neck. So the sleep didn't do me no good. By-and-by I says to myself, I can't live this way; I'm agoing to find out who it is that's here on the island with me; I'll find it out or bust. Well, I felt better, right off.

So I took my paddle and slid out from shore just a step or two, and then let the canoe drop along down amongst the shadows. The moon was shining, and outside of the shadows it made it most as light as day. I poked along well onto an hour, everything still as rocks and sound asleep. Well by this time I was most down to the foot of the island. A little ripply, cool breeze begun to blow, and that was as good as saying the night was about done. I give her a turn with the paddle and brung her nose to shore; then I got my gun and slipped out and into the edge of the woods. I set down there on a log and looked out through the leaves. I see the moon go off watch and the darkness begin to blanket the river. But in a little while I see a pale streak over the tree-tops, and knowed the day was coming. So I took my gun and slipped off towards where I had run across that camp fire, stopping every minute or two to listen. But I hadn't no luck, somehow; I couldn't seem to find the place. But by-and-by, sure enough, I catched a glimpse of fire, away through the trees. I went for it, cautious and slow. By-and-by I was close enough to have a look, and there laid a man on the ground. It most give me the fan-tods.[1] He had a blanket around his head, and his head was nearly in the fire. I set there behind a clump of bushes, in about six foot of him, and kept my eyes on him steady. It was getting gray daylight, now. Pretty soon he gapped, and stretched himself, and hove off the blanket, and it was Miss Watson's Jim! I bet I was glad to see him. I says:

9. The horsemen may be seeking the object of Huck's own search, or they may be left over from a murder plot Clemens discarded as he wrote.
1. The shakes, the willies; slang variant of "fantasy."

"Hello, Jim!" and skipped out.

He bounced up and stared at me wild. Then he drops down on his knees, and puts his hands together and says:

"Doan' hurt me—don't! I hain't ever done no harm to a ghos'. I awluz liked dead people, en done all I could for 'em. You go en git in de river agin, whah you b'longs, en doan' do nuffn to Ole Jim, 'at 'uz awluz yo' fren'."

Well, I warn't long making him understand I warn't dead. I was ever so glad to see Jim. I warn't lonesome, now. I told him I warn't afraid of *him* telling the people where I was. I talked along, but he only set there and looked at me; never said nothing. Then I says:

"It's good daylight. Le's get breakfast. Make up your camp fire good."

"What's de use er makin' up de camp fire to cook strawbries en sich truck? But you got a gun, hain't you? Den we kin git sumfn better den strawbries."

"Strawberries and such truck," I says. "Is that what you live on?"

"I couldn' git nuffn else," he says.

"Why, how long you been on the island, Jim?"

"I come heah de night arter you's killed."

"What, all that time?"

"Yes-indeedy."

"And ain't you had nothing but that kind of rubbage to eat?"

"No, sah—nuffn else."

"Well, you must be most starved, ain't you?"

"I reck'n I could eat a hoss. I think I could. How long you ben on de islan'?"

"Since the night I got killed."

"No! W'y, what has you lived on? But you got a gun. Oh, yes, you got a gun. Dat's good. Now you kill sumfn en I'll make up de fire."

So we went over to where the canoe was, and while he built a fire in a grassy open place amongst the trees, I fetched meal and bacon and coffee, and coffee-pot and frying-pan, and sugar and tin cups, and the nigger was set back considerable, because he reckoned it was all done with witchcraft. I catched a good big cat-fish, too, and Jim cleaned him with his knife, and fried him.

When breakfast was ready, we lolled on the grass and eat it smoking hot. Jim laid it in with all his might, for he was most about starved. Then when we had got pretty well stuffed, we laid off and lazied.

By-and-by Jim says:

"But looky here, Huck, who wuz it dat 'uz killed in dat shanty, ef it warn't you?"

Then I told him the whole thing, and he said it was smart. He said Tom Sawyer couldn't get up no better plan than what I had. Then I says:

"How do you come to be here, Jim, and how'd you get here?"

He looked pretty uneasy, and didn't say nothing for a minute. Then he says:

"Maybe I better not tell."

"Why, Jim?"

"Well, dey's reasons. But you wouldn' tell on me ef I 'uz to tell you, would you, Huck?"

"Blamed if I would, Jim."

"Well, I b'lieve you, Huck. I—I *run off*."

"Jim!"

"But mind, you said you wouldn't tell—you know you said you wouldn't tell, Huck."

"Well, I did. I said I wouldn't, and I'll stick to it. Honest *injun* I will. People would call me a low down Ablitionist and despise me for keeping mum—but that don't make no difference. I ain't agoing to tell, and I ain't agoing back there anyways. So now, le's know all about it."

"Well, you see, it 'uz dis way. Ole Missus—dat's Miss Watson—she pecks on me all de time, en treats me pooty rough, but she awluz said she wouldn' sell me down to Orleans. But I noticed dey wuz a nigger trader roun' de place considable, lately, en I begin to git uneasy. Well, one night I creeps to de do', pooty late, en de do' warn't quite shet, en I hear ole missus tell de widder she gwyne to sell me down to Orleans, but she didn' want to, but she could git eight hund'd dollars for me, en it 'uz sich a big stack o' money she couldn' resis'. De widder she try to git her to say she wouldn' do it, but I never waited to hear de res'. I lit out mighty quick, I tell you.

"I tuck out en shin down de hill en 'spec to steal a skift 'long de sho' som'ers 'bove de town, but dey wuz people a-stirrin' yit, so I hid in de ole tumble-down cooper[2] shop on de bank to wait for everybody to go 'way. Well, I wuz dah all night. Dey wuz somebody roun' all de time. 'Long 'bout six in de mawnin', skifts begin to go by, en 'bout eight er nine every skift dat went 'long wuz talkin' 'bout how yo' pap come over to de town en say you's killed. Dese las' skifts wuz full o' ladies en genlmen agoin' over for to see de place. Sometimes dey'd pull up at de sho' en take a res' b'fo' dey started acrost, so by de talk I got to know all 'bout de killin'. I 'uz powerful sorry you's killed, Huck, but I ain't no mo', now.

"I laid dah under de shavins all day. I 'uz hungry, but I warn't afeared; bekase I knowed ole missus en de widder wuz goin' to start to de camp-meetn' right arter breakfas' en be gone all day, en dey

---

2. Barrelmaker.

knows I goes off wid de cattle 'bout daylight, so dey wouldn' 'spec to see me roun' de place, en so dey wouldn' miss me tell arter dark in de evenin'. De yuther servants wouldn' miss me, kase dey'd shin out en take holiday, soon as de ole folks 'uz out'n de way.

"Well, when it come dark I tuck out up de river road, en went 'bout two mile er more to whah dey warn't no houses. I'd made up my mine 'bout what I's agwyne to do. You see ef I kep' on tryin' to git away afoot, de dogs 'ud track me; ef I stole a skift to cross over, dey'd miss dat skift, you see, en dey'd know 'bout whah I'd lan' on de yuther side en whah to pick up my track. So I says, a raff is what I's arter; it doan' *make* no track.

"I see a light a-comin' roun' de p'int, bymeby, so I wade' in en shove' a log ahead o' me, en swum more'n half-way acrost de river, en got in 'mongst de drift-wood, en kep' my head down low, en kinder swum agin de current tell de raff come along. Den I swum to de stern uv it, en tuck aholt. It clouded up en 'uz pooty dark for a little while. So I clumb up en laid down on de planks. De men 'uz all 'way yonder in de middle, whah de lantern wuz. De river wuz arisin' en dey wuz a good current; so I reck'n'd 'at by fo' in de mawnin' I'd be twenty-five mile down de river, en den I'd slip in, jis' b'fo' daylight, en swim asho' en take to de woods on de Illinoi side.

"But I didn' have no luck. When we 'uz mos' down to de head er de islan', a man begin to come aft wid de lantern. I see it warn't no use fer to wait, so I slid overboad, en struck out fer de islan'.[3] Well, I had a notion I could lan' mos' anywhers, but I couldn't— bank too bluff. I 'uz mos' to de foot er de islan' b'fo' I foun' a good place. I went into de woods en jedged I wouldn' fool wid raffs no mo', long as dey move de lantern roun' so. I had my pipe en a plug er dog-leg,[4] en some matches in my cap, en dey warn't wet, so I 'uz all right."

"And so you ain't had no meat nor bread to eat all this time? Why didn't you get mud-turkles?"

"How you gwyne to git'm? You can't slip up on um en grab um; en how's a body gwyne to hit um wid a rock? How could a body do it in de night? en I warn't gwyne to show myself on de bank in de daytime."

"Well, that's so. You've had to keep in the woods all the time,

3. Huck earlier locates Jackson's Island only a quarter of a mile from the Illinois shore. What is to prevent Jim from later crossing that short space to free soil? By Illinois law, Negroes without freedom papers were subject to arrest and indentured labor. But the risks of going down river into slave territory seem greater still. In Chapter XV, Huck and Jim are said to be heading for the southern tip of Illinois in order to turn northward up the Ohio River. Yet to go against the current, they plan to take a public steamboat past slave territory on the Kentucky side. One answer is that, given the geography, Clemens's narrative would have stalled at the outset without this disguised improbability. Readers forget in the controversy over the ending how skillfully Clemens's art makes them suspend disbelief in the beginning.
4. Chewing tobacco.

of course. Did you heaɪ 'eɪn shooting the cannon?"

"Oh, yes. I knowed dey was aɪteɪ you. I see um go by heah; watched um thoo de bushes."

Some young birds come along, flying a yard or two at a time and lighting. Jim said it was a sign it was going to rain. He said it was a sign when young chickens flew that way, and so he reckoned it was the same way when young birds done it. I was going to catch some of them, but Jim wouldn't let me. He said it was death. He said his father laid mighty sick once, and some of them catched a bird, and his old granny said his father would die, and he did.

And Jim said you mustn't count the things you are going to cook for dinner, because that would bring bad luck. The same if you shook the table-cloth after sundown. And he said if a man owned a bee-hive, and that man died, the bees must be told about it before sun-up next morning, or else the bees would all weaken down and quit work and die. Jim said bees wouldn't sting idiots; but I didn't believe that, because I had tried them lots of times myself, and they wouldn't sting me.

I had heard about some of these things before, but not all of them. Jim knowed all kinds of signs. He said he knowed most everything. I said it looked to me like all the signs was about bad luck, and so I asked him if there warn't any good-luck signs. He says:

"Mighty few—an' *dey* ain' no use to a body. What you want to know when good luck's a-comin' for? want to keep it off?" And he said: "Ef you's got hairy arms en a hairy breas', it's a sign dat you's agwyne to be rich. Well, dey's some use in a sign like dat, 'kase it's so fur ahead. You see, maybe you's got to be po' a long time fust, en so you might git discourage' en kill yo'sef 'f you didn' know by de sign dat you gwyne to be rich bymeby."

"Have you got hairy arms and a hairy breast, Jim?"

"What's de use to ax dat question? don' you see I has?"

"Well, are you rich?"

"No, but I ben rich wunst, and gwyne to be rich agin. Wunst I had foteen dollars, but I tuck to specalat'n', en got busted out."

"What did you speculate in, Jim?"

"Well, fust I tackled stock."

"What kind of stock?"

"Why, live stock. Cattle, you know. I put ten dollars in a cow. But I ain't gwyne to resk no mo' money in stock. De cow up 'n' died on my han's."

"So you lost the ten dollars."

"No, I didn' lose it all. I on'y los' 'bout nine of it. I sole de hide en taller for a dollar en ten cents."

"You had five dollars and ten cents left. Did you speculate any more?"

"Yes. You know dat one-laigged nigger dat b'longs to old Misto

Bradish? well, he sot up a bank, en say anybody dat put in a dollar would git fo' dollars mo' at de en' er de year. Well, all de niggers went in, but dey didn' have much. I wuz de on'y one dat had much. So I stuck out for mo' dan fo' dollars, en I said 'f I didn' git it I'd start a bank myself. Well o' course dat nigger want' to keep me out er de business, bekase he say dey warn't business 'nough for two banks, so he say I could put in my five dollars en he pay me thirty-five at de en' er de year.

"So I done it. Den I reck'n'd I'd inves' de thirty-five dollars right off en keep things a-movin'. Dey wuz a nigger name' Bob, dat had ketched a wood-flat,[5] en his marster didn' know it; en I bought it off'n him en told him to take de thirty-five dollars when de en' er de year come; but somebody stole de wood-flat dat night, en nex' day de one-laigged nigger say de bank 's busted. So dey didn' none uv us git no money."

"What did you do with the ten cents, Jim?"

"Well, I 'uz gwyne to spen' it, but I had a dream, en de dream tole me to give it to a nigger name' Balum—Balum's Ass dey call him for short, he's one er dem chuckle-heads, you know.[6] But he's lucky, dey say, en I see I warn't lucky. De dream say let Balum inves' de ten cents en he'd make a raise for me. Well, Balum he tuck de money, en when he wuz in church he hear de preacher say dat whoever give to de po' len' to de Lord, en boun' to git his money back a hund'd times. So Balum he tuck en give de ten cents to de po', en laid low to see what wuz gwyne to come of it."

"Well, what did come of it, Jim?"

"Nuffn' never come of it. I couldn' manage to k'leck dat money no way; en Balum he couldn'. I ain' gwyne to len' no mo' money 'dout I see de security. Boun' to git yo' money back a hund'd times, de preacher says! Ef I could git de ten *cents* back, I'd call it squah, en be glad er de chanst."

"Well, it's all right, anyway, Jim, long as you're going to be rich again some time or other."

"Yes—en I's rich now, come to look at it. I owns mysef, en I's wuth eight hund'd dollars. I wisht I had de money, I wouldn' want no mo'."

Chapter IX

I wanted to go and look at a place right about the middle of the island, that I'd found when I was exploring; so we started, and soon

5. A flat-bottomed boat for transporting lumber.
6. Sent to curse the Israelites (Numbers 22 : 21–34), Balaam was blind to the presence of God's avenging angel, and the ass was the true seer. Clemens burlesques the prophet's role here, but in Chapter X Jim accurately foretells serious danger.

got to it, because the island was only three miles long and a quarter of a mile wide.

This place was a tolerable long steep hill or ridge, about forty foot high. We had a rough time getting to the top, the sides was so steep and the bushes so thick. We tramped and clumb around all over it, and by-and-by found a good big cavern in the rock, most up to the top on the side towards Illinois. The cavern was as big as two or three rooms bunched together, and Jim could stand up straight in it. It was cool in there. Jim was for putting our traps in there, right away, but I said we didn't want to be climbing up and down there all the time.

Jim said if we had the canoe hid in a good place, and had all the traps in the cavern, we could rush there if anybody was to come to the island, and they would never find us without dogs. And besides, he said them little birds had said it was going to rain, and did I want the things to get wet?

So we went back and got the canoe and paddled up abreast the cavern, and lugged all the traps up there. Then we hunted up a place close by to hide the canoe in, amongst the thick willows. We took some fish off of the lines and set them again, and begun to get ready for dinner.

The door of the cavern was big enough to roll a hogshead in, and on one side of the door the floor stuck out a little bit and was flat and a good place to build a fire on. So we built it there and cooked dinner.

We spread the blankets inside for a carpet, and eat our dinner in there. We put all the other things handy at the back of the cavern. Pretty soon it darkened up and begun to thunder and lighten; so the birds was right about it. Directly it begun to rain, and it rained like all fury, too, and I never see the wind blow so. It was one of these regular summer storms. It would get so dark that it looked all blue-black outside, and lovely; and the rain would thrash along by so thick that the trees off a little ways looked dim and spider-webby; and here would come a blast of wind that would bend the trees down and turn up the pale underside of the leaves; and then a perfect ripper of a gust would follow along and set the branches to tossing their arms as if they was just wild; and next, when it was just about the bluest and blackest—*fst!* it was as bright as glory and you'd have a little glimpse of tree-tops a-plunging about, away off yonder in the storm, hundreds of yards further than you could see before; dark as sin again in a second, and now you'd hear the thunder let go with an awful crash and then go rumbling, grumbling, tumbling down the sky towards the under side of the world, like rolling empty barrels down stairs, where it's long stairs and they bounce a good deal, you know.

"Jim, this is nice," I says. "I wouldn't want to be nowhere else but here. Pass me along another hunk of fish and some hot corn-bread."

"Well, you wouldn't a ben here, 'f it hadn't a ben for Jim. You'd a ben down dah in de woods widout any dinner, en gittn' mos' drownded, too, dat you would, honey. Chickens knows when its gwyne to rain, en so do de birds, chile."

The river went on raising and raising for ten or twelve days, till at last it was over the banks. The water was three or four foot deep on the island in the low places and on the Illinois bottom. On that side it was a good many miles wide; but on the Missouri side it was the same old distance across—a half a mile—because the Missouri shore was just a wall of high bluffs.

Daytimes we paddled all over the island in the canoe. It was mighty cool and shady in the deep woods even if the sun was blazing outside. We went winding in and out amongst the trees; and some-times the vines hung so thick we had to back away and go some other way. Well, on every old broken-down tree, you could see rabbits, and snakes, and such things; and when the island had been overflowed a day or two, they got so tame, on account of being hungry, that you could paddle right up and put your hand on them if you wanted to; but not the snakes and turtles—they would slide off in the water. The ridge our cavern was in, was full of them. We could a had pets enough if we'd wanted them.

One night we catched a little section of a lumber raft—nice pine planks. It was twelve foot wide and about fifteen or sixteen foot long, and the top stood above water six or seven inches, a solid level floor. We could see saw-logs go by in the daylight, sometimes, but we let them go; we didn't show ourselves in daylight.

Another night, when we was up at the head of the island, just before daylight, here comes a frame house down, on the west side. She was a two-story, and tilted over, considerable. We paddled out and got aboard—clumb in at an up-stairs window. But it was too dark to see yet, so we made the canoe fast and set in her to wait for daylight.

The light begun to come before we got to the foot of the island. Then we looked in at the window. We could make out a bed, and a table, and two old chairs, and lots of things around about on the floor; and there was clothes hanging against the wall. There was something laying on the floor in the far corner that looked like a man. So Jim says:

"Hello, you!"

But it didn't budge. So I hollered again, and then Jim says:

"De man ain't asleep—he's dead. You hold still—I'll go en see."

He went and bent down and looked, and says:

"It's a dead man. Yes, indeedy; naked, too. He's ben shot in de back. I reck'n he's ben dead two er three days. Come in, Huck, but doan' look at his face—it's too gashly."

I didn't look at him at all. Jim throwed some old rags over him, but he needn't done it; I didn't want to see him. There was heaps of old greasy cards scattered around over the floor, and old whisky bottles, and a couple of masks made out of black cloth; and all over the walls was the ignorantest kind of words and pictures, made with charcoal. There was two old dirty calico dresses, and a sun-bonnet, and some women's under-clothes, hanging against the wall, and some men's clothing, too. We put the lot into the canoe; it might come good. There was a boy's old speckled straw hat on the floor; I took that too. And there was a bottle that had had milk in it; and it had a rag stopper for a baby to suck. We would a took the bottle, but it was broke. There was a seedy old chest, and an old hair trunk with the hinges broke. They stood open, but there warn't nothing left in them that was any account. The way things was scattered about, we reckoned the people left in a hurry and warn't fixed so as to carry off most of their stuff.

We got an old tin lantern, and a butcher-knife without any handle, and a bran-new Barlow knife[7] worth two bits in any store, and a lot of tallow candles, and a tin candlestick, and a gourd, and a tin cup, and a ratty old bed-quilt off the bed, and a reticule with needles and pins and beeswax and buttons and thread and all such truck in it, and a hatchet and some nails, and a fish-line as thick as my little finger, with some monstrous hooks on it, and a roll of buckskin, and a leather dog-collar, and a horse-shoe, and some vials of medicine that didn't have no label on them; and just as we was leaving I found a tolerable good curry-comb, and Jim he found a ratty old fiddle-bow, and a wooden leg. The straps was broke off of it, but barring that, it was a good enough leg, though it was too long for me and not long enough for Jim, and we couldn't find the other one, though we hunted all around.

And so, take it all around, we made a good haul. When we was ready to shove off, we was a quarter of a mile below the island, and it was pretty broad day; so I made Jim lay down in the canoe and cover up with the quilt, because if he set up, people could tell he was a nigger a good ways off. I paddled over to the Illinois shore, and drifted down most a half a mile doing it. I crept up the dead water under the bank, and hadn't no accidents and didn't see nobody. We got home all safe.

Chapter X

After breakfast I wanted to talk about the dead man and guess out how he come to be killed, but Jim didn't want to. He said it

7. A one-bladed jackknife, named for the inventor.

would fetch bad luck; and besides, he said, he might come and ha'nt us; he said a man that warn't buried was more likely to go a-ha'nting around than one that was planted and comfortable. That sounded pretty reasonable, so I didn't say no more; but I couldn't keep from studying over it and wishing I knowed who shot the man, and what they done it for.

We rummaged the clothes we'd got, and found eight dollars in silver sewed up in the lining of an old blanket overcoat. Jim said he reckoned the people in that house stole the coat, because if they'd a knowed the money was there they wouldn't a left it. I said I reckoned they killed him, too; but Jim didn't want to talk about that. I says:

"Now you think it's bad luck; but what did you say when I fetched in the snake-skin that I found on the top of the ridge day before yesterday? You said it was the worst bad luck in the world to touch a snake-skin with my hands. Well, here's your bad luck! We've raked in all this truck and eight dollars besides. I wish we could have some bad luck like this every day, Jim."

"Never you mind, honey, never you mind. Don't you git too peart. It's a-comin'. Mind I tell you, it's a-comin'."

It did come, too. It was a Tuesday that we had that talk. Well, after dinner Friday, we was laying around in the grass at the upper end of the ridge, and got out of tobacco. I went to the cavern to get some, and found a rattlesnake in there. I killed him, and curled him up on the foot of Jim's blanket, ever so natural, thinking there'd be some fun when Jim found him there. Well, by night I forgot all about the snake, and when Jim flung himself down on the blanket while I struck a light, the snake's mate was there, and bit him.

He jumped up yelling, and the first thing the light showed was the varmint curled up and ready for another spring. I laid him out in a second with a stick, and Jim grabbed pap's whisky jug and began to pour it down.

He was barefooted, and the snake bit him right on the heel. That all comes of my being such a fool as to not remember that wherever you leave a dead snake its mate always comes there and curls around it. Jim told me to chop off the snake's head and throw it away, and then skin the body and roast a piece of it. I done it, and he eat it and said it would help cure him. He made me take off the rattles and tie them around his wrist, too. He said that that would help. Then I slid out quiet and throwed the snakes clear away amongst the bushes; for I warn't going to let Jim find out it was all my fault, not if I could help it.

Jim sucked and sucked at the jug, and now and then he got out of his head and pitched around and yelled; but every time he come to himself he went to sucking at the jug again. His foot swelled up pretty big, and so did his leg; but by-and-by the drunk begun to come, and so I judged he was all right; but I'd druther been bit with a snake than pap's whisky.

Jim was laid up for four days and nights. Then the swelling was all gone and he was around again. I made up my mind I wouldn't ever take aholt of a snake-skin again with my hands, now that I see what had come of it. Jim said he reckoned I would believe him next time. And he said that handling a snake-skin was such awful bad luck that maybe we hadn't got to the end of it yet. He said he druther see the new moon over his left shoulder as much as a thousand times than take up a snake-skin in his hand. Well, I was getting to feel that way myself, though I've always reckoned that looking at the new moon over your left shoulder is one of the carelessest and foolishest things a body can do. Old Hank Bunker done it once, and bragged about it; and in less than two years he got drunk and fell off of the shot tower and spread himself out so that he was just a kind of layer, as you may say; and they slid him edgeways between two barn doors for a coffin, and buried him so, so they say, but I didn't see it. Pap told me. But anyway, it all come of looking at the moon that way, like a fool.

Well, the days went along, and the river went down between its banks again; and about the first thing we done was to bait one of the big hooks with a skinned rabbit and set it and catch a cat-fish that was as big as a man, being six foot two inches long, and weighed over two hundred pounds. We couldn't handle him, of course; he would a flung us into Illinois. We just set there and watched him rip and tear around till he drowned. We found a brass button in his stomach, and a round ball, and lots of rubbage. We split the ball open with the hatchet, and there was a spool in it. Jim said he'd had it there a long time, to coat it over so and make a ball of it. It was as big a fish as was ever catched in the Mississippi, I reckon. Jim said he hadn't ever seen a bigger one. He would a been worth a good deal over at the village. They peddle out such a fish as that by the pound in the market house there; everybody buys some of him; his meat's as white as snow and makes a good fry.

Next morning I said it was getting slow and dull, and I wanted to get a stirring up, some way. I said I reckoned I would slip over the river and find out what was going on. Jim liked that notion; but he said I must go in the dark and look sharp. Then he studied it over and said, couldn't I put on some of them old things and dress up like a girl? That was a good notion, too. So we shortened up one of the calico gowns and I turned up my trowser-legs to my knees and got into it. Jim hitched it behind with the hooks, and it was a fair fit. I put on the sun-bonnet and tied it under my chin, and then for a body to look in and see my face was like looking down a joint of stove-pipe. Jim said nobody would know me, even in the daytime, hardly. I practiced around all day to get the hang of the things, and by-and-by I could do pretty well in them, only Jim said I didn't walk like a girl; and he said I must quit pulling up my gown to get at my britches pocket. I took notice, and done better.

I started up the Illinois shore in the canoe just after dark.

I started across to the town from a little below the ferry landing, and the drift of the current fetched me in at the bottom of the town. I tied up and started along the bank. There was a light burning in a little shanty that hadn't been lived in for a long time, and I wondered who had took up quarters there. I slipped up and peeped in at the window. There was a woman about forty year old in there, knitting by a candle that was on a pine table. I didn't know her face; she was a stranger, for you couldn't start a face in that town that I didn't know. Now this was lucky, because I was weakening; I was getting afraid I had come; people might know my voice and find me out. But if this woman had been in such a little town two days she could tell me all I wanted to know; so I knocked at the door, and made up my mind I wouldn't forget I was a girl.

Chapter XI

"Come in," says the woman, and I did. She says:

"Take a cheer."

I done it. She looked me all over with her little shiny eyes, and says:

"What might your name be?"

"Sarah Williams."

"Where 'bouts do you live? In this neighborhood?"

"No'm. In Hookerville, seven mile below. I've walked all the way and I'm all tired out."

"Hungry, too, I reckon. I'll find you something."

"No'm, I ain't hungry. I was so hungry I had to stop two mile below here at a farm; so I ain't hungry no more. It's what makes me so late. My mother's down sick, and out of money and everything, and I come to tell my uncle Abner Moore. He lives at the upper end of the town, she says. I hain't ever been here before. Do you know him?"

"No; but I don't know everybody yet. I haven't lived here quite two weeks. It's a considerable ways to the upper end of the town. You better stay here all night. Take off your bonnet."

"No," I says, "I'll rest a while, I reckon, and go on. I ain't afeard of the dark."

She said she wouldn't let me go by myself, but her husband would be in by-and-by, maybe in a hour and a half, and she'd send him along with me. Then she got to talking about her husband, and about her relations up the river, and her relations down the river, and about how much better off they used to was, and how they didn't know but they'd made a mistake coming to our town, instead of letting well alone—and so on and so on, till I was afeard *I* had made a mistake coming to her to find out what was going on in the town; but by-and-by she dropped onto pap and the murder, and then I was pretty willing to let her clatter right along. She told about me and Tom Sawyer finding the six thousand dollars[8] (only she got it ten) and all about pap and what a hard lot he was, and what a hard lot I was, and at last she got down to where I was murdered. I says:

"Who done it? We've heard considerable about these goings on, down in Hookerville, but we don't know who 'twas that killed Huck Finn."

"Well, I reckon there's a right smart chance of people *here* that'd like to know who killed him. Some thinks old Finn done it himself."

"No—is that so?"

"Most everybody thought it at first. He'll never know how nigh he come to getting lynched. But before night they changed around and judged it was done by a runaway nigger named Jim."

"Why *he*—"

I stopped. I reckoned I better keep still. She run on, and never noticed I had put in at all.

"The nigger run off the very night Huck Finn was killed. So there's a reward out for him—three hundred dollars. And there's a reward out for old Finn too—two hundred dollars. You see, he come to town the morning after the murder, and told about it, and was out with 'em on the ferry-boat hunt, and right away after he up and left. Before night they wanted to lynch him, but he was gone, you see. Well, next day they found out the nigger was gone; they found out he hadn't ben seen sence ten o'clock the night the murder was done. So then they put it on him, you see, and while they was full of it, next day back comes old Finn and went boo-hooing to Judge Thatcher to get money to hunt for the nigger all over Illinois with. The judge give him some, and that evening he got drunk and was around till after midnight with a couple of mighty hard looking strangers, and then went off with them. Well,

8. Unless he meant $6,000 *each*, Clemens forgot that both Chapter I and *Tom* *Sawyer* fix the amount the boys found at $12,000.

he hain't come back sence, and they ain't looking for him back till this thing blows over a little, for people thinks now that he killed his boy and fixed things so folks would think robbers done it, and then he'd get Huck's money without having to bother a long time with a lawsuit. People do say he warn't any too good to do it. Oh, he's sly, I reckon. If he don't come back for a year, he'll be all right. You can't prove anything on him, you know; everything will be quieted down then, and he'll walk into Huck's money as easy as nothing."

"Yes, I reckon so, 'm. I don't see nothing in the way of it. Has everybody quit thinking the nigger done it?"

"Oh, no, not everybody. A good many thinks he done it. But they'll get the nigger pretty soon, now, and maybe they can scare it out of him."

"Why, are they after him yet?"

"Well, you're innocent, ain't you! Does three hundred dollars lay round every day for people to pick up? Some folks thinks the nigger ain't far from here. I'm one of them—but I hain't talked it around. A few days ago I was talking with an old couple that lives next door in the log shanty, and they happened to say hardly anybody ever goes to that island over yonder that they call Jackson's Island. Don't anybody live there? says I. No, nobody, says they. I didn't say any more, but I done some thinking. I was pretty near certain I'd seen smoke over there, about the head of the island, a day or two before that, so I says to myself, like as not that nigger's hiding over there; anyway, says I, it's worth the trouble to give the place a hunt. I hain't seen any smoke sence, so I reckon maybe he's gone, if it was him; but husband's going over to see—him and another man. He was gone up the river; but he got back to-day and I told him as soon as he got here two hours ago."

I had got so uneasy I couldn't set still. I had to do something with my hands; so I took up a needle off of the table and went to threading it. My hands shook, and I was making a bad job of it. When the woman stopped talking, I looked up, and she was looking at me pretty curious, and smiling a little. I put down the needle and thread and let on to be interested—and I was, too—and says:

"Three hundred dollars is a power of money. I wish my mother could get it. Is your husband going over there to-night?"

"Oh, yes. He went up town with the man I was telling you of, to get a boat and see if they could borrow another gun. They'll go over after midnight."

"Couldn't they see better if they was to wait till daytime?"

"Yes. And couldn't the nigger see better, too? After midnight he'll likely be asleep, and they can slip around through the woods and hunt up his camp fire all the better for the dark, if he's got one."

"I didn't think of that."

The woman kept looking at me pretty curious, and I didn't feel a bit comfortable. Pretty soon she says:

"What did you say your name was, honey?"

"M—Mary Williams."

Somehow it didn't seem to me that I said it was Mary before, so I didn't look up; seemed to me I said it was Sarah; so I felt sort of cornered, and was afeared maybe I was looking it, too. I wished the woman would say something more; the longer she set still, the uneasier I was. But now she says:

"Honey, I thought you said it was Sarah when you first come in?"

"Oh, yes'm, I did. Sarah Mary Williams. Sarah's my first name. Some calls me Sarah, some calls me Mary."

"Oh, that's the way of it?"

"Yes'm."

I was feeling better, then, but I wished I was out of there, anyway. I couldn't look up yet.

Well, the woman fell to talking about how hard times was, and how poor they had to live, and how the rats was as free as if they owned the place, and so forth, and so on, and then I got easy again. She was right about the rats. You'd see one stick his nose out of a hole in the corner every little while. She said she had to have things handy to throw at them when she was alone, or they wouldn't give her no peace. She showed me a bar of lead, twisted up into a knot, and said she was a good shot with it generly, but she'd wrenched her arm a day or two ago, and didn't know whether she could throw true, now. But she watched for a chance, and directly she banged away at a rat, but she missed him wide, and said "Ouch!" it hurt her arm so. Then she told me to try for the next one. I wanted to be getting away before the old man got back, but of course I didn't let on. I got the thing, and the first rat that showed his nose I let drive, and if he'd a stayed where he was he'd a been a tolerable sick rat. She said that that was first-rate, and she reckoned I would hive the next one. She went and got the lump of lead and fetched it back and brought along a hank of yarn, which she wanted me to help her with. I held up my two hands and she put the hank over them and went on talking about her and her husband's matters. But she broke off to say:

"Keep your eye on the rats. You better have the lead in your lap, handy."

So she dropped the lump into my lap, just at that moment, and I clapped my legs together on it and she went on talking. But only about a minute. Then she took off the hank and looked me straight in the face, but very pleasant, and says:

"Come, now—what's your real name?"

"Wh-what, mum?"

"What's your real name? Is it Bill, or Tom, or Bob?—or what is it?"

I reckon I shook like a leaf, and I didn't know hardly what to do. But I says:

"Please to don't poke fun at a poor girl like me, mum. If I'm in the way, here, I'll—"

"No, you won't. Set down and stay where you are. I ain't going to hurt you, and I ain't going to tell on you, nuther. You just tell me your secret, and trust me. I'll keep it; and what's more, I'll help you. So'll my old man, if you want him to. You see, you're a run-away 'prentice—that's all. It ain't anything. There ain't any harm in it. You've been treated bad, and you made up your mind to cut. Bless you, child, I wouldn't tell on you. Tell me all about it, now —that's a good boy."

So I said it wouldn't be no use to try to play it any longer, and I would just make a clean breast and tell her everything, but she mustn't go back on her promise. Then I told her my father and mother was dead, and the law had bound me out to a mean old farmer in the country thirty mile back from the river, and he treated me so bad I couldn't stand it no longer; he went away to be gone a couple of days, and so I took my chance and stole some of his daughter's old clothes, and cleared out, and I had been three nights coming the thirty miles; I traveled nights, and hid day-times and slept, and the bag of bread and meat I carried from home lasted me all the way and I had a plenty. I said I believed my uncle Abner Moore would take care of me, and so that was why I struck out for this town of Goshen."

"Goshen, child? This ain't Goshen. This is St. Petersburg. Goshen's ten mile further up the river. Who told you this was Goshen?"

"Why, a man I met at day-break this morning, just as I was going to turn into the woods for my regular sleep. He told me when the roads forked I must take the right hand, and five mile would fetch me to Goshen."

"He was drunk I reckon. He told you just exactly wrong."

"Well, he did act like he was drunk, but it ain't no matter now. I got to be moving along. I'll fetch Goshen before day-light."

"Hold on a minute. I'll put you up a snack to eat. You might want it."

So she put me up a snack, and says:

"Say—when a cow's laying down, which end of her gets up first?

Answer up prompt, now—don't stop to study over it. Which end gets up first?"

"The hind end, mum."

"Well, then, a horse?"

"The for'rard end, mum."

"Which side of a tree does the most moss grow on?"

"North side."

"If fifteen cows is browsing on a hillside, how many of them eats with their heads pointed the same direction?"

"The whole fifteen, mum."

"Well, I reckon you *have* lived in the country. I thought maybe you was trying to hocus me again. What's your real name, now?"

"George Peters, mum."

"Well, try to remember it, George. Don't forget and tell me it's Elexander before you go, and then get out by saying it's George-Elexander when I catch you. And don't go about women in that old calico. You do a girl tolerable poor, but you might fool men, maybe. Bless you, child, when you set out to thread a needle, don't hold the thread still and fetch the needle up to it; hold the needle still and poke the thread at it—that's the way a woman most always does; but a man always does 'tother way. And when you throw at a rat or anything, hitch yourself up a tip-toe, and fetch your hand up over your head as awkard as you can, and miss your rat about six or seven foot. Throw stiff-armed from the shoulder, like there was a pivot there for it to turn on—like a girl; not from the wrist and elbow, with your arm out to one side, like a boy. And mind you, when a girl tries to catch anything in her lap, she throws her knees apart; she don't clap them together, the way you did when you catched the lump of lead. Why, I spotted you for a boy when you was threading the needle; and I contrived the other things just to make certain. Now trot along to your uncle, Sarah Mary Williams George Elexander Peters, and if you get into trouble you send word to Mrs. Judith Loftus, which is me, and I'll do what I can to get you out of it. Keep the river road, all the way, and next time you tramp, take shoes and socks with you. The river road's a rocky one, and your feet 'll be in a condition when you get to Goshen, I reckon."

I went up the bank about fifty yards, and then I doubled on my tracks and slipped back to where my canoe was, a good piece below the house. I jumped in and was off in a hurry. I went up stream far enough to make the head of the island, and then started across. I took off the sun-bonnet, for I didn't want no blinders on, then. When I was about the middle, I hear the clock begin to strike; so I stops and listens; the sound come faint over the water, but clear —eleven. When I struck the head of the island I never waited to blow, though I was most winded, but I shoved right into the timber where my old camp used to be, and started a good fire there on a high-and-dry spot.

Then I jumped in the canoe and dug out for our place a mile and a half below, as hard as I could go. I landed, and slopped through the timber and up the ridge and into the cavern. There Jim laid, sound asleep on the ground. I roused him out and says:

"Git up and hump yourself, Jim! There ain't a minute to lose. They're after us!"

Jim never asked no questions, he never said a word; but the way he worked for the next half an hour showed about how he was scared. By that time everything we had in the world was on our raft and she was ready to be shoved out from the willow cove where she was hid. We put out the camp fire at the cavern the first thing, and didn't show a candle outside after that.

I took the canoe out from shore a little piece and took a look, but if there was a boat around I couldn't see it, for stars and shadows ain't good to see by. Then we got out the raft and slipped along down in the shade, past the foot of the island dead still, never saying a word.

Chapter XII

It must a been close onto one o'clock when we got below the island at last, and the raft did seem to go mighty slow. If a boat was to come along, we was going to take to the canoe and break for the Illinois shore; and it was well a boat didn't come, for we hadn't ever thought to put the gun into the canoe, or a fishing-line or anything to eat. We was in ruther too much of a sweat to think of so many things. It warn't good judgment to put *everything* on the raft.

If the men went to the island, I just expect they found the camp fire I built, and watched it all night for Jim to come. Anyways, they stayed away from us, and if my building the fire never fooled them it warn't no fault of mine. I played it as low-down on them as I could.

When the first streak of day begun to show, we tied up to a tow-head in a big bend on the Illinois side, and hacked off cotton-wood branches with the hatchet and covered up the raft with them so she looked like there had been a cave-in in the bank there. A tow-head is a sand-bar that has cotton-woods on it as thick as harrow-teeth.

We had mountains on the Missouri shore and heavy timber on the Illinois side, and the channel was down the Missouri shore at that place, so we warn't afraid of anybody running across us. We laid there all day and watched the rafts and steamboats spin down the Missouri shore, and up-bound steamboats fight the big river in the middle. I told Jim all about the time I had jabbering with that woman; and Jim said she was a smart one, and if she was to start after us herself *she* wouldn't set down and watch a camp fire—no, sir, she'd fetch a dog. Well, then, I said, why couldn't she tell her husband to fetch a dog? Jim said he bet she did think of it by the time the men was ready to start, and he believed they must a gone up town to get a dog and so they lost all that time, or else we wouldn't be here on a tow-head sixteen or seventeen mile below the village—no, indeedy, we would be in that same old town again. So I said I didn't care what was the reason they didn't get us, as long as they didn't.

When it was beginning to come on dark, we poked our heads out of the cottonwood thicket and looked up, and down, and across; nothing in sight; so Jim took up some of the top planks of the raft and built a snug wigwam to get under in blazing weather and rainy, and to keep the things dry. Jim made a floor for the wigwam, and raised it a foot or more above the level of the raft, so now the blankets and all the traps was out of the reach of steamboat waves. Right in the middle of the wigwam we made a layer of dirt about five or six inches deep with a frame around it for to hold it to its place; this was to build a fire on in sloppy weather or chilly; the wigwam would keep it from being seen. We made an extra steering oar, too, because one of the others might get broke, on a snag or something. We fixed up a short forked stick to hang the old lantern on; because we must always light the lantern whenever we see a steamboat coming down stream, to keep from getting run over; but we wouldn't have to light it up for upstream boats unless we see we was in what they call a "crossing;" for the river was pretty high yet, very low banks being still a little under water; so up-bound boats didn't always run the channel, but hunted easy water.

This second night we run between seven and eight hours, with a current that was making over four mile an hour. We catched fish, and talked, and we took a swim now and then to keep off sleepiness. It was kind of solemn, drifting down the big still river, laying on our backs looking up at the stars, and we didn't ever feel like talking loud, and it warn't often that we laughed, only a little kind of a low chuckle. We had mighty good weather, as a general thing, and nothing ever happened to us at all, that night, nor the next, nor the next.

Every night we passed towns, some of them away up on black hillsides, nothing but just a shiny bed of lights, not a house could you see. The fifth night we passed St. Louis, and it was like the whole world lit up. In St. Petersburg they used to say there was twenty or thirty thousand people in St. Louis, but I never believed it till I see that wonderful spread of lights at two o'clock that still night. There warn't a sound there; everybody was asleep.

Every night, now, I used to slip ashore, towards ten o'clock, at some little village, and buy ten or fifteen cents' worth of meal or bacon or other stuff to eat; and sometimes I lifted a chicken that warn't roosting comfortable, and took him along. Pap always said, take a chicken when you get a chance, because if you don't want him yourself you can easy find somebody that does, and a good deed ain't ever forgot. I never see Pap when he didn't want the chicken himself, but that is what he used to say, anyway.

Mornings, before daylight, I slipped into corn fields and borrowed a watermelon, or a mushmelon, or a punkin, or some new corn, or things of that kind. Pap always said it warn't no harm to borrow things, if you was meaning to pay them back, sometime; but the widow said it warn't anything but a soft name for stealing, and no decent body would do it. Jim said he reckoned the widow was partly right and pap was partly right; so the best way would be for us to pick out two or three things from the list and say we wouldn't borrow them any more—then he reckoned it wouldn't be no harm to borrow the others. So we talked it over all one night, drifting along down the river, trying to make up our minds whether to drop the watermelons, or the cantelopes, or the mushmelons, or what. But towards daylight we got it all settled satisfactory, and concluded to drop crabapples and p'simmons. We warn't feeling just right, before that, but it was all comfortable now. I was glad the way it come out, too, because crabapples ain't ever good, and the p'simmons wouldn't be ripe for two or three months yet.

We shot a water-fowl, now and then, that got up too early in the morning or didn't go to bed early enough in the evening. Take it all around, we lived pretty high.

The fifth night below St. Louis we had a big storm after midnight, with a power of thunder and lightning, and the rain poured down in a solid sheet. We stayed in the wigwam and let the raft take care of itself. When the lightning glared out we could see a big straight river ahead, and high rocky bluffs on both sides. By-and-by says I, "Hel-*lo*, Jim, looky yonder!" It was a steamboat that had killed herself on a rock. We was drifting straight down for her. The lightning showed her very distinct. She was leaning over, with part of her upper deck above water, and you could see every little chimbly-guy[9] clean and clear, and a chair by the big bell, with an old slouch hat hanging on the back of it when the flashes come.

Well, it being away in the night, and stormy, and all so mysterious-like, I felt just the way any other boy would a felt when I

9. Wires bracing the chimneys.

see that wreck laying there so mournful and lonesome in the middle of the river. I wanted to get aboard of her and slink around a little, and see what there was there. So I says:

"Le's land on her, Jim."

But Jim was dead against it, at first. He says:

"I doan' want to go fool'n 'long er no wrack. We's doin' blame' well, en we better let blame' well alone, as de good book says. Like as not dey's a watchman on dat wrack."

"Watchman your grandmother," I says; "there ain't nothing to watch but the texas[1] and the pilot-house; and do you reckon anybody's going to resk his life for a texas and a pilot-house such a night as this, when it's likely to break up and wash off down the river any minute?" Jim couldn't say nothing to that, so he didn't try. "And besides," I says, "we might borrow something worth having, out of the captain's stateroom. Seegars, I bet you—and cost five cents apiece, solid cash. Steamboat captains is always rich, and get sixty dollars a month, and *they* don't care a cent what a thing costs, you know, long as they want it. Stick a candle in your pocket; I can't rest, Jim, till we give her a rummaging. Do you reckon Tom Sawyer would ever go by this thing? Not for pie, he wouldn't. He'd call it an adventure—that's what he'd call it; and he'd land on that wreck if it was his last act. And wouldn't he throw style into it?—wouldn't he spread himself, nor nothing? Why, you'd think it was Christopher C'lumbus discovering Kingdom-Come. I wish Tom Sawyer *was* here."

Jim he grumbled a little, but give in. He said we mustn't talk any more than we could help, and then talk mighty low. The lightning showed us the wreck again, just in time, and we fetched the starboard derrick, and made fast there.

The deck was high out, here. We went sneaking down the slope of it to labboard, in the dark, towards the texas, feeling our way slow with our feet, and spreading our hands out to fend off the guys, for it was so dark we couldn't see no sign of them. Pretty soon we struck the forward end of the skylight, and clumb onto it; and the next step fetched us in front of the captain's door, which was open, and by Jimminy, away down through the texas-hall we see a light! and all in the same second we seem to hear low voices in yonder!

Jim whispered and said he was feeling powerful sick, and told me to come along. I says, all right; and was going to start for the raft; but just then I heard a voice wail out and say:

"Oh, please don't, boys; I swear I won't ever tell!"

Another voice said, pretty loud:

---

1. Officers' cabin (so-called because it was the largest) on the upper deck of the steamboat, with the pilothouse before or on top.

"It's a lie, Jim Turner. You've acted this way before. You always want more'n your share of the truck, and you've always got it, too, because you've swore 't if you didn't you'd tell. But this time you've said it jest one time too many. You're the meanest, treacherousest hound in this country."

By this time Jim was gone for the raft. I was just a-biling with curiosity; and I says to myself, Tom Sawyer wouldn't back out now, and so I won't either; I'm agoing to see what's going on here. So I dropped on my hands and knees, in the little passage, and crept aft in the dark, till there warn't but about one stateroom betwixt me and the cross-hall of the texas. Then, in there I see a man stretched on the floor and tied hand and foot, and two men standing over him, and one of them had a dim lantern in his hand, and the other one had a pistol. This one kept pointing the pistol at the man's head on the floor and saying—

"I'd *like* to! And I orter, too, a mean skunk!"

The man on the floor would shrivel up, and say: "Oh, please don't, Bill—I hain't ever goin' to tell."

And every time he said that, the man with the lantern would laugh, and say:

" 'Deed you *ain't!* You never said no truer thing 'n that, you bet you." And once he said: "Hear him beg! and yit if we hadn't got the best of him and tied him, he'd a killed us both. And what *for?* Jist for noth'n. Jist because we stood on our *rights*—that's what for. But I lay you ain't agoin' to threaten nobody any more, Jim Turner. Put *up* that pistol, Bill."

Bill says:

"I don't want to, Jake Packard. I'm for killin' him—and didn't he kill old Hatfield jist the same way—and don't he deserve it?"

"But I don't *want* him killed, and I've got my reasons for it."

"Bless yo' heart for them words, Jake Packard! I'll never forgit you, long's I live!" says the man on the floor, sort of blubbering.

Packard didn't take no notice of that, but hung up his lantern on a nail, and started towards where I was, there in the dark, and motioned Bill to come. I crawfished[2] as fast as I could, about two yards, but the boat slanted so that I couldn't make very good time; so to keep from getting run over and catched I crawled into a stateroom on the upper side. The man come a-pawing along in the dark, and when Packard got to my stateroom, he says:

"Here—come in here."

And in he come, and Bill after him. But before they got in, I was up in the upper berth, cornered, and sorry I come. Then they stood there, with their hands on the ledge of the berth, and

2. Crawled backward.

talked. I couldn't see them, but I could tell where they was, by the whisky they'd been having. I was glad I didn't drink whisky; but it wouldn't made much difference, anyway, because most of the time they couldn't a treed me because I didn't breathe. I was too scared. And besides, a body *couldn't* breathe, and hear such talk. They talked low and earnest. Bill wanted to kill Turner. He says:

"He's said he'll tell, and he will. If we was to give both our shares to him *now*, it wouldn't make no difference after the row, and the way we've served him. Shore's you're born, he'll turn State's evidence; now you hear *me*. I'm for putting him out of his troubles."

"So'm I," says Packard, very quiet.

"Blame it, I'd sorter begun to think you wasn't. Well, then, that's all right. Les' go and do it."

"Hold on a minute; I hain't had my say yit. You listen to me. Shooting's good, but there's quieter ways if the thing's *got* to be done. But what *I* say, is this; it ain't good sense to go court'n around after a halter, if you can git at what you're up to in some way that's jist as good and at the same time don't bring you into no resks. Ain't that so?"

"You bet it is. But how you goin' to manage it this time?"

"Well, my idea is this: we'll rustle around and gether up whatever pickins we've overlooked in the staterooms, and shove for shore and hide the truck. Then we'll wait. Now I say it ain't agoin' to be more 'n two hours befo' this wrack breaks up and washes off down the river. See? He'll be drownded, and won't have nobody to blame for it but his own self. I reckon that's a considerble sight better'n killin' of him. I'm unfavorable to killin' a man as long as you can git around it; it ain't good sense, it ain't good morals. Ain't I right?"

"Yes—I reck'n you are. But s'pose she *don't* break up and wash off?"

"Well, we can wait the two hours, anyway, and see, can't we?"

"All right, then; come along."

So they started, and I lit out, all in a cold sweat, and scrambled forward. It was dark as pitch there; but I said in a kind of a coarse whisper, "Jim!" and he answered up, right at my elbow, with a sort of a moan, and I says:

"Quick, Jim, it ain't no time for fooling around and moaning; there's a gang of murderers in yonder, and if we don't hunt up their boat and set her drifting down the river so these fellows can't get away from the wreck, there's one of 'em going to be in a bad fix. But if we find their boat we can put *all* of 'em in a bad fix—for the Sheriff 'll get 'em. Quick—hurry! I'll hunt the labboard side, you hunt the stabboard. You start at the raft, and—"

"Oh, my lordy, lordy! *Raf'?* Dey ain' no raf' no mo', she done broke loose en gone!—'en here we is!"

Chapter XIII

Well, I catched my breath and most fainted. Shut up on a wreck with such a gang as that! But it warn't no time to be sentimentering. We'd *got* to find that boat, now—had to have it for ourselves. So we went a-quaking and shaking down the stabboard side, and slow work it was, too—seemed a week before we got to the stern. No sign of a boat. Jim said he didn't believe he could go any further—so scared he hadn't hardly any strength left, he said. But I said come on, if we get left on this wreck, we are in a fix, sure. So on we prowled, again. We struck for the stern of the texas, and found it, and then scrabbled along forwards on the skylight, hanging on from shutter to shutter, for the edge of the skylight was in the water. When we got pretty close to the cross-hall door there was the skiff, sure enough! I could just barely see her. I felt ever so thankful. In another second I would a been aboard of her; but just then the door opened. One of the men stuck his head out, only about a couple of foot from me, and I thought I was gone; but he jerked it in again, and says:

"Heave that blame lantern out o' sight, Bill!"

He flung a bag of something into the boat, and then got in himself, and set down. It was Packard. Then Bill *he* come out and got in. Packard says, in a low voice:

"All ready—shove off!"

I couldn't hardly hang onto the shutters, I was so weak. But Bill says:

"Hold on—'d you go through him?"

"No. Didn't you?"

"No. So he's got his share o' the cash, yet."

"Well, then, come along—no use to take truck and leave money."

"Say—won't he suspicion what we're up to?"

"Maybe he won't. But we got to have it anyway. Come along."

So they got out and went in.

The door slammed to, because it was on the careened side; and in a half second I was in the boat, and Jim come a tumbling after me. I out with my knife and cut the rope, and away we went!

We didn't touch an oar, and we didn' speak nor whisper, nor hardly even breathe. We went gliding swift along, dead silent, past the tip of the paddle-box, and past the stern; then in a second or two more we was a hundred yards below the wreck, and the darkness soaked her up, every last sign of her, and we was safe, and knowed it.

When we was three or four hundred yards down stream, we see the lantern show like a little spark at the texas door, for a second, and we knowed by that that the rascals had missed their boat, and was beginning to understand that they was in just as much trouble, now, as Jim Turner was.

Then Jim manned the oars, and we took out after our raft. Now was the first time that I begun to worry about the men—I reckon I hadn't had time to before. I begun to think how dreadful it was, even for murderers, to be in such a fix. I says to myself, there ain't no telling but I might come to be a murderer myself, yet, and then how would *I* like it? So says I to Jim:

"The first light we see, we'll land a hundred yards below it or above it, in a place where it's a good hiding-place for you and the skiff, and then I'll go and fix up some kind of a yarn, and get somebody to go for that gang and get them out of their scrape, so they can be hung when their time comes."

But that idea was a failure; for pretty soon it begun to storm again, and this time worse than ever. The rain poured down, and never a light showed; everybody in bed, I reckon. We boomed along down the river, watching for lights and watching for our raft. After a long time the rain let up, but the clouds staid, and the lightning kept whimpering, and by-and-by a flash showed us a black thing ahead, floating, and we made for it.

It was the raft, and mighty glad was we to get aboard of it again. We seen a light, now, away down to the right, on shore. So I said I would go for it. The skiff was half full of plunder which that gang had stole, there on the wreck. We hustled it onto the raft in a pile, and I told Jim to float along down, and show a light when he judged he had gone about two mile, and keep it burning till I come; then I manned my oars and shoved for the light. As I got down towards it, three or four more showed—up on a hillside. It was a village. I closed in above the shore-light, and laid on my oars and floated. As I went by, I see it was a lantern hanging on the jackstaff of a double-hull ferry-boat. I skimmed around for the watchman, a-wondering whereabouts he slept; and by-and-by I found him roosting on the bitts,[3] forward, with his head down between his knees. I give his shoulder two or three little shoves, and begun to cry.

He stirred up, in a kind of startlish way; but when he see it was only me, he took a good gap and stretch, and then he says:

"Hello, what's up? Don't cry, bub. What's the trouble?"

I says:

"Pap, and mam, and sis, and—"

3. Vertical timbers with ropes strung between.

Then I broke down. He says:

"Oh, dang it, now, *don't* take on so, we all has to have our troubles and this'n 'll come out all right. What's the matter with 'em?"

"They're—they're—are you the watchman of the boat?"

"Yes," he says, kind of pretty-well-satisfied like. "I'm the captain and the owner, and the mate, and the pilot, and watchman, and head deck-hand; and sometimes I'm the freight and passengers. I ain't as rich as old Jim Hornback, and I can't be so blame' generous and good to Tom, Dick and Harry as what he is, and slam around money the way he does; but I've told him a many a time 't I wouldn't trade places with him; for, says I, a sailor's life's the life for me, and I'm derned if *I'd* live two mile out o' town, where there ain't nothing ever goin' on, not for all his spondulicks[4] and as much more on top of it. Says I—"

I broke in and says:

"They're in an awful peck of trouble, and—"

"*Who* is?"

"Why, pap, and mam, and sis, and Miss Hooker; and if you'd take your ferry-boat and go up there—"

"Up where? Where are they?"

"On the wreck."

"What wreck?"

"Why, there ain't but one."

"What, you don't mean the *Walter Scott*?"[5]

"Yes."

"Good land! what are they doin' *there*, for gracious sakes?"

"Well, they didn't go there a-purpose."

"I bet they didn't! Why, great goodness, there ain't no chance for 'em if they don't git off mighty quick! Why, how in the nation did they ever git into such a scrape?"

"Easy enough. Miss Hooker was a-visiting, up there to the town—"

"Yes, Booth's Landing—go on."

"She was a-visiting, there at Booth's Landing, and just in the edge of the evening she started over with her nigger woman in the horse-ferry, to stay all night at her friend's house, Miss What-you-may-call-her, I disremember her name, and they lost their steering-oar, and swung around and went a-floating down, stern-first, about two mile, and saddle-baggsed on the wreck, and the

4. Money, cash.
5. In Chapter XLVI of *Life on the Mississippi* (1883), Clemens charged that *Ivanhoe* and "the Sir Walter disease" practically caused the American Civil War by infesting the South with "sham grandeurs, sham gauds, and sham chivalries." Completing *Huckleberry Finn* at the height of the realistic movement in American literature, he hoped that the romances of Scott and James Fenimore Cooper had permanently foundered like a broken-down steamboat or the antebellum culture Huck encounters on the shore.

ferry man and the nigger woman and the horses was all lost, but Miss Hooker she made a grab and got aboard the wreck. Well, about an hour after dark, we come along down in our trading-scow, and it was so dark we didn't notice the wreck till we was right on it; and so *we* saddle-baggsed; but all of us was saved but Bill Whipple—and oh, he *was* the best cretur!—I most wish't it had been me, I do."

"My George! It's the beatenest thing I ever struck. And *then* what did you all do?"

"Well, we hollered and took on, but it's so wide there, we couldn't make nobody hear. So pap said somebody got to get ashore and get help somehow. I was the only one that could swim, so I made a dash for it, and Miss Hooker she said if I didn't strike help sooner, come here and hunt up her uncle, and he'd fix the thing. I made the land about a mile below, and been fooling along ever since, trying to get people to do something, but they said, 'What, in such a night and such a current? there ain't no sense in it; go for the steam-ferry.' Now if you'll go, and—"

"By Jackson, I'd *like* to, and blame it I don't know but I will; but who in the dingnåtion's agoin' to *pay* for it? Do you reckon your pap—"

"Why *that's* all right. Miss Hooker she told me, *particular*, that her uncle Hornback—"

"Great guns! is *he* her uncle? Looky here, you break for that light over yonder-way, and turn out west when you git there, and about a quarter of a mile out you'll come to the tavern; tell 'em to dart you out to Jim Hornback's and he'll foot the bill. And don't you fool around any, because he'll want to know the news. Tell him I'll have his niece all safe before he can get to town. Hump yourself, now; I'm agoing up around the corner here, to roust out my engineer."

I struck for the light, but as soon as he turned the corner I went back and got into my skiff and bailed her out and then pulled up shore in the easy water about six hundred yards, and tucked myself in among some woodboats; for I couldn't rest easy till I could see the ferry-boat start. But take it all around, I was feeling ruther comfortable on accounts of taking all this trouble for that gang, for not many would a done it. I wished the widow knowed about it. I judged she would be proud of me for helping these rapscallions, because rapscallions and dead beats is the kind the widow and good people takes the most interest in.

Well, before long, here comes the wreck, dim and dusky, sliding along down! A kind of cold shiver went through me, and then I struck out for her. She was very deep, and I see in a minute there warn't much chance for anybody being alive in her. I pulled all around her and hollered a little, but there wasn't any answer; all dead still. I felt a little bit heavy-hearted about the gang, but not much, for I reckoned if they could stand it, I could.

Then here comes the ferry-boat; so I shoved for the middle of the river on a long down-stream slant; and when I judged I was out of eye-reach, I laid on my oars, and looked back and see her go and smell around the wreck for Miss Hooker's remainders, because the captain would know her uncle Hornback would want them; and then pretty soon the ferry-boat give it up and went for shore, and I laid into my work and went a-booming down the river.

It did seem a powerful long time before Jim's light showed up; and when it did show, it looked like it was a thousand mile off. By the time I got there the sky was beginning to get a little gray in the east; so we struck for an island, and hid the raft, and sunk the skiff, and turned in and slept like dead people.

Chapter XIV

By-and-by, when we got up, we turned over the truck the gang had stole off of the wreck, and found boots, and blankets, and clothes, and all sorts of other things, and a lot of books, and a spyglass, and three boxes of seegars. We hadn't ever been this rich before, in neither of our lives. The seegars was prime. We laid off all the afternoon in the woods talking, and me reading the books, and having a general good time. I told Jim all about what happened inside the wreck, and at the ferry-boat; and I said these kinds of things was adventures; but he said he didn't want no more adventures. He said that when I went in the texas and he crawled back to get on the raft and found her gone, he nearly died; because he judged it was all up with *him*, anyway it could be fixed; for if he didn't get saved he would get drownded; and if he did get saved, whoever saved him would send him back home so as to get the reward, and then Miss Watson would sell him South, sure. Well, he was right; he was most always right; he had an uncommon level head, for a nigger.

I read considerable to Jim about kings, and dukes, and earls, and such, and how gaudy they dressed, and how much style they put on, and called each other your majesty, and your grace, and your lordship, and so on, 'stead of mister; and Jim's eyes bugged out, and he was interested. He says:

"I didn' know dey was so many un um. I hain't hearn 'bout none un um, skasely, but ole King Sollermun, onless you counts dem kings dat's in a pack er k'yards. How much do a king git?"

"Get?" I says; "why, they get a thousand dollars a month if they want it; they can have just as much as they want; everything belongs to them."

"*Ain'* dat gay? En what dey got to do, Huck?"

"*They* don't do nothing! Why how you talk. They just set around."

"No—is dat so?"

"Of course it is. They just set around. Except maybe when there 's a war; then they go to the war. But other times they just lazy around; or go hawking—just hawking and sp— Sh!—d' you hear a noise?"

We skipped out and looked; but it warn't nothing but the flutter of a steamboat's wheel, away down coming around the point; so we come back.

"Yes," says I, "and other times, when things is dull, they fuss with the parlyment; and if everybody don't go just so he whacks their heads off. But mostly they hang round the harem."

"Roun' de which?"

"Harem."

"What's de harem?"

"The place where he keep his wives. Don't you know about the harem? Solomon had one; he had about a million wives."

"Why, yes, dat's so; I—I'd done forgot it. A harem's a bo'd'n-house, I reck'n. Mos' likely dey has rackety times in de nussery. En I reck'n de wives quarrels considable; en dat 'crease de racket. Yit dey say Sollermun de wises' man dat ever live'. I doan' take no stock in dat. Bekase why: would a wise man want to live in de mids' er sich a blimblammin' all de time? No—'deed he wouldn't. A wise man 'ud take en buil' a biler-factry; en den he could shet *down* de biler-factry when he want to res'."

"Well, but he *was* the wisest man, anyway; because the widow she told me so, her own self."

"I doan k'yer what de widder say, he *warn't* no wise man, nuther. He had some er de dad-fetchedes' ways I ever see. Does you know 'bout dat chile dat he 'uz gwyne to chop in two?"[6]

"Yes, the widow told me all about it."

"*Well*, den! Warn' dat de beatenes' notion in de worl'? You jes' take en look at it a minute. Dah's de stump, dah—dat's one er de women; heah's you— dat's de yuther one; I's Sollermun; en dish-yer dollar bill's de chile. Bofe un you claims it. What does I do? Does I shin aroun' mongs' de neighbors en fine out which un you de bill *do* b'long to, en han' it over to de right one, all safe en soun', de way dat anybody dat had any gumption would? No—I take en whack de bill in *two*, en give half un it to you, en de yuther half to de yuther woman. Dat's de way Sollermun was gwyne to do wid de chile. Now I want to ast you: what's de use er dat half a bill?—

---

6. I Kings 3 : 16–27. When two women claimed the same newborn son, Solomon threatened to divide him with a sword. The true mother begged the king to give the child to the other woman.

can't buy noth'n wid it. En what use is a half a chile? I would'n give a dern for a million un um."

"But hang it, Jim, you've clean missed the point—blame it, you've missed it a thousand mile."

"Who? Me? Go 'long. Doan' talk to *me* 'bout yo' pints. I reck'n I knows sense when I sees it; en dey ain' no sense in sich doin's as dat. De 'spute warn't 'bout a half a chile, de 'spute was 'bout a whole chile; en de man dat think he kin settle a 'spute 'bout a whole chile wid a half a chile, doan' know enough to come in out'n de rain. Doan' talk to me 'bout Sollermun, Huck, I knows him by de back."

"But I tell you you don't get the point."

"Blame de pint! I reck'n I knows what I knows. En mine you, de *real* pint is down furder—it's down deeper. It lays in de way Sollermun was raised. You take a man dat's got on'y one er two chillen; is dat man gwyne to be waseful o' chillen? No, he ain't; he can't 'ford it. *He* know how to value 'em. But you take a man dat's got 'bout five million chillen runnin' roun' de house, en it's diffunt. *He* as soon chop a chile in two as a cat. Dey's plenty mo'. A chile er two, mo' er less, warn't no consekens to Sollermun, dad fetch him!"

I never see such a nigger. If he got a notion in his head once, there warn't no getting it out again. He was the most down on Solomon of any nigger I ever see. So I went to talking about other kings, and let Solomon slide. I told about Louis Sixteenth that got his head cut off in France long time ago; and about his little boy the dolphin,[7] that would a been a king, but they took and shut him up in jail, and some say he died there.

"Po' little chap."

"But some says he got out and got away, and come to America."

"Dat's good! But he'll be pooty lonesome—dey ain' no kings here, is dey, Huck?"

"No."

"Den he cain't git no situation. What he gwyne to do?"

"Well, I don't know. Some of them gets on the police, and some of them learns people how to talk French."

"Why, Huck, doan' de French people talk de same way we does?"

"*No*, Jim; you couldn't understand a word they said—not a single word."

"Well, now, I be ding-busted! How do dat come?"

"*I* don't know; but it's so. I got some of their jabber out of a

7. The Dauphin, Louis Charles (1785–95?) survived the execution of his father, Louis XVI, in 1793, but almost certainly died in prison. Huck alludes to the persistent legends of his escape and survival. The bogus pedigrees of the king and the duke in Chapter XIX derive from such legends.

book. Spose a man was to come to you and say *Polly-voo-franzy*—
what would you think?"

"I wouldn' think nuff'n; I'd take en bust him over de head. Dat
is, if he warn't white. I wouldn't 'low no nigger to call me dat."

"Shucks, it ain't calling you anything. It's only saying do you
know how to talk French."

"Well, den, why couldn't he *say* it?"

"Why, he *is* a-saying it. That's a Frenchman's *way* of saying it."

"Well, it's a blame' ridicklous way, en I doan' want to hear no
mo' 'bout it. Dey ain' no sense in it."

"Looky here, Jim; does a cat talk like we do?"

"No, a cat don't."

"Well, does a cow?"

"No, a cow don't, nuther."

"Does a cat talk like a cow, or a cow talk like a cat?"

"No, dey don't."

"It's natural and right for 'em to talk different from each other,
ain't it?"

" 'Course."

"And ain't it natural and right for a cat and a cow to talk different from *us?*"

"Why, mos' sholy it is."

"Well, then, why ain't it natural and right for a *Frenchman* to
talk different from us? You answer me that."

"Is a cat a man, Huck?"

"No."

"Well, den, dey ain't no sense in a cat talkin' like a man. Is a
cow a man?—er is a cow a cat?"

"No, she ain't either of them."

"Well, den, she ain' got no business to talk like either one er
the yuther of 'em. Is a Frenchman a man?"

"Yes."

"*Well*, den! Dad blame it, why doan' he *talk* like a man? You
answer me *dat!*"

I see it warn't no use wasting words—you can't learn a nigger to
argue. So I quit.

Chapter XV

We judged that three nights more would fetch us to Cairo,[8] at
the bottom of Illinois, where the Ohio River comes in, and that was
what we was after. We would sell the raft and get on a steamboat
and go way up the Ohio amongst the free States, and then be out
of trouble.

8. Pronounced "Kay-row."

Well, the second night a fog begun to come on, and we made for a tow-head to tie to, for it wouldn't do to try to run in fog; but when I paddled ahead in the canoe, with the line, to make fast, there warn't anything but little saplings to tie to. I passed the line around one of them right on the edge of the cut bank, but there was a stiff current, and the raft come booming down so lively she tore it out by the roots and away she went. I see the fog closing down, and it made me so sick and scared I couldn't budge for most a half a minute it seemed to me—and then there warn't no raft in sight; you couldn't see twenty yards. I jumped into the canoe and run back to the stern and grabbed the paddle and set her back a stroke. But she didn't come. I was in such a hurry I hadn't untied her. I got up and tried to untie her, but I was so excited my hands shook so I couldn't hardly do anything with them.

As soon as I got started I took out after the raft, hot and heavy, right down the tow-head. That was all right as far as it went, but the tow-head warn't sixty yards long, and the minute I flew by the foot of it I shot out into the solid white fog, and hadn't no more idea which way I was going than a dead man.

Thinks I, it won't do to paddle; first I know I'll run into the bank or a tow-head or something; I got to set still and float, and yet it's mighty fidgety business to have to hold your hands still at such a time. I whooped and listened. Away down there, somewheres, I hears a small whoop, and up comes my spirits. I went tearing after it, listening sharp to hear it again. The next time it come, I see I warn't heading for it but heading away to the right of it. And the next time, I was heading away to the left of it—and not gaining on it much, either, for I was flying around, this way and that and 'tother, but it was going straight ahead all the time.

I did wish the fool would think to beat a tin pan, and beat it all the time, but he never did, and it was the still places between the whoops that was making the trouble for me. Well, I fought along, and directly I hears the whoop *behind* me. I was tangled good, now. That was somebody else's whoop, or else I was turned around.

I throwed the paddle down. I heard the whoop again; it was behind me yet, but in a different place; it kept coming, and kept changing its place, and I kept answering, till by-and-by it was in front of me again and I knowed the current had swung the canoe's head down stream and I was all right, if that was Jim and not some other raftsman hollering. I couldn't tell nothing about voices in a fog, for nothing don't look natural nor sound natural in a fog.

The whooping went on, and in about a minute I come a booming down on a cut bank with smoky ghosts of big trees on it, and the current throwed me off to the left and shot by, amongst a lot of snags that fairly roared, the current was tearing by them so swift.

In another second or two it was solid white and still again. I set perfectly still, then, listening to my heart thump, and I reckon I didn't draw a breath while it thumped a hundred.

I just give up, then. I knowed what the matter was. That cut bank was an island, and Jim had gone down 'tother side of it. It warn't no tow-head, that you could float by in ten minutes. It had the big timber of a regular island; it might be five or six mile long and more than a half a mile wide.

I kept quiet, with my ears cocked, about fifteen minutes, I reckon. I was floating along, of course, four or five mile an hour; but you don't ever think of that. No, you *feel* like you are laying dead still on the water; and if a little glimpse of a snag slips by, you don't think to yourself how fast *you're* going, but you catch your breath and think, my! how that snag's tearing along. If you think it ain't dismal and lonesome out in a fog that way, by yourself, in the night, you try it once—you'll see.

Next, for about a half an hour, I whoops now and then; at last I hears the answer a long ways off, and tries to follow it, but I couldn't do it, and directly I judged I'd got into a nest of tow-heads, for I had little dim glimpses of them on both sides of me, sometimes just a narrow channel between; and some that I couldn't see, I knowed was there, because I'd hear the wash of the current against the old dead brush and trash that hung over the banks. Well, I warn't long losing the whoops, down amongst the tow-heads; and I only tried to chase them a little while, anyway, because it was worse than chasing a Jack-o-lantern. You never knowed a sound dodge around so, and swap places so quick and so much.

I had to claw away from the bank pretty lively, four or five times, to keep from knocking the islands out of the river; and so I judged the raft must be butting into the bank every now and then, or else it would get further ahead and clear out of hearing—it was floating a little faster than what I was.

Well, I seemed to be in the open river again, by-and-by, but I couldn't hear no sign of a whoop nowheres. I reckoned Jim had fetched up on a snag, maybe, and it was all up with him. I was good and tired, so I laid down in the canoe and said I wouldn't bother no more. I didn't want to go to sleep, of course; but I was so sleepy I couldn't help it; so I thought I would take just one little cat-nap.

But I reckon it was more than a cat-nap, for when I waked up the stars was shining bright, the fog was all gone, and I was spinning down a big bend stern first. First I didn't know where I was; I thought I was dreaming; and when things begun to come back to me, they seemed to come up dim out of last week.

It was a monstrous big river here, with the tallest and the thickest kind of timber on both banks; just a solid wall, as well as I could see, by the stars. I looked away down stream, and seen a black speck on the water. I took out after it; but when I got to it it warn't nothing but a couple of saw-logs made fast together. Then I see another speck, and chased that; then another, and this time I was right. It was the raft.

When I got to it Jim was setting there with his head down between his knees, asleep, with his right arm hanging over the steering oar. The other oar was smashed off, and the raft was littered up with leaves and branches and dirt. So she'd had a rough time.

I made fast and laid down under Jim's nose on the raft, and begun to gap, and stretch my fists out against Jim, and says:

"Hello, Jim, have I been asleep? Why didn't you stir me up?"

"Goodness gracious, is dat you, Huck? En you ain' dead—you ain' drowned—you's back agin? It's too good for true, honey, it's too good for true. Lemme look at you, chile, lemme feel o' you. No, you ain' dead! you's back agin, 'live en soun', jis de same ole Huck —de same ole Huck, thanks to goodness!"

"What's the matter with you, Jim? You been a drinking?"

"Drinkin'? Has I ben a drinkin'? Has I had a chance to be a drinkin'?"

"Well, then, what makes you talk so wild?"

"How does I talk wild?"

"*How?* why, hain't you been talking about my coming back, and all that stuff, as if I'd been gone away?"

"Huck—Huck Finn, you look me in de eye; look me in de eye. *Hain't* you ben gone away?"

"Gone away? Why, what in the nation do you mean? *I* hain't been gone anywheres. Where would I go to?"

"Well, looky here, boss, dey's sumf'n wrong, dey is. Is I *me*, or who *is* I? Is I heah, or whah *is* I? Now dat's what I wants to know?"

"Well, I think you're here, plain enough, but I think you're a tangle-headed old fool, Jim."

"I is, is I? Well you answer me dis. Didn't you tote out de line in de canoe, fer to make fas' to de tow-head?"

"No, I didn't. What tow-head? I hain't seen no tow-head."

"You hain't seen no tow-head? Looky here—didn't de line pull loose en de raf' go a hummin' down de river, en leave you en de canoe behine in de fog?"

"What fog?"

"Why *de* fog. De fog dat's ben aroun' all night. En didn't you whoop, en didn't I whoop, tell we got mix' up in de islands en one un us got los' en 'tother one was jis' as good as los', 'kase he didn' know whah he wuz? En didn't I bust up agin a lot er dem islands

en have a turrible time en mos' git drownded? Now ain' dat so, boss
—ain't it so? You answer me dat."

"Well, this is too many for me, Jim. I hain't seen no fog, nor no
islands, nor no troubles, nor nothing. I been setting here talking
with you all night till you went to sleep about ten minutes ago, and
I reckon I done the same. You couldn't a got drunk in that time, so
of course you've been dreaming."

"Dad fetch it, how is I gwyne to dream all dat in ten minutes?"

"Well, hang it all, you did dream it, because there didn't any of
it happen."

"But Huck, it's all jis' as plain to me as—"

"It don't make no difference how plain it is, there ain't nothing
in it. I know, because I've been here all the time."

Jim didn't say nothing for about five minutes, but set there studying over it. Then he says:

"Well, den, I reck'n I did dream it, Huck; but dog my cats ef it
ain't de powerfullest dream I ever see. En I hain't ever had no
dream b'fo' dat's tired me like dis one."

"Oh, well, that's all right, because a dream does tire a body like
everything, sometimes. But this one was a staving[9] dream—tell me
all about it, Jim."

So Jim went to work and told me the whole thing right through,
just as it happened, only he painted it up considerable. Then he
said he must start in and " 'terpret" it, because it was sent for a
warning. He said the first tow-head stood for a man that would try
to do us some good, but the current was another man that would get
get us away from him. The whoops was warnings that would come
to us every now and then, and if we didn't try hard to make out to
understand them they'd just take us into bad luck, 'stead of keeping
us out of it. The lot of tow-heads was troubles we was going to get
into with quarrelsome people and all kinds of mean folks, but if
we minded our business and didn't talk back and aggravate them,
we would pull through and get out of the fog and into the big
clear river, which was the free States, and wouldn't have no more
trouble.

It had clouded up pretty dark just after I got onto the raft, but
it was clearing up again, now.

"Oh, well, that's all interpreted well enough, as far as it goes,
Jim," I says; "but what does *these* things stand for?"

It was the leaves and rubbish on the raft, and the smashed oar.
You could see them first rate, now.

Jim looked at the trash, and then looked at me, and back at the
trash again. He had got the dream fixed so strong in his head that
he couldn't seem to shake it loose and get the facts back into its

9. Smashing, vivid.

place again, right away. But when he did get the thing straightened around, he looked at me steady, without ever smiling, and says:

"What do dey stan' for? I's gwyne to tell you. When I got all wore out wid work, en wid de callin' for you, en went to sleep, my heart wuz mos' broke bekase you wuz los', en I didn' k'yer no mo' what become er me en de raf'. En when I wake up en fine you back agin', all safe en soun', de tears come en I could a got down on my knees en kiss yo' foot I's so thankful. En all you wuz thinkin' 'bout wuz how you could make a fool uv ole Jim wid a lie. Dat truck dah is *trash*; en trash is what people is dat puts dirt on de head er dey fren's en makes 'em ashamed."

Then he got up slow, and walked to the wigwam, and went in there, without saying anything but that. But that was enough. It made me feel so mean I could almost kissed *his* foot to get him to take it back.

It was fifteen minutes before I could work myself up to go and humble myself to a nigger—but I done it, and I warn't ever sorry for it afterwards, neither. I didn't do him no more mean tricks, and I wouldn't done that one if I'd a knowed it would make him feel that way.

Chapter XVI

We slept most all day, and started out at night, a little ways behind a monstrous long raft that was as long going by as a procession. She had four long sweeps[1] at each end, so we judged she carried as many as thirty men, likely. She had five big wigwams aboard, wide apart, and an open camp fire in the middle, and a tall flagpole at each end. There was a power of style about her. It *amounted* to something being a raftsman on such a craft as that.

We went drifting down into a big bend, and the night clouded up and got hot. The river was very wide, and was walled with solid timber on both sides; you couldn't see a break in it hardly ever, or a light. We talked about Cairo, and wondered whether we would know it when we got to it. I said likely we wouldn't, because I had heard say there warn't but about a dozen houses there, and if they didn't happen to have them lit up, how was we going to know we was passing a town? Jim said if the two big rivers joined together there, that would show. But I said maybe we might think we was passing the foot of an island and coming into the same old river again. That disturbed Jim—and me too. So the question was, what to do? I said, paddle ashore the first time a light showed, and tell them pap was behind, coming along with a trading-scow, and was

---

1. Oars used with a sweeping motion to propel or steer.

a green hand at the business, and wanted to know how far it was to Cairo. Jim thought it was a good idea, so we took a smoke on it and waited.[2]

There warn't nothing to do, now, but to look out sharp for the town, and not pass it without seeing it. He said he'd be mighty sure to see it, because he'd be a free man the minute he seen it, but if he missed it he'd be in the slave country again and no more show for freedom. Every little while he jumps up and says:

"Dah she is!"

But it warn't. It was Jack-o-lanterns, or lightning-bugs; so he set down again, and went to watching, same as before. Jim said it made him all over trembly and feverish to be so close to freedom. Well, I can tell you it made me all over trembly and feverish, too, to hear him, because I begun to get it through my head that he *was* most free—and who was to blame for it? Why, *me*. I couldn't get that out of my conscience, no how nor no way. It got to troubling me so I couldn't rest; I couldn't stay still in one place. It hadn't ever come home to me before, what this thing was that I was doing. But now it did; and it staid with me, and scorched me more and more. I tried to make out to myself that I warn't to blame, because I didn't run Jim off from his rightful owner; but it warn't no use, conscience up and says, every time, "But you knowed he was running for his freedom, and you could a paddled ashore and told somebody." That was so—I couldn't get around that, noway. That was where it pinched. Conscience says to me, "What had poor Miss Watson done to you, that you could see her nigger go off right under your eyes and never say one single word? What did that poor old woman do to you, that you could treat her so mean? Why, she tried to learn you your book, she tried to learn you your manners, she tried to be good to you every way she knowed how. *That's* what she done."

I got to feeling so mean and so miserable I most wished I was dead. I fidgeted up and down the raft, abusing myself to myself, and Jim was fidgeting up and down past me. We neither of us could keep still. Every time he danced around and says, "Dah's Cairo!" it went through me like a shot, and I thought if it *was* Cairo I reckoned I would die of miserableness.

Jim talked out loud all the time while I was talking to myself. He was saying how the first thing he would do when he got to a free State he would go to saving up money and never spend a single cent, and when he got enough he would buy his wife, which was

---

2. A long passage describing life on the "monstrous" raft followed here in the manuscript. Already published in *Life on the Mississippi*, it was cut to shorten *Huckleberry Finn*. The original "Raftsmen's Passage," as it is now known, may be found beginning on page 233.

owned on a farm close to where Miss Watson lived; and then they would both work to buy the two children, and if their master wouldn't sell them, they'd get an Ab'litionist to go and steal them.

It most froze me to hear such talk. He wouldn't ever dared to talk such talk in his life before. Just see what a difference it made in him the minute he judged he was about free. It was according to the old saying, "give a nigger an inch and he'll take an ell." Thinks I, this is what comes of my not thinking. Here was this nigger which I had as good as helped to run away, coming right out flat-footed and saying he would steal his children—children that belonged to a man I didn't even know; a man that hadn't ever done me no harm.

I was sorry to hear Jim say that, it was such a lowering of him. My conscience got to stirring me up hotter than ever, until at last I says to it, "Let up on me—it ain't too late, yet—I'll paddle ashore at the first light, and tell." I felt easy, and happy, and light as a feather, right off. All my troubles was gone. I went to looking out sharp for a light, and sort of singing to myself. By-and-by one showed. Jim sings out:

"We's safe, Huck, we's safe! Jump up and crack yo' heels, dat's de good ole Cairo at las', I jis knows it!"

I says:

"I'll take the canoe and go see, Jim. It mightn't be, you know."

He jumped and got the canoe ready, and put his old coat in the bottom for me to set on, and give me the paddle; and as I shoved off, he says:

"Pooty soon I'll be a-shout'n for joy, en I'll say, it's all on accounts o' Huck; I's a free man, en I couldn't ever ben free ef it hadn' ben for Huck; Huck done it. Jim won't ever forgit you, Huck; you's de bes' fren' Jim's ever had; en you's de *only* fren' ole Jim's got now."

I was paddling off, all in a sweat to tell on him; but when he says this, it seemed to kind of take the tuck all out of me. I went along slow then, and I warn't right down certain whether I was glad I started or whether I warn't. When I was fifty yards off, Jim says:

"Dah you goes, de ole true Huck; de on'y white genlman dat ever kep' his promise to ole Jim."

Well, I just felt sick. But I says, I *got* to do it—I can't get *out* of it. Right then, along comes a skiff with two men in it, with guns, and they stopped and I stopped. One of them says:

"What's that, yonder?"

"A piece of a raft," I says.

"Do you belong on it?"

"Yes, sir."

"Any men on it?"

"Only one, sir."

"Well, there's five niggers run off to-night, up yonder above the head of the bend. Is your man white or black?"

I didn't answer up prompt. I tried to, but the words wouldn't come. I tried, for a second or two, to brace up and out with it, but I warn't man enough—hadn't the spunk of a rabbit. I see I was weakening; so I just give up trying, and up and says—

"He's white."[3]

"I reckon we'll go and see for ourselves."

"I wish you would," says I, "because it's pap that's there, and maybe you'd help me tow the raft ashore where the light is. He's sick—and so is mam and Mary Ann."

"Oh, the devil! we're in a hurry, boy. But I s'pose we've got to. Come—buckle to your paddle, and let's get along."

I buckled to my paddle and they laid to their oars. When we had made a stroke or two, I says:

"Pap'll be mighty much obleeged to you, I can tell you. Everybody goes away when I want them to help me tow the raft ashore, and I can't do it by myself."

"Well, that's infernal mean. Odd, too. Say, boy, what's the matter with your father?"

"It's the—a—the—well, it ain't anything, much."

They stopped pulling. It warn't but a mighty little ways to the raft, now. One says:

"Boy, that's a lie. What *is* the matter with your pap? Answer up square, now, and it'll be the better for you."

"I will, sir, I will, honest—but don't leave us, please. It's the—the—gentlemen, if you'll only pull ahead, and let me heave you the head-line, you won't have to come a-near the raft—please do."

"Set her back, John, set her back!" says one. They backed water. "Keep away, boy—keep to looard.[4] Confound it, I just expect the wind has blowed it to us. Your pap's got the small-pox, and you know it precious well. Why didn't you come out and say so? Do you want to spread it all over?"

"Well," says I, a-blubbering, "I've told everybody before, and then they just went away and left us."

"Poor devil, there's something in that. We are right down sorry for you, but we—well, hang it, we don't want the small-pox, you see. Look here, I'll tell you what to do. Don't you try to land by yourself, or you'll smash everything to pieces. You float along down about twenty miles and you'll come to a town on the left-hand side of the river. It will be long after sun-up, then, and when you ask for help, you tell them your folks are all down with chills and fever.

3. Huck's triumph over his shore-trained conscience anticipates the great crisis of conscience he will face in Chapter XXXI.
4. Leeward, the side toward which the wind is blowing.

Don't be a fool again, and let people guess what is the matter. Now we're trying to do you a kindness; so you just put twenty miles between us, that's a good boy. It wouldn't do any good to land yonder where the light is—it's only a wood-yard. Say—I reckon your father's poor, and I'm bound to say he's in pretty hard luck. Here —I'll put a twenty dollar gold piece on this board, and you get it when it floats by. I feel mighty mean to leave you, but my kingdom! it won't do to fool with small-pox, don't you see?"

"Hold on, Parker," says the other man, "here's a twenty to put on the board for me. Good-bye boy, you do as Mr. Parker told you, and you'll be all right."

"That's so, my boy—good-bye, good-bye. If you see any runaway niggers, you get help and nab them, and you can make some money by it."

"Good-bye, sir," says I, "I won't let no runaway niggers get by me if I can help it."

They went off, and I got aboard the raft, feeling bad and low, because I knowed very well I had done wrong, and I see it warn't no use for me to try to learn to do right; a body that don't get *started* right when he's little, ain't got no show—when the pinch comes there ain't nothing to back him up and keep him to his work, and so he gets beat. Then I thought a minute, and says to myself, hold on,—s'pose you'd a done right and give Jim up; would you felt better than what you do now? No, says I, I'd feel bad—I'd feel just the same way I do now. Well, then, says I, what's the use you learning to do right, when it's troublesome to do right and ain't no trouble to do wrong, and the wages is just the same? I was stuck. I couldn't answer that. So I reckoned I wouldn't bother no more about it, but after this always do whichever come handiest at the time.

I went into the wigwam; Jim warn't there. I looked all around; he warn't anywhere. I says:

"Jim!"

"Here I is, Huck. Is dey out o' sight yit? Don't talk loud."

He was in the river, under the stern oar, with just his nose out. I told him they was out of sight, so he come aboard. He says:

"I was a-listenin' to all de talk, en I slips into de river en was gwyne to shove for sho' if dey come aboard. Den I was gwyne to swim to de raf' agin when dey was gone. But lawsy, how you did fool 'em, Huck! Dat *wuz* de smartes' dodge! I tell you, chile, I 'speck it save' ole Jim—ole Jim ain't gwyne to forgit you for dat, honey."

Then we talked about the money. It was a pretty good raise, twenty dollars apiece. Jim said we could take deck passage on a steamboat now, and the money would last us as far as we wanted to go in the free States. He said twenty mile more warn't far for the raft to go, but he wished we was already there.

Towards daybreak we tied up, and Jim was mighty particular about hiding the raft good. Then he worked all day fixing things in bundles, and getting all ready to quit rafting.

That night about ten we hove in sight of the lights of a town away down in a left-hand bend.

I went off in the canoe, to ask about it. Pretty soon I found a man out in the river with a skiff, setting a trot-line. I ranged up and says:

"Mister, is that town Cairo?"

"Cairo? no. You must be a blame' fool."

"What town is it, mister?"

"If you want to know, go and find out. If you stay here botherin' around me for about a half a minute longer, you'll get something you won't want."

I paddled to the raft. Jim was awful disappointed, but I said never mind, Cairo would be the next place, I reckoned.

We passed another town before daylight, and I was going out again; but it was high ground, so I didn't go. No high ground about Cairo, Jim said. I had forgot it. We laid up for the day, on a towhead tolerable close to the left-hand bank. I begun to suspicion something. So did Jim. I says:

"Maybe we went by Cairo in the fog that night."

He says:

"Doan' less' talk about it, Huck. Po' niggers can't have no luck. I awluz 'spected dat rattle-snake skin warn't done wid it's work."

"I wish I'd never seen that snake-skin, Jim—I do wish I'd never laid eyes on it."

"It ain't yo' fault, Huck; you didn' know. Don't you blame yo'self 'bout it."

When it was daylight, here was the clear Ohio water in shore, sure enough, and outside was the old regular Muddy! So it was all up with Cairo.[5]

We talked it all over. It wouldn't do to take to the shore; we couldn't take the raft up the stream, of course. There warn't no way but to wait for dark, and start back in the canoe and take the chances. So we slept all day amongst the cotton-wood thicket, so as to be fresh for the work, and when we went back to the raft about dark the canoe was gone!

5. Cairo lies at the point where the relatively clear Ohio flows into the muddy Mississippi. Since they now see water from both rivers, Huck and Jim know they have gone too far. Why did the author abandon his stated plan to send Jim up the Ohio toward freedom instead of down river toward slavery? To prolong the escape theme was to make escape increasingly hopeless. This problem seems to have perplexed Clemens himself, and he broke off composition a few paragraphs later.

We didn't say a word for a good while. There warn't anything to say. We both knowed well enough it was some more work of the rattle-snake skin; so what was the use to talk about it? It would only look like we was finding fault, and that would be bound to fetch more bad luck—and keep on fetching it, too, till we knowed enough to keep still.

By-and-by we talked about what we better do, and found there warn't no way but just to go along down with the raft till we got a chance to buy a canoe to go back in. We warn't going to borrow it when there warn't anybody around, the way pap would do, for that might set people after us.

So we shoved out, after dark, on the raft.

Anybody that don't believe yet, that it's foolishness to handle a snake-skin, after all that that snake-skin done for us, will believe it now, if they read on and see what more it done for us.

The place to buy canoes is off of rafts laying up at shore. But we didn't see no rafts laying up; so we went along during three hours and more. Well, the night got gray, and ruther thick, which is the next meanest thing to fog. You can't tell the shape of the river, and you can't see no distance. It got to be very late and still, and then along comes a steamboat up the river. We lit the lantern, and judged she would see it. Up-stream boats didn't generly come close to us; they go out and follow the bars and hunt for easy water under the reefs; but nights like this they bull right up the channel against the whole river.

We could hear her pounding along, but we didn't see her good till she was close. She aimed right for us. Often they do that and try to see how close they can come without touching; sometimes the wheel bites off a sweep, and then the pilot sticks his head out and laughs, and thinks he's mighty smart. Well, here she comes, and we said she was going to try to shave us; but she didn't seem to be sheering off a bit. She was a big one, and she was coming in a hurry, too, looking like a black cloud with rows of glow-worms around it; but all of a sudden she bulged out, big and scary, with a long row of wide-open furnace doors shining like red-hot teeth, and her monstrous bows and guards hanging right over us. There was a yell at us, and a jingling of bells to stop the engines, a pow-wow of cussing, and whistling of steam—and as Jim went overboard on one side and I on the other, she come smashing straight through the raft.[6]

I dived—and I aimed to find the bottom, too, for a thirty-foot wheel had got to go over me, and I wanted it to have plenty of

6. After composing about 400 manuscript pages in the summer of 1876, Clemens stopped writing at approximately this point. He resumed three years later, producing only chapters XVII–XX and part of XXI between autumn 1879 and summer 1883.

room. I could always stay under water a minute; this time I reckon
I staid under water a minute and a half. Then I bounced for the top
in a hurry, for I was nearly busting. I popped out to my arm-pits
and blowed the water out of my nose, and puffed a bit. Of course
there was a booming current; and of course that boat started her
engines again ten seconds after she stopped them, for they never
cared much for raftsmen; so now she was churning along up the
river, out of sight in the thick weather, though I could hear her.

I sung out for Jim about a dozen times, but I didn't get any
answer; so I grabbed a plank that touched me while I was "treading
water," and struck out for shore, shoving it ahead of me. But I
made out to see that the drift of the current was towards the left-
hand shore,[7] which meant that I was in a crossing; so I changed off
and went that way.

It was one of these long, slanting, two-mile crossings; so I was a
good long time in getting over. I made a safe landing, and clum
up the bank. I couldn't see but a little ways, but I went poking
along over rough ground for a quarter of a mile or more, and then
I run across a big old-fashioned double log house before I noticed
it. I was going to rush by and get away, but a lot of dogs jumped
out and went to howling and barking at me, and I knowed better
than to move another peg.

Chapter XVII

In about half a minute somebody spoke out of a window, without
putting his head out, and says:

"Be done, boys! Who's there?"

I says:

"It's me."

"Who's me?"

"George Jackson, sir."

"What do you want?"

"I don't want nothing, sir. I only want to go along by, but the
dogs won't let me."

"What are you prowling around here this time of night, for—
hey?"

"I warn't prowling around, sir; I fell overboard off of the steamboat."

"Oh, you did, did you? Strike a light there, somebody. What did
you say your name was?"

"George Jackson, sir. I'm only a boy."

"Look here; if you're telling the truth, you needn't be afraid—

---

7. Probably Kentucky, where the feud in the following chapters takes place.

nobody'll hurt you. But don't try to budge; stand right where you are. Rouse out Bob and Tom, some of you, and fetch the guns. George Jackson, is there anybody with you?"

"No, sir, nobody."

I heard the people stirring around in the house, now, and see a light. The man sung out:

"Snatch that light away, Betsy, you old fool—ain't you got any sense? Put it on the floor behind the front door. Bob, if you and Tom are ready, take your places."

"All ready."

"Now, George Jackson, do you know the Shepherdsons?"

"No, sir—I never heard of them."

"Well, that may be so, and it mayn't. Now, all ready. Step forward, George Jackson. And mind, don't you hurry—come mighty slow. If there's anybody with you, let him keep back—if he shows himself he'll be shot. Come along, now. Come slow; push the door open, yourself—just enough to squeeze in, d' you hear?"

I didn't hurry, I couldn't if I'd a wanted to. I took one slow step at a time, and there warn't a sound, only I thought I could hear my heart. The dogs were as still as the humans, but they followed a little behind me. When I got to the three log door-steps, I heard them unlocking and unbarring and unbolting. I put my hand on the door and pushed it a little and a little more, till somebody said, "There, that's enough—put your head in." I done it, but I judged they would take it off.

The candle was on the floor, and there they all was, looking at me, and me at them, for about a quarter of a minute. Three big men with guns pointed at me, which made me wince, I tell you; the oldest, gray and about sixty, the other two thirty or more—all of them fine and handsome—and the sweetest old gray-headed lady, and back of her two young women which I couldn't see right well. The old gentleman says:

"There—I reckon it's all right. Come in."

As soon as I was in, the old gentleman he locked the door and barred it and bolted it, and told the young men to come in with their guns, and they all went in a big parlor that had a new rag carpet on the floor, and got together in a corner that was out of range of the front windows—there warn't none on the side. They held the candle, and took a good look at me, and all said, "Why *he* ain't a Shepherdson—no, there ain't any Shepherdson about him." Then the old man said he hoped I wouldn't mind being searched for arms, because he didn't mean no harm by it—it was only to make sure. So he didn't pry into my pockets, but only felt outside with his hands, and said it was all right. He told me to make myself easy and at home, and tell all about myself; but the old lady says:

"Why bless you, Saul, the poor thing's as wet as he can be; and don't you reckon it may be he's hungry?"

"True for you, Rachel—I forgot."

So the old lady says:

"Betsy" (this was a nigger woman), "you fly around and get him something to eat, as quick as you can, poor thing; and one of you girls go and wake up Buck and tell him— Oh, here he is himself. Buck, take this little stranger and get the wet clothes off from him and dress him up in some of yours that's dry."

Buck looked about as old as me—thirteen or fourteen or along there,[8] though he was a little bigger than me. He hadn't on anything but a shirt, and he was very frowsy-headed. He come in gaping and digging one fist into his eyes, and he was dragging a gun along with the other one. He says:

"Ain't they no Shepherdsons around?"

They said, no, 'twas a false alarm.

"Well," he says, "if they'd a ben some, I reckon I'd a got one."

They all laughed, and Bob says:

"Why, Buck, they might have scalped us all, you've been so slow in coming."

"Well, nobody come after me, and it ain't right. I'm always kep' down; I don't get no show."

"Never mind, Buck, my boy," says the old man, "you'll have show enough, all in good time, don't you fret about that. Go 'long with you now, and do as your mother told you."

When we got up stairs to his room, he got me a coarse shirt and a roundabout[9] and pants of his, and I put them on. While I was at it he asked me what my name was, but before I could tell him, he started to telling me about a blue jay and a young rabbit he had catched in the woods day before yesterday, and he asked me where Moses was when the candle went out. I said I didn't know; I hadn't heard about it before, no way.

"Well, guess," he says.

"How'm I going to guess," says I, "when I never heard tell about it before?"

"But you can guess, can't you? It's just as easy."

"*Which* candle?" I says.

"Why, any candle," he says.

"I don't know where he was," says I; "where was he?"

"Why he was in the *dark!* That's where he was!"

"Well, if you knowed where he was, what did you ask me for?"

"Why, blame it, it's a riddle, don't you see? Say, how long are you going to stay here? You got to stay always. We can just have

8. In a notebook entry, Clemens placed Huck's age at fourteen.

9. A short, close jacket.

booming times—they don't have no school now. Do you own a dog?
I've got a dog—and he'll go in the river and bring out chips that
you throw in. Do you like to comb up, Sundays, and all that kind
of foolishness? You bet I don't, but ma she makes me. Confound
these ole britches, I reckon I'd better put 'em on, but I'd ruther
not, it's so warm. Are you all ready? All right—come along, old
hoss."

Cold corn-pone, cold corn-beef, butter and butter-milk—that is
what they had for me down there, and there ain't nothing better
that ever I've come across yet. Buck and his ma and all of them
smoked cob pipes, except the nigger woman, which was gone, and
the two young women. They all smoked and talked, and I eat and
talked. The young women had quilts around them, and their hair
down their backs. They all asked me questions, and I told them how
pap and me and all the family was living on a little farm down at
the bottom of Arkansaw, and my sister Mary Ann run off and got
married and never was heard of no more, and Bill went to hunt
them and he warn't heard of no more, and Tom and Mort died,
and then there warn't nobody but just me and pap left, and he was
just trimmed down to nothing, on account of his troubles; so when
he died I took what there was left, because the farm didn't belong
to us, and started up the river, deck passage, and fell overboard;
and that was how I come to be here. So they said I could have a
home there as long as I wanted it. Then it was most daylight, and
everybody went to bed, and I went to bed with Buck, and when I
waked up in the morning, drat it all, I had forgot what my name
was. So I laid there about an hour trying to think, and when Buck
waked up, I says:

"Can you spell, Buck?"

"Yes," he says.

"I bet you can't spell my name," says I.

"I bet you what you dare I can," says he.

"All right," says I, "go ahead."

"G-o-r-g-e J-a-x-o-n—there now," he says.

"Well," says I, "you done it, but I didn't think you could. It
ain't no slouch of a name to spell—right off without studying."

I set it down, private, because somebody might want *me* to spell
it, next, and so I wanted to be handy with it and rattle it off like
I was used to it.

It was a mighty nice family, and a mighty nice house, too. I
hadn't seen no house out in the country before that was so nice
and had so much style. It didn't have an iron latch on the front
door, nor a wooden one with a buckskin string, but a brass knob
to turn, the same as houses in a town. There warn't no bed in the
parlor, not a sign of a bed; but heaps of parlors in towns has beds in

them. There was a big fireplace that was bricked on the bottom, and the bricks was kept clean and red by pouring water on them and scrubbing them with another brick; sometimes they washed them over with red water-paint that they call Spanish-brown, same as they do in town. They had big brass dog-irons that could hold up a saw-log. There was a clock on the middle of the mantel-piece, with a picture of a town painted on the bottom half of the glass front, and a round place in the middle of it for the sun, and you could see the pendulum swing behind it. It was beautiful to hear that clock tick; and sometimes when one of these peddlers had been along and scoured her up and got her in good shape, she would start in and strike a hundred and fifty before she got tuckered out. They wouldn't took any money for her.

Well, there was a big outlandish parrot on each side of the clock, made out of something like chalk, and painted up gaudy. By one of the parrots was a cat made of crockery, and a crockery dog by the other; and when you pressed down on them they squeaked, but didn't open their mouths nor look different nor interested. They squeaked through underneath. There was a couple of big wild-turkey-wing fans spread out behind those things. On a table in the middle of the room was a kind of a lovely crockery basket that had apples and oranges and peaches and grapes piled up in it which was much redder and yellower and prettier than real ones is, but they warn't real because you could see where pieces had got chipped off and showed the white chalk or whatever it was, underneath.

This table had a cover made out of beautiful oil-cloth, with a red and blue spread-eagle painted on it, and a painted border all around. It come all the way from Philadelphia, they said. There was some books too, piled up perfectly exact, on each corner of the table. One was a big family Bible, full of pictures. One was "Pilgrim's Progress,"[1] about a man that left his family it didn't say why. I read considerable in it now and then. The statements was interesting, but tough. Another was "Friendship's Offering,"[2] full of beautiful stuff and poetry; but I didn't read the poetry. Another was Henry Clay's Speeches, and another was Dr. Gunn's Family Medicine,[3] which told you all about what to do if a body was sick or dead. There was a Hymn Book, and a lot of other books. And there was nice split-bottom chairs, and perfectly sound, too—not bagged down in the middle and busted, like an old basket.

1. *The Pilgrim's Progress* (1678), a religious allegory by John Bunyan. Christian, followed later by his family, journeys from the City of Destruction to the Celestial City. One of the few books routinely found in rural American households before the Civil War.
2. First published in Boston in 1843, one of many successful annual collections of sentimental poetry and prose designed as gift books.
3. An early American popular household medical encyclopedia, it was first published in 1830 under the title, *Domestic Medicine or Poor Man's Friend, in the House of Affliction, Pain and Sickness*.

They had pictures hung on the walls—mainly Washingtons and Lafayettes, and battles, and Highland Marys,[4] and one called "Signing the Declaration." There was some that they called crayons, which one of the daughters which was dead made her own self when she was only fifteen years old. They was different from any pictures I ever see before; blacker, mostly, than is common. One was a woman in a slim black dress, belted small under the armpits, with bulges like a cabbage in the middle of the sleeves, and a large black scoop-shovel bonnet with a black veil, and white slim ankles crossed about with black tape, and very wee black slippers, like a chisel, and she was leaning pensive on a tombstone on her right elbow, under a weeping willow, and her other hand hanging down her side holding a white handkerchief and a reticule, and underneath the picture it said "Shall I Never See Thee More Alas." Another one was a young lady with her hair all combed up straight to the top of her head, and knotted there in front of a comb like a chair-back, and she was crying into a handkerchief and had a dead bird laying on its back in her other hand with its heels up, and underneath the picture it said "I Shall Never Hear Thy Sweet Chirrup More Alas." There was one where a young lady was at a window looking up at the moon, and tears running down her cheeks; and she had an open letter in one hand with black sealing-wax showing on one edge of it, and she was mashing a locket with a chain to it against her mouth, and underneath the picture it said "And Art Thou Gone Yes Thou Art Gone Alas." These was all nice pictures, I reckon, but I didn't somehow seem to take to them, because if ever I was down a little, they always give me the fan-tods. Everybody was sorry she died, because she had laid out a lot more of these pictures to do, and a body could see by what she had done what they had lost. But I reckoned, that with her disposition, she was having a better time in the graveyard. She was at work on what they said was her greatest picture when she took sick, and every day and every night it was her prayer to be allowed to live till she got it done, but she never got the chance. It was a picture of a young woman in a long white gown, standing on the rail of a bridge all ready to jump off, with her hair all down her back, and looking up to the moon, with the tears running down her face, and she had two arms folded across her breast, and two arms stretched out in front, and two more reaching up towards the moon—and the idea was, to see which pair would look best and then scratch out all the other arms; but, as I was saying, she died before she got her mind made up, and now they kept this picture over the head of the bed in her room, and every time her birthday come they hung

---

4. Mary Campbell, the first sweetheart of Scottish poet Robert Burns, a fitting subject of pathetic painting and verse because she died soon after they met.

flowers on it. Other times it was hid with a little curtain. The young woman in the picture had a kind of a nice sweet face, but there was so many arms it made her look too spidery, seemed to me.

This young girl kept a scrap-book when she was alive, and used to paste obituaries and accidents and cases of patient suffering in it out of the *Presbyterian Observer,* and write poetry after them out of her own head. It was very good poetry. This is what she wrote about a boy by the name of Stephen Dowling Bots that fell down a well and was drownded:

ODE TO STEPHEN DOWLING BOTS, DEC'D.[5]

And did young Stephen sicken,
   And did young Stephen die?
And did the sad hearts thicken,
   And did the mourners cry?

No; such was not the fate of
   Young Stephen Dowling Bots;
Though sad hearts round him thickened,
   'Twas not from sickness' shots.

No whooping-cough did rack his frame,
   Nor measles drear, with spots;
Not these impaired the sacred name
   Of Stephen Dowling Bots.

Despised love struck not with woe
   That head of curly knots,
Nor stomach troubles laid him low,
   Young Stephen Dowling Bots.

O no. Then list with tearful eye,
   Whilst I his fate do tell.
His soul did from this cold world fly,
   By falling down a well.

They got him out and emptied him;
   Alas it was too late;
His spirit was gone for to sport aloft
   In the realms of the good and great.

If Emmeline Grangerford could make poetry like that before she was fourteen, there ain't no telling what she could a done by-and-by. Buck said she could rattle off poetry like nothing. She didn't

5. Deceased. Emmeline's tin ear is inherited from such poetasters as Julia A. Moore, the "Sweet Singer of Michigan" (1847–1920) and Bloodgood Cutter (1819–1906), the "poet lariat" of *Innocents Abroad.* Examples of their stricken verse are included in "Backgrounds and Sources."

ever have to stop to think. He said she would slap down a line, and if she couldn't find anything to rhyme with it she would just scratch it out and slap down another one, and go ahead. She warn't particular, she could write about anything you choose to give her to write about, just so it was sadful. Every time a man died, or a woman died, or a child died, she would be on hand with her "tribute" before he was cold. She called them tributes. The neighbors said it was the doctor first, then Emmeline, then the undertaker— the undertaker never got in ahead of Emmeline but once, and then she hung fire on a rhyme for the dead person's name, which was Whistler. She warn't ever the same, after that; she never complained, but she kind of pined away and did not live long. Poor thing, many's the time I made myself go up to the little room that used to be hers and get out her poor old scrapbook and read in it when her pictures had been aggravating me and I had soured on her a little. I liked all that family, dead ones and all, and warn't going to let anything come between us. Poor Emmeline made poetry about all the dead people when she was alive, and it didn't seem right that there warn't nobody to make some about her, now she was gone; so I tried to sweat out a verse or two myself, but I couldn't seem to make it go, somehow. They kept Emmeline's room trim and nice and all the things fixed in it just the way she liked to have them when she was alive, and nobody ever slept there. The old lady took care of the room herself, though there was plenty of niggers, and she sewed there a good deal and read her Bible there, mostly.

Well, as I was saying about the parlor, there was beautiful curtains on the windows: white, with pictures painted on them, of castles with vines all down the walls, and cattle coming down to drink. There was a little old piano, too, that had tin pans in it, I reckon, and nothing was ever so lovely as to hear the young ladies sing, "The Last Link is Broken" and play "The Battle of Prague"[6] on it. The walls of all the rooms was plastered, and most had carpets on the floors, and the whole house was whitewashed on the outside.

It was a double house, and the big open place betwixt them was roofed and floored, and sometimes the table was set there in the middle of the day, and it was a cool, comfortable place. Nothing couldn't be better. And warn't the cooking good, and just bushels of it too!

Chapter XVIII

Col. Grangerford was a gentleman, you see. He was a gentleman all over; and so was his family. He was well born, as the saying is,

6. Published about 1840, by William Clifton, the first is the lament of a re-signed lover who gives up a "mislead-ing" and "unheeding" partner. Clemens first heard the second jarring composition, by Franz Kotswara, in 1878.

and that's worth as much in a man as it is in a horse, so the Widow
Douglas said, and nobody ever denied that she was of the first
aristocracy in our town; and pap he always said it, too, though he
warn't no more quality than a mudcat,[7] himself. Col. Grangerford
was very tall and very slim, and had a darkish-paly complexion, not
a sign of red in it anywheres; he was clean-shaved every morning,
all over his thin face, and he had the thinnest kind of lips, and
the thinnest kind of nostrils, and a high nose, and heavy eyebrows,
and the blackest kind of eyes, sunk so deep back that they seemed
like they was looking out of caverns at you, as you may say. His forehead was high, and his hair was black and straight, and hung to his
shoulders. His hands was long and thin, and every day of his life he
put on a clean shirt and a full suit from head to foot made out of
linen so white it hurt your eyes to look at it; and on Sundays he
wore a blue tail-coat with brass buttons on it. He carried a mahogany cane with a silver head to it. There warn't no frivolishness about
him, not a bit, and he warn't ever loud. He was as kind as he
could be—you could feel that, you know, and so you had confidence.
Sometimes he smiled, and it was good to see; but when he straightened himself up like a liberty-pole, and the lightning begun to
flicker out from under his eyebrows you wanted to climb a tree first,
and find out what the matter was afterwards. He didn't ever have
to tell anybody to mind their manners—everybody was always good
mannered where he was. Everybody loved to have him around, too;
he was sunshine most always—I mean he made it seem like good
weather. When he turned into a cloud-bank it was awful dark for
a half a minute and that was enough; there wouldn't nothing go
wrong again for a week.

When him and the old lady come down in the morning, all the
family got up out of their chairs and give them good-day, and didn't
set down again till they had set down. Then Tom and Bob went
to the sideboard where the decanters was, and mixed a glass of
bitters and handed it to him, and he held it in his hand and waited
till Tom's and Bob's was mixed, and then they bowed and said
"Our duty to you, sir, and madam;" and *they* bowed the least bit
in the world and said thank you, and so they drank, all three, and
Bob and Tom poured a spoonful of water on the sugar and the
mite of whisky or apple brandy in the bottom of their tumblers,
and give it to me and Buck, and we drank to the old people too.

Bob was the oldest, and Tom next. Tall, beautiful men with very
broad shoulders and brown faces, and long black hair and black eyes.
They dressed in white linen from head to foot, like the old gentleman, and wore broad Panama hats.

Then there was Miss Charlotte, she was twenty-five, and tall and
proud and grand, but as good as she could be, when she warn't

7. A type of catfish.

stirred up; but when she was, she had a look that would make you wilt in your tracks, like her father. She was beautiful

So was her sister, Miss Sophia, but it was a different kind. She was gentle and sweet, like a dove, and she was only twenty.

Each person had their own nigger to wait on them—Buck, too. My nigger had a monstrous easy time, because I warn't used to having anybody do anything for me, but Buck's was on the jump most of the time.

This was all there was of the family, now; but there used to be more—three sons; they got killed; and Emmeline that died.

The old gentleman owned a lot of farms, and over a hundred niggers. Sometimes a stack of people would come there, horseback, from ten or fifteen mile around, and stay five or six days, and have such junketings round about and on the river, and dances and picnics in the woods, day-times, and balls at the house, nights. These people was mostly kin-folks of the family The men brought their guns with them. It was a handsome lot of quality, I tell you.

There was another clan of aristocracy around there—five or six families—mostly of the name of Shepherdson. They was as high-toned, and well born, and rich and grand, as the tribe of Grangerfords. The Shepherdsons and the Grangerfords used the same steamboat landing, which was about two mile above our house; so sometimes when I went up there with a lot of our folks I used to see a lot of the Shepherdsons there, on their fine horses.

One day Buck and me was away out in the woods, hunting, and heard a horse coming. We was crossing the road. Buck says:

"Quick! Jump for the woods!"

We done it, and then peeped down the woods through the leaves. Pretty soon a splendid young man come galloping down the road, setting his horse easy and looking like a soldier. He had his gun across his pommel. I had seen him before. It was young Harney Shepherdson. I heard Buck's gun go off at my ear, and Harney's hat tumbled off from his head. He grabbed his gun and rode straight to the place where we was hid. But we didn't wait. We started through the woods on a run. The woods warn't thick, so I looked over my shoulder, to dodge the bullet, and twice I seen Harney cover Buck with his gun; and then he rode away the way he come—to get his hat, I reckon, but I couldn't see. We never stopped running till we got home. The old gentleman's eyes blazed a minute—'twas pleasure, mainly, I judged—then his face sort of smoothed down, and he says, kind of gentle:

"I don't like that shooting from behind a bush. Why didn't you step into the road, my boy?"

"The Shepherdsons don't, father. They always take advantage."

Miss Charlotte she held her head up like a queen while Buck

was telling his tale, and her nostrils spread and her eyes snapped. The two young men looked dark, but never said nothing. Miss Sophia she turned pale, but the color come back when she found the man warn't hurt.

Soon as I could get Buck down by the corn-cribs under the trees by ourselves, I says:

"Did you want to kill him, Buck?"

"Well, I bet I did."

"What did he do to you?"

"Him? He never done nothing to me."

"Well, then, what did you want to kill him for?"

"Why nothing—only it's on account of the feud."

"What's a feud?"

"Why, where was you raised? Don't you know what a feud is?"

"Never heard of it before—tell me about it."

"Well," says Buck, "a feud is this way. A man has a quarrel with another man, and kills him; then that other man's brother kills *him*; then the other brothers, on both sides, goes for one another; then the *cousins* chip in—and by-and-by everybody's killed off, and there ain't no more feud. But it's kind of slow, and takes a long time."

"Has this one been going on long, Buck?"

"Well I should *reckon!* it started thirty year ago, or som'ers along there. There was trouble 'bout something and then a lawsuit to settle it; and the suit went agin one of the men, and so he up and shot the man that won the suit—which he would naturally do, of course. Anybody would."

"What was the trouble about, Buck?—land?"

"I reckon maybe—I don't know."

"Well, who done the shooting?—was it a Grangerford or a Shepherdson?"

"Laws, how do *I* know? it was so long ago."

"Don't anybody know?"

"Oh, yes, pa knows, I reckon, and some of the other old folks; but they don't know, now, what the row was about in the first place."

"Has there been many killed, Buck?"

"Yes—right smart chance of funerals. But they don't always kill. Pa's got a few buck-shot in him; but he don't mind it 'cuz he don't weigh much anyway. Bob's been carved up some with a bowie, and Tom's been hurt once or twice."

"Has anybody been killed this year, Buck?"

"Yes, we got one and they got one. 'Bout three months ago, my cousin Bud, fourteen year old, was riding through the woods, on t'other side of the river, and didn't have no weapon with him, which was blame' foolishness, and in a lonesome place he hears a horse a-coming behind him, and sees old Baldy Shepherdson a-linkin' after him with his gun in his hand and his white hair a-flying in the wind; and 'stead of jumping off and taking to the brush, Bud 'lowed he could outrun him; so they had it, nip and tuck, for five mile or more, the old man a-gaining all the time; so at last Bud seen it warn't any use, so he stopped and faced around so as to have the bullet holes in front, you know, and the old man he rode up and shot him down. But he didn't git much chance to enjoy his luck, for inside of a week our folks laid *him* out."

"I reckon that old man was a coward, Buck."

"I reckon he *warn't* a coward. Not by a blame' sight. There ain't a coward amongst them Shepherdsons—not a one. And there ain't no cowards amongst the Grangerfords, either. Why, that old man kep' up his end in a fight one day, for a half an hour, against three Grangerfords, and come out winner. They was all a-horseback; he lit off of his horse and got behind a little wood-pile, and kep' his horse before him to stop the bullets; but the Grangerfords staid on their horses and capered around the old man, and peppered away at him, and he peppered away at them. Him and his horse both went home pretty leaky and crippled, but the Grangerfords had to be *fetched* home—and one of 'em was dead, and another died the next day. No, sir, if a body's out hunting for cowards, he don't want to fool away any time amongst them Shepherdsons, be-cuz they don't breed any of that *kind*."

Next Sunday we all went to church, about three mile, every-body a-horseback. The men took their guns along, so did Buck, and kept them between their knees or stood them handy against the wall. The Shepherdsons done the same. It was pretty ornery preach-ing—all about brotherly love, and such-like tiresomeness; but every-body said it was a good sermon, and they all talked it over going home, and had such a powerful lot to say about faith, and good works, and free grace, and preforeordestination,[8] and I don't know what all, that it did seem to me to be one of the roughest Sundays I had run across yet.

About an hour after dinner everybody was dozing around, some in their chairs and some in their rooms, and it got to be pretty dull. Buck and a dog was stretched out on the grass in the sun, sound asleep. I went up to our room, and judged I would take a nap myself. I found that sweet Miss Sophia standing in her door, which was next to ours, and she took me in her room and shut the door very soft, and asked me if I liked her, and I said I did; and she asked me if I would do something for her and not tell any-

8. Huck combines two cardinal doctrines foreordination.
of Presbyterianism: predestination and

body, and I said I would. Then she said she'd forgot her Testament, and left it in the seat at church, between two other books and would I slip out quiet and go there and fetch it to her, and not say nothing to nobody. I said I would. So I slid out and slipped off up the road, and there warn't anybody at the church, except maybe a hog or two, for there warn't any lock on the door, and hogs likes a puncheon floor[9] in summer-time because it's cool. If you notice, most folks don't go to church only when they've got to; but a hog is different.

Says I to myself something's up—it ain't natural for a girl to be in such a sweat about a Testament; so I give it a shake, and out drops a little piece of paper with *"Half-past two"* wrote on it with a pencil. I ransacked it, but couldn't find anything else. I couldn't make anything out of that, so I put the paper in the book again, and when I got home and up stairs, there was Miss Sophia in her door waiting for me. She pulled me in and shut the door; then she looked in the Testament till she found the paper, and as soon as she read it she looked glad; and before a body could think, she grabbed me and give me a squeeze, and said I was the best boy in the world, and not to tell anybody. She was mighty red in the face, for a minute, and her eyes lighted up and it made her powerful pretty. I was a good deal astonished, but when I got my breath I asked her what the paper was about, and she asked me if I had read it, and I said no, and she asked me if I could read writing, and I told her "no, only coarse-hand,"[1] and then she said the paper warn't anything but a book-mark to keep her place, and I might go and play now.

I went off down to the river, studying over this thing, and pretty soon I noticed that my nigger was following along behind. When we was out of sight of the house, he looked back and around a second, and then comes a-running, and says:

"Mars Jawge, if you'll come down into de swamp, I'll show you a whole stack o' water-moccasins."

Thinks I, that's mighty curious; he said that yesterday. He oughter know a body don't love water-moccasins enough to go around hunting for them. What is he up to anyway? So I says—

"All right, trot ahead."

I followed a half a mile, then he struck out over the swamp and waded ankle deep as much as another half mile. We come to a little flat piece of land which was dry and very thick with trees and bushes and vines, and he says—

"You shove right in dah, jist a few steps, Mars Jawge, dah's whah dey is. I's seed 'm befo', I don't k'yer to see 'em no mo'."

9. Male of log slabs with the rounded   1. Printing.
sides downward.

Then he slopped right along and went away, and pretty soon the trees hid him. I poked into the place a-ways, and come to a little open patch as big as a bedroom, all hung around with vines, and found a man laying there asleep—and by jings it was my old Jim!

I waked him up, and I reckoned it was going to be a grand surprise to him to see me again, but it warn't. He nearly cried, he was so glad, but he warn't surprised. Said he swum along behind me, that night, and heard me yell every time, but dasn't answer, because he didn't want nobody to pick *him* up, and take him into slavery again. Says he—

"I got hurt a little, en couldn't swim fas', so I wuz a considable ways behine you, towards de las'; when you landed I reck'ned I could ketch up wid you on de lan' 'dout havin' to shout at you, but when I see dat house I begin to go slow. I 'uz off too fur to hear what dey say to you—I wuz 'fraid o' de dogs—but when it 'uz all quiet agin, I knowed you's in de house, so I struck out for de woods to wait for day. Early in de mawnin' some er de niggers come along, gwyne to de fields, en dey tuck me en showed me dis place, whah de dogs can't track me on accounts o' de water, en dey brings me truck to eat every night, en tells me how you's a gitt'n along."

"Why didn't you tell my Jack to fetch me here sooner, Jim?"

"Well, 'twarn't no use to 'sturb you, Huck, tell we could do sumfn—but we's all right, now. I ben a-buyin' pots en pans en vittles, as I got a chanst, en a patchin' up de raf', nights, when—"

"*What* raft, Jim?"

"Our ole raf'."

"You mean to say our old raft warn't smashed all to flinders?"

"No, she warn't. She was tore up a good deal—one en' of her was—but dey warn't no great harm done, on'y our traps was mos' all los'. Ef we hadn' dive' so deep en swum so fur under water, en de night hadn' ben so dark, en we warn't so sk'yerd, en ben sich punkin-heads, as de sayin' is, we'd a seed de raf'. But it's jis' as well we didn't, 'kase now she's all fixed up agin mos' as good as new, en we's got a new lot o' stuff, too, in de place o' what 'uz los'."

"Why, how did you get hold of the raft again, Jim—did you catch her?"

"How I gwyne to ketch her, en I out in de woods? No, some er de niggers foun' her ketched on a snag, along heah in de ben', en dey hid her in a crick, 'mongst de willows, en dey wuz so much jawin' 'bout which un 'um she b'long to de mos', dat I come to heah 'bout it pooty soon, so I ups en settles de trouble by tellin' 'um she don't b'long to none uv um, but to you en me; en I ast 'm if dey gwyne to grab a young white genlman's propaty, en git a hid'n for it? Den I gin 'm ten cents apiece, en dey 'uz mighty well satisfied, en wisht some mo' raf's 'ud come along en make 'm rich agin. Dey's mighty good to me, dese niggers is, en whatever I wants 'm to do fur me, I doan' have to ast 'm twice, honey. Dat Jack's a good nigger, en pooty smart."

"Yes, he is. He ain't ever told me you was here; told me to come, and he'd show me a lot of water-moccasins. If anything happens, *he* ain't mixed up in it. He can say he never seen us together, and it'll be the truth."

I don't want to talk much about the next day. I reckon I'll cut it pretty short. I waked up about dawn, and was agoing to turn over and go to sleep again, when I noticed how still it was—didn't seem to be anybody stirring. That warn't usual. Next I noticed that Buck was up and gone. Well, I gets up, a-wondering, and goes down stairs—nobody around; everything as still as a mouse. Just the same outside; thinks I, what does it mean? Down by the wood-pile I comes across my Jack, and says:

"What's it all about?"

Says he:

"Don't you know, Mars Jawge?"

"No," says I, "I don't."

"Well, den, Miss Sophia's run off! 'deed she has. She run off in de night, sometime—nobody don't know jis' when—run off to git married to dat young Harney Shepherdson, you know—leastways, so dey 'spec. De fambly foun' it out, 'bout half an hour ago—maybe a little mo'—en' I *tell* you dey warn't no time los'. Sich another hurryin' up guns en hosses *you* never see! De women folks has gone for to stir up de relations, en ole Mars Saul en de boys tuck dey guns en rode up de river road for to try to ketch dat young man en kill him 'fo' he kin git acrost de river wid Miss Sophia. I reck'n dey's gwyne to be mighty rough times."

"Buck went off 'thout waking me up."

"Well I reck'n he *did!* Dey warn't gwyne to mix you up in it. Mars Buck he loaded up his gun en 'lowed he's gwyne to fetch home a Shepherdson or bust. Well, dey'll be plenty un 'm dah, I reck'n, en you bet you he'll fetch one ef he gits a chanst."

I took up the river road as hard as I could put. By-and-by I begin to hear guns a good ways off. When I come in sight of the log store and the wood-pile where the steamboats lands, I worked along under the trees and brush till I got to a good place, and then I clumb up into the forks of a cotton-wood that was out of reach, and watched. There was a wood-rank four foot high, a little ways in front of the tree, and first I was going to hide behind that; but maybe it was luckier I didn't.

There was four or five men cavorting around on their horses in the open place before the log store, cussing and yelling, and trying to get at a couple of young chaps that was behind the wood-rank alongside of the steamboat landing—but they couldn't come it. Every time one of them showed himself on the river side of the wood-pile he got shot at. The two boys was squatting back to back behind the pile, so they could watch both ways.

By-and-by the men stopped cavorting around and yelling. They started riding towards the store; then up gets one of the boys, draws a steady bead over the wood-rank, and drops one of them out of his saddle. All the men jumped off of their horses and grabbed the hurt one and started to carry him to the store; and that minute the two boys started on the run. They got half-way to the tree I was in before the men noticed. Then the men see them, and jumped on their horses and took out after them. They gained on the boys, but it didn't do no good, the boys had too good a start; they got to the wood-pile that was in front of my tree, and slipped in behind it, and so they had the bulge on the men again. One of the boys was Buck, and the other was a slim young chap about nineteen years old.

The men ripped around awhile, and then rode away. As soon as they was out of sight, I sung out to Buck and told him. He didn't know what to make of my voice coming out of the tree, at first. He was awful surprised. He told me to watch out sharp and let him know when the men come in sight again; said they was up to some devilment or other—wouldn't be gone long. I wished I was out of that tree, but I dasn't come down. Buck begun to cry and rip, and 'lowed that him and his cousin Joe (that was the other young chap) would make up for this day, yet. He said his father and his two brothers was killed, and two or three of the enemy. Said the Shepherdsons laid for them, in ambush. Buck said his father and brothers ought to waited for their relations—the Shepherdsons was too strong for them. I asked him what was become of young Harney and Miss Sophia. He said they'd got across the river and was safe. I was glad of that; but the way Buck did take on because he didn't manage to kill Harney that day he shot at him—I hain't ever heard anything like it.

All of a sudden, bang! bang! bang! goes three or four guns—the men had slipped around through the woods and come in from behind without their horses! The boys jumped for the river—both of them hurt—and as they swum down the current the men run along the bank shooting at them and singing out, "Kill them, kill them!" It made me so sick I most fell out of the tree. I ain't agoing to tell *all* that happened—it would make me sick again if I was to do that. I wished I hadn't ever come ashore that night, to see such things. I ain't ever going to get shut of them—lots of times I dream about them.

I staid in the tree till it begun to get dark, afraid to come down. Sometimes I heard guns away off in the woods; and twice I seen little gangs of men gallop past the log store with guns; so I reckoned the trouble was still agoing on. I was mighty down-hearted; so I made up my mind I wouldn't ever go anear that house again, because I reckoned I was to blame, somehow. I judged that that piece of paper meant that Miss Sophia was to meet Harney somewheres at half-past two and run off; and I judged I ought to told her father about that paper and the curious way she acted, and then maybe he would a locked her up and this awful mess wouldn't ever happened.

When I got down out of the tree, I crept along down the river bank a piece, and found the two bodies laying in the edge of the water, and tugged at them till I got them ashore; then I covered up their faces, and got away as quick as I could. I cried a little when I was covering up Buck's face, for he was mighty good to me.

It was just dark, now. I never went near the house, but struck through the woods and made for the swamp. Jim warn't on his is-land, so I tramped off in a hurry for the crick, and crowded through the willows, red-hot to jump aboard and get out of that awful coun-try—the raft was gone! My souls, but I was scared! I couldn't get my breath for most a minute. Then I raised a yell. A voice not twenty-five foot from me, says—

"Good lan'! is dat you, honey? Doan' make no noise."

It was Jim's voice—nothing ever sounded so good before. I run along the bank a piece and got aboard, and Jim he grabbed me and hugged me, he was so glad to see me. He says—

"Laws bless you, chile, I 'uz right down sho' you's dead agin. Jack's been heah, he say he reck'n you's ben shot, kase you didn' come home no mo'; so I's jes' dis minute a startin' de raf' down towards de mouf er de crick, so's to be all ready for to shove out en leave soon as Jack comes agin en tells me for certain you *is* dead. Lawsy, I's mighty glad to git you back agin, honey."

I says—

"All right—that's mighty good; they won't find me, and they'll think I've been killed, and floated down the river—there's some-thing up there that'll help them to think so—so don't you lose no time, Jim, but just shove off for the big water as fast as ever you can."

I never felt easy till the raft was two mile below there and out in the middle of the Mississippi. Then we hung up our signal lan-tern, and judged that we was free and safe once more. I hadn't had a bite to eat since yesterday; so Jim he got out some corn-dodgers and buttermilk, and pork and cabbage, and greens—there ain't nothing in the world so good, when it's cooked right—and whilst I eat my supper we talked, and had a good time. I was powerful glad to get away from the feuds, and so was Jim to get away from the swamp. We said there warn't no home like a raft, after all. Other places do seem so cramped up and smothery, but a raft don't. You feel mighty free and easy and comfortable on a raft.

Chapter XIX

Two or three days and nights went by; I reckon I might say they swum by, they slid along so quiet and smooth and lovely. Here is the way we put in the time. It was a monstrous big river down there—sometimes a mile and a half wide; we run nights, and laid up and hid day-times; soon as night was most gone, we stopped navigating and tied up—nearly always in the dead water under a tow-head; and then cut young cottonwoods and willows and hid the raft with them. Then we set out the lines. Next we slid into the river and had a swim, so as to freshen up and cool off; then we set down on the sandy bottom where the water was about knee deep, and watched the daylight come. Not a sound, anywheres— perfectly still—just like the whole world was asleep, only some- times the bull-frogs a-cluttering, maybe. The first thing to see, looking away over the water, was a kind of dull line—that was the woods on t'other side—you couldn't make nothing else out; then a pale place in the sky; then more paleness, spreading around; then the river softened up, away off, and warn't black any more, but gray; you could see little dark spots drifting along, ever so far away —trading scows, and such things; and long black streaks—rafts; sometimes you could hear a sweep screaking; or jumbled up voices, it was so still, and sounds come so far; and by-and-by you could see a streak on the water which you know by the look of the streak that there's a snag there in a swift current which breaks on it and makes that streak look that way; and you see the mist curl up off of the water, and the east reddens up, and the river, and you make out a log cabin in the edge of the woods, away on the bank on t'other side of the river, being a wood-yard, likely, and piled by them cheats so you can throw a dog through it anywheres;[2] then the nice breeze springs up, and comes fanning you from over there, so cool and fresh, and sweet to smell, on account of the woods and the flowers; but sometimes not that way, because they've left dead fish laying around, gars, and such, and they do get pretty rank; and next you've got the full day, and everything smiling in the sun, and the song-birds just going it!

2. The yard's customers were cheated because stacks of wood were sold by vol- ume, gaps included.

A little smoke couldn't be noticed, now, so we would take some fish off of the lines, and cook up a hot breakfast. And afterwards we would watch the lonesomeness of the river, and kind of lazy along, and by-and-by lazy off to sleep. Wake up, by-and-by, and look to see what done it, and maybe see a steamboat coughing along up stream, so far off towards the other side you couldn't tell nothing about her only whether she was stern-wheel or side-wheel; then for about an hour there wouldn't be nothing to hear nor nothing to see—just solid lonesomeness. Next you'd see a raft sliding by, away off yonder, and maybe a galoot on it chopping, because they're almost always doing it on a raft; you'd see the ax flash, and come down—you don't hear nothing; you see that ax go up again, and by the time it's above the man's head, then you hear the *k'chunk!*—it had took all that time to come over the water. So we would put in the day, lazying around, listening to the stillness. Once there was a thick fog, and the rafts and things that went by was beating tin pans so the steamboats wouldn't run over them. A scow or a raft went by so close we could hear them talking and cussing and laughing—heard them plain; but we couldn't see no sign of them; it made you feel crawly, it was like spirits carrying on that way in the air. Jim said he believed it was spirits; but I says:

"No, spirits wouldn't say, 'dern the dern fog.' "

Soon as it was night, out we shoved; when we got her out to about the middle, we let her alone, and let her float wherever the current wanted her to; then we lit the pipes, and dangled our legs in the water and talked about all kinds of things—we was always naked, day and night, whenever the mosquitoes would let us—the new clothes Buck's folks made for me was too good to be comfortable, and besides I didn't go much on clothes, nohow.

Sometimes we'd have that whole river all to ourselves for the longest time. Yonder was the banks and the islands, across the water; and maybe a spark—which was a candle in a cabin window —and sometimes on the water you could see a spark or two—on a raft or a scow, you know; and maybe you could hear a fiddle or a song coming over from one of them crafts. It's lovely to live on a raft. We had the sky, up there, all speckled with stars, and we used to lay on our backs and look up at them, and discuss about whether they was made, or only just happened—Jim he allowed they was made, but I allowed they happened; I judged it would have took too long to *make* so many. Jim said the moon could a *laid* them; well, that looked kind of reasonable, so I didn't say nothing against it, because I've seen a frog lay most as many, so of course it could be done. We used to watch the stars that fell, too, and see them streak down. Jim allowed they'd got spoiled and was hove out of the nest.

Once or twice of a night we would see a steamboat slipping along in the dark, and now and then she would belch a whole world of sparks up out of her chimbleys, and they would rain down in the river and look awful pretty; then she would turn a corner and her lights would wink out and her pow-wow[3] shut off and leave the river still again; and by-and-by her waves would get to us, a long time after she was gone, and joggle the raft a bit, and after that you wouldn't hear nothing for you couldn't tell how long, except maybe frogs or something.

After midnight the people on shore went to bed, and then for two or three hours the shores was black—no more sparks in the cabin windows. These sparks was our clock—the first one that showed again meant morning was coming, so we hunted a place to hide and tie up, right away.

One morning about day-break, I found a canoe and crossed over a chute[4] to the main shore—it was only two hundred yards—and paddled about a mile up a crick amongst the cypress woods, to see if I couldn't get some berries. Just as I was passing a place where a kind of a cow-path crossed the crick, here comes a couple of men tearing up the path as tight as they could foot it. I thought I was a goner, for whenever anybody was after anybody I judged it was *me*—or maybe Jim. I was about to dig out from there in a hurry, but they was pretty close to me then, and sung out and begged me to save their lives—said they hadn't been doing nothing, and was being chased for it—said there was men and dogs a-coming. They wanted to jump right in, but I says—

"Don't you do it. I don't hear the dogs and horses yet; you've got time to crowd through the brush and get up the crick a little ways; then you take to the water and wade down to me and get in —that'll throw the dogs off the scent."

They done it, and soon as they was aboard I lit out for our tow-head, and in about five or ten minutes we heard the dogs and the men away off, shouting. We heard them come along towards the crick, but couldn't see them; they seemed to stop and fool around a while; then, as we got further and further away all the time, we couldn't hardly hear them at all; by the time we had left a mile of woods behind us and struck the river, everything was quiet, and we paddled over to the tow-head and hid in the cotton-woods and was safe.

One of these fellows was about seventy, or upwards, and had a bald head and very gray whiskers. He had an old battered-up slouch hat on, and a greasy blue woolen shirt, and ragged old blue jeans

3. Clemens uses the word several times in *Huckleberry Finn* to mean racket or commotion.

4. A narrow, swift-flowing channel to the mainland.

britches stuffed into his boot tops, and home-knit galluses⁵—no, he only had one. He had an old long-tailed blue jeans coat with slick brass buttons, flung over his arm, and both of them had big fat ratty-looking carpet-bags.

The other fellow was about thirty and dressed about as ornery. After breakfast we all laid off and talked, and the first thing that come out was that these chaps didn't know one another.

"What got you into trouble?" says the baldhead to t'other chap.

"Well, I'd been selling an article to take the tartar off the teeth —and it does take it off, too, and generly the enamel along with it—but I staid about one night longer than I ought to, and was just in the act of sliding out when I ran across you on the trail this side of town, and you told me they were coming, and begged me to help you to get off. So I told you I was expecting trouble myself and would scatter out *with* you. That's the whole yarn—what's yourn?"

"Well, I'd ben a-runnin' a little temperance revival thar, 'bout a week, and was the pet of the women-folks, big and little, for I was makin' it mighty warm for the rummies, I *tell* you, and takin' as much as five or six dollars a night—ten cents a head, children and niggers free—and business a growin' all the time; when somehow or another a little report got around, last night, that I had a way of puttin' in my time with a private jug, on the sly. A nigger rousted me out this morning', and told me the people was getherin' on the quiet, with their dogs and horses, and they'd be along pretty soon and give me 'bout half an hour's start, and then run me down, if they could; and if they got me they'd tar and feather me and ride me on a rail, sure. I didn't wait for no breakfast—I warn't hungry."

"Old man," says the young one, "I reckon we might double-team it together; what do you think?"

"I ain't undisposed. What's your line—mainly?"

"Jour printer,⁶ by trade; do a little in patent medicines; theatre-actor—tragedy, you know; take a turn at mesmerism and phrenology⁷ when there's a chance; teach singing-geography school for a change; sling a lecture, sometimes—oh, I do lots of things—most anything that comes handy, so it ain't work. What's your lay?"

"I've done considerble in the doctoring way in my time. Layin' on o' hands is my best holt—for cancer, and paralysis, and sich things; and I k'n tell a fortune pretty good, when I've got somebody along to find out the facts for me. Preachin's my line, too; and workin' camp-meetin's; and missionaryin' around."

Nobody never said anything for a while; then the young man hove a sigh and says—

---

5. Suspenders.
6. Journeyman printer, one who worked by the day.

7. Hypnotism and the pseudo science of reading character from the natural bumps and ridges of the skull.

"Alas!"

"What 're you alassin' about?" says the baldhead.

"To think I should have lived to be leading such a life, and be degraded down into such company." And he begun to wipe the corner of his eye with a rag.

"Dern your skin, ain't the company good enough for you?" says the baldhead, pretty pert and uppish.

"Yes, it *is* good enough for me; it's as good as I deserve; for who fetched me so low, when I was so high? *I* did myself. I don't blame *you*, gentlemen—far from it; I don't blame anybody. I deserve it all. Let the cold world do its worst; one thing I know—there's a grave somewhere for me. The world may go on just as its always done, and take everything from me—loved ones, property, everything—but it can't take that. Some day I'll lie down in it and forget it all, and my poor broken heart will be at rest." He went on a-wiping.

"Drot your pore broken heart," says the baldhead; "what are you heaving your pore broken heart at *us* f'r? *We* hain't done nothing."

"No, I know you haven't. I ain't blaming you, gentlemen. I brought myself down—yes, I did it myself. It's right I should suffer—perfectly right—I don't make any moan."

"Brought you down from whar? Whar was you brought down from?"

"Ah, you would not believe me; the world never believes—let it pass—'tis no matter. The secret of my birth—"

"The secret of your birth? Do you mean to say—"

"Gentlemen," says the young man, very solemn, "I will reveal it to you, for I feel I may have confidence in you. By rights I am a duke!"

Jim's eyes bugged out when he heard that; and I reckon mine did, too. Then the baldhead says: "No! you can't mean it?"

"Yes. My great-grandfather, eldest son of the Duke of Bridgewater, fled to this country about the end of the last century, to breathe the pure air of freedom; married here, and died, leaving a son, his own father dying about the same time. The second son of the late duke seized the title and estates—the infant real duke was ignored. I am the lineal descendant of that infant—I am the rightful Duke of Bridgewater; and here am I, forlorn, torn from my high estate, hunted of men, despised by the cold world, ragged, worn, heart-broken, and degraded to the companionship of felons on a raft!"

Jim pitied him ever so much ,and so did I. We tried to comfort him, but he said it warn't much use, he couldn't be much comforted; said if we was a mind to acknowledge him, that would do him more good than most anything else; so we said we would, if he would tell us how. He said we ought to bow, when we spoke to him, and say "Your Grace," or "My Lord," or "Your Lordship"—and he wouldn't mind it if we called him plain "Bridgewater," which he said was a title, anyway, and not a name; and one of us ought to wait on him at dinner, and do any little thing for him he wanted done.

Well, that was all easy, so we done it. All through dinner Jim stood around and waited on him, and says, "Will yo' Grace have some o' dis, or some o' dat?" and so on, and a body could see it was mighty pleasing to him.

But the old man got pretty silent, by-and-by—didn't have much to say, and didn't look pretty comfortable over all that petting that was going on around that duke. He seemed to have something on his mind. So, along in the afternoon, he says:

"Looky here, Bilgewater," he says, "I'm nation sorry for you, but you ain't the only person that's had troubles like that."

"No?"

"No, you ain't. You ain't the only person that's ben snaked down wrongfully out'n a high place."

"Alas!"

"No, you ain't the only person that's had a secret of his birth." And by jings, *he* begins to cry.

"Hold! What do you mean?"

"Bilgewater, kin I trust you?" says the old man, still sort of sobbing.

"To the bitter death!" He took the old man by the hand and squeezed it, and says, "The secret of your being: speak!"

"Bilgewater, I am the late Dauphin!"

You bet you Jim and me stared, this time. Then the duke says: "You are what?"

"Yes, my friend, it is too true—your eyes is lookin' at this very moment on the pore disappeared Dauphin, Looy the Seventeen, son of Looy the Sixteen and Marry Antonette."

"You! At your age! No! You mean you're the late Charlemagne;[8] you must be six or seven hundred years old, at the very least."

"Trouble has done it, Bilgewater, trouble has done it; trouble has brung these gray hairs and this premature balditude. Yes, gentlemen, you see before you, in blue jeans and misery, the wanderin', exiled, trampled-on and sufferin' rightful King of France."

Well, he cried and took on so, that me and Jim didn't know hardly what to do, we was so sorry—and so glad and proud we'd got him with us, too. So we set in, like we done before with the duke, and tried to comfort *him*. But he said it warn't no use, noth-

8. See Chapter XIV, note 7; had the real Dauphin lived, he would have been in his mid-fifties. Charlemagne died in 814.

ing but to be dead and done with it all could do him any good; though he said it often made him feel easier and better for a while if people treated him according to his rights, and got down on one knee to speak to him, and always called him "Your Majesty," and waited on him first at meals, and didn't set down in his presence till he asked them. So Jim and me set to majestying him, and doing this and that and t'other for him, and standing up till he told us we might set down. This done him heaps of good, and so he got cheerful and comfortable. But the duke kind of soured on him, and didn't look a bit satisfied with the way things was going; still, the king acted real friendly towards him, and said the duke's great-grandfather and all the other Dukes of Bilgewater was a good deal thought of by *his* father and was allowed to come to the palace considerable; but the duke staid huffy a good while, till by-and-by the king says:

"Like as not we got to be together a blamed long time, on this h-yer raft, Bilgewater, and so what's the use o' your bein' sour? It'll only make things oncomfortable. It ain't my fault I warn't born a duke, it ain't your fault you warn't born a king—so what's the use to worry? Make the best o' things the way you find 'em, says I—that's my motto. This ain't no bad thing that we've struck here—plenty grub and an easy life—come, give us your hand, Duke, and less all be friends."

The duke done it, and Jim and me was pretty glad to see it. It took away all the uncomfortableness, and we felt mighty good over it, because it would a been a miserable business to have any un-friendliness on the raft; for what you want, above all things, on a raft, is for everybody to be satisfied, and feel right and kind to-wards the others.

It didn't take me long to make up my mind that these liars warn't no kings nor dukes, at all, but just low-down humbugs and frauds. But I never said nothing, never let on; kept it to myself; it's the best way; then you don't have no quarrels, and don't get into no trouble. If they wanted us to call them kings and dukes, I hadn't no objections, 'long as it would keep peace in the family; and it warn't no use to tell Jim, so I didn't tell him. If I never learnt nothing else out of pap, I learnt that the best way to get along with his kind of people is to let them have their own way.

Chapter XX

They asked us considerable many questions; wanted to know what we covered up the raft that way for, and laid by in the day-time instead of running—was Jim a runaway nigger? Says I—

"Goodness sakes, would a runaway nigger run *south?*"

No, they allowed he wouldn't. I had to account for things some way, so I says:

"My folks was living in Pike County, in Missouri, where I was born, and they all died off but me and pa and my brother Ike. Pa, he 'lowed he'd break up and go down and live with Uncle Ben, who's got a little one-horse place on the river, forty-four mile below Orleans. Pa was pretty poor, and had some debts; so when he'd squared up there warn't nothing left but sixteen dollars and our nigger, Jim. That warn't enough to take us fourteen hundred mile, deck passage nor no other way. Well, when the river rose, pa had a streak of luck one day; he ketched this piece of a raft; so we reckoned we'd go down to Orleans on it. Pa's luck didn't hold out; a steamboat run over the forrard corner of the raft, one night, and we all went overboard and dove under the wheel; Jim and me come up, all right, but pa was drunk, and Ike was only four years old, so they never come up no more. Well, for the next day or two we had considerable trouble, because people was always coming out in skiffs and trying to take Jim away from me, saying they believed he was a runaway nigger. We don't run day-times no more, now; nights they don't bother us."

The duke says—

"Leave me alone to cipher out a way so we can run in the day-time if we want to. I'll think the thing over—I'll invent a plan that'll fix it. We'll let it alone for to-day, because of course we don't want to go by that town yonder in daylight—it mightn't be healthy."

Towards night it begun to darken up and look like rain; the heat lightning was squirting around, low down in the sky, and the leaves was beginning to shiver—it was going to be pretty ugly, it was easy to see that. So the duke and the king went to overhauling our wigwam, to see what the beds was like. My bed was a straw tick—better than Jim's, which was a corn-shuck tick; there's always cobs around about in a shuck tick, and they poke into you and hurt; and when you roll over, the dry shucks sound like you was rolling over in a pile of dead leaves; it makes such a rustling that you wake up. Well, the duke allowed he would take my bed; but the king allowed he wouldn't. He says—

"I should a reckoned the difference in rank would a sejested to you that a corn-shuck bed warn't just fitten for me to sleep on. Your Grace'll take the shuck bed yourself."

Jim and me was in a sweat again, for a minute, being afraid there was going to be some more trouble amongst them; so we was pretty glad when the duke says—

" 'Tis my fate to be always ground into the mire under the iron heel of oppression. Misfortune has broken my once haughty spirit;

I yield, I submit; 'tis my fate. I am alone in the world—let me suffer; I can bear it."

We got away as soon as it was good and dark. The king told us to stand well out towards the middle of the river, and not show a light till we got a long ways below the town. We come in sight of the little bunch of lights by-and-by—that was the town, you know —and slid by, about a half a mile out, all right. When we was three-quarters of a mile below, we hoisted up our signal lantern; and about ten o'clock it come on to rain and blow and thunder and lighten like everything; so the king told us to both stay on watch till the weather got better; then him and the duke crawled into the wigwam and turned in for the night. It was my watch below, till twelve, but I wouldn't a turned in, anyway, if I'd had a bed; because a body don't see such a storm as that every day in the week, not by a long sight. My souls, how the wind did scream along! And every second or two there'd come a glare that lit up the white-caps for a half a mile around, and you'd see the islands looking dusty through the rain, and the trees thrashing around in the wind; then comes a *h-wack!*—bum! bum! bumble-umble-um-bum-bum-bum-bum—and the thunder would go rumbling and grumbling away, and quit—and then *rip* comes another flash and another sockdolager.[9] The waves most washed me off the raft, sometimes, but I hadn't any clothes on, and didn't mind. We didn't have no trouble about snags; the lightning was glaring and flittering around so constant that we could see them plenty soon enough to throw her head this way or that and miss them.

I had the middle watch, you know, but I was pretty sleepy by that time, so Jim he said he would stand the first half of it for me; he was always mighty good, that way, Jim was. I crawled into the wigwam, but the king and the duke had their legs sprawled around so there warn't no show for me; so I laid outside—I didn't mind the rain, because it was warm, and the waves warn't running so high, now. About two they come up again, though, and Jim was going to call me, but he changed his mind because he reckoned they warn't high enough yet to do any harm; but he was mistaken about that, for pretty soon all of a sudden along comes a regular ripper, and washed me overboard. It most killed Jim a-laughing. He was the easiest nigger to laugh that ever was, anyway.

I took the watch, and Jim he laid down and snored away; and by-and-by the storm let up for good and all; and the first cabin-light that showed, I rousted him out and we slid the raft into hiding-quarters for the day.

The king got out an old ratty deck of cards, after breakfast, and him and the duke played seven-up[1] a while, five cents a game. Then

9. A humdinger, a finisher.
1. A trumping game won by the first   player to score seven points, also called "All Fours" and "Old Sledge."

they got tired of it, and allowed they would "lay out a campaign," as they called it. The duke went down into his carpet bag and fetched up a lot of little printed bills, and read them out loud. One bill said "The celebrated Dr. Armand de Montalban of Paris," would "lecture on the Science of Phrenology" at such and such a place, on the blank day of blank, at ten cents admission, and "furnish charts of character at twenty-five cents apiece." The duke said that was *him*. In another bill he was the "world renowned Shaksperean tragedian, Garrick the Younger,[2] of Drury Lane, London." In other bills he had a lot of other names and done other wonderful things, like finding water and gold with a "divining rod," "dissipating witch-spells," and so on. By-and-by he says—

"But the histrionic muse is the darling. Have you ever trod the boards, Royalty?"

"No," says the king.

"You shall, then, before you're three days older, Fallen Grandeur," says the duke. "The first good town we come to, we'll hire a hall and do the sword-fight in Richard III. and the balcony scene in Romeo and Juliet. How does that strike you?"

"I'm in, up to the hub, for anything that will pay, Bilgewater, but you see I don't know nothing about play-actn', and hain't ever seen much of it. I was too small when pap used to have 'em at the palace. Do you reckon you can learn me?"

"Easy!"

"All right. I'm jist a-freezn' for something fresh, anyway. Less commence, right away."

So the duke he told him all about who Romeo was, and who Juliet was, and said he was used to being Romeo, so the king could be Juliet.

"But if Juliet's such a young gal, Duke, my peeled head and my white whiskers is goin' to look oncommon odd on her, maybe."

"No, don't you worry—these country jakes won't ever think of that. Besides, you know, you'll be in costume, and that makes all the difference in the world; Juliet's in a balcony, enjoying the moonlight before she goes to bed, and she's got on her night-gown and her ruffled night-cap. Here are the costumes for the parts."

He got out two or three curtain-calico suits, which he said was meedyevil armor for Richard III. and t'other chap, and a long white cotton night-shirt and a ruffled night-cap to match. The king was satisfied; so the duke got out his book and read the parts over in the most splendid spread-eagle way, prancing around and acting at the same time, to show how it had got to be done; then he give the book to the king and told him to get his part by heart.

2. Here and in the next two chapters, the duke confuses three famous British actors: David Garrick (1717–79), Edmund Kean (1787–1833), and his son Charles John Kean (1811?–68). The original Theatre Royal in Drury Lane was built in 1663.

There was a little one-horse town about three mile down the bend, and after dinner the duke said he had ciphered out his idea about how to run in daylight without it being dangersome for Jim; so he allowed he would go down to the town and fix that thing. The king allowed he would go too, and see if he couldn't strike something. We was out of coffee, so Jim said I better go along with them in the canoe and get some.

When we got there, there warn't nobody stirring; streets empty, and perfectly dead and still, like Sunday. We found a sick nigger sunning himself in a back yard, and he said everybody that warn't too young or too sick or too old, was gone to camp-meeting, about two mile back in the woods. The king got the directions, and allowed he'd go and work that camp-meeting for all it was worth, and I might go, too.

The duke said what he was after was a printing office. We found it; a little bit of a concern, up over a carpenter shop—carpenters and printers all gone to the meeting, and no doors locked. It was a dirty, littered-up place, and had ink marks, and handbills with pictures of horses and runaway niggers on them, all over the walls. The duke shed his coat and said he was all right, now. So me and the king lit out for the camp-meeting.

We got there in about a half an hour, fairly dripping, for it was a most awful hot day. There was as much as a thousand people there, from twenty mile around. The woods was full of teams and wagons, hitched everywheres, feeding out of the wagon troughs and stomping to keep off the flies. There was sheds made out of poles and roofed over with branches, where they had lemonade and gingerbread to sell, and piles of watermelons and green corn and such-like truck.

The preaching was going on under the same kinds of sheds, only they was bigger and held crowds of people. The benches was made out of outside slabs of logs, with holes bored in the round side to drive sticks into for legs. They didn't have no backs. The preachers had high platforms to stand on, at one end of the sheds. The women had on sunbonnets; and some had linsey-woolsey[3] frocks, some gingham ones, and a few of the young ones had on calico. Some of the young men was barefooted, and some of the children didn't have on any clothes but just a tow-linen shirt. Some of the old women was knitting, and some of the young folks was courting on the sly.

The first shed we come to, the preacher was lining out a hymn. He lined out two lines, everybody sung it, and it was kind of grand to hear it, there was so many of them and they done it in such a

3. Coarse cloth made of linen and wool or cotton and wool.

rousing way; then he lined out two more for them to sing—and so on. The people woke up more and more, and sung louder and louder; and towards the end, some begun to groan, and some begun to shout. Then the preacher begun to preach; and begun in earnest, too; and went weaving first to one side of the platform and then the other, and then a leaning down over the front of it, with his arms and his body going all the time, and shouting his words out with all his might; and every now and then he would hold up his Bible and spread it open, and kind of pass it around this way and that, shouting, "It's the brazen serpent in the wilderness! Look upon it and live!" And people would shout out, "Glory! —A-a-*men!*" And so he went on, and the people groaning and crying and saying amen:

"Oh, come to the mourners' bench![4] come, black with sin! (*amen!*) come, sick and sore! (*amen!*) come, lame and halt, and blind! (*amen!*) come, pore and needy, sunk in shame! (*a-a-men!*) come all that's worn, and soiled, and suffering!—come with a broken spirit! come with a contrite heart! come in your rags and sin and dirt! the waters that cleanse is free, the door of heaven stands open—oh, enter in and be at rest!" (*a-a-men! glory, glory hallelujah!*)

And so on. You couldn't make out what the preacher said, any more, on account of the shouting and crying. Folks got up, everywheres in the crowd, and worked their way, just by main strength, to the mourners' bench, with the tears running down their faces; and when all the mourners had got up there to the front benches in a crowd, they sung, and shouted, and flung themselves down on the straw, just crazy and wild.

Well, the first I knowed, the king got agoing; and you could hear him over everybody; and next he went a-charging up on to the platform and the preacher he begged him to speak to the people, and he done it. He told them he was a pirate—been a pirate for thirty years, out in the Indian Ocean, and his crew was thinned out considerable, last spring, in a fight, and he was home now, to take out some fresh men, and thanks to goodness he'd been robbed last night, and put ashore off of a steamboat without a cent, and he was glad of it, it was the blessedest thing that ever happened to him, because he was a changed man now, and happy for the first time in his life; and poor as he was, he was going to start right off and work his way back to the Indian Ocean and put in the rest of his life trying to turn the pirates into the true path; for he could do it better than anybody else, being acquainted with all the pirate crews in that ocean; and though it would take him a long time to

4. Front-row seats reserved for penitents.

get there, without money, he would get there anyway, and every time he convinced a pirate he would say to him, "Don't you thank me, don't you give me no credit, it all belongs to them dear people in Pokeville camp-meeting, natural brothers and benefactors of the race—and that dear preacher there, the truest friend a pirate ever had!"

And then he busted into tears, and so did everybody. Then somebody sings out, "Take up a collection for him, take up a collection!" Well, a half a dozen made a jump to do it, but somebody sings out, "Let *him* pass the hat around!" Then everybody said it, the preacher too.

So the king went all through the crowd with his hat, swabbing his eyes, and blessing the people and praising them and thanking them for being so good to the poor pirates away off there; and every little while the prettiest kind of girls, with the tears running down their cheeks, would up and ask him would he let them kiss him, for to remember him by; and he always done it; and some of them he hugged and kissed as many as five or six times—and he was invited to stay a week; and everybody wanted him to live in their houses, and said they'd think it was an honor; but he said as this was the last day of the camp-meeting he couldn't do no good, and besides he was in a sweat to get to the Indian Ocean right off and go to work on the pirates.

When we got back to the raft and he come to count up, he found he had collected eighty-seven dollars and seventy-five cents. And then he had fetched away a three-gallon jug of whisky, too, that he found under a wagon when we was starting home through the woods. The king said, take it all around, it laid over any day he'd ever put in in the missionarying line. He said it warn't no use talking, heathens don't amount to shucks, alongside of pirates, to work a campmeeting with.

The duke was thinking *he'd* been doing pretty well, till the king come to show up, but after that he didn't think so so much. He had set up and printed off two little jobs for farmers, in that printing office—horse bills—and took the money, four dollars. And he had got in ten dollars worth of advertisements for the paper, which he said he would put in for four dollars if they would pay in advance—so they done it. The price of the paper was two dollars a year, but he took in three subscriptions for half a dollar apiece on condition of them paying him in advance; they were going to pay in cordwood and onions, as usual. but he said he had just bought the concern and knocked down the price as low as he could afford it, and was going to run it for cash. He set up a little piece of poetry, which he made, himself, out of his own head—three verses—kind of sweet and saddish—the name of it was, "Yes, crush, cold world, this breaking heart"—and he left that all set up and ready to print in the paper and didn't charge nothing for it. Well, he took in nine

dollars and a half, and said he'd done a pretty square day's work for
it.

Then he showed us another little job he'd printed and hadn't
charged for, because it was for us. It had a picture of a runaway
nigger, with a bundle on a stick, over his shoulder, and "$200 re-
ward" under it. The reading was all about Jim, and just described
him to a dot. It said he run away from St. Jacques' plantation, forty
mile below New Orleans, last winter, and likely went north, and
whoever would catch him and send him back, he could have the
reward and expenses.

"Now," says the duke, "after to-night we can run in the daytime
if we want to. Whenever we see anybody coming, we can tie Jim
hand and foot with a rope, and lay him in the wigwam and show
this handbill and say we captured him up the river, and were too
poor to travel on a steamboat, so we got this little raft on credit
from our friends and are going down to get the reward. Handcuffs
and chains would look still better on Jim, but it wouldn't go well
with the story of us being so poor. Too much like jewelry. Ropes
are the correct thing—we must preserve the unities, as we say on
the boards."

We all said the duke was pretty smart, and there couldn't be no
trouble about running daytimes. We judged we could make miles
enough that night to get out of the reach of the pow-wow we reckoned the duke's work in the printing office was going to make in that
little town—then we could boom right along, if we wanted to.

We laid low and kept still, and never shoved out till nearly ten
o'clock; then we slid by, pretty wide away from the town, and didn't
hoist our lantern till we was clear out of sight of it.

When Jim called me to take the watch at four in the morning,
he says—

"Huck, does you reck'n we gwyne to run acrost any mo' kings on
dis trip?"

"No," I says, "I reckon not."

"Well," says he, "dat's all right, den. I doan' mine one er two
kings, but dat's enough. Dis one's powerful drunk, en de duke ain'
much better."

I found Jim had been trying to get him to talk French, so he
could hear what it was like; but he said he had been in this country
so long, and had so much trouble, he'd forgot it.

Chapter XXI [5]

It was after sun-up, now, but we went right on, and didn't tie up.
The king and the duke turned out, by-and-by, looking pretty rusty;

5. Somewhere in this chapter—perhaps
at the point where the canoe reaches the
town—Clemens picked up his manuscript
after having added only a little over four
chapters in four years. In a creative
burst he finished a first draft of the
book between summer and autumn, 1883.

but after they'd jumped overboard and took a swim, it chippered them up a good deal. After breakfast the king he took a seat on a corner of the raft, and pulled off his boots and rolled up his britches, and let his legs dangle in the water, so as to be comfortable, and lit his pipe, and went to getting his Romeo and Juliet by heart. When he had got it pretty good, him and the duke begun to practice it together. The duke had to learn him over and over again, how to say every speech; and he made him sigh, and put his hand on his heart, and after while he said he done it pretty well; "only," he says, "you mustn't bellow out *Romeo!* that way, like a bull— you must say it soft, and sick, and languishy, so—R-o-o-meo! that is the idea; for Juliet's a dear sweet mere child of a girl, you know, and she don't bray like a jackass."

Well, next they got out a couple of long swords that the duke made out of oak laths, and begun to practice the sword-fight—the duke called himself Richard III.; and the way they laid on, and pranced around the raft was grand to see. But by-and-by the king tripped and fell overboard, and after that they took a rest, and had a talk about all kinds of adventures they'd had in other times along the river.

After dinner, the duke says:

"Well, Capet,[6] we'll want to make this a first-class show, you know, so I guess we'll add a little more to it. We want a little something to answer encores with, anyway."

"What's onkores, Bilgewater?"

The duke told him, and then says:

"I'll answer by doing the Highland fling or the sailor's hornpipe; and you—well, let me see—oh, I've got it—you can do Hamlet's soliloquy."

"Hamlet's which?"

"Hamlet's soliloquy, you know; the most celebrated thing in Shakespeare. Ah, it's sublime, sublime! Always fetches the house. I haven't got it in the book—I've only got one volume—but I reckon I can piece it out from memory. I'll just walk up and down a minute, and see if I can call it back from recollection's vaults."

So he went to marching up and down, thinking, and frowning horrible every now and then; then he would hoist up his eyebrows; next he would squeeze his hand on his forehead and stagger back and kind of moan; next he would sigh, and next he'd let on to drop a tear. It was beautiful to see him. By-and-by he got it. He told us to give attention. Then he strikes a most noble attitude, with one leg shoved forwards, and his arms stretched away up, and his head tilted back, looking up at the sky; and then he begins to rip and rave and grit his teeth; and after that, all through his speech he

6. When convicting Louis XVI, the National Convention used his family name, Louis Capet. The duke may also be garbling Juliet's family name, Capulet.

howled, and spread around, and swelled up his chest, and just
knocked the spots out of any acting ever I see before. This is the
speech—I learned it, easy enough, while he was learning it to the
king:[7]

To be, or not to be; that is the bare bodkin
That makes calamity of so long life;
For who would fardels bear, till Birnam Wood do come to Dun-
    sinane,
But that the fear of something after death
Murders the innocent sleep,
Great nature's second course,
And makes us rather sling the arrows of outrageous fortune
Than fly to others that we know not of.
There's the respect must give us pause:
Wake Duncan with thy knocking! I would thou couldst;
For who would bear the whips and scorns of time,
The oppressor's wrong, the proud man's contumely,
The law's delay, and the quietus which his pangs might take,
In the dead waste and middle of the night, when churchyards yawn
In customary suits of solemn black,
But that the undiscovered country from whose bourne no traveler
    returns,
Breathes forth contagion on the world,
And thus the native hue of resolution, like the poor cat i' the adage,
Is sicklied o'er with care,
And all the clouds that lowered o'er our housetops,
With this regard their currents turn awry,
And lose the name of action.
'Tis a consummation devoutly to be wished. But soft you, the fair
    Ophelia:
Ope not thy ponderous and marble jaws,
But get thee to a nunnery—go!

Well, the old man he liked that speech, and he mighty soon got
it so he could do it first rate. It seemed like he was just born for it;
and when he had his hand in and was excited, it was perfectly lovely
the way he would rip and tear and rair up behind when he was getting it off.

The first chance we got, the duke he had some show bills printed;
and after that, for two or three days as we floated along, the raft
was a most uncommon lively place, for there warn't nothing but
sword-fighting and rehearsing—as the duke called it—going on all
the time. One morning, when we was pretty well down the State

7. The duke is supposed to be reciting
the soliloquy from *Hamlet*, Act III,
scene ii, but his fractured Shakespeare
distorts famous lines from several other
plays, particularly *Macbeth*.

of Arkansaw, we come in sight of a little one-horse town in a big bend; so we tied up about three-quarters of a mile above it, in the mouth of a crick which was shut in like a tunnel by the cypress trees, and all of us but Jim took the canoe and went down there to see if there was any chance in that place for our show.

We struck it mighty lucky; there was going to be a circus there that afternoon, and the country people was already beginning to come in, in all kinds of old shackly wagons, and on horses. The circus would leave before night, so our show would have a pretty good chance. The duke he hired the court house, and we went around and stuck up our bills. They read like this:

Shaksperean Revival! ! !
Wonderful Attraction!
For One Night Only!
The world renowned tragedians,
David Garrick the younger, of Drury Lane Theatre, London,
and
Edmund Kean the elder, of the Royal Haymarket Theatre, White-
chapel, Pudding Lane, Piccadilly, London, and the
Royal Continental Theatres, in their sublime
Shaksperean Spectacle entitled
The Balcony Scene
in
Romeo and Juliet! ! !

Romeo . . . . Mr. Garrick.
Juliet . . . . Mr. Kean.

Assisted by the whole strength of the company!
New costumes, new scenery, new appointments!
Also:
The thrilling, masterly, and blood-curdling
Broad-sword conflict
In Richard III.! ! !

Richard III . . . . Mr. Garrick.
Richmond . . . . Mr. Kean.

also:
(by special request,)
Hamlet's Immortal Soliloquy! !
By the Illustrious Kean!
Done by him 300 consecutive nights in Paris!
For One Night Only,
On account of imperative European engagements!
Admission 25 cents; children and servants, 10 cents.

Then we went loafing around the town. The stores and houses was most all old shackly dried-up frame concerns that hadn't ever been painted; they was set up three or four foot above ground on stilts, so as to be out of reach of the water when the river was over-flowed. The houses had little gardens around them, but they didn't seem to raise hardly anything in them but jimpson weeds, and sun-flowers, and ash-piles, and old curled-up boots and shoes, and pieces

of bottles, and rags, and played-out tin-ware. The fences was made
of different kinds of boards, nailed on at different times; and they
leaned every which-way, and had gates that didn't generly have but
one hinge—a leather one. Some of the fences had been whitewashed, some time or another, but the duke said it was in Clum-
bus's time, like enough. There was generly hogs in the garden, and
people driving them out.

All the stores was along one street. They had white-domestic
awnings in front, and the country people hitched their horses to
the awning-posts. There was empty dry-goods boxes under the awnings, and loafers roosting on them all day long, whittling them with
their Barlow knives; and chawing tobacco, and gaping and yawning
and stretching—a mighty ornery lot. They generly had on yellow
straw hats most as wide as an umbrella, but didn't wear no coats
nor waistcoats; they called one another Bill, and Buck, and Hank,
and Joe, and Andy, and talked lazy and drawly, and used considerable many cuss-words. There was as many as one loafer leaning up
against every awning-post, and he most always had his hands in his
britches pockets, except when he fetched them out to lend a chaw
of tobacco or scratch. What a body was hearing amongst them, all
the time was—

"Gimme a chaw 'v tobacker, Hank."

"Cain't—I hain't got but one chaw left. Ask Bill."

Maybe Bill he gives him a chaw; maybe he lies and says he ain't
got none. Some of them kinds of loafers never has a cent in the
world, nor a chaw of tobacco of their own. They get all their chawing by borrowing—they say to a fellow, "I wisht you'd len' me a
chaw, Jack, I jist this minute give Ben Thompson the last chaw I
had"—which is a lie, pretty much every time; it don't fool nobody
but a stranger; but Jack ain't no stranger, so he says—

"*You* give him a chaw, did you? so did your sister's cat's grandmother. You pay me back the chaws you've awready borry'd off'n
me, Lafe Buckner, then I'll loan you one or two ton of it, and won't
charge you no back intrust, nuther."

"Well, I *did* pay you back some of it wunst."

"Yes, you did—'bout six chaws. You borry'd store tobacker and
paid back nigger-head."

Store tobacco is flat black plug, but these fellows mostly chaws
the natural leaf twisted. When they borrow a chaw, they don't
generly cut it off with a knife, but they set the plug in between their
teeth, and gnaw with their teeth and tug at the plug with their
hands till they get it in two—then sometimes the one that owns the
tobacco looks mournful at it when it's handed back, and says, sarcastic—

"Here, gimme the *chaw*, and you take the *plug*."

All the streets and lanes was just mud, they warn't nothing else *but* mud—mud as black as tar, and nigh about a foot deep in some places; and two or three inches deep in *all* the places. The hogs loafed and grunted around, everywheres. You'd see a muddy sow and a litter of pigs come lazying along the street and whollop herself right down in the way, where folks had to walk around her, and she'd stretch out, and shut her eyes, and wave her ears, whilst the pigs was milking her, and look as happy as if she was on salary. And pretty soon you'd hear a loafer sing out, "Hi! *so* boy! sick him, Tige!" and away the sow would go, squealing most horrible, with a dog or two swinging to each ear, and three or four dozen more a-coming; and then you would see all the loafers get up and watch the thing out of sight, and laugh at the fun and look grateful for the noise. Then they'd settle back again till there was a dog-fight. There couldn't anything wake them up all over, and make them happy all over, like a dog-fight—unless it might be putting turpentine on a stray dog and setting fire to him, or tying a tin pan to his tail and see him run himself to death.

On the river front some of the houses was sticking out over the actual bank, and they was bowed and bent, and about ready to tumble in. The people had moved out of them. The bank was caved away under one corner of some others, and that corner was hanging over. People lived in them yet, but it was dangersome, because sometimes a strip of land as wide as a house caves in at a time. Sometimes a belt of land a quarter of a mile deep will start in and cave along and cave along till it all caves into the river in one summer. Such a town as that has to be always moving back, and back, and back, because the river's always gnawing at it.

The nearer it got to noon that day, the thicker and thicker was the wagons and horses in the streets, and more coming all the time. Families fetched their dinners with them, from the country, and eat them in the wagons. There was considerable whiskey drinking going on, and I seen three fights. By-and-by somebody sings out—

"Here comes old Boggs![8]—in from the country for his little old monthly drunk—here he comes, boys!"

All the loafers looked glad—I reckoned they was used to having fun out of Boggs. One of them says—

"Wonder who he's a gwyne to chaw up this time. If he'd a chawed up all the men he's ben a gwyne to chaw up in the last twenty year, he'd have considerble ruputation, now."

Another one says, "I wisht old Boggs'd threaten me, 'cuz then I'd know I warn't gwyne to die for a thousan' year."

8. The following episode is based on an actual murder committed in Hannibal in 1845 when Clemens was ten years old. His father, John M. Clemens, Justice of the Peace, took down twenty-eight depositions by witnesses, for which labor he was paid $13.50.

Boggs comes a-tearing along on his horse, whooping and yelling like an Injun, and singing out—

"Cler the track, thar. I'm on the waw-path, and the price uv coffins is a gwyne to raise."

He was drunk, and weaving about in his saddle; he was over fifty year old, and had a very red face. Everybody yelled at him, and laughed at him, and sassed him, and he sassed back, and said he'd attend to them and lay them out in their regular turns, but he couldn't wait now, because he'd come to town to kill old Colonel Sherburn, and his motto was, "meat first, and spoon vittles to top off on."

He see me, and rode up and says—

"Whar'd you come f'm, boy? You prepared to die?"

Then he rode on. I was scared; but a man says—

"He don't mean nothing; he's always a carryin' on like that, when he's drunk. He's the best-naturedest old fool in Arkansaw—never hurt nobody, drunk nor sober."

Boggs rode up before the biggest store in town and bent his head down so he could see under the curtain of the awning, and yells—

"Come out here, Sherburn! Come out and meet the man you've swindled. You're the houn' I'm after, and I'm a gwyne to have you, too!"

And so he went on, calling Sherburn everything he could lay his tongue to, and the whole street packed with people listening and laughing and going on. By-and-by a proud-looking man about fifty-five—and he was a heap the best dressed man in that town, too—steps out of the store, and the crowd drops back on each side to let him come. He says to Boggs, mighty ca'm and slow—he says:

"I'm tired of this; but I'll endure it till one o'clock. Till one o'clock, mind—no longer. If you open your mouth against me only once, after that time, you can't travel so far but I will find you."

Then he turns and goes in. The crowd looked mighty sober; nobody stirred, and there warn't no more laughing. Boggs rode off blackguarding Sherburn as loud as he could yell, all down the street; and pretty soon back he comes and stops before the store, still keeping it up. Some men crowded around him and tried to get him to shut up, but he wouldn't; they told him it would be one o'clock in about fifteen minutes, and so he *must* go home—he must go right away. But it didn't do no good. He cussed away, with all his might, and throwed his hat down in the mud and rode over it, and pretty soon away he went a-raging down the street again, with his gray hair a-flying. Everybody that could get a chance at him tried their best to coax him off of his horse so they could lock him up and get him sober; but it warn't no use—up the street he would tear again, and give Sherburn another cussing. By-and-by somebody says—

"Go for his daughter!—quick, go for his daughter; sometimes he'll listen to her. If anybody can persuade him, she can."

So somebody started on a run. I walked down street a ways, and stopped. In about five or ten minutes, here comes Boggs again— but not on his horse. He was a-reeling across the street towards me, bareheaded, with a friend on both sides of him aholt of his arms and hurrying him along. He was quiet, and looked uneasy; and he warn't hanging back any, but was doing some of the hurrying himself. Somebody sings out—

"Boggs!"

I looked over there to see who said it, and it was that Colonel Sherburn. He was standing perfectly still, in the street, and had a pistol raised in his right hand—not aiming it, but holding it out with the barrel tilted up towards the sky. The same second I see a young girl coming on the run, and two men with her. Boggs and the men turned round, to see who called him, and when they see the pistol the men jumped to one side, and the pistol barrel come down slow and steady to a level—both barrels cocked. Boggs throws up both of his hands, and says, "O Lord, don't shoot!" Bang! goes the first shot, and he staggers back clawing at the air—bang! goes the second one, and he tumbles backwards onto the ground, heavy and solid, with his arms spread out. That young girl screamed out, and comes rushing, and down she throws herself on her father, crying, and saying, "Oh, he's killed him, he's killed him!" The crowd closed up around them, and shouldered and jammed one another, with their necks stretched, trying to see, and people on the inside trying to shove them back, and shouting, "Back, back! give him air, give him air!"

Colonel Sherburn he tossed his pistol onto the ground, and turned around on his heels and walked off.

They took Boggs to a little drug store, the crowd pressing around, just the same, and the whole town following, and I rushed and got a good place at the window, where I was close to him and could see in. They laid him on the floor, and put one large Bible under his head, and opened another one and spread it on his breast—but they tore open his shirt first, and I seen where one of the bullets went in. He made about a dozen long gasps, his breast lifting the Bible up when he drawed in his breath, and letting it down again when he breathed it out—and after that he laid still; he was dead. Then they pulled his daughter away from him, screaming and crying, and took her off. She was about sixteen, and very sweet and gentle-looking, but awful pale and scared.

Well, pretty soon the whole town was there, squirming and scrouging and pushing and shoving to get at the window and have a look, but people that had the places wouldn't give them up, and folks behind them was saying all the time, "Say, now, you've looked enough, you fellows; 'taint right and 'taint fair, for you to stay thar all the time, and never give nobody a chance; other folks has their rights as well as you."

There was considerable jawing back, so I slid out, thinking maybe there was going to be trouble. The streets was full, and everybody was excited. Everybody that seen the shooting was telling how it happened, and there was a big crowd packed around each one of these fellows, stretching their necks and listening. One long lanky man, with long hair and a big white fur stove-pipe hat on the back of his head, and a crooked-handled cane, marked out the places on the ground where Boggs stood, and where Sherburn stood, and the people following him around from one place to t'other and watching everything he done, and bobbing their heads to show they understood, and stooping a little and resting their hands on their thighs to watch him mark the places on the ground with his cane; and then he stood up straight and stiff where Sherburn had stood, frowning and having his hat-brim down over his eyes, and sung out, "Boggs!" and then fetched his cane down slow to a level, and says "Bang!" staggered backwards, says "Bang!" again, and fell down flat on his back. The people that had seen the thing said he done it perfect; said it was just exactly the way it all happened. Then as much as a dozen people got out their bottles and treated him.

Well, by-and-by somebody said Sherburn ought to be lynched. In about a minute everybody was saying it; so away they went, mad and yelling, and snatching down every clothes-line they come to, to do the hanging with.

Chapter XXII

They swarmed up the street towards Sherburn's house, a-whooping and yelling and raging like Injuns, and everything had to clear the way or get run over and tromped to mush, and it was awful to see. Children was heeling it ahead of the mob, screaming and trying to get out of the way; and every window along the road was full of women's heads, and there was nigger boys in every tree, and bucks and wenches looking over every fence; and as soon as the mob would get nearly to them they would break and skaddle back out of reach. Lots of the women and girls was crying and taking on, scared most to death.

They swarmed up in front of Sherburn's palings as thick as they could jam together, and you couldn't hear yourself think for the noise. It was a little twenty-foot yard. Some sung out "Tear down the fence! tear down the fence!" Then there was a racket of ripping and tearing and smashing, and down she goes, and the front wall of the crowd begins to roll in like a wave.

Just then Sherburn steps out on to the roof of his little front porch, with a double-barrel gun in his hand, and takes his stand, perfectly ca'm and deliberate, not saying a word. The racket stopped, and the wave sucked back.

Sherburn never said a word—just stood there, looking down. The stillness was awful creepy and uncomfortable. Sherburn run his eye slow along the crowd; and wherever it struck, the people tried a little to outgaze him, but they couldn't; they dropped their eyes and looked sneaky. Then pretty soon Sherburn sort of laughed; not the pleasant kind, but the kind that makes you feel like when you are eating bread that's got sand in it.

Then he says, slow and scornful:

"The idea of *you* lynching anybody! It's amusing. The idea of you thinking you had pluck enough to lynch a *man!* Because you're brave enough to tar and feather poor friendless cast-out women that come along here, did that make you think you had grit enough to lay your hands on a *man?* Why, a *man's* safe in the hands of ten thousand of your kind—as long as it's day-time and you're not behind him.

"Do I know you? I know you clear through. I was born and raised in the South, and I've lived in the North; so I know the average all around. The average man's a coward. In the North he lets anybody walk over him that wants to, and goes home and prays for a humble spirit to bear it. In the South one man, all by himself, has stopped a stage full of men, in the day-time, and robbed the lot. Your newspapers call you a brave people so much that you think you *are* braver than any other people—whereas you're just *as* brave, and no braver. Why don't your juries hang murderers? Because they're afraid the man's friends will shoot them in the back, in the dark—and it's just what they *would* do.

"So they always acquit; and then a *man* goes in the night, with a hundred masked cowards at his back, and lynches the rascal. Your mistake is, that you didn't bring a man with you; that's one mistake, and the other is that you didn't come in the dark, and fetch your masks. You brought *part* of a man—Buck Harkness, there—and if you hadn't had him to start you, you'd a taken it out in blowing.

"You didn't want to come. The average man don't like trouble and danger. *You* don't like trouble and danger. But if only *half* a man—like Buck Harkness, there—shouts 'Lynch him, lynch him!' you're afraid to back down—afraid you'll be found out to be what you are—*cowards*—and so you raise a yell, and hang yourselves onto that half-a-man's coat tail, and come raging up here, swearing what big things you're going to do. The pitifulest thing out is a mob; that's what an army is—a mob; they don't fight with courage that's born in them, but with courage that's borrowed from their mass, and from their officers. But a mob without any *man* at the head of it, is *beneath* pitifulness. Now the thing for you to do, is to droop your tails and go home and crawl in a hole. If any real lynching's going to be done, it will be done in the dark, Southern fashion; and when they come they'll bring their masks, and fetch a *man* along. Now *leave*—and take your half-a-man with you"—tossing his gun up across his left arm and cocking it, when he says this.

The crowd washed back sudden, and then broke all apart and went tearing off every which way, and Buck Harkness he heeled it after them, looking tolerable cheap. I could a staid, if I'd a wanted to, but I didn't want to.

I went to the circus, and loafed around the back side till the watchman went by, and then dived in under the tent. I had my twenty-dollar gold piece and some other money, but I reckoned I better save it, because there ain't no telling how soon you are going to need it, away from home and amongst strangers, that way. You can't be too careful. I ain't opposed to spending money on circuses, when there ain't no other way, but there ain't no use in *wasting* it on them.

It was a real bully circus. It was the splendidest sight that ever was, when they all come riding in, two and two, a gentleman and lady, side by side, the men just in their drawers and under-shirts, and no shoes nor stirrups, and resting their hands on their thighs, easy and comfortable—there must a' been twenty of them—and every lady with a lovely complexion, and perfectly beautiful, and looking just like a gang of real sure-enough queens, and dressed in clothes that cost millions of dollars, and just littered with diamonds. It was a powerful fine sight; I never see anything so lovely. And then one by one they got up and stood, and went a-weaving around the ring so gentle and wavy and graceful, the men looking ever so tall and airy and straight, with their heads bobbing and skimming along, away up there under the tent-roof, and every lady's rose-leafy dress flapping soft and silky around her hips, and she looking like the most loveliest parasol.

And then faster and faster they went, all of them dancing, first one foot stuck out in the air and then the other, the horses leaning more and more, and the ring-master going round and round the centre-pole, cracking his whip and shouting "hi!—hi!" and the clown cracking jokes behind him; and by-and-by all hands dropped the reins, and every lady put her knuckles on her hips and every gentleman folded his arms, and then how the horses did lean over and hump themselves! And so, one after the other they all skipped off into the ring, and made the sweetest bow I ever see, and then scampered out, and everybody clapped their hands and went just about wild.

Well, all through the circus they done the most astonishing

things; and all the time that clown carried on so it most killed the people. The ring-master couldn't ever say a word to him but he was back at him quick as a wink with the funniest things a body ever said; and how he ever *could* think of so many of them, and so sudden and so pat, was what I couldn't noway understand. Why, I couldn't a thought of them in a year. And by-and-by a drunk man tried to get into the ring—said he wanted to ride; said he could ride as well as anybody that ever was. They argued and tried to keep him out, but he wouldn't listen, and the whole show come to a standstill. Then the people begun to holler at him and make fun of him, and that made him mad, and he begun to rip and tear; so that stirred up the people, and a lot of men began to pile down off of the benches and swarm towards the ring, saying, "Knock him down! throw him out!" and one or two women begun to scream. So, then, the ring-master he made a little speech, and said he hoped there wouldn't be no disturbance, and if the man would promise he wouldn't make no more trouble, he would let him ride, if he thought he could stay on the horse. So everybody laughed and said all right, and the man got on. The minute he was on, the horse begun to rip and tear and jump and cavort around, with two circus men hanging onto his bridle trying to hold him, and the drunk man hanging onto his neck, and his heels flying in the air every jump, and the whole crowd of people standing up shouting and laughing till the tears rolled down. And at last, sure enough, all the circus men could do, the horse broke loose, and away he went like the very nation, round and round the ring, with that sot laying down on him and hanging to his neck, with first one leg hanging most to the ground on one side, and then t'other one on t'other side, and the people just crazy. It warn't funny to me, though; I was all of a tremble to see his danger. But pretty soon he struggled up astraddle and grabbed the bridle, a-reeling this way and that; and the next minute he sprung up and dropped the bridle and stood! and the horse agoing like a house afire too. He just stood up there, a-sailing around as easy and comfortable as if he warn't ever drunk in his life —and then he begun to pull off his clothes and sling them. He shed them so thick they kind of clogged up the air, and altogether he shed seventeen suits. And then, there he was, slim and handsome, and dressed the gaudiest and prettiest you ever saw, and he lit into that horse with his whip and made him fairly hum—and finally skipped off, and made his bow and danced off to the dressing-room, and everybody just a-howling with pleasure and astonishment.

Then the ring-master he see how he had been fooled, and he *was* the sickest ring-master you ever see, I reckon. Why, it was one of his own men! He had got up that joke all out of his own head, and never let on to nobody. Well, I felt sheepish enough, to be took in so, but I wouldn't a been in that ring-master's place, not for a thousand dollars. I don't know; there may be bullier circuses than what that one was, but I never struck them yet. Anyways it was plenty good enough for *me*; and wherever I run across it, it can have all of *my* custom, every time.

Well, that night we had *our* show; but there warn't only about twelve people there; just enough to pay expenses. And they laughed all the time, and that made the duke mad; and everybody left, anyway, before the show was over, but one boy which was asleep. So the duke said these Arkansaw lunkheads couldn't come up to Shakspeare; what they wanted was low comedy—and may be something ruther worse than low comedy, he reckoned. He said he could size their style. So next morning he got some big sheets of wrapping-paper and some black paint, and drawed off some handbills and stuck them up all over the village. The bills said:

AT THE COURT HOUSE!
FOR 3 NIGHTS ONLY!
The World-Renowned Tragedians
DAVID GARRICK THE YOUNGER
AND
EDMUND KEAN THE ELDER!
*Of the London and Continental
Theatres,*
In their Thrilling Tragedy of
THE KING'S CAMELOPARD
OR
THE ROYAL NONESUCH! ! !
Admission 50 cents.

Then at the bottom was the biggest line of all—which said:

LADIES AND CHILDREN NOT ADMITTED.

"There," says he, "if that line don't fetch them, I dont know Arkansaw!"

Chapter XXIII

Well, all day him and the king was hard at it, rigging up a stage, and a curtain, and a row of candles for footlights; and that night the house was jam full of men in no time. When the place couldn't hold no more, the duke he quit tending door and went around the back way and come onto the stage and stood up before the curtain, and made a little speech, and praised up this tragedy, and said it was the most thrillingest one that ever was; and so he went on a-bragging about the tragedy and about Edmund Kean the Elder, which was to play the main principal part in it; and at last when he'd got everybody's expectations up high enough, he rolled up the curtain, and the next minute the king come a-prancing out on all fours, naked; and he was painted all over, ring-streaked-and-striped, all sorts of colors, as splendid as a rainbow. And—but never mind the rest of his outfit, it was just wild, but it was awful funny. The people most killed themselves laughing; and when the king got done caper-ing, and capered off behind the scenes, they roared and clapped and stormed and haw-hawed till he come back and done it over again; and after that, they made him do it another time. Well, it would a made a cow laugh to see the shines that old idiot cut.[9]

Then the duke he lets the curtain down, and bows to the people, and says the great tragedy will be performed only two nights more, on accounts of pressing London engagements, where the seats is all sold aready for it in Drury Lane; and then he makes them another bow, and says if he has succeeded in pleasing them and instructing them, he will be deeply obleeged if they will mention it to their friends and get them to come and see it.

Twenty people sings out:

"What, is it over? Is that *all?*"

The duke says yes. Then there was a fine time. Everybody sings out "sold," and rose up mad, and was agoing for that stage and them tragedians. But a big fine-looking man jumps up on a bench, and shouts:

"Hold on! Just a word, gentlemen." They stopped to listen. "We are sold—mighty badly sold. But we don't want to be the laughing-stock of this whole town, I reckon, and never hear the last of this thing as long as we live. *No.* What we want, is to go out of here quiet, and talk this show up, and sell the *rest* of the town! Then we'll all be in the same boat. Ain't that sensible?" ("You bet it is! —the jedge is right!" everybody sings out.) "All right, then—not a word about any sell. Go along home, and advise everybody to come and see the tragedy."

Next day you couldn't hear nothing around that town but how splendid that show was. House was jammed again, that night, and we sold this crowd the same way. When me and the king and the duke got home to the raft, we all had a supper; and by-and-by, about midnight, they made Jim and me back her out and float her down the middle of the river and fetch her in and hide her about two mile below town.

The third night the house was crammed again—and they warn't new-comers, this time, but people that was at the show the other two nights. I stood by the duke at the door, and I see that every

9. Clemens's *Autobiography* mentions "The Tragedy of the Burning Shame," an "unprintable" story he first heard in the 1860s from a gifted raconteur named Jim Gillis. A "pale" version appeared in *Huckleberry Finn,* Clemens recalled. This lusty, probably phallic yarn was one model for the duke's performance.

man that went in had his pockets bulging, or something muffled up under his coat—and I see it warn't no perfumery neither, not by a long sight. I smelt sickly eggs by the barrel, and rotten cabbages. and such things; and if I know the signs of a dead cat being around. and I bet I do, there was sixty-four of them went in. I shoved in there for a minute, but it was too various for me, I couldn't stand it. Well, when the place couldn't hold no more people, the duke he give a fellow a quarter and told him to tend door for him a minute, and then he started around for the stage door, I after him; but the minute we turned the corner and was in the dark, he says:

"Walk fast, now, till you get away from the houses, and then shin for the raft like the dickens was after you!"

I done it, and he done the same. We struck the raft at the same time, and in less than two seconds we was gliding down stream, all dark and still, and edging towards the middle of the river, nobody saying a word. I reckoned the poor king was in for a gaudy time of it with the audience; but nothing of the sort; pretty soon he crawls out from under the wigwam, and says:

"Well, how'd the old thing pan out this time, Duke?"

He hadn't been up town at all.

We never showed a light till we was about ten mile below that village. Then we lit up and had a supper, and the king and the duke fairly laughed their bones loose over the way they'd served them people. The duke says:

"Greenhorns, flatheads! I knew the first house would keep mum and let the rest of the town get roped in; and I knew they'd lay for us the third night, and consider it was *their* turn now. Well, it *is* their turn, and I'd give something to know how much they'd take for it. I *would* just like to know how they're putting in their opportunity. They can turn it into a picnic, if they want to—they brought plenty provisions."

Them rapscallions took in four hundred and sixty-five dollars in that three nights. I never see money hauled in by the wagon-load like that, before.

By-and-by, when they was asleep and snoring, Jim says:

"Don't it 'sprise you, de way dem kings carries on, Huck?"

"No," I says, "it don't."

"Why don't it, Huck?"

"Well, it don't, because it's in the breed. I reckon they're all alike."

"But, Huck, dese kings o' ourn is regular rapscallions; dat's jist what dey is; dey's reglar rapscallions."

"Well, that's what I'm a-saying; all kings is mostly rapscallions, as fur as I can make out."

"Is dat so?"

"You read about them once—you'll see. Look at Henry the Eight; this'n 's a Sunday-School Superintendent to *him*. And look at Charles Second, and Louis Fourteen, and Louis Fifteen, and James Second, and Edward Second, and Richard Third, and forty more; besides all them Saxon heptarchies that used to rip around so in old times and raise Cain. My, you ought to seen old Henry the Eight when he was in bloom.[1] He *was* a blossom. He used to marry a new wife every day, and chop off her head next morning. And he would do it just as indifferent as if he was ordering up eggs. 'Fetch up Nell Gwynn,' he says. They fetch her up. Next morning, 'Chop off her head!' And they chop it off. 'Fetch up Jane Shore,' he says; and up she comes. Next morning 'Chop off her head'—and they chop it off. 'Ring up Fair Rosamun.' Fair Rosamun answers the bell. Next morning, 'Chop off her head.' And he made every one of them tell him a tale every night; and he kept that up till he had hogged a thousand and one tales that way, and then he put them all in a book, and called it Domesday Book—which was a good name and stated the case. You don't know kings, Jim, but I know them; and this old rip of ourn is one of the cleanest I've struck in history. Well, Henry he takes a notion he wants to get up some trouble with this country. How does he go at it—give notice? —give the country a show? No. All of a sudden he heaves all the tea in Boston Harbor overboard, and whacks out a declaration of independence, and dares them to come on. That was *his* style—he never give anybody a chance. He had suspicions of his father, the Duke of Wellington. Well, what did he do?—ask him to show up? No—drownded him in a butt of mamsey, like a cat. Spose people left money laying around where he was—what did he do? He collared it. Spose he contracted to do a thing; and you paid him, and didn't set down there and see that he done it—what did he do? He always done the other thing. Spose he opened his mouth—what then? If he didn't shut it up powerful quick, he'd lose a lie, every time. That's the kind of a bug Henry was; and if we'd a had him along 'stead of our kings, he'd a fooled that town a heap worse than ourn done. I don't say that ourn is lambs, because they ain't, when you come right down to the cold facts; but they ain't nothing to *that* old ram, anyway. All I say is, kings is kings, and you got to make allowances. Take them all around, they're a mighty ornery lot. It's the way they're raised."

---

1. Huck's description of Henry VIII (1509–47) grandly confuses the historical *Domesday Book* with the fictional *Arabian Nights' Entertainments,* and it conflates persons, incidents, and even centuries that had no connection with Henry. He makes the sixteenth-century king the son of the nineteenth-century Duke of Wellington, whom he confuses with the fifteenth-century Duke of Clarence (supposedly drowned in a butt of malmsey wine). Fair Rosamond was mistress to twelfth-century Henry II, Jane Shore to fifteenth-century Edward IV, Nell Gwyn to seventeenth-century Charles II.

"But dis one do *smell* so like de nation, Huck."

"Well, they all do, Jim. We can't help the way a king smells; history don't tell no way."

"Now de duke, he's a tolerble likely man, in some ways."

"Yes, a duke's different. But not very different. This one's a middling hard lot, for a duke. When he's drunk, there ain't no near-sighted man could tell him from a king."

"Well, anyways, I doan' hanker for no mo' un um, Huck. Dese is all I kin stan'."

"It's the way I feel, too, Jim. But we've got them on our hands, and we got to remember what they are, and make allowances. Sometimes I wish we could hear of a country that's out of kings."

What was the use to tell Jim these warn't real kings and dukes? It wouldn't a done no good; and besides, it was just as I said; you couldn't tell them from the real kind.

I went to sleep, and Jim didn't call me when it was my turn. He often done that. When I waked up, just at day-break, he was setting there with his head down betwixt his knees, moaning and mourning to himself. I didn't take notice, nor let on. I knowed what it was about. He was thinking about his wife and his children, away up yonder, and he was low and homesick; because he hadn't ever been away from home before in his life; and I do believe he cared just as much for his people as white folks does for their'n. It don't seem natural, but I reckon it's so. He was often moaning and mourning that way, nights, when he judged I was asleep, and saying, "Po' little 'Lizabeth! po' little Johnny! its mighty hard; I spec' I ain't ever gwyne to see you no mo', no mo'!" He was a mighty good nigger, Jim was.

But this time I somehow got to talking to him about his wife and young ones; and by-and-by he says:

"What makes me feel so bad dis time, 'uz bekase I hear sumpn over yonder on de bank like a whack, er a slam, while ago, en it mine me er de time I treat my little 'Lizabeth so ornery. She warn't on'y 'bout fo' year ole, en she tuck de sk'yarlet-fever, en had a powful rough spell; but she got well, en one day she was a-stannin' aroun', en I says to her, I says:

" 'Shet de do'.'

"She never done it; jis' stood dah, kiner smilin' up at me. It make me mad; en I says agin, mighty loud, I says:

" 'Doan' you hear me?—shet de do'!'

"She jis' stood de same way, kiner smilin' up. I was a-bilin'! I says:

" 'I lay I *make* you mine!'

"En wid dat I fetch' her a slap side de head dat sont her a-sprawlin'. Den I went into de yuther room, en 'uz gone 'bout ten minutes; en when I come back, dah was dat do' a-stannin' open *yit*, en dat chile stannin' mos' right in it, a-lookin' down and mournin', en de tears runnin' down. My, but I *wuz* mad, I was agwyne for de chile, but jis' den—it was a do' dat open innerds—jis' den, 'long come de wind en slam it to, behine de chile, ker-*blam!* —en my lan', de chile never move'! My breff mos' hop outer me; en I feel so—so—I doan' know *how* I feel. I crope out, all a-tremblin', en crope aroun' en open de do' easy en slow, en poke my head in behine de chile, sof' en still, en all uv a sudden, I says *pow!* jis' as loud as I could yell. *She never budge!* Oh, Huck, I bust out a-cryin' en grab her up in my arms, en say, 'Oh, de po' little thing! de Lord God Amighty fogive po' ole Jim, kaze he never gwyne to fogive hisself as long's he live!' Oh, she was plumb deef en dumb, Huck, plumb deef en dumb—en I'd ben a'treat'n her so!"

Chapter XXIV

Next day, towards night, we laid up under a little willow towhead out in the middle, where there was a village on each side of the river, and the duke and the king begun to lay out a plan for working them towns. Jim he spoke to the duke, and said he hoped it wouldn't take but a few hours, because it got mighty heavy and tiresome to him when he had to lay all day in the wigwam tied with the rope. You see, when we left him all alone we had to tie him, because if anybody happened on him all by himself and not tied, it wouldn't look much like he was a runaway nigger, you know. So the duke said it *was* kind of hard to have to lay roped all day, and he'd cipher out some way to get around it.

He was uncommon bright, the duke was, and he soon struck it. He dressed Jim up in King Lear's outfit—it was a long curtain-calico gown, and a white horse-hair wig and whiskers; and then he took his theatre-paint and painted Jim's face and hands and ears and neck all over a dead dull solid blue, like a man that's been drownded nine days. Blamed if he warn't the horriblest looking outrage I ever see. Then the duke took and wrote out a sign on a shingle so—

Sick Arab—but harmless when not out of his head.

And he nailed that shingle to a lath, and stood the lath up four or five foot in front of the wigwam. Jim was satisfied. He said it was a sight better than laying tied a couple of years every day and trembling all over every time there was a sound. The duke told him to make himself free and easy, and if anybody ever come meddling around, he must hop out of the wigwam, and carry on a little, and fetch a howl or two like a wild beast, and he reckoned they would light out and leave him alone. Which was sound enough judgment; but you take the average man, and he wouldn't wait for him to howl. Why, he didn't only look like he was dead, he looked considerable more than that.

These rapscallions wanted to try the Nonesuch again, because there was so much money in it, but they judged it wouldn't be safe, because maybe the news might a worked along down by this time. They couldn't hit no project that suited, exactly; so at last the duke said he reckoned he'd lay off and work his brains an hour or two and see if he couldn't put up something on the Arkansaw village; and the king he allowed he would drop over to t'other village, without any plan, but just trust in Providence to lead him the profitable way —meaning the devil, I reckon. We had all bought store clothes where we stopped last; and now the king put his'n on, and he told me to put mine on. I done it, of course. The king's duds was all black, and he did look real swell and starchy. I never knowed how clothes could change a body before. Why, before, he looked like the orneriest old rip that ever was; but now, when he'd take off his new white beaver and make a bow and do a smile, he looked that grand and good and pious that you'd say he had walked right out of the ark, and maybe was old Leviticus[2] himself. Jim cleaned up the canoe, and I got my paddle ready. There was a big steamboat laying at the shore away up under the point, about three mile above town—been there a couple of hours, taking on freight. Says the king:

"Seein' how I'm dressed, I reckon maybe I better arrive down from St. Louis or Cincinnati, or some other big place. Go for the steamboat, Huckleberry; we'll come down to the village on her."

I didn't have to be ordered twice, to go and take a steamboat ride. I fetched the shore a half a mile above the village, and then went scooting along the bluff bank in the easy water. Pretty soon we come to a nice innocent-looking young country jake setting on a log swabbing the sweat off of his face, for it was powerful warm weather; and he had a couple of big carpet-bags by him.

"Run her nose in shore," says the king. I done it. "Wher' you bound for, young man?"

"For the steamboat; going to Orleans."

"Git aboard," says the king. "Hold on a minute, my servant 'll he'p you with them bags. Jump out and he'p the gentleman, Adolphus"—meaning me, I see.

I done so, and then we all three started on again. The young chap was mighty thankful; said it was tough work toting his baggage such weather. He asked the king where he was going, and the king told him he'd come down the river and landed at the other village this morning, and now he was going up a few mile to see an old friend

---

2. A book of the Old Testament.

on a farm up there. The young fellow says:

"When I first see you, I says to myself, 'It's Mr. Wilks, sure, and he come mighty near getting here in time.' But then I says again, 'No, I reckon it ain't him, or else he wouldn't be paddling up the river.' You *ain't* him, are you?"

"No, my name's Blodgett—Elexander Blodgett—*Reverend* Elexander Blodgett, I spose I must say, as I'm one o' the Lord's poor servants. But still I'm jist as able to be sorry for Mr. Wilks for not arriving in time, all the same, if he's missed anything by it—which I hope he hasn't."

"Well, he don't miss any property by it, because he'll get that all right; but he's missed seeing his brother Peter die—which he mayn't mind, nobody can tell as to that—but his brother would a give anything in this world to see *him* before he died; never talked about nothing else all these three weeks; hadn't seen him since they was boys together—and hadn't ever seen his brother William at all— that's the deef and dumb one—William ain't more than thirty or thirty-five. Peter and George was the only ones that come out here; George was the married brother; him and his wife both died last year. Harvey and William's the only ones that's left now; and, as I was saying, they haven't got here in time."

"Did anybody send 'em word?"

"Oh, yes; a month or two ago, when Peter was first took; because Peter said then that he sorter felt like he warn't going to get well this time. You see, he was pretty old, and George's g'yirls was too young to be much company for him, except Mary Jane the red-headed one; and so he was kinder lonesome after George and his wife died, and didn't seem to care much to live. He most desperately wanted to see Harvey—and William too, for that matter—because he was one of them kind that can't bear to make a will. He left a letter behind for Harvey, and said he'd told in it where his money was hid, and how he wanted the rest of the property divided up so George's g'yirls would be all right—for George didn't leave nothing. And that letter was all they could get him to put a pen to."

"Why do you reckon Harvey don't come? Wher' does he live?"

"Oh, he lives in England—Sheffield—preaches there—hasn't ever been in this country. He hasn't had any too much time—and besides he mightn't a got the letter at all, you know."

"Too bad, too bad he couldn't a lived to see his brothers, poor soul. You going to Orleans, you say?"

"Yes, but that ain't only a part of it. I'm going in a ship, next Wednesday, for Ryo Janeero,[3] where my uncle lives."

"It's a pretty long journey. But it'll be lovely; I wisht I was agoing.

3. Presumably Rio de Janeiro in southeastern Brazil.

Is Mary Jane the oldest? How old is the others?"

"Mary Jane's nineteen, Susan's fifteen, and Joanna's about fourteen—that's the one that gives herself to good works and has a hare-lip."

"Poor things! to be left alone in the cold world so."

"Well, they could be worse off. Old Peter had friends, and they ain't going to let them come to no harm. There's Hobson, the Babtis' preacher; and Deacon Lot Hovey, and Ben Rucker, and Abner Shackleford, and Levi Bell, the lawyer; and Dr. Robinson, and their wives, and the widow Bartley, and—well, there's a lot of them; but these are the ones that Peter was thickest with, and used to write about sometimes, when he wrote home; so Harvey'll know where to look for friends when he gets here."

Well, the old man he went on asking questions till he just fairly emptied that young fellow. Blamed if he didn't inquire about everybody and everything in that blessed town, and all about all the Wilkses; and about Peter's business—which was a tanner; and about George's—which was a carpenter; and about Harvey's— which was a dissentering minister; and so on, and so on. Then he says:

"What did you want to walk all the way up to the steamboat for?"

"Because she's a big Orleans boat, and I was afeard she mightn't stop there. When they're deep they won't stop for a hail. A Cincinnati boat will, but this is a St. Louis one."

"Was Peter Wilks well off?"

"Oh, yes, pretty well off. He had houses and land, and it's reckoned he left three or four thousand in cash hid up som'ers."

"When did you say he died?"

"I didn't say, but it was last night."

"Funeral to-morrow, likely?"

"Yes, 'bout the middle of the day."

"Well, it's all terrible sad; but we've all got to go, one time or another. So what we want to do is to be prepared; then we're all right."

"Yes, sir, it's the best way. Ma used to always say that."

When we struck the boat, she was about done loading, and pretty soon she got off. The king never said nothing about going aboard, so I lost my ride, after all. When the boat was gone, the king made me paddle up another mile to a lonesome place, and then he got ashore, and says:

"Now hustle back, right off, and fetch the duke up here, and the new carpet-bags. And if he's gone over to t'other side, go over there and git him. And tell him to git himself up regardless. Shove along, now."

I see what *he* was up to; but I never said nothing, of course. When I got back with the duke, we hid the canoe and then they set down on a log, and the king told him everything, just like the young fellow had said it—every last word of it. And all the time he was a doing it, he tried to talk like an Englishman; and he done it pretty well too, for a slouch. I can't imitate him, and so I ain't agoing to try to; but he really done it pretty good. Then he says:

"How are you on the deef and dumb, Bilgewater?"

The duke said, leave him alone for that; said he had played a deef and dumb person on the histrionic boards. So then they waited for a steamboat.

About the middle of the afternoon a couple of little boats come along, but they didn't come from high enough up the river; but at last there was a big one, and they hailed her. She sent out her yawl, and we went aboard, and she was from Cincinnati; and when they found we only wanted to go four or five mile, they was booming mad, and give us a cussing, and said they wouldn't land us. But the king was ca'm. He says:

"If gentlemen kin afford to pay a dollar a mile apiece, to be took on and put off in a yawl, a steamboat kin afford to carry 'em, can't it?"

So they softened down and said it was all right; and when we got to the village, they yawled us ashore. About two dozen men flocked down, when they see the yawl a coming; and when the king says—

"Kin any of you gentlemen tell me wher' Mr. Peter Wilks lives?" they give a glance at one another, and nodded their heads, as much as to say, "What d' I tell you?" Then one of them says, kind of soft and gentle:

"I'm sorry, sir, but the best we can do is to tell you where he *did* live yesterday evening."

Sudden as winking, the ornery old cretur went all to smash, and fell up against the man, and put his chin on his shoulder, and cried down his back, and says:

"Alas, alas, our poor brother—gone, and we never got to see him; oh, it's too, *too* hard!"

Then he turns around, blubbering, and makes a lot of idiotic signs to the duke on his hands, and blamed if *he* didn't drop a carpet-bag and bust out a-crying. If they warn't the beatenest lot, them two frauds, that ever I struck.

Well, the men gethered around, and sympathized with them, and said all sorts of kind things to them, and carried their carpet-bags up the hill for them, and let them lean on them and cry, and told the king all about his brother's last moments, and the king he told it all over again on his hands to the duke, and both of them

took on about that dead tanner like they'd lost the twelve disciples.
Well, if ever I struck anything like it, I'm a nigger. It was enough
to make a body ashamed of the human race.

Chapter XXV

The news was all over town in two minutes, and you could see
the people tearing down on the run, from every which way, some
of them putting on their coats as they come. Pretty soon we was
in the middle of a crowd, and the noise of the tramping was like a
soldier-march. The windows and dooryards was full; and every
minute somebody would say, over a fence:

"Is it *them?*"

And somebody trotting along with the gang would answer back
and say,

"You bet it is."

When we got to the house, the street in front of it was packed,
and the three girls was standing in the door. Mary Jane *was* red-
headed, but that don't make no difference, she was most awful
beautiful, and her face and her eyes was all lit up like glory, she was
so glad her uncles was come. The king he spread his arms, and
Mary Jane she jumped for them, and the hare-lip jumped for the
duke, and there they *had* it! Everybody most, leastways women, cried
for joy to see them meet again at last and have such good times.

Then the king he hunched the duke, private—I see him do it—
and then he looked around and see the coffin, over in the corner on
two chairs; so then, him and the duke, with a hand across each
other's shoulder, and t'other hand to their eyes, walked slow and
solemn over there, everybody dropping back to give them room, and
all the talk and noise stopping, people saying "Sh!" and all the men
taking their hats off and drooping their heads, so you could a heard
a pin fall. And when they got there, they bent over and looked
in the coffin, and took one sight, and then they bust out a crying
so you could a heard them to Orleans, most; and then they put
their arms around each other's necks, and hung their chins over
each other's shoulders; and then for three minutes, or maybe four,
I never see two men leak the way they done. And mind you, everybody was doing the same; and the place was that damp I never see
anything like it. Then one of them got on one side of the coffin,
and t'other on t'other side, and they kneeled down and rested their
foreheads on the coffin, and let on to pray all to theirselves. Well,
when it come to that, it worked the crowd like you never see anything like it, and so everybody broke down and went to sobbing
right out loud—the poor girls, too; and every woman, nearly, went
up to the girls, without saying a word, and kissed them, solemn,

on the forehead, and then put their hand on their head, and looked up towards the sky, with the tears running down, and then busted out and went off sobbing and swabbing, and give the next woman a show. I never see anything so disgusting.

Well, by-and-by the king he gets up and comes forward a little, and works himself up and slobbers out a speech, all full of tears and flapdoodle about its being a sore trial for him and his poor brother to lose the diseased, and to miss seeing diseased alive, after the long journey of four thousand mile, but its a trial that's sweetened and sanctified to us by this dear sympathy and these holy tears, and so he thanks them out of his heart and out of his brother's heart, because out of their mouths they can't, words being too weak and cold, and all that kind of rot and slush, till it was just sickening; and then he blubbers out a pious goody-goody Amen, and turns himself loose and goes to crying fit to bust.

And the minute the words was out of his mouth somebody over in the crowd struck up the doxolojer,[4] and everybody joined in with all their might, and it just warmed you up and made you feel as good as church letting out. Music *is* a good thing; and after all that soul-butter and hogwash, I never see it freshen up things so, and sound so honest and bully.

Then the king begins to work his jaw again, and says how him and his nieces would be glad if a few of the main principal friends of the family would take supper here with them this evening, and help set up with the ashes of the diseased; and says if his poor brother laying yonder could speak, he knows who he would name, for they was names that was very dear to him, and mentioned often in his letters; and so he will name the same, to-wit, as follows, vizz: —Rev. Mr. Hobson, and Deacon Lot Hovey, and Mr. Ben Rucker, and Abner Shackleford, and Levi Bell, and Dr. Robinson, and their wives, and the widow Bartley.

Rev. Hobson and Dr. Robinson was down to the end of the town, a-hunting together; that is, I mean the doctor was shipping a sick man to t'other world, and the preacher was pinting him right. Lawyer Bell was away up to Louisville on some business. But the rest was on hand, and so they all come and shook hands with the king and thanked him and talked to him; and then they shook hands with the duke, and didn't say nothing but just kept a-smiling and bobbing their heads like a passel of sapheads whilst he made all sorts of signs with his hands and said "Goo-goo—goo-goo-goo," all the time, like a baby that can't talk.

So the king he blatted along, and managed to inquire about pretty much everybody and dog in town, by his name, and mentioned all sorts of little things that happened one time or another in the town,

4. The Doxology, beginning "Praise God, from whom all blessings flow."

or to George's family, or to Peter; and he always let on that Peter wrote him the things, but that was a lie, he got every blessed one of them out of that young flathead that we canoed up to the steamboat.

Then Mary Jane she fetched the letter her father left behind, and the king he read it out loud and cried over it. It give the dwelling-house and three thousand dollars, gold, to the girls; and it give the tanyard (which was doing a good business), along with some other houses and land (worth about seven thousand), and three thousand dollars in gold to Harvey and William, and told where the six thousand cash was hid, down cellar. So these two frauds said they'd go and fetch it up, and have everything square and above-board; and told me to come with a candle. We shut the cellar door behind us, and when they found the bag they spilt it out on the floor, and it was a lovely sight, all them yallerboys. My, the way the king's eyes did shine! He slaps the duke on the shoulder, and says:

"Oh, *this* ain't bully, nor noth'n! Oh, no, I reckon not! Why, Biljy, it beats the Nonesuch, *don't* it!"

The duke allowed it did. They pawed the yaller-boys,[5] and sifted them through their fingers and let them jingle down on the floor; and the king says:

"It ain't no use talkin'; bein' brothers to a rich dead man, and representatives of furrin heirs that's got left, is the line for you and me, Bilge. Thish-yer comes of trust'n to Providence. It's the best way, in the long run. I've tried 'em all, and ther' ain't no better way."

Most everybody would a been satisfied with the pile, and took it on trust; but no, they must count it. So they counts it, and it comes out four hundred and fifteen dollars short. Says the king:

"Dern him, I wonder what he done with that four hundred and fifteen dollars?"

They worried over that a while, and ransacked all around for it. Then the duke says:

"Well, he was a pretty sick man, and likely he made a mistake —I reckon that's the way of it. The best way's to let it go, and keep still about it. We can spare it."

"Oh, shucks, yes, we can *spare* it. I don't k'yer noth'n 'bout that —it's the *count* I'm thinkin' about. We want to be awful square and open and aboveboard, here, you know. We want to lug this h-yer money up stairs and count it before everybody—then ther' ain't noth'n suspicious. But when the dead man says ther's six thous'n dollars, you know, we don't want to—"

"Hold on," says the duke. "Less make up the deffisit"—and he

5. Gold coins.

begun to haul out yallerboys out of his pocket.

"It's a most amaz'n' good idea, duke—you *have* got a rattlin' clever head on you," says the king. "Blest if the old Nonesuch ain't a heppin' us out agin"—and *he* begun to haul out yallerjackets and stack them up.

It most busted them, but they made up the six thousand clean and clear.

"Say," says the duke, "I got another idea. Le's go up stairs and count this money, and then take and *give it to the girls.*"

"Good land, duke, lemme hug you! It's the most dazzling idea 'at ever a man struck. You have cert'nly got the most astonishin' head I ever see. Oh, this is the boss dodge, ther' ain't no mistakè 'bout it. Let 'em fetch along their suspicions now, if they want to—this'll lay 'em out."

When we got up stairs, everybody gethered around the table, and the king he counted it and stacked it up, three hundred dollars in a pile—twenty elegant little piles. Everybody looked hungry at it, and licked their chops. Then they raked it into the bag again, and I see the king begin to swell himself up for another speech. He says:

"Friends all, my poor brother that lays yonder, has done generous by them that's left behind in the vale of sorrers. He has done generous by these-yer poor little lambs that he loved and sheltered, and that's left fatherless and motherless. Yes, and we that knowed him, knows that he would a done *more* generous by 'em if he hadn't been afeard o' woundin' his dear William and me. Now, *wouldn't* he? Ther' ain't no question 'bout it, in *my* mind. Well, then— what kind o' brothers would it be, that 'd stand in his way at sech a time? And what kind o' uncles would it be that 'd rob—yes, *rob* —sech poor sweet lambs as these 'at he loved so, at sech a time? If I know William—and I *think* I do—he—well, I'll jest ask him." He turns around and begins to make a lot of signs to the duke with his hands; and the duke he looks at him stupid and leather-headed a while, then all of a sudden he seems to catch his meaning, and jumps for the king, goo-gooing with all his might for joy, and hugs him about fifteen times before he lets up. Then the king says, "I knowed it; I reckon *that* 'll convince anybody the way *he* feels about it. Here, Mary Jane, Susan, Joanner, take the money—take it *all.* It's the gift of him that lays yonder, cold but joyful."

Mary Jane she went for him, Susan and the hare-lip went for the duke, and then such another hugging and kissing I never see yet. And everybody crowded up with the tears in their eyes, and most shook the hands off of them frauds, saying all the time:

"You *dear* good souls!—how *lovely!*—how *could* you!"

Well, then, pretty soon all hands got to talking about the diseased again, and how good he was, and what a loss he was, and all that; and before long a big iron-jawed man worked himself in there from outside, and stood a listening and looking, and not saying anything; and nobody saying anything to him either, because the king was talking and they was all busy listening. The king was saying—in the middle of something he'd started in on—

"—they bein' partickler friends o' the diseased. That's why they're invited here this evenin'; but to-morrow we want *all* to come—everybody; for he respected everybody, he liked everybody, and so it's fitten that his funeral orgies sh'd be public."

And so he went a-mooning on and on, liking to hear himself talk, and every little while he fetched in his funeral orgies again, till the duke he couldn't stand it no more; so he writes on a little scrap of paper, "*obsequies*, you old fool," and folds it up and goes to goo-gooing and reaching it over people's heads to him. The king he reads it, and puts it in his pocket, and says:

"Poor William, afflicted as he is, his *heart's* aluz right. Asks me to invite everybody to come to the funeral—wants me to make 'em all welcome. But he needn't a worried—it was jest what I was at."

Then he weaves along again, perfectly ca'm, and goes to dropping in his funeral orgies again every now and then, just like he done before. And when he done it the third time, he says:

"I say orgies, not because it's the common term, because it ain't —obsequies bein' the common term—but because orgies is the right term. Obsequies ain't used in England no more, now—it's gone out. We say orgies now, in England. Orgies is better, because it means the thing you're after, more exact. It's a word that's made up out'n the Greek *orgo*, outside, open, abroad; and the Hebrew *jeesum*, to plant, cover up; hence in*ter*. So, you see, funeral orgies is an open er public funeral."

He was the *worst* I ever struck. Well, the iron-jawed man he laughed right in his face. Everybody was shocked. Everybody says, "Why *doctor!*" and Abner Shackleford says:

"Why, Robinson, hain't you heard the news? This is Harvey Wilks."

The king he smiled eager, and shoved out his flapper, and says:

"*Is* it my poor brother's dear good friend and physician? I—"

"Keep your hands off of me!" says the doctor. "*You* talk like an Englishman—*don't* you? It's the worse imitation I ever heard. *You* Peter Wilks's brother. You're a fraud, that's what you are!"

Well, how they all took on! They crowded around the doctor, and tried to quiet him down, and tried to explain to him, and tell him how Harvey'd showed in forty ways that he *was* Harvey, and knowed everybody by name, and the names of the very dogs, and begged and *begged* him not to hurt Harvey's feelings and the poor girls' feelings, and all that; but it warn't no use, he stormed right along, and said any man that pretended to be an Englishman and couldn't imitate the lingo no better than what he did, was a fraud and a liar. The poor girls was hanging to the king and crying; and all of a sudden the doctor ups and turns on *them*. He says:

"I was your father's friend, and I'm your friend; and I warn you *as* a friend, and an honest one, that wants to protect you and keep you out of harm and trouble, to turn your backs on that scoundrel, and have nothing to do with him, the ignorant tramp, with his idiotic Greek and Hebrew as he calls it. He is the thinnest kind of an impostor—has come here with a lot of empty names and facts which he has picked up somewheres, and you take them for *proofs*, and are helped to fool yourselves by these foolish friends here, who ought to know better. Mary Jane Wilks, you know me for your friend, and for your unselfish friend, too. Now listen to me; turn this pitiful rascal out—I *beg* you to do it. Will you?"

Mary Jane straightened herself up, and my, but she was handsome! She says:

"*Here* is my answer." She hove up the bag of money and put it in the king's hands, and says, "Take this six thousand dollars, and invest it for me and my sisters any way you want to, and don't give us no receipt for it."

Then she put her arm around the king on one side, and Susan and the hare-lip done the same on the other. Everybody clapped their hands and stomped on the floor like a perfect storm, whilst the king held up his head and smiled proud. The doctor says:

"All right, I wash *my* hands of the matter. But I warn you all that a time's coming when you're going to feel sick whenever you think of this day"—and away he went.

"All right, doctor," says the king, kinder mocking him, "we'll try and get 'em to send for you"—which made them all laugh, and they said it was a prime good hit.

Chapter XXVI

Well, when they was all gone, the king he asks Mary Jane how they was off for spare rooms, and she said she had one spare room, which would do for Uncle William, and she'd give her own room to Uncle Harvey, which was a little bigger, and she would turn into the room with her sisters and sleep on a cot; and up garret was a little cubby, with a pallet in it. The king said the cubby would do for his valley—meaning me.

So Mary Jane took us up, and she showed them their rooms, which was plain but nice. She said she'd have her frocks and a lot of other traps took out of her room if they was in Uncle Harvey's way, but he said they warn't. The frocks was hung along the wall, and before them was a curtain made out of calico that hung down to the floor. There was an old hair trunk in one corner, and a guitar box in another, and all sorts of little knickknacks and jimcracks around, like girls brisken up a room with. The king said it was all the more homely and more pleasanter for these fixings, and so don't disturb them. The duke's room was pretty small, but plenty good enough, and so was my cubby.

That night they had a big supper, and all them men and women was there, and I stood behind the king and the duke's chairs and waited on them, and the niggers waited on the rest. Mary Jane she set at the head of the table, with Susan along side of her, and said how bad the biscuits was, and how mean the preserves was, and how ornery and tough the fried chickens was—and all that kind of rot, the way women always do for to force out compliments; and the people all knowed everything was tip-top, and said so—said "How *do* you get biscuits to brown so nice?" and "Where, for the land's sake *did* you get these amaz'n pickles?" and all that kind of humbug talky-talk, just the way people always does at a supper, you know.

And when it was all done, me and the hare-lip had supper in the kitchen off of the leavings, whilst the others was helping the niggers clean up the things. The hare-lip she got to pumping me about England, and blest if I didn't think the ice was getting mighty thin, sometimes. She says:

"Did you ever see the king?"

"Who? William Fourth? Well, I bet I have—he goes to our church." I knowed he was dead years ago, but I never let on. So when I says he goes to our church, she says:

"What—regular?"

"Yes—regular. His pew's right over opposite ourn—on 'tother side the pulpit."

"I thought he lived in London?"

"Well, he does. Where *would* he live?"

"But I thought *you* lived in Sheffield?"

I see I was up a stump. I had to let on to get choked with a chicken bone, so as to get time to think how to get down again. Then I says:

"I mean he goes to our church regular when he's in Sheffield. That's only in the summer-time, when he comes there to take the sea baths."

"Why, how you talk—Sheffield ain't on the sea."

"Well, who said it was?"

"Why, you did."

"I *didn't*, nuther."

"You did!"

"I didn't."

"You did."

"I never said nothing of the kind."

"Well, what *did* you say, then?"

"Said he come to take the sea *baths*—that's what I said."

"Well, then! how's he going to take the sea baths if it ain't on the sea?"

"Looky here," I says; "did you ever see any Congress water?"[6]

"Yes."

"Well, did you have to go to Congress to get it?"

"Why, no."

"Well, neither does William Fourth have to go to the sea to get a sea bath."

"How does he get it, then?"

"Gets it the way people down here gets Congress water—in barrels. There in the palace at Sheffield they've got furnaces, and he wants his water hot. They can't bile that amount of water away off there at the sea. They haven't got no conveniences for it."

"Oh, I see, now. You might a said that in the first place and saved time."

When she said that, I see I was out of the woods again, and so I was comfortable and glad. Next, she says:

"Do you go to church, too?"

"Yes—regular."

"Where do you set?"

"Why, in our pew."

"*Whose* pew?"

"Why, *ourn*—your Uncle Harvey's."

"His'n? What does *he* want with a pew?"

"Wants it to set in. What did you *reckon* he wanted with it?"

"Why, I thought he'd be in the pulpit."

Rot him, I forgot he was a preacher. I see I was up a stump again, so I played another chicken bone and got another think. Then I says:

"Blame it, do you suppose there ain't but one preacher to a church?"

"Why, what do they want with more?"

"What!—to preach before a king? I never see such a girl as you. They don't have no less than seventeen."

"Seventeen! My land! Why, I wouldn't set out such a string as that, not if I *never* got to glory. It must take 'em a week."

"Shucks, they don't *all* of 'em preach the same day—only *one* of 'em."

"Well, then, what does the rest of 'em do?"

"Oh, nothing much. Loll around, pass the plate—and one thing

6. Mineral water from the Congress Spring at Saratoga, New York.

or another. But mainly they don't do nothing."

"Well, then, what are they *for?*"

"Why, they're for *style*. Don't you know nothing?"

"Well, I don't *want* to know no such foolishness as that. How is servants treated in England? Do they treat 'em better 'n we treat our niggers?"

"*No!* A servant ain't nobody there. They treat them worse than dogs."

"Don't they give 'em holidays, the way we do, Christmas and New Year's week, and Fourth of July?"

"Oh, just listen! A body could tell *you* hain't ever been to England, by that. Why, Hare-l—why, Joanna, they never see a holiday from year's end to year's end; never go to the circus, nor theatre, nor nigger shows, nor nowheres."

"Nor church?"

"Nor church."

"But *you* always went to church."

Well, I was gone up again. I forgot I was the old man's servant. But next minute I whirled in on a kind of an explanation how a valley was different from a common servant, and *had* to go to church whether he wanted to or not, and set with the family, on account of it's being the law. But I didn't do it pretty good, and when I got done I see she warn't satisfied. She says:

"Honest injun, now, hain't you been telling me a lot of lies?"

"Honest injun," says I.

"None of it at all?"

"None of it at all. Not a lie in it," says I.

"Lay your hand on this book and say it."

I see it warn't nothing but a dictionary, so I laid my hand on it and said it. So then she looked a little better satisfied, and says:

"Well, then, I'll believe some of it; but I hope to gracious if I'll believe the rest."

"What is it you won't believe, Joe?" says Mary Jane, stepping in with Susan behind her. "It ain't right nor kind for you to talk so to him, and him a stranger and so far from his people. How would you like to be treated so?"

"That's always your way, Maim—always sailing in to help somebody before they're hurt. I hain't done nothing to him. He's told some stretchers, I reckon; and I said I wouldn't swallow it all; and that's every bit and grain I *did* say. I reckon he can stand a little think like that, can't he?"

"I don't care whether 'twas little or whether 'twas big, he's here in our house and a stranger, and it wasn't good of you to say it. If you was in his place, it would make you feel ashamed; and so you ought'nt to say a thing to another person that will make *them* feel ashamed."

"Why, Maim, he said—"

"It don't make no difference what he *said*—that ain't the thing. The thing is for you to treat him *kind*, and not be saying things to make him remember he ain't in his own country and amongst his own folks."

I says to myself, *this* is a girl that I'm letting that old reptle rob her of her money!

Then Susan *she* waltzed in; and if you'll believe me, she did give Hare-lip hark from the tomb![7]

Says I to myself, And this is *another* one that I'm letting him rob her of her money!

Then Mary Jane she took another inning, and went in sweet and lovely again—which was her way—but when she got done there warn't hardly anything left o' poor Hare-lip. So she hollered.

"All right, then," says the other girls, "you just ask his pardon."

She done it, too. And she done it beautiful. She done it so beautiful it was good to hear; and I wished I could tell her a thousand lies, so she could do it again.

I says to myself, this is *another* one that I'm letting him rob her of her money. And when she got through, they all jest laid theirselves out to make me feel at home and know I was amongst friends. I felt so ornery and low down and mean, that I says to myself, My mind's made up; I'll hive[8] that money for them or bust.

So then I lit out—for bed, I said, meaning some time or another. When I got by myself, I went to thinking the thing over. I says to myself, shall I go to that doctor, private, and blow on these frauds? No—that won't do. He might tell who told him; then the king and the duke would make it warm for me. Shall I go, private, and tell Mary Jane? No—I dasn't do it. Her face would give them a hint, sure; they've got the money, and they'd slide right out and get away with it. If she was to fetch in help, I'd get mixed up in the business, before it was done with, I judge. No, there ain't no good way but one. I got to steal that money, somehow; and I got to steal it some way that they won't suspicion that I done it. They've got a good thing, here; and they ain't agoing to leave till they've played this family and this town for all they're worth, so I'll find a chance time enough. I'll steal it, and hide it; and by-and-by, when I'm away down the river, I'll write a letter and tell Mary Jane where it's hid. But I better hive it to-night, if I can, because the doctor maybe hasn't let up as much as he lets on he has; he might scare them out of here, yet.

So, thinks I, I'll go and search them rooms. Up stairs the hall was dark, but I found the duke's room, and started to paw around it with my hands; but I recollected it wouldn't be much like the

7. A talking-to, a scolding.   8. Store up, secure.

king to let anybody else take care of that money but his own self; so then I went to his room and begun to paw around there. But I see I couldn't do nothing without a candle, and I dasn't light one, of course. So I judged I'd got to do the other thing—lay for them, and eavesdrop. About that time, I hears their footsteps coming, and was going to skip under the bed; I reached for it, but it wasn't where I thought it would be; but I touched the curtain that hid Mary Jane's frocks, so I jumped in behind that and snuggled in amongst the gowns, and stood there perfectly still.

They come in and shut the door; and the first thing the duke done was to get down and look under the bed. Then I was glad I hadn't found the bed when I wanted it. And yet, you know, it's kind of natural to hide under the bed when you are up to anything private. They sets down, then, and the king says:

"Well, what is it? and cut it middlin' short, because it's better for us to be down there a whoopin'-up the mournin', than up here givin' 'em a chance to talk us over."

"Well, this is it, Capet. I ain't easy; I ain't comfortable. That doctor lays on my mind. I wanted to know your plans. I've got a notion, and I think it's a sound one."

"What is it, duke?"

"That we better glide out of this, before three in the morning, and clip it down the river with what we've got. Specially, seeing we got it so easy—*given* back to us, flung at our heads, as you may say, when of course we allowed to have to steal it back. I'm for knocking off and lighting out."

That made me feel pretty bad. About an hour or two ago, it would a been a little different, but now it made me feel bad and disappointed. The king rips out and says:

"What! And not sell out the rest o' the property? March off like a passel o' fools and leave eight or nine thous'n' dollars' worth o' property layin' around jest sufferin' to be scooped in?—and all good salable stuff, too."

The duke he grumbled; said the bag of gold was enough, and he didn't want to go no deeper—didn't want to rob a lot of orphans of *everything* they had.

"Why, how you talk!" says the king. "We shan't rob 'em of nothing at all but jest this money. The people that *buys* the property is the suff'rers; because as soon's it's found out 'at we didn't own it—which won't be long after we've slid—the sale won't be valid, and it'll all go back to the estate. These-yer orphans 'll git their house back agin, and that's enough for *them*; they're young and spry, and k'n easy earn a livin'. *They* ain't agoing to suffer. Why, jest think—there's thous'n's and thous'n's that ain't nigh so well off. Bless you, *they* ain't got noth'n to complain of."

Well, the king he talked him blind; so at last he give in, and said all right, but said he believed it was blame foolishness to stay, and that doctor hanging over them. But the king says:

"Cuss the doctor! What do we k'yer for *him?* Hain't we got all the fools in town on our side? and ain't that a big enough majority in any town?"

So they got ready to go down stairs again. The duke says:

"I don't think we put that money in a good place."

That cheered me up. I'd begun to think I warn't going to get a hint of no kind to help me. The king says:

"Why?"

"Because Mary Jane 'll be in mourning from this out; and first you know the nigger that does up the rooms will get an order to box these duds up and put 'em away; and do you reckon a nigger can run across money and not borrow some of it?"

"Your head's level, agin, duke," says the king; and he come a fumbling under the curtain two or three foot from where I was. I stuck tight to the wall, and kept mighty still, though quivery; and I wondered what them fellows would say to me if they catched me; and I tried to think what I'd better do if they did catch me. But the king he got the bag before I could think more than about a half a thought, and he never suspicioned I was around. They took and shoved the bag through a rip in the straw tick that was under the feather bed, and crammed it in a foot or two amongst the straw and said it was all right, now, because a nigger only makes up the feather bed, and don't turn over the straw tick only about twice a year, and so it warn't in no danger of getting stole, now.

But I knowed better. I had it out of there before they was half-way down stairs. I groped along up to my cubby, and hid it there till I could get a chance to do better. I judged I better hide it outside of the house somewheres, because if they missed it they would give the house a good ransacking. I knowed that very well. Then I turned in, with my clothes all on; but I couldn't a gone to sleep, if I'd a wanted to, I was in such a sweat to get through with the business. By-and-by I heard the king and the duke come up; so I rolled off of my pallet and laid with my chin at the top of my ladder and waited to see if anything was going to happen. But nothing did.

So I held on till all the late sounds had quit and the early ones hadn't begun, yet; and then I slipped down the ladder.

Chapter XXVII

I crept to their doors and listened; they was snoring, so I tip-toed along, and got down stairs all right. There warn't a sound any-wheres. I peeped through a crack of the dining-room door, and see the men that was watching the corpse all sound asleep on their chairs. The door was open into the parlor, where the corpse was laying, and there was a candle in both rooms, I passed along, and the parlor door was open; but I see there warn't nobody in there but the remainders of Peter; so I shoved on by; but the front door was locked, and the key wasn't there. Just then I heard somebody coming down the stairs, back behind me. I run in the parlor, and took a swift look around, and the only place I see to hide the bag was in the coffin. The lid was shoved along about a foot, showing the dead man's face down in there, with a wet cloth over it, and his shroud on. I tucked the money-bag in under the lid, just down beyond where his hands was crossed, which made me creep, they was so cold, and then I run back across the room and in behind the door.

The person coming was Mary Jane. She went to the coffin, very soft, and kneeled down and looked in; then she put up her hand-kerchief and I see she begun to cry, though I couldn't hear her, and her back was to me. I slid out, and as I passed the dining-room I thought I'd make sure them watchers hadn't seen me; so I looked through the crack and everything was all right. They hadn't stirred.

I slipped up to bed, feeling ruther blue, on accounts of the thing playing out that way after I had took so much trouble and run so much resk about it. Says I, if it could stay where it is, all right; because when we get down the river a hundred mile or two, I could write back to Mary Jane, and she could dig him up again and get it; but that ain't the thing that's going to happen; the thing that's going to happen is, the money 'll be found when they come to screw on the lid. Then the king 'll get it again, and it 'll be a long day before he gives anybody another chance to smouch it from him. Of course I *wanted* to slide down and get it out of there, but I dasn't try it. Every minute it was getting earlier, now, and pretty soon some of them watchers would begin to stir, and I might get catched—catched with six thousand dollars in my hands that no-body hadn't hired me to take care of. I don't wish to be mixed up in no such business as that, I says to myself.

When I got down stairs in the morning, the parlor was shut up, and the watchers was gone. There warn't nobody around but the family and the widow Bartley and our tribe. I watched their faces to see if anything had been happening, but I couldn't tell.

Towards the middle of the day the undertaker come, with his man, and they set the coffin in the middle of the room on a couple of chairs, and then set all our chairs in rows, and borrowed more from the neighbors till the hall and the parlor and the dining-room was full. I see the coffin lid was the way it was before, but I dasn't go to look in under it, with folks around.

Then the people begun to flock in, and the beats[9] and the girls took seats in the front row at the head of the coffin, and for a half an hour the people filed around slow, in single rank, and looked down at the dead man's face a minute, and some dropped in a tear, and it was all very still and solemn, only the girls and the beats holding handkerchiefs to their eyes and keeping their heads bent, and sobbing a little. There warn't no other sound but the scraping of the feet on the floor, and blowing noses—because people always blows them more at a funeral than they do at other places except church.

When the place was packed full, the undertaker he slid around in his black gloves with his softy soothering ways, putting on the last touches, and getting people and things all shipshape and comfortable, and making no more sound than a cat. He never spoke; he moved people around, he squeezed in late ones, he opened up passage-ways, and done it all with nods, and signs with his hands. Then he took his place over against the wall. He was the softest, glidingest, stealthiest man I ever see; and there warn't no more smile to him than there is to a ham.

They had borrowed a melodeum[1]—a sick one; and when everything was ready, a young woman set down and worked it, and it was pretty skreeky and colicky, and everybody joined in and sung, and Peter was the only one that had a good thing, according to my notion. Then the Reverend Hobson opened up, slow and solemn, and begun to talk; and straight off the most outrageous row busted out in the cellar a body ever heard; it was only one dog, but he made a most powerful racket, and he kept it up, right along; the parson he had to stand there, over the coffin, and wait—you couldn't hear yourself think. It was right down awkward, and nobody didn't seem to know what to do. But pretty soon they see that long-legged undertaker make a sign to the preacher as much as to say, "Don't you worry—just depend on me." Then he stooped down and begun to glide along the wall, just his shoulders showing over the people's heads. So he glided along, and the pow-wow and racket getting more and more outrageous all the time; and at last, when he had gone around two sides of the room, he disappears down cellar. Then, in about two seconds we heard a whack, and the dog he finished up with a most amazing howl or two, and then everything was dead still, and the parson begun his solemn talk where he left off. In a minute or two here comes this undertaker's back and shoulders gliding along the wall again; and so he glided, and glided, around three sides of the room, and then rose up, and shaded his mouth with his hands, and stretched his neck out to-

9. Dead beats, cheats; the duke and the king.   1. Melodeon, a small reed organ.

wards the preacher, over the people's heads, and says, in a kind of a coarse whisper, "*He had a rat!*" Then he drooped down and glided along the wall again to his place. You could see it was a great satisfaction to the people, because naturally they wanted to know. A little thing like that don't cost nothing, and it's just the little things that makes a man to be looked up to and liked. There warn't no more popular man in town than what that undertaker was.

Well, the funeral sermon was very good, but pison long and tiresome; and then the king he shoved in and got off some of his usual rubbage, and at last the job was through, and the undertaker begun to sneak up on the coffin with his screw-driver. I was in a sweat then, and watched him pretty keen. But he never meddled at all; just slid the lid along, as soft as mush, and screwed it down tight and fast. So there I was! I didn't know whether the money was in there, or not. So, says I, spose somebody has hogged that bag on the sly?—now how do *I* know whether to write to Mary Jane or not? 'Spose she dug him up and didn't find nothing—what would she think of me? Blame it, I says, I might get hunted up and jailed; I'd better lay low and keep dark, and not write at all; the thing's awful mixed, now; trying to better it, I've worsened it a hundred times, and I wish to goodness I'd just let it alone, dad fetch the whole business!

They buried him, and we come back home, and I went to watching faces again—I couldn't help it, and I couldn't rest easy. But nothing come of it; the faces didn't tell me nothing.

The king he visited around, in the evening, and sweetened every body up, and made himself ever so friendly; and he give out the idea that his congregation over in England would be in a sweat about him, so he must hurry and settle up the estate right away, and leave for home. He was very sorry he was so pushed, and so was everybody; they wished he could stay longer, but they said they could see it couldn't be done. And he said of course him and William would take the girls home with them; and that pleased everybody too, because then the girls would be well fixed, and amongst their own relations; and it pleased the girls, too—tickled them so they clean forgot they ever had a trouble in the world; and told him to sell out as quick as he wanted to, they would be ready. Them poor things was that glad and happy it made my heart ache to see them getting fooled and lied to so, but I didn't see no safe way for me to chip in and change the general tune.

Well, blamed if the king didn't bill the house and the niggers and all the property for auction straight off—sale two days after the funeral; but anybody could buy private beforehand if they wanted to.

So the next day after the funeral, along about noontime, the girls'
joy got the first jolt; a couple of nigger traders come along, and the
king sold them the niggers reasonable, for three-day drafts as they
called it, and away they went, the two sons up the river to Memphis,
and their mother down the river to Orleans. I thought them poor
girls and them niggers would break their hearts for grief; they cried
around each other, and took on so it most made me down sick to see
it. The girls said they hadn't ever dreamed of seeing the family
separated or sold away from the town. I can't ever get it out of my
memory, the sight of them poor miserable girls and niggers hanging around each other's necks and crying; and I reckon I couldn't
a stood it all but would a had to bust out and tell on our gang if I
hadn't knowed the sale warn't no account and the niggers would
be back home in a week or two.

The thing made a big stir in the town, too, and a good many
come out flatfooted and said it was scandalous to separate the
mother and the children that way. It injured the frauds some; but
the old fool he bulled right along, spite of all the duke could say
or do, and I tell you the duke was powerful uneasy.

Next day was auction day. About broad-day in the morning, the
king and the duke come up in the garret and woke me up, and I
see by their look that there was trouble. The king says:

"Was you in my room night before last?"

"No, your majesty"—which was the way I always called him when
nobody but our gang warn't around.

"Was you in there yesterday er last night?"

"No, your majesty."

"Honor bright, now—no lies."

"Honor bright, your majesty, I'm telling you the truth. I hain't
been anear your room since Miss Mary Jane took you and the duke
and showed it to you."

The duke says:

"Have you seen anybody else go in there?"

"No, your grace, not as I remember, I believe."

"Stop and think."

I studied a while, and see my chance, then I says:

"Well, I see the niggers go in there several times."

Both of them give a little jump; and looked like they hadn't
ever expected it, and then like they *had*. Then the duke says:

"What, *all* of them?"

"No—leastways not all at once. That is, I don't think I ever see
them all come *out* at once but just one time."

"Hello—when was that?"

"It was the day we had the funeral. In the morning. It warn't
early, because I overslept. I was just starting down the ladder, and

I see them."

"Well, go on, go on—what did they do? How'd they act?"

"They didn't do nothing. And they didn't act anyway, much, as fur as I see. They tip-toed away; so I seen, easy enough, that they'd shoved in there to do up your majesty's room, or something, sposing you was up; and found you *warn't* up, and so they was hoping to slide out of the way of trouble without waking you up, if they hadn't already waked you up."

"Great guns, *this* is a go!" says the king; and both of them looked pretty sick, and tolerable silly. They stood there a thinking and scratching their heads, a minute, and then the duke he bust into a kind of a little raspy chuckle, and says:

"It does beat all, how neat the niggers played their hand. They let on to be *sorry* they was going out of this region! and I believed they *was* sorry. And so did you, and so did everybody. Don't ever tell *me* any more that a nigger ain't got any histrionic talent. Why, the way they played that thing, it would fool *anybody*. In my opinion there's a fortune in 'em. If I had capital and a theatre, I wouldn't want a better lay out than that—and here we've gone and sold 'em for a song. Yes, and ain't privileged to sing the song, yet. Say, where *is* that song?—that draft."

"In the bank for to be collected. Where *would* it be?"

"Well, *that's* all right then, thank goodness."

Says I, kind of timid-like:

"Is something gone wrong?"

The king whirls on me and rips out:

"None o' your business! You keep your head shet, and mind y'r own affairs—if you got any. Long as you're in this town, don't you forget *that*, you hear?" Then he says to the duke, "We got to jest swaller it, and say noth'n: mum's the word for *us*."

As they was starting down the ladder, the duke he chuckles again, and says:

"Quick sales *and* small profits! It's a good business—yes."

The king snarls around on him and says,

"I was trying to do for the best, in sellin' 'm out so quick. If the profits has turned out to be none, lackin' considable, and none to carry, is it my fault any more'n it's yourn?"

"Well, *they'd* be in this house yet, and we *wouldn't* if I could a got my advice listened to."

The king sassed back, as much as was safe for him, and then swapped around and lit into *me* again. He give me down the banks for not coming and *telling* him I see the niggers come out of his room acting that way—said any fool would a *knowed* something was up. And then waltzed in and cussed *himself* a while; and said it all come of him not laying late and taking his natural rest that morning, and he'd be blamed if he'd ever do it again. So they went off a jawing; and I felt dreadful glad I'd worked it all off onto the niggers and yet hadn't done the niggers no harm by it.

Chapter XXVIII

By-and-by it was getting-up time; so I come down the ladder and started for down stairs, but as I come to the girls' room, the door was open, and I see Mary Jane setting by her old hair trunk, which was open and she'd been packing things in it—getting ready to go to England. But she had stopped now, with a folded gown in her lap, and had her face in her hands, crying. I felt awful bad to see it; of course anybody would. I went in there, and says:

"Miss Mary Jane, you can't abear to see people in trouble, and *I* can't—most always. Tell me about it."

So she done it. And it was the niggers—I just expected it. She said the beautiful trip to England was most about spoiled for her; she didn't know *how* she was ever going to be happy there, knowing the mother and the children warn't ever going to see each other no more—and then busted out bitterer than ever, and flung up her hands, and says

"Oh, dear, dear, to think they ain't *ever* going to see each other any more!"

"But they *will*—and inside of two weeks—and I *know* it!" says I.

Laws it was out before I could think!—and before I could budge, she throws her arms around my neck, and told me to say it *again*, say it *again*, say it *again!*

I see I had spoke too sudden, and said too much, and was in a close place. I asked her to let me think a minute; and she set there, very impatient and excited, and handsome, but looking kind of happy and eased-up, like a person that's had a tooth pulled out. So I went to studying it out. I says to myself, I reckon a body that ups and tells the truth when he is in a tight place, is taking considerable many resks, though I ain't had no experience, and can't say for certain; but it looks so to me, anyway; and yet here's a case where I'm blest if it don't look to me like the truth is better, and actuly *safer*, than a lie. I must lay it by in my mind, and think it over some time or other, it's so kind of strange and unregular. I never see nothing like it. Well, I says to myself at last, I'm agoing to chance it; I'll up and tell the truth this time, though it does seem most like setting down on a kag of powder and touching it off just to see where you'll go to. Then I says:

"Miss Mary Jane, is there any place out of town a little ways, where you could go and stay three or four days?"

"Yes—Mr. Lothrop's. Why?"

"Never mind why, yet. If I'll tell you how I know the niggers will see each other again—inside of two weeks—here in this house—and *prove* how I know it—will you go to Mr. Lothrop's and stay four days?"

"Four days!" she says; "I'll stay a year!"

"All right," I says, "I don't want nothing more out of *you* than just your word—I druther have it than another man's kiss-the-Bible." She smiled, and reddened up very sweet, and I says, "If you don't mind it, I'll shut the door—and bolt it."

Then I come back and set down again, and says:

"Don't you holler. Just set still, and take it like a man. I got to tell the truth, and you want to brace up, Miss Mary, because it's a bad kind, and going to be hard to take, but there ain't no help for it. These uncles of yourn ain't no uncles at all—they're a couple of frauds—regular dead-beats. There, now we're over the worst of it—you can stand the rest middling easy."

It jolted her up like everything, of course; but I was over the shoal water now, so I went right along, her eyes a blazing higher and higher all the time, and told her every blame thing, from where we first struck that young fool going up to the steamboat, clear through to where she flung herself onto the king's breast at the front door and he kissed her sixteen or seventeen times—and then up she jumps, with her face afire like sunset, and says:

"The brute! Come—don't waste a minute—not a *second*—we'll have them tarred and feathered, and flung in the river!"

Says I:

"Cert'nly. But do you mean, *before* you go to Mr. Lothrop's, or—"

"Oh," she says, "what am I *thinking* about!" she says, and set right down again. "Don't mind what I said—please don't—you *won't*, now, *will* you?" Laying her silky hand on mine in that kind of a way that I said I would die first. "I never thought, I was so stirred up," she says; "now go on, and I won't do so any more. You tell me what to do, and whatever you say, I'll do it."

"Well," I says, "it's a rough gang, them two frauds, and I'm fixed so I got to travel with them a while longer, whether I want to or not—I druther not tell you why—and if you was to blow on them this town would get me out of their claws, and I'd be all right, but there'd be another person that you don't know about who'd be in big trouble. Well, we got to save *him*, hain't we? Of course. Well, then, we won't blow on them."

Saying them words put a good idea in my head. I see how maybe I could get me and Jim rid of the frauds; get them jailed here, and then leave. But I didn't want to run the raft in day-time, without anybody aboard to answer questions but me; so I didn't want the plan to begin working till pretty late to-night. I says:

"Miss Mary Jane, I'll tell you what we'll do—and you won't have to stay at Mr. Lothrop's so long, nuther. How fur is it?"

"A little short of four miles—right out in the country, back here."

"Well, that'll answer. Now you go along out there, and lay low till nine or half-past, to-night, and then get them to fetch you home again—tell them you've thought of something. If you get here before eleven, put a candle in this window, and if I don't turn up, wait *till* eleven, and *then* if I don't turn up it means I'm gone, and out of the way, and safe. Then you come out and spread the news around, and get these beats jailed."

"Good," she says, "I'll do it."

"And if it just happens so that I don't get away, but get took up along with them, you must up and say I told you the whole thing beforehand, and you must stand by me all you can."

"Stand by you, indeed I will. They sha'n't touch a hair of your head!" she says, and I see her nostrils spread and her eyes snap when she said it, too.

"If I get away, I sha'n't be here," I says, "to prove these rapscallions ain't your uncles, and I couldn't do it if I *was* here. I could swear they was beats and bummers, that's all; though that's worth something. Well, there's others can do that better than what I can—and they're people that ain't going to be doubted as quick as I'd be. I'll tell you how to find them. Gimme a pencil and a piece of paper. There—'*Royal Nonesuch, Bricksville.*' Put it away, and don't lose it. When the court wants to find out something about these two, let them send up to Bricksville and say they've got the men that played the Royal Nonesuch, and ask for some witnesses—why, you'll have that entire town down here before you can hardly wink, Miss Mary. And they'll come a-biling, too."

I judged we had got everything fixed about right, now. So I says:

"Just let the auction go right along, and don't worry. Nobody don't have to pay for the things they buy till a whole day after the auction, on accounts of the short notice, and they ain't going out of this till they get that money—and the way we've fixed it the sale ain't going to count, and they ain't going to *get* no money. It's just like the way it was with the niggers—it warn't no sale, and the niggers will be back before long. Why, they can't collect the money for the *niggers,* yet—they're in the worst kind of a fix, Miss Mary."

"Well," she says, "I'll run down to breakfast now, and then I'll start straight for Mr. Lothrop's."

"'Deed, *that* ain't the ticket, Miss Mary Jane," I says, "by no manner of means; go *before* breakfast."

"Why?"

"What did you reckon I wanted you to go at all for, Miss Mary?"

"Well, I never thought—and come to think, I don't know. What was it?"

"Why, it's because you ain't one of these leather-face people. I don't want no better book than what your face is. A body can set down and read it off like coarse print. Do you reckon you can go and face your uncles, when they come to kiss you good-morning, and never—"

"There, there, don't! Yes, I'll go before breakfast—I'll be glad to. And leave my sisters with them?"

"Yes—never mind about them. They've got to stand it yet a while. They might suspicion something if all of you was to go. I don't want you to see them, nor your sisters, nor nobody in this town—if a neighbor was to ask how is your uncles this morning, your face would tell something. No, you go right along, Miss Mary Jane, and I'll fix it with all of them. I'll tell Miss Susan to give your love to your uncles and say you've went away for a few hours for to get a little rest and change, or to see a friend, and you'll be back to-night or early in the morning."

"Gone to see a friend is all right, but I won't have my love given to them."

"Well, then, it sha'n't be." It was well enough to tell *her* so—no harm in it. It was only a little thing to do, and no trouble; and it's the little things that smoothes people's roads the most, down here below; it would make Mary Jane comfortable, and it wouldn't cost nothing. Then I says: "There's one more thing—that bag of money."

"Well, they've got that; and it makes me feel pretty silly to think *how* they got it."

"No, you're out, there. They hain't got it."

"Why, who's got it?"

"I wish I knowed, but I don't. I *had* it, because I stole it from them: and I stole it to give to you; and I know where I hid it, but I'm afraid it ain't there no more. I'm awful sorry, Miss Mary Jane, I'm just as sorry as I can be; but I done the best I could; I did, honest. I come nigh getting caught, and I had to shove it into the first place I come to, and run—and it warn't a good place."

"Oh, stop blaming yourself—it's too bad to do it, and I won't allow it—you couldn't help it; it wasn't you fault. Where did you hide it?"

I didn't want to set her to thinking about her troubles again; and I couldn't seem to get my mouth to tell her what would make her see that corpse laying in the coffin with that bag of money on his stomach. So for a minute I didn't say nothing—then I says:

"I'd ruther not *tell* you where I put it, Miss Mary Jane, if you don't mind letting me off; but I'll write it for you on a piece of paper, and you can read it along the road to Mr. Lothrop's, if you want to. Do you reckon that'll do?"

"Oh, yes."

So I wrote: "I put it in the coffin. It was in there when you was crying there, away in the night. I was behind the door, and I was mighty sorry for you, Miss Mary Jane."

It made my eyes water a little, to remember her crying there all by herself in the night, and them devils laying there right under her own roof, shaming her and robbing her; and when I folded it up and give it to her, I see the water come into her eyes, too; and she shook me by the hand, hard, and says:

"Good-bye—I'm going to do everything just as you've told me; and if I don't ever see you again, I sha'n't ever forget you, and I'll think of you a many and a many a time, and I'll *pray* for you, too!"—and she was gone.

Pray for me! I reckoned if she knowed me she'd take a job that was more nearer her size. But I bet she done it, just the same—she was just that kind. She had the grit to pray for Judus if she took the notion—there warn't no backdown to her, I judge. You may say what you want to, but in my opinion she had more sand in her than any girl I ever see; in my opinion she was just full of sand. It sounds like flattery, but it ain't no flattery. And when it comes to beauty—and goodness too—she lays over them all. I hain't ever seen her since that time that I see her go out of that door; no, I hain't ever seen her since, but I reckon I've thought of her a many and a many a million times, and of her saying she would pray for me; and if ever I'd a thought it would do any good for me to pray for *her*, blamed if I wouldn't a done it or bust.

Well, Mary Jane she lit out the back way, I reckon; because nobody see her go. When I struck Susan and the hare-lip, I says:

"What's the name of them people over on t'other side of the river that you all goes to see sometimes?"

They says:

"There's several; but it's the Proctors, mainly."

"That's the name," I says; "I most forgot it. Well, Miss Mary Jane she told me to tell you she's gone over there in a dreadful hurry—one of them's sick."

"Which one?"

"I don't know; leastways I kinder forget; but I think it's—"

"Sakes alive, I hope it ain't *Hanner?*"

"I'm sorry to say it," I says, "but Hanner's the very one."

"My goodness—and she so well only last week! Is she took bad?"

"It ain't no name for it. They set up with her all night, Miss Mary Jane said, and they don't think she'll last many hours."

"Only think of that, now! What's the matter with her!"

I couldn't think of anything reasonable, right off that way, so I says:

"Mumps."

"Mumps your granny! They don't set up with people that's got the mumps."

"They don't, don't they? You better bet they do with *these* mumps. These mumps is different. It's a new kind, Miss Mary Jane said."

"How's it a new kind?"

"Because it's mixed up with other things."

"What other things?"

"Well, measles, and whooping-cough, and erysiplas, and consumption, and yaller janders, and brain fever, and I don't know what all."[2]

"My land! And they call it the *mumps?*"

"That's what Miss Mary Jane said."

"Well, what in the nation do they call it the *mumps* for?"

"Why, because it *is* the mumps. That's what it starts with."

"Well, ther' ain't no sense in it. A body might stump his toe, and take pison, and fall down the well, and break his neck, and bust his brains out, and somebody come along and ask what killed him, and some numskull up and say, 'Why, he stumped his *toe.*' Would ther' be any sense in that? *No.* And ther' ain't no sense in *this*, nuther. Is it ketching?"

"Is it *ketching?* Why, how you talk. Is a *harrow* catching?—in the dark? If you don't hitch onto one tooth, you're bound to on another, ain't you? And you can't get away with that tooth without fetching the whole harrow along, can you? Well, these kind of mumps is a kind of a harrow, as you may say—and it ain't no slouch of a harrow, nuther, you come to get it hitched on good."

"Well, it's awful, I think," says the hare-lip. "I'll go to Uncle Harvey and—"

"Oh, yes," I says, "I *would.* Of *course* I would. I wouldn't lose no time."

"Well, why wouldn't you?"

"Just look at it a minute, and maybe you can see. Hain't your uncles obleeged to get along home to England as fast as they can? And do you reckon they'd be mean enough to go off and leave you to go all that journey by yourselves? *You* know they'll wait for you. So fur, so good. Your uncle Harvey's a preacher, ain't he? Very well, then; is a *preacher* going to deceive a steamboat clerk? is he going to deceive a *ship clerk?*—so as to get them to let Miss Mary Jane go aboard? Now *you* know he ain't. What *will* he do, then?

2. Erysipelas, a severe skin disease; consumption, tuberculosis; yellow jaundice, a liver disease.

Why, he'll say, 'It's a great pity, but my church matters has got to get along the best way they can; for my niece has been exposed to the dreadful pluribus-unum³ mumps, and so it's my bounden duty to set down here and wait the three months it takes to show on her if she's got it.' But never mind, if you think it's best to tell your uncle Harvey—"

"Shucks, and stay fooling around here when we could all be having good times in England whilst we was waiting to find out whether Mary Jane's got it or not? Why, you talk like a muggins."⁴

"Well, anyway, maybe you better tell some of the neighbors."

"Listen at that, now. You do beat all, for natural stupidness. Can't you *see* that *they'd* go and tell? Ther' ain't no way but just to not tell anybody at *all*."

"Well, maybe you're right—yes, I judge you *are* right."

"But I reckon we ought to tell Uncle Harvey she's gone out a while, anyway, so he wont be uneasy about her?"

"Yes, Miss Mary Jane she wanted you to do that. She says, 'Tell them to give Uncle Harvey and William my love and a kiss, and say I've run over the river to see Mr.—Mr.—what *is* the name of that rich family your uncle Peter used to think so much of?—I mean the one that—"

"Why, you must mean the Apthorps, ain't it?"

"Of course; bother them kind of names, a body can't ever seem to remember them, half the time, somehow. Yes, she said, say she has run over for to ask the Apthorps to be sure and come to the auction and buy this house, because she allowed her uncle Peter would ruther they had it than anybody else; and she's going to stick to them till they say they'll come, and then, if she ain't too tired, she's coming home; and if she is, she'll be home in the morning anyway. She said, don't say nothing about the Proctors, but only about the Apthorps—which'll be perfectly true, because she *is* going there to speak about their buying the house; I know it, because she told me so, herself."

"All right," they said, and cleared out to lay for their uncles, and give them the love and the kisses, and tell them the message.

Everything was all right now. The girls wouldn't say nothing because they wanted to go to England; and the king and the duke would ruther Mary Jane was off working for the auction than around in reach of Doctor Robinson. I felt very good; I judged I had done it pretty neat—I reckoned Tom Sawyer couldn't a done it no neater himself. Of course he would a throwed more style into it, but I can't do that very handy, not being brung up to it.

Well, they held the auction in the public square, along towards

3. Like the United States, whose motto Huck misappropriates, this fearful dis- ease makes "one out of many." 4. A fool.

the end of the afternoon, and it strung along, and strung along, and the old man he was on hand and looking his level piousest, up there longside of the auctioneer, and chipping in a little Scripture, now and then, or a little goody-goody saying, of some kind, and the duke he was around goo-gooing for sympathy all he knowed how, and just spreading himself generly.

But by-and-by the thing dragged through, and everything was sold. Everything but a little old trifling lot in the graveyard. So they'd got to work *that* off—I never see such a girafft as the king was for wanting to swallow *everything*. Well, whilst they was at it, a steamboat landed, and in about two minutes up comes a crowd a whooping and yelling and laughing and carrying on, and singing out:

"*Here's* your opposition line! here's your two sets o' heirs to old Peter Wilks—and you pays your money and you takes your choice!"

Chapter XXIX

They was fetching a very nice looking old gentleman along, and a nice looking younger one, with his right arm in a sling. And my souls, how the people yelled, and laughed, and kept it up. But I didn't see no joke about it, and I judged it would strain the duke and the king some to see any. I reckoned they'd turn pale. But no, nary a pale did *they* turn. The duke he never let on he suspicioned what was up, but just went a goo-gooing around, happy and satisfied, like a jug that's googling out buttermilk; and as for the king, he just gazed and gazed down sorrowful on them newcomers like it give him the stomach-ache in his very heart to think there could be such frauds and rascals in the world. Oh, he done it admirable. Lots of the principal people gethered around the king, to let him see they was on his side. That old gentleman that had just come looked all puzzled to death. Pretty soon he begun to speak, and I see, straight off, he pronounced *like* an Englishman, not the king's way, though the king's *was* pretty good, for an imitation. I can't give the old gent's words, nor I can't imitate him; but he turned around to the crowd, and says, about like this:

"This is a surprise to me which I wasn't looking for; and I'll acknowledge, candid and frank, I ain't very well fixed to meet it and answer it; for my brother and me has had misfortunes, he's broke his arm, and our baggage got put off at a town above here, last night in the night by a mistake. I am Peter Wilks's brother Harvey, and this is his brother William, which can't hear nor speak—and can't even make signs to amount to much, now 't he's only got one hand to work them with. We are who we say we are; and in a day or two, when I get the baggage, I can prove it. But, up till then, I won't say nothing more, but go to the hotel and wait."

So him and the new dummy started off; and the king he laughs, and blethers out:

"Broke his arm—*very* likely *ain't* it?—and very convenient, too, for a fraud that's got to make signs, and hain't learnt how. Lost their baggage! That's *mighty* good!—and mighty ingenious—under the *circumstances!*"

So he laughed again; and so did everybody else, except three or four, or maybe half a dozen. One of these was that doctor; another one was a sharp looking gentleman, with a carpet-bag of the old-fashioned kind made out of carpet-stuff, that had just come off of the steamboat and was talking to him in a low voice, and glancing towards the king now and then and nodding their heads—it was Levi Bell, the lawyer that was gone up to Louisville; and another one was a big rough husky that come along and listened to all the old gentleman said, and was listening to the king now. And when the king got done, this husky up and says:

"Say, looky here; if you are Harvey Wilks, when'd you come to this town?"

"The day before the funeral, friend," says the king.

"But what time o' day?"

"In the evenin'—'bout an hour er two before sundown."

"*How'd* you come?"

"I come down on the *Susan Powell*, from Cincinnati."

"Well, then, how'd you come to be up at the Pint in the *mornin'* —in a canoe?"

"I warn't up at the Pint in the mornin'."

"It's a lie."

Several of them jumped for him and begged him not to talk that way to an old man and a preacher.

"Preacher be hanged, he's a fraud and a liar. He was up at the Pint that mornin'. I live up there, don't I? Well, I was up there, and he was up there. I *see* him there. He come in a canoe, along with Tim Collins and a boy."

The doctor he up and says:

"Would you know the boy again if you was to see him, Hines?"

"I reckon I would, but I don't know. Why, yonder he is, now. I know him perfectly easy."

It was me he pointed at. The doctor says:

"Neighbors, 1 don't know whether the new couple is frauds or not; but if *these* two ain't frauds, I am an idiot, that's all. I think it's our duty to see that they don't get away from here till we've looked into this thing. Come along, Hines; come along, the rest of you. We'll take these fellows to the tavern and affront them with t'other couple, and I reckon we'll find out *something* before we get through."

It was nuts for the crowd, though maybe not for the king's friends; so we all started. It was about sundown. The doctor he led me along by the hand, and was plenty kind enough, but he never let *go* my hand.

We all got in a big room in the hotel, and lit up some candles, and fetched in the new couple. First, the doctor says:

"I don't wish to be too hard on these two men, but I think they're frauds, and they may have complices that we don't know nothing about. If they have, won't the complices get away with that bag of gold Peter Wilks left? It ain't unlikely. If these men ain't frauds, they won't object to sending for that money and letting us keep it till they prove they're all right—ain't that so?"

Everybody agreed to that. So I judged they had our gang in a pretty tight place, right at the outstart. But the king he only looked sorrowful, and says:

"Gentlemen, I wish the money was there, for I ain't got no disposition to throw anything in the way of a fair, open, out-and-out investigation o' this misable business; but alas, the money ain't there; you k'n send and see, if you want to."

"Where is it, then?"

"Well, when my niece give it to me to keep for her, I took and hid it inside o' the straw tick o' my bed, not wishin' to bank it for the few days we'd be here, and considerin' the bed a safe place, we not bein' used to niggers, and suppos'n' 'em honest, like servants in England. The niggers stole it the very next mornin' after I had went down stairs; and when I sold 'em, I hadn't missed the money yit, so they got clean away with it. My servant here k'n tell you 'bout it gentlemen."

The doctor and several said "Shucks!" and I see nobody didn't altogether believe him. One man asked me if I see the niggers steal it. I said no, but I see them sneaking out of the room and hustling away, and I never thought nothing, only I reckoned they was afraid they had waked up my master and was trying to get away before he made trouble with them. That was all they asked me. Then the doctor whirls on me and says:

"Are *you* English too?"

I says yes; and him and some others laughed, and said, "Stuff!"

Well, then they sailed in on the general investigation, and there we had it, up and down, hour in, hour out, and nobody never said a word about supper, nor ever seemed to think about it—and so they kept it up, and kept it up; and it *was* the worst mixed-up thing you ever see. They made the king tell his yarn, and they made the old gentleman tell his'n; and anybody but a lot of prejudiced chuckleheads would a *seen* that the old gentleman was spinning truth and t'other one lies. And by-and-by they had me up to tell what I knowed. The king he give me a left-handed look out of the corner of his eye, and so I knowed enough to talk on the right side. I begun to tell about Sheffield, and how we lived there, and all about the English Wilkses, and so on; but I didn't get pretty fur till the doctor begun to laugh; and Levi Bell, the lawyer, says:

"Set down, my boy, I wouldn't strain myself, if I was you. I reckon you ain't used to lying, it don't seem to come handy; what you want is practice. You do it pretty awkward."

I didn't care nothing for the compliment, but I was glad to be let off, anyway.

The doctor he started to say something, and turns and says:

"If you'd been in town at first, Levi Bell—"

The king broke in and reached out his hand, and says:

"Why, is this my poor dead brother's old friend that he's wrote so often about?"

The lawyer and him shook hands, and the lawyer smiled and looked pleased, and they talked right along a while, and then got to one side and talked low; and at last the lawyer speaks up and says:

"That'll fix it. I'll take the order and send it, along with your brother's, and then they'll know it's all right."

So they got some paper and a pen, and the king he set down and twisted his head to one side, and chawed his tongue, and scrawled off something; and then they give the pen to the duke—and then for the first time, the duke looked sick. But he took the pen and wrote. So then the lawyer turns to the new old gentleman and says:

"You and your brother please write a line or two and sign your names."

The old gentleman wrote, but nobody couldn't read it. The lawyer looked powerful astonished, and says:

"Well, it beats *me*"—and snaked a lot of old letters out of his pocket, and examined them, and then examined the old man's writing, and then *them* again; and then says: "These old letters is from Harvey Wilks; and here's *these* two's handwritings, and anybody can see *they* didn't write them" (the king and the duke looked sold and foolish, I tell you, to see how the lawyer had took them in), "and here's *this* old gentleman's handwriting, and anybody can tell, easy enough, *he* didn't write them—fact is, the scratches he makes ain't properly *writing*, at all. Now here's some letters from—"

The new old gentleman says:

"If you please, let me explain. Nobody can read my hand but my brother there—so he copies for me. It's *his* hand you've got there, not mine."

"Well!" says the lawyer, "this *is* a state of things. I've got some of William's letters too; so if you'll get him to write a line or so we can com—"

"He *can't* write with his left hand," says the old gentleman. "If he could use his right hand, you would see that he wrote his own letters and mine too. Look at both, please—they're by the same hand."

The lawyer done it, and says:

"I believe it's so—and if it ain't so, there's a heap stronger resemblance than I'd noticed before, anyway. Well, well, well! I thought we was right on the track of a slution, but it's gone to grass, partly. But anyway, *one* thing is proved—*these* two ain't either of 'em Wilkses"—and he wagged his head towards the king and the duke.

Well, what do you think?—that muleheaded old fool wouldn't give in *then!* Indeed he wouldn't. Said it warn't no fair test. Said his brother William was the cussedest joker in the world, and hadn't *tried* to write—he see William was going to play one of his jokes the minute he put the pen to paper. And so he warmed up and went warbling and warbling right along, till he was actuly beginning to believe what he was saying, *himself*—but pretty soon the new old gentleman broke in, and says:

"I've thought of something. Is there anybody here that helped to lay out my br—helped to lay out the late Peter Wilks for burying?"

"Yes," says somebody, "me and Ab Turner done it. We're both here."

Then the old man turns towards the king, and says:

"Peraps this gentleman can tell me what was tatooed on his breast?"

Blamed if the king didn't have to brace up mighty quick, or he'd a squshed down like a bluff bank that the river has cut under, it took him so sudden—and mind you, it was a thing that was calculated to make most *anybody* sqush to get fetched such a solid one as that without any notice—because how was *he* going to know what was tatooed on the man? He whitened a little; he couldn't help it; and it was mighty still in there, and everybody bending a little forwards and gazing at him. Says I to myself, *Now* he'll throw up the sponge—there ain't no more use. Well, did he? A body can't hardly believe it, but he didn't. I reckon he thought he'd keep the thing up till he tired them people out, so they'd thin out, and him and the duke could break loose and get away. Anyway, he set there, and pretty soon he begun to smile, and says:

"Mf! It's a *very* tough question, *ain't* it! *Yes,* sir, I k'n tell you what's tatooed on his breast. It's jest a small, thin, blue arrow—that's what it is; and if you don't look clost, you can't see it. *Now* what do you say—hey?"

Well, *I* never see anything like that old blister for clean out-and-out cheek.

The new old gentleman turns brisk towards Ab Turner and his pard, and his eye lights up like he judged he'd got the king *this* time, and says:

"There—you've heard what he said! Was there any such mark on Peter Wilks's breast?"

Both of them spoke up and says:

"We didn't see no such mark."

"Good!" says the old gentleman. "Now, what you *did* see on his breast was a small dim P, and a B (which is an initial he dropped when he was young), and a W, with dashes between them, so: P—B—W"—and he marked them that way on a piece of paper. "Come—ain't that what you saw?"

Both of them spoke up again, and says:

"No, we *didn't.* We never seen any marks at all."

Well, everybody *was* in a state of mind, now; and they sings out:

"The whole *bilin'* of 'm 's frauds! Le's duck 'em! le's drown 'em! le's ride 'em on a rail!" and everybody was whooping at once, and there was a rattling pow-wow. But the lawyer he jumps on the table and yells, and says:

"Gentlemen—gentle*men!* Hear me just a word—just a *single* word—if you PLEASE! There's one way yet—let's go and dig up the corpse and look."

That took them.

"Hooray!" they all shouted, and was starting right off; but the lawyer and the doctor sung out:

"Hold on, hold on! Collar all these four men and the boy, and fetch *them* along, too!"

"We'll do it!" they all shouted: "and if we don't find them marks we'll lynch the whole gang!"

I *was* scared, now, I tell you. But there warn't no getting away, you know. They gripped us all, and marched us right along, straight for the graveyard, which was a mile and a half down the river, and the whole town at our heels, for we made noise enough, and it was only nine in the evening.

As we went by our house I wished I hadn't sent Mary Jane out of town; because now if I could tip her the wink, she'd light out and save me, and blow on our dead-beats.

Well, we swarmed along down the river road, just carrying on like wild-cats, and to make it more scary, the sky was darking up, and the lightning beginning to wink and flitter, and the wind to shiver amongst the leaves. This was the most awful trouble and most dangersome I ever was in; and I was kinder stunned; everything was going so different from what I had allowed for; stead of being fixed so I could take my own time, if I wanted to, and see all the fun, and have Mary Jane at my back to save me and set me free when the close-fit come, here was nothing in the world betwixt me and sudden death but just them tatoo-marks. If they didn't find them—

I couldn't bear to think about it; and yet, somehow, I couldn't think about nothing else. It got darker and darker, and it was a beautiful time to give the crowd the slip; but that big husky had me by the wrist—Hines—and a body might as well try to give Goliar[5] the slip. He dragged me right along, he was so excited; and I had to run to keep up.

When they got there they swarmed into the graveyard and washed over it like an overflow. And when they got to the grave, they found they had about a hundred times as many shovels as they wanted, but nobody hadn't thought to fetch a lantern. But they sailed into digging, anyway, by the flicker of the lightning, and sent a man to the nearest house a half a mile off, to borrow one.

So they dug and dug, like everything; and it got awful dark, and the rain started, and the wind swished and swushed along, and the lightning come brisker and brisker, and the thunder boomed; but them people never took no notice of it, they was so full of this business; and one minute you could see everything and every face in that big crowd, and the shovelfuls of dirt sailing up out of the grave, and the next second the dark wiped it all out, and you couldn't see nothing at all.

At last they got out the coffin, and begun to unscrew the lid, and then such another crowding, and shouldering, and shoving as there was, to scrouge in and get a sight, you never see; and in the dark, that way, it was awful. Hines he hurt my wrist dreadful, pulling and tugging so, and I reckon he clean forgot I was in the world, he was so excited and panting.

All of a sudden the lightning let go a perfect sluice of white glare, and somebody sings out:

"By the living jingo, here's the bag of gold on his breast!"

Hines let out a whoop, like everybody else, and dropped my wrist and give a big surge to bust his way in and get a look, and the way I lit out and shinned for the road in the dark, there ain't nobody can tell.

5. Goliath.

I had the road all to myself, and I fairly flew—leastways I had it all to myself except the solid dark, and the now-and-then glares, and the buzzing of the rain, and the thrashing of the wind, and the splitting of the thunder; and sure as you are born I did clip it along!

When I struck the town, I see there warn't nobody out in the storm, so I never hunted for no back streets, but humped it straight through the main one; and when I begun to get towards our house I aimed my eye and set it. No light there; the house all dark—which made me feel sorry and disappointed, I didn't know why. But at last, just as I was sailing by, *flash* comes the light in Mary Jane's window! and my heart swelled up sudden, like to bust; and the same second the house and all was behind me in the dark, and wasn't ever going to be before me no more in this world. She *was* the best girl I ever see, and had the most sand.

The minute I was far enough above the town to see I could make the tow-head, I begun to look sharp for a boat to borrow; and the first time the lightning showed me one that wasn't chained, I snatched it and shoved. It was a canoe, and warn't fastened with nothing but a rope. The tow-head was a rattling big distance off, away out there in the middle of the river, but I didn't lose no time; and when I struck the raft at last, I was so fagged I would a just laid down to blow and gasp if I could afforded it. But I didn't. As I sprung aboard I sung out:

"Out with you Jim, and set her loose! Glory be to goodness, we're shut of them!"

Jim lit out, and was a coming for me with both arms spread, he was so full of joy; but when I glimpsed him in the lightning, my heart shot up in my mouth, and I went overboard backwards; for I forgot he was old King Lear and a drownded A-rab all in one, and it most scared the livers and lights out of me. But Jim fished me out, and was going to hug me and bless me, and so on, he was so glad I was back and we was shut of the king and the duke, but I says:

"Not now—have it for breakfast, have it for breakfast! Cut loose and let her slide!"

So, in two seconds, away we went, a sliding down the river, and it *did* seem so good to be free again and all by ourselves on the big river and nobody to bother us. I had to skip around a bit, and jump up and crack my heels a few times, I couldn't help it; but about the third crack, I noticed a sound that I knowed mighty well—and held my breath and listened and waited—and sure enough, when the next flash busted out over the water, here they come!—and just a laying to their oars and making their skiff hum! It was the king and the duke.

So I wilted right down onto the planks, then, and give up, and it was all I could do to keep from crying.

Chapter XXX

When they got aboard, the king went for me, and shook me by the collar, and says:

"Tryin' to give us the slip, was ye, you pup! Tired of our company—hey?"

I says:

"No, your majesty, we warn't—*please* don't, your majesty!"

"Quick, then, and tell us what *was* your idea, or I'll shake the insides out o' you!"

"Honest, I'll tell you everything, just as it happened, your majesty. The man that had aholt of me was very good to me, and kept saying he had a boy about as big as me that died last year, and he was sorry to see a boy in such a dangerous fix; and when they was all took by surprise by finding the gold, and made a rush for the coffin, he lets go of me and whispers, 'Heel it, now, or they'll hang ye, sure!' and I lit out. It didn't seem no good for *me* to stay—I couldn't do nothing, and I didn't want to be hung if I could get away. So I never stopped running till I found the canoe; and when I got here I told Jim to hurry, or they'd catch me and hang me yet, and said I was afeard you and the duke wasn't alive, now, and I was awful sorry, and so was Jim, and was awful glad when we see you coming, you may ask Jim if I didn't."

Jim said it was so; and the king told him to shut up, and said, "Oh, yes, it's *mighty* likely!" and shook me up again, and said he reckoned he'd drownd me. But the duke says:

"Leggo the boy, you old idiot! Would *you* a done any different? Did you inquire around for *him*, when you got loose? *I* don't remember it."

So the king let go of me, and begun to cuss that town and everybody in it. But the duke says:

"You better a blame sight give *yourself* a good cussing, for you're the one that's entitled to it most. You hain't done a thing, from the start, that had any sense in it, except coming out so cool and cheeky with that imaginary blue-arrow mark. That *was* bright —it was right down bully; and it was the thing that saved us. For if it hadn't been for that, they'd a jailed us till them Englishmen's baggage come—and then—the penitentiary, you bet! But that trick took 'em to the graveyard, and the gold done us a still bigger kindness; for if the excited fools hadn't let go all holts and

made that rush to get a look, we'd a slept in our cravats to-night—
cravats warranted to *wear*,[6] too—longer than *we'd* need 'em."

They was still a minute—thinking—then the king says, kind
of absent-minded like:

"Mf! And we reckoned the *niggers* stole it!"

That made me squirm!

"Yes," says the duke, kinder slow, and deliberate, and sarcastic,
"*We* did."

After about a half a minute, the king drawls out:

"Leastways—*I* did."

The duke says, the same way:

"On the contrary—*I* did."

The king kind of ruffles up, and says:

"Looky here, Bilgewater, what'r you referrin' to?"

The duke says, pretty brisk:

"When it comes to that, maybe you'll let me ask, what was *you*
referring to?"

"Shucks!" says the king, very sarcastic; "but *I* don't know—
maybe you was asleep, and didn't know what you was about."

The duke bristles right up, now, and says:

"Oh, let *up* on this cussed nonsense—do you take me for a
blame' fool? Don't you reckon *I* know who hid that money in that
coffin?"

"*Yes*, sir! I know you *do* know—because you done it yourself!"

"It's a lie!"—and the duke went for him. The king sings out:

"Take y'r hands off!—leggo my throat!—I take it all back!"

The duke says:

"Well, you just own up, first, that you *did* hide that money
there, intending to give me the slip one of these days, and come
back and dig it up, and have it all to yourself."

"Wait jest a minute, duke—answer me this one question, honest and fair; if you didn't put the money there, say it, and I'll
b'lieve you, and take back everything I said."

"You old scoundrel, I didn't, and you know I didn't. There,
now!"

"Well, then, I b'lieve you. But answer me only jest this one
more—now *don't* git mad; didn't you have it in your *mind* to
hook the money and hide it?"

The duke never said nothing for a little bit; then he says:

"Well—I don't care if I *did*, I didn't *do* it, anyway. But you
not only had it in mind to do it, but you *done* it."

"I wisht I may never die if I done it, duke, and that's honest. I
won't say I warn't *goin'* to do it, because I *was*; but you—I mean
somebody—got in ahead o' me."

6. Hangman's nooses.

"It's a lie! You done it, and you got to *say* you done it, or—"

The king begun to gurgle, and then he gasps out:

" 'Nough!—*I own up!*"

I was very glad to hear him say that, it made me feel much more easier than what I was feeling before. So the duke took his hands off, and says:

"If you ever deny it again, I'll drown you. It's *well* for you to set there and blubber like a baby—it's fitten for you, after the way you've acted. I never see such an old ostrich for wanting to gobble everything—and I a trusting you all the time, like you was my own father. You ought to been ashamed of yourself to stand by and hear it saddled onto a lot of poor niggers and you never say a word for 'em. It makes me feel ridiculous to think I was soft enough to *believe* that rubbage. Cuss you, I can see, now, why you was so anxious to make up the deffesit—you wanted to get what money I'd got out of the Nonesuch and one thing or another, and scoop it *all!*"

The king says, timid, and still a snuffling:

"Why, duke, it was you that said make up the deffersit, it warn't me."

"Dry up! I don't want to hear no more *out* of you!" says the duke. "And *now* you see what you *got* by it. They've got all their own money back, and all of *ourn* but a shekel or two, *besides*. G'long to bed—and don't you deffersit *me* no more deffersits, long 's *you* live!"

So the king sneaked into the wigwam, and took to his bottle for comfort; and before long the duke tackled *his* bottle; and so in about a half an hour they was as thick as thieves again, and the tighter they got, the lovinger they got; and went off a snoring in each other's arms. They both got powerful mellow, but I noticed the king didn't get mellow enough to forget to remember to not deny about hiding the money-bag again. That made me feel easy and satisfied. Of course when they got to snoring, we had a long gabble, and I told Jim everything.

/ *Chapter* XXXI

We dasn't stop again at any town, for days and days; kept right along down the river. We was down south in the warm weather, now, and a mighty long ways from home. We begun to come to trees with Spanish moss on them, hanging down from the limbs like long gray beards. It was the first I ever see it growing, and it made the woods look solemn and dismal. So now the frauds reckoned they was out of danger, and they begun to work the villages again.

First they done a lecture on temperance; but they didn't make enough for them both to get drunk on. Then in another village they started a dancing school; but they didn't know no more how to dance than a kangaroo does; so the first prance they made, the general public jumped in and pranced them out of town. Another time they tried a go at yellocution; but they didn't yellocute long till the audience got up and give them a solid good cussing and made them skip out. They tackled missionarying, and mesmerizering, and doctoring, and telling fortunes, and a little of everything; but they couldn't seem to have no luck. So at last they got just about dead broke, and laid around the raft, as she floated along, thinking, and thinking, and never saying nothing, by the half a day at a time, and dreadful blue and desperate.

And at last they took a change, and begun to lay their heads together in the wigwam and talk low and confidential two or three hours at a time. Jim and me got uneasy. We didn't like the look of it. We judged they was studying up some kind of worse deviltry than ever. We turned it over and over, and at last we made up our minds they was going to break into somebody's house or store, or was going into the counterfeit-money business, or something. So then we was pretty scared, and made up an agreement that we wouldn't have nothing in the world to do with such actions, and if we ever got the least show we would give them the cold shake, and clear out and leave them behind. Well, early one morning we hid the raft in a good safe place about two mile below a little bit of a shabby village, named Pikesville, and the king he went ashore, and told us all to stay hid whilst he went up to town and smelt around to see if anybody had got any wind of the Royal Nonesuch there yet. ("House to rob, you *mean*," says I to myself; "and when you get through robbing it you'll come back here and wonder what's become of me and Jim and the raft—and you'll have to take it out in wondering.") And he said if he warn't back by midday, the duke and me would know it was all right, and we was to come along.

So we staid where we was. The duke he fretted and sweated around, and was in a mighty sour way. He scolded us for everything, and we couldn't seem to do nothing right; he found fault with every little thing. Something was a-brewing, sure. I was good and glad when midday come and no king; we could have a change, anyway—and maybe a chance for *the* change, on top of it. So me and the duke went up to the village, and hunted around there for the king, and by-and-by we found him in the back room of a little low doggery,[7] very tight, and a lot of loafers bullyragging him

---

7. Saloon.

for sport, and he a cussing and threatening with all his might, and so tight he couldn't walk, and couldn't do nothing to them. The duke he begun to abuse him for an old fool, and the king begun to sass back; and the minute they was fairly at it, I lit out, and shook the reefs[8] out of my hind legs, and spun down the river road like a deer—for I see our chance; and I made up my mind that it would be a long day before they ever see me and Jim again. I got down there all out of breath but loaded up with joy, and sung out—

"Set her loose, Jim, we're all right, now!"

But there warn't no answer, and nobody come out of the wigwam. Jim was gone! I set up a shout—and then another—and then another one; and run this way and that in the woods, whooping and screeching; but it warn't no use—old Jim was gone. Then I set down and cried; I couldn't help it. But I couldn't set still long. Pretty soon I went out on the road, trying to think what I better do, and I run across a boy walking, and asked him if he'd seen a strange nigger, dressed so and so, and he says:

"Yes."

"Whereabouts?" says I.

"Down to Silas Phelps's place, two mile below here. He's a runaway nigger, and they've got him. Was you looking for him?"

"You bet I ain't! I run across him in the woods about an hour or two ago, and he said if I hollered he'd cut my livers out—and told me to lay down and stay where I was; and I done it. Been there ever since; afeard to come out."

"Well," he says, "you needn't be afeard no more, becuz they've got him. He run off f'm down South, som'ers."

"It's a good job they got him."

"Well, I *reckon!* There's two hunderd dollars reward on him. It's like picking up money out'n the road."

"Yes, it is—and *I* could a had it if I'd been big enough; I see him *first.* Who nailed him?"

"It was an old fellow—a stranger—and he sold out his chance in him for forty dollars, becuz he's got to go up the river and can't wait. Think o' that, now! You bet *I'd* wait, if it was seven year."

"That's me, every time," says I. "But maybe his chance ain't worth no more than that, if he'll sell it so cheap. Maybe there's something ain't straight about it."

"But it *is*, though—straight as a string. I see the handbill myself. It tells all about him, to a dot—paints him like a picture, and tells the plantation he's frum, below Newr*leans*. No-siree-*bob*, they ain't no trouble 'bout *that* speculation, you bet you. Say, gimme a chaw tobacker, won't ye?"

8. Folds, kinks.

I didn't have none, so he left. I went to the raft, and set down in the wigwam to think. But I couldn't come to nothing. I thought till I wore my head sore, but I couldn't see no way out of the trouble. After all this long journey, and after all we'd done for them scoundrels, here was it all come to nothing, everything all busted up and ruined, because they could have the heart to serve Jim such a trick as that, and make him a slave again all his life, and amongst strangers, too, for forty dirty dollars.

Once I said to myself it would be a thousand times better for Jim to be a slave at home where his family was, as long as he'd *got* to be a slave, and so I'd better write a letter to Tom Sawyer and tell him to tell Miss Watson where he was. But I soon give up that notion, for two things: she'd be mad and disgusted at his rascality and ungratefulness for leaving her, and so she'd sell him straight down the river again; and if she didn't, everybody naturally despises an ungrateful nigger, and they'd make Jim feel it all the time, and so he'd feel ornery and disgraced. And then think of *me!* It would get all around, that Huck Finn helped a nigger to get his freedom; and if I was to ever see anybody from that town again, I'd be ready to get down and lick his boots for shame. That's just the way: a person does a low-down thing, and then he don't want to take no consequences of it. Thinks as long as he can hide it, it ain't no disgrace. That was my fix exactly. The more I studied about this, the more my conscience went to grinding me, and the more wicked and low-down and ornery I got to feeling. And at last, when it hit me all of a sudden that here was the plain hand of Providence slapping me in the face and letting me know my wickedness was being watched all the time from up there in heaven, whilst I was stealing a poor old woman's nigger that hadn't ever done me no harm, and now was showing me there's One that's always on the lookout, and ain't agoing to allow no such miserable doings to go only just so fur and no further, I most dropped in my tracks I was so scared. Well, I tried the best I could to kinder soften it up somehow for myself, by saying I was brung up wicked, and so I warn't so much to blame; but something inside of me kept saying, "There was the Sunday school, you could a gone to it; and if you'd a done it they'd a learnt you, there, that people that acts as I'd been acting about that nigger goes to everlasting fire."

It made me shiver. And I about made up my mind to pray; and see if I couldn't try to quit being the kind of a boy I was, and be better. So I kneeled down. But the words wouldn't come. Why wouldn't they? It warn't no use to try and hide it from Him. Nor from *me*, neither. I knowed very well why they wouldn't come. It was because my heart warn't right; it was because I warn't square; it was because I was playing double. I was letting *on* to give up sin, but away inside of me I was holding on to the biggest one of all. I was trying to make my mouth *say* I would do the right thing and the clean thing, and go and write to that nigger's owner and tell where he was; but deep down in me I knowed it was a lie—and He knowed it. You can't pray a lie—I found that out.

So I was full of trouble, full as I could be; and didn't know what to do. At last I had an idea; and I says, I'll go and write the letter—and *then* see if I can pray. Why, it was astonishing, the way I felt as light as a feather, right straight off, and my troubles all gone. So I got a piece of paper and a pencil, all glad and excited, and set down and wrote:

Miss Watson your runaway nigger Jim is down here two mile below Pikesville and Mr. Phelps has got him and he will give him up for the reward if you send.   HUCK FINN.

I felt good and all washed clean of sin for the first time I had ever felt so in my life, and I knowed I could pray now. But I didn't do it straight off, but laid the paper down and set there thinking—thinking how good it was all this happened so, and how near I come to being lost and going to hell. And went on thinking. And got to thinking over our trip down the river; and I see Jim before me, all the time, in the day, and in the night-time, sometimes moonlight, sometimes storms, and we a floating along, talking, and singing, and laughing. But somehow I couldn't seem to strike no places to harden me against him, but only the other kind. I'd see him standing my watch on top of his'n, stead of calling me, so I could go on sleeping; and see him how glad he was when I come back out of the fog; and when I come to him again in the swamp, up there where the feud was; and such-like times; and would always call me honey, and pet me, and do everything he could think of for me, and how good he always was; and at last I struck the time I saved him by telling the men we had small-pox aboard, and he was so grateful, and said I was the best friend old Jim ever had in the world, and the *only* one he's got now; and then I happened to look around, and see that paper.

It was a close place. I took it up, and held it in my hand. I was a trembling, because I'd got to decide, forever, betwixt two things, and I knowed it. I studied a minute, sort of holding my breath, and then says to myself:

"All right, then, I'll *go* to hell"—and tore it up.[9]

9. This is Huck's famous crisis of conscience. Clemens apparently worked on the passage with great care, lengthening it by about 150 words when revising the manuscript. By pushing Huck the "wrong" way in a tug of war between conscience and temptation, Clemens inverts a stock device of Christian rhetoric that goes back at least to St. Augustine's *Confessions* (c. 399).

It was awful thoughts, and awful words, but they was said. And I let them stay said; and never thought no more about reforming. I shoved the whole thing out of my head; and said I would take up wickedness again, which was in my line, being brung up to it, and the other warn't. And for a starter, I would go to work and steal Jim out of slavery again; and if I could think up anything worse, I would do that, too; because as long as I was in, and in for good, I might as well go the whole hog.

Then I set to thinking over how to get at it, and turned over considerable many ways in my mind; and at last fixed up a plan that suited me. So then I took the bearings of a woody island that was down the river a piece, and as soon as it was fairly dark I crept out with my raft and went for it, and hid it there, and then turned in. I slept the night through, and got up before it was light, and had my breakfast, and put on my store clothes, and tied up some others and one thing or another in a bundle, and took the canoe and cleared for shore. I landed below where I judged was Phelps's place, and hid my bundle in the woods, and then filled up the canoe with water, and loaded rocks into her and sunk her where I could find her again when I wanted her, about a quarter of a mile below a little steam sawmill that was on the bank.

Then I struck up the road, and when I passed the mill I see a sign on it, "Phelps's Sawmill," and when I come to the farm-houses, two or three hundred yards further along, I kept my eyes peeled, but didn't see nobody around, though it was good daylight, now. But I didn't mind, because I didn't want to see nobody just yet—I only wanted to get the lay of the land. According to my plan, I was going to turn up there from the village, not from below. So I just took a look, and shoved along, straight for town. Well, the very first man I see, when I got there, was the duke. He was sticking up a bill for the Royal Nonesuch—three-night performance—like that other time. *They* had the cheek, them frauds! I was right on him, before I could shirk. He looked astonished, and says:

"Hel-*lo!* Where'd *you* come from?" Then he says, kind of glad and eager, "Where's the raft?—got her in a good place?"

I says:

"Why, that's just what I was agoing to ask your grace."

Then he didn't look so joyful—and says:

"What was your idea for asking *me*?" he says.

"Well," I says, "when I see the king in that doggery yesterday, I says to myself, we can't get him home for hours, till he's soberer; so I went a loafing around town to put in the time, and wait. A man up and offered me ten cents to help him pull a skiff over the river and back to fetch a sheep, and so I went along; but when we was dragging him to the boat, and the man left me aholt of the

rope and went behind him to shove him along, he was too strong
for me, and jerked loose and run, and we after him. We didn't have
no dog, and so we had to chase him all over the country till we
tired him out. We never got him till dark, then we fetched him
over, and I started down for the raft. When I got there and see
it was gone, I says to myself, 'they've got into trouble and had to
leave; and. they've took my nigger, which is the only nigger I've got
in the world, and now I'm in a strange country, and ain't got no
property no more, nor nothing, and no way to make my living;' so
I set down and cried. I slept in the woods all night. But what *did*
become of the raft then?—and Jim, poor Jim!"

"Blamed if *I* know—that is, what's become of the raft. That old
fool had made a trade and got forty dollars, and when we found
him in the doggery the loafers had matched half dollars with him
and got every cent but what he'd spent for whisky; and when I got
him home late last night and found the raft gone, we said, 'That
little rascal has stole our raft and shook us, and run off down the
river.' "

"I wouldn't shake my *nigger*, would I?—the only nigger I had in
the world, and the only property."

"We never thought of that. Fact is, I reckon we'd come to
consider him *our* nigger; yes, we did consider him so—goodness
knows we had trouble enough for him. So when we see the raft was
gone, and we flat broke, there warn't anything for it but to try the
Royal Nonesuch another shake. And I've pegged along ever since,
dry as a powderhorn. Where's that ten cents? Give it here."

I had considerable money, so I give him ten cents, but begged
him to spend it for something to eat, and give me some, because
it was all the money I had, and I hadn't had nothing to eat since
yesterday. He never said nothing. The next minute he whirls on
me and says:

"Do you reckon that nigger would blow on us? We'd skin him
if he done that!"

"How can he blow? Hain't he run off?"

"No! That old fool sold him, and never divided with me, and
the money's gone."

"*Sold* him?" I says, and begun to cry; "why, he was *my* nigger,
and that was my money. Where is he?—I want my nigger."

"Well, you can't *get* your nigger, that's all—so dry up your
blubbering. Looky here—do you think *you'd* venture to blow on
us? Blamed if I think I'd trust you. Why, if you *was* to blow on
us—"

He stopped, but I never see the duke look so ugly out of his eyes
before. I went on a-whimpering, and says:

"I don't want to blow on nobody; and I ain't got no time to blow, nohow. I got to turn out and find my nigger."

He looked kinder bothered, and stood there with his bills fluttering on his arm, thinking, and wrinkling up his forehead. At last he says:

"I'll tell you something. We got to be here three days. If you'll promise you won't blow, and won't let the nigger blow, I'll tell you where to find him."

So I promised, and he says:

"A farmer by the name of Silas Ph——" and then he stopped. You see he started to tell me the truth; but when he stopped, that way, and begun to study and think again, I reckoned he was changing his mind. And so he was. He wouldn't trust me; he wanted to make sure of having me out of the way the whole three days. So pretty soon he says: "The man that bought him is named Abram Foster—Abram G. Foster—and he lives forty mile back here in the country, on the road to Lafayette."

"All right," I says, "I can walk it in three days. And I'll start this very afternoon."

"No you won't, you'll start *now*; and don't you lose any time about it, neither, nor do any gabbling by the way. Just keep a tight tongue in your head and move right along, and then you won't get into trouble with *us*, d'ye hear?"

That was the order I wanted, and that was the one I played for. I wanted to be left free to work my plans.

"So clear out," he says; "and you can tell' Mr. Foster whatever you want to. Maybe you can get him to believe that Jim *is* your nigger—some idiots don't require documents—leastways I've heard there's such down South here. And when you tell him the handbill and the reward's bogus, maybe he'll believe you when you explain to him what the idea was for getting 'em out. Go 'long, now, and tell him anything you want to; but mind you don't work your jaw any *between* here and there."

So I left, and struck for the back country. I didn't look around, but I kinder felt like he was watching me. But I knowed I could tire him out at that. I went straight out in the country as much as a mile, before I stopped; then I doubled back through the woods towards Phelps's. I reckoned I better start in on my plan straight off, without fooling around, because I wanted to stop Jim's mouth till these fellows could get away. I didn't want no trouble with their kind. I'd seen all I wanted to of them, and wanted to get entirely shut of them.

Chapter XXXII

When I got there it was all still and Sunday-like, and hot and sunshiny—the hands was gone to the fields; and there was them kind of faint dronings of bugs and flies in the air that makes it seem so lonesome and like everybody's dead and gone; and if a breeze fans along and quivers the leaves, it makes you feel mournful, because you feel like it's spirits whispering—spirits that's been dead ever so many years—and you always think they're talking about *you*. As a general thing it makes a body wish *he* was dead, too, and done with it all.

Phelps's was one of these little one-horse cotton plantations; and they all look alike.[1] A rail fence round a two-acre yard; a stile, made out of logs sawed off and up-ended, in steps, like barrels of a different length, to climb over the fence with, and for the women to stand on when they are going to jump onto a horse; some sickly grass-patches in the big yard, but mostly it was bare and smooth, like an old hat with the nap rubbed off; big double log house for the white folks—hewed logs, with the chinks stopped up with mud or mortar, and these mud-stripes been whitewashed some time or another; round-log kitchen, with a big broad, open but roofed passage joining it to the house; log smoke-house back of the kitchen; three little log nigger-cabins in a row t'other side the smokehouse; one little hut all by itself away down against the back fence, and some outbuildings down a piece the other side; ash-hopper,[2] and big kettle to bile soap in, by the little hut; bench by the kitchen door, with bucket of water and a gourd; hound asleep there, in the sun; more hounds asleep, round about; about three shade-trees away off in a corner; some currant bushes and gooseberry bushes in one place by the fence; outside of the fence a garden and a water-melon patch; then the cotton fields begins; and after the fields, the woods.

I went around and clumb over the back stile by the ash-hopper, and started for the kitchen. When I got a little ways, I heard the dim hum of a spinning-wheel wailing along up and sinking along down again; and then I knowed for certain I wished I was dead—for that *is* the lonesomest sound in the whole world.

I went right along, not fixing up any particular plan, but just trusting to Providence to put the right words in my mouth when the time come; for I'd noticed that Providence always did put the right words in my mouth, if I left it alone.

When I got half-way, first one hound and then another got up and went for me, and of course I stopped and faced them, and kept still. And such another pow-wow as they made! In a quarter of a minute I was a kind of a hub of a wheel, as you may say—spokes made out of dogs—circle of fifteen of them packed together around me, with their necks and noses stretched up towards me, a barking and howling; and more a coming; you could see them sailing over

1. This plantation resembles the farm near Hannibal of Clemens's uncle, John Quarles. The Phelps place becomes the chief locale and Aunt Sally and Uncle Silas important characters in *Tom Sawyer, Detective*.
2. Containing lye for making soap.

fences and around corners from everywheres.

A nigger woman come tearing out of the kitchen with a rolling-pin in her hand, singing out, "Begone! *you* Tige! you Spot! begone, sah!" and she fetched first one and then another of them a clip and sent him howling, and then the rest followed; and the next second, half of them come back, wagging their tails around me and making friends with me. There ain't no harm in a hound, nohow.

And behind the woman comes a little nigger girl and two little nigger boys, without anything on but tow-linen shirts, and they hung onto their mother's gown, and peeped out from behind her at me, bashful, the way they always do. And here comes the white woman running from the house, about forty-five or fifty year old, bare-headed, and her spinning-stick in her hand; and behind her comes her little white children, acting the same way the little niggers was doing. She was smiling all over so she could hardly stand—and says:

"It's *you*, at last!—*ain't* it?"

I out with a "Yes'm," before I thought.

She grabbed me and hugged me tight; and then gripped me by both hands and shook and shook; and the tears come in her eyes, and run down over; and she couldn't seem to hug and shake enough, and kept saying, "You don't look as much like your mother as I reckoned you would, but law sakes, I don't care for that, I'm *so* glad to see you! Dear, dear, it does seem like I could eat you up! Childern, it's your cousin Tom!—tell him howdy."

But they ducked their heads, and put their fingers in their mouths, and hid behind her. So she run on:

"Lize, hurry up and get him a hot breakfast, right away—or did you get your breakfast on the boat?"

I said I had got it on the boat. So then she started for the house, leading me by the hand, and the children tagging after. When we got there, she set me down in a split-bottomed chair, and set herself down on a little low stool in front of me, holding both of my hands, and says:

"Now I can have a *good* look at you; and laws-a-me, I've been hungry for it a many and a many a time, all these long years, and it's come at last! We been expecting you a couple of days and more. What's kep' you?—boat get aground?"

"Yes'm—she—"

"Don't say yes'm—say Aunt Sally. Where'd she get aground?"

I didn't rightly know what to say, because I didn't know whether the boat would be coming up the river or down. But I go a good deal on instinct; and my instinct said she would be coming up—from down towards Orleans. That didn't help me much, though; for I didn't know the names of bars down that way. I see I'd got to invent a bar, or forget the name of the one we got aground on—or—

Now I struck an idea, and fetched it out:

"It warn't the grounding—that didn't keep us back but a little. We blowed out a cylinder-head."

"Good gracious! anybody hurt?"

"No'm. Killed a nigger."

"Well, it's lucky; because sometimes people do get hurt. Two years ago last Christmas, your uncle Silas was coming up from Newrleans on the old *Lally Rook*,[3] and she blowed out a cylinder-head and crippled a man. And I think he died afterwards. He was a Babtist. Your uncle Silas knowed a family in Baton Rouge that knowed his people very well. Yes, I remember, now he *did* die. Mortification set in, and they had to amputate him. But it didn't save him. Yes, it was mortification—that was it. He turned blue all over, and died in the hope of a glorious resurrection. They say he was a sight to look at. Your uncle's been up to the town every day to fetch you. And he's gone again, not more'n an hour ago; he'll be back any minute, now. You must a met him on the road, didn't you?—oldish man, with a—"

"No, I didn't see nobody, Aunt Sally. The boat landed just at daylight, and I left my baggage on the wharf-boat and went looking around the town and out a piece in the country, to put in the time and not get here too soon; and so I come down the back way."

"Who'd you give the baggage to?"

"Nobody."

"Why, child, it'll be stole!"

"Not where I hid it I reckon it won't," I says.

"How'd you get your breakfast so early on the boat?"

It was kinder thin ice, but I says:

"The captain see me standing around, and told me I better have something to eat before I went ashore; so he took me in the texas to the officers' lunch, and give me all I wanted."

I was getting so uneasy I couldn't listen good. I had my mind on the children all the time; I wanted to get them out to one side, and pump them a little, and find out who I was. But I couldn't get no show, Mrs. Phelps kept it up and run on so. Pretty soon she made the cold chills streak all down my back, because she says:

"But here we're a running on this way, and you hain't told me a word about Sis, nor any of them. Now I'll rest my works a little, and you start up yourn; just tell me *everything*—tell me all about 'm all—every one of 'm; and how they are, and what they're doing, and what they told you to tell me; and every last thing you can think of."

Well, I see I was up a stump—and up it good. Providence had

3. Named after the oriental emperor's *Rookh* (1817).
daughter in Thomas Moore's *Lalla*

stood by me this fur, all right, but I was hard and tight aground, now. I see it warn't a bit of use to try to go ahead—I'd *got* to throw up my hand. So I says to myself, here's another place where I got to resk the truth. I opened my mouth to begin; but she grabbed me and hustled me in behind the bed, and says:

"Here he comes! stick your head down lower—there, that'll do; you can't be seen, now. Don't you let on you're here. I'll play a joke on him. Children, don't you say a word."

I see I was in a fix, now. But it warn't no use to worry; there warn't nothing to do but just hold still, and try and be ready to stand from under when the lightning struck.

I had just one little glimpse of the old gentleman when he come in, then the bed hid him. Mrs. Phelps she jumps for him and says:

"Has he come?"

"No," says her husband.

"Good-*ness* gracious!" she says, "what in the world *can* have become of him?"

"I can't imagine," says the old gentleman; "and I must say, it makes me dreadful uneasy."

"Uneasy!" she says, "I'm ready to go distracted! He *must* a come; and you've missed him along the road. I *know* it's so— something *tells* me so."

"Why Sally, I *couldn't* miss him along the road—*you* know that."

"But oh, dear, dear, what *will* Sis say! He must a come! You must a missed him. He—"

"Oh, don't distress me any more'n I'm already distressed. I don't know what in the world to make of it. I'm at my wit's end, and I don't mind acknowledging 't I'm right down scared. But there's no hope that he's come; for he *couldn't* come and me miss him. Sally, it's terrible—just terrible—something's happened to the boat, sure!"

"Why, Silas! Look yonder!—up the road!—ain't that somebody coming?"

He sprung to the window at the head of the bed, and that give Mrs. Phelps the chance she wanted. She stooped down quick, at the foot of the bed, and give me a pull, and out I come; and when he turned back from the window, there she stood, a-beaming and a-smiling like a house afire, and I standing pretty meek and sweaty alongside. The old gentleman stared, and says:

"Why, who's that?"

"Who do you reckon 't is?"

"I haint no idea. Who *is* it?"

"It's *Tom Sawyer!*"

By jings, I most slumped through the floor. But there warn't no

time to swap knives; the old man grabbed me by the hand and
shook, and kept on shaking; and all the time, how the woman did
dance around and laugh and cry; and then how they both did fire
off questions about Sid, and Mary, and the rest of the tribe.

But if they was joyful, it warn't nothing to what I was; for it was
like being born again, I was so glad to find out who I was. Well,
they froze to me for two hours; and at last when my chin was so
tired it couldn't hardly go, any more, I had told them more about
my family—I mean the Sawyer family—than ever happened to any
six Sawyer families. And I explained all about how we blowed out
a cylinder-head at the mouth of White River and it took us three
days to fix it. Which was all right, and worked first rate; because
they didn't know but what it would take three days to fix it. If
I'd a called it a bolt-head it would a done just as well.

Now I was feeling pretty comfortable all down one side, and
pretty uncomfortable all up the other. Being Tom Sawyer was
easy and comfortable; and it stayed easy and comfortable till by-
and-by I hear a steamboat coughing along down the river—then I
says to myself, spose Tom Sawyer come down on that boat?—and
spose he steps in here, any minute, and sings out my name before
I can throw him a wink to keep quiet? Well, I couldn't *have* it that
way—it wouldn't do at all. I must go up the road and waylay him.
So I told the folks I reckoned I would go up to the town and fetch
down my baggage. The old gentleman was for going along with
me, but I said no, I could drive the horse myself, and I druther
he wouldn't take no trouble about me.

Chapter XXXIII

So I started for town, in the wagon, and when I was half-way I
see a wagon coming, and sure enough it was Tom Sawyer, and I
stopped and waited till he come along. I says "Hold on!" and it
stopped alongside, and his mouth opened up like a trunk, and
staid so; and he swallowed two or three times like a person that's
got a dry throat, and then says:

"I hain't ever done you no harm. You know that. So then, what
you want to come back and ha'nt *me* for?"

I says:

"I hain't come back—I hain't been *gone*."

When he heard my voice, it righted him up some, but he warn't
quite satisfied yet. He says:

"Don't you play nothing on me, because I wouldn't on you.
Honest injun, now, you ain't a ghost?"

"Honest injun, I ain't," I says.

"Well—I—I—well, that ought to settle it, of course; but I can't somehow seem to understand it, no way. Looky here, warn't you ever murdered *at all?*"

"No. I warn't ever murdered at all—I played it on them. You come in here and feel of me if you don't believe me."

So he done it; and it satisfied him; and he was that glad to see me again, he didn't know what to do. And he wanted to know all about it right off; because it was a grand adventure, and mysterious, and so it hit him where he lived. But I said, leave it alone till by-and-by; and told his driver to wait, and we drove off a little piece, and I told him the kind of a fix I was in, and what did he reckon we better do? He said, let him alone a minute, and don't disturb him. So he thought and thought, and pretty soon he says:

"It's all right, I've got it. Take my trunk in your wagon, and let on it's your'n; and you turn back and fool along slow, so as to get to the house about the time you ought to; and I'll go towards town a piece, and take a fresh start, and get there a quarter or a half an hour after you; and you needn't let on to know me, at first."

I says:

"All right; but wait a minute. There's one more thing—a thing that *nobody* don't know but me. And that is, there's a nigger here that I'm a trying to steal out of slavery—and his name is *Jim*—old Miss Watson's Jim."

He says:

"What! Why Jim is—"

He stopped and went to studying. I says:

"*I* know what you'll say. You'll say it's dirty low-down business; but what if it is?—*I*'m low down; and I'm agoing to steal him, and I want you to keep mum and not let on. Will you?"

His eye lit up, and he says:

"I'll *help* you steal him!"

Well, I let go all holts then, like I was shot. It was the most astonishing speech I ever heard—and I'm bound to say Tom Sawyer fell, considerable, in my estimation. Only I couldn't believe it. Tom Sawyer a *nigger stealer!*

"Oh, shucks," I says, "you're joking."

"I ain't joking, either."

"Well, then," I says, "joking or no joking, if you hear anything said about a runaway nigger, don't forget to remember that *you* don't know nothing about him, and *I* don't know nothing about him."

Then we took the trunk and put it in my wagon, and he drove off his way, and I drove mine. But of course I forgot all about driving slow, on accounts of being glad and full of thinking; so I got home a heap too quick for that length of a trip. The old gentleman was at the door, and he says:

"Why, this is wonderful. Who ever would a thought it was in that mare to do it. I wish we'd a timed her. And she hain't sweated a hair—not a hair. It's wonderful. Why, I wouldn't take a hunderd dollars for that horse now; I wouldn't, honest; and yet I'd a sold her for fifteen before, and thought 'twas all she was worth."

That's all he said. He was the innocentest, best old soul I ever see. But it warn't surprising; because he warn't only just a farmer, he was a preacher, too, and had a little one-horse log church down back of the plantation, which he built it himself at his own expense, for a church and school-house, and never charged nothing for his preaching, and it was worth it, too. There was plenty other farmer-preachers like that, and done the same way, down South.

In about half an hour Tom's wagon drove up to the front stile, and Aunt Sally she see it through the window because it was only about fifty yards, and says:

"Why, there's somebody come! I wonder who 'tis? Why, I do believe it's a stranger. Jimmy" (that's one of the children), "run and tell Lize to put on another plate for dinner."

Everybody made a rush for the front door, because, of course, a stranger don't come *every* year, and so he lays over the yaller fever, for interest, when he does come. Tom was over the stile and starting for the house; the wagon was spinning up the road for the village, and we was all bunched in the front door. Tom had his store clothes on, and an audience—and that was always nuts for Tom Sawyer. In them circumstances it warn't no trouble to him to throw in an amount of style that was suitable. He warn't a boy to meeky[4] along up that yard like a sheep; no, he come ca'm and important, like the ram. When he got afront of us, he lifts his hat ever so gracious and dainty, like it was the lid of a box that had butterflies asleep in it and he didn't want to disturb them, and says:

"Mr. Archibald Nichols, I presume?"

"No, my boy," says the old gentleman, "I'm sorry to say 't your driver has deceived you; Nichols's place is down a matter of three mile more. Come in, come in."

Tom he took a look back over his shoulder, and says, "Too late— he's out of sight."

"Yes, he's gone, my son, and you must come in and eat your dinner with us; and then we'll hitch up and take you down to Nichols's."

"Oh, I *can't* make you so much trouble; I couldn't think of it. I'll walk—I don't mind the distance."

"But we won't *let* you walk—it wouldn't be Southern hospitality

4. Come meekly.

to do it. Come right in."

"Oh, *do*," says Aunt Sally; "it ain't a bit of trouble to us, not a bit in the world. You *must* stay. It's a long, dusty three mile, and we *can't* let you walk. And besides, I've already told 'em to put on another plate, when I see you coming; so you mustn't disappoint us. Come right in, and make yourself at home."

So Tom he thanked them very hearty and handsome, and let himself be persuaded, and come in; and when he was in, he said he was a stranger from Hicksville, Ohio, and his name was William Thompson—and he made another bow.

Well, he run on, and on, and on, making up stuff about Hicksville and everybody in it he could invent, and I getting a little nervous, and wondering how this was going to help me out of my scrape; and at last, still talking along, he reached over and kissed Aunt Sally right on the mouth, and then settled back again in his chair, comfortable, and was going on talking; but she jumped up and wiped it off with the back of her hand, and says:

"You owdacious puppy!"

He looked kind of hurt, and says:

"I'm surprised at you, m'am."

"You're s'rp— Why, what do you reckon *I* am? I've a good notion to take and—say, what do you mean by kissing me?"

He looked kind of humble, and says:

"I didn't mean nothing, m'am. I didn't mean no harm. I—I—thought you'd like it."

"Why, you born fool!" She took up the spinning-stick, and it looked like it was all she could do to keep from giving him a crack with it. "What made you think I'd like it?"

"Well, I don't know. Only, they—they—told me you would."

"*They* told you I would. Whoever told you's *another* lunatic. I never heard the beat of it. Who's *they?*"

"Why—everybody. They all said so, m'am."

It was all she could do to hold in; and her eyes snapped, and her fingers worked like she wanted to scratch him; and she says:

"Who's 'everybody?' Out with their names—or ther'll be an idiot short."

He got up and looked distressed, and fumbled his hat, and says:

"I'm sorry, and I warn't expecting it. They told me to. They all told me to. They all said kiss her; and said she'll like it. They all said it—every one of them. But I'm sorry, m'am, and I won't do it no more—I won't, honest."

"You won't, won't you? Well, I sh'd *reckon* you won't!"

"No'm, I'm honest about it; I won't ever do it again. Till you ask me."

"Till I *ask* you! Well, I never see the beat of it in my born days!

I lay you'll be the Methusalem-numskull[5] of creation before ever I ask you—or the likes of you."

"Well," he says, "it does surprise me so. I can't make it out, somehow. They said you would, and I thought you would. But—" He stopped and looked around slow, like he wished he could run across a friendly eye, somewhere's; and fetched up on the old gentleman's, and says, "Didn't *you* think she'd like me to kiss her, sir?"

"Why, no, I—I—well, no, I b'lieve I didn't."

Then he looks on around, the same way, to me—and says:

"Tom, didn't *you* think Aunt Sally 'd open out her arms and say, 'Sid Sawyer—' "

"My land!" she says, breaking in and jumping for him, "you impudent young rascal, to fool a body so—" and was going to hug him, but he fended her off, and says:

"No, not till you've asked me, first."

So she didn't lose no time, but asked him; and hugged him and kissed him, over and over again, and then turned him over to the old man, and he took what was left. And after they got a little quiet again, she says:

"Why, dear me, I never see such a surprise. We warn't looking for *you*, at all, but only Tom. Sis never wrote to me about anybody coming but him."

"It's because it warn't *intended* for any of us to come but Tom," he says; "but I begged and begged, and at the last minute she let me come, too; so, coming down the river, me and Tom thought it would be a first-rate surprise for him to come here to the house first, and for me to by-and-by tag along and drop in and let on to be a stranger. But it was a mistake, Aunt Sally. This ain't no healthy place for a stranger to come."

"No—not impudent whelps, Sid. You ought to had your jaws boxed; I hain't been so put out since I don't know when. But I don't care, I don't mind the terms—I'd be willing to stand a thousand such jokes to have you here. Well, to think of that performance! I don't deny it, I was most putrified with astonishment when you give me that smack."

We had dinner out in that broad open passage betwixt the house and the kitchen; and there was things enough on that table for seven families—and all hot, too; none of your flabby tough meat that's laid in a cupboard in a damp cellar all night and tastes like a hunk of old cold cannibal in the morning. Uncle Silas he asked a pretty long blessing over it, but it was worth it; and it didn't cool it a bit, neither, the way I've seen them kind of interruptions do,

5. An idiot as old as Methusaleh.

lots of times.

There was a considerable good deal of talk, all the afternoon, and me and Tom was on the lookout all the time, but it warn't no use, they didn't happen to say nothing about any runaway nigger, and we was afraid to try to work up to it. But at supper, at night, one of the little boys says:

"Pa, mayn't Tom and Sid and me go to the show?"

"No," says the old man, "I reckon there ain't going to be any; and you couldn't go if there was; because the runaway nigger told Burton and me all about that scandalous show, and Burton said he would tell the people; so I reckon they've drove the owdacious loafers out of town before this time."

So there it was!—but *I* couldn't help it. Tom and me was to sleep in the same room and bed; so, being tired, we bid good-night and went up to bed, right after supper, and clumb out of the window and down the lightning-rod, and shoved for the town; for I didn't believe anybody was going to give the king and the duke a hint, and so, if I didn't hurry up and give them one they'd get into trouble sure.

On the road Tom he told me all about how it was reckoned I was murdered, and how pap disappeared, pretty soon, and didn't come back no more, and what a stir there was when Jim run away; and I told Tom all about our Royal Nonesuch rapscallions, and as much of the raft-voyage as I had time to; and as we struck into the town and up through the middle of it—it was as much as half-after eight, then—here comes a raging rush of people, with torches, and an awful whooping and yelling, and banging tin pans and blowing horns; and we jumped to one side to let them go by; and as they went by, I see they had the king and the duke astraddle of a rail—that is, I knowed it *was* the king and the duke, though they was all over tar and feathers, and didn't look like nothing in the world that was human—just looked like a couple of monstrous big soldier-plumes. Well, it made me sick to see it; and I was sorry for them poor pitiful rascals, it seemed like I couldn't ever feel any hardness against them any more in the world. It was a dreadful thing to see. Human beings *can* be awful cruel to one another.

We see we was too late—couldn't do no good. We asked some stragglers about it, and they said everybody went to the show looking very innocent; and laid low and kept dark till the poor old king was in the middle of his cavortings on the stage; then somebody give a signal, and the house rose up and went for them.

So we poked along back home, and I warn't feeling so brash as I was before, but kind of ornery, and humble, and to blame, somehow—though I hadn't done nothing. But that's always the way;

it don't make no difference whether you do right or wrong, a
person's conscience ain't got no sense, and just goes for him *anyway*. If I had a yaller dog that didn't know no more than a person's
conscience does, I would pison him. It takes up more room than all
the rest of a person's insides, and yet ain't no good, nohow. Tom
Sawyer he says the same.

Chapter XXXIV

We stopped talking, and got to thinking. By-and-by Tom says:
"Looky here, Huck, what fools we are, to not think of it before!
I bet I know where Jim is."

"No! Where?"

"In that hut down by the ash-hopper. Why, looky here. When
we was at dinner, didn't you see a nigger man go in there with
some vittles?"

"Yes."

"What did you think the vittles was for?"

"For a dog."

"So'd I. Well, it wasn't for a dog."

"Why?"

"Because part of it was watermelon."

"So it was—I noticed it. Well, it does beat all, that I never
thought about a dog not eating watermelon. It shows how a body
can see and don't see at the same time."

"Well, the nigger unlocked the padlock when he went in, and
he locked it again when he come out. He fetched uncle a key, about
the time we got up from table—same key, I bet. Watermelon shows
man, lock shows prisoner; and it ain't likely there's two prisoners on
such a little plantation, and where the people's all so kind and
good. Jim's the prisoner. All right—I'm glad we found it out
detective fashion; I wouldn't give shucks for any other way. Now
you work your mind and study out a plan to steal Jim, and I will
study out one, too; and we'll take the one we like the best."

What a head for just a boy to have! If I had Tom Sawyer's
head, I wouldn't trade it off to be a duke, nor mate of a steamboat, nor clown in a circus, nor nothing I can think of. I went to
thinking out a plan, but only just to be doing something; I knowed
very well where the right plan was going to come from. Pretty
soon, Tom says:

"Ready?"

"Yes," I says.

"All right—bring it out."

"My plan is this," I says. "We can easy find out if it's Jim in
there. Then get up my canoe to-morrow night, and fetch my raft

over from the island. Then the first dark night that comes, steal the key out of the old man's britches, after he goes to bed, and shove off down the river on the raft, with Jim, hiding daytimes and running nights, the way me and Jim used to do before. Wouldn't that plan work?"

"*Work?* Why cert'nly, it would work, like rats a fighting. But it's too blame' simple; there ain't nothing *to* it. What's the good of a plan that ain't no more trouble than that? It's as mild as goose-milk. Why, Huck, it wouldn't make no more talk than breaking into a soap factory."

I never said nothing, because I warn't expecting nothing different; but I knowed mighty well that whenever he got *his* plan ready it wouldn't have none of them objections to it.

And it didn't. He told me what it was, and I see in a minute it was worth fifteen of mine, for style, and would make Jim just as free a man as mine would, and maybe get us all killed besides. So I was satisfied, and said we would waltz in on it. I needn't tell what it was, here, because I knowed it wouldn't stay the way it was. I knowed he would be changing it around, every which way, as we went along, and heaving in new bullinesses wherever he got a chance. And that is what he done.

Well, one thing was dead sure; and that was, that Tom Sawyer was in earnest and was actly going to help steal that nigger out of slavery. That was the thing that was too many for me. Here was a boy that was respectable, and well brung up; and had a character to lose; and folks at home that had characters; and he was bright and not leather-headed; and knowing and not ignorant; and not mean, but kind; and yet here he was, without any more pride, or rightness, or feeling, than to stoop to this business, and make himself a shame, and his family a shame, before everybody. I *couldn't* understand it, no way at all. It was outrageous, and I knowed I ought to just up and tell him so; and so be his true friend, and let him quit the thing right where he was, and save himself. And I *did* start to tell him; but he shut me up, and says:

"Don't you reckon I know what I'm about? Don't I generly know what I'm about?"

"Yes."

"Didn't I *say* I was going to help steal the nigger?"

"Yes."

"*Well* then."

That's all he said, and that's all I said. It warn't no use to say any more; because when he said he'd do a thing, he always done it. But *I* couldn't make out how he was willing to go into this thing; so I just let it go, and never bothered no more about it. If he was bound to have it so, *I* couldn't help it.

When we got home, the house was all dark and still; so we went on down to the hut by the ash-hopper, for to examine it. We went through the yard, so as to see what the hounds would do. They knowed us, and didn't make no more noise than country dogs is always doing when anything comes by in the night. When we got to the cabin, we took a look at the front and the two sides; and on the side I warn't acquainted with—which was the north side—we found a square window-hole, up tolerable high, with just one stout board nailed across it. I says:

"Here's the ticket. This hole's big enough for Jim to get through, if we wrench off the board."

Tom says:

"It's as simple as tit-tat-toe, three-in-a-row, and as easy as playing hooky. I should *hope* we can find a way that's a little more complicated than *that*, Huck Finn."

"Well then," I says, "how'll it do to saw him out, the way I done before I was murdered, that time?"

"That's more *like*," he says. "It's real mysterious, and troublesome, and good," he says; "but I bet we can find a way that's twice as long. There ain't no hurry; le's keep on looking around."

Betwixt the hut and the fence, on the back side, was a lean to, that joined the hut at the eaves, and was made out of plank. It was as long as the hut, but narrow—only about six foot wide. The door to it was at the south end, and was padlocked. Tom he went to the soap kettle, and searched around and fetched back the iron thing they lift the lid with; so he took it and prized out one of the staples. The chain fell down, and we opened the door and went in, and shut it, and struck a match, and see the shed was only built against the cabin and hadn't no connection with it; and there warn't no floor to the shed, nor nothing in it but some old rusty played-out hoes, and spades, and picks, and a crippled plow. The match went out, and so did we, and shoved in the staple again, and the door was locked as good as ever. Tom was joyful. He says:

"Now we're all right. We'll *dig* him out. It'll take about a week!"

Then we started for the house, and I went in the back door—you only have to pull a buckskin latch-string, they don't fasten the doors—but that warn't romantical enough for Tom Sawyer: no way would do him but he must climb up the lightning-rod. But after he got up half-way about three times, and missed fire and fell every time, and the last time most busted his brains out, he thought he'd got to give it up; but after he was rested, he allowed he would give her one more turn for luck, and this time he made the trip.

In the morning we was up at break of day, and down to the nigger cabins to pet the dogs and make friends with the nigger that fed Jim—if it *was* Jim that was being fed. The niggers was just getting through breakfast and starting for the fields; and Jim's nigger was piling up a tin pan with bread and meat and things; and whilst the others was leaving, the key come from the house.

This nigger had a good-natured, chuckle-headed face, and his wool was all tied up in little bunches with thread. That was to keep witches off. He said the witches was pestering him awful, these nights, and making him see all kinds of strange things, and hear all kinds of strange words and noises, and he didn't believe he was ever witched so long, before, in his life. He got so worked up, and got to running on so about his troubles, he forgot all about what he'd been agoing to do. So Tom says:

"What's the vittles for? Going to feed the dogs?"

The nigger kind of smiled around graduly over his face, like when you heave a brickbat in a mud puddle, and he says:

"Yes, Mars Sid, *a* dog. Cur'us dog, too. Does you want to go en look at 'im?"

"Yes."

I hunched Tom, and whispers:

"You going, right here in the day-break? *That* warn't the plan."

"No, it warn't—but it's the plan *now*."

So, drat him, we went along, but I didn't like it much. When we got in, we couldn't hardly see anything, it was so dark; but Jim was there, sure enough, and could see us; and he sings out:

"Why, *Huck!* En good *lan'!* ain' dat Misto Tom?"

I just knowed how it would be; I just expected it. *I* didn't know nothing to do; and if I had, I couldn't a done it; because that nigger busted in and says:

"Why, de gracious sakes! do he know you genlmen?"

We could see pretty well, now. Tom he looked at the nigger, steady and kind of wondering, and says:

"Does *who* know us?"

"Why, dish-yer runaway nigger."

"I don't reckon he does; but what put that into your head?"

"What *put* it dar? Didn' he jis' dis minute sing out like he knowed you?"

Tom says, in a puzzled-up kind of way:

"Well, that's mighty curious. *Who* sung out? *When* did he sing out. *What* did he sing out?" And turns to me, perfectly ca'm, and says, "Did *you* hear anybody sing out?"

Of course there warn't nothing to be said but the one thing; so I says:

"No; *I* ain't heard nobody say nothing."

Then he turns to Jim, and looks him over like he never see him before; and says:

"Did you sing out?"

"No, sah," says Jim; "*I* hain't said nothing, sah."

"Not a word?"

"No, sah, I hain't said a word."

"Did you ever see us before?"

"No, sah; not as *I* knows on."

So Tom turns to the nigger, which was looking wild and distressed, and says, kind of severe:

"What do you reckon's the matter with you, anyway? What made you think somebody sung out?"

"Oh, it's de dad-blame' witches, sah, en I wisht I was dead, I do. Dey's awluz at it, sah, en dey do mos' kill me, dey sk'yers me so. Please to don't tell nobody 'bout it sah, er ole Mars Silas he'll scole me; 'kase he say dey *ain't* no witches. I jis' wish to goodness he was heah now—*den* what would he say! I jis' bet he couldn' fine no way to git aroun' it *dis* time. But it's awluz jis' so; people dat's *sot*, stays sot; dey won't look into nothn' en fine it out f'r deyselves, en when *you* fine it out en tell um 'bout it, dey doan' b'lieve you."

Tom give him a dime, and said we wouldn't tell nobody; and told him to buy some more thread to tie up his wool with; and then looks at Jim, and says:

"I wonder if Uncle Silas is going to hang this nigger. If I was to catch a nigger that was ungrateful enough to run away, *I* wouldn't give him up, I'd hang him." And whilst the nigger stepped to the door to look at the dime and bite it to see if it was good, he whispers to Jim, and says:

"Don't ever let on to know us. And if you hear any digging going on nights, it's us: we're going to set you free."

Jim only had time to grab us by the hand and squeeze it, then the nigger come back, and we said we'd come again some time if the nigger wanted us to; and he said he would, more particular if it was dark, because the witches went for him mostly in the dark, and it was good to have folks around then.

Chapter XXXV

It would be most an hour, yet, till breakfast, so we left, and struck down into the woods; because Tom said we got to have *some* light to see how to dig by, and a lantern makes too much, and might get us into trouble; what we must have was a lot of them rotten chunks that's called fox-fire and just makes a soft kind of a glow when you lay them in a dark place. We fetched an armful and hid it in the weeds, and set down to rest, and Tom says, kind of dissatisfied:

"Blame it, this whole thing is just as easy and awkard as it can be. And so it makes it so rotten difficult to get up a difficult plan. There ain't no watchman to be drugged—now there *ought* to be a watchman. There ain't even a dog to give a sleeping-mixture to. And there's Jim chained by one leg, with a ten-foot chain, to the leg of his bed: why, all you got to do is to lift up the bedstead and slip off the chain. And Uncle Silas he trusts everybody; sends the key to the punkin-headed nigger, and don't send nobody to watch the nigger. Jim could a got out of that window hole before this, only there wouldn't be no use trying to travel with a ten-foot chain on his leg. Why, drat it, Huck, it's the stupidest arrangement I ever see. You got to invent *all* the difficulties. Well, we can't help it, we got to do the best we can with the materials we've got. Anyhow, there's one thing—there's more honor in getting him out through a lot of difficulties and dangers, where there warn't one of them furnished to you by the people who it was their duty to furnish them, and you had to contrive them all out of your own head. Now look at just that one thing of the lantern. When you come down to the cold facts, we simply got to *let on* that a lantern's resky. Why, we could work with a torchlight procession if we wanted to, I believe. Now, whilst I think of it, we got to hunt up something to make a saw out of, the first chance we get."

"What do we want of a saw?"

"What do we *want* of it? Hain't we got to saw the leg of Jim's bed off, so as to get the chain loose?"

"Why, you just said a body could lift up the bedstead and slip the chain off."

"Well, if that ain't just like you, Huck Finn. You *can* get up the infant-schooliest ways of going at a thing. Why, hain't you ever read any books at all?—Baron Trenck, nor Casanova, nor Benvenuto Chelleeny, nor Henri IV., nor none of them heroes?[6] Whoever heard of getting a prisoner loose in such an old-maidy way as that? No; the way all the best authorities does, is to saw the bed-leg in two, and leave it just so, and swallow the sawdust, so it can't be found, and put some dirt and grease around the sawed place so the very keenest seneskal[7] can't see no sign of it's being sawed, and thinks the bed-leg is perfectly sound. Then, the night you're ready, fetch the leg a kick, down she goes; slip off your chain, and there you are. Nothing to do but hitch your rope-ladder to the battlements, shin down it, break your leg in the moat—because a rope-ladder is nineteen foot too short, you know—and there's your horses

---

6. All of Tom's models attempted daring escapes—Friedrich von der Trenck (1726–94), staff-officer of Frederick the Great; Giovanni Jacopo Casanova (1725–98), Italian lover-adventurer; Benvenuto Cellini (1500–71), goldsmith and sculptor; and King Henry IV of France (1553–1610).

7. Seneschal, powerful steward of a medieval lord.

and your trusty vassles, and they scoop you up and fling you across a saddle and away you go, to your native Langudoc,[8] or Navarre, or wherever it is. It's gaudy, Huck. I wish there was a moat to this cabin. If we get time, the night of the escape, we'll dig one."

I says:

"What do we want of a moat, when we're going to snake him out from under the cabin?"

But he never heard me. He had forgot me and everything else. He had his chin in his hand, thinking. Pretty soon, he sighs, and shakes his head; then sighs again, and says:

"No, it wouldn't do—there ain't necessity enough for it."

"For what?" I says.

"Why, to saw Jim's leg off," he says.

"Good land!" I says, "why, there ain't *no* necessity for it. And what would you want to saw his leg off for, anyway?"

"Well, some of the best authorities has done it. They couldn't get the chain off, so they just cut their hand off, and shoved. And a leg would be better still. But we got to let that go. There ain't necessity enough in this case; and besides, Jim's a nigger and wouldn't understand the reasons for it, and how it's the custom in Europe; so we'll let it go. But there's one thing—he can have a rope-ladder; we can tear up our sheets and make him a rope-ladder easy enough. And we can send it to him in a pie; it's mostly done that way. And I've et worse pies."

"Why, Tom Sawyer, how you talk," I says; "Jim ain't got no use for a rope-ladder."

"He *has* got use for it. How *you* talk, you better say; you don't know nothing about it. He's *got* to have a rope ladder; they all do."

"What in the nation can he *do* with it?"

"*Do* with it? He can hide it in his bed, can't he? That's what they all do; and *he's* got to, too. Huck, you don't ever seem to want to do anything that's regular; you want to be starting something fresh all the time. Spose he *don't* do nothing with it? ain't it there in his bed, for a clew, after he's gone? and don't you reckon they'll want clews? Of course they will. And you wouldn't leave them any? That would be a *pretty* howdy-do, *wouldn't* it! I never heard of such a thing."

"Well," I says, "if it's in the regulations, and he's got to have it, all right, let him have it; because I don't wish to go back on no regulations; but there's one thing, Tom Sawyer—if we go to tearing up our sheets to make Jim a rope-ladder, we're going to get into trouble with Aunt Sally, just as sure as you're born. Now, the way I look at it, a hickry-bark ladder don't cost nothing, and don't waste nothing, and is just as good to load up a pie with, and hide

8. Languedoc, formerly a province in southern France.

in a straw tick, as any rag ladder you can start; and as for Jim, he ain't had no experience, and so *he* don't care what kind of a—"

"Oh, shucks, Huck Finn, if I was as ignorant as you, I'd keep still—that's what *I'd* do. Who ever heard of a state prisoner escaping by a hickry-bark ladder? Why, it's perfectly ridiculous."

"Well, all right, Tom, fix it your own way; but if you'll take my advice, you'll let me borrow a sheet off of the clothes-line."

He said that would do. And that give him another idea, and he says:

"Borrow a shirt, too."

"What do we want of a shirt, Tom?"

"Want it for Jim to keep a journal on."

"Journal your granny—*Jim* can't write."

"Spose he *can't* write—he can make marks on the shirt, can't he, if we make him a pen out of an old pewter spoon or a piece of an old iron barrel-hoop?"

"Why, Tom, we can pull a feather out of a goose and make him a better one; and quicker, too."

"*Prisoners* don't have geese running around the donjon-keep to pull pens out of, you muggins. They *always* make their pens out of the hardest, toughest, troublesomest piece of old brass candlestick or something like that they can get their hands on; and it takes them weeks and weeks, and months and months to file it out, too, because they've got to do it by rubbing it on the wall. *They* wouldn't use a goose-quill if they had it. It ain't regular."

"Well, then, what'll we make him the ink out of?"

"Many makes it out of iron-rust and tears; but that's the common sort and women; the best authorities uses their own blood. Jim can do that; and when he wants to send any little common ordinary mysterious message to let the world know where he's captivated, he can write it on the bottom of a tin plate with a fork and throw it out of the window. The Iron Mask[9] always done that, and it's a blame' good way, too."

"Jim ain't got no tin plates. They feed him in a pan."

"That aint' anything; we can get him some."

"Can't nobody *read* his plates."

"That ain't got nothing to *do* with it, Huck Finn. All *he's* got to do is to write on the plate and throw it out. You don't *have* to be able to read it. Why, half the time you can't read anything a prisoner writes on a tin plate, or anywhere else."

"Well, then, what's the sense in wasting the plates?"

"Why, blame it all, it ain't the *prisoner's* plates."

"But it's *somebody's* plates, ain't it?"

---

9. The mysterious masked prisoner in Alexandre Dumas's *Le Vicomte de Bra-* *gelonne* (1848–50), translated in part as *The Man in the Iron Mask.*

"Well, spos'n it is? What does the *prisoner* care whose—"

He broke off there, because we heard the breakfast-horn blowing. So we cleared out for the house.

Along during that morning I borrowed a sheet and a white shirt off of the clothes-line; and I found an old sack and put them in it, and we went down and got the fox-fire, and put that in too. I called it borrowing, because that was what pap always called it; but Tom said it warn't borrowing, it was stealing. He said we was representing prisoners; and prisoners don't care how they get a thing so they get it, and nobody don't blame them for it, either. It ain't no crime in a prisoner to steal the thing he needs to get away with, Tom said; it's his right; and so, as long as we was representing a prisoner, we had a perfect right to steal anything on this place we had the least use for, to get ourselves out of prison with. He said if we warn't prisoners it would be a very different thing, and nobody but a mean ornery person would steal when he warn't a prisoner. So we allowed we would steal everything there was that come handy. And yet he made a mighty fuss, one day, after that, when I stole a watermelon out of the nigger patch and eat it; and he made me go and give the niggers a dime, without telling them what it was for. Tom said that what he meant was, we could steal anything we *needed*. Well, I says, I needed the watermelon. But he said I didn't need it to get out of prison with, there's where the difference was. He said if I'd a wanted it to hide a knife in, and smuggle it to Jim to kill the seneskal with, it would a been all right. So I let it go at that, though I couldn't see no advantage in my representing a prisoner, if I got to set down and chaw over a lot of gold-leaf distinctions like that, every time I see a chance to hog a watermelon.

Well, as I was saying, we waited that morning till everybody was settled down to business, and nobody in sight around the yard; then Tom he carried the sack into the lean-to whilst I stood off a piece to keep watch. By-and-by he come out, and we went and set down on the wood-pile, to talk. He says:

"Everything's all right, now, except tools; and that's easy fixed."

"Tools?" I says.

"Yes."

"Tools for what?"

"Why, to dig with. We ain't agoing to *gnaw* him out, are we?"

"Ain't them old crippled picks and things in there good enough to dig a nigger out with?" I says.

He turns on me looking pitying enough to make a body cry, and says:

"Huck Finn, did you *ever* hear of a prisoner having picks and shovels, and all the modern conveniences in his wardrobe to dig

himself out with? Now I want to ask you—if you got any reason-
ableness in you at all—what kind of a show would *that* give him
to be a hero? Why, they might as well lend him the key, and done
with it. Picks and shovels—why they wouldn't furnish 'em to a
king."

"Well, then," I says, "if we don't want the picks and shovels,
what do we want?"

"A couple of case-knives."

"To dig the foundations out from under that cabin with?"

"Yes."

"Confound it, it's foolish, Tom."

"It don't make no difference how foolish it is, it's the *right* way
—and it's the regular way. And there ain't no *other* way, that ever
I heard of, and I've read all the books that gives any information
about these things. They always dig out with a case-knife—and not
through dirt, mind you; generly it's through solid rock. And it takes
them weeks and weeks and weeks, and for ever and ever. Why, look
at one of them prisoners in the bottom dungeon of the Castle
Deef,[1] in the harbor of Marseilles, that dug himself out that way;
how long was *he* at it, you reckon?"

"I don't know."

"Well, guess."

"I don't know. A month and a half?"

"*Thirty-seven year*—and he come out in China. *That's* the kind.
I wish the bottom of *this* fortress was solid rock."

"*Jim* don't know nobody in China."

"What's *that* got to do with it? Neither did that other fellow.
But you're always a-wandering off on a side issue. Why can't you
stick to the main point?"

"All right—*I* don't care where he comes out, so he *comes* out;
and Jim don't, either, I reckon. But there's one thing, anyway—
Jim's too old to be dug out with a case-knife. He won't last."

"Yes he will *last*, too. You don't reckon it's going to take thirty-
seven years to dig out through a *dirt* foundation, do you?"

"How long will it take, Tom?"

"Well, we can't resk being as long as we ought to, because it
mayn't take very long for Uncle Silas to hear from down there by
New Orleans. He'll hear Jim ain't from there. Then his next move
will be to advertise Jim, or something like that. So we can't resk
being as long digging him out as we ought to. By rights I reckon
we ought to be a couple of years; but we can't. Things being so
uncertain, what I recommend is this: that we really dig right in,
as quick as we can; and after that, we can *let on*, to ourselves, that

1. Chateau d'If; the hero of Dumas's *Count of Monte Cristo* was imprisoned there.

we was at it thirty-seven years. Then we can snatch him out and rush him away the first time there's an alarm. Yes, I reckon that'll be the best way."

"Now, there's *sense* in that," I says. "Letting on don't cost nothing; letting on ain't no trouble; and if it's any object, I don't mind letting on we was at it a hundred and fifty year. It wouldn't strain me none, after I got my hand in. So I'll mosey along now, and smouch a couple of case-knives."

"Smouch three," he says; "we want one to make a saw out of."

"Tom, if it ain't unregular and irreligious to sejest it," I says, "there's an old rusty saw-blade around yonder sticking under the weatherboarding behind the smoke-house."

He looked kind of weary and discouraged-like, and says:

"It ain't no use to try to learn you nothing, Huck. Run along and smouch the knives—three of them." So I done it.

Chapter XXXVI

As soon as we reckoned everybody was asleep, that night, we went down the lightning-rod, and shut ourselves up in the lean-to, and got out our pile of fox-fire, and went to work. We cleared everything out of the way, about four or five foot along the middle of the bottom log. Tom said he was right behind Jim's bed now, and we'd dig in under it, and when we got through there couldn't nobody in the cabin ever know there was any hole there, because Jim's counterpin[2] hung down most to the ground, and you'd have to raise it up and look under to see the hole. So we dug and dug, with the case-knives, till most midnight; and then we was dog-tired, and our hands was blistered, and yet you couldn't see we'd done anything, hardly. At last I says:

"This ain't no thirty-seven year job, this is a thirty-eight year job, Tom Sawyer."

He never said nothing. But he sighed, and pretty soon he stopped digging, and then for a good little while I knowed he was thinking. Then he says:

"It ain't no use, Huck, it ain't agoing to work. If we was prisoners it would, because then we'd have as many years as we wanted, and no hurry; and we wouldn't get but a few minutes to dig, every day, while they was changing watches, and so our hands wouldn't get blistered, and we could keep it up right along, year in and year out, and do it right, and the way it ought to be done. But *we* can't fool along, we got to rush; we ain't got no time to spare. If we was to put in another night this way, we'd have to knock off for a week

2. Counterpane, bedspread.

to let our hands get well—couldn't touch a case-knife with them sooner."

"Well, then, what we going to do, Tom?"

"I'll tell you. It ain't right, and it ain't moral, and I wouldn't like it to get out—but there ain't only just the one way; we got to dig him out with the picks, and *let on* it's case-knives."

"*Now* you're *talking!*" I says; "your head gets leveler and leveler all the time, Tom Sawyer," I says. "Picks is the thing, moral or no moral; and as for me, I don't care shucks for the morality of it, nohow. When I start in to steal a nigger, or a watermelon, or a Sunday-school book, I ain't no ways particular how it's done so it's done. What I want is my nigger; or what I want is my watermelon; or what I want is my Sunday-school book; and if a pick's the handiest thing, that's the thing I'm agoing to dig that nigger or that watermelon or that Sunday-school book out with; and I don't give a dead rat what the authorities thinks about it nuther."

"Well," he says, "there's excuse for picks and letting-on in a case like this; if it warn't so, I wouldn't approve of it, nor I wouldn't stand by and see the rules broke—because right is right, and wrong is wrong, and a body ain't got no business doing wrong when he ain't ignorant and knows better. It might answer for *you* to dig Jim out with a pick, *without* any letting-on, because you don't know no better; but it wouldn't for me, because I do know better. Gimme a case-knife."

He had his own by him, but I handed him mine. He flung it down, and says:

"Gimme a *case-knife.*"

I didn't know just what to do—but then I thought. I scratched around amongst the old tools, and got a pick-ax and give it to him, and he took it and went to work, and never said a word.

He was always just that particular. Full of principle.

So then I got a shovel, and then we picked and shoveled, turn about, and made the fur fly. We stuck to it about a half an hour, which was as long as we could stand up; but we had a good deal of a hole to show for it. When I got up stairs, I looked out at the window and see Tom doing his level best with the lightning-rod, but he couldn't come it, his hands was so sore. At last he says:

"It ain't no use, it can't be done. What you reckon I better do? Can't you think up no way?"

"Yes," I says, "but I reckon it ain't regular. Come up the stairs, and let on it's a lightning-rod."

So he done it.

Next day Tom stole a pewter spoon and a brass candlestick in the house, for to make some pens for Jim out of, and six tallow candles; and I hung around the nigger cabins, and laid for a chance, and stole three tin plates. Tom said it wasn't enough; but I said nobody wouldn't ever see the plates that Jim throwed out, because they'd fall in the dog-fennel and jimpson weeds under the window-hole—then we could tote them back and he could use them over again. So Tom was satisfied. Then he says:

"Now, the thing to study out is, how to get the things to Jim."

"Take them in through the hole," I says, "when we get it done."

He only just looked scornful, and said something about nobody ever heard of such an idiotic idea, and then he went to studying. By-and-by he said he had ciphered out two or three ways, but there warn't no need to decide on any of them yet. Said we'd got to post Jim first.

That night we went down the lightning-rod a little after ten, and took one of the candles along, and listened under the window-hole, and heard Jim snoring; so we pitched it in, and it didn't wake him. Then we whirled in with the pick and shovel, and in about two hours and a half the job was done. We crept in under Jim's bed and into the cabin, and pawed around and found the candle and lit it, and stood over Jim a while, and found him looking hearty and healthy, and then we woke him up gentle and gradual. He was so glad to see us he most cried; and called us honey, and all the pet names he could think of; and was for having us hunt up a cold chisel to cut the chain off of his leg with, right away, and clearing out without losing any time. But Tom he showed him how unregular it would be, and set down and told him all about our plans, and how we could alter them in a minute any time there was an alarm; and not to be the least afraid, because we would see he got away, *sure*. So Jim he said it was all right, and we set there and talked over old times a while, and then Tom asked a lot of questions, and when Jim told him Uncle Silas come in every day or two to pray with him, and Aunt Sally come in to see if he was comfortable and had plenty to eat, and both of them was kind as they could be, Tom says:

"*Now* I know how to fix it. We'll send you some things by them."

I said, "Don't do nothing of the kind; it's one of the most jackass ideas I ever struck;" but he never paid no attention to me; went right on. It was his way when he'd got his plans set.

So he told Jim how we'd have to smuggle in the rope-ladder pie, and other large things, by Nat, the nigger that fed him, and he must be on the lookout, and not be surprised, and not let Nat see him open them; and we would put small things in uncle's coat pockets and he must steal them out; and we would tie things to aunt's apron strings or put them in her apron pocket, if we got a chance; and told him what they would be and what they was for. And told him how to keep a journal on the shirt with his blood, and all that. He told him everything. Jim he couldn't see no sense in the most of it, but he allowed we was white folks and knowed better than him; so he was satisfied, and said he would do it all just as Tom said.

Jim had plenty corn-cob pipes and tobacco; so we had a right down good sociable time; then we crawled out through the hole, and so home to bed, with hands that looked like they'd been chawed. Tom was in high spirits. He said it was the best fun he ever had in his life, and the most intellectural; and said if he only could see his way to it we would keep it up all the rest of our lives and leave Jim to our children to get out; for he believed Jim would come to like it better and better the more he got used to it. He said that in that way it could be strung out to as much as eighty year, and would be the best time on record. And he said it would make us all celebrated that had a hand in it.

In the morning we went out to the wood-pile and chopped up the brass candlestick into handy sizes, and Tom put them and the pewter spoon in his pocket. Then we went to the nigger cabins, and while I got Nat's notice off, Tom shoved a piece of candlestick into the middle of a corn-pone that was in Jim's pan, and we went along with Nat to see how it would work, and it just worked noble; when Jim bit into it it most mashed all his teeth out; and there warn't ever anything could a worked better. Tom said so himself. Jim he never let on but what it was only just a piece of rock or something like that that's always getting into bread, you know; but after that he never bit into nothing but what he jabbed his fork into it in three or four places, first.

And whilst we was a standing there in the dimmish light, here comes a couple of the hounds bulging in, from under Jim's bed; and they kept on piling in till there was eleven of them, and there warn't hardly room in there to get your breath. By jings, we forgot to fasten that lean-to door. The nigger Nat he only just hollered "witches!" once, and keeled over onto the floor amongst the dogs, and begun to groan like he was dying. Tom jerked the door open and flung out a slab of Jim's meat, and the dogs went for it, and in two seconds he was out himself and back again and shut the door, and I knowed he'd fixed the other door too. Then he went to work on the nigger, coaxing him and petting him, and asking him if he'd been imagining he saw something again. He raised up, and blinked his eyes around, and says:

"Mars Sid, you'll say I's a fool, but if I didn't b'lieve I see most a million dogs, er devils, er some'n, I wisht I may die right heah in dese tracks. I did, mos' sholy. Mars Sid, I *felt* um—I *felt* um, sah; dey was all over me. Dad fetch it, I jis' wisht I could git my han's on one er dem witches jis' wunst—on'y jis' wunst—it's all I'd ast.

But mos'ly I wisht dey'd lemme 'lone, I does."

Tom says:

"Well, I tell you what I think. What makes them come here just at this runaway nigger's breakfast-time? It's because they're hungry; that's the reason. You make them a witch pie; that's the thing for *you* to do."

"But my lan', Mars Sid, how's *I* gwyne to make 'm a witch pie? I doan' know how to make it. I hain't ever hearn er sich a thing b'fo.' "

"Well, then, I'll have to make it myself."

"Will you do it, honey?—will you? I'll wusshup de groun' und' yo' foot, I will!"

"All right, I'll do it, seeing it's you, and you've been good to us and showed us the runaway nigger. But you got to be mighty careful. When we come around, you turn your back; and then whatever we've put in the pan, don't you let on you see it at all. And don't you look, when Jim unloads the pan—something might happen, I don't know what. And above all, don't you *handle* the witch-things."

"*Hannel* 'm Mars Sid? What *is* you a talkin' 'bout? I wouldn' lay de weight er my finger on um, not f'r ten hund'd thous'n' billion dollars, I wouldn't."

Chapter XXXVII

That was all fixed. So then we went away and went to the rubbage-pile in the back yard where they keep the old boots, and rags, and pieces of bottles, and wore-out tin things, and all such truck, and scratched around and found an old tin washpan and stopped up the holes as well as we could, to bake the pie in, and took it down cellar and stole it full of flour, and started for breakfast and found a couple of shingle-nails that Tom said would be handy for a prisoner to scrabble his name and sorrows on the dungeon walls with, and dropped one of them in Aunt Sally's apron pocket which was hanging on a chair, and t'other we stuck in the band of Uncle Silas's hat, which was on the bureau, because we heard the children say their pa and ma was going to the runaway nigger's house this morning, and then went to breakfast, and Tom dropped the pewter spoon in Uncle Silas's coat pocket, and Aunt Sally wasn't come yet, so we had to wait a little while.

And when she come she was hot, and red, and cross, and couldn't hardly wait for the blessing; and then she went to sluicing out coffee with one hand and cracking the handiest child's head with her thimble with the other, and says:

"I've hunted high, and I've hunted low, and it does beat all, what *has* become of your other shirt."

My heart fell down amongst my lungs and livers and things, and a hard piece of corn-crust started down my throat after it and got met on the road with a cough and was shot across the table and took one of the children in the eye and curled him up like a fishing-worm, and let a cry out of him the size of a war-whoop, and Tom he turned kinder blue around the gills, and it all amounted to a considerable state of things for about a quarter of a minute or as much as that, and I would a sold out for half price if there was a bidder. But after that we was all right again—it was the sudden surprise of it that knocked us so kind of cold. Uncle Silas he says:

"It's most uncommon curious, I can't understand it. I know perfectly well I took it *off*, because——"

"Because you hain't got but one *on*. Just *listen* at the man! *I* know you took it off, and know it by a better way than your wool-gethering memory, too, because it was on the clo'es-line yester-day—I see it there myself. But it's gone—that's the long and the short of it, and you'll just have to change to a red flann'l one till I can get time to make a new one. And it'll be the third I've made in two years; it just keeps a body on the jump to keep you in shirts; and whatever you do manage to *do* with 'm all, is more'n *I* can make out. A body'd think you *would* learn to take some sort of care of 'em, at your time of life."

"I know it, Sally, and I do try all I can. But it oughtn't to be altogether my fault, because you know I don't see them nor have nothing to do with them except when they're on me; and I don't believe I've ever lost one of them *off* of me."

"Well, it ain't *your* fault if you haven't, Silas—you'd a done it if you could, I reckon. And the shirt ain't all that's gone, nuther. Ther's a spoon gone; and *that* ain't all. There was ten, and now ther's only nine. The calf got the shirt I reckon, but the calf never took the spoon, *that's* certain."

"Why, what else is gone, Sally?"

"Ther's six *candles* gone—that's what. The rats could a got the candles, and I reckon they did; I wonder they don't walk off with the whole place, the way you're always going to stop their holes and don't do it; and if they warn't fools they'd sleep in your hair, Silas—*you'd* never find it out; but you can't lay the *spoon* on the rats, and that I *know*."

"Well, Sally, I'm in fault, and I acknowledge it; I've been remiss; but I won't let to-morrow go by without stopping up them holes."

"Oh, I wouldn't hurry, next year'll do. Matilda Angelina Araminta *Phelps!*"

Whack comes the thimble, and the child snatches her claws out of the sugar-bowl without fooling around any. Just then, the nigger woman steps onto the passage, and says:

"Missus, dey's a sheet gone."

"A *sheet* gone! Well, for the land's sake!"

"I'll stop up them holes *to-day*," says Uncle Silas, looking sorrowful.

"Oh, *do* shet up!—spose the rats took the *sheet? Where's* it gone, Lize?"

"Clah to goodness I hain't no notion, Miss Sally. She wuz on de clo's-line yistiddy, but she done gone; she ain' dah no mo', now."

"I reckon the world *is* coming to an end. I *never* see the beat of it, in all my born days. A shirt, and a sheet, and a spoon, and six can—"

"Missus," comes a young yaller wench, "dey's a brass cannel-stick miss'n."

"Cler out from here, you hussy, er I'll take a skillet to ye!"

Well, she was just a biling. I begun to lay for a chance; I reckoned I would sneak out and go for the woods till the weather moderated. She kept a raging right along, running her insurrection all by herself, and everybody else mighty meek and quiet; and at last Uncle Silas, looking kind of foolish, fishes up that spoon out of his pocket. She stopped, with her mouth open and her hands up; and as for me, I wished I was in Jeruslem or somewheres. But not long; because she says:

"It's *just* as I expected. So you had it in your pocket all the time; and like as not you've got the other things there, too. How'd it get there?"

"I reely don't know, Sally," he says, kind of apologizing, "or you know I would tell. I was a-studying over my text in Acts Seventeen,[3] before breakfast, and I reckon I put it in there, not noticing, meaning to put my Testament in, and it must be so, because my Testament ain't in, but I'll go and see, and if the Testament is where I had it, I'll know I didn't put it in, and that will show that I laid the Testament down and took up the spoon, and——"

"Oh, for the land's sake! Give a body a rest! Go 'long now, the whole kit and biling of ye; and don't come nigh me again till I've got back my peace of mind."

I'd a heard her, if she'd a said it to herself, let alone speaking it out; and I'd a got up and obeyed her, if I'd a been dead. As we was passing through the setting-room, the old man he took up his

3. Modest Uncle Silas has been reading about himself. In Acts 17, Silas and Paul are persecuted for their eloquent preaching. The namesake who imprisons Jim seems not to have lingered, however, over the preceding book, in which the biblical Silas is himself imprisoned by slaveholders.

hat, and the shingle-nail fell out on the floor, and he just merely picked it up and laid it on the mantel-shelf, and never said nothing, and went out. Tom see him do it, and remembered about the spoon, and says:

"Well, it ain't no use to send things by *him* no more, he ain't reliable." Then he says: "But he done us a good turn with the spoon, anyway, without knowing it, and so we'll go and do him one without *him* knowing it—stop up his rat-holes."

There was a noble good lot of them, down cellar, and it took us a whole hour, but we done the job tight and good, and ship-shape. Then we heard steps on the stairs, and blowed out our light, and hid; and here comes the old man, with a candle in one hand and a bundle of stuff in t'other, looking as absent-minded as year before last. He went a mooning around, first to one rat-hole and then another, till he'd been to them all. Then he stood about five minutes, picking tallow-drip off of his candle and thinking. Then he turns off slow and dreamy towards the stairs, saying:

"Well, for the life of me I can't remember when I done it. I could show her now that I warn't to blame on account of the rats. But never mind—let it go. I reckon it wouldn't do no good."

And so he went on a mumbling up stairs, and then we left. He was a mighty nice old man. And always is.

Tom was a good deal bothered about what to do for a spoon, but he said we'd got to have it; so he took a think. When he had ciphered it out, he told me how we was to do; then we went and waited around the spoon-basket till we see Aunt Sally coming, and then Tom went to counting the spoons and laying them out to one side, and I slid one of them up my sleeve, and Tom says:

"Why, Aunt Sally, there ain't but nine spoons, *yet*."

She says:

"Go 'long to your play, and don't bother me. I know better, I counted 'm myself."

"Well, I've counted them twice, Aunty, and *I* can't make but nine."

She looked out of all patience, but of course she come to count —anybody would.

"I declare to gracious ther' *ain't* but nine!" she says. "Why, what in the world—plague *take* the things, I'll count 'm again."

So I slipped back the one I had, and when she got done counting, she says:

"Hang the troublesome rubbage, ther's *ten*, now!" and she looked huffy and bothered both. But Tom says:

"Why, Aunty, I don't think there's ten."

"You numskull, didn't you see me *count* 'm?"

"I know, but—"

"Well, I'll count 'm *again.*"

So I smouched one, and they come out nine same as the other time. Well, she *was* in a tearing way—just a trembling all over, she was so mad. But she counted and counted, till she got that addled she'd start to count-in the *basket* for a spoon, sometimes; and so, three times they come out right, and three times they come out wrong. Then she grabbed up the basket and slammed it across the house and knocked the cat galley-west;[4] and she said cle'r out and let her have some peace, and if we come bothering around her again betwixt that and dinner, she'd skin us. So we had the odd spoon; and dropped it in her apron pocket whilst she was a giving us our sailing-orders, and Jim got it all right, along with her shingle-nail, before noon. We was very well satisfied with this business, and Tom allowed it was worth twice the trouble it took, because he said *now* she couldn't ever count them spoons twice alike again to save her life; and wouldn't believe she'd counted them right, if she *did;* and said that after she'd about counted her head off, for the next three days, he judged she'd give it up and offer to kill anybody that wanted her to ever count them any more.

So we put the sheet back on the line, that night, and stole one out of her closet; and kept on putting it back and stealing it again, for a couple of days, till she didn't know how many sheets she had, any more, and said she didn't *care,* and warn't agoing to bullyrag[5] the rest of her soul out about it, and wouldn't count them again not to save her life, she druther die first.

So we was all right now, as to the shirt and the sheet and the spoon and the candles, by the help of the calf and the rats and the mixed-up counting; and as to the candlestick, it warn't no consequence, it would blow over by-and-by.

But that pie was a job; we had no end of trouble with that pie. We fixed it up away down in the woods, and cooked it there; and we got it done at last, and very satisfactory, too; but not all in one day; and we had to use up three washpans full of flour, before we got through, and we got burnt pretty much all over, in places, and eyes put out with the smoke; because, you see, we didn't want nothing but a crust, and we couldn't prop it up right, and she would always cave in. But of course we thought of the right way at last; which was to cook the ladder, too, in the pie. So then we laid in with Jim, the second night, and tore up the sheet all in little strings, and twisted them together, and long before daylight we had a lovely rope, that you could a hung a person with. We let on it took nine months to make it.

And in the forenoon we took it down to the woods, but it

4. Out of kilter, cockeyed.   5. Abuse, threaten.

wouldn't go in the pie. Being made of a whole sheet, that way, there was rope enough for forty pies, if we'd a wanted them, and plenty left over for soup, or sausage, or anything you choose. We could a had a whole dinner.

But we didn't need it. All we needed was just enough for the pie, and so we throwed the rest away. We didn't cook none of the pies in the washpan, afraid the solder would melt; but Uncle Silas he had a noble brass warming-pan which he thought considerable of, because it belonged to one of his ancestors with a long wooden handle that come over from England with William the Conqueror in the *Mayflower* or one of them early ships and was hid away up garret with a lot of other old pots and things that was valuable, not on acount of being any account because they warn't, but on account of them being relicts, you know, and we snaked her out, private, and took her down there, but she failed on the first pies, because we didn't know how, but she come up smiling on the last one. We took and lined her with dough, and set her in the coals, and loaded her up with rag-rope, and put on a dough roof, and shut down the lid, and put hot embers on top, and stood off five foot, with the long handle, cool and comfortable, and in fifteen minutes she turned out a pie that was a satisfaction to look at. But the person that et it would want to fetch a couple of kags of toothpicks along, for if that rope-ladder wouldn't cramp him down to business, I don't know nothing what I'm talking about, and lay him in enough stomach-ache to last him till next time, too.

Nat didn't look, when we put the witch-pie in Jim's pan; and we put the three tin plates in the bottom of the pan under the vittles; and so Jim got everything all right, and as soon as he was by himself he busted into the pie and hid the rope-ladder inside of his straw tick, and scratched some marks on a tin plate and throwed it out of the window-hole.

Chapter XXXVIII

Making them pens was a distressid-tough job, and so was the saw; and Jim allowed the inscription was going to be the toughest of all. That's the one which the prisoner has to scrabble on the wall. But we had to have it; Tom said we'd *got* to; there warn't no case of a state prisoner not scrabbling his inscription to leave behind, and his coat of arms.

"Look at Lady Jane Grey," he says; "look at Gilford Dudley; look at old Northumberland![6] Why, Huck, spose it *is* considerble

---

6. Lady Jane Grey (1537–54), briefly a claimant to the British throne, was imprisoned in the Tower of London along with her husband, Guildford Dudley, and his father, the Duke of Northumberland. All three were executed.

trouble?—what you going to do?—how you going to get around it? Jim's got to do his inscription and coat of arms. They all do."

Jim says:

"Why, Mars Tom, I hain't got no coat o' arms; I hain't got nuffn but dish-yer ole shirt, en you knows I got to keep de journal on dat."

"Oh, you don't understand, Jim; a coat of arms is very different."

"Well," I says, "Jim's right, anyway, when he says he hain't got no coat of arms, because he hain't."

"I reckon I knowed that," Tom says, "but you bet he'll have one before he goes out of this—because he's going out *right*, and there ain't going to be no flaws in his record."

So whilst me and Jim filed away at the pens on a brickbat apiece, Jim a making his'n out of the brass and I making mine out of the spoon, Tom set to work to think out the coat of arms. By-and-by he said he'd struck so many good ones he didn't hardly know which to take, but there was one which he reckoned he'd decide on. He says:

"On the scutcheon we'll have a bend *or* in the dexter base, a saltire *murrey* in the fess, with a dog, couchant, for common charge, and under his foot a chain embattled, for slavery, with a chevron *vert* in a chief engrailed, and three invected lines on a field *azure*, with the nombril points rampant on a dancette indented; crest, a runaway nigger, *sable*, with his bundle over his shoulder on a bar sinister: and a couple of gules for supporters, which is you and me; motto, *Maggiore fretta, minore atto.*[7] Got it out of a book—means, the more haste, the less speed."

"Geewhillikins," I says, "but what does the rest of it mean?"

"We ain't got no time to bother over that," he says, "we got to dig in like all git-out."

"Well, anyway," I says, "what's *some* of it? What's a fess?"

"A fess—a fess is—*you* don't need to know what a fess is. I'll show him how to make it when he gets to it."

"Shucks, Tom," I says, "I think you might tell a person. What's a bar sinister?"

"Oh, I don't know. But he's got to have it. All the nobility does."

That was just his way. If it didn't suit him to explain a thing to you, he wouldn't do it. You might pump at him a week, it wouldn't make no difference.

He'd got all that coat of arms business fixed, so now he started in to finish up the rest of that part of the work, which was to plan out a mournful inscription—said Jim got to have one, like they

7. Jim's shield is a little crowded. Divided into thirds (chief, fess, base), it is crisscrossed with bars and emblazoned with six colors, the figures of dog and slave, and a motto appropriate to Tom's leisurely conduct of the escape.

all done. He made up a lot, and wrote them out on a paper, and read them off, so:

1. *Here a captive heart busted.*
2. *Here a poor prisoner, forsook by the world and friends, fretted out his sorrowful life.*
3. *Here a lonely heart broke, and a worn spirit went to its rest, after thirty-seven years of solitary captivity.*
4. *Here, homeless and friendless, after thirty-seven years of bitter captivity, perished a noble stranger, natural son of Louis XIV.*

Tom's voice trembled, whilst he was reading them, and he most broke down. When he got done, he couldn't no way make up his mind which one for Jim to scrabble onto the wall, they was all so good; but at last he allowed he would let him scrabble them all on. Jim said it would take him a year to scrabble such a lot of truck onto the logs with a nail, and he didn't know how to make letters, besides; but Tom said he would block them out for him, and then he wouldn't have nothing to do but just follow the lines. Then pretty soon he says:

"Come to think, the logs ain't agoing to do; they don't have log walls in a dungeon: we got to dig the inscriptions into a rock. We'll fetch a rock."

Jim said the rock was worse than the logs; he said it would take him such a pison long time to dig them into a rock, he wouldn't ever get out. But Tom said he would let me help him do it. Then he took a look to see how me and Jim was getting along with the pens. It was most pesky tedious hard work and slow, and didn't give my hands no show to get well of the sores, and we didn't seem to make no headway, hardly. So Tom says:

"I know how to fix it. We got to have a rock for the coat of arms and mournful inscriptions, and we can kill two birds with that same rock. There's a gaudy big grindstone down at the mill, and we'll smouch it, and carve the things on it, and file out the pens and the saw on it, too."

It warn't no slouch of an idea; and it warn't no slouch of a grindstone nuther; but we allowed we'd tackle it. It warn't quite midnight, yet, so we cleared out for the mill, leaving Jim at work. We smouched the grindstone, and set out to roll her home, but it was a most nation tough job. Sometimes, do what we could, we couldn't keep her from falling over, and she come mighty near mashing us, every time. Tom said she was going to get one of us, sure, before we got through. We got her half way; and then we was plumb played out, and most drownded with sweat. We see it warn't no use, we got to go and fetch Jim. So he raised up his bed and slid the chain off of the bed-leg, and wrapt it round and round his neck, and we crawled out through our hole and down there, and Jim and me laid into that grindstone and walked her along like nothing; and Tom superintended. He could out-superintend any boy I ever see. He knowed how to do everything.

Our hole was pretty big, but it warn't big enough to get the grindstone through; but Jim he took the pick and soon made it big enough. Then Tom marked out them things on it with the nail, and set Jim to work on them, with the nail for a chisel and an iron bolt from the rubbage in the lean-to for a hammer, and told him to work till the rest of his candle quit on him, and then he could go to bed, and hide the grindstone under his straw tick and sleep on it. Then we helped him fix his chain back on the bed-leg, and was ready for bed ourselves. But Tom thought of something, and says:

"You got any spiders in here, Jim?"

"No, sah, thanks to goodness I hain't, Mars Tom."

"All right, we'll get you some."

"But bless you, honey, I doan' *want* none. I's afeard un um. I jis' 's soon have rattlesnakes aroun'."

Tom thought a minute or two, and says:

"It's a good idea. And I reckon it's been done. It *must* a been done; it stands to reason. Yes, it's a prime good idea. Where could you keep it?"

"Keep what, Mars Tom?"

"Why, a rattlesnake."

"De goodness gracious alive, Mars Tom! Why, if dey was a rattlesnake to come in heah, I'd take en bust right out thoo dat log wall, I would, wid my head."

"Why, Jim, you wouldn't be afraid of it, after a little. You could tame it."

"*Tame* it!"

"Yes—easy enough. Every animal is grateful for kindness and petting, and they wouldn't *think* of hurting a person that pets them. Any book will tell you that. You try—that's all I ask; just try for two or three days. Why, you can get him so, in a little while, that he'll love you; and sleep with you; and won't stay away from you a minute; and will let you wrap him round your neck and put his head in your mouth."

"*Please*, Mars Tom—*doan'* talk so! I can't *stan'* it! He'd *let* me shove his head in my mouf—fer a favor, hain't it? I lay he'd wait a pow'ful long time 'fo' I *ast* him. En mo' en dat, I doan' *want* him to sleep wid me."

"Jim, don't act so foolish. A prisoner's *got* to have some kind of a dumb pet, and if a rattlesnake hain't ever been tried, why, there's more glory to be gained in your being the first to ever try it than any other way you could ever think of to save your life."

"Why, Mars Tom, I doan' *want* no sich glory. Snake take 'n bite Jim's chin off, den *whah* is de glory? No, sah, I doan' want no sich doin's."

"Blame it, can't you *try?* I only *want* you to try—you needn't keep it up if it don't work."

"But de trouble all *done,* ef de snake bite me while I's a tryin' him. Mars Tom, I's willin' to tackle mos' anything 'at ain't onreasonable, but ef you en Huck fetches a rattlesnake in heah for me to tame, I's gwyne to *leave,* dat's *shore.*"

"Well, then, let it go, let it go, if you're so bullheaded about it. We can get you some garter-snakes and you can tie some buttons on their tails, and let on they're rattlesnakes, and I reckon that'll have to do."

"I k'n stan' *dem,* Mars Tom, but blame' 'f I couldn' get along widout um, I tell you dat. I never knowed b'fo', 't was so much bother and trouble to be a prisoner."

"Well, it *always* is, when it's done right. You got any rats around here?"

"No, sah, I hain't seed none."

"Well, we'll get you some rats."

"Why, Mars Tom, I doan' *want* no rats. Dey's de dad-blamedest creturs to sturb a body, en rustle roun' over 'im, en bite his feet, when he's tryin' to sleep, I ever see. No, sah, gimme g'yartersnakes, 'f I's got to have 'm, but doan' gimme no rats, I ain' got no use f'r um, skasely."

"But Jim, you *got* to have 'em—they all do. So don't make no more fuss about it. Prisoners ain't ever without rats. There ain't no instance of it. And they train them, and pet them, and learn them tricks, and they get to be as sociable as flies. But you got to play music to them. You got anything to play music on?"

"I ain't got nuffn but a coase comb en a piece o' paper, en a juice-harp; but I reck'n dey wouldn' take no stock in a juice-harp."

"Yes they would. *They* don't care what kind of music 'tis. A jews-harp's plenty good enough for a rat. All animals likes music— in a prison they dote on it. Specially, painful music; and you can't get no other kind out of a jews-harp. It always interests them; they come out to see what's the matter with you. Yes, you're all right; you're fixed very well. You want to set on your bed, nights, before you go to sleep, and early in the mornings, and play your jews-harp; play The Last Link is Broken—that's the thing that'll scoop a rat, quicker'n anything else: and when you've played about two minutes, you'll see all the rats, and the snakes, and spiders, and things begin to feel worried about you, and come. And they'll just fairly swarm over you, and have a noble good time."

"Yes, *dey* will, I reck'n, Mars Tom, but what kine er time is *Jim* havin'? Blest if I kin see de pint. But I'll do it ef I got to. I reck'n I better keep de animals satisfied, en not have no trouble in de house."

Tom waited to think over, and see if there wasn't nothing else; and pretty soon he says:

"Oh—there's one thing I forgot. Could you raise a flower here, do you reckon?"

"I doan' know but maybe I could, Mars Tom; but it's tolable dark in heah, en I ain' got no use f'r no flower, nohow, en she'd be a pow'ful sight o' trouble."

"Well, you try it, anyway. Some other prisoners has done it."

"One er dem big cat-tail-lookin' mullen-stalks would grow in heah, Mars Tom, I reck'n, but she wouldn' be wuth half de trouble she'd coss."

"Don't you believe it. We'll fetch you a little one, and you plant it in the corner, over there, and raise it. And don't call it mullen, call it Pitchiola—that's its right name, when it's in a prison.[8] And you want to water it with your tears."

"Why, I got plenty spring water, Mars Tom."

"You don't *want* spring water; you want to water it with your tears. It's the way they always do."

"Why, Mars Tom, I lay I kin raise one er dem mullen-stalks twyste wid spring water whiles another man's a *start'n* one wid tears."

"That ain't the idea. You *got* to do it with tears."

"She'll die on my han's, Mars Tom, she sholy will; kase I doan' skasely ever cry."

So Tom was stumped. But he studied it over, and then said Jim would have to worry along the best he could with an onion. He promised he would go to the nigger cabins and drop one, private, in Jim's coffee-pot, in the morning. Jim said he would "jis' 's soon have tobacker in his coffee;" and found so much fault with it, and with the work and bother of raising the mullen, and jews-harping the rats, and petting and flattering up the snakes and spiders and things, on top of all the other work he had to do on pens, and inscriptions, and journals, and things, which made it more trouble and worry and responsibility to be a prisoner than anything he ever undertook, that Tom most lost all patience with him; and said he was just loadened down with more gaudier chances than a prisoner ever had in the world to make a name for himself, and yet he didn't know enough to appreciate them, and they was

---

8. A plant sustains a noble prisoner in Joseph Xavier Boniface's *Picciola* (1836).

just about wasted on him. So Jim he was sorry, and said he wouldn't behave so no more, and then me and Tom shoved for bed.

Chapter XXXIX

In the morning we went up to the village and bought a wire rat trap and fetched it down, and unstopped the best rat hole, and in about an hour we had fifteen of the bulliest kind of ones; and then we took it and put it in a safe place under Aunt Sally's bed. But while we was gone for spiders, little Thomas Franklin Benjamin Jefferson Elexander Phelps found it there, and opened the door of it to see if the rats would come out, and they did; and Aunt Sally she come in, and when we got back she was a standing on top of the bed raising Cain, and the rats was doing what they could to keep off the dull times for her. So she took and dusted us both with the hickry, and we was as much as two hours catching another fifteen or sixteen, drat that meddlesome cub, and they warn't the likeliest, nuther, because the first haul was the pick of the flock. I never see a likelier lot of rats than what that first haul was.

We got a splendid stock of sorted spiders, and bugs, and frogs, and caterpillars, and one thing or another; and we like-to got a hornet's nest, but we didn't. The family was at home. We didn't give it right up, but staid with them as long as we could; because we allowed we'd tire them out or they'd got to tire us out, and they done it. Then we got allycumpain[9] and rubbed on the places, and was pretty near all right again, but couldn't set down convenient. And so we went for the snakes, and grabbed a couple of dozen garters and house-snakes, and put them in a bag, and put it in our room, and by that time it was supper time, and a rattling good honest day's work; and hungry?—oh, no, I reckon not! And there warn't a blessed snake up there, when we went back—we didn't half tie the sack, and they worked out, somehow, and left. But it didn't matter much, because they was still on the premises somewheres. So we judged we could get some of them again. No, there warn't no real scarcity of snakes about the house for a considerble spell. You'd see them dripping from the rafters and places, every now and then; and they generly landed in your plate, or down the back of your neck, and most of the time where you didn't want them. Well, they was handsome, and striped, and there warn't no harm in a million of them; but that never made no difference to Aunt Sally, she despised snakes, be the breed what they might, and she couldn't stand them no way you could fix it; and every time one of them flopped down on her, it didn't make no difference what she was doing, she would just lay that work

9. Elecampane, a medicinal herb.

down and light out. I never see such a woman. And you could hear
her whoop to Jericho. You couldn't get her to take aholt of one
of them with the tongs. And if she turned over and found one in
bed, she would scramble out and lift a howl that you would think
the house was afire. She disturbed the old man so, that he said he
could most wish there hadn't ever been no snakes created. Why,
after every last snake had been gone clear out of the house for as
much as a week, Aunt Sally warn't over it yet; she warn't near over
it; when she was setting thinking about something, you could touch
her on the back of her neck with a feather and she would jump
right out of her stockings. It was very curious. But Tom said all
women was just so. He said they was made that way; for some reason or other.

We got a licking every time one of our snakes come in her way;
and she allowed these lickings warn't nothing to what she would
do if we ever loaded up the place again with them. I didn't mind
the lickings, because they didn't amount to nothing; but I minded
the trouble we had, to lay in another lot. But we got them laid in,
and all the other things; and you never see a cabin as blithesome as
Jim's was when they'd all swarm out for music and go for him.
Jim didn't like the spiders, and the spiders didn't like Jim; and so
they'd lay for him and make it mighty warm for him. And he said
that between the rats, and the snakes, and the grindstone, there
warn't no room in bed for him, skasely; and when there was, a
body couldn't sleep, it was so lively, and it was always lively, he
said, because *they* never all slept at one time, but took turn about, so
when the snakes was asleep the rats was on deck, and when the
rats turned in the snakes come on watch, so he always had one
gang under him, in his way, and t'other gang having a circus over
him, and if he got up to hunt a new place, the spiders would take
a chance at him as he crossed over. He said if he ever got out, this
time, he wouldn't ever be a prisoner again, not for a salary.

Well, by the end of three weeks, everything was in pretty good
shape. The shirt was sent in early, in a pie, and every time a rat bit
Jim he would get up and write a little in his journal whilst the ink
was fresh; the pens was made, the inscriptions and so on was all
carved on the grindstone; the bed-leg was sawed in two, and we
had et up the sawdust, and it give us a most amazing stomach-
ache. We reckoned we was all going to die, but didn't. It was the
most undigestible sawdust I ever see; and Tom said the same. But
as I was saying, we'd got all the work done, now, at last; and we
was all pretty much fagged out, too, but mainly Jim. The old man
had wrote a couple of times to the plantation below Orleans to
come and get their runaway nigger, but hadn't got no answer, because there warn't no such plantation; so he allowed he would ad-

vertise Jim in the St. Louis and New Orleans papers; and when he mentioned the St. Louis ones, it give me the cold shivers, and I see we hadn't no time to lose. So Tom said, now for the nonnamous letters.

"What's them?" I says.

"Warnings to the people that something is up. Sometimes it's done one way, sometimes another. But there's always somebody spying around, that gives notice to the governor of the castle. When Louis XVI was going to light out of the Tooleries,[1] a servant girl done it. It's a very good way, and so is the nonnamous letters. We'll use them both. And it's usual for the prisoner's mother to change clothes with him, and she stays in, and he slides out in her clothes. We'll do that too."

"But looky here, Tom, what do we want to *warn* anybody for, that something's up? Let them find it out for themselves—it's their lookout."

"Yes, I know; but you can't depend on them. It's the way they've acted from the very start—left us to do *everything*. They're so confiding and mullet-headed[2] they don't take notice of nothing at all. So if we don't *give* them notice, there won't be nobody nor nothing to interfere with us, and so after all our hard work and trouble this escape 'll go off perfectly flat: won't amount to nothing—won't be nothing *to* it."

"Well, as for me, Tom, that's the way I'd like."

"Shucks," he says, and looked disgusted. So I says:

"But I ain't going to make no complaint. Anyway that suits you suits me. What you going to do about the servant-girl?"

"You'll be her. You slide in, in the middle of the night, and hook that yaller girl's frock."

"Why, Tom, that'll make trouble next morning; because of course she prob'bly hain't got any but that one."

"I know; but you don't want it but fifteen minutes, to carry the nonnamous letter and shove it under the front door."

"All right, then, I'll do it; but I could carry it just as handy in my own togs."

"You wouldn't look like a servant-girl *then*, would you?"

"No, but there won't be nobody to see what I look like, *anyway*."

"That ain't got nothing to do with it. The thing for us to do, is just to do our *duty*, and not worry about whether anybody *sees* us do it or not. Hain't you got no principle at all?"

"All right, I ain't saying nothing; I'm the servant-girl. Who's Jim's mother?"

<hr>

1. The Tuileries, a royal palace in Paris, burned in 1871; now the site of a park near the Louvre.
2. Trusting and stupid.

"I'm his mother. I'll hook a gown from Aunt Sally."

"Well, then, you'll have to stay in the cabin when me and Jim leaves."

"Not much. I'll stuff Jim's clothes full of straw and lay it on his bed to represent his mother in disguise, and Jim 'll take Aunt Sally's gown off of me and wear it, and we'll all evade together. When a prisoner of style escapes, it's called an evasion.[3] It's always called so when a king escapes, f'rinstance. And the same with a king's son; it don't make no difference whether he's a natural one or an unnatural one."

So Tom he wrote the nonamous letter, and I smouched the yaller wench's frock, that night, and put it on, and shoved it under the front door, the way Tom told me to. It said:

Beware. Trouble is brewing. Keep a sharp lookout.

UNKNOWN FRIEND.

Next night we stuck a picture which Tom drawed in blood, of a skull and crossbones, on the front door; and next night another one of a coffin, on the back door. I never see a family in such a sweat. They couldn't a been worse scared if the place had a been full of ghosts laying for them behind everything and under the beds and shivering through the air. If a door banged, Aunt Sally she jumped, and said "ouch!" if anything fell, she jumped and said "ouch!" if you happened to touch her, when she warn't noticing, she done the same; she couldn't face noway and be satisfied, because she allowed there was something behind her every time—so she was always a whirling around, sudden, and saying "ouch," and before she'd get two-thirds around, she'd whirl back again, and say it again; and she was afraid to go to bed, but she dasn't set up. So the thing was working very well, Tom said; he said he never see a thing work more satisfactory. He said it showed it was done right.

So he said, now for the grand bulge! So the very next morning at the streak of dawn we got another letter ready, and was wondering what we better do with it, because we heard them say at supper they was going to have a nigger on watch at both doors all night. Tom he went down the lightning-rod to spy around; and the nigger at the back door was asleep, and he stuck it in the back of his neck and come back. This letter said:

Don't betray me, I wish to be your friend. There is a desprate gang of cutthroats from over in the Ingean Territory[4] going to steal your runaway nigger to-night, and they have been trying to scare you so as you will stay in the house and not bother them. I

---

3. As in the title of Dumas's romance, *L'évasion du duc de Beaufort.*

4. Land in present-day Oklahoma granted to the Indians by the federal government.

am one of the gang, but have got religgion and wish to quit it and lead a honest life again, and will betray the helish design. They will sneak down from northards, along the fence, at midnight exact, with a false key, and go in the nigger's cabin to get him. I am to be off a piece and blow a tin horn if I see any danger; but stead of that, I will BA like a sheep soon as they get in and not blow at all; then whilst they are getting his chains loose, you slip there and lock them in, and can kill them at your leasure. Don't do anything but just the way I am telling you, if you do they will suspicion something and raise whoopjamboreehoo. I do not wish any reward but to know I have done the right thing.

UNKNOWN FRIEND.

Chapter XL

We was feeling pretty good, after breakfast, and took my canoe and went over the river a fishing, with a lunch, and had a good time, and took a look at the raft and found her all right, and got home late to supper, and found them in such a sweat and worry they didn't know which end they was standing on, and made us go right off to bed the minute we was done supper, and wouldn't tell us what the trouble was, and never let on a word about the new letter, but didn't need to, because we knowed as much about it as anybody did, and as soon as we was half up stairs and her back was turned, we slid for the cellar cubboard and loaded up a good lunch and took it up to our room and went to bed, and got up about half-past eleven, and Tom put on Aunt Sally's dress that he stole and was going to start with the lunch, but says:

"Where's the butter?"

"I laid out a hunk of it," I says, "on a piece of a corn-pone."

"Well, you *left* it laid out, then—it ain't here."

"We can get along without it," I says.

"We can get along *with* it, too," he says; "just you slide down cellar and fetch it. And then mosey right down the lightning-rod and come along. I'll go and stuff the straw into Jim's clothes to represent his mother in disguise, and be ready to *ba* like a sheep and shove soon as you get there."

So out he went, and down cellar went I. The hunk of butter, big as a person's fist, was where I had left it, so I took up the slab of corn-pone with it on, and blowed out my light, and started up stairs, very stealthy, and got up to the main floor all right, but here comes Aunt Sally with a candle, and I clapped the truck in my hat, and clapped my hat on my head, and the next second she see me; and she says:

"You been down cellar?"

"Yes'm."

"What you been doing down there?"

"Noth'n."

"*Noth'n!*"

"No'm.".

"Well, then, what possessed you to go down there, this time of night?"

"I don't know'm."

"You don't *know?* Don't answer me that way, Tom, I want to know what you been *doing* down there?"

"I hain't been doing a single thing, Aunt Sally, I hope to gracious if I have."

I reckoned she'd let me go, now, and as a generl thing she would; but I spose there was so many strange things going on she was just in a sweat about every little thing that warn't yard-stick straight; so she says, very decided:

"You just march into that setting-room and stay there till I come. You been up to something you no business to, and I lay I'll find out what it is before *I'm* done with you."

So she went away as I opened the door and walked into the setting-room. My, but there was a crowd there! Fifteen farmers, and every one of them had a gun. I was most powerful sick, and slunk to a chair and set down. They was setting around, some of them talking a little, in a low voice, and all of them fidgety and uneasy, but trying to look like they warn't; but I knowed they was, because they was always taking off their hats, and putting them on, and scratching their heads, and changing their seats, and fumbling with their buttons. I warn't easy myself, but I didn't take my hat off, all the same.

I did wish Aunt Sally would come, and get done with me, and lick me, if she wanted to, and let me get away and tell Tom how we'd overdone this thing, and what a thundering hornet's nest we'd got ourselves into, so we could stop fooling around, straight off, and clear out with Jim before these rips got out of patience and come for us.

At last she come, and begun to ask me questions, but I *couldn't* answer them straight, I didn't know which end of me was up; because these men was in such a fidget now, that some was wanting to start right *now* and lay for them desperadoes, and saying it warn't but a few minutes to midnight; and others was trying to get them to hold on and wait for the sheep-signal; and here was aunty pegging away at the questions, and me a shaking all over and ready to sink down in my tracks I was that scared; and the place getting hotter and hotter, and the butter beginning to melt and run down my neck and behind my ears: and pretty soon, when one of them says, "*I'm* for going and getting in the cabin *first*, and right *now*, and catching them when they come," I most dropped; and a streak of butter come a trickling down my forehead, and Aunt Sally she see it, and turns white as a sheet, and says:

"For the land's sake what *is* the matter with the child!—he's got the brain fever as shore as you're born, and they're oozing out!"

And everybody runs to see, and she snatches off my hat, and out comes the bread, and what was left of the butter, and she grabbed me, and hugged me, and says:

"Oh, what a turn you did give me! and how glad and grateful I am it ain't no worse; for luck's against us, and it never rains but it pours, and when I see that truck I thought we'd lost you, for I knowed by the color and all, it was just like your brains would be if— Dear, dear, whyd'nt you *tell* me that was what you'd been down there for, I wouldn't a cared. Now cler out to bed, and don't lemme see no more of you till morning!"

I was up stairs in a second, and down the lightning-rod in another one, and shinning through the dark for the lean-to. I couldn't hardly get my words out, I was so anxious; but I told Tom as quick as I could, we must jump for it, now, and not a minute to lose—the house full of men, yonder, with guns!

His eyes just blazed; and he says:

"No!—is that so? *Ain't* it bully! Why, Huck, if it was to do over again, I bet I could fetch two hundred! If we could put it off till—"

"Hurry! *hurry!*" I says. "Where's Jim?"

"Right at your elbow; if you reach out your arm you can touch him. He's dressed, and everything's ready. Now we'll slide out and give the sheep-signal."

But then we heard the tramp of men, coming to the door, and heard them begin to fumble with the padlock; and heard a man say:

"I *told* you we'd be too soon; they haven't come—the door is locked. Here, I'll lock some of you into the cabin and you lay for 'em in the dark and kill 'em when they come; and the rest scatter around a piece, and listen if you can hear 'em coming."

So in they come, but couldn't see us in the dark, and most trod on us whilst we was hustling to get under the bed. But we got under all right, and out through the hole, swift but soft—Jim first, me next, and Tom last, which was according to Tom's orders. Now we was in the lean-to, and heard trampings close by outside. So we crept to the door, and Tom stopped us there and put his eye to the crack, but couldn't make out nothing, it was so dark; and whispered and said he would listen for the steps to get further, and when he nudged us Jim must glide out first, and him last. So he set his ear to the crack and listened, and listened, and listened, and the steps a scraping around, out there, all the time; and at last he nudged us, and we slid out, and stooped down, not breathing, and not making the least noise, and slipped stealthy towards the fence, in Injun file, and got to it, all right, and me and Jim over it; but Tom's britches catched fast on a splinter on the top rail, and then he hear the steps coming, so he had to pull loose, which snapped the splinter and made a noise; and as he dropped in our tracks and started, somebody sings out:

"Who's that? Answer, or I'll shoot!"

But we didn't answer; we just unfurled our heels and shoved. Then there was a rush, and a *bang, bang, bang!* and the bullets fairly whizzed around us! We heard them sing out:

"Here they are! They've broke for the river! after 'em, boys! And turn loose the dogs!"

So here they come, full tilt. We could hear them, because they wore boots, and yelled, but we didn't wear no boots, and didn't yell. We was in the path to the mill; and when they got pretty close onto us, we dodged into the bush and let them go by, and then dropped in behind them. They'd had all the dogs shut up, so they wouldn't scare off the robbers; but by this time somebody had let them loose, and here they come, making pow-wow enough for a million; but they was our dogs; so we stopped in our tracks till they catched up; and when they see it warn't nobody but us, and no excitement to offer them, they only just said howdy, and tore right ahead towards the shouting and clattering; and then we up steam again and whizzed along after them till we was nearly to the mill, and then struck up through the bush to where my canoe was tied, and hopped in and pulled for dear life towards the middle of the river, but didn't make no more noise than we was obleeged to. Then we struck out, easy and comfortable, for the island where my raft was; and we could hear them yelling and barking at each other all up and down the bank, till we was so far away the sounds got dim and died out. And when we stepped onto the raft, I says:

"Now, old Jim, you're a free man *again*, and I bet you won't ever be a slave no more."

"En a mighty good job it wuz, too, Huck. It 'uz planned beautiful, en it 'uz *done* beautiful; en dey ain't *nobody* kin git up a plan dat's mo' mixed-up en splendid den what dat one wuz."

We was all as glad as we could be, but Tom was the gladdest of all, because he had a bullet in the calf of his leg.

When me and Jim heard that, we didn't feel so brash as what we did before. It was hurting him considerble, and bleeding; so we laid him in the wigwam and tore up one of the duke's shirts for to bandage him, but he says:

"Gimme the rags, I can do it myself. Don't stop, now; don't fool around here, and the evasion booming along so handsome; man the sweeps, and set her loose! Boys, we done it elegant!—'deed we did. I wish *we'd* a had the handling of Louis XVI, there wouldn't a been no 'Son of Saint Louis, ascend to heaven!'[5] wrote down in *his* biography: no, sir, we'd a whooped him over the *border*— that's what we'd a done with *him*—and done it just as slick as nothing at all, too. Man the sweeps—man the sweeps!"

But me and Jim was consulting—and thinking. And after we'd thought a minute, I says:

"Say it, Jim."

So he says:

"Well, den, dis is de way it look to me, Huck. Ef it wuz *him* dat 'uz bein' sot free, en one er de boys wuz to git shot, would he say, 'Go on en save me, nemmine 'bout a doctor f'r to save dis one? Is dat like Mars Tom Sawyer? Would he say dat? You *bet* he wouldn't! *Well*, den, is *Jim* gwyne to say it? No, sah—I doan' budge a step out'n dis place, 'dout a *doctor*; not if it's forty year!"

I knowed he was white inside, and I reckoned he'd say what he did say—so it was all right, now, and I told Tom I was agoing for a doctor. He raised considerble row about it, but me and Jim stuck to it and wouldn't budge; so he was for crawling out and setting the raft loose himself; but we wouldn't let him. Then he give us a piece of his mind—but it didn't do no good.

So when he see me getting the canoe ready, he says:

"Well, then, if you're bound to go, I'll tell you the way to do, when you get to the village. Shut the door, and blindfold the doctor tight and fast, and make him swear to be silent as the grave, and put a purse full of gold in his hand, and then take and lead him all around the back alleys and everywheres, in the dark, and then fetch him here in the canoe, in a roundabout way amongst the islands, and search him and take his chalk away from him, and don't give it back to him till you get him back to the village, or else he will chalk this raft so he can find it again. It's the way they all do."

So I said I would, and left, and Jim was to hide in the woods when he see the doctor coming, till he was gone again.

Chapter XLI

The doctor was an old man; a very nice, kind-looking old man, when I got him up. I told him me and my brother was over on Spanish Island hunting, yesterday afternoon, and camped on a

5. Tom borrows this admonition from Thomas Carlyle's account of Louis XVI's execution in *The French Revolution* (1837), a book Clemens knew well.

piece of a raft we found, and about midnight he must a kicked his gun in his dreams, for it went off and shot him in the leg, and we wanted him to go over there and fix it and not say nothing about it, nor let anybody know, because we wanted to come home this evening, and surprise the folks.

"Who is your folks?" he says.

"The Phelpses, down yonder."

"Oh," he says. And after a minute, he says: "How'd you say he got shot?"

"He had a dream," I says, "and it shot him."

"Singular dream," he says.

So he lit up his lantern, and got his saddle-bags, and we started. But when he see the canoe, he didn't like the look of her—said she was big enough for one, but didn't look pretty safe for two. I says:

"Oh, you needn't be afeard, sir, she carried the three of us, easy enough."

"What three?"

"Why, me and Sid, and—and—and *the guns*; that's what I mean."

"Oh," he says.

But he put his foot on the gunnel, and rocked her; and shook his head, and said he reckoned he'd look around for a bigger one. But they was all locked and chained; so he took my canoe, and said for me to wait till he come back, or I could hunt around further, or maybe I better go down home and get them ready for the surprise, if I wanted to. But I said I didn't; so I told him just how to find the raft, and then he started.

I struck an idea, pretty soon. I says to myself, spos'n he can't fix that leg just in three shakes of a sheep's tail, as the saying is? spos'n it takes him three or four days? What are we going to do?—lay around there till he lets the cat out of the bag? No, sir, I know what *I'll* do. I'll wait, and when he comes back, if he says he's got to go any more, I'll get down there, too, if I swim; and we'll take and tie him, and keep him, and shove out down the river; and when Tom's done with him, we'll give him what it's worth, or all we got, and then let him get shore.

So then I crept into a lumber pile to get some sleep; and next time I waked up the sun was away up over my head! I shot out and went for the doctor's house, but they told me he'd gone away in the night, some time or other, and warn't back yet. Well, thinks I, that looks powerful bad for *Tom*, and I'll dig out for the island, right off. So away I shoved, and turned the corner, and nearly rammed my head into Uncle Silas's stomach! He says:

"Why, Tom! Where you been, all this time, you rascal?"

"I hain't been nowheres," I says, "only just hunting for the runaway nigger—me and Sid."

"Why, where ever did you go?" he says. "Your aunt's been mighty uneasy."

"She needn't," I says, "because we was all right. We followed the men and the dogs, but they out-run us, and we lost them; but we thought we heard them on the water, so we got a canoe and took out after them, and crossed over but couldn't find nothing of them; so we cruised along up-shore till we got kind of tired and beat out; and tied up the canoe and went to sleep, and never waked up till about an hour ago, then we paddled over here to hear the news, and Sid's at the post-office to see what he can hear, and I'm a branching out to get something to eat for us, and then we're going home."

So then we went to the post-office to get "Sid"; but just as I suspicioned, he warn't there; so the old man he got a letter out of the office, and we waited a while longer but Sid didn't come; so the old man said come along, let Sid foot it home, or canoe-it, when he got done fooling around—but we would ride. I couldn't get him to let me stay and wait for Sid; and he said there warn't no use in it, and I must come along, and let Aunt Sally see we was all right.

When we got home, Aunt Sally was that glad to see me she laughed and cried both, and hugged me, and give me one of them lickings of hern that don't amount to shucks, and said she'd serve Sid the same when he come.

And the place was plumb full of farmers and farmers' wives, to dinner; and such another clack a body never heard. Old Mrs. Hotchkiss was the worst; her tongue was agoing all the time. She says:

"Well, Sister Phelps, I've ransacked that-air cabin over an' I b'lieve the nigger was crazy. I says so to Sister Damrell—didn't I, Sister Damrell?—s'I, he's crazy, s'I—them's the very words I said. You all hearn me: he's crazy, s'I; everything shows it, s'I. Look at that-air grindstone, s'I; want to tell *me* 't any cretur 'ts in his right mind 's agoin' to scrabble all them crazy things onto a grindstone, s'I? Here sich 'n' sich a person busted his heart; 'n' here so 'n' so pegged along for thirty-seven year, 'n' all that—natcherl son o' Louis somebody, 'n' sich everlast'n rubbage. He's plumb crazy, s'I; it's what I says in the fust place, it's what I says in the middle, 'n' it's what I says last 'n' all the time—the nigger's crazy—crazy's Nebokoodneezer,[6] s'I."

"An' look at that-air ladder made out'n rags, Sister Hotchkiss," says old Mrs. Damrell, "what in the name o' goodness *could* he ever want of—"

"The very words I was a-sayin' no longer ago th'n this minute to Sister Utterback, 'n' she'll tell you so herself. Sh-she, look at that-

6. Nebuchadnezzar, king of Babylon, loses his sanity in Daniel 4:33.

air rag ladder, sh-she; 'n' s'I, yes, *look* at it, s'I—what *could* he a wanted of it, s'I. Sh-she, Sister Hotchkiss, sh-she—"

"But how in the nation'd thcy ever *git* that grindstone *in* there, anyway? 'n' who dug that-air *hole?* 'n' who—"

"My very *words,* Brer Penrod! I was a-sayin'—pass that-air sasser o' m'lasses, won't ye?—I was a-sayin' to Sister Dunlap, jist this minute, how *did* they git that grindstone in there, s'I. Without *help,* mind you—'thout *help!* Thar's wher' 'tis. Don't tell *me,* s'I; there *wuz* help, s'I; 'n' ther' wuz a *plenty* help, too, s'I; ther's ben a *dozen* a-helpin' that nigger, 'n' I lay I'd skin every last nigger on this place, but *I'd* find out who done it, s'I; 'n' moreover, s'I—"

"A *dozen* says you!—*forty* couldn't a done everything that's been done. Look at them case-knife saws and things, how tedious they've been made; look at that bed-leg sawed off with 'em, a week's work for six men; look at that nigger made out'n straw on the bed; and look at—"

"You may *well* say it, Brer Hightower! It's jist as I was a-sayin' to Brer Phelps, his own sel S'e, what do *you* think of it, Sister Hotchkiss, s'e? think o' what, Brer Phelps, s'I? think o' that bed-leg sawed off that a way, s'e? *think* of it, s'I? I lay it never sawed *itself* off, s'I—somebody *sawed* it, s'I; that's my opinion, take it or leave it, it mayn't be no 'count, s'I, but sich as 't is, it's my opinion, s'I, 'n' if anybody k'n start a better one, s'I, let him *do* it, s'I, that's all. I says to Sister Dunlap, s'I—"

"Why, dog my cats, they must a ben a house-full o' niggers in there every night for four weeks, to a done all that work, Sister Phelps. Look at that shirt—every last inch of it kivered over with secret African writ'n done with blood! Must a ben a raft uv 'm at it right along, all the time, amost. Why, I'd give two dollars to have it read to me; 'n' as for the niggers that wrote it, I 'low I'd take 'n' lash 'm t'll—"

"People to *help* him, Brother Marples! Well, I reckon you'd *think* so, if you'd a been in this house for a while back. Why, they've stole everything they could lay their hands on—and we a watching, all the time, mind you. They stole that shirt right off o' the line! and as for that sheet they made the rag ladder out of ther' ain't no telling how many times they *didn't* steal that; and flour, and candles, and candlesticks, and spoons, and the old warming-pan, and most a thousand things that I disremember, now, and my new calico dress; and me, and Silas, and my Sid and Tom on the constant watch day *and* night, as I was a telling you, and not a one of us could catch hide nor hair, nor sight nor sound of them; and here at the last minute, lo and behold you, they slides right in under our noses, and fools us, and not only fools *us* but the Injun Territory robbers too, and actly gets *away* with that nigger, safe and sound, and that with sixteen men and twenty-two dogs right on their very heels at that very time! I tell you, it just bangs anything I ever *heard* of. Why, *sperits* couldn't a done better, and been no smarter. And I reckon they must a *been* sperits—because, *you* know our dogs, and ther' ain't no better; well, them dogs never even got on the *track* of 'm, once! You explain *that* to me, if you can!—*any* of you!"

"Well, it does beat—"

"Laws alive, I never—"

"So help me, I wouldn't a be—"

"*House* thieves as well as—"

"Goodnessgracioussakes, I'd a ben afeard to *live* in sich a—"

" 'Fraid to *live!*—why, I was that scared I dasn't hardly go to bed, or get up, or lay down, or *set* down, Sister Ridgeway. Why, they'd steal the very—why, goodness sakes, you can guess what kind of a fluster I was in by the time midnight come, last night. I hope to gracious if I warn't afraid they'd steal some o' the family! I was just to that pass, I didn't have no reasoning faculties no more. It looks foolish enough, *now*, in the day-time; but I says to myself, there's my two poor boys asleep, 'way up stairs in that lonesome room, and I declare to goodness I was that uneasy 't I crep' up there and locked 'em in! I *did*. And anybody would. Because, you know, when you get scared, that way, and it keeps running on, and getting worse and worse, all the time, and your wits gets to addling, and you get to doing all sorts o' wild things, and by-and-by you think to yourself, spos'n I was a boy, and was away up there, and the door ain't locked, and you—" She stopped, looking kind of wondering, and then she turned her head around slow, and when her eye lit on me—I got up and took a walk.

Says I to myself, I can explain better how we come to not be in that room this morning, if I go out to one side and study over it a little. So I done it. But I dasn't go fur, or she'd a sent for me. And when it was late in the day, the people all went, and then I come in and told her the noise and shooting waked up me and "Sid," and the door was locked, and we wanted to see the fun, so we went down the lightning-rod, and both of us got hurt a little, and we didn't never want to try *that* no more. And then I went on and told her all what I told Uncle Silas before; and then she said she'd forgive us, and maybe it was all right enough anyway, and about what a body might expect of boys, for all boys was a pretty harum-scarum[7] lot, as fur as she could see; and so, as long as no harm hadn't come of it, she judged she better put in her time being grateful we was alive and well and she had us still, stead of fretting

7. Reckless, wild.

over what was past and done. So then she kissed me, and patted me on the head, and dropped into a kind of a brown study; and pretty soon jumps up, and says:

"Why, lawsamercy, it's most night, and Sid not come yet! What *has* become of that boy?"

I see my chance; so I skips up and says:

"I'll run right up to town and get him," I says.

"No you won't," she says. "You'll stay right wher' you are; *one's* enough to be lost at a time. If he ain't here to supper, your uncle 'll go."

Well, he warn't there to supper; so right after supper uncle went.

He come back about ten, a little bit uneasy; hadn't run across Tom's track. Aunt Sally was a good *deal* uneasy; but Uncle Silas he said there warn't no occasion to be—boys will be boys, he said, and you'll see this one turn up in the morning, all sound and right. So she had to be satisfied. But she said she'd set up for him a while, anyway, and keep a light burning, so he could see it.

And then when I went up to bed she come up with me and fetched her candle, and tucked me in, and mothered me so good I felt mean, and like I couldn't look her in the face; and she set down on the bed and talked with me a long time, and said what a splendid boy Sid was, and didn't seem to want to ever stop talking about him; and kept asking me every now and then, if I reckoned he could a got lost, or hurt, or maybe drownded, and might be laying at this minute, somewheres, suffering or dead, and she not by him to help him, and so the tears would drip down, silent, and I would tell her that Sid was all right, and would be home in the morning, sure; and she would squeeze my hand, or maybe kiss me, and tell me to say it again, and keep on saying it, because it done her good, and she was in so much trouble. And when she was going away, she looked down in my eyes, so steady and gentle, and says:

"The door ain't going to be locked, Tom; and there's the window and the rod; but you'll be good, *won't* you? And you won't go? For *my* sake."

Laws knows I *wanted* to go, bad enough, to see about Tom, and was all intending to go; but after that, I wouldn't a went, not for kingdoms.

But she was on my mind, and Tom was on my mind; so I slept very restless. And twice I went down the rod, away in the night, and slipped around front, and see her setting there by her candle in the window with her eyes towards the road and the tears in them; and I wished I could do something for her, but I couldn't, only to swear that I wouldn't never do nothing to grieve her any more.

And the third time, I waked up at dawn, and slid down, and she was there yet, and her candle was most out, and her old gray head was resting on her hand, and she was asleep.

Chapter XLII

The old man was up town again, before breakfast, but couldn't get no track of Tom; and both of them set at the table, thinking, and not saying nothing, and looking mournful, and their coffee getting cold, and not eating anything. And by-and-by the old man says:

"Did I give you the letter?"

"What letter?"

"The one I got yesterday out of the post-office."

"No, you didn't give me no letter."

"Well, I must a forgot it."

So he rummaged his pockets, and then went off somewheres where he had laid it down, and fetched it, and give it to her. She says:

"Why, it's from St. Petersburg—it's from Sis."

I allowed another walk would do me good; but I couldn't stir. But before she could break it open, she dropped it and run—for she see something. And so did I. It was Tom Sawyer on a mattress; and that old doctor; and Jim, in *her* calico dress, with his hands tied behind him; and a lot of people. I hid the letter behind the first thing that come handy, and rushed. She flung herself at Tom, crying, and says:

"Oh, he's dead, he's dead, I know he's dead!"

And Tom he turned his head a little, and muttered something or other, which showed he warn't in his right mind; then she flung up her hands, and says:

"He's alive, thank God! And that's enough!" and she snatched a kiss of him, and flew for the house to get the bed ready, and scattering orders right and left at the niggers and everybody else, as fast as her tongue could go, every jump of the way.

I followed the men to see what they was going to do with Jim; and the old doctor and Uncle Silas followed after Tom into the house. The men was very huffy, and some of them wanted to hang Jim, for an example to all the other niggers around there, so they wouldn't be trying to run away, like Jim done, and making such a raft of trouble, and keeping a whole family scared most to death for days and nights. But the others said, don't do it, it wouldn't answer at all, he ain't our nigger, and his owner would turn up and make us pay for him, sure. So that cooled them down a little, because the people that's always the most anxious for to hang a nigger that hain't done just right, is always the very ones that ain't the most anxious to pay for him when they've got their satisfaction out of him.

They cussed Jim considerble, though, and give him a cuff or two, side the head, once in a while, but Jim never said nothing, and he never let on to know me, and they took him to the same cabin, and put his own clothes on him, and chained him again, and not to no bed-leg, this time, but to a big staple drove into the bottom log, and chained his hands, too, and both legs, and said he warn't to have nothing but bread and water to eat, after this, till his owner come or he was sold at auction, because he didn't come in a certain length of time, and filled up our hole, and said a couple of farmers with guns must stand watch around about the cabin every night, and a bull-dog tied to the door in the day time; and about this time they was through with the job and was tapering off with a kind of generl good-bye cussing, and then the old doctor comes and takes a look and says:

"Don't be no rougher on him than you're obleeged to, because he ain't a bad nigger. When I got to where I found the boy, I see I couldn't cut the bullet out without some help, and he warn't in no condition for me to leave, to go and get help; and he got a little worse and a little worse, and after a long time he went out of his head, and wouldn't let me come anigh him, any more, and said if I chalked his raft he'd kill me, and no end of wild foolishness like that, and I see I couldn't do anything at all with him; so I says, I got to have *help*, somehow; and the minute I says it, out crawls this nigger from somewheres, and says he'll help, and he done it, too, and done it very well. Of course I judged he must be a runaway nigger, and there I *was!* and there I had to stick, right straight along all the rest of the day, and all night. It was a fix, I tell you! I had a couple of patients with the chills, and of course I'd of liked to run up to town and see them, but I dasn't, because the nigger might get away, and then I'd be to blame; and yet never a skiff come close enough for me to hail. So there I had to stick, plumb till daylight this morning; and I never see a nigger that was a better nuss or faithfuller, and yet he was resking his freedom to do it, and was all tired out, too, and I see plain enough he'd been worked main hard, lately. I liked the nigger for that; I tell you, gentlemen, a nigger like that is worth a thousand dollars—and kind treatment, too. I had everything I needed, and the boy was doing as well there as he would a done at home— better, maybe, because it was so quiet; but there I *was*, with both of 'm on my hands; and there I had to stick, till about dawn this morning; then some men in a skiff come by, and as good luck would have it, the nigger was setting by the pallet with his head propped on his knees, sound asleep; so I motioned them in, quiet, and they slipped up on him and grabbed him and tied him before he knowed what he was about, and we never had no trouble. And the boy being in a kind of a flighty sleep, too, we muffled the oars and hitched the raft on, and towed her over very nice and quiet, and the nigger never made the least row nor said a word, from the start. He ain't no bad nigger, gentlemen; that's what I think about him."

Somebody says:

"Well, it sounds very good, doctor, I'm obleeged to say."

Then the others softened up a little, too, and I was mighty thankful to that old doctor for doing Jim that good turn; and I was glad it was according to my judgment of him, too; because I thought he had a good heart in him and was a good man, the first time I see him. Then they all agreed that Jim had acted very well, and was deserving to have some notice took of it, and reward. So every one of them promised, right out and hearty, that they wouldn't cuss him no more.

Then they come out and locked him up. I hoped they was going to say he could have one or two of the chains took off, because they was rotten heavy, or could have meat and greens with his bread and water, but they didn't think of it, and I reckoned it warn't best for me to mix in, but I judged I'd get the doctor's yarn to Aunt Sally, somehow or other, as soon as I'd got through the breakers that was laying just ahead of me. Explanations, I mean, of how I forgot to mention about Sid being shot, when I was telling how him and me put in that dratted night paddling around hunting the runaway nigger.

But I had plenty time. Aunt Sally she stuck to the sick-room all day and all night; and every time I see Uncle Silas mooning around, I dodged him.

Next morning I heard Tom was a good deal better, and they said Aunt Sally was gone to get a nap. So I slips to the sick-room, and if I found him awake I reckoned we could put up a yarn for the family that would wash. But he was sleeping, and sleeping very peaceful, too; and pale, not fire-faced the way he was when he come. So I set down and laid for him to wake. In about a half an hour, Aunt Sally comes gliding in, and there I was, up a stump again! She motioned me to be still, and set down by me, and begun to whisper, and said we could all be joyful now, because all the symptoms was first rate, and he'd been sleeping like that for ever so long, and looking better and peacefuller all the time, and ten to one he'd wake up in his right mind.

So we set there watching, and by-and-by he stirs a bit, and opened his eyes very natural, and takes a look, and says:

"Hello, why I'm at *home!* How's that? Where's the raft?"

"It's all right," I says.

"And *Jim?*"

"The same," I says, but couldn't say it pretty brash. But he never noticed, but says:

"Good! Splendid! *Now* we're all right and safe! Did you tell Aunty?"

I was going to say yes; but she chipped in and says:

"About what, Sid?"

"Why, about the way the whole thing was done."

"What whole thing?"

"Why, *the* whole thing. There ain't but one; how we set the runaway nigger free—me and Tom."

"Good land! Set the run— What *is* the child talking about! Dear, dear, out of his head again!"

"No, I ain't out of my HEAD; I know all what I'm talking about. We *did* set him free—me and Tom. We laid out to do it, and we *done* it. And we done it elegant, too." He'd got a start, and she never checked him up, just set and stared and stared, and let him clip along, and I see it warn't no use for *me* to put in. "Why, Aunty, it cost us a power of work—weeks of it—hours and hours, every night, whilst you was all asleep. And we had to steal candles, and the sheet, and the shirt, and your dress, and spoons, and tin plates, and case-knives, and the warming-pan, and the grindstone, and flour, and just no end of things, and you can't think what work it was to make the saws, and pens, and inscriptions, and one thing or another, and you can't think *half* the fun it was. And we had to make up the pictures of coffins and things, and nonnamous letters from the robbers, and get up and down the lightning-rod, and dig the hole into the cabin, and make the rope-ladder and send it in cooked up in a pie, and send in spoons and things to work with, in your apron pocket"—

"Mercy sakes!"

—"and load up the cabin with rats and snakes and so on, for company for Jim; and then you kept Tom here so long with the butter in his hat that you come near spiling the whole business, because the men come before we was out of the cabin, and we had to rush, and they heard us and let drive at us, and I got my share, and we dodged out of the path and let them go by, and when the dogs come they warn't interested in us, but went for the most noise, and we got our canoe, and made for the raft, and was all safe, and Jim was a free man, and we done it all by ourselves, and *wasn't* it bully, Aunty!"

"Well, I never heard the likes of it in all my born days! So it was *you*, you little rapscallions, that's been making all this trouble, and turn everybody's wits clean inside out and scared us all most to death. I've as good a notion as ever I had in my life, to take it out o' you this very minute. To think, here I've been, night after night, a—*you* just get well once, you young scamp, and I lay

I'll tan the Old Harry out o' both o' ye!"

But Tom, he *was* so proud and joyful, he just *couldn't* hold in, and his tongue just *went* it—she a-chipping in, and spitting fire all along, and both of them going it at once, like a cat-convention; and she says:

"*Well*, you get all the enjoyment you can out of it *now*, for mind I tell you if I catch you meddling with him again—"

"Meddling with *who?*" Tom says, dropping his smile and looking surprised.

"With *who?* Why, the runaway nigger, of course. Who'd you reckon?"

Tom looks at me very grave, and says:

"Tom, didn't you just tell me he was all right? Hasn't he got away?"

"*Him?*" says Aunt Sally; "the runaway nigger? 'Deed he hasn't. They've got him back, safe and sound, and he's in that cabin again, on bread and water, and loaded down with chains, till he's claimed or sold!"

Tom rose square up in bed, with his eye hot, and his nostrils opening and shutting like gills, and sings out to me:

"They hain't no *right* to shut him up! *Shove!*—and don't you lose a minute. Turn him loose! he ain't no slave; he's as free as any cretur that walks this earth!"

"What *does* the child mean?"

"I mean every word I *say*, Aunt Sally, and if somebody don't go, *I'll* go. I've knowed him all his life, and so has Tom, there. Old Miss Watson died two months ago, and she was ashamed she ever was going to sell him down the river, and *said* so; and she set him free in her will."

"Then what on earth did *you* want to set him free for, seeing he was already free?"

"Well, that *is* a question, I must say; and *just* like women! Why, I wanted the *adventure* of it; and I'd a waded neck-deep in blood to—goodness alive, Aunt Polly!"

If she warn't standing right there, just inside the door, looking as sweet and contented as an angel half-full of pie, I wish I may never!

Aunt Sally jumped for her, and most hugged the head off of her, and cried over her, and I found a good enough place for me under the bed, for it was getting pretty sultry for *us*, seemed to me. And I peeped out, and in a little while Tom's Aunt Polly shook herself loose and stood there looking across at Tom over her spectacles—kind of grinding him into the earth, you know. And then she says:

"Yes, you *better* turn y'r head away—I would if I was you, Tom."

"Oh, deary me!" says Aunt Sally; "*is* he changed so? Why, that ain't *Tom* it's Sid; Tom's—Tom's—why, where *is* Tom? He was here a minute ago."

"You mean where's Huck *Finn*—that's what you mean! I reckon I hain't raised such a scamp as my Tom all these years, not to know him when I *see* him. That *would* be a pretty howdy-do. Come out from under that bed, Huck Finn."

So I done it. But not feeling brash.

Aunt Sally she was one of the mixed-upest looking persons I ever see; except one, and that was Uncle Silas, when he come in, and they told it all to him. It kind of made him drunk, as you may say, and he didn't know nothing at all the rest of the day, and preached a prayer-meeting sermon that night that give him a rattling ruputation, because the oldest man in the world couldn't a understood it. So Tom's Aunt Polly, she told all about who I was, and what; and I had to up and tell how I was in such a tight place that when Mrs. Phelps took me for Tom Sawyer—she chipped in and says, "Oh, go on and call me Aunt Sally, I'm used to it, now, and 'tain't no need to change"—that when Aunt Sally took me for Tom Sawyer, I had to stand it—there warn't no other way, and I knowed he wouldn't mind, because it would be nuts for him, being a mystery, and he'd make an adventure out of it and be perfectly satisfied. And so it turned out, and he let on to be Sid, and made things as soft as he could for me.

And his Aunt Polly she said Tom was right about old Miss Watson setting Jim free in her will; and so, sure enough, Tom Sawyer had gone and took all that trouble and bother to set a free nigger free! and I couldn't ever understand, before, until that minute and that talk, how he *could* help a body set a nigger free, with his bringing-up.

Well, Aunt Polly she said that when Aunt Sally wrote to her that Tom and *Sid* had come, all right and safe, she says to herself:

"Look at that, now! I might have expected it, letting him go off that way without anybody to watch him. So now I got to go and trapse all the way down the river, eleven hundred mile, and find out what that creetur's up to, *this* time; as long as I couldn't seem to get any answer out of you about it."

"Why, I never heard nothing from you," says Aunt Sally.

"Well, I wonder! Why, I wrote to you twice, to ask you what you could mean by Sid being here."

"Well, I never got 'em, Sis."

Aunt Polly, she turns around slow and severe, and says:

"You, Tom!"

"Well—*what?*" he says, kind of pettish.

"Don't you what *me*, you impudent thing—hand out them 'etters."

"What letters?"

"*Them* letters. I be bound, if I have to take aholt of you I'll—"

"They're in the trunk. There, now. And they're just the same as they was when I got them out of the office. I hain't looked into them, I hain't touched them. But I knowed they'd make trouble, and I thought if you warn't in no hurry, I'd—"

"Well, you *do* need skinning, there ain't no mistake about it. And I wrote another one to tell you I was coming; and I spose he—"

"No, it come yesterday; I hain't read it yet, but *it's* all right, I've got that one."

I wanted to offer to bet two dollars she hadn't, but I reckoned maybe it was just as safe to not to. So I never said nothing.

Chapter the Last

The first time I catched Tom, private, I asked him what was his idea, time of the evasion?—what it was he'd planned to do if the evasion worked all right and he managed to set a nigger free that was already free before? And he said, what he had planned in his head, from the start, if we got Jim out all safe, was for us to run him down the river, on the raft, and have adventures plumb to the mouth of the river, and then tell him about his being free, and take him back up home on a steamboat, in style, and pay him for his lost time, and write word ahead and get out all the niggers around, and have them waltz him into town with a torchlight procession and a brass band, and then he would be a hero, and so would we. But I reckened it was about as well the way it was.

We had Jim out of the chains in no time, and when Aunt Polly and Uncle Silas and Aunt Sally found out how good he helped the doctor nurse Tom, they made a heap of fuss over him, and fixed him up prime, and give him all he wanted to eat, and a good time, and nothing to do. And we had him up to the sickroom; and had a high talk; and Tom give Jim forty dollars for being prisoner for us so patient, and doing it up so good, and Jim was pleased most to death, and busted out, and says:

"*Dah*, now, Huck, what I tell you?—what I tell you up dah on Jackson islan'? I *tole* you I got a hairy breas', en what's de sign un it; en I *tole* you I ben rich wunst, en gwineter to be rich *agin*; en it's come true; en heah she *is*! *Dah*, now! doan' talk to *me*— signs is *signs*, mine I tell you; en I knowed jis' 's well 'at I 'uz gwineter be rich agin as I's a stannin' heah dis minute!"

And then Tom he talked along, and talked along, and says, le's all three slide out of here, one of these nights, and get an outfit, and go for howling adventures amongst the Injuns, over in the

Territory, for a couple of weeks or two; and I says, all right, that suits me, but I aint got no money for to buy the outfit, and I reckon I couldn't get none from home, because it's likely pap's been back before now, and got it all away from Judge Thatcher and drunk it up.

"No he hain't," Tom says; "it's all there, yet—six thousand dollars and more; and your pap hain't ever been back since. Hadn't when I come away, anyhow."

Jim says, kind of solemn:

"He ain't a comin' back no mo', Huck."

I says:

"Why, Jim?"

"Nemmine why, Huck—but he ain't comin' back no mo'."

But I kept at him; so at last he says:

"Doan' you 'member de house dat was float'n down de river, en dey wuz a man in dah, kivered up, en I went in en unkivered him and didn' let you come in? Well, den, you k'n git yo' money when you wants it; kase dat wuz him."

Tom's most well, now, and got his bullet around his neck on a watch-guard for a watch, and is always seeing what time it is, and so there ain't nothing more to write about, and I am rotten glad of it, because if I'd a knowed what a trouble it was to make a book I wouldn't a tackled it and ain't agoing to no more. But I reckon I got to light out for the Territory ahead of the rest, because Aunt Sally she's going to adopt me and sivilize me and I can't stand it. I been there before.

THE END. YOURS TRULY, HUCK FINN.

A Note on the Text

Adventures of Huckleberry Finn was first published in England in December 1884. The present edition follows the first American edition, February 1885. The list which follows gives the typographical and other errors in the 1885 edition that have been silently corrected in the current text. The words and phrases in boldface (with page and line numbers) are as given in this Norton Critical Edition; they are followed by the words and phrases as they appeared in the 1885 edition.

18.05	**by-and-by**	by and-by
19.40	**I**	I I
31.40	**saw**	was
33.14	**let**	le
66.26	**ago**	age
87.02	**Douglas**	Douglass
118.15	**you're**	you re
129.13	**gets**	get's
134.10	**orgies sh'd**	orgiess h'd
136.22	**invest it for**	invest for
149.14	**couple**	couples
151.05	**than**	that
155.02	**piousest**	pisonest
162.02	**now-and-then**	now and-then
168.45	**it**	is
174.43	**didn't**	did'nt
186.11	**running**	runinng
206.36	**jews-harp's**	jew-sharp's
211.06–7	**Aunt Sally's gown**	the nigger woman's gown
220.13	**dasn't**	das'nt
229.23	**ain't**	aint't

The Raftsmen's Passage: Should It Remain?

SAMUEL LANGHORNE CLEMENS

From *Life on the Mississippi*

[*The Raftsmen's Passage*]†

By way of illustrating keelboat talk and manners, and that now departed and hardly remembered raft life, I will throw in, in this place, a chapter from a book which I have been working at, by fits and starts, during the past five or six years, and may possibly finish in the course of five or six more. The book is a story which details some passages in the life of an ignorant village boy, Huck Finn, son of the town drunkard of my time out West, there. He has run away from his persecuting father, and from a persecuting good widow who wishes to make a nice, truth-telling, respectable boy of him; and with him a slave of the widow's has also escaped. They have found a fragment of a lumber-raft (it is high water and dead summer-time), and are floating down the river by night, and hiding in the willows by day—bound for Cairo,[1] whence the negro will seek freedom in the heart of the free states. But, in a fog, they pass Cairo without knowing it. By and by they begin to suspect the truth, and Huck Finn is persuaded to end the dismal suspense by swimming down to a huge raft which they have seen in the distance ahead of them, creeping aboard under cover of the darkness, and gathering the needed information by eavesdropping:

But you know a young person can't wait very well when he is impatient to find a thing out. We talked it over, and by and by Jim said it was such a black night, now, that it wouldn't be no risk to swim down to the big raft and crawl aboard and listen—they would talk about Cairo, because they would be calculating to go ashore there for a spree, maybe; or anyway they would send boats ashore to buy whisky or fresh meat or something. Jim had a wonderful level head, for a nigger: he could most always start a good plan when you wanted one.

I stood up and shook my rags off and jumped into the river, and struck out for the raft's light. By and by, when I got down nearly to her, I eased up and went slow and cautious. But everything was all right—nobody at

† The so-called "Raftsmen's Passage" was part of the 1876 draft of *Huckleberry Finn*, where it appeared in present Chapter XVI, following the second paragraph. In 1883 Clemens inserted it in *Life on the Mississippi*, Chapter III; but in 1884 the passage was omitted from *Huckleberry Finn* at the suggestion of Clemens's publisher. Because Clemens's final intention seems to have been to omit the passage and because the book to most readers over the last ninety years has meant the novel as published in 1884–85 *without* the passage, it is reprinted here in an appendix rather than in the text proper. Recently, however, the argument that the Raftsmen's Passage should be restored is gaining ground; see the essay by Peter G. Beidler.

1. At the southern tip of Illinois, where the Mississippi is joined by the Ohio River.

the sweeps. So I swum down along the raft till I was most abreast the camp-fire in the middle, then I crawled aboard and inched along and got in among some bundles of shingles on the weather side of the fire. There was thirteen men there—they was the watch on deck of course. And a mighty rough-looking lot, too. They had a jug, and tin cups, and they kept the jug moving. One man was singing—roaring, you may say; and it wasn't a nice song—for a parlor, anyway. He roared through his nose, and strung out the last word of every line very long. When he was done they all fetched a kind of Injun war-whoop, and then another was sung. It begun:

> "There was a woman in our towdn,
>   In our towdn did dwed'l [dwell],
> She loved her husband dear-i-lee,
>   But another man twyste as wed'l.

> "Singing too, riloo, riloo, riloo,
>   Ri-too, riloo, rilay - - - e,
> She loved her husband dear-i-lee,
>   But another man twyste as wed'l."

And so on—fourteen verses. It was kind of poor, and when he was going to start on the next verse one of them said it was the tune the old cow died on; and another one said: "Oh, give us a rest!" And another one told him to take a walk. They made fun of him till he got mad and jumped up and begun to cuss the crowd, and said he could lam any thief in the lot.

They was all about to make a break for him, but the biggest man there jumped up and says:

"Set whar you are, gentlemen. Leave him to me; he's my meat."

Then he jumped up in the air three times, and cracked his heels together every time. He flung off a buckskin coat that was all hung with fringes, and says, "You lay thar tell the chawin-up's done"; and flung his hat down, which was all over ribbons, and says, "You lay thar tell his sufferin's is over."

Then he jumped up in the air and cracked his heels together again, and shouted out:

"Whoo-oop! I'm the old original iron-jawed, brass-mounted, copper-bellied corpse-maker from the wilds of Arkansaw! Look at me! I'm the man they call Sudden Death and General Desolation! Sired by a hurricane, dam'd by an earthquake, half-brother to the cholera, nearly related to the smallpox on the mother's side! Look at me! I take nineteen alligators and a bar'l of whisky for breakfast when I'm in robust health, and a bushel of rattlesnakes and a dead body when I'm ailing. I split the everlasting rocks with my glance, and I squench the thunder when I speak! Whoo-oop! Stand back and give me room according to my strength! Blood's my natural drink, and the wails of the dying is music to my ear. Cast your eye on me, gentlemen! and lay low and hold your breath, for I'm 'bout to turn myself loose![2]

All the time he was getting this off, he was shaking his head and looking fierce, and kind of swelling around in a little circle, tucking up his wrist-bands, and now and then straightening up and beating his breast with his fist, saying, "Look at me, gentlemen!" When he got through, he jumped up and cracked his heels together three times, and let off a roaring "Whoo-

---

2. This tall talk is the boast of the ring-tailed roarer, a figure in his prime in the   Old Southwest humor of 1830–65.

oop! I'm the bloodiest son of a wildcat that lives!"

Then the man that had started the row tilted his old slouch·hat down over his right eye; then he bent stooping forward, with his back sagged and his south end sticking out far, and his fists a-shoving out and drawing in in front of him, and so went around in a little circle about three times, swelling himself up and breathing hard. Then he straightened, and jumped up and cracked his heels together three times before he lit again (that made them cheer), and he began to shout like this:

"Whoo-oop! bow your neck and spread, for the kingdom of sorrow's a-coming! Hold me down to the earth, for I feel my powers a-working! whoo-oop! I'm a child of sin, *don't* let me get a start! Smoked glass, here, for all! Don't attempt to look at me with the naked eye, gentlemen! When I'm playful I use the meridians of longitude and parallels of latitude for a seine, and drag the Atlantic Ocean for whales! I scratch my head with the lightning and purr myself to sleep with the thunder! When I'm cold, I bile the Gulf of Mexico and bathe in it; when I'm hot I fan myself with an equinoctial storm; when I'm thirsty I reach up and suck a cloud dry like a sponge; when I range the earth hungry, famine follows in my tracks! Whoo-oop! Bow your neck and spread! I put my hand on the sun's face and make it night in the earth; I bite a piece out of the moon and hurry the seasons; I shake myself and crumble the mountains! Contemplate me through leather—*don't* use the naked eye! I'm the man with a petrified heart and biler-iron bowels! The massacre of isolated communities is the pastime of my idle moments, the destruction of nationalities the serious business of my life! The boundless vastness of the great American desert is my inclosed property, and I bury my dead on my own premises!" He jumped up and cracked his heels together three times before he lit (they cheered him again), and as he come down he shouted out: "Whoo-oop! bow your neck and spread, for the Pet Child of Calamity's a-coming!"

Then the other one went to swelling around and blowing again—the first one—the one they called Bob; next, the Child of Calamity chipped in again, bigger than ever; then they both got at it at the same time, swelling round and round each other and punching their fists most into each other's faces, and whooping and jawing like Injuns; then Bob called the Child names, and the Child called him names back again; next, Bob called him a heap rougher names, and the Child come back at him with the very worst kind of language; next, Bob knocked the Child's hat off, and the Child picked it up and kicked Bob's ribbony hat about six foot; Bob went and got it and said never mind, this warn't going to be the last of this thing, because he was a man that never forgot and never forgive, and so the Child better look out, for there was a time a-coming, just as sure as he was a living man, that he would have to answer to him with the best blood in his body. The Child said no man was willinger than he for that time to come, and he would give Bob fair warning, *now*, never to cross his path again, for he could never rest till he had waded in his blood, for such was his nature, though he was sparing him now on account of his family, if he had one.

Both of them was edging away in different directions, growling and shaking their heads and going on about what they was going to do; but a little black-whiskered chap skipped up and says:

"Come back here, you couple of chicken-livered cowards, and I'll thrash the two of ye!"

And he done it, too. He snatched them, he jerked them this way and that, he booted them around, he knocked them sprawling faster than they could get up. Why, it warn't two minutes till they begged like dogs—and how the other lot did yell and laugh and clap their hands all the way through, and shout, "Sail in, Corpse-Maker!" "Hi! at him again, Child of Calamity!" "Bully for you, little Davy!" Well, it was a perfect pow-wow for a while. Bob and the Child had red noses and black eyes when they got through. Little Davy made them own up that they was sneaks and cowards and not fit to eat with a dog or drink with a nigger; then Bob and the Child shook hands with each other, very solemn, and said they had always respected each other and was willing to let bygones be bygones. So then they washed their faces in the river; and just then there was a loud order to stand by for a crossing, and some of them went forward to man the sweeps there, and the rest went aft to handle the after sweeps.

I laid still and waited for fifteen minutes, and had a smoke out of a pipe that one of them left in reach; then the crossing was finished, and they stumped back and had a drink around and went to talking and singing again. Next they got out an old fiddle, and one played, and another patted juba, and the rest turned themselves loose on a regular old-fashioned keelboat breakdown.[3] They couldn't keep that up very long without getting winded, so by and by they settled around the jug again.

They sung "Jolly, Jolly Raftsman's the Life for Me," with a rousing chorus, and then they got to talking about differences betwixt hogs, and their different kind of habits; and next about women and their different ways; and next about the best ways to put out houses that was afire; and next about what ought to be done with the Injuns; and next about what a king had to do, and how much he got; and next about how to make cats fight; and next about what to do when a man has fits; and next about differences betwixt clear-water rivers and muddy-water ones. The man they called Ed said the muddy Mississippi water was wholesomer to drink than the clear water of the Ohio; he said if you let a pint of this yaller Mississippi water settle, you would have about a half to three-quarters of an inch of mud in the bottom, according to the stage of the river, and then it warn't no better than Ohio water—what you wanted to do was to keep it stirred up—and when the river was low, keep mud on hand to put in and thicken the water up the way it ought to be.

The Child of Calamity said that was so; he said there was nutritiousness in the mud, and a man that drunk Mississippi water could grow corn in his stomach if he wanted to. He says:

"You look at the graveyards; that tells the tale. Trees won't grow worth shucks in a Cincinnati graveyard, but in a Sent Louis graveyard they grow upwards of eight hundred foot high. It's all on account of the water the people drunk before they laid up. A Cincinnati corpse don't richen a soil any."

And they talked about how Ohio water didn't like to mix with Mississippi water. Ed said if you take the Mississippi on a rise when the Ohio is low, you'll find a wide band of clear water all the way down the east side of the Mississippi for a hundred mile or more, and the minute you get out a quarter of a mile from shore and pass the line, it is all thick and yaller the rest of the way across. Then they talked about how to keep tobacco from getting moldy, and from that they went into ghosts and told about a lot that other folks had seen; but Ed says:

"Why don't you tell something that you've seen yourselves? Now let me have a say. Five years ago I was on a raft as big as this, and right along here it was a bright moonshiny night, and I was on watch and boss of the stabboard oar forrard, and one of my pards was a man named Dick Allbright,

3. Juba: a lively tap dance accompanied   dance in very rapid rhythm.
by clapping; breakdown: a shuffling

and he come along to where I was sitting, forrard—gaping and stretching, he was—and stooped down on the edge of the raft and washed his face in the river, and come and set down by me and got out his pipe, and had just got it filled, when he looks up and says:

" 'Why looky-here,' he says, 'ain't that Buck Miller's place, over yander in the bend?'

" 'Yes,' says I, 'it is—why?' He laid his pipe down and leaned his head on his hand, and says:

" 'I thought we'd be furder down.' I says:

" 'I thought it, too, when I went off watch'—we was standing six hours on and six off—'but the boys told me,' I says, 'that the raft didn't seem to hardly move, for the last hour,' says I, 'though she's a-slipping along all right now,' says I. He give a kind of a groan, and says:

" 'I've seed a raft act so before, along here,' he says. ' 'pears to me the current has most quit above the head of this bend durin' the last two years,' he says.

"Well, he raised up two or three times, and looked away off and around on the water. That started me at it, too. A body is always doing what he sees somebody else doing, though there mayn't be no sense in it. Pretty soon I see a black something floating on the water away off to stabboard and quartering behind us. I see he was looking at it, too. I says:

" 'What's that?' He says, sort of pettish:

" ' 'Tain't nothing but an old empty bar'l.'

" 'An empty bar'l!' says I, 'why,' says I, 'a spy-glass is a fool to *your* eyes. How can you tell it's an empty bar'l?' He says:

" 'I don't know; I reckon it ain't a bar'l, but I thought it might be,' says he.

" 'Yes,' I says, 'so it might be, and it might be anything else too; a body can't tell nothing about it, such a distance as that,' I says.

"We hadn't nothing else to do, so we kept on watching it. By and by I says:

" 'Why, looky-here, Dick Allbright, that thing's a-gaining on us, I believe.'

"He never said nothing. The thing gained and gained, and I judged it must be a dog that was about tired out. Well, we swung down into the crossing, and the thing floated across the bright streak of the moonshine, and by George, it *was* a bar'l. Says I:

" 'Dick Allbright, what made you think that thing was a bar'l, when it was half a mile off?' says I. Says he:

" 'I don't know.' Says I:

" 'You tell me, Dick Allbright.' Says he:

" 'Well, I knowed it was a bar'l; I've seen it before; lots has seen it; they says it's a ha'nted bar'l.'

"I called the rest of the watch, and they come and stood there, and I told them what Dick said. It floated right along abreast, now, and didn't gain any more. It was about twenty foot off. Some was for having it aboard, but the rest didn't want to. Dick Allbright said rafts that had fooled with it had got bad luck by it. The captain of the watch said he didn't believe in it. He said he reckoned the bar'l gained on us because it was in a little better current than what we was in. He said it would leave by and by.

"So then we went to talking about other things, and we had a song, and then a breakdown; and after that the captain of the watch called for another song; but it was clouding up now, and the bar'l stuck right thar in the same place, and the song didn't seem to have much warm-up to it, somehow, and so they didn't finish it, and there warn't any cheers, but it sort of dropped flat, and nobody said anything for a minute. Then every-body tried to talk at once, and one chap got off a joke, but it warn't no use, they didn't laugh, and even the chap that made the joke didn't laugh at it, which ain't usual. We all just settled down glum, and watched the bar'l, and was oneasy and oncomfortable. Well, sir, it shut down black and still, and then the wind began to moan around, and next the lightning began to play and the thunder to grumble. And pretty soon there was a regular storm, and in the middle of it a man that was running aft stumbled and fell and sprained his ankle so that he had to lay up. This made the boys shake their heads. And every time the lightning come, there was that bar'l, with the blue lights winking around it. We was always on the lookout for it. But by and by, toward dawn, she was gone. When the day come we couldn't see her anywhere, and we warn't sorry, either.

"But next night about half-past nine, when there was songs and high jinks going on, here she comes again, and took her old roost on the stab-board side. There warn't no more high jinks. Everybody got solemn; no-body talked; you couldn't get anybody to do anything but set around moody and look at the bar'l. It begun to cloud up again. When the watch changed, the off watch stayed up, 'stead of turning in. The storm ripped and roared around all night, and in the middle of it another man tripped and sprained his ankle, and had to knock off. The bar'l left toward day, and nobody see it go.

"Everybody was sober and down in the mouth all day. I don't mean the kind of sober that comes of leaving liquor alone—not that. They was quiet, but they all drunk more than usual—not together, but each man sidled off and took it private, by himself.

"After dark the off watch didn't turn in; nobody sung, nobody talked; the boys didn't scatter around, neither; they sort of huddled together, forrard; and for two hours they set there, perfectly still, looking steady in the one direction, and heaving a sigh once in a while. And then, here comes the bar'l again. She took up her old place. She stayed there all night; no-body turned in. The storm come on again, after midnight. It got awful dark; the rain poured down; hail, too; the thunder boomed and roared and bellowed; the wind blowed a hurricane; and the lightning spread over every-thing in big sheets of glare, and showed the whole raft as plain as day; and the river lashed up white as milk as far as you could see for miles, and there was that bar'l jiggering along, same as ever. The captain ordered the watch to man the after sweeps for a crossing, and nobody would go—no more sprained ankles for them, they said. They wouldn't even *walk* aft. Well, then, just then the sky split wide open, with a crash, and the light-ning killed two men of the after watch, and crippled two more. Crippled them how, say you? Why, *sprained their ankles!*

"The bar'l left in the dark betwixt lightnings, toward dawn. Well, not a body eat a bite at breakfast that morning. After that the men loafed around, in twos and threes, and talked low together. But none of them herded with Dick Allbright. They all give him the cold shake. If he come around where any of the men was, they split up and sidled away. They wouldn't man the sweeps with him. The captain had all the skiffs hauled up on the raft, alongside of his wigwam, and wouldn't let the dead men be took ashore to be planted; he didn't believe a man that got ashore would come back; and he was right.

"After night come, you could see pretty plain that there was going to be trouble if that bar'l come again; there was such a muttering going on. A good many wanted to kill Dick Allbright, because he'd seen the bar'l on other trips, and that had an ugly look. Some wanted to put him ashore.

Some said: 'Let's all go ashore in a pile, if the bar'l comes again.'

"This kind of whispers was still going on, the men being bunched to-gether forrard watching for the bar'l, when lo and behold you! here she comes again. Down she comes, slow and steady, and settles into her old tracks. You could 'a' heard a pin drop. Then up comes the captain, and says:

"'Boys, don't be a pack of children and fools; I don't want this bar'l to be dogging us all the way to Orleans, and *you* don't: Well, then, how's the best way to stop it? Burn it up—that's the way. I'm going to fetch it aboard,' he says. And before anybody could say a word, in he went.

"He swum to it, and as he come pushing it to the raft, the men spread to one side. But the old man got it aboard and busted in the head, and there was a baby in it! Yes, sir; a stark-naked baby. It was Dick Allbright's baby; he owned up and said so.

"'Yes,' he says, a-leaning over it, 'yes, it is my own lamented darling, my poor lost Charles William Allbright deceased,' says he—for he could curl his tongue around the bulliest words in the language when he was a mind to, and lay them before you without a jint started anywheres.[4] Yes, he said, he used to live up at the head of this bend, and one night he choked his child, which was crying, not intending to kill it—which was prob'ly a lie—and then he was scared, and buried it in a bar'l, before his wife got home, and off he went, and struck the northern trail and went to rafting; and this was the third year that the bar'l had chased him. He said the bad luck always begun light, and lasted till four men was killed, and then the bar'l didn't come any more after that. He said if the men would stand it one more night—and was a-going on like that—but the men had got enough. They started to get out a boat to take him ashore and lynch him, but he grabbed the little child all of a sudden and jumped overboard with it, hugged up to his breast and shedding tears, and we never see him again in this life, poor old suffering soul, nor Charles William neither."

"*Who* was shedding tears?" says Bob; "was it Allbright or the baby?"

"Why, Allbright, of course; didn't I tell you the baby was dead? Been dead three years—how could it cry?"

"Well, never mind how it could cry—how could it *keep* all that time?" says Davy. "You answer me that."

"I don't know how it done it," says Ed. "It done it, though—that's all I know about it."

"Say—what did they do with the bar'l?" says the Child of Calamity.

"Why, they hove it overboard, and it sunk like a chunk of lead."

"Edward, did the child look like it was choked?" says one.

"Did it have its hair parted?" says another.

"What was the brand on that bar'l, Eddy?" says a fellow they called Bill.

"Have you got the papers for them statistics, Edmund?" says Jimmy.

"Say, Edwin, was you one of the men that was killed by the lightning?" says Davy.

"Him? Oh, no! he was both of 'em," says Bob. Then they all haw-hawed.

"Say, Edward, don't you reckon you'd better take a pill? You look bad—don't you feel pale?" says the Child of Calamity.

"Oh, come, now, Eddy," says Jimmy, "show up; you must 'a' kept part of that bar'l to prove the thing by. Show us the bung-hole—do—and we'll all believe you."

"Say, boys," says Bill, "less divide it up. Thar's thirteen of us. I can

4. Without spreading a joint, bursting a seam.

swaller a thirteenth of the yarn, if you can worry down the rest."

Ed got up mad and said they could all go to some place which he ripped out pretty savage, and then walked off aft, cussing to himself, and they yelling and jeering at him, and roaring and laughing so you could hear them a mile.

"Boys, we'll split a watermelon on that," says the Child of Calamity; and he came rummaging around in the dark amongst the shingle bundles where I was, and put his hand on me. I was warm and soft and naked; so he says "Ouch!" and jumped back.

"Fetch a lantern or a chunk of fire here, boys—there's a snake here as big as a cow!"

So they run there with a lantern, and crowded up and looked in on me.

"Come out of that, you beggar!" says one.

"Who are you?" says another.

"What are you after here? Speak up prompt, or overboard you go."

"Snake him out, boys. Snatch him out by the heels."

I began to beg, and crept out amongst them trembling. They looked me over, wondering, and the Child of Calamity says:

"A cussed thief! Lend a hand and less heave him overboard!"

"No," says Big Bob, "less get out the paint-pot and paint him a sky-blue all over from head to heel, and *then* heave him over."

"Good! that's it. Go for the paint, Jimmy."

When the paint come, and Bob took the brush and was just going to begin, the others laughing and rubbing their hands, I begun to cry, and that sort of worked on Davy, and he says:

" 'Vast there. He's nothing but a cub. I'll paint the man that teches him!"

So I looked around on them, and some of them grumbled and growled, and Bob put down the paint, and the others didn't take it up.

"Come here to the fire, and less see what you're up to here," says Davy. "Now set down there and give an account of yourself. How long have you been aboard here?"

"Not over a quarter of a minute, sir," says I.

"How did you get dry so quick?"

"I don't know, sir. I'm always that way, mostly."

"Oh, you are, are you? What's your name?"

I warn't going to tell my name. I didn't know what to say, so I just says:

"Charles William Allbright, sir."

Then they roared—the whole crowd; and I was mighty glad I said that, because, maybe, laughing would get them in a better humor.

When they got done laughing, Davy says:

"It won't hardly do, Charles William. You couldn't have growed this much in five year, and you was a baby when you come out of the bar'l, you know, and dead at that. Come, now, tell a straight story, and nobody'll hurt you, if you ain't up to anything wrong. What *is* your name?"

"Aleck Hopkins, sir. Aleck James Hopkins."

"Well, Aleck, where did you come from, here?"

"From a trading-scow. She lays up the bend yonder. I was born on her. Pap has traded up and down here all his life; and he told me to swim off here, because when you went by he said he would like to get some of you to speak to a Mr. Jonas Turner, in Cairo, and tell him—"

"Oh, come!"

"Yes, sir, it's as true as the world. Pap he says—"

"Oh, your grandmother!"

They all laughed, and I tried again to talk, but they broke in on me and stopped me.

"Now, looky-here," says Davy; "you're scared, and so you talk wild. Honest, now, do you live in a scow, or is it a lie?"

"Yes, sir, in a trading-scow. She lays up at the head of the bend. But I warn't born in her. It's our first trip."

"Now you're talking! What did you come aboard here for? To steal?"

"No sir, I didn't. It was only to get a ride on the raft. All boys does that."

"Well, I know that. But what did you hide for?"

"Sometimes they drive the boys off."

"So they do. They might steal. Looky-here; if we let you off this time, will you keep out of these kind of scrapes hereafter?"

" 'Deed I will, boss. You try me."

"All right, then. You ain't but little ways from shore. Overboard with you, and don't you make a fool of yourself another time this way. Blast it, boy, some raftsmen would rawhide you till you were black and blue!"

I didn't wait to kiss good-by, but went overboard and broke for shore. When Jim come along by and by, the big raft was away out of sight around the point. I swum out and got aboard, and was mighty glad to see home again.

PETER G. BEIDLER

The Raft Episode in *Huckleberry Finn*†

Included in the original manuscript of *Huckleberry Finn* was the "raft episode," a fifteen-page passage recording Huck's visit to a large raft to discover how far he and Jim were from Cairo. Twain had previously lifted the passage from the unfinished novel and printed it in *Life on the Mississippi,* for it was interesting in itself as an account of river life and the bragging and tall tales that river men are fond of. Before he sent the manuscript of his completed novel to Charles Webster, his nephew and publisher, he restored the passage to its original position after the second paragraph of Chapter XVI. Webster, however, persuaded Twain to leave the passage out of the final published version of the novel, and most subsequent editors have printed *Huckleberry Finn* as he did. The purpose of the present paper is to question Twain's decision to allow the deletion of the raft episode and then to consider briefly the editorial problem that has resulted.

Since Twain was determined not to let Webster publish *Huckleberry Finn* until at least 40,000 copies had been ordered, he impressed upon his nephew the need for forceful canvassing and a well-selected "canvassing book." Apparently afraid that prospective

† From *Modern Fiction Studies*, XIV, 1 (Spring, 1968), 11–20. Reprinted by permission of the Purdue Research Foundation.

242 · *Peter G. Beidler*

buyers would recognize the passage from *Life on the Mississippi*,
Twain, in a letter written on April 14, 1884, specifically cautioned
Webster to "Be particular & don't get any of that *old* matter into
your canvassing book—(the *raft* episode.)" A week later, on April
21, Webster wrote to Twain suggesting that the episode be left out
of the novel altogether: "The book is so *much* larger than Tom
Sawyer would it not be better to omit that old Mississippi matter? I
think it would improve it." Since the letter was postmarked in New
York at 6 P.M., we may assume that Twain did not receive it in
Hartford until the next day. He answered promptly that same day,
April 22: "Yes, I think that raft chapter can be left wholly out, by
heaving in a paragraph to say Huck visited the raft to find out how
far it might be to Cairo, but got no satisfaction. Even *this* is not
necessary unless that raft-visit is referred to later in the book. I
think it is, but am not certain."[1]

These letters make clear two important facts. First, it was Webster who suggested dropping the raft episode from the published
novel, apparently only because he wanted the new novel to be short
enough to look like a companion to *Tom Sawyer*. Second, Twain's
decision to approve Webster's suggestion was made rapidly and
apparently without his having checked a manuscript of the novel;
he was not even sure whether a possible later reference to the visit
to the raft would necessitate a new paragraph. Twain's failure to
remember very clearly the details of his narrative is not surprising
when we recall that much of the novel had been written eight years
earlier in 1876.[2] Under these circumstances we need not consider
the author's rapid editorial decision as necessarily artistically justified. We have the time and the materials, which Twain apparently
did not have, to examine the function of the passage in its original
context, and we are not being pressed, as Twain was, by a publisher
who is more interested in counting words than in reading them.

That Twain so readily permitted the deletion of the raft episode
testifies apparently to his awareness of the basically episodic nature
of *Huckleberry Finn*: eliminate a passage here and there and no real
harm is done. This attitude toward the episodes, however, is incon-
sistent with the second of his "nineteen rules governing literary
art": "the episodes of a tale shall be necessary parts of the tale and

1. Excerpts from the two letters by
Twain are quoted from *Mark Twain,
Business Man*, ed. Samuel Charles Webster (Boston, 1946), pp. 249–50. For his
assistance in locating the letter by Webster, I am indebted to Frederick Anderson, Editor of the Mark Twain Papers
in the General Library of the University
of California in Berkeley. I have decided
to refer to what is usually called the
"raftsmen's passage" as the "raft episode" because that is what Twain himself called it, not only in the first letter

quoted above, but also in a letter written
to Howells on July 20, 1883. Twain mentioned that he was at work on "a kind
of companion to Tom Sawyer. There's a
raft episode from it in second or third
chapter of Life on the Mississippi" (see
Mark Twain-Howells Letters, ed. Henry
Nash Smith et al. [Cambridge, Mass.,
1960], I, 435).
2. For a full discussion of the writing of
the novel, see Walter Blair, *Mark Twain
and Huck Finn* (Berkeley and Los Angeles, 1960).

shall help to develop it."[3] I believe that the raft episode *is* a necessary part of the novel and *does* help to develop it, and I believe that it should not have been removed.

In the first place, the deletion of the raft episode leaves a curious narrative gap in the novel, for Twain never did "heave in" a paragraph about Huck's unsuccessful visit to the large raft to find out about Cairo. In the second paragraph of Chapter XVI Huck and Jim discuss how they might recognize Cairo when they do come to it. Huck fears they may drift right on past it if they go by at night, and so he determines to paddle ashore the first time they see a light and ask how far ahead Cairo is. In the published version this paragraph is immediately followed by a paragraph beginning, "There warn't nothing to do now but to look out sharp for the town and not pass it without seeing it." Such a statement is puzzling indeed when it follows immediately Huck's resolution *not* to count on recognizing the town when they come to it but to make an attempt to discover before they get there how far ahead it is. In the original manuscript, of course, the lengthy raft episode came between the second and third paragraphs, and, because Huck's attempt to discover the location of Cairo by swimming to the raft had not only failed but had nearly gotten him into serious trouble, it fully explained his statement that now there was nothing to do but wait and hope they would recognize the town when they came to it. Huck was not anxious to make a second dangerous inquiry that night.

The raft episode serves other functions than that of a bridge between two otherwise awkwardly juxtaposed paragraphs. It gives us, for example, just as it gives Huck himself, technical information about the place where the two rivers come together. In the second paragraph of the chapter, as I have said, Huck and Jim discuss how they will know when they reach Cairo: "Jim said if the two big rivers joined together there, that would show. But I said maybe we might think we was passing the foot of an island and coming into the same old river again. That disturbed Jim—and me too." Huck is apparently unaware that the two rivers will be distinguishable or that any difference between them will show up after they have joined at Cario. After all, he has never been down the river before; how could he know? A few pages later in the originally published volume, however, Huck somehow *does* know enough about the condition of the two rivers to recognize that he has passed Cairo. He and Jim have tied up for the day on a towhead near the left (east) shore of the river. When daylight comes, Huck sees that "here was the clear Ohio water inshore, sure enough, and outside was the old regular Muddy! So it was all up with Cairo." That Huck can now

3. From "Fenimore Cooper's Literary Offenses" in *The Portable Mark Twain*, ed. Bernard DeVoto (New York, 1946), pp. 541–42.

recognize the difference between the two rivers and interpret the difference correctly shows that since the second paragraph he must have learned about the merging of the rivers below Cairo. In the published version, however, we are not told how he learned this.

The mystery is, of course, cleared up if we reinsert the raft episode. While hidden on the raft, Huck overhears Ed say that "the muddy Mississippi water was wholesomer to drink than the clear water of the Ohio," so he would now know that the rivers were not of identical consistency. And Huck would also have learned that the difference between the two rivers would be apparent for some distance below Cairo, for the raftsmen talk about "how Ohio water didn't like to mix with Mississippi water. Ed said if you take the Mississippi on a rise [and the Mississippi now *is* on a rise] when the Ohio is low, you'll find a wide band of clear water all the way down the east side of the Mississippi for a hundred mile or more, and the minute you get out a quarter of a mile from shore and pass the line, it is all thick and yaller the rest of the way across." Twain clearly used the raft episode as a device to give Huck and the equally naive reader the technical background to interpret properly the condition of the river below Cairo. Twain apparently forgot that, in permitting the excision of the episode, he was leaving unexplained Huck's sudden ability to understand the phenomenon and was leaving unanswered for many readers the question of why the inshore water on the left bank was clearer than the water further out, and what that difference had to do with the location of Cairo.

The raft episode also provides the careful reader with a different kind of information about the location of Cairo, information which this time Huck himself does not get. Twain subtly tells us that Huck and Jim have already drifted past the destination they seek. I suspect that the very fact that the raftmen are discussing the mixing of the two rivers in the first place is a hint that they have passed the point where the two rivers come together. The real clue comes, however, when Huck is being questioned by the raftsmen about why he has come to their raft. Huck quickly makes up a lie about how his pap, who had "traded up and down here all his life," had told him to swim to the raft to ask one of them "to speak to a Mr. Jonas Turner, in Cairo, and tell him—" Here, after he mentions Cairo, Huck is interrupted by the raftsmen and accused of lying. I suggest that they are already past Cairo and so could not deliver a message to anyone there. They therefore know Huck is lying when he mentions Cairo because no one who knows as much about the region as Huck says his pap knows could possibly *not* know that they were below Cairo. Huck himself never understands how they know he is lying, but we readers can see that this is the only possible inconsistency in his lie.

Dramatic irony, then, is made possible by the raft episode. When Jim thinks every light he sees is Cairo, we know he will be disappointed; when Huck asks the fisherman if that town up ahead is Cairo, we know why the man thinks Huck "must be a blame' fool"; and when Huck wrestles with his "conscience" because he thinks he has helped bring Jim to the town where Jim will be free, we know that they are already well south into slave territory and are beyond the place where Jim could have found his freedom. In letting us know ahead of time what Jim and Huck have yet to find out, Twain makes sure that our chief interest is not in the location of Cairo but in the states of mind of Jim and, especially, Huck as they anticipate an event which we know will not happen. If we read the novel without the raft episode, this dramatic irony is lost. We learn the location of Cairo no sooner than Huck and Jim do, and our interest is more likely to be in the suspense of the action than in the psychology of the characters.

It is, of course, Huck's psychological nature that is our chief interest in the novel, and no attempt to justify the raft episode can be finally convincing unless it can show that the episode is important for its development of, or its contribution to our understanding of, Huck's character. Huck plays only a small part in the action of the raft episode. During most of it he is hidden and listening to the others talking. What he hears, however, makes a deep impression on him, and his reaction to what he hears is significant. The account of Ed's story of Dick Allbright and the haunted barrel, like the immediately preceding account of the "fight" between the two raftsmen, is valuable for its addition to Twain's fictional version of life on the Mississippi; it is also important for its effect on Huck. Before we can refer in detail to Ed's story and its effect on Huck, however, it is necessary to examine Huck's generally morbid outlook on life, his repeated identification with dead and suffering human beings.

Huck's many lies on his downward journey are, I feel, central to an understanding of his character. I cannot agree with Wyatt Blessingame that Twain used the lie, "simply a variation of the old vaudeville gag," merely as an excuse to "release his full flamboyant genius" by setting up "a situation which he wished to described [sic] in detail." In other words, Blessingame feels that Huck's lies are not an organic part of the novel, are usually not necessary, and represent merely Twain's indulging his desire to write scenes which "he could get his teeth into."[4] If we examine Huck's lies carefully, however, we find a pattern emerging from them which reveals something of Huck's psychological nature: in many of them Huck casts

4. Wyatt Blessingame, "The Use of the Lie in *Huckleberry Finn* as a Technical Device," *Mark Twain Quarterly,* IX (Winter, 1953), 11–12.

himself in the role of a boy who is alone in the world and whose family is dead, sick, or in grave danger.

Let us look at some of those lies Huck tells Mrs. Loftus that "my mother's down sick and out of money and everything." A moment later he tells her that "my father and mother was dead and the law had bound me out to a mean old farmer . . . and he treated me so bad I couldn't stand it no longer." He tells the ferryboat captain about the "awful peck of trouble" his family is in up on the wrecked *Walter Scott*. He lets the two men in the skiff believe that his father and mother and sister all have the smallpox and that "I've told everybody before, and they just went away and left us." He tells the Grangerfords that his sister "run off and got married and never was heard of no more, and Bill went to hunt them and he warn't heard of no more, and Tom and Mort died, and then there warn't nobody but just me and pap left, and he was just trimmed down to nothing, on account of his troubles; so when he died I took what there was left, because the farm didn't belong to us, and started up the river, deck passage, and fell overboard." He tells the King and the Duke that his folks "all died off but me and pa and my brother Ike." When their raft collided with the steamboat, "pa was drunk, and Ike was only four years old, so they never come up no more."

It might be argued that these lies show us nothing about Huck except that he was extremely adept at making up convincing stories to explain his being where he was without any family. Huck's lies certainly do show his ability to explain his way out of difficult situations, but it seems to me that Huck's lies are identifiably *Huck's*, and that Tom Sawyer, for example, under similar conditions, would have dreamed up equally effective but very different lies. The particular lies Huck tells are prescribed not only by circumstances but also by Huck's own character and background. If Huck were not, in effect, an orphan, and if he had known no loneliness and brutality, I doubt that he would have come up with such mournful imaginary accounts of his past.

As evidence for my contention I refer to an instance where Huck's lying is quite unnecessary and even cumbersome when only the demands of the situation are considered. When the King accuses Huck of trying to give him and the Duke the slip at Peter Wilks's grave, Huck might simply have told the truth: the man who held him let go his arm in the excitement of the discovery of the gold. This explanation would surely have sufficed, for that is exactly the way the King and the Duke themselves escaped. Instead, Huck fabricates a lie that the man who held him prisoner took a liking to him because Huck reminded him of his own "boy about as big as me that died last year." Since the lie cannot be explained by the circumstances under which Huck told it, it can be explained only by Huck's character. In saying that the man identified him with his dead son, Huck is identifying *himself* with the imaginary dead son, since it is Huck who quite unnecessarily makes up the lie. Huck's lies, then, make real to others, and perhaps temporarily to himself, the fantasy world of his imagination. It can hardly be accidental that in his stories Huck takes on the role of the suffering child, separated through sickness, accident, or death from his family.

It is important to note before we go on that when Huck is cast in a different role, he convinces no one with his lies. In trying to be the English "valley," for example, Huck almost immediately has "the hare-lip" suspecting that he has been telling her "a lot of lies." When Huck gives his account of himself in the tavern, the lawyer Levi Bell does not even let him finish: "I reckon you ain't used to lying, it don't seem to come handy; what you want is practice. You do it pretty awkward." Huck is usually anything but an awkward liar, and he has certainly had plenty of practice. Perhaps one of the reasons why his lies are usually not questioned is that if his ficitious role is psychologically congenial to him, he *lives* the role as he plays it, and so he is being true, if not to actual fact, then to his own nature.

Huck's lie about his escape from the graveyard, revealing his identification with a dead boy, leads us directly into another important matter: Huck's almost obsessive concern with death. It is necessary that we be aware of this concern if we are to understand why the raft episode belongs in *Huckleberry Finn*. Throughout the novel we find evidence of the darkness of Huck's imagination and his intuitive awareness of death. In the first chapter, for example, when Huck hears an owl in the woods, he imagines that it is "who-whooing about somebody that was dead." When he hears a dog and a "whippowill," he imagines that they are "crying about somebody that was going to die." He hears another sound in the woods, the "kind of a sound that a ghost makes when it wants to tell about something that's on its mind and can't make itself understood, and so can't rest easy in its grave." The house in which he sits is "as still as death." Often Huck's intense concern with death is more obviously related to himself. After his experience with the *Walter Scott*, for example, he tells us that he and Jim "slept like dead people." When he loses his way in the fog he finds that he has no more idea which way he is going "than a dead man," and feels that he is "laying dead still on the water."

One aspect of Huck's obsessive concern with death is his desire for it. I suspect that Huck's elaborate efforts to have his pap and the townspeople think he has been murdered are more an expression of his own desire for death than of any real fear that they might attempt to follow him. He must know that if he just runs away the townspeople will not care enough to stage much of a search, even if they have any idea where to look, and he knows his pap well enough to know that he will not wander far from the six thousand dollars. If this is so, then the "murder" is at least in part an outward manifestation of Huck's desire for death.

The plausibility of such an interpretation is supported by Huck's many explicit statements of his desire for death and his envy of those who are dead. In the first chapter of the novel, for example, Huck's reaction to Miss Watson's description of "the bad place" is "I wished I was there." Later, as Huck sits in his room, he tells us that "I felt so lonesome I most wished I was dead." When he describes the plight of those who are stranded on the wrecked *Walter Scott*, he adds as part of his lie the information—quite unnecessary to his story, it must be remembered—that Bill Whipple had been killed when the scow had "saddle-baggsed" on the wreck. What we are chiefly interested in here is Huck's comment about the imaginary Bill Whipple's death: "I most wisht it had been me, I do." When Huck's conscience begins to bother him about his part in helping Jim to escape, Huck "got to feeling so mean and so miserable I most wished I was dead. . . . I reckoned I would die of miserableness." Later he thinks that Emmeline Grangerford had had such a death-centered disposition that she was better off dead than alive: "I reckoned . . . she was having a better time in the graveyard." And I wonder if it is just a coincidence that the poem he chooses to quote as an example of her "very good poetry" is the "Ode to Stephen Dowling Bots, Dec'd," a poem about a boy "that fell down a well and was drownded." At any rate, when he makes his escape from the Grangerfords after the fighting, Huck seems pleased that "they'll think I've been killed, and floated down the river." During Peter Wilks's funeral Huck reflects that the dead man "was the only one that had a good thing, according to my notion." When he approaches the Phelps place to find out about Jim, Huck finds that the droning of insects and the gentle breezes make "a body wish *he* was dead . . . and done with it all." As he gets closer to the house he hears the mournful hum of a spinning wheel, "and then I knowed for certain I wished I was dead—for that *is* the lonesomest sound in the whole world." In view of such explicit and repeated expressions there can be little question that Huck, whether fully aware of it or not, is attracted to death as a release from the cruelty and suffering that is life—at least "sivilized" life.

With this much background, then, on the nature of Huck's lying and his yearning for death, we can get to the matter at hand: how these motifs figure in the raft episode. In the part of the passage with which we are concerned, Ed tells the story of his experience with Dick Allbright and the haunted barrel. It seems that Dick All-bright had had a son named Charles William Allbright. One night the child had cried, and in a rage the father had choked him to death and buried him in a barrel and run away to take up rafting. For three years the floating barrel had haunted Dick Allbright along a certain stretch of the river as he went by on a raft, bringing bad luck in the form of sprained ankles and death to other men on the raft with him. On one trip the captain of the raft, wondering what was in the barrel and why it seemed to bring bad luck, brought the barrel aboard, opened it, and found the baby. Dick Allbright con-fessed that the baby was his and told how he had choked it, "not intending to kill it." Then, before the crew could lynch him, Dick Allbright grabbed the baby, jumped into the river with it, and was never seen again.

It is not important whether the story is true or false, or whether the other raftsmen believe Ed. What is important is that Huck, from his dark hiding place on the raft, hears the story and is appar-ently much affected by it. A moment after the story is completed, Huck is discovered, brought out into the light, and questioned. When asked what his name is Huck "didn't know what to say, so I just says: 'Charles William Allbright' "—the name of the dead baby.[5]

Can there be any doubt, in view of what we have seen about the psychological revelations of Huck's other lies and about his desire for death, that in blurting out the name of the mistreated child whose sufferings have been ended by death, Huck is unconsciously identifying with the child? Both boys have been mistreated by their fathers. Both are alone and naked in the dark when they are discov-ered and brought into the light by raftsmen. And it can be no coin-cidence when Huck later lies to them and tells them that he lives in a scow "up at the head of the bend"; Charles William had lived "up at the head of this bend" when he was killed. The raftsmen are amused at Huck's lies, and so, perhaps, are we, but surely there is a psychologically significant meaning in them. They tell us, I am sure, much more than Huck thinks they do.

The raft episode, then, very much belongs in its original context

5. Kenneth S. Lynn thinks Huck replies "jokingly," but I find no evidence that the frightened Huck intended "the re-lease of laughter triggered by this su-perbly timed response." Lynn is the only critic I have read who has seriously at-tempted to explain the function of the raft episode. He finds it "an episode of extraordinary richness, of great beauty and humor, which takes us to the heart of the novel." Lynn connects the episode with the "parenthood problem" (Charles William Allbright and Huck both search for fathers on the river), with the theme of death and rebirth ("having died, both boys have come alive again in the flow-ing waters of the great Mississippi"), and with "the novel's grand theme . . . , the Mosaic drama of liberation." My quotations are from pages 212–13 of Lynn's *Mark Twain and Southwestern Humor* (Boston, 1959); see also his ear-lier article "Huck and Jim" in *Yale Re-view,* XLVII (Spring 1958), 421–31.

in Chapter XVI. It supplies narrative connections which are otherwise rather conspicuously missing. It affects our reading of the rest of the chapter by giving information about Cairo which Huck and Jim do not yet have. And most important, it helps us to understand Huck by bringing into sharp focus his identification with suffering children and his desire for refuge in death. To read the novel without all this is to miss a great deal.

The problem is finally an editorial one. Ought we to respect Twain's "final intention" and print the novel as he finally permitted it to be printed—without the raft episode? Hamlin Hill thinks so: "To add the raftsmen passage to the body of Mark Twain's text is a literary tampering as serious as removing the *Walter Scott* passage would be; the former belongs out (good or bad) because Mark Twain left it out and the latter belongs in (good or bad) because Twain put it in."[6] There is some merit in this argument, but I wonder if the question is quite so simple as Hill makes it sound. Twain did not, we must remember, leave the episode out of the manuscript he sent to his publisher. It was Webster who suggested the deletion, and then only because he wanted to make the book smaller in size. Twain's decision to permit the deletion was made rapidly and apparently without his having consulted the manscript. I have tried to show that that was an ill-advised and unfortunate decision, and I wonder if we are right, under the circumstances, to hold Twain to it. In printing the novel without the raft episode, an editor is insisting that the reader read what Charles Webster published, not what Mark Twain wrote.

6. See Hill's "Introduction" to the Facsimile of the First Edition of the novel   (San Francisco, 1962), p. xii.

Backgrounds and Sources

JOHNSON JONES HOOPER

From *Some Adventures of Captain Simon Suggs*†

Chapter the Tenth. *The Captain Attends a Camp-Meeting*

* * * Captain Suggs drew on his famous old green-blanket over-coat, and ordered his horse, and within five minutes was on his way to a camp-meeting, then in full blast on Sandy creek, twenty miles distant, where he hoped to find amusement, at least. When he arrived there, he found the hollow square of the encampment filled with people, listening to the mid-day sermon and its dozen accompanying "exhortations." * * * Men and women rolled about on the ground, or lay sobbing or shouting in promiscuous heaps. More than all, the negroes sang and screamed and prayed. Several, under the influence of what is technically called "the jerks," were plunging and pitching about with convulsive energy. * * *

"Keep the thing warm!" roared a sensual seeming man, of stout mould and florid countenance, who was exhorting among a bevy of young women, upon whom he was lavishing caresses. "Keep the thing warm, breethring!—come to the Lord, honey!" he added, as he vigorously hugged one of the damsels he sought to save.

"Oh, I've got him!" said another in exulting tones, as he led up a gawky youth among the mourners— "I've got him—he tried to git off, but—ha! Lord!"—shaking his head as much as to say, it took a smart fellow to escape him—"ha! Lord!"—and he wiped the perspiration from his face with one hand, and with the other, patted his neophyte on the shoulder—"he couldn't do it! No!" * * *

In another part of the square a dozen old women were singing. They were in a state of absolute extasy, as their shrill pipes gave forth,

> "I rode on the sky,
> Quite ondestified[1] I,
> And the moon it was under my feet!"

* * *

Amid all this confusion and excitement Suggs stood un-moved. * * *

† From *Some Adventures of Captain Simon Suggs,* by Johnson Jones Hooper, published in Philadelphia in 1845. Hooper's book imposed the picaresque tradition of Cervantes upon frontier life in the old American Southwest, a region which produced a roguish literature of oral anecdote. Clemens knew the book in his youth, and he knew the Mississippi Valley customs and folklore that it portrayed. When the king "works" a camp meeting in Chapter XX of *Huckleberry Finn,* his tactics might have been learned from Simon Suggs.

1. Frontier humor typically coined outlandish words; perhaps a combination of "unsanctified" and "predestined."

"Well, now," said he, as he observed the full-faced brother who was "officiating," among the women, "that ere feller takes *my* eye! —thar he's been this half-hour, a-figurin amongst them galls, and's never said the fust word to nobody else. Wonder what's the reason these here preachers never hugs up the old, ugly women? Never seed one do it in my life—the sperrit never moves 'em that way! It's nater[2] tho'; and the women, *they* never flocks round one o' the old dried-up breethring—bet two to one old splinter-legs thar,"— nodding at one of the ministers—"won't git a chance to say turkey to a good-lookin gall to-day! Well! who blames 'em? Nater will be nater, all the world over; and I judge ef I was a preacher, I should save the purtiest souls fust, myself!"

While the Captain was in the middle of this conversation with himself, he caught the attention of the preacher in the pulpit, who inferring from an indescribable something about his appearance that he was a person of some consequence, immediately determined to add him at once to the church if it could be done; and to that end began a vigorous, direct personal attack.

"Breethring," he exclaimed, "I see yonder a man that's a sinner; I *know* he's a sinner! Thar he stands," pointing at Simon, "a mis-subble old crittur, with his head a-blossomin for the grave! A few more short years, and d-o-w-n he'll go to perdition, lessen the Lord have mer-cy on him! Come up here, you old hoary-headed sinner, a-n-d git down upon your knees, a-n-d put up your cry for the Lord to snatch you from the bottomless pit! You're ripe for the devil— you're b-o-u-n-d for hell, and the Lord only knows what'll become on you!"

"D——n it," thought Suggs, "*ef* I only had you down in the krick swamp for a minit or so, *I'd* show you who's *old*! *I'd* alter your tune *mighty* sudden, you sassy, 'saitful[3] 'old rascal!" But he judiciously held his tongue and gave no utterance to the thought.

The attention of many having been directed to the Captain by the preacher's remarks, he was soon surrounded by numerous well-meaning, and doubtless very pious persons, each one of whom seemed bent on the application of his own particular recipe for the salvation of souls. For a long time the Captain stood silent, or answered the incessant stream of exhortation only with a sneer; but at length, his countenance began to give token of inward emotion. First his eye-lids twitched—then his upper lip quivered—next a transparent drop formed on one of his eyelashes and a similar one on the tip of his nose—and, at last, a sudden bursting of air from nose and mouth, told that Captain Suggs was overpowered by his emotions. At the moment of the explosion, he made a feint as if to rush from the crowd, but he was in experienced hands, who well

2. Nature.   3. Deceitful.

knew that the battle was more than half won.

"Hold to him!" said one—"it's a-working in him as strong as a Dick horse!"

"Pour it into him," said another, "it'll all come right directly!"

"That's the way I love to see 'em do," observed a third; "when you begin to draw water from their eyes, taint gwine to be long afore you'll have 'em on their knees!"

And so they clung to the Captain manfully, and half dragged, half led him to the mourner's bench; by which he threw himself down, altogether unmanned, and bathed in tears. Great was the rejoicing of the brethren, as they sang, shouted, and prayed around him—for by this time it had come to be generally known that the "convicted" old man was Captain Simon Suggs, the very "chief of sinners" in all that region.

The Captain remained grovelling in the dust during the usual time, and gave vent to even more than the requisite number of sobs, and groans, and heart-piercing cries. At length, when the proper time had arrived, he bounced up, and with a face radiant with joy commenced a series of vaultings and tumblings, which "laid in the shade" all previous performances of the sort at that camp-meeting. The brethren were in extasies at this demonstrative evidence of completion of the work; and whenever Suggs shouted "Gloree!" at the top of his lungs, every one of them shouted it back, until the woods rang with echoes. * * *

"Friends," he said, "it don't take long to curry a short horse, accordin' to the old sayin', and I'll give you the perticklers of the way I was brought to a knowledge"—here the Captain wiped his eyes, brushed the tip of his nose and snuffled a little—"in less'n no time."

"Praise the Lord!" ejaculated a bystander.

"You see I come here full o' romancin' and devilment, and jist to make game of all the purceedins. Well, sure enough, I done so for some time, and was a-thinkin how I should play some trick * * * to turn it all into redecule, when they began to come round me and talk. Long at fust I didn't mind it, but arter a little that brother"—pointing to the reverend gentleman who * * * Simon was convinced was the "big dog of the tanyard"—"that brother spoke a word that struck me kleen to the heart, and run all over me, like fire in dry grass——"

"I-I-I can bring 'em!" cried the preacher alluded to, in a tone of exultation—"Lord thou knows ef thy servant can't stir 'em up, nobody else needn't try—but the glory aint mine! I'm a poor worrum of the dust," he added, with ill-managed affectation.[4]

"And so from that I felt somethin' a-pullin' me inside——"

4. The object of a camp-meeting revival was to convert the sinner by bringing him to feel the presence of divine grace.

"Grace! grace! nothin' but grace!" exclaimed one; meaning that "grace" had been operating in the Captain's gastric region.

"And then," continued Suggs, "I wanted to git off, but they hilt me, and bimeby I felt so missuble, I had to go yonder"—pointing to the mourners' seat—"and when I lay down thar it got wuss and wuss, and 'peared like somethin' was a-mashin' down on my back—"

"That was his load o' sin," said one of the brethren—"never mind, it'll tumble off presently, see ef it don't!" and he shook his head professionally and knowingly.

"And it kept a-gittin heavier and heavier, ontwell[5] it looked like it might be a four year old steer, or a big pine log, or somethin' of that sort—" * * *

"And arter awhile," Suggs went on, " 'peared like I fell into a trance, like, and I seed—"

"Now we'll git the good on it" cried one of the sanctified.

"And I seed the biggest, longest, rip-roarenest, blackest, scaliest—" Captain Suggs paused, wiped his brow, and ejaculated "Ah, L-o-r-d!" so as to give full time for curiosity to become impatience to know what he saw.

"*Sarpent!* warn't it?" asked one of the preachers.

"No, not a sarpent," replied Suggs, blowing his nose.

"Do tell us *what* it war, soul alive!—whar *is* John?" said Mrs. Dobbs.

"Allegator!" said the Captain.

"Alligator!" repeated every woman present, and screamed for very life. * * *

"Well," said the Captain in continuation, "the allegator kept a-comin' and a-comin' to'ards me, with his great long jaws a-gapin' open like a ten-foot pair o' tailors' shears—"

"Oh! oh! oh! Lord! gracious above!" cried the woman.

"SATAN!" was the laconic ejaculation of the oldest preacher present, who thus informed the congregation that it was the devil which had attacked Suggs in the shape of an alligator.

"And then I concluded the jig was up, 'thout I could block his game some way; for I seed his idee was to snap off my head—"

The women screamed again.

"So I fixed myself jist like I was purfectly willin' for him to take my head, and rather he'd do it as not"—here the women shuddered perceptibly—"and so I hilt my head straight out"—the Captain illustrated by elongating his neck—"and when he come up and was a gwine to *shet down* on it, I jist pitched in a big rock which choked him to death, and that minit I felt the weight slide off, and

5. Until.

I had the best feelins—sorter like you'll have from *good* sperrits—
any body ever had!"

"Didn't I *tell* you so? Didn't I *tell* you so?" asked the brother
who had predicted the off-tumbling of the load of sin. "Ha, Lord!
fool *who?* I've been *all* along thar!—yes, *all along thar!* and I know
every inch of the way jist as good as I do the road home!" and then
he turned round and round, and looked at all, to receive a silent
tribute to his superior penetration.

Captain Suggs was now the "lion of the day." Nobody could
pray so well, or exhort so movingly, as "brother Suggs." Nor did
his natural modesty prevent the performance of appropriate exercises. With the reverend Bela Bugg (him to whom, under providence, he ascribed his conversion) he was a most especial favourite.
They walked, sang, and prayed together for hours. * * *

The next morning, when the preacher of the day first entered
the pulpit, he announced that "brother Simon Suggs," mourning
over his past iniquities, and desirous of going to work in the cause
as speedily as possible, would take up a collection to found a church
in his own neighborhood, at which he hoped to make himself use-
ful as soon as he could prepare himself for the ministry, which the
preacher didn't doubt, would be in a very few weeks, as brother
Suggs was "a man of mighty good *judgment,* and of a *great dis-
corse.*" The funds were to be collected by "brother Suggs," and
held in trust by brother Bela Bugg, who was the financial officer of
the circuit, until some arrangement could be made to build a
suitable house.

"Yes, breethring," said the Captain, rising to his feet; "I want
to start a little 'sociation close to me, and I want you all to help.
I'm mighty poor myself, as poor as any of you—don't leave breethring"—observing that several of the well-to-do were about to go
off—"don't leave; ef you aint able to afford any thing, jist give us
your blessin' and it'll be all the same!"

This insinuation did the business, and the sensitive individuals
re-seated themselves.

"It's mighty little of this world's goods I've got," resumed
Suggs, pulling off his hat and holding it before him; "but I'll bury
that in the cause any how," and he deposited his last five-dollar
bill in the hat.

There was a murmur of approbation at the Captain's liberality
throughout the assembly.

Suggs now commenced collecting, and very prudently attacked
first the gentlemen who had shown a disposition to escape. These,
to exculpate themselves from any thing like poverty, contributed
handsomely.

"Look here, breethring," said the Captain, displaying the bank-notes thus received, "brother Snooks has drapt a five wi' me, and brother Snodgrass a ten! In course 'taint expected that you *that aint as well off as them*, will give *as much*; let every one give *accordin'* to ther means."

This was another chain-shot that raked as it went! "Who so low" as not to be able to contribute as much as Snooks and Snodgrass?

"Here's all the *small* money I've got about me," said a burly old fellow, ostentatiously handing to Suggs, over the heads of a half dozen, a ten dollar bill.

"That's what I call maganimus!" exclaimed the Captain; "that's the way *every* rich man ought to do!"

These examples were followed, more or less closely, by almost all present, for Simon had excited the pride of purse of the congregation, and a very handsome sum was collected in a very short time.

The reverend Mr. Bugg, as soon as he observed that our hero had obtained all that was to be had at that time, went to him and inquired what amount had been collected. The Captain replied that it was still uncounted, but that it couldn't be much under a hundred.

"Well, brother Suggs, you'd better count it and turn it over to me now. I'm goin' to leave presently."

"No!" said Suggs—"can't do it!"

"Why?—what's the matter?" inquired Bugg.

"It's got to be *prayed over*, fust!" said Simon, a heavenly smile illuminating his whole face.

"Well," replied Bugg, "less go one side and do it!"

"No!" said Simon, solemnly.

Mr. Bugg gave a look of inquiry,

"You see that krick swamp?" asked Suggs—"I'm gwine down in *thar*, and I'm gwine to lay this money down *so*"—showing how he would place it on the ground—"and I'm gwine to git on these here knees"—slapping the right one—"and I'm n-e-v-e-r gwine to quit the grit ontwell I feel it's got the blessin'! And nobody aint got to be thar but me!"

Mr. Bugg greatly admired the Captain's fervent piety, and bidding him God-speed, turned off.

Captain Suggs "struck for" the swamp sure enough, where his horse was already hitched. "Ef them fellers ain't done to a cracklin,"[6] he muttered to himself as he mounted, "*I'll* never bet on two pair agin! They're peart at the snap game, theyselves; but they're badly lewed[7] this hitch! Well, Live and let live is a good old motter, and it's my sentiments adzactly!" And giving the spur to his horse, off he cantered.

---

6. Done to a crisp.   7. Brought low, outwitted.

DAN DE QUILLE

From *The Big Bonanza*†

Chapter LXXII. The Comical Story of Pike. Tom sings—The joke successful—Pike vanishes—A pretty big story—Doubtful dreams—Self-deceived—Our journey's end

As soon as we were left to ourselves we built a roaring fire, in spite of all Pike's remonstrances. "It's jist as good a thing as the Injuns want," said he. "It's jist showin' 'em whar we are. We'll lose our skelps afore mornin'."

When we began to think of supper, we found that we had played a little joke on ourselves, in our hurry to get the other fellows away in order to make sure of Pike. We had nothing in the shape of provision except a few pounds of rice, which happened to be on Tom's horse. We put some of this into a gold-pan and boiled it, but it was rather poor eating without either butter or salt. As we were sitting about the pan scooping up this rice with knives and wooden paddles, Pike said: "I allers knowed I didn't like rice as well as I thought I did, and now I'm sure of it." But we had plenty of tobacco and what we lacked in "grub" we made up in smoke. As soon as it grew dark Pike became very restless.

"What was that?" he would say. "Did you hear the rocks rattle up on the hillside?" and he would peer out into the darkness.

Tom now began to sing as loud as he could roar:

"My name it is Joe Bowers, I've got a brother Ike,
I come from old Missouri, yes, all the way from Pike."

"Stop singin' so loud, Tom," cried Pike in alarm. "Don't!" But Tom roared the louder:

"I'll tell you why I left thar, and how I came to roam,
And leave my poor old mammy, so far away from home."

"Tom! Tom! Good Lord, don't!" begged Pike.

"I used to love a gal thar, they called her Sally Black,
I axed her for to marry me, she said it was a whack,

---

† From *History of the Big Bonanza, An Authentic Account of the Discovery, History, and Working of the * * * Comstock Lode of Nevada * * ***, by Dan De Quille, Hartford, 1877. Dan De Quille was the pen name of William Wright (1829–98), who, like Mark Twain and Artemus Ward, followed the lure of gold to Nevada and California as prospector, newspaper man, and humorist. Associates in 1862 on the *Territorial Enterprise*, Virginia City, Nevada, all three remained lifelong friends and influenced each other's writing. Huck's attempt in Chapter XV of *Huckleberry Finn* to delude Jim into thinking he has been dreaming during the fog is a version of the western hoax perpetrated upon Pike in the following story.

But says she to me: 'Joe Bowers, before we hitch for life,
You'd orter have a little home, to keep your little wife.' "

"If you've got a little home, Tom," said Pike, "I wish to God you
was now in it!"

"Says I, 'My dearest Sally, O Sally, for your sake,
I'll go to Californy and try to raise a stake.' "

"That thar's a fool song," said Pike, "and nobody but a fool
would sing it!"

"But one day I got a letter from my dear brother Ike,
It came from old Missouri, sent all the way from Pike."

"Whar I wish to the Lord I was now!" groaned Pike.

"It brought the goldarndest news that ever you did hear.
My heart is almost bustin', so pray excuse this tear.
It said my Sal was fickle, that her love for me had fled,
That she'd married with a butcher, whose har was orful red."

"Thar'll be butchers here 'fore long," groaned Pike.

"It told me more than that, oh! it's enough to make one swear
It said Sally had a baby, and the baby had red hair."

"Now, cuss yer pictur!" said Pike. "Yer done, air yer? I'll bet
thar'll be red har enough here before mornin'. Your singin' has
played thunder with us, sure as thar's wool on a nigger, but you'll
not have a bit on the—"

"Top of his head, where the wool had orter be,"[1] roared Tom.

Pike was now at his wits' end and went off a rod or two from the
fire and sat down by a dark clump of bushes, sullen and thoroughly
disgusted. Tom called out to him: "Say, Pike, are you loadin' that
revolver o' your'n?" but Pike had the sulks and would not condescend to answer. It was soon time to turn in for the night, and each
man took his blankets and sought the smoothest place to be found.
Pike and one of our party known as "Hank" spread their blankets
together at some distance from the fire, which was now quite low,
while the rest of us found places for our beds among some willows.

Pike lay awake a long time listening for Indians and would rise to
his knees at the slightest sound, pulling the blankets off Hank, who
was trying to make him lie still, so that he could get to sleep. There
was a high hill on the east side of the canyon, covered on the side
next to us with shelly slate rock, and whenever a fox, coyote, or even
a rat ran over this it caused a great clatter, the scales of slate ringing
like pieces of pottery. This was a place fruitful of alarms and caused

1. In a folk song then familiar, the "old Negro, Uncle Ned, had no wool on the
top of his head."

Pike to be upon his knees about every five minutes, but about midnight he could keep his eyes open no longer. Hank made the signal agreed upon, by holding up his hat, when two of the boys crept cautiously out of the camp with six-shooters in their hands. By following up a little ravine they were able to gain the summit of the slaty hill without making the slightest noise, as there was no loose rock except on the slope. Presently they started down the slope through the loose rock, leaping and making as much noise as though old Winnemucca and half the Piute tribe were coming down the mountain. At the same time they began yelling and firing their revolvers. At the first racket made on the hill Pike was on his feet and came running toward us, who were returning the fire of the supposed Indians, and yelling as we fired, making altogether enough noise for half a dozen small battles. When Pike reached us, two or three of our men fell, crying out that they were killed, and at the same time Hank fell and caught him about the legs, crying: "I'm wounded. Carry me off and hide me in the bushes!"

"Let go of me, Hank, there's five hundred of 'em comin'!"

"I'll never let go of you," said Hank. "Carry me off!"

Pike then lifted Hank, who was groaning at a terrible rate, and carrying him about two rods, pitched him, neck and heels, into a clump of thorny bushes. This done, Pike rushed down the canyon at the speed of an antelope. Tom rolled on the ground and laughed until he almost smothered himself. "I'm even with Pike on the prickly-pear business!" cried he as soon as he was able to speak. "He shall never hear the last of this Injun fight!" For my part, now that the fun was all over, I began to feel quite miserable over the whole affair. I feared that in his great fright Pike might dash his brains out against a tree or break his neck among the rocks. I firmly resolved never to take part in another affair of the kind, calling to mind several sham fights and other deviltry in California that had been attended by fatal results to the victims.

In the morning we were ready for a start at sunrise. The first thing I saw was Pike's hat, lying near the place where he had spread his blankets the night before. The sight gave me quite a shock, as it seemed to be the hat of a dead man. I soon found that the others were beginning to feel much as I did about the matter, for as Pike's blankets were being rolled up to be packed on Tom's horse, one of the boys said: "I hope nothing has happened to Pike." Another said: "Oh, he's all right!" but at the same time it was easy to see that the speaker feared that he was not "all right."

As we passed down the canyon, I could not help thinking that we should presently find Pike lying wounded or already dead in some rocky pit or pile of boulders near the trail, and most of our party looked quite solemn. The man who carried Pike's hat looked as though he were in a funeral procession, carrying a portion of the corpse. At length we were through the canyon, and having reached the level plain without finding Pike's remains, we all felt quite jolly again and immediately set to work and planned another surprise for him when we should find him. Instead of fording the river, as we had done in going out, we went some two miles farther down and crossed at a ferry. We inquired of the colored man in charge if anyone had crossed during the night. He assured us that no one had crossed, as he found the boat tied up on the west bank as he had left it the evening before.

We now knew that Pike must have crossed at the ford and again began to feel uneasy, fearing that, reaching the river in a state of exhaustion, he had plunged in and had been swept under by the current. One of two things was certain: he was either safe across or was drowned, as the Mississippi itself would not have stayed his flight. On turning into the main street of Chinatown we came suddenly upon a group of men with Minié muskets in their hands and in their midst stood Pike, with a handkerchief tied about his head. He had a musket in his hand and was the center of attraction. We could see that he was telling those about him of the dreadful affair of the previous night. All those surrounding him were listening so intently that we approached without being observed. Pike was just saying: "Yes, Hank may be alive. I carried him about two miles on my back, with the red cusses yellin' at my heels, then laid him down and kivered him up with brush. But all the rest—" Here Pike turned and saw our party. His jaw dropped, and his eyes almost started from their sockets.

"Well, what of the rest?" said one of his auditors.

"Why, my God! They are all here!" said Pike. "There they all stand!"

The crowd now turned to us and began to ask: "Who was killed?" "Were there many Indians?" and many other like questions. Not a word of this, however, could we be made to understand. We had seen no Indians; we had never dreamed of any danger from Indians. The whole crowd at once turned to Pike for an explanation. Some of the men hinted that unless he gave a pretty satisfactory explanation of his strange stories he would get into trouble. Pike was thunderstruck and gazed at us with a look of utter helplessness. At last he stammered: "Tom, wasn't you killed?"

"If I was killed I wouldn't be here, would I?"

"I thought I saw you fall," and Pike's face wore the most puzzled look imaginable. His fingers sought the yellowish tuft of hair on his chin and, gazing at one and another of us, he sighed: "I don't understand it at all."

"We none of us understand it," said one of the crowd sneeringly.

"All here—all here!" said Pike, his countenance wearing the look of an insane person.

"Pike," said I, "you must have dreamt all this about Indians."

Pike's face brightened for a moment, but soon resumed its old look of despair. "No, no," said he, "no dream. I saw them all killed."

"But, Pike, look at us; we are all here—all alive and well!"

Pike looked vacantly about him at the boys, and said: "Yes, I know, but I don't understand it at all."

"Well," said I, "all there is about it is that you were dreaming and suddenly rose up shouting: 'Injuns! Injuns!' and before we could stop you, you ran away down the canyon."

"Yes," said Pike, "it must have been a dream. You are all here—it must have been a dream. But it don't seem that way at all."

"Don't seem what way?"

"Why, the way you tell it."

"Well, how does it seem? Let us hear you tell it. Let us have your dream."

"Give us the dream!" "Let's have yer dream!" cried the crowd.

"Well, you see I was a-layin' thar in my blankets— But I'll be doggoned ef I believe I did dream it!" cried Pike. "I can almost hear the guns crack now!"

"Of course you dreamt it. Ain't we all here?"

"Yes, I know. But how did I act—what did I do?"

"Why, I've just told you all you did. You know that after you went to bed you was bouncing up on your knees every five minutes, and at last you bounced up and took to your heels."

"Yes, I know I was a little oneasy like. I kept a-hearin' somethin' rattle up on that hill, so I kinder kept on my guard like."

"Well, let us have the dream," all again cried.

"Well," began Pike, "at first I was a-dreamin' along kinder nice and easy like, when all at once I heard the rocks clatter—I mean I thought I heard 'em clatter. Then bang, bang! pop, pop! went the guns, and oh, sich yells—sich yells! I thought my hair riz straight on end, and I seed more'n five hundred Injuns, all a-hoppin' down the hill like turkeys. All this time I thought that you fellers was a-blazin' away at about two hundred of 'em that was all round you and about five hundred on the hill. Then I thought I grabbed up a pick and went right inter the thick of the cusses and fit and fit till I'd wore out the pick, and then fit a long time with the handle. By this time I thought you fellers was all killed and I thought I'd git up and dust. But jist then I thought that Hank got holt round my legs and said he was wounded, and wouldn't let go of me 'thout I'd carry him off. I thought I tuck him on my back and carried him 'bout four miles, and hid him in some brush. Then I thought I run on and waded across the river—"

"No, no! You didn't dream that! You did actually wade across

264 · *Dan De Quille*

the river."

"Well, then, what part of it did I dream? Can anybody tell me that?" and poor Pike looked more puzzled than ever.

"You must have waded the river, you know, or you would not be here."

"Well, yes; I s'pose I did, but that don't seem a bit plainer, nor hardly half as plain as the shootin' and yellin' part. That was the doggonest plainest dream I ever did hev!"

"Yet, as we are all here, alive and well, it must have been a dream?"

"Oh, yes, it was a dream, sartain and sure, but what gits me was its bein' so astonishin' plain—jist the same as bein' wide awake!"

Pike continued to tell his dream for some years, constantly adding new matter, till at last it was a wonderful yarn. He enlarged greatly on the part he took in the fight, and after wearing out the pick on the skulls of the Indians, wound up by thrusting the handle down the throat of a brave, as his last act before beating a retreat. Tom more than once told him the truth about the whole affair, bringing in half a dozen of the "boys" to corroborate what he said, but not a word of it would Pike believe.

"Do you think," he would say, "that I was fool enough to believe that sich things actually happened? No, it was all a dream from fust to last, and the biggest and plainest dream I ever had!"

* * *

THE "POET LARIAT" and THE "SWEET SINGER OF MICHIGAN"†

BLOODGOOD H. CUTTER: On the Death of His Beloved Wife, March 24, 1881

The tyrant, Death did my home invade,
In his cold embrace my wife he laid;

† Emmeline Grangerford's "Ode to Stephen Dowling Bots, Dec'd." imitates the sentimental and only semiliterate effusions of such versifiers as Bloodgood Haviland Cutter (1817–1906) and Julia A. Moore (1847–1920). Cutter, the "poet lariat" of the *Quaker City* excursion to the Holy Land as reported in *Innocents Abroad* (1869), was inspired by every aspect of the trip, including seasickness, the health authorities at Naples, and his fellow passengers. Of these last, he wrote: "One droll person there was on board / The passengers called him 'Mark Twain;' / He'd talk and write all sort of stuff, / In his queer way, would it explain." Clemens gleefully encouraged Cutter to publish *The Long Island Farmer's Poems, Lines Written on the "Quaker City" Excursion to Palestine, and other Poems* (New York, 1886), the source of the present selection. Julia A. Moore, known as the "Sweet Singer of Michigan," was moved to verse by the deaths of little children, such perils as choking on roast beef, and the Ashtabula bridge disaster. One of her "admirers," Clemens said that she had "the touch that makes an intentionally humorous episode pathetic and an intentionally pathetic one funny." "Little Andrew" is taken from *The Sentimental Song Book* (Cleveland, 1877).

So sudden and fatal was the blow,
She had to yield and from me go.

When the doctor said her end was near,
It did affect me so severe;
It seemed to paralyze my brains,
And the circulation of my veins.

When I went up into her room,
I quickly did perceive her doom;
So fatal, then, did seem her case,
The mark of death was in her face.

Oh! 'twas the sad agony of my life,
To see the death gasping of my wife;
Then calmly yielding up her breath,
There in the cold embrace of death.

So quietly she seemed to rest,
With her cold hands across her breast;
Free from all pain and sorrow too,
Her face still looked lovely to my view.

As if her spirit was at rest
In the pure regions of the blest;
That, I sincerely do believe,
Though for my loss I sadly grieve.

In sadness now I mourn! I mourn,
For her who never will return;
Wife of my youth, my heart's delight,
Forever banished from my sight.

After I bade my last adieu,
The grave soon hid her from my view;
Tears from my eyes like fountains run,
When I did lose this faithful one.

If the Lord who gave took her away,
I must submit and to Him pray;
To enable me this trial to bear,
And trust to His Almighty care.

For forty years He did her spare,
And in my trials she did share;
When sick, to me she was so kind,
To ease my pain, to cheer my mind.

Bind up my wounds, to bathe my head,
Sit up by night by my sick bed;
Try many ways to me relieve—
Till that was done, would sit and grieve.

Now she is taken from the earth,
More keenly I do feel her worth!
On none like her I can depend,
I've lost! I've lost my dearest friend.

Perhaps my loss is now her gain:
She's free from sickness, care and pain;
But the debt of nature all must pay,
At a sooner or a later day.

Her spirit seems whispering in my ear,
"Weep not for me, my husband dear;
O! do your duty there below,
Until the Lord call you also."

    (Little Neck, L. I., April, 1881)

JULIA A. MOORE: Little Andrew

Andrew was a little infant,
And his life was two years old;
He was his parents' eldest boy,
And he was drowned, I was told.
His parents never more can see him
In this world of grief and pain,
And Oh! they will not forget him
While on earth they do remain.

On one bright and pleasant morning
His uncle thought it would be nice
To take his dear little nephew
Down to play upon a raft,
Where he was to work upon it,
And this little child would company be—
The raft the water rushed around it,
Yet he the danger did not see.
This little child knew no danger—
Its little soul was free from sin—
He was looking in the water,
When, alas, this child fell in.
Beneath the raft the water took him,
For the current was so strong,
And before they could rescue him
He was drowned and was gone.

Oh! how sad were his kind parents
When they saw their drowned child,
As they brought him from the water,
It almost made their hearts grow wild.

Oh! how mournful was the parting
From that little infant son.
Friends, I pray you, all take warning,
Be careful of your little ones.

SAMUEL LANGHORNE CLEMENS

From *Life on the Mississippi*†

[*The House Beautiful*]

* * *

Every town and village along that vast stretch of double river-frontage had a best dwelling, finest dwelling, mansion—the home of its wealthiest and most conspicuous citizen. It is easy to describe it: large grassy yard, with paling fence painted white—in fair repair; brick walk from gate to door; big, square, two-story "frame" house, painted white and porticoed like a Grecian temple—with this difference, that the imposing fluted columns and Corinthian capitals were a pathetic sham, being made of white pine, and painted; iron knocker; brass door-knob—discolored, for lack of polishing. Within, an uncarpeted hall, of planed boards; opening out of it, a parlor, fifteen feet by fifteen—in some instances five or ten feet larger; ingrain carpet; mahogany center-table; lamp on it, with green-paper shade—standing on a gridiron, so to speak, made of high-colored yarns, by the young ladies of the house, and called a lamp-mat; several books, piled and disposed, with cast-iron exactness, according to an inherited and unchangeable plan; among them, Tupper, much penciled; also, *Friendship's Offering*, and *Affection's Wreath*, with their sappy inanities illustrated in die-away mezzotints; also, Ossian; *Alonzo and Melissa*; maybe *Ivanhoe*; also "Album," full of original "poetry" of the Thou-hast-wounded-the-spirit-that-loved-thee breed; two or three goody-goody works—*Shepherd of Salisbury Plain*, etc.; current number of the chaste and innocuous *Godey's Lady's Book*, with painted fashion-plate of wax-figure women with

† From Samuel Langhorne Clemens, *Life on the Mississippi* (Osgood: Boston, 1883).

The first of the two excerpts (in which Clemens sketches the typical residence of the chief citizen of innumerable river towns along the Mississippi) is one model for the description of the Grangerford plantation in Chapter XVII of *Huckleberry Finn*. The disparity between Clemens's sense of shabby pretension and Huck's awe and wonder over fundamentally the same house is a measure of Huck's innocence and the distance he stands from the "realistic" point of view of his creator.

The second excerpt from *Life on the Mississippi* is an old-timer's account in Chapter XXVI of a lingering family feud that was later to supply Clemens with the essentials of the lethal quarrel between Grangerfords and Shepherdsons.

mouths all alike—lips and eyelids the same size—each five-foot woman with a two-inch wedge sticking from under her dress and letting on to be half of her foot. Polished air-tight stove (new and deadly invention), with pipe passing through a board which closes up the discarded good old fireplace. On each end of the wooden mantel, over the fireplace, a large basket of peaches and other fruits, natural size, all done in plaster, rudely, or in wax, and painted to resemble the originals—which they don't. Over middle of mantel, engraving— "Washington Crossing the Delaware"; on the wall by the door, copy of it done in thunder-and-lightning crewels by one of the young ladies—work of art which would have made Washington hesitate about crossing, if he could have foreseen what advantage was going to be taken of it. Piano—kettle in disguise— with music, bound and unbound, piled on it, and on a stand near by: "Battle of Prague"; "Bird Waltz"; "Arkansas Traveler"; "Rosin the Bow"; "Marseillaise Hymn"; "On a Lone Barren Isle" (St. Helena); "The Last Link Is Broken"; "She Wore a Wreath of Roses the Night When Last We Met"; "Go, Forget Me, Why Should Sorrow o'er That Brow a Shadow Fling"; "Hours That Were to Memory Dearer"; "Long, Long Ago"; "Days of Absence"; "A Life on the Ocean Wave, a Home on the Rolling Deep"; "Bird at Sea"; and spread open on the rack where the plaintive singer has left it, "Ro-holl on, silver *moo*-hoon, guide the *trav*-el-err on his *way*," etc. Tilted pensively against the piano, a guitar— guitar capable of playing the Spanish fandango by itself, if you give it a start. Frantic work of art on the wall—pious motto, done on the premises, sometimes in colored yarns, sometimes in faded grasses: progenitor of the "God Bless Our Home" of modern commerce. Framed in black moldings on the wall, other works of art, conceived and committed on the premises, by the young ladies; being grim black-and-white crayons; landscapes, mostly: lake, solitary sailboat, petrified clouds, pregeological trees on shore, anthracite precipice; name of criminal conspicuous in the corner. Lithograph, "Napoleon Crossing the Alps." Lithograph, "The Grave at St. Helena." Steel plates, Trumbull's "Battle of Bunker Hill," and the "Sally from Gibraltar." Copper plates, "Moses Smiting the Rock," and "Return of the Prodigal Son." In big gilt frame, slander of the family in oil: papa holding a book ("Constitution of the United States"); guitar leaning against mamma, blue ribbons fluttering from its neck; the young ladies, as children, in slippers and scalloped pantalettes, one embracing toy horse, the other beguiling kitten with ball of yarn, and both simpering up at mamma, who simpers back. These persons all fresh, raw, and red—apparently skinned. Opposite, in gilt frame, grandpa and grandma, at thirty and twenty-two, stiff, old-fashioned, high-collared, puff-sleeved, glaring pallidly out from a background of solid Egyptian night. Under a glass French clock dome, large bouquet of stiff flowers done in corpsy-white wax. Pyramidal what-not in the corner, the shelves occupied chiefly with bric-à-brac of the period, disposed with an eye to best effect: shell, with the Lord's Prayer carved on it; another shell—of the long-oval sort, narrow, straight orifice, three inches long, running from end to end—portrait of Washington carved on it; not well done; the shell had Washington's mouth, originally—artist should have built to that. These two are memorials of the long-ago bridal trip to New Orleans and the French Market. Other bric-à-brac: Californian "specimens"—quartz, with gold wart adhering; old Guinea-gold locket, with circlet of ancestral hair in it; Indian arrow-heads, of flint; pair of bead moccasins, from uncle who crossed the Plains; three "alum" baskets of various colors— being skeleton-frame of wire, clothed on with cubes of crystallized alum in the rock-candy style—works of art which were achieved by the young ladies; their doubles and duplicates to be found upon all what-nots in the land; convention of desiccated bugs and butter-flies pinned to a card; painted toy dog, seated upon bellows attach-ment—drops its under-jaw and squeaks when pressed upon; sugar-candy rabbit—limbs and features merged together, not strongly defined; pewter presidential-campaign medal; miniature cardboard wood-sawyer, to be attached to the stovepipe and operated by the heat; small Napoleon, done in wax; spread-open daguerreotypes of dim children, parents, cousins, aunts, and friends, in all attitudes but customary ones; no templed portico at back, and manufactured landscape stretching away in the distance—that came in later, with the photograph; all these vague figures lavishly chained and ringed— metal indicated and secured from doubt by stripes and splashes of vivid gold bronze; all of them too much combed, too much fixed up; and all of them uncomfortable in inflexible Sunday clothes of a pattern which the spectator cannot realize could ever have been in fashion; husband and wife generally grouped together—husband sitting, wife standing, with hand on his shoulder—and both preserv-ing, all these fading years, some traceable effect of the daguerreo-typist's brisk "Now smile, if you please!" Bracketed over what-not— place of special sacredness—an outrage in water-color, done by the young niece that came on a visit long ago, and died. Pity, too; for she might have repented of this in time. Horsehair chairs, horse-hair sofa which keeps sliding from under you. Window-shades, of oil stuff, with milkmaids and ruined castles stenciled on them in fierce colors. Lambrequins dependent from gaudy boxings of beaten tin, gilded. Bedrooms with rag carpets; bedsteads of the "corded" sort, with a sag in the middle, the cords needing tightening; snuffy feather-bed—not aired often enough; cane-seat chairs, splint-bottomed rocker; looking-glass on wall, school-slate size, veneered frame; inherited bureau; wash-bowl and pitcher, possibly—but not certainly; brass candlestick, tallow candle, snuffers. Nothing else in the room. Not a bathroom in the house; and no visitor likely to come along who has ever seen one.

That was the residence of the principal citizen, all the way from the suburbs of New Orleans to the edge of St. Louis. * * *

[The Darnell-Watson Feud]

"There's been more than one feud around here, in old times, but I reckon the worst one was between the Darnells and the Watsons. Nobody don't know now what the first quarrel was about, it's so long ago; the Darnells and the Watsons don't know, if there's any of them living, which I don't think there is. Some says it was about a horse or a cow—anyway, it was a little matter; the money in it wasn't of no consequence—none in the world—both families was rich. The thing could have been fixed up, easy enough; but no, that wouldn't do. Rough words had been passed; and so, nothing but blood could fix it up after that. That horse or cow, whichever it was, cost sixty years of killing and crippling! Every year or so somebody was shot, on one side or the other; and as fast as one generation was laid out, their sons took up the feud and kept it a-going. And it's just as I say; they went on shooting each other, year in and year out—making a kind of a religion of it, you see—till they'd done forgot, long ago, what it was all about. Wherever a Darnell caught a Watson, or a Watson caught a Darnell, one of 'em was going to get hurt—only question was, which of them got the drop on the other. They'd shoot one another down, right in the presence of the family. They did n't *hunt* for each other, but when they happened to meet, they pulled and begun. Men would shoot boys, boys would shoot men. A man shot a boy twelve years old—happened on him in the woods, and did n't give him no chance. If he *had* 'a' given him a chance, the boy'd 'a' shot *him*. Both families belonged to the same church (everybody around here is religious); through all this fifty or sixty years' fuss, both tribes was there every Sunday, to worship. They lived each side of the line, and the church was at a landing called Compromise. Half the church and half the aisle was in Kentucky, the other half in Tennessee. Sundays you'd see the families drive up, all in their Sunday clothes, men, women, and children, and file up the aisle, and set down, quiet and orderly, one lot on the Tennessee side of the church and the other on the Kentucky side; and the men and boys would lean their guns up against the wall, handy, and then all hands would join in with the prayer and praise; though they say the man next the aisle did n't kneel down, along with the rest of the family; kind of stood guard. I don't know; never was at that church in my life; but I remember that that's what used to be said.

"Twenty or twenty-five years ago, one of the feud families caught a young man of nineteen out and killed him. Don't remember whether it was the Darnells and Watsons, or one of the other feuds; but anyway, this young man rode up—steamboat laying there at the time—and the first thing he saw was a whole gang of the enemy. He jumped down behind a wood-pile, but they rode around and begun on him, he firing back, and they galloping and cavorting and yelling and banging away with all their might. Think he wounded a couple of them; but they closed in on him and chased him into the river; and as he swum along down stream, they followed along the bank and kept on shooting at him; and when he struck shore he was dead. Windy Marshall told me about it. He saw it. He was captain of the boat.

"Years ago, the Darnells was so thinned out that the old man and his two sons concluded they'd leave the country. They started to take steamboat just above No. 10; but the Watsons got wind of it; and they arrived just as the two young Darnells was walking up the companion-way with their wives on their arms. The fight begun then, and they never got no further—both of them killed. After that, old Darnell got into trouble with the man that run the ferry, and the ferry-man got the worst of it—and died. But his friends shot old Darnell through and through—filled him full of bullets, and ended him."

DIXON WECTER

From *Sam Clemens of Hannibal*†

[*The Prototype of Jim*]

But the most memorable servant of the Quarleses[1] was middle-aged Uncle Dan'l, sensible, honest, patient, the children's comrade in adventure, their adviser and ally in time of trouble. "It was on the farm that I got my strong liking for his race," wrote Mark, "and my appreciation of certain of its fine qualities." Mark made a trial

---

† From Dixon Wecter, *Sam Clemens of Hannibal*, Boston, 1952. The selections from the Wecter biography (pp. 100, 106–9, 147–51, 186–89) are reprinted by permission of and arrangement with Houghton Mifflin, the authorized publishers

1. The family of Clemens's uncle, John Quarles, of Florida, Missouri [*Editors*].

sketch of him, under that name, in *The Gilded Age*. Later he became the acknowledged original of Huck Finn's friend "Nigger Jim," whose unshakable loyalty, generous heart, and unconscious dignity—even when Huck makes game of his credulity—raise him to the rank of Mark Twain's noblest creation. He probably intended Joan of Arc for that niche; in his hands she turns to plaster saint. But Nigger Jim is as vital and earth-bound as one of the lofty hickories that towered over the old farmstead.

[Murder at Bricksville]

On January 24, 1845, Hannibal witnessed its first premeditated murder, which left among its relics twenty-eight depositions set down by the hand of John M. Clemens, J.P., and the recollection which his son recaptured in one of *Huckleberry Finn*'s most vivid episodes—the shooting of old Boggs by Colonel Sherburn.[2] The village shoemaker named Boggs may have furnished this name, but the real victim was "Uncle Sam" Smarr, "as honest a man as any in the state" a neighbor testified to Judge Clemens, but "when drinking he was a little turbulent," yet "I did not consider him a dangerous man at all." Curiously enough, one of the "damned rascals" against whom Uncle Sam liked to rail when in his cups was "big Ira Stout," of unhappy association with John M. Clemens' business affairs. Another target was a prosperous merchant named William Owsley, whom old Smarr when drinking liked to describe to all within earshot as "a damned pickpocket . . . a damned son of a bitch . . . if he ever does cross my path I will kill him." He believed that Owsley "had stole" two thousand dollars from a friend at Palmyra named Thompson, and had also swindled old Smarr's drinking crony Tom Davis, "and for that he intended to have Owsley whipped." Two or three weeks before the shooting, "Smarr and Davis had been in town, spreeing around and cutting up smart . . . and shooting off pistols." Probably on this same evening, stated another witness named Caldwell, "when on my way home, when opposite to Judge Clemens' office, I heard Mr. Smarr five times call out at different points in the street 'O yes! O yes, here is Bill Owsley, has got a big stack of goods here, and stole two thousand dollars from Thompson in Palmyra.' . . . I returned and went to Mr. Selms' store—Mr. Davis and Mr. Smarr were in there —Davis then went out and I heard the report of a pistol—Mr. Davis and Jimmy Finn then both came in, Jim remarked, 'that would have made a hole in a man's belly. . . .'" (Jimmy Finn, original of Huck's pappy who slept with the hogs in the tanyard, held the distinction of being the village drunkard.) Other witnesses

2. The episode occurs in Chapters XXI and XXII. The town is identified as Bricksville in Chapter XXVIII [*Editors*].

called Smarr sober, "as kind and good a neighbor as any man amongst us," and doubted that he ever carried a pistol, but agreed that he had walked or ridden up in front of Owsley's store shouting drunken abuse, while Owsley within, hearing these words in the presence of his customers, "had a kind of twitching and turned white around the mouth—and said it was insufferable."

The general forecast that "Smarr would catch hell" was fulfilled at noon a few days later, when Smarr came back to town to sell some beef. At the corner of Hill and Main—a few steps from the Clemens doorway—Owsley came up behind Smarr and a friend named Brown, and as the latter told Judge Clemens, the merchant cried out,

" 'You Sam Smarr'—Mr. Smarr turned around, seeing Mr. Owsley in the act of drawing a pistol from his pocket, said Mr. Owsley don't fire, or something to that effect. Mr. Owsley was within about four paces of Mr. Smarr when he drew the pistol and fired twice in succession, after the second fire, Mr. Smarr fell, when Mr. Owsley turned on his heel and walked off. After Mr. Smarr fell he raised his head and called, 'Brown come take me up I am shot and will soon be a dead man.' Dr. Grant then came up and invited us to take him to his store. We did so. The while he was begging us to lay him on his back. He then begged me not to leave him saying he must soon die. In about a half an hour from the time he was shot he expired."

Another witness added the detail that Smarr fell backward when shot, while "the gentleman that I saw shoot" kept his arm extended as he fired a second time. Thus, almost without a hairsbreadth of variation, the description in *Huckleberry Finn* of how the Colonel dispatched old Boggs.

In the depositions taken by Judge Clemens no mention is made of the heavy Bible laid by some pious fool upon the dying man's chest, though this "torture of its leaden weight" haunted young Sam's dreams and figured long afterward in his inspired retelling of the story. But Dr. Orville Grant, over whose drugstore at Hill and Main the Clemenses soon took up their abode, attested that the dying man was carried into this shop—where he and a fellow physician opened the victim's clothing and made hasty examination of the wounds, but "he then shewed signs of fainting and we . . . then stood by to see him die."

Owsley, a proud Kentuckian who smoked "fragrant cigars—regalias" and was regarded as something of a swell, may have repelled the threat of mob violence with the same cold contempt displayed by the fictitious Colonel Sherburn. Of this the court record makes no mention, but clearly the first deliberate murder on Hannibal's streets caused uproar and feverish excitement. Long afterward, in writing about the cowardice of lynch mobs, Mark reflected that in such a group "of a certainty there are never ten men in it who would not prefer to be somewhere else—and would be, if they had but the courage to go. When I was a boy I saw a brave gentleman deride and insult a mob and drive it away." Whatever threats Owsley may have faced down in the heat of the hour, he was not brought to trial until more than a year later. A man of wealth and influence, he had friends who were ready from the start to swear that his provocation had been great. At Palmyra on March 14, 1846, a jury returned a verdict of acquittal. Mark Twain's notes tell the sequel: "His party brought him huzzaing in from Palmyra at midnight. But there was a cloud upon him—a social chill—and he presently moved away."

The paltriness of a justice's fees is shown well enough by a note on the docket of papers which John M. Clemens prepared in this case—revealing that his fee for writing these 13,500 words was $13.50, and for administering oaths to twenty-nine witnesses, $1.81. Clerical drudgery, in fact, seems to have become the essence of his life. To his daughter Pamela, now helping to support the family by giving piano and guitar lessons in Florida and Paris, in adjoining Monroe County, he wrote a letter on May 5, 1845: "I have removed my office of Justice to Messrs McCune & Holliday's counting room where I have taken Mr. Dawes' place as clerk—I did not succeed in making such arrangements as would enable me to go into business advantageously on my acct—and thought it best therefore not to attempt it at present." The tradition that John M. Clemens "obtained employment for a time in a commission-house on the levee" doubtless belongs to this stage in his ill fortunes.

But under all the batterings of poverty Judge Clemens clung to his pride, his intellectual fastidiousness, and his sense of civic duty. Every letter that survives from his pen is redolent of an old-fashioned dignity. With the loose grammar and slovenly speech of river towns and backwoods—"the fruit of careless habit, not ignorance," as his famous son described it in Life on the Mississippi —the Judge made no truce or concession. In August 1845 he began to attend a course of "twenty oral lectures on Grammar . . . by Professor Hull," and made a careful précis of "Rules for Parsing by Transposition" for the benefit of Orion, the prentice printer in St. Louis.

[The Prototype of Huck]

* * * In Life on the Mississippi Mark observes that if, in one of his penitential moods he had dared to carry a basket of victuals to the poor, "I knew we had none so poor but they would smash the basket over my head for my pains."

One such family, whose invincible cheerfulness seemed no less a communal scandal than its indolence, is thus sketched in Mark's reminiscent notes: "Blankenships. The parents paupers and drunkards; the girls charged with prostitution—not proven. Tom, a kindly young heathen. Bence, a fisherman. These children were never sent to school or church. Played out and disappeared." They lived in a ramshackle old barn of a house on Hill Street—a distance quickly covered by Sam when summoned with stealthy catcalls from Tom.[3] The site is now cherished by the Chamber of Commerce as that of "Huck Finn's home," although the house no longer stands, following several generations of habitation by Negro families whose petty thefts, cutting scrapes, and the didos of a one-time denizen called Cocaine Nell Smith lent it a repute still more dubious than it enjoyed in the Blankenships' day.

Head of the family was Woodson Blankenship, a ne'er-do-well from South Carolina, who fitfully worked at the old sawmill but drank whenever possessed of cash to jingle in his jeans. In 1845 he appears on the roll of tax delinquents as owing twenty-nine cents. His eldest boy Benson, called Bence, did odd jobs but preferred to angle for catfish and tease the playmates of Sam Clemens by knotting their clothes when they went swimming, or clodding them when they came ashore. But he had a kind streak too—probably furnishing the original for Tom and Huck's friend Muff Potter,[4] who loafed and drank, but shared his catch if they were hungry, and mended their kites. In the summer of 1847 Bence befriended secretly a runaway Negro whom he found hiding among the swampy thickets of Sny Island, a part of Illinois's Pike County that hugged the opposite bank of the river from Hannibal. Ignoring the reward posted for the black man, Bence carried food to him week after week and kept mum about his hiding place—thus inspiring that rare tribute to loyalty in *Huckleberry Finn*, in which the homeless river rat rejects all temptations of gain and even elects to "go to Hell" rather than betray his friend Nigger Jim. But one day woodchoppers flushed the fugitive and chased him into a morass called Bird Slough, where he disappeared. Some days later, Sam Clemens, John Briggs, and the Bowen boys were fishing and roaming about the island as they often did—for the sake of its berries, and a fine grove of Illinois pecans such as the woods behind Hannibal did not bear—and made a discovery thus reported in the Hannibal *Journal* of August 19: "While some of our citizens were fishing a few days since on the Sny Island, they discovered in what is called Bird Slough the body of a negro man. On examination of

3. Tom Blankenship was the real-life prototype of the fictional Huck Finn [*Editors*].

4. A character in *Tom Sawyer* [*Editors*].

the body, they found it to answer the description of a negro recently advertised in handbills as a runaway from Neriam Todd, of Howard County. He had on a brown jeans frock coat, home-made linen pants, and a new pair of lined and bound shoes. The body when discovered was much mutilated." One account says that the gruesome thing, released from a snag by their poling about in the drift, rose headfirst like an apparition before their eyes. Endless seem the variations upon terror in the boyhood of Sam Clemens.

Among the Blankenships, whose society was a forbidden pleasure and therefore sought as often as possible, Sam's special joy was the younger brother Tom. Like Huck Finn, whose image Mark Twain repeatedly identified with him, Tom was ill-fed, an outrageous wreck of rags, dirty, ignorant, cheerful, carefree, and altogether enviable, being "the only really independent person—boy or man—in the community." Tom went barefoot all the time, both from freedom and necessity, whereas boys from "quality" families were forbidden by parents to "come out barefoot" until warm weather—meanwhile often mocked as "Miss Nancys" by the more emancipated. The woods and the waters around Hannibal were his education. Living by his wits, suspicious of every attempt to civilize him, "to comb him all to hell," he had none of the unimportant virtues and all the essential ones. The school of hard knocks had given him a tenacious grasp on reality, despite his faith in dreams, omens, and superstitions. But it had not toughened him into cynicism or crime, and "he had as good a heart as ever any boy had." The testimony of another witness is interesting, a lad named Ayres, grandson of a pioneer Hannibal settler named Richmond. Younger than Sam Clemens, he knew him slightly and was his fellow member in the Cadets of Temperance, but Tom he knew well and admiringly:

"My grandmother told us that Tom Blankenship was a bad boy and we were forbidden to play with him, but when we went on a rabbit chase he joined us. . . . Black John (a half-grown negro belonging to my grandmother) and Tom Blankenship were naturally leading spirits and they led us younger 'weaker' ones through all our sports. Both were 'talented,' bold, kind, and just, and we all liked them both and were easily led by them. We also played down around the old Robards mill and the school house in the city park."

Long years after, in 1902, Mark heard that his old crony Tom had become justice of the peace and a respected citizen "in a remote village in Montana."

Objects of equal juvenile interest with the Blankenship boys, but naturally less comradeship, were those ultimate dregs of Hannibal society, the village drunkards. Besides old Blankenship himself, the list began with "General" Gaines—an ancient and disreputable relic of the Indian wars, who when full of rotgut used to fancy himself one of the half-man, half-alligator breed, and roar, "Whoop! bow your neck and spread!" like one of the raftmen whose mixture of cockalorum with cowardice Mark hit off in the third chapter of *Life on the Mississippi*. From him the title of town drunkard, "an exceedingly well-defined and unofficial office of those days," descended to Jimmy Finn, who furnished the name and most of the attributes for Huck's pappy. "He was a monument of rags and dirt; he was the profanest man in town; he had bleary eyes, and a nose like a mildewed cauliflower; he slept with the hogs in an abandoned tanyard." Judge Clemens once tried without success to reform him; the Judge's son merely enjoyed him. To Will Bowen in later years Sam recalled how "we stole his dinner while he slept in the vat and fed it to the hogs in order to keep them still till we could mount them and have a ride." It was probably with Jimmy Finn in mind that a town ordinance passed in the spring of 1845 made it a misdemeanor to be "found drunk or intoxicated in any streat, alley, avinue, market place, or public square . . . or found a sleep in any such place not his own." But Finn was not long destined to plague the good citizens of Hannibal. On November 6 of that year, among the county records we find the sum of $8.25 allowed "for making a coffin, furnishing a shroud and burying James Finn a pauper." Mark insisted that he died a natural death in a tan vat, from delirium tremens combined with spontaneous combustion— "I mean it was a natural death for Jimmy Finn to die."

[The Burning Shame]

Mark recalls how in his school days a couple of young Englishmen sojourning in Hannibal "one day . . . got themselves up in cheap royal finery and did the Richard III sword-fight with maniac energy and prodigious powwow, in the presence of the village boys" —another favorite in the repertory of Huck's renegades. A cryptic note among further Hannibal memories, "Uncle Tom Cabin '53" may refer to some wandering troupe's offering a year after the appearance of Mrs. Stowe's novel—though its theme could hardly have been popular in slave-owning Hannibal.

In 1845 Hannibal's city fathers penalized anyone daring to "exhibit any indecent or lewd book, picture, statute [sic] or other things, or who shall exhibit or perform any immoral or lewd play or other representation." Probably, as one Mark Twain expert has suggested, "The Royal Nonesuch" or "The Burning Shame," as originally called—from which all details are suppressed in *Huckleberry Finn* save that the king came prancing out on all fours as the "cameleopard," naked save for rings and stripes of many-colored paint, and capered to the base instincts of the Arkansas loafers—

had to do with a mythical phallic beast known to the old southwest frontier as the "Gyascutus." Although the king and duke "fetched" their loafers by handbills barring ladies and children, the beast was sometimes exhibited a shade more decently. In Palmyra, the *Whig* on October 9, 1845, announced that the Gyascutus is "loose" and the public should be warned. It related that a couple of Yankees roving through the South, finding themselves short of cash and "determined to take advantage of the passion for shows which possessed our people," decided that one should "personate a rare beast, for which they invented the name of 'Gyascutus,' while the other was to be keeper or showman." At the next village they advertised their find, "captured . . . in the wilds of the Arostook . . . more ferocious and terrible than the gnu, the hyena, or ant-eater of the African desert! Admittance 25 cents, children and servants half price." A great crowd gathered, all agog. Beneath the curtain stretched across a corner of the hall could be seen "four horrible feet, which to less excited fancies would have born a wonderful resemblance to the feet and hands of a live Yankee, with strips of coonskin sewed round his wrists and ankles." While this monster flapped about and growled, the keeper Jonathan—his pockets heavy with silver—started a lecture on the beast's ferocity, all the while prodding him behind the curtain with a stick. Then came a savage roar, and the warning cry, "Ladies and gentlemen— *save yourselves—the Gyascutus is loose!*" In the pell-mell flight, Jonathan and the Gyascutus retired through the back door. From the old frontier of Missouri, the legendary beast later traveled to the Far West, as newspaper witticisms show. Out there in January 1865 Mark saw some miners on Jackass Hill enact a ribald skit, and jotted cautiously in his notebook in phonetic shorthand, "The 'Tragedians' and the Burning Shame. No Women admitted."

A similar "sell" in Hannibal is reported by Orion Clemens' *Journal* on March 18, 1852, captioned "The ——— Troupe." Sam Clemens' playful touch may be suspected in this account, rather than the heavy hand of Orion. It relates how a few days earlier the town had suddenly blossomed with posters announcing that wonders were imminent at Benton Hall.

"All the little boys in town gazed on the groups of astonishing pictures which appeared on the above mentioned bills, and were thereby wrought up to an intense pitch of excitement. It was to be a real theatre, and the 'troupe' (which nobody had ever heard of before,) was so 'celebrated.' Well, the momentous evening came. Those who enjoyed the felicity of paying a quarter, to see the show, found a large man on the first story, who received the money, and a small man at the top of the second pair of steps, who received the tickets . . . the very persons who were afterwards transformed into heroes and soldiers by the power of paint. In the hall we found forty or fifty of our citizens, sitting in front of a striped curtain, be hind which was all the mysterious paraphernalia of the theatre.

When the curtain was pulled to one side, the first appearance on the stage was the large man. . . . He was evidently a novice, and acted his part about as you have seen boys, in a thespian society. He was intended to be a lover of the distinguished danseuse, who played the part of a miss in short dresses, though her apparent age would have justified her in wearing them longer, and we have seen spectacles on younger people. Then the small man, who came in first as a corporal in the army, and then pretended to be drunk, for the amusement of the audience, made up the third character in this burlesque of a farce, the dullness of which was not relieved even by the disgusting blackguardisms with which it was profusely inter-larded."

Beyond much doubt, the antics of the king and the duke in *Huckleberry Finn* owe something to the experiences of that night in Benton Hall.

SAMUEL LANGHORNE CLEMENS

From *Mark Twain's Autobiography*†

In *Huckleberry Finn* I have drawn Tom Blankenship exactly as he was. He was ignorant, unwashed, insufficiently fed; but he had as good a heart as ever any boy had. His liberties were totally unrestricted. He was the only really independent person—boy or man—in the community, and by consequence he was tranquilly and continuously happy, and was envied by all the rest of us. We liked him; we enjoyed his society. And as his society was forbidden us by our parents, the prohibition trebled and quadrupled its value, and therefore we sought and got more of his society than of any other boy's. I heard, four years ago, that he was justice of the peace in a remote village in Montana, and was a good citizen and greatly respected.

[II, 174–75]

My uncle, John A. Quarles, was a farmer, and his place was in the country four miles from Florida. He had eight children and fifteen or twenty negroes, and was also fortunate in other ways, par-ticularly in his character. I have not come across a better man

† From *Mark Twain's Autobiography*, ed. Albert Bigelow Paine (New York, 1924). Copyright 1924 by Clara Gabri-lowitsch. Reprinted by permission of Harper and Brothers. The bracketed vol-ume and page numbers following each excerpt refer to this edition.

than he was. I was his guest for two or three months every year, from the fourth year after we removed to Hannibal till I was eleven or twelve years old. I have never consciously used him or his wife in a book, but his farm has come very handy to me in literature once or twice. In *Huck Finn* and in *Tom Sawyer, Detective* I moved it down to Arkansas. It was all of six hundred miles, but it was no trouble; it was not a very large farm—five hundred acres, perhaps—but I could have done it if it had been twice as large. And as for the morality of it, I cared nothing for that; I would move a state if the exigencies of literature required it.

It was a heavenly place for a boy, that farm of my uncle John's. The house was a double log one, with a spacious floor (roofed in) connecting it with the kitchen. In the summer the table was set in the middle of that shady and breezy floor, and the sumptuous meals—well, it makes me cry to think of them. Fried chicken, roast pig; wild and tame turkeys, ducks, and geese; venison just killed; squirrels, rabbits, pheasants, partridges, prairie-chickens; biscuits, hot batter cakes, hot buckwheat cakes, hot "wheat bread," hot rolls, hot corn pone; fresh corn boiled on the ear, succotash, butter-beans, stringbeans, tomatoes, peas, Irish potatoes, sweet potatoes; buttermilk, sweet milk, "clabber"; watermelons, muskmelons, cantaloupes—all fresh from the garden; apple pie, peach pie, pumpkin pie, apple dumplings, peach cobbler—I can't remember the rest. The way that the things were cooked was perhaps the main splendor—particularly a certain few of the dishes. For instance, the corn bread, the hot biscuits and wheat bread, and the fried chicken. These things have never been properly cooked in the North—in fact, no one there is able to learn the art, so far as my experience goes. The North thinks it knows how to make corn bread, but this is mere superstition. Perhaps no bread in the world is quite so good as Southern corn bread, and perhaps no bread in the world is quite so bad as the Northern imitation of it. The North seldom tries to fry chicken, and this is well; the art cannot be learned north of the line of Mason and Dixon, nor anywhere in Europe. This is not hearsay; it is experience that is speaking. In Europe it is imagined that the custom of serving various kinds of bread blazing hot is "American," but that is too broad a spread; it is custom in the South, but is much less than that in the North. In the North and in Europe hot bread is considered unhealthy. This is probably another fussy superstition, like the European superstition that ice-water is unhealthy. Europe does not need ice-water and does not drink it; and yet, notwithstanding this, its word for it is better than ours, because it describes it, whereas ours doesn't. Europe calls it "iced" water. Our word describes water made from melted ice—a drink which has a characterless taste and which we have but little acquaintance with.

It seems a pity that the world should throw away so many good things merely because they are unwholesome. I doubt if God has given us any refreshment which, taken in moderation, is unwholesome, except microbes. Yet there are people who strictly deprive themselves of each and every eatable, drinkable, and smokable which has in any way acquired a shady reputation. They pay this price for health. And health is all they get for it. How strange it is! It is like paying out your whole fortune for a cow that has gone dry.

The farmhouse stood in the middle of a very large yard, and the yard was fenced on three sides with rails and on the rear side with high palings; against these stood the smoke-house; beyond the palings was the orchard; beyond the orchard were the negro quarters and the tobacco fields. The front yard was entered over a stile made of sawed-off logs of graduated heights; I do not remember any gate. In a corner of the front yard were a dozen lofty hickory trees and a dozen black walnuts, and in the nutting season riches were to be gathered there.

Down a piece, abreast the house, stood a little log cabin against the rail fence; and there the woody hill fell sharply away, past the barns, the corn-crib, the stables, and the tobacco-curing house, to a limpid brook which sang along over its gravelly bed and curved and frisked in and out and here and there and yonder in the deep shade of overhanging foliage and vines—a divine place for wading, and it had swimming pools, too, which were forbidden to us and therefore much frequented by us. For we were little Christian children and had early been taught the value of forbidden fruit.

[I, 96–99]

W. D. HOWELLS

From *My Mark Twain*†

* * * Even now I think he should rather be called a romancer, though such a book as *Huckleberry Finn* takes itself out of the order of romance and places itself with the great things in picaresque fiction. Still, it is more poetic than picaresque, and of a deeper psychology. The probable and credible soul that the author divines

† From *My Mark Twain*, by William Dean Howells, New York, 1910. Reprinted by permission of Harper and Brothers. Author of *The Rise of Silas Lapham* (1885), *A Hazard of New Fortunes* (1890), and many other novels, editor of the *Atlantic Monthly* and *Harper's*, Howells was Clemens's closest literary friend. It was Howells who called Clemens "sole, incomparable, the Lincoln of our literature."

in the son of the town-drunkard is one which we might each own brother, and the art which portrays this nature at first hand in the person and language of the hero, without pose or affectation, is fine art. In the boy's history the author's fancy works realistically to an end as high as it has reached elsewhere, if not higher; and I who like *The Connecticut Yankee in King Arthur's Court* so much have half a mind to give my whole heart to *Huckleberry Finn*.

Both *Huckleberry Finn* and *Tom Sawyer* wander in episodes loosely related to the main story, but they are of a closer and more logical advance from the beginning to the end than the fiction which preceded them, and which I had almost forgotten to name before them. * * *

SAMUEL LANGHORNE CLEMENS

[Letters About *Huckleberry Finn*]†

To W. D. Howells

[Hartford] July 5, [1875]

I have finished the story [*Tom Sawyer*] & didn't take the chap beyond boyhood. I believe it would be fatal to do it in any shape but autobiographically—like Gil Blas.[1] I perhaps made a mistake in not writing it in the first person. If I went on, now, & took him into manhood, he would just be like all the one-horse men in literature & the reader would conceive a hearty contempt for him. It is *not* a boy's book, at all. It will only be read by adults. It is only written for adults.

* * *

By & by I shall take a boy of twelve & run him on through life (in the first person) but not Tom Sawyer—he would not be a good character for it.

* * *

† The following excerpts from letters about the composition and publication of *Huckleberry Finn* are reprinted in chronological order. "Letter to W. D. Howells, Aug. 9 [1876]" and "Letter to Orion Clemens and family, in Keokuk, Ia., Elmira, July 21, '83," ("Private—Dear Ma and Orion and Mollie") in *Mark Twain's Letters*, Vol I, arranged by Albert Bigelow Paine. Copyright 1917 by Mark Twain Company. By permission of Harper & Row, Publishers, Inc. The letter to Charles L. Webster is quoted from Hamlin Hill, ed., *Mark Twain's Letters to His Publishers* (Berkeley and Los Angeles: University of California Press, 1967). Copyright © 1967 by The Mark Twain Company; reprinted by permission of the University of California Press. The rest, to Howells, appear in Frederick Anderson, William M. Gibson, and Henry Nash Smith, eds., *Selected Mark Twain-Howells Letters: 1872–1910* (Cambridge, Massachusetts: Harvard University Press, 1967). Reprinted by permission of the trustees under the will of Clara Clemens Samossoud.
1. Hero of Alain René Le Sage's picaresque classic, *The History of Gil Blas de Santillane* (1715–35). This letter indicates that Clemens was concerned with narrative point of view from the inception of *Huckleberry Finn* [Editors].

Elmira, Aug[ust] 9, [1876]

⋏ ⋏ ⋏

The double-barreled novel [perhaps *The Prince and the Pauper*] lies torpid. I found I could not go on with it. The chapters I had written were still too new and familiar to me. I may take it up next winter, but cannot tell yet; I waited and waited to see if my interest in it would not revive, but gave it up a month ago and began another boys' book—more to be at work than anything else. I have written 400 pages on it—therefore it is very nearly half done. It is Huck Finn's Autobiography. I like it only tolerably well, as far as I have got, and may possibly pigeonhole or burn the MS when it is done.

* * *

Elmira, July 21, [18]83

* * *

I haven't piled up MS so in years as I have done since we came here to the farm three weeks & a half ago. Why, it's like old times, to step straight into the study, damp from the breakfast table, & sail right in & sail right on, the whole day long, without thought of running short of stuff or words. I wrote 4000 words to-day & I touch 3000 & upwards pretty often, & don't fall below 2600 on any working day. And when I get fagged out, I lie abed a couple of days & read & smoke, & then go it again for 6 or 7 days. I have finished one small book, & am away along in a big one that I half-finished two or three years ago. I expect to complete it in a month or six weeks or two months more. And *I* shall *like* it, whether anybody else does or not. It's a kind of companion to Tom Sawyer. There's a raft episode from it in second or third chapter of Life on the Mississippi.

* * *

To Jane Lampton Clemens

Elmira, July 21, [18]83

* * * I haven't had such booming working-days for many years. I am piling up manuscript in a really astonishing way. I believe I shall complete, in two months, a book which I have been fooling over for 7 years. This summer it is no more trouble to me to write than it is to lie.

* * *

To W. D. Howells

Elmira, Aug[ust] 22, [18]83

How odd it seems, to sit down to write a letter with the feeling

that you've got *time* to do it. But I'm done work, for this season, &
so have got time. I've done two seasons' work in one, & haven't anything left to do, now, but revise. I've written eight or nine hundred
MS pages in such a brief space of time that I mustn't name the
number of days; *I* shouldn't believe it myself, & therefore of course
couldn't expect you to. I used to restrict myself to 4 & 5 hours a day
& 5 days in the week; but this time I've wrought from breakfast till
5.15 p.m. six days in the week; & once or twice I smouched a
Sunday when the boss wasn't looking. Nothing is half so good as literature hooked on Sunday on the sly.

* * *

Hartford, Ap[ri]l 8, [18]84

It took my breath away, & I haven't recovered it yet, entirely—I
mean the generosity of your proposal to read the proofs of Huck
Finn.

Now if you *mean* it, old man—if you are in *earnest*—proceed, in
God's name, & be by me forever blest. I cannot conceive of a
rational man deliberately piling such an atrocious job upon himself;
but if there is such a man, & you be that man, why then *pile it on*.
It will cost me a pang every time I think of it. * * * The proof-
reading on the P & Pauper [*The Prince and the Pauper*] cost me
the last rags of my religion.

* * *

To Charles L. Webster[2]

[Hartford], April 14, 1884

* * *

Get at your canvassing early, and drive it with all your might,
with the intent and purpose of issuing on the 10th (or 15th) of
next December (the best time in the year to tumble a big pile into
the trade)—but if we haven't 40,000 orders then, we simply postpone publication till we've *got* them. It is a plain, simple policy,
and would have saved both of my last books if it had been followed.
There is not going to be any reason whatever, why this book should
not succeed—and it shall and *must*.

* * *

2. Clemens's nephew, and manager of
the publishing company he established in
New York under Webster's name. The
firm sold books by subscription, a
method some writers considered unfash-
ionable but which helped make Mark
Twain the best-paid writer of his day
[*Editors*].

To W.D. Howells

Elmira, Aug[ust] 31, [18]84

Thank you ever so much for reading that batch of the proof. It was a relief & respite, & I cursed my way through the rest & survived. I was most heavenly glad to get done with it. The sight of a proof-slip is always exasperating to me; but on this book it was maddening.

* * *

[Banned in Boston: The Concord Public Library Uproar]†

Boston *Transcript*, March 1885

The Concord (Mass.) Public Library committee has decided to exclude Mark Twain's latest book from the library. One member of the committee says that, while he does not wish to call it immoral, he thinks it contains but little humor, and that of a very coarse type. He regards it as the veriest trash. The librarian and the other members of the committee entertain similar views, characterizing it as rough, coarse and inelegant, dealing with a series of experiences not elevating, the whole book being more suited to the slums than to intelligent, respectable people.

Springfield *Republican*, March 1885

The Concord public library committee deserves well of the public by their action in banishing Mark Twain's new book, 'Huckleberry Finn,' on the ground that it is trashy and vicious. It is time that this influential pseudonym should cease to carry into homes and libraries unworthy productions. Mr. Clemens is a genuine and powerful humorist, with a bitter vein of satire on the weaknesses of humanity which is sometimes wholesome, sometimes only grotesque, but in certain of his works degenerates into a gross trifling with every fine feeling. The trouble with Mr. Clemens is that he has no reliable sense of propriety. His notorious speech at an *Atlantic* dinner, marshalling Longfellow and Emerson and Whittier in vulgar parodies in a Western miner's cabin, illustrated this, but not in much more relief than the 'Adventures of Tom Sawyer' did, or these Huckleberry Finn stories, do. . . . They are no better in tone

---

† Soon after the publication of *Huckleberry Finn* and just when sales were lagging, a committee of the Concord Public Library, in Clemens's words, "condemned and excommunicated my last book—and doubled its sale." The committee's prudish "case" is summarized in these typical newspaper extracts from the fracas.

than the dime novels which flood the blood-and-thunder reading population. Mr. Clemens has made them smarter, for he has an inexhaustible fund of 'quips and cranks and wanton wiles,' and his literary skill is, of course, superior; but their moral level is low, and their perusal cannot be anything less than harmful.

SAMUEL LANGHORNE CLEMENS

[A Reply to the Newspapers]†

Huckleberry Finn is not an imaginary person. He still lives; or rather, *they* still live; for Huckleberry Finn is two persons in one—namely, the author's two uncles, the present editors of the Boston *Advertiser* and the Springfield *Republican*. In character, language, clothing, education, instinct, and origin, he is the painstakingly and truthfully drawn photograph and counterpart of these two gentlemen as they were in the time of their boyhood, forty years ago. The work has been most carefully and conscientiously done, and is exactly true to the originals, in even the minutest particulars, with but one exception, and that a trifling one: this boy's language has been toned down and softened, here and there, in deference to the taste of a more modern and fastidious day.

---

† On April 4, 1885, Clemens instructed Charles L. Webster to include in future editions of *Huckleberry Finn* a "Prefatory Remark" aimed at newspaper attacks like those quoted above. Mrs. Clemens, however, vetoed the retort, reprinted here from Hamlin Hill, ed., *Mark Twain's Letters to His Publishers: 1867–1894* (Berkeley and Los Angeles, University of California Press, 1967). Copyright © 1967 by The Mark Twain Company; reprinted by permission of the University of California Press.

Criticism

Early Views

THOMAS SERGEANT PERRY

[The First American Review] †

Mark Twain's "Tom Sawyer" is an interesting record of boyish adventure; but, amusing as it is, it may yet be fair to ask whether its most marked fault is not too strong adherence to conventional literary models? A glance at the book certainly does not confirm this opinion, but those who recall the precocious affection of Tom Sawyer, at the age when he is losing his first teeth, for a little girl whom he has seen once or twice, will confess that the modern novel exercises a very great influence. What is best in the book, what one remembers, is the light we get into the boy's heart. The romantic devotion to the little girl, the terrible adventures with murderers and in huge caves, have the air of concessions to jaded readers. But when Tom gives the cat Pain-Killer, is restless in church, and is recklessly and eternally deceiving his aunt, we are on firm ground— the author is doing sincere work.

This later book, "Huckleberry Finn," has the great advantage of being written in autobiographical form. This secures a unity in the narration that is most valuable; every scene is given, not described; and the result is a vivid picture of Western life forty or fifty years ago. While "Tom Sawyer" is scarcely more than an apparently fortuitous collection of incidents, and its thread is one that has to do with murders, this story has a more intelligible plot. Huckleberry, its immortal hero, runs away from his worthless father, and floats down the Mississippi on a raft, in company with Jim, a runaway negro. This plot gives great opportunity for varying incidents. The travelers spend some time on an island; they outwit every one they meet; they acquire full knowledge of the hideous fringe of civilization that then adorned that valley; and the book is a most valuable record of an important part of our motley American civilization.

What makes it valuable is the evident truthfulness of the narrative, and where this is lacking and its place is taken by ingenious

† From *Century*, XXX, 1 (May, 1885), 171-72. The first review of any significance published in America and the first to question the ending of the novel. Versed in European languages and literature, Perry wrote regularly for the *Nation* and the *Atlantic*. His works include a history of Greek literature and a biography of John Fiske.

invention, the book suffers. What is inimitable, however, is the reflection of the whole varied series of adventures in the mind of the young scapegrace of a hero. His undying fertility of invention, his courage, his manliness in every trial, are an incarnation of the better side of the ruffianism that is one result of the independence of Americans, just as hypocrisy is one result of the English respect for civilization. The total absence of morbidness in the book—for the *mal du siècle* has not yet reached Arkansas—gives it a genuine charm; and it is interesting to notice the art with which this is brought out. The best instance is perhaps to be found in the account of the feud between the Shepherdsons and the Grangerfords, which is described only as it would appear to a semi-civilized boy of fourteen, without the slightest condemnation or surprise,—either of which would be bad art,—and yet nothing more vivid can be imagined. That is the way that a story is best told, by telling it, and letting it go to the reader unaccompanied by sign-posts or directions how he shall understand it and profit by it. Life teaches its lessons by implication, not by didactic preaching; and literature is at its best when it is an imitation of life and not an excuse for instruction.

As to the humor of Mark Twain, it is scarcely necessary to speak. It lends vividness to every page. The little touch in "Tom Sawyer," where, after the murder of which Tom was an eye-witness, it seemed "that his school-mates would never get done holding inquests on dead cats and thus keeping the trouble present to his mind," and that in the account of the spidery six-armed girl of Emmeline's picture in "Huckleberry Finn," are in the author's happiest vein. Another admirable instance is to be seen in Huckleberry Finn's mixed feelings about rescuing Jim, the negro, from slavery. His perverted views regarding the unholiness of his actions are most instructive and amusing. It is possible to feel, however, that the fun in the long account of Tom Sawyer's artificial imitation of escapes from prison is somewhat forced; everywhere simplicity is a good rule, and while the account of the Southern *vendetta* is a masterpiece, the caricature of books of adventure leaves us cold. In one we have a bit of life; in the other Mark Twain is demolishing something that has no place in the book.

Yet the story is capital reading, and the reason of its great superiority to "Tom Sawyer" is that it is, for the most part, a consistent whole. If Mark Twain would follow his hero through manhood, he would condense a side of American life that, in a few years, will have to be delved out of newspapers, government reports, county histories, and misleading traditions by unsympathetic sociologists.

BRANDER MATTHEWS

[*Huckleberry Finn:* A Review] †

The boy of to-day is fortunate indeed, and, of a truth, he is to be congratulated. While the boy of yesterday had to stay his stomach with the unconscious humour of *Sandford and Merton*, the boy of to-day may get his fill of fun and of romance and of adventure in *Treasure Island* and in *Tom Brown* and in *Tom Sawyer*, and now in a sequel to *Tom Sawyer*, wherein Tom himself appears in the very nick of time, like a young god from the machine. Sequels of stories which have been widely popular are not a little risky. *Huckleberry Finn* is a sharp exception to this general rule. Although it is a sequel, it is quite as worthy of wide popularity as *Tom Sawyer*. An American critic once neatly declared that the late G. P. R. James hit the bull's-eye of success with his first shot, and that for ever thereafter he went on firing through the same hole. Now this is just what Mark Twain has not done. *Huckleberry Finn* is not an attempt to do *Tom Sawyer* over again. It is a story quite as unlike its predecessor as it is like. Although Huck Finn appeared first in the earlier book, and although Tom Sawyer reappears in the later, the scenes and the characters are otherwise wholly different. Above all, the atmosphere of the story is different. *Tom Sawyer* was a tale of boyish adventure in a village in Missouri, on the Mississippi river, and it was told by the author. *Huckleberry Finn* is autobiographic; it is a tale of boyish adventure along the Mississippi river told as it appeared to Huck Finn. There is not in *Huckleberry Finn* any one scene quite as funny as those in which Tom Sawyer gets his friends to whitewash the fence for him, and then uses the spoils thereby acquired to attain the highest situation of the Sunday school the next morning. Nor is there any distinction quite as thrilling as that awful moment in the cave when the boy and the girl are lost in the darkness, and when Tom Sawyer suddenly sees a human hand bearing a light, and then finds that the hand is the hand of Indian Joe, his one mortal enemy; we have always thought that the vision of the hand in the cave in *Tom Sawyer* is one of the very finest things in the literature of adventure since Robinson Crusoe first saw a single footprint in the sand of the seashore. But though *Huckleberry Finn* may not quite reach these two highest points of *Tom Sawyer*, we incline to the opinion that the general

† Published in the *Saturday Review* (London), January 31, 1885, p. 153. The earliest review recorded, this dealt with the English release of the novel, which antedated the American issue. Brander Matthews, an American, then thirty-three and author of two plays and several books on the theater, was contributing to both British and American periodicals, and later became a professor at Columbia University.

level of the later story is perhaps higher than that of the earlier. For one thing, the skill with which the character of Huck Finn is maintained is marvellous. We see everything through his eyes— and they are his eyes and not a pair of Mark Twain's spectacles. And the comments on what he sees are his comments—the comments of an ignorant, superstitious, sharp, healthy boy, brought up as Huck Finn had been brought up; they are not speeches put into his mouth by the author. One of the most artistic things in the book— and that Mark Twain is a literary artist of a very high order all who have considered his later writings critically cannot but confess— one of the most artistic things in *Huckleberry Finn* is the sober self-restraint with which Mr. Clemens lets Huck Finn set down, without any comment at all, scenes which would have afforded the ordinary writer matter for endless moral and political and socio-logical disquisition. We refer particularly to the account of the Grangerford-Shepherdson feud, and of the shooting of Boggs by Colonel Sherburn. Here are two incidents of the rough old life of the South-Western States, and of the Mississippi Valley forty or fifty years ago, of the old life which is now rapidly passing away under the influence of advancing civilization and increasing com-mercial prosperity, but which has not wholly disappeared even yet, although a slow revolution in public sentiment is taking place. The Grangerford-Shepherdson feud is a vendetta as deadly as any Cor-sican could wish, yet the parties to it were honest, brave, sincere, good Christian people, probably people of deep religious sentiment. Not the less we see them taking their guns to church, and, when occasion serves, joining in what is little better than a general mas-sacre. The killing of Boggs by Colonel Sherburn is told with equal sobriety and truth; and the later scene in which Colonel Sherburn cows and lashes the mob which has set out to lynch him is one of the most vigorous bits of writing Mark Twain has done.

In *Tom Sawyer* we saw Huckleberry Finn from the outside; in the present volume we see him from the inside. He is almost as much a delight to any one who has been a boy as was Tom Sawyer. But only he or she who has been a boy can truly enjoy this record of his adventures, and of his sentiments and of his sayings. Old maids of either sex will wholly fail to understand him or to like him, or to see his significance and his value. Like Tom Sawyer, Huck Finn is a genuine boy; he is neither a girl in boy's clothes like many of the modern heroes of juvenile fiction, nor is he a "little man," a full-grown man cut down; he is a boy, just a boy, only a boy. And his ways and modes of thought are boyish. As Mr. F. Anstey understands the English boy, and especially the English boy of the middle classes, so Mark Twain understands the American boy, and especially the American boy of the Mississippi Valley of forty or fifty years ago. The contrast between Tom Sawyer, who is the child of respectable parents, decently brought up, and Huckleberry Finn, who is the child of the town drunkard, not brought up at all, is made distinct by a hundred artistic touches, not the least natural of which is Huck's constant reference to Tom as his ideal of what a boy should be. When Huck escapes from the cabin where his drunken and worthless father had confined him, carefully manufacturing a mass of very circumstantial evidence to prove his own murder by robbers, he cannot help saying, "I did wish Tom Sawyer was there, I knowed he would take an interest in this kind of business, and throw in the fancy touches. Nobody could spread himself like Tom Sawyer in such a thing as that." Both boys have their full share of boyish imagination; and Tom Sawyer, being given to books, lets his imagination run on robbers and pirates and genies, with a perfect understanding with himself that, if you want to get fun out of this life, you must never hesitate to make believe very hard; and, with Tom's youth and health, he never finds it hard to make believe and to be a pirate at will, or to summon an attendant spirit, or to rescue a prisoner from the deepest dungeon 'neath the castle moat. But in Huck this imagination has turned to superstition; he is a walking repository of the juvenile folklore of the Mississippi Valley —a folklore partly traditional among the white settlers, but largely influenced by intimate association with the negroes. When Huck was in his room at night all by himself waiting for the signal Tom Sawyer was to give him at midnight, he felt so lonesome he wished he was dead:—

"The stars was shining and the leaves rustled in the woods ever so mournful; and I heard an owl, away off, who-whooing about somebody that was dead, and a whippowill and a dog crying about somebody that was going to die; and the wind was trying to whisper something to me, and I couldn't make out what it was, and so it made the cold shivers run over me. Then away out in the woods I heard that kind of a sound that a ghost makes when it wants to tell about something that's on its mind and can't make itself understood, and so can't rest easy in its grave, and has to go about that way every night grieving. I got so downhearted and scared I did wish I had some company. Pretty soon a spider went crawling up my shoulders, and I flipped it off and it lit in the candle; and before I could budge it was all shrivelled up. I didn't need anybody to tell me that that was an awful bad sign and would fetch me some bad luck, so I was scared and most shook the clothes off me. I got up and turned around in my tracks three times and crossed my breast every time; and then I tied up a little lock of my hair with a thread to keep witches away. But I hadn't no confidence. You do that when you've lost a horse-shoe that you've found, instead of nailing it up over the door, but I hadn't ever heard anybody say it was any way to keep off bad luck when you'd killed a spider."

And, again, later in the story, not at night this time, but in broad daylight, Huck walks along a road:—

"When I got there it was all still and Sunday-like, and hot and sunshiny—the hands was gone to the fields; and there was them kind of faint dronings of bugs and flies in the air that makes it seem so lonesome and like everybody's dead and gone; and if a breeze fans along and quivers the leaves, it makes you feel mournful, because you feel like it's spirits whispering—spirits that's been dead ever so many years—and you always think they're talking about *you*. As a general thing it makes a body wish *he* was dead, too, and done with it all."

Now, none of these sentiments are appropriate to Tom Sawyer, who had none of the feeling for nature which Huck Finn had caught during his numberless days and nights in the open air. Nor could Tom Sawyer either have seen or set down this instantaneous photograph of a summer storm:—

"It would get so dark that it looked all blue-black outside, and lovely; and the rain would thrash along by so thick that the trees off a little ways looked dim and spider-webby; and here would come a blast of wind that would bend the trees down and turn up the pale underside of the leaves; and then a perfect ripper of a gust would follow along and set the branches to tossing their arms as if they was just wild; and next, when it was just about the bluest and blackest—fst! it was as bright as glory, and you'd have a little glimpse of tree-tops a-plunging about, away off yonder in the storm, hundreds of yards further than you could see before; dark as sin again in a second, and now you'd hear the thunder let go with an awful crash, and then go rumbling, grumbling, tumbling down the sky towards the under side of the world, like rolling empty barrels down stairs, where it's long stairs and they bounce a good deal, you know."

The romantic side of Tom Sawyer is shown in most delightfully humorous fashion in the account of his difficult devices to aid in the easy escape of Jim, a runaway negro. Jim is an admirably drawn character. There have been not a few fine and firm portraits of negroes in recent American fiction, of which Mr. Cable's Bras-Coupé in the *Grandissimes* is perhaps the most vigorous, and Mr. Harris's Mingo and Uncle Remus and Blue Dave are the most gentle. Jim is worthy to rank with these; and the essential simplicity and kindliness and generosity of the Southern negro have never been better shown than here by Mark Twain. Nor are Tom Sawyer and Huck Finn and Jim the only fresh and original figures in Mr. Clemens's new book; on the contrary, there is scarcely a character of the many introduced who does not impress the reader at once as true to life—and therefore as new, for life is so varied that a portrait from life is sure to be as good as new. That Mr. Clemens draws from life, and yet lifts his work from the domain of the photograph to the region of art, is evident to any one who will give his work the honest attention which it deserves. Mr. John T. Raymond, the American comedian, who performs the character of Colonel Sellers to perfection, is wont to say that there is scarcely a town in the West and South-West where some man did not claim to be the original of the character. And as Mark Twain made Colonel Sellers, so has he made the chief players in the present drama of boyish adventure; they are taken from life, no doubt, but they are so aptly chosen and so broadly drawn that they are quite as typical as they are actual. They have one great charm, all of them—they are not written about and about; they are not described and dissected and analysed; they appear and play their parts and disappear; and yet they leave a sharp impression of indubitable vitality and individuality. No one, we venture to say, who reads this book will readily forget the Duke and the King, a pair of as pleasant "confidence operators" as one may meet in a day's journey, who leave the story in the most appropriate fashion, being clothed in tar and feathers and ridden on a rail. Of the more broadly humorous passages—and they abound—we have not left ourselves space to speak; they are to the full as funny as in any of Mark Twain's other books; and, perhaps, in no other book has the humourist shown so much artistic restraint, for there is in *Huckleberry Finn* no mere "comic copy," no straining after effect; one might almost say that there is no waste word in it * * *

VAN WYCK BROOKS

From *The Ordeal of Mark Twain*†

There was a reason for Mark Twain's pessimism, a reason for that chagrin, that fear of solitude, that tortured conscience, those fantastic self-accusations, that indubitable self-contempt. It is an established fact, if I am not mistaken, that these morbid feelings of sin, which have no evident cause, are the result of having trans-

† From the book *The Ordeal of Mark Twain*, by Van Wyck Brooks. Copyright, 1920, by E. P. Dutton & Co. Inc. Renewal, 1948, by Van Wyck Brooks. Reprinted by permission of the publishers. The editors have selected, *cursim* from the volume, passages intended to represent the so-called "Brooks thesis." This supported certain controversial ideas of the period: namely, that the American experience, especially that of the frontier, and the genteel tradition as reportedly represented in the attitudes of Mark's mother, his wife, and his editorial friend, Howells, would handicap the creative freedom of the artist. (Bracketed page numbers follow each selection.)

gressed some inalienable life-demand peculiar to one's nature. It is as old as Milton that there are talents which are "death to hide," and I suggest that Mark Twain's "talent" was just so hidden. That bitterness of his was the effect of a certain miscarriage in his creative life, a balked personality, an arrested development of which he himself was almost wholly unaware, but which for him destroyed the meaning of life. The spirit of the artist in him, like the genie at last released from the bottle, overspread in a gloomy vapor the mind it had never quite been able to possess. [p. 14]

He was, as Arnold Bennett says, a "divine amateur"; his appeal is, on the whole, what Henry James called it, an appeal to rudimentary minds. But is not that simply another way of saying, in the latter case, that his was a mind that had not developed, and in the former, that his was a splendid genius which had never found itself? [p. 17]

The life of a Mississippi pilot had, in some special way, satisfied the instinct of the artist in him; in quite his way, the instinct of the artist in him had never been satisfied again. We do not have to look beyond this in order to interpret, if not the fact, at least the obsession. He felt that, in some way, he had been as a pilot on the right track; and he felt that he had lost this track. * * * Is it possible that he had, in fact, found himself in his career as a pilot and lost himself with that career? It is a bold hypothesis, and yet I think a glance at Mark Twain's childhood will bear it out. * * *

What a social setting it was, that little world into which Mark Twain was born! It was drab, it was tragic. In *Huckleberry Finn* and *Tom Sawyer* we see it in the color of rose; and besides, we see there only a later phase of it, after Mark Twain's family had settled in Hannibal, on the Mississippi. He was five at the time; his eyes had opened on such a scene as we find in the early pages of *The Gilded Age*. That weary, discouraged father, struggling against conditions amid which, as he says, a man can do nothing but rot away, that kind, worn, wan, desperately optimistic, fanatically energetic mother, those ragged, wretched little children, sprawling on the floor, "sopping corn-bread in some gravy left in the bottom of a frying-pan"—it is the epic not only of Mark Twain's infancy but of a whole phase of American civilization. [pp. 28–29]

If Jane Clemens had been a woman of wide experience and independent mind, in proportion to the strength of her character, Mark Twain's career might have been wholly different. Had she been catholic in her sympathies, in her understanding of life, then, no matter how more than maternal her attachment to her son was, she might have placed before him and encouraged him to pursue interests and activities amid which he could eventually have re-covered his balance, reduced the filial bond to its normal measure and stood on his own feet. But that is to wish for a type of woman our old pioneer society could never have produced. We are told that the Aunt Polly of *Tom Sawyer* is a speaking portrait of Jane Clemens, and Aunt Polly, as we know, was the symbol of all the taboos. The stronger her will was, the more comprehensive were her repressions, the more certainly she became the inflexible guardian of tradition in a social regime where tradition was inalterably opposed to every sort of personal deviation from the accepted type. [p. 34]

Already, I think we divine what was bound to happen in the soul of Mark Twain. The story of Huckleberry Finn turns, as we remem-ber, upon a conflict: "The author," says Mr. Paine, "makes Huck's struggle a psychological one between conscience and the law, on one side, and sympathy on the other." In the famous episode of Nigger Jim, "sympathy," the cause of individual freedom, wins. "We found," says the boy who tells the story [of "The Mysterious Stranger"], "that we were not manly enough nor brave enough to do a generous action when there was a chance that it could get us into trouble." Conscience and the law, we see, had long prevailed in the spirit of Mark Twain, but what is the conscience of a boy who checks a humane impulse but "boy terror," as Mr. Paine calls it, an instinctive fear of custom, of tribal authority? The conflict in *Huckleberry Finn* is simply the conflict of Mark Twain's own child-hood. He solved it successfully, he fulfilled his desire, in the book, as an author can. In actual life he did not solve it at all; he sur-rendered. [pp. 35–36]

As we can see now, it was affection rather than material self-interest that was leading Mark Twain onward and upward. It had always been affection! He had never at bottom wanted to "make good" for any other reason than to please his mother, and in order to get on he had had to adopt his mother's values of life; he had had to repress the deepest instinct in him and accept the guidance of those who knew the ropes of success. As the ward of his mother, he had never consciously broken with the traditions of Western society. Now, a candidate for gentility on terms wholly foreign to his nature, he found the filial bond of old renewed with tenfold intensity in a fresh relationship. He had to "make good" in his wife's eyes, and that was a far more complicated obligation. As we shall see, Mark Twain rebelled against her will, just as he had rebelled against his mother's, yet could not seriously or finally question anything she thought or did. "He adored her as little less than a saint," we are told: which is only another way of saying that, automatically, her gods had become his. [p. 106]

It was, this marriage, as we perceive, a case of the blind leading the blind. Mark Twain had thrown himself into the hands of his wife; she, in turn, was merely the echo of her environment. "She was very sensitive about me," he wrote in his Autobiography. "It distressed her to see me do heedless things which could bring me under criticism." That was partly, of course, because she wished him to succeed for his own sake, but it was also because she was not sure of herself. We can see, between the lines of Mr. Paine's record, not only what a shy little provincial body she was, how easily thrown out of her element, how ill-at-ease in their journeyings about the world, but how far from unambitious she was also. It was for her own sake, therefore, that she trimmed him and tried to turn Caliban into a gentleman. [p. 116]

Profane art, the mature expression of life, in short, was outside Mrs. Clemens's circle of ideas; she could not breathe in that atmosphere with any comfort; her instinctive notion of literature was of something that is read at the fireside, out loud, under the lamp, a family institution, vaguely associated with the Bible and a father tempering the wind of King James's English to the sensitive ears and blushing cheek of the youngest daughter. Her taste, in a word, was quite infantile. "Mrs. Clemens says my version of the blindfold novelette, *A Murder and a Marriage*, is 'good.' Pretty strong language for her," writes Mark Twain in 1876; and we know that when he was at work on *Huckleberry Finn* and *The Prince and the Pauper*, she so greatly preferred the latter that Mark Twain really felt it was rather discreditable of him to pay any attention to *Huckleberry Finn* at all. [pp. 120–21]

It was *The Prince and the Pauper*, a book that anybody might have written but whose romantic medievalism was equally respectable in its tendency and infantile in its appeal, that Mrs. Clemens felt so proud of: "Nobody," adds Mr. Paine, "appears to have been especially concerned about Huck, except, possibly the publisher." Plainly it was very little encouragement that Mark Twain's natural genius received from these relentless critics to whom he stood in such subjection, to whom he offered such devotion; for Mr. Howells, too, if we are to accept Mr. Paine's record, seconded him as often as not in these innocuous, infantile ventures, abetting him in the production of "blindfold novelettes" and plays of an abysmal foolishness. As for Mark Twain's unique masterpiece, *Huckleberry Finn*, "I like it only tolerably well, as far as I have got," he writes, "and may possibly pigeonhole or burn the MS when it is done"; to which Mr. Paine adds: "It did not fascinate him as did the story of the wandering prince. He persevered only as the story moved him. * * * Apparently, he had not yet acquired confidence or pride enough in poor Huck to exhibit him, even to friends." [p. 121]

Through the character of Huck, that disreputable, illiterate little boy, as Mrs. Clemens no doubt thought him, he was licensed to let himself go. We have seen how indifferent his sponsors were to the writing and the fate of this book. * * * The more indifferent they were, the freer was Mark Twain! Anything that little vagabond said might be safely trusted to pass the censor, just because he was a little vagabond, just because, as an irresponsible boy, he could not, in the eyes of the mighty ones of this world, know anything in any case about life, morals and civilization. That Mark Twain was almost, if not quite, conscious of his opportunity, we can see from his introductory note to the book: "Persons attempting to find a motive in this narrative will be prosecuted; persons attempting to find a moral in it will be banished; persons attempting to find a plot in it will be shot." He feels so secure of himself that he can actually challenge the censor to accuse him of having a motive! Huck's illiteracy, Huck's disreputableness and general outrageousness are so many shields behind which Mark Twain can let all the cats out of the bag with impunity. He must, I say, have had a certain sense of his unusual security when he wrote some of the more cynically satirical passages of the book, when he permitted Colonel Sherburn to taunt the mob, when he drew that picture of the audience who had been taken in by the Duke proceeding to sell the rest of their townspeople, when he had the King put up the notice, "Ladies and Children not Admited," and add: "There, if that line don't fetch them, I don't know Arkansaw!" The withering contempt for humankind expressed in these episodes was of the sort that Mark Twain expressed more and more openly, as time went on, in his own person; but he was not indulging in that costly kind of cynicism in the days when he wrote *Huckleberry Finn*. He must, therefore, have appreciated the license that little vagabond, like the puppet on the lap of a ventriloquist, afforded him. This, however, was only a trivial detail in his general sense of happy expansion, of ecstatic liberation. "Other places do seem so cramped up and smothery, but a raft don't," says Huck, on the river; "you feel mighty free and easy and comfortable on a raft." Mark Twain himself was free at last!—that raft and river to him were something more than mere material facts. His whole unconscious life, the pent-up river on his own soul, had burst its bonds and rushed forth, a joyous torrent! Do we need any other explanation of the abandon, the beauty, the eternal freshness of *Huckleberry Finn*? Perhaps we can say that a lifetime of moral slavery and repression was not too much to pay for it. Certainly, if it flies like a gay, bright, shining arrow through the tepid atmosphere of American literature, it is because of the straining of the bow, the tautness of the string, that gave it its momentum.

Yes, if we did not know, if we did not feel, that Mark Twain was intended for a vastly greater destiny, for the role of a demiurge, in fact, we might have been glad of all those pretty restrictions and misprisions he had undergone, restrictions that had prepared the way for this joyous release. No smoking on Sundays! No "swearing" allowed! Neckties having to be bothered over! That everlasting diet of Ps and Qs, petty Ps and pettier Qs, to which Mark Twain had had to submit, the domestic diet of Mrs. Clemens, the literary diet of Mr. Howells, those second parents who had taken the place of his first—we have to thank it, after all, for the vengeful solace we find in the promiscuous and general revolt of Huckleberry Finn. [pp. 194–96]

BERNARD DeVOTO

[Mark Twain: The Artist as American]†

* * *

As an accessory of literature, American journalism attained its highest reach in the February or Midwinter number of the *Century Magazine* for 1885. That issue carried "Royalty on the Mississippi" the last of three selections from *The Adventures of Huckleberry Finn*. It had also the ninth and tenth chapters of *The Rise of Silas Lapham* and began the serialization of *The Bostonians*. No comparable enterprise has ever been undertaken by a magazine.

To Mark, Howells's novel seemed "dazzling—masterly—incomparable." But as for Henry James's, he "would rather be damned to John Bunyan's heaven than read that." Both judgments were in-

† The selection from Bernard DeVoto, *Mark Twain's America*, copyright 1932, is reprinted by permission of and arrangement with Houghton Mifflin Company, the authorized publishers. Pp. 308, 310–20. By emphasizing the creative inspiration which Twain derived from his frontier origins and his knowledge of common American life, DeVoto opposed the hypothesis of Van Wyck Brooks (see *The Ordeal of Mark Twain*, 1920, quoted above) and the official biography by Twain's secretary, Albert Bigelow Paine (1912); the latter portrayed the author and man in the image of Hartford gentility, whereas Brooks suggested that Twain as an artist was betrayed by genteel censorship and the traumatic effect of his frontier boyhood.

evitable to him, but they neglect to understand a coincidence that joined the two novels with his in the climax of the national literature which followed the Civil War. The coincidence provides a yardstick for comparative measurements.

The two studies of amenities in the Back Bay are a chapter in the amiable difference between Howells and James which seems to have been, through the course of several novels on intersecting themes, an almost deliberate debate. Neither went beyond this chapter. *The Rise of Silas Lapham* is the most effective of Howells's stenotypes. After *The Bostonians* James began to submerge in the psychological perplexity through which only members of a school can follow him with complete belief; it was his last confrontation of an objective world. In the two books, two realisms, each in its way formidable, deal with American theorems—in so far as there remained, on the water side of Beacon Street, something recognizable as American.

* * *

Both novels are exquisitely conceived and written. Both employ a more mature technique than our fiction had experienced before them. Both, to the full extent of their powers, embody the truth about their themes sensitively studied and imaginatively projected. But both are wonderfully innocent of the world, their time and their nation. They are insulated from America. They are the genteel tradition attaining its complete expression in fiction but also irrevocably revealing its anæmia. Their impotence could be no more dramatically exhibited than by Gilder's accompanying them with selections from the novel in which nineteenth-century America exists with a vitality, a finality, and a greatness it has had nowhere else.

The kernel of *Huckleberry Finn* is in a speech of Huck's toward the end of *Tom Sawyer*. At the foot of the dead-limb tree t'other side of Still-House branch, he doubts the value of finding buried treasure. "Pap would come back to thish yer town some day and get his claws on it if I didn't hurry up, and I tell you he'd clean it out pretty quick." *Old Times on the Mississippi*, contains a passage as integral with Huck's journey as anything in his book, and *Life on the Mississippi*, written over the period when Huck was gestated, has many incidents on their way to fruition.[1] The Darnell-Watson feud is the Grangerford-Shepherdson trouble in chrysalis, a desultory tale told by a passenger as the *Gold Dust* passes through the chute of Island Number 8. On the upstream voyage as yet anonymous

1. Critics who enjoy dealing with the unconscious mind as the womb of art are offered such passages for amusement. I reluctantly confess, however, my fear that they will not indicate a father fixation, Mark's incestuous love of his sister, a forgotten reading of Nathaniel Wanley, or zoöphily.

strollers forecast David Garrick the younger and Edmund Keen the elder. John A. Murrell's inheritors hint at revenge in the state-rooms of a wrecked steamboat and other creatures of midnight presage the turmoil of search and escape through underbrush. Nor are these volumes the only ones in which pupal stages of incidents in *Huckleberry Finn* may be observed: most of the books that precede have passages of premonition. Why not? It was a book he was foreordained to write: it brought harmoniously to a focus everything that had a basic reality in his mind.

The opening is just *Tom Sawyer* and pretty poor *Tom Sawyer* at that. Huck's report of his emotions while ghosts are talking to him in the wind is a promise of what is to come, but Tom Sawyer's gang commenting on *Don Quixote* lacks the fineness of its predecessor. Discussions of ransom and Tom's exposition of Aladdin's lamp are feeble; such finish as they have comes from Huck's tolerant but obstinate common sense, here making its first experiments. But no flavor of the real Odyssey appears until Miss Watson forbids him to avert by magic the bad luck made inevitable by spilled salt, thus precipitating his trouble, and he immediately finds in the snow the impression of a boot heel in which nails make a cross to keep off the devil. . . . It is expedient to list here the book's obvious faults. After a first half in which, following the appearance of old man Finn, no touch is unsure, Mark's intuition begins to falter occasionally. When the Duke has Louis XVII learn a Shakespearian speech compounded out of Sol Smith and George Ealer, high and poetic reality lapses into farce. (Predictably. The humorist's necessity to write burlesque had frequently ruined fine things in the earlier books.) The King's conversion is weakened by his use of pirates instead of the neighborhood church which his predecessor Simon Suggs had more persuasively employed. (Predictably. The necessity to carry a joke into cosmic reaches had betrayed him often enough before.) Huck's discourse on the domestic manners of royalty is a blemish. (Extravaganza had diluted satire in many earlier contexts.) Huck's confusion when he tries to lie to the hare-lipped girl is perfunctory. (Improvisation had substituted for structure sufficiently often in Mark's previous fiction.) The concluding episodes of the attempted fraud on the Wilks family are weak in their technical devices—the manipulation required to postpone the detection of imposture, for instance, is annoying. Thereafter the narrative runs downhill through a steadily growing incredibility. The use of ghosts, the deceptions practiced on Aunt Sally and Uncle Silas, the whole episode built around the delivery of Jim from prison—all these are far below the accomplishment of what has gone before. Mark was once more betrayed. He intended a further chapter in his tireless attack on romanticism, especially Southern romanticism, and nothing in his mind or training enabled him to understand that this extemporized burlesque was a defacement of his purer work. His boundless gusto expended itself equally on the true and the false. . . . Predictably. It has been observed that he was incapable of sustained and disciplined imagination. One could expect it no more reasonably here than in *The Innocents Abroad.*

So, though I regard comparisons as worthless in æsthetics, the obligation of a critic of Mark Twain rests on me to point out these selfsame faults in the only American novel which even enthusiasm can offer to dispute the preëminence of *The Adventures of Huckleberry Finn.* Much more identity than has ever been noticed in print exists in the careers of Mark Twain and Herman Melville, whose minds were as antipathetic as religion and reality or the subjective and the objective world can be. Similarly, Jonathan Edwards's successor, when he came to write his masterpiece, plentifully anticipated the errors of Mark Twain and went beyond them. *Moby Dick* has, as fiction, no structure whatever. Its lines of force mercilessly intercept one another. Its improvisations are commoner and falser than those in Huck Finn. It does not suffer from burlesque (exuberant vitality had no place in Melville's nature) but its verbal humor is sometimes more vicariously humiliating than such passages as Huck's discussion of kings—a miracle, no doubt, withheld Mark Twain from the mere jokes habitual to him. And, though Melville could write great prose, his book frequently escapes into a passionately swooning rhetoric that is unconscious burlesque. He was no surer than Mark, he was in fact less sure, of the true object of his book, and much less sure of the technical instruments necessary to achieve it. That much of weakness the two novels have in common. It is convenient to point out, this much having been said, that they are otherwise antipathies. *Moby Dick* opposes metaphysics to the objective reality of *Huckleberry Finn.* It is a study in demonology, bound to the world of experience by no more durable threads than a few passages in the lives of mates, harpooners and sailors who are otherwise mostly symbol or mist. They were the book's disregarded possibility of great realism. Melville preferred to sigh through eternity after the infinite. It is a search which has an eternal value for some minds. Other minds, if they look to fiction for values of time instead of eternity and of the finite instead of the infinite, are likely to relinquish the *Pequod's* voyage toward fulfillment of man's destiny and prefer a lumber raft's voyage down inland waters after no more ambitious purpose than to see what the world is like.

The title announces the structure: a picaresque novel concerned with the adventures of Huckleberry Finn. The form is the one most native to Mark Twain and so best adapted to his use. No more than

Huck and the river's motion gives continuity to a series of episodes which are in essence only developed anecdotes. They originate in the tradition of newspaper humor, but the once uncomplicated form becomes here the instrument of great fiction. The lineage goes back to a native art; the novel derives from the folk and embodies their mode of thought more purely and more completely than any other ever written. Toward the beginning of this preface it was asserted that the life of the southwestern frontier was umbilical to the mind of Mark Twain. The blood and tissue of *Huckleberry Finn* have been formed in no other way. That life here finds issue more memorably than it has anywhere else, and since the frontier is a phase through which most of the nation has passed, the book comes nearer than any other to identity with the national life. The gigantic amorphousness of our past makes impossible, or merely idle, any attempt to fix in the form of idea the meaning of nationality. But more truly with *Huckleberry Finn* than with any other book, inquiry may satisfy itself: here is America.

The book has the fecundity, the multiplicity, of genius. It is the story of a wandering—so provocative a symbol that it moved Rudyard Kipling to discover another sagacious boy beneath a cannon and conduct him down an endless road, an enterprise that enormously fell short of its model. It is a passage through the structure of the nation. It is an exploration of the human race, whose adjective needs no explicit recording. It is an adventure of pageantry, horror, loveliness, and the tropisms of the mind. It is a faring-forth with inexhaustible delight through the variety of America. It is the restlessness of the young democracy borne southward on the river—the energy, the lawlessness, the groping ardor of the flux perfectly comprehended in a fragment of lumber raft drifting on the June flood. In a worn phrase—it is God's plenty.

The arrival of Huck's father lifts the narrative from the occupations of boyhood to as mature intelligence as fiction has anywhere. The new interest begins on a major chord, for old man Finn is the perfect portrait of the squatter. Behind him are the observations of hundreds of anonymous or forgotten realists who essayed to present the clay eaters or piney-woods people, as well as a lifelong interest of Mark Twain's. It is amazing how few pages of type he occupies; the effect is as of a prolonged, minute analysis. There is no analysis; a clear light is focused on him and the dispassionate, final knowledge of his creator permits him to reveal himself. We learn of him only that he had heard about Huck's money "away down the river," but a complete biography shines through his speech. This rises to the drunken monologue about a government that can't take a-hold of a prowling, thieving, white-shirted free nigger. The old man subsides to an attack of snakes, is heard rowing his skiff in darkness, and then is just a frowsy corpse, shot in the back, which drifts downstream with the flood

Something exquisite and delicate went into that creation—as into the casuals of the riverside. Mrs. Judith Loftus is employed to start Huck and Jim upon their voyage. She is just a device, but she outtops a hundred-odd patient attempts of fiction to sketch the pioneer wife. In her shrewdness, curiosity, initiative and brusque humanity one reads an entire history. Mere allusions—the ferryboat owner, the oarsmen who flee from smallpox, even raftsmen heard joking in the dark—have an incomparable authenticity. There is also the crowd. The loafers of Bricksville whittle under the store fronts. They set a dog upon a sow that has "wholloped" herself right down in the way and "laugh and look grateful for the noise." Presently a bubble rises through this human mire: the drunken Boggs, the best-naturedest old fool in Arkansaw, comes riding into Bricksville, on the warpath. Colonel Sherburn finds it necessary to shoot him; and then, in one of the most blinding flashlights in all fiction, a "long, lanky man, with long hair and a big white fur stovepipe hat on the back of his head" rehearses the murder. "The people that had seen the thing said he done it perfect." So Buck Harkness leads a mob to Sherburn's house for a lynching but the Colonel breaks up the mob with a speech in which contempt effervesces like red nitric.

But in such passages as this, the clearly seen individuals merge into something greater, a social whole, a civilization, seen just as clearly. Pokeville, where the King is converted at the camp meeting, Bricksville, and the town below the P'int where a tanner has died are one with Dawson's Landing and Napoleon—but more concentrated and thereby more final. It seems unnecessary to linger in consideration of this society. At the time of its appearance in 1885 a number of other novelists, perhaps fecundated by *The Gilded Age*, were considering similar themes. The name of any one of them—Charles Egbert Craddock or Mary E. Wilkins or Edward Eggleston will do—is enough to distinguish honest talent from genius. The impulse weakened under the æstheticism of the Nineties, and it was not till after the World War that the countryside again received consideration in these terms. To set Bricksville against Gopher Prairie or Winesburg is to perceive at once the finality of Mark Twain. The long lanky man in a white stovepipe hat who rehearses the death of Boggs has recorded this society with an unemotional certainty beside which either Mr. Lewis's anger or Mr. Anderson's misery seems a transitory hysterics.

The completeness of the society must be insisted upon. One should scrutinize the family of the dead tanner and their friends and neighbors, and orient them by reference to the family of Colonel

Grangerford. The Wilkses belong to the industrious respectability of the towns. Their speech and thinking, the objects of their desire, the circumstances of their relationships are the totality of their kind. The funeral of Peter Wilks is, as fiction, many themes blended together; it is, among them, a supreme exhibition of the mid-continental culture of its time—almost an archæological display. When the undertaker tiptoes among the mourners to silence a howling dog and returns to whisper "He had a rat," something final has been said about this life. But Colonel Grangerford is a gentle-man. Incidentally to the feud, which is the principal occupation of this episode, Southern gentility is examined. James's Basil Ransom was an embraced tradition; Colonel Grangerford is a reality. His daughter's elopement, a device for the precipitation of the plot, is out of fiction; the feud itself, with all the lovingly studied details of the scene, are from life. Gentility decorates the parlor with Em-maline Grangerford's verse and sketches. Its neurons show in the management of more than a hundred niggers quite as positively as in the parlor, or in the ceremonies of family intercourse and the simple code of honor, so indistinguishable from that of the Iroquois, which results in mass murder.

The portraiture which begins among the dregs with old man Finn ends with the Grangerfords. Between these strata has come every level of the South. What is the integrity of an artist? It would seem to consist in an intelligence which holds itself to the statement of a perceived truth, refusing to color it with an emotion of the artist's consequent to the truth. . . . These scenes are warm with an originality and a gusto that exist nowhere else in American fiction, and yet they are most notable for Mark Twain's detachment. There is no coloration, no resentment, no comment of any kind. The thing itself is rendered. If repudiation is complete, it exists im-plicitly in the thing.[2]

The differentiation of the speech these people use is so subtly done that Mark had to defend himself against an accusation of carelessness. He did not want readers to "suppose that all these characters were trying to talk alike and not succeeding." Superla-tives are accurate once more: no equal sensitiveness to American speech has ever been brought to fiction. But a triumph in dialect is after all one of the smaller triumphs of novel-writing, and the important thing to be observed about Huckleberry's speech is its achievement in making the vernacular a perfect instrument for all the necessities of fiction. Like Melville, Mark Twain could write

2. Criticism has spent some pain on Mark Twain's deletion from *Life on the Mississippi* of a passage which, he was persuaded, might affect sales in the South. Apparently those who were out-raged by this pandering to prejudice did not bother to read the suppressed passage. It is considerably less offensive to Southern sensibilities than several passages which remain in *Life on the Mississippi* and beside a good half of *Huckleberry Finn* it is innocuous.

empty rhetoric enough when the mood was on him, and the set pieces of description in the travel books are as trying as the Mc-Guffey selections which may have influenced them, while a willingness to let tears flow menaces a good many effects elsewhere. Yet his writing is never mediocre and is mostly, even in the least pretentious efforts, a formidable strength. Beginning with *Life on the Mississippi* it becomes, as Mr. Ford has remarked, one of the great styles of English literature. No analysis need be made here: its basis is simplicity, adaptability, an intimate liaison with the senses, and fidelity to the idioms of speech. Against the assertions of criticism, it should be remembered that such a style is not developed inattentively, nor are infants born with one by God's providence. Mark's lifelong pleasure in the peculiarities of language, which has distressed commentators, was the interest of any artist in his tools. . . . The successful use of an American vernacular as the sole prose medium of a masterpiece is a triumph in technique. Such attempts have been common in two and a half centuries of English fiction, but no other attempt on the highest level has succeeded. In this respect, too, *Huckleberry Finn* is unique. Patently, American literature has nothing to compare with it. Huck's language is a sensitive, subtle, and versatile instrument—capable of every effect it is called upon to manage. Whether it be the purely descriptive necessity of recording the river's mystery, or the notation of psychological states so minute and transitory as the effect on a boy of ghosts crying in the wind, or the fixation of individuality in dialogue, or the charged finality that may be typified by the King's "Hain't we got all the fools in town on our side? And ain't that a big enough majority in any town?"—the prose fulfills its obligation with the casual competence of genius. The fiction of Mark Twain had brought many innovations to the national literature—themes, lives, and interests of the greatest originality. This superb adaptation of vernacular to the purposes of art is another innovation, one which has only in the last few years begun to have a dim and crude but still perceptible fruition.

A tradition almost as old as prose narrative joins to the novel another tributary of world literature when a purely American wandering brings two further creatures of twilight to the raft. The Duke of Bilgewater and the Lost Dauphin were born of Mark's inexhaustible delight in worthlessness, but are many-sided. Pretension of nobility is one of his commonest themes, here wrought into pure comedy. The Duke is akin to characters in the other books; the King embodies a legend widespread and unimaginably glorious on the frontier. The ambiguity surrounding the death of Louis XVII gave to history riots, dynasties and social comedies that still absorb much reverence in Florence and Paris. It gave mythology a superb legend, which at once accommodated itself to American belief. Up the river from New Orleans, one of the most pious repositories of allegiance, stories of the dethroned Bourbon gratified believers during three generations. The legend must have entertained Mark's boyhood but the circumstances of his Dauphin suggest that he more enjoyed the appearance of Eleazar Williams, who became an international celebrity in 1853. The whole course of his life probably gave him no more satisfying exhibition of the race's folly than the discovery of a Bourbon king in the person of this Mohawk half-breed turned Christian and missionary, who had systematically defrauded his church and his people. The story is one of the occasional ecstasies with which history rewards the patient mind.

The two rogues are formed from the nation's scum. They are products of chance and opportunity, drifters down rivers and across the countryside in the service of themselves. The Duke has sold medicines, among them a preparation to remove tartar from the teeth; he has acted tragedy and can sling a lecture sometimes; he can teach singing-geography school or take a turn to mesmerism or phrenology when there's a chance. The King can tell fortunes and can cure cancer or paralysis by the laying on of hands; but preaching, missionarying, and the temperance revival are his best lines. American universals meet here; once more, this is a whole history, and into these drifters is poured an enormous store of the nation's experience. They have begotten hordes of successors since 1885 but none that joins their immortality. They belong with Colonel Sellers: they are the pure stuff of comedy. Their destiny is guile: to collect the tax which freedom and wit levy on respectability. Their voyage is down a river deep in the American continent; they are born of a purely American scene. Yet the river becomes one of the world's roads and these disreputables join, of right, a select fellowship. They are Diana's foresters: the brotherhood that receives them, approving their passage, is immortal in the assenting dreams of literature. Such freed spirits as Panurge, Falstaff, Gil Blas and the Abbé Coignard are of that fellowship; no Americans except the Duke and the Dauphin have joined it. None seems likely to.

Yet the fabric on which all this richness is embroidered is the journey of Huck and Jim down the Mississippi on the June rise. There, finally, the book's glamour resides. To discuss that glamour would be futile. In a sense, Huck speaks to the national shrewdness, facing adequately what he meets, succeeding by means of native intelligence whose roots are ours—and ours only. In a sense, he exists for a delight or wonder inseparable from the American race. This passage down the flooded river, through pageantry and spectacle, amidst an infinite variety of life, something of surprise or gratification surely to be met with each new incident—it is the heritage of a nation not unjustly symbolized by the river's flow. Huck sleeping under the stars or wakefully drifting through an immensity dotted only by far lights or scurrying to a cave while the forest bends under a cloudburst satisfies blind gropings of the mind. The margin widens to obscurity. Beyond awareness, a need for freedom, an insatiable hunger for its use, finds in him a kind of satisfaction. At the margin, too, the endless flow speaks for something quite as immediate. It is movement, not quiet. By day or darkness the current is unceasing; its rhythm, at the obscure margin, speaks affirmatively. For life is movement—a down-river voyage amidst strangeness.

Go warily in the obscurity. One does not care to leave Huck in the twilight at such a threshold, among the dim shapes about which no one can speak with authority. Unquestionably something of him is resident there—with something of Tom, the disreputables, Colonel Sellers and some others. But first he is a shrewd boy who takes a raft down the Mississippi, through a world incomparably alive. With him goes a fullness made and shaped wholly of America. It is only because the world he passes through is real and only because it is American that his journey escapes into universals and is immortal. His book is American life formed into great fiction.

Somewhere in the person of Mark Twain, who wrote it, must have been an artist—as American.

* * *

DeLANCEY FERGUSON

Huck Finn Aborning†

No American critical theory has taken deeper root than Mr. Van Wyck Brooks's thesis that Mark Twain was a thwarted satirist whose bitterness toward the damned human race was the fruit of a lifelong prostitution of his talents. Despite the counter-attacks of Bernard DeVoto and others, it flourishes everywhere from the London *Times Literary Supplement* to the last semester paper turned in by an English major at the University of Middletown. Past question, it is picturesque and dramatic, but—as Braxfield said of the clever chiel who would be none the worse for a hanging—it would be better if it were supported by a few facts.

A new interpretation of a great writer cannot have too many facts to stand on. The books published by the man himself or his literary executors are not enough; one must study him in his un-

† Published in *Colophon*, III, N. S. (Spring 1938), 171–80. Among the earliest critical articles substantiated by the evidence of the Mark Twain manuscripts. Reprinted by permission of DeLancey Ferguson.

guarded moments, in the letters withheld from his biography and in the first drafts of his books. Had Mr. Brooks thus studied Mark Twain, he would have found out many things. But he could not have written his book.

If a writer either consciously or unconsciously withholds anything of himself in his public utterances, traces of the buried talents are bound to show in the early drafts that are not yet groomed and sleeked for print. If nothing appears there which is not in the finished book, then the author is not censored, either by himself, his wife, or his literary advisors.

Everyone, including Mr. Brooks, agrees that *Huckleberry Finn* is Mark Twain's masterpiece. Written at the height of his creative power, it includes all he had to say, for good and ill, of the Mississippi world of his boyhood. Mr. DeVoto, while rejecting the Brooks thesis, admits it is impossible to pass final judgment on Mark Twain as an artist until we know, among other things, what was deleted from the early drafts of Huck, and why. For here, if Mark Twain had any more to say about the damned human race than he admitted to print, is where he would have said it.

It speaks little for the enterprise of the critics that a large part of the original manuscript of *Huck Finn* has for the past fifty years lain in the Buffalo Public Library without attracting the least notice. Its author gave it to James Fraser Gluck of Buffalo in 1886; soon afterward Mr. Gluck gave it to the library, along with a lot of other literary documents. It has been there ever since, most of the time on public exhibition.

True, the manuscript represents a little less than three-fifths of the book. Beginning in the middle of Chapter XII, it extends to the end of Chapter XIV, resumes at Chapter XXII, and is complete from there on. (The manuscript chapters are not numbered, and the few signs of division seldom coincide with those in the book.) Nevertheless, incomplete as it is, it is fully representative. Some strong scenes are missing, among them the Shepherdson-Grangerford feud, the camp meeting, and the shooting of Boggs, but it includes the attempt to lynch Col. Sherburn, "The Royal Nonesuch," the whole Wilks episode, and Huck's struggle with his conscience over surrendering Jim. The presence of the weak Tom Sawyer chapters at the end is offset by the absence of those at the beginning.

Furthermore, it is genuinely the *original* manuscript, not a specially revised fair copy. Though it bears no printer's marks, it must be the text from which the book was set up, for it includes the original title page, with the author's instructions to the printer, and similar instructions are written here and there in the margins. Without counting the innumerable differences in punctuation, the manuscript contains more than nine hundred textual changes, ranging from single words to whole paragraphs added or deleted, and shows, moreover, several distinct layers of correction, done at different times. Some changes were made at first writing, or almost immediately afterward; others indicate the direction taken in rejected passages not now in the manuscript; still others must have been made in proof. Besides these, a number of penciled marginalia show a critical reading intermediate between first composition and proofs.

But whatever their date, nature, or extent, all the revisions are the same sort. They are not the excision of scathing passages which Mrs. Clemens or Howells would disapprove of, neither are they the dilution of grim realism to make it meat for babes. They are the work of a skilled craftsman removing the unessential, adding vividness to dialog and description, and straightening out incongruities. Not more than two or three of the lot are the sort Olivia Clemens is reputed to have insisted on, and these two or three are so trifling that Mark may well have made them himself, without his wife's orders.

The only clear evidence of change of plan in a main section of the story will scarcely hearten the believers in censorship. When Huck and Tom arrived at Silas Phelps's plantation their creator originally intended them to find there a boy and a girl about their own age, named Phil and Mat. Fragmentary deleted passages, on renumbered pages, show that Mark Twain had developed this idea as far as where Tom passes himself off as Sid. Huck had confided Tom's impending arrival to Phil and Mat. But about that time Mark plainly realized that Tom and Huck, unaided, were going to furnish quite as many complications as the story would hold. He destroyed the older children, leaving only the brood of youngsters who were too small to share in the excitement. But he neglected to revise downward the ages of Silas and Sally (at first called Ruth) Phelps, who therefore appear in the book as somewhat elderly for the parents of so young a family.

So far, then, as the surviving manuscript shows, the general plan was little altered. Most of the changes are of detail. Thus when Huck and Jim visit the wrecked steamboat, Huck talks down Jim's fears by pointing out the untold riches, in five-cent cigars and other things, of steamboat captains. This whole long speech was added overleaf in the manuscript, to replace the unimaginative sentence, "Steamboat captains is always rich, and have everything they want, you know." Some of the best phrases were inserted in proof. The King's "soul-butter and hogwash" was only "humbug and hogwash" in the manuscript. Later on, when the King has "to brace up mighty quick, or he'd 'a squshed down like a bluff bank that the river has cut under," the simile was an afterthought. In the manuscript he merely "kerflummoxed." Again, the mob tears down Sherburn's fence, and begins "to roll in like a wave." When the Colonel appears with his shotgun, the book says, "The racket stopped, and the wave sucked back." For the last phrase, the manuscript has only "the crowd fell back." In the next paragraph, the book says, "Then pretty soon Sherburn sort of laughed; not the pleasant kind, but the kind that makes you feel like when you are eating bread that's got sand in it." This replaces, "not the kind of laugh you hear at the circus, but the kind that's fitten for a funeral—the kind that makes you feel crawly."

Many substitutions are dramatic. The first thoughts may be picturesque, but are out of character. Huck's summing up of Mary Jane Wilks was first, "She *was* the best girl that ever was! and you could depend on her like the everlasting sun and the stars, every time."—The speech might have fitted the mouth of the Playboy of the Western World, but not Huck's. It was changed in proof to, "She *was* the best girl I ever see, and had the most sand." A sentimental reference to "the big friendly river stretching out so homelike before us" was deleted entirely. Huck, telling Jim of the ways and works of kings, at first said that Henry VIII made each wife tell him a tale every night, "and he kept that up till he had hogged a thousand and one tales that way, and then he got out a copyright and published them all in a book, and called it Domesday Book—which was a good name and stated the case. Of course most any publisher would do that, but you wouldn't think a king would. If you didn't know kings." . . . But copyright is outside Huck's range of knowledge. Mark Twain, author and publisher, had taken his place. The passage was struck out of the proofs.

Remarks, again, might be right in character, but wrong in tone. Some of the more serious persons tended at first to orate in the style of Drury Lane melodrama. Col. Sherburn's speeches are full of passages like the one here italicised: "Because you're brave enough to tar and feather poor friendless cast-out women that come along here *lowering themselves to your level to earn a bite of bitter bread to eat, did it fool you into thinking you had courage enough to lay your hands on a* MAN?" And when Dr. Robinson denounces the King and Duke as imposters, his oration originally wound up thus:

"He is the thinnest of thin imposters—has come here with a lot of empty names and facts which he picked up somewhere; and you weakly take them for proofs, and are assisted in deceiving yourselves by these thoughtless unreasoning friends here, who ought to know better. Mary Jane Wilks, you know me for your friend, and your honest and unselfish friend. Now listen to me: cast this paltry villain out—I beg you, I beseech you to do it. Will you?"

As any reader of Victorian novels knows, this was a natural literary idiom in the 1870's. But even if Dr. Robinson had really talked that way, it was not the natural idiom for Huck to report him in.

Another sort of revision marks the King's two speeches, "all full of tears and flapdoodle," over Peter Wilks's coffin. Their permanent form, like the immortal phrase which introduces them, was an afterthought. They were first written in direct discourse, thus:

"Friends, good friends of the deceased, and ourn too, I trust—it's indeed a sore trial to lose him, and a sore trial to miss seeing him alive, after the wearisome long journey of four thousand mile; but it's a trial that's sweetened and sanctified to us by this dear sympathy and these holy tears; and so, out of our hearts we thank you, for out of our mouths we cannot, words being too weak and cold. May you find such friends and such sympathy yourselves, when your own time of trial comes, and may this affliction be softened to you as ourn is today, by the soothing ba'm of earthly love and the healing of heavenly grace. Amen."

In this speech and its companion, every phrase in the draft is carried over into the final text, but the indirect reporting, by implying compression from much greater length, immeasurably heightens the effect. It also gives Stephen Leacock, who says that Mark Twain never could convey the idea of prolixity except by getting prolix, something to ponder.

For still other effects, entire situations are expanded or reduced. Apparently almost the whole plan of the Wilks auction and its consequences came to Mark Twain as he wrote. After reporting the sale of the slaves, he at first went on with merely, "Next day was auction. They sold off the girls' house, and the tanyard and the rest of the property, but the prices wasn't the very highest." He immediately struck this out, and developed the narrative much as it stands in the book. Mark's invention, like most people's, did not always run smooth. Some passages, such as the chapter recording Huck's efforts to warn Mary Jane of impending trouble with the King and the Duke, have as many as twenty or twenty-five textual changes on a single page of print; at other times, whole pages of the book stand unchanged from the manuscript. There is no relation between the level of the work and the number of changes: Tom's arrival at the Phelps's is almost as much revised as Huck's interview with Mary Jane, and more than the attempted lynching of Sherburn.

Earlier in the Wilks episode, at the opening of Chapter XXVI, Mark originally began:

"Well, when they was all gone the king asked Mary Jane how they was off for spare rooms, and she said they had two; so he said they

could put his valley in the same bed with him—meaning me. He
said in England it warn't usual for a valley to sleep with his master,
but in Rome he always done the way the Romans done, and besides he warn't proud, and reckoned he could stand Adolphus very
well. Maybe he could; but I couldn't a stood him, only I was long
ago used to sleeping with the other kind of hogs. So Mary Jane
showed us all up, and they was plain rooms but nice."

Here again deletion was immediate. Huck's nocturnal prowls, and
his hiding the Wilks gold, would have been impossible had he slept
in the same room with the King. This, like the auction passage,
shows Mark composing as he went along, with only the vaguest
general plan in mind.

In the earlier adventure on the wrecked steamboat some changes
are in the manuscript; others were not made until the proofs. At
first writing, when Huck and Jim board the wreck, "rip comes a
flash of lightning out of the sky, and shows us a skiff tied to the
skylight pretty close beyond the door, for all that side was under
water." This was struck out at once; it destroyed both the surprise
of discovering the ruffians on the boat and the suspense when the
raft went adrift. But later in the chapter the manuscript elaborates
the plans of Bill and Jake for silencing their treacherous companion,
Jim Turner. They are going to gag him, to keep him quiet till the
wreck breaks up and drowns him. Bill objects,

" 'But s'pose she don't break up and wash off?'
" 'Well, we can wait the two hours, can't we? Then, if the thing
don't work, it'll still be long enough befo' daylight, and we'll come
back and do the next best thing—tie a rock to him and dump him
into the river.'
" 'All right, then: come along and less gag him.' "

And later, when the ruffians come out just as Huck and Jim are
getting away in the skiff, a wail from Turner calls them back to
replace the gag he has worked loose. In the book, all references to
the gagging disappear, apparently because it merely complicated
the action without intensifying it.

In this same episode appears the first of the marginalia indicating
critical revision between first writing and sending to press. When
Huck cuts the skiff loose, his creator has penciled in the margin,
"Provide him with a knife." This reminder is no doubt what allowed
Huck to find, among the junk in the wrecked house floating down
river in Chapter IX, "a bran-new Barlow knife worth two bits in
any store."

Several such notes appear on the pages telling of the flight after
the Wilks fiasco. When the crooks are plotting to sell Jim, the
Duke, says Huck, "found fault with every little thing, and he even

cussed Jim for being a fool and keeping his blue paint and King Lear clothes on, and made him take them off and wash himself off; and yet it warn't no fault of Jim's, for nobody hadn't ever told him he might do it." This passage is scored through, and a note says, "This is lugged—shove it back yonder to where they escape lynching and regain raft." But Mark failed to shove it, and so never told how or when Jim shed his "sick Arab" make-up. But the next note was acted on. When Huck, trying to find what the scoundrels have done with Jim, arrives at the Phelps's, a penciled note says, "Has good clothes on." Consequently, in the previous chapter, when Huck leaves the raft, the book has him putting on his store clothes, instead of "some old rough clothes" that he wore in the manuscript. There also, when he is going ashore in the canoe, one note says, "The skiff being new and worth advertising;" another, "Go back and [*sink* deleted] burn the skiff when they escape lynching;" a third, on the next leaf, "Go back and put on old clothes after escape from lynching." All these were finally ignored. So were a couple during Tom's elaborate schemes to free Jim. Where Tom instructs Huck about famous escapes, his author added in the margin, "Edmond Dantes," but let the book text stand as "them prisoners in the bottom dungeon of the Castle Deef." In the next chapter, when the boys are working in Jim's shack, a note says, "They always take along a lunch." But no change was made, and so far as the book reveals they carried on their night work without extra nourishment.

Most interesting of all is the note on the leaf which describes the King's make-up in "The Royal Nonesuch." It is the single word, scored through, "scandalous." Here, if anywhere, we might expect censorship. No one acquainted with fraternity initiations and other gatherings where Greek phallic comedy survives, has ever been in doubt as to the sort of show the King provided for the male population of Bricksville, Arkansas. Mark's canceled comment shows that he knew it was dangerous ground; the text shows exactly how much censorship he—or possibly Olivia—exercised. One phrase is deleted: the King originally "said he judged he could caper to their base instincts; 'lowed he could size their style." The title of the "play" is changed: throughout the manuscript it is "The Burning Shame" instead of "The Royal Nonesuch." The description of the King's makeup is modified in two places. In the manuscript he is "stark naked;" in the book merely "naked." The next sentence was first, "And—but I won't describe the rest of his outfit, because it was just outrageous, although it was awful funny." In the book Huck says, "And—but never mind the rest of his outfit; it was just wild, but it was awful funny." Out of the vast laboring mountain of charges that Mark Twain was a blighted Hemingway emerges this tiny and ineffectual mouse. If this was the utmost he suffered in revising what by implication is probably the bawdiest passage he ever conceived for publication, he was one of the freest authors who ever lived, instead of one of the most repressed.

The complete list of other changes which were, or may have been, made for decorum's sake bears out the impression from "The Royal Nonesuch." "Drunk," used twice in one paragraph, becomes "tight" and "mellow." Kings "hang," instead of "wallow," round the harem. "Rotten eggs" is changed to "sickly eggs," but since "rotten cabbages" stands in the same line, the change may be mere avoidance of repetition. The smells "too various" for Huck in the book were "too rancid" in the manuscript, and "the signs of a dead cat being around" replace "the smell of a dead cat." In several other places Mark's second thought modified his unhappy fondness for seeking humor in death, decay, and viscera. Jim, made up as the sick Arab, "didn't only look like he was dead, he looked considerably more than that." It may be doubted if realism would have gained much had the phrase been let stand as "he looked like he was mortified." It would be a questionable improvement to describe unappetizing meat as "a hunk of your old cold grandfather" instead of the "hunk of old cold cannibal," which again was second thought. And is it any better to say your conscience "takes up more room than a person's bowels" instead of "all the rest of a person's insides"?

A very few alterations considered the feelings of the churchly. Huck first said that the King rigged out in his store clothes looked as if "he had walked right out of the Bible;" this was changed to "the ark," but he still might be "old Leviticus himself." "Judas Iscarott" is softened to "Judus"; the King looks up towards the sky instead of the Throne. Two of Tom's jibes are altered, "mild as Sunday School" becoming "mild as goose-milk," and "Sunday-schooliest ways" becoming "infant-schooliest." On the other hand, when Huck trusts "to Providence to put the right words in [his] mouth when the time come," Mark changed "Providence" to "luck" in the manuscript, but restored the original reading in the proofs. And once he inadvertently wrote "damn," but immediately changed it to "dern."

In the Wilks episode, the manuscript allows the King and Duke to be a trifle more goatish towards Mary Jane and her sisters than the book does. The description of their welcome by the girls originally included this:

"Soon as he could, the duke shook the hair-lip, and sampled Susan, which was better looking. After the king had kissed Mary Jane fourteen or fifteen times, he give the duke a show, and tapered off on the others."

When Huck is getting Mary Jane away as the show-down approaches, he asks, "Do you reckon you can face your uncles, and take your regular three or four good-morning smacks?" The earlier passage was deleted, and this one softened. The motive is obviously artistic, not prudish. Mary Jane is a heroine, Huck's ideal of spirited young womanhood. The canceled passages are esthetically out of key with his feelings towards her.

Out of all the hundreds of changes, just one deletion is sincerely to be regretted as a masterly sample of Mark Twain's invective. When the scoundrels quarrel after the Wilks fisasco, the Duke's denunciation of the King originally ended as here italicised: "You wanted to get what money I'd got out of the 'Burning Shame' and one thing or another, and scoop it *all, you unsatisfiable, tunnel-bellied old sewer!*" Mark may well have canceled it himself, without his wife's help, but it is the sole instance in the entire manuscript which gives her critics a chance to score, and they had better make the most of it.

In short, the Mark Twain who emerges from this study is a man of letters practising his art, a humorist who knows what he is doing and making the most of his materials. Of the thwarted Swift invented by Mr. Brooks and his followers there is not a trace. Mark Twain didn't write humor because his wife forced him to prostitute his genius; he wrote it because he was Mark Twain.

Form and Symbol: The River and the Shore

LIONEL TRILLING

The Greatness of *Huckleberry Finn*

In 1876 Mark Twain published *The Adventures of Tom Sawyer* and in the same year he began what he called "another boys' book." He set little store by the new venture and said that he had undertaken it "more to be at work than anything else." His heart was not in it—"I like it only tolerably well as far as I have got," he said, "and may possibly pigeonhole or burn the MS when it is done." He pigeonholed it long before it was done and for as much as four years. In 1880 he took it out and carried it forward a little, only to abandon it again. He had a theory of unconscious composition and believed that a book must write itself; the book which he referred to as "Huck Finn's Autobiography" refused to do the job of its own creation and he would not coerce it.

But then in the summer of 1882 Mark Twain was possessed by a charge of literary energy which, as he wrote to a friend, was more intense than any he had experienced for many years. He worked all day and every day, and periodically he so fatigued himself that he had to recruit his strength by a day or two of smoking and reading in bed. It is impossible not to suppose that this great creative drive was connected with—was perhaps the direct result of—the visit to the Mississippi he had made earlier in the year, the trip which forms the matter of the second part of *Life on the Mississippi*. His boyhood and youth on the river he so profoundly loved had been at once the happiest and most significant part of Mark Twain's life; his return to it in middle age stirred vital memories which revived and refreshed the idea of *Huckleberry Finn*. Now at last the book was not only ready but eager to write itself. But it was not to receive much conscious help from its author. He was always full of second-rate literary schemes and now, in the early weeks of the

† From Lionel Trilling's Introduction to *The Adventures of Huckleberry Finn*, Rinehart Editions. Copyright 1948 by Lionel Trilling. Reprinted by permission of the publishers, Holt, Rinehart and Winston, Inc. Collected in *The Liberal Imagination*, by Lionel Trilling, New York, 1950.

summer, with *Huckleberry Finn* waiting to complete itself, he turned his hot energy upon several of these sorry projects, the completion of which gave him as much sense of satisfying productivity as did his eventual absorption in *Huckleberry Finn*.

When at last *Huckleberry Finn* was completed and published and widely loved, Mark Twain became somewhat aware of what he had accomplished with this book that had been begun as journeywork and depreciated, postponed, threatened with destruction. It is his masterpiece, and perhaps he learned to know that. But he could scarcely have estimated it for what it is, one of the world's great books and one of the central documents of American culture.

2

Wherein does its greatness lie? Primarily in its power of telling the truth. An awareness of this quality as it exists in *Tom Sawyer* once led Mark Twain to say of the earlier work that "it is *not* a boys' book at all. It will be read only by adults. It is written only for adults." But this was only a manner of speaking, Mark Twain's way of asserting, with a discernible touch of irritation, the degree of truth he had achieved. It does not represent his usual view either of boys' books or of boys. No one, as he well knew, sets a higher value on truth than a boy. Truth is the whole of a boy's conscious demand upon the world of adults. He is likely to believe that the adult world is in a conspiracy to lie to him, and it is this belief, by no means unfounded, that arouses Tom and Huck and all boys to their moral sensitivity, their everlasting concern with justice, which they call fairness. At the same time it often makes them skillful and profound liars in their own defense, yet they do not tell the ultimate lie of adults: they do not lie to themselves. That is why Mark Twain felt that it was impossible to carry Tom Sawyer beyond boyhood—in maturity "he would lie just like all the other one-horse men of literature and the reader would conceive a hearty contempt for him."

Certainly one element in the greatness of *Huckleberry Finn*—as also in the lesser greatness of *Tom Sawyer*—is that it succeeds first as a boys' book. One can read it at ten and then annually ever after, and each year find that it is as fresh as the year before, that it has changed only in becoming somewhat larger. To read it young is like planting a tree young—each year adds a new growth-ring of meaning, and the book is as little likely as the tree to become dull. So, we may imagine, an Athenian boy grew up together with the *Odyssey*. There are few other books which we can know so young and love so long.

The truth of *Huckleberry Finn* is of a different kind from that of *Tom Sawyer*. It is a more intense truth, fiercer and more complex. *Tom Sawyer* has the truth of honesty—what it says about things and feelings is never false and always both adequate and beautiful. *Huckleberry Finn* has this kind of truth, too, but it has also the truth of moral passion; it deals directly with the virtue and depravity of man's heart.

Perhaps the best clue to the greatness of *Huckleberry Finn* has been given to us by a writer who is as different from Mark Twain as it is possible for one Missourian to be from another. T. S. Eliot's poem, "The Dry Salvages," the third of his *Four Quartets*, begins with a meditation on the Mississippi, which Mr. Eliot knew in his St. Louis boyhood. These are the opening lines:

> I do not know much about gods; but I think that the river
> Is a strong brown god . . .

And the meditation goes on to speak of the god as

>   almost forgotten
> By the dwellers in cities—ever, however, implacable,
> Keeping his seasons and rages, destroyer, reminder of
> What men choose to forget. Unhonoured, unpropitiated
> By worshippers of the machine, but waiting, watching and waiting.[1]

Huckleberry Finn is a great book because it is about a god—about, that is, a power which seems to have a mind and will of its own, and which, to men of moral imagination, appears to embody a great moral idea.

Huck himself is the servant of the river-god, and he comes very close to being aware of the divine nature of the being he serves. The world he inhabits is perfectly equipped to accommodate a deity, for it is full of presences and meanings which it conveys by natural signs and also by preternatural omens and taboos: to look at the moon over the left shoulder, to shake the tablecloth after sundown, to handle a snakeskin, are ways of offending the obscure and prevalent spirits. Huck is at odds, on moral and aesthetic grounds, with the only form of Christianity he knows, and his very intense moral life may be said to derive from his love of the river. He lives in a perpetual adoration of the Mississippi's power and charm. Huck, of course, always expresses himself better than he can know, but nothing draws upon his gift of speech like his response to his deity. After every sally into the social life of the shore, he returns to the river with relief and thanksgiving; and at each return, regular and explicit as a chorus in a Greek tragedy, there is a hymn of praise to the god's beauty, mystery, and strength, and to his noble grandeur in contrast with the pettiness of men.

Generally the god is benign, a being of long sunny days and spa-

---

1. Copyright, 1943, by T. S. Eliot, reprinted by permission of Harcourt, Brace and Company.

cious nights. But, like any god, he is also dangerous and deceptive. He generates fogs which bewilder, and he contrives echoes and false distances which confuse. His sandbars can ground and his hidden snags can mortally wound a great steamboat. He can cut away the solid earth from under a man's feet and take his house with it. The sense of the danger of the river is what saves the book from any touch of the sentimentality and moral ineptitude of most works of the imagination which contrast the life of nature with the life of society.

The river itself is only divine; it is not ethical and good. But its nature seems to foster the goodness of those who love it and try to fit themselves to its ways. And we must observe that we cannot make —that Mark Twain does not make—an absolute opposition between the river and human society. To Huck much of the charm of the river life is human: it is the raft and the wigwam and Jim. He has not run away from Miss Watson and the Widow Douglas and his brutal father to a completely individualistic liberty, for in Jim he finds his true father, very much as Stephen Dedalus in James Joyce's *Ulysses* finds his true father in Leopold Bloom.[2] The boy and the Negro slave form a family, a primitive community—and it is a community of saints.

Huck's intense and even complex moral quality may possibly not appear on a first reading, for one may be caught and convinced by his own estimate of himself, by his brags about his lazy hedonism, his avowed preference for being alone, his dislike of civilization. The fact is, of course, that he is involved in civilization up to his ears. His escape from society is but his way of reaching what society ideally dreams of for itself. Responsibility is the very essence of his character, and it is perhaps to the point that the original of Huck, a boyhood companion of Mark Twain's named Tom Blankenship, did, like Huck, "light out for the Territory," only to become a justice of the peace in Montana, "a good citizen and greatly respected."

Huck does indeed have all the capacities for simple happiness he says he has, but circumstances and his own moral nature make him the least carefree of boys—he is always "in a sweat" over the predicament of someone else. He has a great sense of the sadness of human life, and although he likes to be alone, the words "lonely" and "loneliness" are frequent with him. The note of his special sensibility is struck early in the story: "Well, when Tom and me got to the edge of the hilltop we looked away down into the village and

2. In Joyce's *Finnegans Wake* both Mark Twain and Huckleberry Finn appear frequently. The theme of rivers is, of course, dominant in the book; and Huck's name suits Joyce's purpose, as so many names do, for Finn is one of the many names of his hero. Mark Twain's love of and gift for the spoken language makes another reason for Joyce's interest in him.

could see three or four lights twinkling where there were sick folks, maybe; and the stars over us was sparkling ever so fine; and down by the village was the river, a whole mile broad, and awful still and grand." The identification of those three or four lonely lights as the lamps of sick-watches defines Huck's character.

His sympathy is quick and immediate. When the circus audience laughs at the supposedly drunken man who tries to ride the horse, Huck is only miserable: "It wasn't funny to me . . . ; I was all of a tremble to see his danger." When he imprisons the intending murderers on the wrecked steamboat, his first thought is of how to get someone to rescue them, for he considers "how dreadful it was, even for murderers, to be in such a fix. I says to myself, there ain't no telling but I might come to be a murderer myself yet, and then how would I like it?" But his sympathy is never sentimental. When at last he knows that the murderers are beyond help, he has no inclination to false pathos. "I felt a little bit heavy-hearted about the gang, but not much, for I reckoned that if they could stand it I could." His will is genuinely good and therefore he has no need to torture himself with guilty second thoughts.

Not the least remarkable thing about Huck's feeling for people is that his tenderness goes along with the assumption that his fellow men are likely to be dangerous and wicked. He travels incognito, never telling the truth about himself and never twice telling the same lie, for he trusts no one and the lie comforts him even when it is not necessary. He instinctively knows that the best way to keep a party of men away from Jim on the raft is to beg them to come aboard to help his family stricken with smallpox. And if he had not already had the knowledge of human weakness and stupidity and cowardice, he would soon have acquired it, for all his encounters forcibly teach it to him—the insensate feud of the Grangerfords and Shepherdsons, the invasion of the raft by the Duke and the King, the murder of Boggs, the lynching party, and the speech of Colonel Sherburn. Yet his profound and bitter knowledge of human depravity never prevents him from being a friend to man.

No personal pride interferes with his well-doing. He knows what status is and on the whole he respects it—he is really a very *respectable* person and inclines to like "quality folks"—but he himself is unaffected by it. He himself has never had status, he has always been the lowest of the low, and the considerable fortune he had acquired in *The Adventures of Tom Sawyer* is never real to him. When the Duke suggests that Huck and Jim render him the personal service that accords with his rank, Huck's only comment is, "Well, that was easy so we done it." He is injured in every possible way by the Duke and the King, used and exploited and manipulated, yet when he hears that they are in danger from a mob, his natural impulse is to warn them. And when he fails of his purpose and the two men are tarred and feathered and ridden on a rail, his only thought is, "Well, it made me sick to see it; and I was sorry for them poor pitiful rascals, it seemed like I couldn't ever feel any hardness against them any more in the world."

And if Huck and Jim on the raft do indeed make a community of saints, it is because they do not have an ounce of pride between them. Yet this is not perfectly true, for the one disagreement they ever have is over a matter of pride. It is on the occasion when Jim and Huck have been separated by the fog. Jim has mourned Huck as dead, and then, exhausted, has fallen asleep. When he awakes and finds that Huck has returned, he is overjoyed; but Huck convinces him that he has only dreamed the incident, that there has been no fog, no separation, no chase, no reunion, and then allows him to make an elaborate "interpretation" of the dream he now believes he has had. Then the joke is sprung, and in the growing light of the dawn Huck points to the debris of leaves on the raft and the broken oar.

"Jim looked at the trash, and then looked at me, and back at the trash again. He had got the dream fixed so strong in his head that he couldn't seem to shake it loose and get the facts back into its place again right away. But when he did get the thing straightened around he looked at me steady without ever smiling, and says:

"'What do dey stan' for? I'se gwyne to tell you. When I got all wore out wid work, en wid de callin' for you, en went to sleep, my heart wuz mos' broke bekase you wuz los', en I didn' k'yer no mo' what became er me en de raf'. En when I wake up en fine you back agin, all safe en soun', de tears come, en I could a got down on my knees en kiss yo' foot, I's so thankful. En all you wuz thinkin' 'bout wuz how you could make a fool uv ole Jim wid a lie. Dat truck dah is *trash*; en trash is what people is dat puts dirt on de head er dey fren's en makes 'em ashamed.'

"Then he got up slow and walked to the wigwam, and went in there without saying anything but that."

The pride of human affection has been touched, one of the few prides that has any true dignity. And at its utterance, Huck's one last dim vestige of pride of status, his sense of his position as a white man, wholly vanishes: "It was fifteen minutes before I could work myself up to go and humble myself to a nigger; but I done it, and I warn't sorry for it afterward, neither."

This incident is the beginning of the moral testing and development which a character so morally sensitive as Huck's must inevitably undergo. And it becomes an heroic character when, on the urging of affection, Huck discards the moral code he has always taken for granted and resolves to help Jim in his escape from slavery.

The intensity of his struggle over the act suggests how deeply he is involved in the society which he rejects. The satiric brilliance of the episode lies, of course, in Huck's solving his problem not by doing "right" but by doing "wrong." He has only to consult his conscience, the conscience of a Southern boy in the middle of the last century, to know that he ought to return Jim to slavery. And as soon as he makes the decision according to conscience and decides to inform on Jim, he has all the warmly gratifying emotions of conscious virtue. "Why, it was astonishing, the way I felt as light as a feather right straight off, and my troubles all gone . . . I felt good and all washed clean of sin for the first time I had ever felt so in my life, and I knowed I could pray now." And when at last he finds that he cannot endure his decision but must change it and help Jim in his escape, it is not because he has acquired any new ideas about slavery—he believes that he detests Abolitionists; he himself answers when he is asked if the explosion of a steamboat boiler had hurt anyone, "No'm, killed a nigger," and of course he finds nothing wrong in the responsive comment, "Well, it's lucky because sometimes people do get hurt." Ideas and ideals can be of no help to him in his moral crisis. He no more condemns slavery than Tristram and Lancelot condemn marriage; he is as consciously *wicked* as any illicit lover of romance and he consents to be damned for a personal devotion, never questioning the justice of the punishment he has incurred.

Huckleberry Finn was once barred from certain libraries and schools for its alleged subversion of morality. The authorities had in mind the book's endemic lying, the petty thefts, the denigrations of respectability and religion, the bad language and the bad grammar. We smile at that excessive care, yet in point of fact *Huckleberry Finn* is indeed a subversive book—no one who reads thoughtfully the dialectic of Huck's great moral crisis will ever again be wholly able to accept without some question and some irony the assumptions of the respectable morality by which he lives, nor will ever again be certain that what he considers the clear dictates of moral reason are not merely the engrained customary beliefs of his time and place.

3

We are not likely to miss in *Huckleberry Finn* the subtle, implicit moral meaning of the great river. But we are likely to understand these moral implications as having to do only with personal and individual conduct. And since the sum of individual pettiness is on the whole pretty constant, we are likely to think of the book as applicable to mankind in general and at all times and in all places, and we praise it by calling it "universal." And so it is; but like many books to which that large adjective applies, it is also local and par-

ticular. It has a particular moral reference to the United States in
the period after the Civil War. It was then when, in Mr. Eliot's
phrase, the river was forgotten, and precisely by the "dwellers in
cities," by the "worshippers of the machine."

The Civil War and the development of the railroads ended the
great days when the river was the central artery of the nation. No
contrast could be more moving than that between the hot, turbulent
energy of the river life of the first part of *Life on the Mississippi*
and the melancholy reminiscence of the second part. And the war
that brought the end of the rich Mississippi days also marked a
change in the quality of life in America which, to many men, con-
sisted of a deterioration of American moral values. It is of course a
human habit to look back on the past and to find it a better and
more innocent time than the present. Yet in this instance there
seems to be an objective basis for the judgment. We cannot disregard the testimony of men so diverse as Henry Adams, Walt Whitman, William Dean Howells, and Mark Twain himself, to mention
but a few of the many who were in agreement on this point. All
spoke of something that had gone out of American life after the
war, some simplicity, some innocence, some peace. None of them
was under any illusion about the amount of ordinary human wickedness that existed in the old days, and Mark Twain certainly was not.
The difference was in the public attitude, in the things that were
now accepted and made respectable in the national ideal. It was,
they all felt, connected with new emotions about money. As Mark
Twain said, where formerly "the people had desired money," now
they "fall down and worship it." The new gospel was, "Get money.
Get it quickly. Get it in abundance. Get it in prodigious abundance.
Get it dishonestly if you can, honestly if you must."[3]

With the end of the Civil War capitalism had established itself.
The relaxing influence of the frontier was coming to an end. Americans increasingly became "dwellers in cities" and "worshippers of
the machine." Mark Twain himself became a notable part of this
new dispensation. No one worshipped the machine more than he
did, or thought he did—he ruined himself by his devotion to the
Paige typesetting machine by which he hoped to make a fortune
even greater than he had made by his writing, and he sang the
praises of the machine age in *A Connecticut Yankee in King
Arthur's Court*. He associated intimately with the dominant figures
of American business enterprise. Yet at the same time he hated
the new way of life and kept bitter memoranda of his scorn, commenting on the low morality or the bad taste or the smugness and
dullness of the men who were shaping the national ideal and di-

3. *Mark Twain in Eruption*, edited by Bernard De Voto, p. 77.

recting the destiny of the nation.

Mark Twain said of *Tom Sawyer* that it "is simply a hymn, put into prose form to give it a worldly air." He might have said the same, and with even more reason, of *Huckleberry Finn*, which is a hymn to an older America forever gone, an America which had its great national faults, which was full of violence and even of cruelty, but which still maintained its sense of reality, for it was not yet enthralled by money, the father of ultimate illusion and lies. Against the money-god stands the river-god, whose comments are silent— sunlight, space, uncrowded time, stillness and danger. It was quickly forgotten once its practical usefulness had passed, but, as Mr. Eliot's poem says, "The river is within us. . . ."

4

In form and style *Huckleberry Finn* is an almost perfect work. Only one mistake has ever been charged against it, that it concludes with Tom Sawyer's elaborate, too elaborate, game of Jim's escape. Certainly this episode is too long—in the original draft it was much longer—and certainly it is a falling-off, as almost anything would have to be, from the incidents of the river. Yet it has a certain formal aptness—like, say, that of the Turkish initiation which brings Molière's *Le Bourgeois Gentilhomme* to its close. It is a rather mechanical development of an idea, and yet some device is needed to permit Huck to return to his anonymity, to give up the role of hero, to fall into the background which he prefers, for he is modest in all things and could not well endure the attention and glamour which attend a hero at a book's end. For this purpose nothing could serve better than the mind of Tom Sawyer with its literary furnishings, its conscious romantic desire for experience and the hero's part, and its ingenious schematization of life to achieve that aim.

The form of the book is based on the simplest of all novel-forms, the so-called picaresque novel, or novel of the road, which strings its incidents on the line of the hero's travels. But, as Pascal says, "rivers are roads that move," and the movement of the road in its own mysterious life transmutes the primitive simplicity of the form: the road itself is the greatest character in this novel of the road, and the hero's departures from the river and his returns to it compose a subtle and significant pattern. The linear simplicity of the picaresque novel is further modified by the story's having a clear dramatic organization: it has a beginning, a middle and an end, and a mounting suspense of interest.

As for the style of the book, it is not less than definitive in American literature. The prose of *Huckleberry Finn* established for written prose the virtues of American colloquial speech. This has nothing to do with pronunciation or grammar. It has something to do with ease and freedom in the use of language. Most of all it has to do with the structure of the sentence, which is simple, direct, and fluent, maintaining the rhythm of the word-groups of speech and the intonations of the speaking voice.

In the matter of language, American literature had a special problem. The young nation was inclined to think that the mark of the truly literary product was a grandiosity and elegance not to be found in the common speech. It therefore encouraged a greater breach between its vernacular and its literary language than, say, English literature of the same period ever allowed. This accounts for the hollow ring one now and then hears even in the work of our best writers in the first half of the last century. English writers of equal stature would never have made the lapses into rhetorical excess that are common in Cooper and Poe and that are to be found even in Melville and Hawthorne.

Yet at the same time that the language of ambitious literature was high and thus always in danger of falseness, the American reader was keenly interested in the actualities of daily speech. No literature, indeed, was ever so taken up with matters of speech as ours was. "Dialect," which attracted even our serious writers, was the accepted common ground of our popular humorous writing. Nothing in social life seemed so remarkable as the different forms which speech could take—the brogue of the immigrant Irish or the mispronunciation of the German, the "affectation" of the English, the reputed precision of the Bostonian, the legendary twang of the Yankee farmer, and the drawl of the Pike County man. Mark Twain, of course, was in the tradition of humor that exploited this interest, and no one could play with it nearly so well. Although today the carefully spelled-out dialects of nineteenth-century American humor are likely to seem dull enough, the subtle variations of speech of *Huckleberry Finn*, of which Mark Twain was justly proud, are still part of the liveliness and flavor of the book.

Out of his knowledge of the actual speech of America Mark Twain forged a classic prose. The adjective may seem a strange one, yet it is apt. Forget the misspellings and the faults of grammar, and the prose will be seen to move with the greatest simplicity, directness, lucidity, and grace. These qualities are by no means accidental. Mark Twain, who read widely, was passionately interested in the problems of style; the mark of the strictest literary sensibility is everywhere to be found in the prose of *Huckleberry Finn*.

It is this prose that Ernest Hemingway had chiefly in mind when he said that "all modern American literature comes from one book by Mark Twain called *Huckleberry Finn*." Hemingway's own prose stems from it directly and consciously; so does the prose of the two modern writers who most influenced Hemingway's early style, Gertrude Stein and Sherwood Anderson (although neither of them could maintain the robust purity of their model); so, too, does the best of William Faulkner's prose, which, like Mark Twain's own, reinforces the colloquial tradition with the literary tradition. Indeed, it may be said that almost every contemporary writer who deals conscientiously with the problems and possibility of prose must feel, directly or indirectly, the influence of Mark Twain. He is the master of the style that escapes the fixity of the printed page, that sounds in our ears with the immediacy of the heard voice, the very voice of unpretentious truth.

T. S. ELIOT

[An Introduction to *Huckleberry Finn*]†

The Adventures of Huckleberry Finn is the only one of Mark Twain's various books which can be called a masterpiece. I do not suggest that it is his only book of permanent interest; but it is the only one in which his genius is completely realized, and the only one which creates its own category. There are pages in *Tom Sawyer* and in *Life on the Mississippi* which are, within their limits, as good as anything with which one can compare them in *Huckleberry Finn*; and in other books there are drolleries just as good of their kind. But when we find one book by a prolific author which is very much superior to all the rest, we look for the peculiar accident or concourse of accidents which made that book possible. In the writing of *Huckleberry Finn* Mark Twain had two elements which, when treated with his sensibility and his experience, formed a great book: these two are the Boy and the River.

Huckleberry Finn is, no doubt, a book which boys enjoy. I cannot speak from memory: I suspect that a fear on the part of my parents lest I should acquire a premature taste for tobacco, and perhaps other habits of the hero of the story, kept the book out of my way. But *Huckleberry Finn* does not fall into the category of juvenile fiction. The opinion of my parents that it was a book unsuitable for boys left me, for most of my life, under the impression that it was a book suitable only for boys. Therefore it was only a few years ago that I read for the first time, and in that order, *Tom Sawyer* and *Huckleberry Finn*.

Tom Sawyer did not prepare me for what I was to find its sequel to be. *Tom Sawyer* seems to me to be a boys' book, and a very good

† From T. S. Eliot's Introduction to *The Adventures of Huckleberry Finn*. The Cresset Press, London, 1950, pp. vii–xvi. Published in the U. S. by Chanticleer Press, New York, 1950. Reprinted by permission of T. S. Eliot.

one. The River and *the* Boy make their appearance in it; the narrative is good; and there is also a very good picture of society in a small mid-Western river town (for St. Petersburg is more Western than Southern) a hundred years ago. But the point of view of the narrator is that of an adult observing a boy. And Tom is the ordinary boy, though of quicker wits, and livelier imagination, than most. Tom is, I suppose, very much the boy that Mark Twain had been: he is remembered and described as he seemed to his elders, rather than created. Huck Finn, on the other hand, is the boy that Mark Twain still was, at the time of writing his adventures. We look at Tom as the smiling adult does: Huck we do not look at— we see the world through his eyes. The two boys are not merely different types; they were brought into existence by different processes. Hence in the second book their roles are altered. In the first book Huck is merely the humble friend—almost a variant of the traditional valet of comedy; and we see him as he is seen by the conventional respectable society to which Tom belongs, and of which, we feel sure, Tom will one day become an eminently respectable and conventional member. In the second book their nominal relationship remains the same; but here it is Tom who has the secondary role. The author was probably not conscious of this, when he wrote the first two chapters: *Huckleberry Finn* is not the kind of story in which the author knows, from the beginning, what is going to happen. Tom then disappears from our view; and when he returns, he has only two functions. The first is to provide a foil for Huck. Huck's persisting admiration for Tom only exhibits more clearly to our eyes the unique qualities of the former and the commonplaceness of the latter. Tom has the imagination of a lively boy who has read a good deal of romantic fiction: he might, of course, become a writer—he might become Mark Twain. Or rather, he might become the more commonplace aspect of Mark Twain. Huck has not imagination, in the sense in which Tom has it: he has, instead, vision. He sees the real world; and he does not judge it—he allows it to judge itself.

Tom Sawyer is an orphan. But he has his aunt; he has, as we learn later, other relatives; and he has the environment into which he fits. He is wholly a social being. When there is a secret band to be formed, it is Tom who organizes it and prescribes the rules. Huck Finn is alone: there is no more solitary character in fiction. The fact that he has a father only emphasizes his loneliness; and he views his father with a terrifying detachment. So we come to see Huck himself in the end as one of the permanent symbolic figures of fiction; not unworthy to take a place with Ulysses, Faust, Don Quixote, Don Juan, Hamlet and other great discoveries that man has made about himself.

It would seem that Mark Twain was a man who—perhaps like most of us—never became in all respects mature. We might even say that the adult side of him was boyish, and that only the boy in him, that was Huck Finn, was adult. As Tom Sawyer grown up, he wanted success and applause (Tom himself always needs an audience). He wanted prosperity, a happy domestic life of a conventional kind, universal approval, and fame. All of these things he obtained. As Huck Finn he was indifferent to all these things; and being composite of the two, Mark Twain both strove for them, and resented their violation of his integrity. Hence he became the humorist and even clown: with his gifts, a certain way to success, for everyone could enjoy his writings without the slightest feeling of discomfort, self-consciousness or self-criticism. And hence, on the other hand, his pessimism and misanthropy. To be a misanthrope is to be in some way divided; or it is a sign of an uneasy conscience. The pessimism which Mark Twain discharged into *The Man That Corrupted Hadleyburg* and *What is Man?* springs less from observation of society, than from his hatred of himself for allowing society to tempt and corrupt him and give him what he wanted. There is no wisdom in it. But all this personal problem has been diligently examined by Mr. Van Wyck Brooks; and it is not Mark Twain, but *Huckleberry Finn*, that is the subject of this introduction.

You cannot say that Huck himself is either a humorist or a misanthrope. He is the impassive observer: he does not interfere, and, as I have said, he does not judge. Many of the episodes that occur on the voyage down the river, after he is joined by the Duke and the King (whose fancies about themselves are akin to the kind of fancy that Tom Sawyer enjoys) are in themselves farcical; and if it were not for the presence of Huck as the reporter of them, they would be no more than farce. But, seen through the eyes of Huck, there is a deep human pathos in these scoundrels. On the other hand, the story of the feud between the Grangerfords and the Shepherdsons is a masterpiece in itself: yet Mark Twain could not have written it so, with that economy and restraint, with just the right details and no more, and leaving to the reader to make his own moral reflections, unless he had been writing in the person of Huck. And the *style* of the book, which is the style of Huck, is what makes it a far more convincing indictment of slavery than the sensationalist propaganda of *Uncle Tom's Cabin*. Huck is passive and impassive, apparently always the victim of events; and yet, in his acceptance of his world and of what it does to him and others, he is more powerful than his world, because he is more *aware* than any other person in it.

Repeated readings of the book only confirm and deepen one's admiration of the consistency and perfect adaptation of the writing.

This is a style which at the period, whether in America or in England, was an innovation, a new discovery in the English language. Other authors had achieved natural speech in relation to particular characters—Scott with characters talking Lowland Scots, Dickens with cockneys: but no one else had kept it up through the whole of a book. Thackeray's Yellowplush, impressive as he is, is an obvious artifice in comparison. In *Huckleberry Finn* there is no exaggeration of grammar or spelling or speech, there is no sentence or phrase to destroy the illusion that these are Huck's own words. It is not only in the way in which he tells his story, but in the details he remembers, that Huck is true to himself. There is, for instance, the description of the Grangerford interior as Huck sees it on his arrival; there is the list of the objects which Huck and Jim salvaged from the derelict house:

> "We got an old tin lantern, and a butcher-knife without any handle, and a bran-new Barlow knife worth two bits in any store, and a lot of tallow candles, and a tin candlestick, and a gourd, and a tin cup, and a ratty old bedquilt off the bed, and a reticule with needles and pins and beeswax and buttons and thread and all such truck in it, and a hatchet and some nails, and a fish-line as thick as my little finger, with some monstrous hooks on it, and a roll of buckskin, and a leather dog-collar, and a horseshoe, and some vials of medicine that didn't have no label on them; and just as we was leaving I found a tolerable good curry-comb, and Jim he found a ratty old fiddle-bow, and a wooden leg. The straps was broke off of it, but barring that, it was a good enough leg, though it was too long for me and not long enough for Jim, and we couldn't find the other one, though we hunted all round.
> "And so, take it all round, we made a good haul."

This is the sort of list that a boy reader should pore over with delight; but the paragraph performs other functions of which the boy reader would be unaware. It provides the right counterpoise to the horror of the wrecked house and the corpse; it has a grim precision which tells the reader all he needs to know about the way of life of the human derelicts who had used the house; and (especially the wooden leg, and the fruitless search for its mate) reminds us at the right moment of the kinship of mind and the sympathy between the boy outcast from society and the negro fugitive from the injustice of society.

Huck in fact would be incomplete without Jim, who is almost as notable a creation as Huck himself. Huck is the passive observer of men and events, Jim the submissive sufferer from them; and they are equal in dignity. There is no passage in which their relationship is brought out more clearly than the conclusion of the chapter in which, after the two have become separated in the fog, Huck in the canoe and Jim on the raft, Huck, in his impulse of boyish mischief, persuades Jim for a time that the latter had dreamt the whole episode.

". . . my heart wuz mos' broke bekase you wuz los', en I didn' k'yer no mo' what become er me en de raf'. En when I wake up en fine you back agin', all safe en soun', de tears come en I could a got down on my knees en kiss' yo' foot, I's so thankful. En all you wuz thinkin' 'bout wuz how you could make a fool uv ole Jim wid a lie. Dat truck dah is *trash*; en trash is what people is dat puts dirt on de head er dey fren's en makes 'em ashamed.' . . .

"It was fifteen minutes before I could work myself up to go and humble myself to a nigger—but I done it, and I warn't ever sorry for it afterwards, neither."

This passage has been quoted before; and if I quote it again, it is because I wish to elicit from it one meaning that is, I think, usually overlooked. What is obvious in it is the pathos and dignity of Jim, and this is moving enough; but what I find still more disturbing, and still more unusual in literature, is the pathos and dignity of the boy, when reminded so humbly and humiliatingly, that his position in the world is not that of other boys, entitled from time to time to a practical joke; but that he must bear, and bear alone, the responsibility of a man.

It is Huck who gives the book style. The River gives the book its form. But for the River, the book might be only a sequence of adventures with a happy ending. A river, a very big and powerful river, is the only natural force that can wholly determine the course of human peregrination. At sea, the wanderer may sail or be carried by winds and currents in one direction or another; a change of wind or tide may determine fortune. In the prairie, the direction of movement is more or less at the choice of the caravan; among mountains there will often be an alternative, a guess at the most likely pass. But the river with its strong, swift current is the dictator to the raft or to the steamboat. It is a treacherous and capricious dictator. At one season, it may move sluggishly in a channel so narrow that, encountering it for the first time at that point, one can hardly believe that it has travelled already for hundreds of miles, and has yet many hundreds of miles to go; at another season, it may obliterate the low Illinois shore to a horizon of water, while in its bed it runs with a speed such that no man or beast can survive in it. At such times, it carries down human bodies, cattle and houses. At least twice, at St. Louis, the western and the eastern shores have been separated by the fall of bridges, until the designer of the great Eads Bridge devised a structure which could resist the floods. In my own childhood, it was not unusual for the spring freshet to interrupt railway travel; and then the traveller to the East had to take steamboat from the levee up to Alton, at a higher level on the Illinois shore, before he could begin his rail journey. The river is never wholly chartable; it changes its pace, it shifts its channel, unaccountably; it may suddenly efface a sandbar, and throw up another bar where before was navigable water.

It is the River that controls the voyage of Huck and Jim; that will not let them land at Cairo, where Jim could have reached freedom; it is the River that separates them and deposits Huck for a time in the Grangerford household; the River that re-unites them, and then compels upon them the unwelcome company of the King and the Duke. Recurrently we are reminded of its presence and its power.

"When I woke up, I didn't know where I was for a minute. I set up and looked around, a little scared. Then I remembered. The river looked miles and miles across. The moon was so bright I could a counted the drift-logs that went a-slipping along, black and still, hundreds of yards out from shore. Everything was dead quiet, and it looked late, and *smelt* late. You know what I mean— I don't know the words to put it in.

"It was kind of solemn, drifting down the big still river, laying on our backs looking up at the stars, and we didn't ever feel like talking loud, and it warn't often that we laughed, only a little kind of a low chuckle. We had mighty good weather as a general thing, and nothing ever happened to us at all, that night, nor the next, nor the next.

"Every night we passed towns, some of them away up on black hillsides, nothing but just a shiny bed of lights, not a house could you see. The fifth night we passed St. Louis, and it was like the whole world lit up. In St. Petersburg they used to say there was twenty or thirty thousand people in St. Louis, but I never believed it till I see that wonderful spread of lights at two o'clock that still night. There warn't a sound there; everybody was asleep."

We come to understand the River by seeing it through the eyes of the Boy; but the Boy is also the spirit of the River. *Huckleberry Finn*, like other great works of imagination, can give to every reader whatever he is capable of taking from it. On the most superficial level of observation, Huck is convincing as a boy. On the same level, the picture of social life on the shores of the Mississippi a hundred years ago is, I feel sure, accurate. On any level, Mark Twain makes you see the River, as it is and was and always will be, more clearly than the author of any other description of a river known to me. But you do not merely see the River, you do not merely become acquainted with it through the senses: you experience the River. Mark Twain, in his later years of success and fame, referred to his early life as a steamboat pilot as the happiest he had known. With all allowance for the illusions of age, we can agree that those years were the years in which he was most fully alive. Certainly, but for his having practised that calling, earned his living by that profession, he would never have gained the understanding which his genius for expression communicates in this book. In the pilot's daily struggle with the River, in the satisfaction of activity, in the constant attention to the River's unpredictable vagaries, his consciousness was fully occupied, and he absorbed knowledge of which, as an artist, he later made use. There are, perhaps, only two ways in which a writer can acquire the understanding of environment which he can later turn to account: by having spent his childhood in that environment—that is, living in it at a period of life in which one experiences much more than one is aware of; and by having had to struggle for a livelihood in that environment—a livelihood bearing no direct relation to any intention of writing about it, of *using* it as literary material. Most of Joseph Conrad's understanding came to him in the latter way. Mark Twain knew the Mississippi in both ways: he had spent his childhood on its banks, and he had earned his living matching his wits against its currents.

Thus the River makes the book a great book. As with Conrad, we are continually reminded of the power and terror of Nature, and the isolation and feebleness of Man. Conrad remains always the European observer of the tropics, the white man's eye contemplating the Congo and its black gods. But Mark Twain is a native, and the River God is his God. It is as a native that he accepts the River God, and it is the subjection of Man that gives to Man his dignity. For without some kind of God, Man is not even very interesting.

Readers sometimes deplore the fact that the story descends to the level of *Tom Sawyer* from the moment that Tom himself re-appears. Such readers protest that the escapades invented by Tom, in the attempted "rescue" of Jim, are only a tedious development of themes with which we were already too familiar—even while admitting that the escapades themselves are very amusing, and some of the incidental observations memorable.[1] But it is right that the mood of the end of the book should bring us back to that of the beginning. Or, if this was not the right ending for the book, what ending would have been right?

In *Huckleberry Finn* Mark Twain wrote a much greater book than he could have known he was writing. Perhaps all great works of art mean much more than the author could have been aware of meaning: certainly, *Huckleberry Finn* is the one book of Mark Twain's which, as a whole, has this unconsciousness. So what seems to be the rightness, of reverting at the end of the book to the mood of *Tom Sawyer*, was perhaps unconscious art. For Huckleberry Finn,

1. *e.g.*, "*Jim* don't know anybody in China."

neither a tragic nor a happy ending would be suitable. No worldly success or social satisfaction, no domestic consummation would be worthy of him; a tragic end also would reduce him to the level of those whom we pity. Huck Finn must come from nowhere and be bound for nowhere. His is not the independence of the typical or symbolic American Pioneer, but the independence of the vagabond. His existence questions the values of America as much as the values of Europe; he is as much an affront to the "pioneer spirit" as he is to "business enterprise"; he is in a state of nature as detached as the state of the saint. In a busy world, he represents the loafer; in an acquisitive and competitive world, he insists on living from hand to mouth. He could not be exhibited in any amorous encounters or engagements, in any of the juvenile affections which are appropriate to Tom Sawyer. He belongs neither to the Sunday School nor to the Reformatory. He has no beginning and no end. Hence, he can only disappear; and his disappearance can only be accomplished by bringing forward another performer to obscure the disappearance in a cloud of whimsicalities.

Like Huckleberry Finn, the River itself has no beginning or end. In its beginning, it is not yet the River; in its end, it is no longer the River. What we call its headwaters is only a selection from among the innumerable sources which flow together to compose it. At what point in its course does the Mississippi become what the Mississippi *means?* It is both one and many; it is the Mississippi of this book only after its union with the Big Muddy—the Missouri; it derives some of its character from the Ohio, the Tennessee and other confluents. And at the end it merely disappears among its deltas: it is no longer there, but it is still where it was, hundreds of miles to the North. The River cannot tolerate any design, to a story which is its story, that might interfere with its dominance. Things must merely happen, here and there, to the people who live along its shores or who commit themselves to its current. And it is as impossible for Huck as for the River to have a beginning or end —a *career.* So the book has the right, the only possible concluding sentence. I do not think that any book ever written ends more certainly with the right words:

"But I reckon I got to light out for the Territory ahead of the rest, because Aunt Sally she's going to adopt me and civilize me, and I can't stand it. I been there before."

The Problem of the Ending

LEO MARX

Mr. Eliot, Mr. Trilling, and *Huckleberry Finn*†

In the losing battle that the plot fights with the characters, it often takes a cowardly revenge. Nearly all novels are feeble at the end. This is because the plot requires to be wound up. Why is this necessary? Why is there not a convention which allows a novelist to stop as soon as he feels muddled or bored? Alas, he has to round things off, and usually the characters go dead while he is at work, and our final impression of them is through deadness.—E. M. Forster

The *Adventures of Huckleberry Finn* has not always occupied its present high place in the canon of American literature. When it was first published in 1885, the book disturbed and offended many reviewers, particularly spokesmen for the genteel tradition.[1] In fact, a fairly accurate inventory of the narrow standards of such critics might be made simply by listing epithets they applied to Clemens' novel. They called it vulgar, rough, inelegant, irreverent, coarse, semi-obscene, trashy and vicious.[2] So much for them. Today (we like to think) we know the true worth of the book. Everyone now agrees that *Huckleberry Finn* is a masterpiece: it is probably the one book in our literature about which highbrows and lowbrows can agree. Our most serious critics praise it. Nevertheless, a close look at what two of the best among them have recently written will likewise reveal, I believe, serious weaknesses in current criticism. Today the problem of evaluating the book is as much obscured by unqualified praise as it once was by parochial hostility.

I have in mind essays by Lionel Trilling and T. S. Eliot.[3] Both praise the book, but in praising it both feel obligated to say some-

† Reprinted from *The American Scholar*, Vol. 22, No. 4 (Autumn 1953), pp. 423–40. Copyright © 1953 by the United Chapters of Phi Beta Kappa. By permission of the publishers.

1. I use the term "genteel tradition" as George Santayana characterized it in his famous address "The Genteel Tradition in American Philosophy," first delivered in 1911 and published the following year in his *Winds of Doctrine*. Santayana described the genteel tradition as an "old mentality" inherited from Europe. It consists of the various dilutions of Christian theology and morality, as in transcendentalism—a fastidious and stale philosophy of life no longer relevant to the thought and activities of the United States. "America," he said, "is a young country with an old mentality." (Later references to Santayana also refer to this essay.)

2. For an account of the first reviews, see A. L. Vogelback, "The Publication and Reception of *Huckleberry Finn* in America," *American Literature*, XI (November, 1939), 260–272.

3. Mr. Eliot's essay is the introduction to the edition of *Huckleberry Finn* published by Chanticleer Press, New York, 1950. Mr. Trilling's is the introduction to an edition of the novel published by Rinehart, New York, 1948, and later reprinted in his *The Liberal Imagination*, Viking, New York, 1950.

thing in justification of what so many readers have felt to be its great flaw: the disappointing "ending," the episode which begins when Huck arrives at the Phelps place and Tom Sawyer reappears. There are good reasons why Mr. Trilling and Mr. Eliot should feel the need to face this issue. From the point of view of scope alone, more is involved than the mere "ending"; the episode comprises almost one-fifth of the text. The problem, in any case, is unavoidable. I have discussed *Huckleberry Finn* in courses with hundreds of college students, and I have found only a handful who did not confess their dissatisfaction with the extravagant mock rescue of Nigger Jim and the denouement itself. The same question always comes up: "What went wrong with Twain's novel?" Even Bernard De Voto, whose wholehearted commitment to Clemens' genius is well known, has said of the ending that "in the whole reach of the English novel there is no more abrupt or more chilling descent."[4] Mr. Trilling and Mr. Eliot do not agree. They both attempt, and on similar grounds, to explain and defend the conclusion.

Of the two, Mr. Trilling makes the more moderate claim for Clemens' novel. He does admit that there is a "falling off" at the end; nevertheless he supports the episode as having "a certain formal aptness." Mr. Eliot's approval is without serious qualification. He allows no objections, asserts that "it is right that the mood of the end of the book should bring us back to the beginning." I mean later to discuss their views in some detail, but here it is only necessary to note that both critics see the problem as one of form. And so it is. Like many questions of form in literature, however, this one is not finally separable from a question of "content," of value, or, if you will, of moral insight. To bring *Huckleberry Finn* to a satisfactory close, Clemens had to do more than find a neat device for ending a story. His problem, though it may never have occurred to him, was to invent an action capable of placing in focus the meaning of the journey down the Mississippi.

I believe that the ending of *Huckleberry Finn* makes so many readers uneasy because they rightly sense that it jeopardizes the significance of the entire novel. To take seriously what happens at the Phelps farm is to take lightly the entire downstream journey. What is the meaning of the journey? With this question all discussion of *Huckleberry Finn* must begin. It is true that the voyage down the river has many aspects of a boy's idyl. We owe much of its hold upon our imagination to the enchanting image of the raft's unhurried drift with the current. The leisure, the absence of constraint, the beauty of the river—all these things delight us. "It's lovely to live on a raft." And the multitudinous life of the great valley we see through Huck's eyes has a fascination of its own. Then, of

4. *Mark Twain at Work* (Cambridge, 1942), p 92.

course, there is humor—laughter so spontaneous, so free of bitterness present almost everywhere in American humor that readers often forget how grim a spectacle of human existence Huck contemplates. Humor in this novel flows from a bright joy of life as remote from our world as living on a raft.

Yet along with the idyllic and the epical and the funny in *Huckleberry Finn,* there is a coil of meaning which does for the disparate elements of the novel what a spring does for a watch. The meaning is not in the least obscure. It is made explicit again and again. The very words with which Clemens launches Huck and Jim upon their voyage indicate that theirs is not a boy's lark but a quest for freedom. From the electrifying moment when Huck comes back to Jackson's Island and rouses Jim with the news that a search party is on the way, we are meant to believe that Huck is enlisted in the cause of freedom. "Git up and hump yourself, Jim!" he cries. "There ain't a minute to lose. They're after us!" What particularly counts here is the *us.* No one is after Huck; no one but Jim knows he is alive. In that small word Clemens compresses the exhilarating power of Huck's instinctive humanity. His unpremeditated identification with Jim's flight from slavery is an unforgettable moment in American experience, and it may be said at once that any culmination of the journey which detracts from the urgency and dignity with which it begins will necessarily be unsatisfactory. Huck realizes this himself, and says so when, much later, he comes back to the raft after discovering that the Duke and the King have sold Jim:

"After all this long journey . . . here it was all come to nothing, everything all busted up and ruined, because they could have the heart to serve Jim such a trick as that, and make him a slave again all his life, and amongst strangers, too, for forty dirty dollars."

Huck knows that the journey will have been a failure unless it takes Jim to freedom. It is true that we do discover, in the end, that Jim is free, but we also find out that the journey was not the means by which he finally reached freedom.

The most obvious thing wrong with the end, then, is the flimsy contrivance by which Clemens frees Jim. In the end we not only discover that Jim has been a free man for two months, but that his freedom has been granted by old Miss Watson. If this were only a mechanical device for terminating the action, it might not call for much comment. But it is more than that: it is a significant clue to the import of the last ten chapters. Remember who Miss Watson is. She is the Widow's sister whom Huck introduces in the first pages of the novel. It is she who keeps "pecking" at Huck, who tries to teach him to spell and to pray and to keep his feet off the furniture. She is an ardent proselytizer for piety and good manners, and her greed provides the occasion for the journey in the first place. She is Jim's owner, and he decides to flee only when he realizes that she is about to break her word (she cannot resist a slave trader's offer of eight hundred dollars) and sell him down the river away from his family.

→ Miss Watson, in short, is the Enemy. If we except a predilection for physical violence, she exhibits all the outstanding traits of the valley society. She pronounces the polite lies of civilization that suffocate Huck's spirit. The freedom which Jim seeks, and which Huck and Jim temporarily enjoy aboard the raft, is accordingly freedom *from* everything for which Miss Watson stands. Indeed, the very intensity of the novel derives from the discordance between the aspirations of the fugitives and the respectable code for which she is a spokesman. Therefore, her regeneration, of which the death-bed freeing of Jim is the unconvincing sign, hints a resolution of the novel's essential conflict. Perhaps because this device most transparently reveals that shift in point of view which he could not avoid, and which is less easily discerned elsewhere in the concluding chapters, Clemens plays it down. He makes little attempt to account for Miss Watson's change of heart, a change particularly surprising in view of Jim's brazen escape. Had Clemens given this episode dramatic emphasis appropriate to its function, Miss Watson's bestowal of freedom upon Jim would have proclaimed what the rest of the ending actually accomplishes—a vindication of persons and attitudes Huck and Jim had symbolically repudiated when they set forth downstream.

It may be said, and with some justice, that a reading of the ending as a virtual reversal of meanings implicit in the rest of the novel misses the point—that I have taken the final episode too seriously. I agree that Clemens certainly did not intend us to read it so solemnly. The ending, one might contend, is simply a burlesque upon Tom's taste for literary romance. Surely the tone of the episode is familiar to readers of Mark Twain. The preposterous monkey business attendant upon Jim's "rescue," the careless improvisation, the nonchalant disregard for common-sense plausibility—all these things should not surprise readers of Twain or any low comedy in the tradition of "Western humor." However, the trouble is, first, that the ending hardly comes off as burlesque: it is *too* fanciful, *too* extravagant; and it is tedious. For example, to provide a "gaudy" atmosphere for the escape, Huck and Tom catch a couple of dozen snakes. Then the snakes escape.

"No, there warn't no real scarcity of snakes about the house for a considerable spell. You'd see them dripping from the rafters and places every now and then; and they generly landed in your plate, or down the back of your neck. . . ."

Even if this were *good* burlesque, which it is not, what is it doing here? It is out of keeping; the slapstick tone jars with the underlying seriousness of the voyage.

Huckleberry Finn is a masterpiece because it brings Western humor to perfection and yet transcends the narrow limits of its conventions. But the ending does not. During the final extravaganza we are forced to put aside many of the mature emotions evoked earlier by the vivid rendering of Jim's fear of capture, the tenderness of Huck's and Jim's regard for each other, and Huck's excruciating moments of wavering between honesty and respectability. None of these emotions are called forth by the anticlimactic final sequence. I do not mean to suggest that the inclusion of low comedy per se is a flaw in *Huckleberry Finn*. One does not object to the shenanigans of the rogues; there is ample precedent for the place of extravagant humor even in works of high seriousness. But here the case differs from most which come to mind: the major characters themselves are forced to play low comedy roles. Moreover, the most serious motive in the novel, Jim's yearning for freedom, is made the object of nonsense. The conclusion, in short, is farce, but the rest of the novel is not.

That Clemens reverts in the end to the conventional manner of Western low comedy is most evident in what happens to the principals. Huck and Jim become comic characters; that is a much more serious ground for dissatisfaction than the unexplained regeneration of Miss Watson. Remember that Huck has grown in stature throughout the journey. By the time he arrives at the Phelps place, he is not the boy who had been playing robbers with Tom's gang in St. Petersburg the summer before. All he has seen and felt since he parted from Tom has deepened his knowledge of human nature and of himself. Clemens makes a point of Huck's development in two scenes which occur just before he meets Tom again. The first describes Huck's final capitulation to his own sense of right and wrong: "All right, then, I'll go to Hell." This is the climactic moment in the ripening of his self-knowledge. Shortly afterward, when he comes upon a mob riding the Duke and the King out of town on a rail, we are given his most memorable insight into the nature of man. Although these rogues had subjected Huck to every indignity, what he sees provokes this celebrated comment:

"Well, it made me sick to see it; and I was sorry for them poor pitiful rascals, it seemed like I couldn't ever feel any hardness against them any more in the world. It was a dreadful thing to see. Human beings can be awful cruel to one another."

The sign of Huck's maturity here is neither the compassion nor the skepticism, for both had been marks of his personality from the first. Rather, the special quality of these reflections is the extraordinary combination of the two, a mature blending of his instinctive suspicion of human motives with his capacity for pity.

But at this point Tom reappears. Soon Huck has fallen almost completely under his sway once more, and we are asked to believe that the boy who felt pity for the rogues is now capable of making Jim's capture the occasion for a game. He becomes Tom's helpless accomplice, submissive and gullible. No wonder that Clemens has Huck remark, when Huck first realizes Aunt Sally has mistaken him for Tom, that "it was like being born again." Exactly. In the end, Huck regresses to the subordinate role in which he had first appeared in *The Adventures of Tom Sawyer*. Most of those traits which made him so appealing a hero now disappear. He had never, for example, found pain or misfortune amusing. At the circus, when a clown disguised as a drunk took a precarious ride on a prancing horse, the crowd loved the excitement and danger; "it warn't funny to me, though," said Huck. But now, in the end, he submits in awe to Tom's notion of what is amusing. To satisfy Tom's hunger for adventure he makes himself a party to sport which aggravates Jim's misery.

It should be added at once that Jim doesn't mind too much. The fact is that he has undergone a similar transformation. On the raft he was an individual, man enough to denounce Huck when Huck made him the victim of a practical joke. In the closing episode, however, we lose sight of Jim in the maze of farcical invention. He ceases to be a man. He allows Huck and "Mars Tom" to fill his hut with rats and snakes, "and every time a rat bit Jim he would get up and write a line in his journal whilst the ink was fresh." This creature who bleeds ink and feels no pain is something less than human. He has been made over in the image of a flat stereotype: the submissive stage-Negro. These antics divest Jim, as well as Huck, of much of his dignity and individuality.[5]

What I have been saying is that the flimsy devices of plot, the discordant farcical tone, and the disintegration of the major characters all betray the failure of the ending. These are not aspects merely of form in a technical sense, but of meaning. For that matter. I would maintain that this book has little or no formal unity independent of the joint purpose of Huck and Jim. What components of the novel, we may ask, provide the continuity which links one adventure with another? The most important is the unifying consciousness of Huck, the narrator. and the fact that we follow the same principals through the entire string of adventures. Events, moreover, occur in a temporal sequence. Then there is the river; after each adventure Huck and Jim return to the raft and the river. Both Mr. Trilling and Mr. Eliot speak eloquently of the river as a

---

5. For these observations on the transformation of Jim in the closing episodes, I am indebted to the excellent unpublished essay by Mr. Chadwick Hansen on the subject of Clemens and Western humor.

source of unity, and they refer to the river as a god. Mr. Trilling says that Huck is "the servant of the river-god." Mr. Eliot puts it this way: "The River gives the book its form. But for the River, the book might be only a sequence of adventures with a happy ending." This seems to me an extravagant view of the function of the neutral agency of the river. Clemens had a knowledgeable respect for the Mississippi and, without sanctifying it, was able to provide excellent reasons for Huck's and Jim's intense relation with it. It is a source of food and beauty and terror and serenity of mind. But above all, it provides motion; it is the means by which Huck and Jim move away from a menacing civilization. They return to the river to continue their journey. The river cannot, does not, supply purpose. That purpose is a facet of their consciousness, and without the motive of escape from society, *Huckleberry Finn* would indeed "be only a sequence of adventures." Mr. Eliot's remark indicates how lightly he takes the quest for freedom. His somewhat fanciful exaggeration of the river's role is of a piece with his neglect of the theme at the novel's center.

That theme is heightened by the juxtaposition of sharp images of contrasting social orders: the microcosmic community Huck and Jim establish aboard the raft and the actual society which exists along the Mississippi's banks. The two are separated by the river, the road to freedom upon which Huck and Jim must travel. Huck tells us what the river means to them when, after the Wilks episode, he and Jim once again shove their raft into the current: "It *did* seem so good to be free again and all by ourselves on the big river, and nobody to bother us." The river is indifferent. But its sphere is relatively uncontaminated by the civilization they flee, and so the river allows Huck and Jim some measure of freedom at once, the moment they set foot on Jackson's Island or the raft. Only on the island and the raft do they have a chance to practice that idea of brotherhood to which they are devoted. "Other places do seem so cramped and smothery," Huck explains, "but a raft don't. You feel mighty free and easy and comfortable on a raft." The main thing is freedom.

On the raft the escaped slave and the white boy try to practice their code: "What you want, above all things, on a raft, is for everybody to be satisfied, and feel right and kind towards the others." This human credo constitutes the paramount affirmation of *The Adventures of Huckleberry Finn*, and it obliquely aims a devastating criticism at the existing social order. It is a creed which Huck and Jim bring to the river. It neither emanates from nature nor is it addressed to nature. Therefore I do not see that it means much to talk about the river as a god in this novel. The river's connection with this high aspiration for man is that it provides a means of escape, a place where the code can be tested. The truly profound meanings of the novel are generated by the impingement of the actual world of slavery, feuds, lynching, murder, and a spurious Christian morality upon the ideal of the raft. The result is a tension which somehow demands release in the novel's ending.

But Clemens was unable to effect this release and at the same time control the central theme. The unhappy truth about the ending of *Huckleberry Finn* is that the author, having revealed the tawdry nature of the culture of the great valley, yielded to its essential complacency. The general tenor of the closing scenes, to which the token regeneration of Miss Watson is merely one superficial clue, amounts to just that. In fact, this entire reading of *Huckleberry Finn* merely confirms the brilliant insight of George Santayana, who many years ago spoke of American humorists, of whom he considered Mark Twain an outstanding representative, as having only "half escaped" the genteel tradition. Santayana meant that men like Clemens were able to "point to what contradicts it in the facts; but not in order to abandon the genteel tradition, for they have nothing solid to put in its place." This seems to me the real key to the failure of *Huckleberry Finn*. Clemens had presented the contrast between the two social orders but could not, or would not, accept the tragic fact that the one he had rejected was an image of solid reality and the other an ecstatic dream. Instead he gives us the cozy reunion with Aunt Polly in a scene fairly bursting with approbation of the entire family, the Phelpses included.

Like Miss Watson, the Phelpses are almost perfect specimens of the dominant culture. They are kind to their friends and relatives; they have no taste for violence; they are people capable of devoting themselves to their spectacular dinners while they keep Jim locked in the little hut down by the ash hopper, with its lone window boarded up. (Of course Aunt Sally visits Jim to see if he is "comfortable," and Uncle Silas comes in "to pray with him.") These people, with their comfortable Sunday-dinner conviviality and the runaway slave padlocked nearby, are reminiscent of those solid German citizens we have heard about in our time who tried to maintain a similarly *gemütlich* way of life within virtual earshot of Buchenwald. I do not mean to imply that Clemens was unaware of the shabby morality of such people. After the abortive escape of Jim, when Tom asks about him, Aunt Sally replies: "Him? . . . the runaway nigger? . . . They've got him back, safe and sound, and he's in the cabin again, on bread and water, and loaded down with chains, till he's claimed or sold!" Clemens understood people like the Phelpses, but nevertheless he was forced to rely upon them to provide his happy ending. The satisfactory outcome of Jim's quest for freedom must be attributed to the benevolence of the very people whose inhumanity first made it necessary.

But to return to the contention of Mr. Trilling and Mr. Eliot that the ending is more or less satisfactory after all. As I have said, Mr. Trilling approves of the "formal aptness" of the conclusion. He says that "some device is needed to permit Huck to return to his anonymity, to give up the role of hero," and that therefore "nothing could serve better than the mind of Tom Sawyer with its literary furnishings, its conscious romantic desire for experience and the hero's part, and its ingenious schematization of life. . . ." Though more detailed, this is essentially akin to Mr. Eliot's blunt assertion that "it is right that the mood at the end of the book should bring us back to that of the beginning." I submit that it is wrong for the end of the book to bring us back to that mood. The mood of the beginning of *Huckleberry Finn* is the mood of Huck's attempt to accommodate himself to the ways of St. Petersburg. It is the mood of the end of *The Adventures of Tom Sawyer*, when the boys had been acclaimed heroes, and when Huck was accepted as a candidate for respectability. That is the state in which we find him at the beginning of *Huckleberry Finn*. But Huck cannot stand the new way of life, and his mood gradually shifts to the mood of rebellion which dominates the novel until he meets Tom again. At first, in the second chapter, we see him still eager to be accepted by the nice boys of the town. Tom leads the gang in re-enacting adventures he has culled from books, but gradually Huck's pragmatic turn of mind gets him in trouble. He has little tolerance for Tom's brand of make-believe. He irritates Tom. Tom calls him a "numbskull," and finally Huck throws up the whole business:

"So then I judged that all that stuff was only just one of Tom Sawyer's lies. I reckoned he believed in the A-rabs and the elephants, but as for me I think different. It had all the marks of a Sunday school."

With this statement, which ends the third chapter, Huck parts company with Tom. The fact is that Huck has rejected Tom's romanticizing of experience; moreover, he has rejected it as part of the larger pattern of society's make-believe, typified by Sunday school. But if he cannot accept Tom's harmless fantasies about the A-rabs, how are we to believe that a year later Huck is capable of awestruck submission to the far more extravagant fantasies with which Tom invests the mock rescue of Jim?

After Huck's escape from his "pap," the drift of the action, like that of the Mississippi's current, is *away* from St. Petersburg. Huck leaves Tom and the A-rabs behind, along with the Widow, Miss Watson, and all the pseudo-religious ritual in which nice boys must partake. The return, in the end, to the mood of the beginning therefore means defeat—Huck's defeat; to return to that mood *joyously* is to portray defeat in the guise of victory.

Mr. Eliot and Mr. Trilling deny this. The overriding consideration for them is form—form which seems largely to mean symmetry of structure. It is fitting, Mr. Eliot maintains, that the book should come full circle and bring Huck once more under Tom's sway. Why? Because it begins that way. But it seems to me that such structural unity is *imposed* upon the novel, and therefore is meretricious. It is a jerry-built structure, achieved only by sacrifice of characters and theme. Here the controlling principle of form apparently is unity, but unfortunately a unity much too superficially conceived. Structure, after all, is only one element—indeed, one of the more mechanical elements—of unity. A unified work must surely manifest coherence of meaning and clear development of theme, yet the ending of *Huckleberry Finn* blurs both. The eagerness of Mr. Eliot and Mr. Trilling to justify the ending is symptomatic of that absolutist impulse of our critics to find reasons, once a work has been admitted to the highest canon of literary reputability, for admiring every bit of it.

What is perhaps most striking about these judgments of Mr. Eliot's and Mr. Trilling's is that they are so patently out of harmony with the basic standards of both critics. For one thing, both men hold far more complex ideas of the nature of literary unity than their comments upon *Huckleberry Finn* would suggest. For another, both critics are essentially moralists, yet here we find them turning away from a moral issue in order to praise a dubious structural unity. Their efforts to explain away the flaw in Clemens' novel suffer from a certain narrowness surprising to anyone who knows their work. These facts suggest that we may be in the presence of a tendency in contemporary criticism which the critics themselves do not fully recognize.

Is there an explanation? How does it happen that two of our most respected critics should seem to treat so lightly the glaring lapse of moral imagination in *Huckleberry Finn?* Perhaps—and I stress the conjectural nature of what I am saying—perhaps the kind of moral issue raised by *Huckleberry Finn* is not the kind of moral issue to which today's criticism readily addresses itself. Today our critics, no less than our novelists and poets, are most sensitively attuned to moral problems which arise in the sphere of individual behavior. They are deeply aware of sin, of individual infractions of our culture's Christian ethic. But my impression is that they are, possibly because of the strength of the reaction against the mechanical sociological criticism of the thirties, less sensitive to questions of what might be called social or political morality.

By social or political morality I refer to the values implicit in a social system, values which may be quite distinct from the personal morality of any given individual within the society. Now *The Adventures of Huckleberry Finn*, like all novels, deals with the behavior of individuals. But one mark of Clemens' greatness is his deft presentation of the disparity between what people do when they behave as individuals and what they do when forced into roles imposed upon them by society. Take, for example, Aunt Sally and Uncle Silas Phelps, who consider themselves Christians, who are by impulse generous and humane, but who happen also to be staunch upholders of certain degrading and inhuman social institutions. When they are confronted with an escaped slave, the imperatives of social morality outweigh all pious professions.

The conflict between what people think they stand for and what social pressure forces them to do is central to the novel. It is present to the mind of Huck and, indeed, accounts for his most serious inner conflicts. He knows how he feels about Jim, but he also knows what he is expected to do about Jim. This division within his mind corresponds to the division of the novel's moral terrain into the areas represented by the raft on the one hand and society on the other. His victory over his "yaller dog" conscience therefore assumes heroic size: it is a victory over the prevailing morality. But the last fifth of the novel has the effect of diminishing the importance and uniqueness of Huck's victory. We are asked to assume that somehow freedom can be achieved in spite of the crippling power of what I have called the social morality. Consequently the less importance we attach to that force as it operates in the novel, the more acceptable the ending becomes.

Moreover, the idea of freedom, which Mr. Eliot and Mr. Trilling seem to slight, takes on its full significance only when we acknowledge the power which society exerts over the minds of men in the world of *Huckleberry Finn*. For freedom in this book specifically means freedom from society and its imperatives. This is not the traditional Christian conception of freedom. Huck and Jim seek freedom not from a burden of individual guilt and sin, but from social constraint. That is to say, evil in *Huckleberry Finn* is the product of civilization, and if this is indicative of Clemens' rather too simple view of human nature, nevertheless the fact is that Huck, when he can divest himself of the taint of social conditioning (as in the incantatory account of sunrise on the river), is entirely free of anxiety and guilt. The only guilt he actually knows arises from infractions of a social code. (The guilt he feels after playing the prank on Jim stems from his betrayal of the law of the raft.) Huck's and Jim's creed is secular. Its object is harmony among men, and so Huck is not much concerned with his own salvation. He repeatedly renounces prayer in favor of pragmatic solutions to his problems. In other words, the central insights of the novel belong to the tradition of the Enlightenment. The meaning of the quest itself is hardly reconcilable with that conception of human nature embodied in the myth of original sin. In view of the current fashion of reaffirming man's innate depravity, it is perhaps not surprising to find the virtues of *Huckleberry Finn* attributed not to its meaning but to its form.

But "if this was not the right ending for the book," Mr. Eliot asks, "what ending would have been right?" Although this question places the critic in an awkward position (he is not always equipped to rewrite what he criticizes), there are some things which may justifiably be said about the "right" ending of *Huckleberry Finn*. It may be legitimate, even if presumptuous, to indicate certain conditions which a hypothetical ending would have to satisfy if it were to be congruent with the rest of the novel. If the conclusion is not to be something merely tacked on to close the action, then its broad outline must be immanent in the body of the work.

It is surely reasonable to ask that the conclusion provide a plausible outcome to the quest. Yet freedom, in the ecstatic sense that Huck and Jim knew it aboard the raft, was hardly to be had in the Mississippi Valley in the 1840's, or, for that matter, in any other known human society. A satisfactory ending would inevitably cause the reader some frustration. That Clemens felt such disappointment to be inevitable is borne out by an examination of the novel's clear, if unconscious, symbolic pattern. Consider, for instance, the inferences to be drawn from the book's geography. The river, to whose current Huck and Jim entrust themselves, actually carries them to the heart of slave territory. Once the raft passes Cairo, the quest is virtually doomed. Until the steamboat smashes the raft, we are kept in a state of anxiety about Jim's escape. (It may be significant that at this point Clemens found himself unable to continue work on the manuscript, and put it aside for several years.) Beyond Cairo, Clemens allows the intensity of that anxiety to diminish, and it is probably no accident that the fainter it becomes, the more he falls back upon the devices of low comedy. Huck and Jim make no serious effort to turn north, and there are times (during the Wilks episode) when Clemens allows Huck to forget all about Jim. It is as if the author, anticipating the dilemma he had finally to face, instinctively dissipated the power of his major theme.

Consider, too, the circumscribed nature of the raft as a means of moving toward freedom. The raft lacks power and maneuverability. It can only move easily with the current—southward into slave country. Nor can it evade the mechanized power of the steamboat. These impotencies of the raft correspond to the innocent helplessness of its occupants. Unresisted, the rogues invade and take over the raft. Though it is the symbolic locus of the novel's central affirmations, the raft provides an uncertain and indeed precarious mode of traveling toward freedom. This seems another confirmation of Santayana's perception. To say that Clemens only half escaped the genteel tradition is not to say that he failed to note any of the creed's inadequacies, but rather that he had "nothing solid" to put in its place. The raft patently was not capable of carrying the burden of hope Clemens placed upon it.[6] (Whether this is to be attributed to the nature of his vision or to the actual state of American society in the nineteenth century is another interesting question.) In any case, the geography of the novel, the raft's powerlessness, the goodness and vulnerability of Huck and Jim, all prefigure a conclusion quite different in tone from that which Clemens gave us. These facts constitute what Hart Crane might have called the novel's "logic of metaphor," and this logic—probably inadvertent—actually takes us to the underlying meaning of *The Adventures of Huckleberry Finn*. Through the symbols we reach a truth which the ending obscures: the quest cannot succeed.

Fortunately, Clemens broke through to this truth in the novel's last sentences:

"But I reckon I got to light out for the territory ahead of the rest, because Aunt Sally she's going to adopt me and civilize me, and I can't stand it. I been there before."

Mr. Eliot properly praises this as "the only possible concluding sentence." But one sentence can hardly be advanced, as Mr. Eliot advances this one, to support the rightness of ten chapters. Moreover, if this sentence is right, then the rest of the conclusion is wrong, for its meaning clashes with that of the final burlesque. Huck's decision to go west ahead of the inescapable advance of civilization is a confession of defeat. It means that the raft is to be abandoned. On the other hand, the jubilation of the family reunion and the proclaiming of Jim's freedom create a quite different mood. The tone, except for these last words, is one of unclouded success. I believe this is the source of the almost universal dissatisfaction with the conclusion. One can hardly forget that a bloody civil war did not resolve the issue.

Should Clemens have made Huck a tragic hero? Both Mr. Eliot and Mr. Trilling argue that that would have been a mistake, and they are very probably correct. But between the ending as we have it and tragedy in the fullest sense, there was vast room for invention.

6. Gladys Bellamy (*Mark Twain as a Literary Artist*, Norman, Oklahoma, 1950, p. 221) has noted the insubstantial, dream-like quality of the image of the raft. Clemens thus discusses travel by raft in *A Tramp Abroad:* "the motion of the raft is . . . gentle, and gliding, and smooth. and noiseless; it calms down all feverish activities, it soothes to sleep all nervous . . . impatience; under its restful influence all the troubles and vexations and sorrows that harass the mind vanish away, and existence becomes a dream . . . a deep and tranquil ecstasy."

Clemens might have contrived an action which left Jim's fate as much in doubt as Huck's. Such an ending would have allowed us to assume that the principals were defeated but alive, and the quest unsuccessful but not abandoned. This, after all, would have been consonant with the symbols, the characters, and the theme as Clemens had created them—and with history.

Clemens did not acknowledge the truth his novel contained. He had taken hold of a situation in which a partial defeat was inevitable, but he was unable to—or unaware of the need to—give imaginative substance to that fact. If an illusion of success was indispensable, where was it to come from? Obviously Huck and Jim could not succeed by their own efforts. At this point Clemens, having only half escaped the genteel tradition, one of whose preeminent characteristics was an optimism undaunted by disheartening truth, returned to it. *Why* he did so is another story, having to do with his parents and his boyhood, with his own personality and his wife's, and especially with the character of his audience. But whatever the explanation, the faint-hearted ending of *The Adventures of Huckleberry Finn* remains an important datum in the record of American thought and imagination. It has been noted before, both by critics and non-professional readers. It should not be forgotten now.

To minimize the seriousness of what must be accounted a major flaw in so great a work is, in a sense, to repeat Clemens' failure of nerve. This is a disservice to criticism. Today we particularly need a criticism alert to lapses of moral vision. A measured appraisal of the failures and successes of our writers, past and present, can show us a great deal about literature and about ourselves. That is the critic's function. But he cannot perform that function if he substitutes considerations of technique for considerations of truth. Not only will such methods lead to errors of literary judgment, but beyond that, they may well encourage comparable evasions in other areas. It seems not unlikely, for instance, that the current preoccupation with matters of form is bound up with a tendency, by no means confined to literary quarters, to shy away from painful answers to complex questions of political morality. The conclusion to *The Adventures of Huckleberry Finn* shielded both Clemens and his audience from such an answer. But we ought not to be as tender-minded. For Huck Finn's besetting problem, the disparity between his best impulses and the behavior the community attempted to impose upon him, is as surely ours as it was Twain's.

JAMES M. COX

[The Uncomfortable Ending of *Huckleberry Finn*]†

Probably the most formidable attack ever made on the ending of the book is found in Leo Marx's extremely interesting essay, "Mr. Eliot, Mr. Trilling, and Huckleberry Finn." Exposing Trilling's and Eliot's rather perfunctory and evasive approvals of the ending, Marx presents a rigorous analysis of Mark Twain's failure in the closing chapters of his masterpiece. Mark Twain failed, Marx believes, because he refused the responsibilities which went with the vision of the journey. For the journey was, according to Marx, the Quest —the great voyage toward freedom which Huck and Jim had so precariously made. But in the last ten chapters, Marx feels that Mark Twain simply turns the book over to the high jinks of Tom Sawyer, while Huck shrinkingly assumes the stature of a little straight man, observing the burlesque antics of his companion, but apparently unmoved by them. The cause of this slump on Mark Twain's part, Marx concludes, is simply that the journey, the Quest, *cannot* succeed. The drifting river has taken Huck and Jim ever deeper into slavery, and Mark Twain, unable to resolve the paradox of this reality which defeats his wish, simply evades the entire issue by shifting to burlesque.[1]

Persuasive though this argument is, Mark Twain's form rules out the possibilities which Marx insists on. Since Huck's entire identity is based upon an inverted order of values just as his style is based upon "incorrect" usage, he cannot have any recognition of his own virtue. Failure to acknowledge this necessity causes Marx to see the journey as a quest, whereas it simply is not at any time a quest. A quest is a positive journey, implying an effort, a struggle to reach a goal. But Huck is escaping. His journey is primarily a negation, a flight *from* tyranny, not a flight toward freedom.

In fact, Huck's central mode of being is that of escape and evasion. He forgets much more than he remembers; he lies, steals, and in general participates in as many confidence tricks as the King and the Duke. But the two cardinal facts—that he is a boy and is involved in helping a runaway slave—serve endlessly to sustain the reader's approval. It is precisely this approval which, putting the reader's moral censor to sleep, provides the central good humor per-

† Selections from James M. Cox, *Mark Twain: The Fate of Humor* (copyright © 1966 by Princeton University Press), pp. 172–84. Reprinted by permission of Princeton University Press. The author's notes have been renumbered.
1. Leo Marx, "Mr. Eliot, Mr. Trilling, and Huckleberry Finn," *American Scholar*, XXII (Autumn 1953), 423–39.

vading the incongruities, absurdities, and cruelties through which the narrative beautifully makes its way. The vernacular inversion, which so surely evokes the feeling of approval and indulgence, is narratively embodied in the very drift of the great river on which the raft miraculously rides.[2]

To be sure, at the fateful moment when Huck determines to set Jim free, he finds himself in open rebellion against Negro slavery. But he comes reluctantly, not gloriously, forward; even as he makes his famous declaration to go to hell, he is looking for a way out. He is certainly not a rebel; he is in a tight place and does the *easiest* thing. The role of Abolitionist is not comfortable nor comforting to him and in turning over to Tom Sawyer the entire unpleasant business of freeing Jim, Huck is surely not acting out of but remarkably *in* character.

Marx's inversion of Huck's escape into a quest drives him to the position of saying that Mark Twain could not "acknowledge the truth his novel contained" and thus evaded the central moral responsibilities of his vision. Yet for Marx the "truth" amounts to nothing more than Huck's perceiving that Negro slavery is wrong and involving himself in a quest for *political* freedom. In saying that the ending of the book discloses a failure of nerve and a retreat to the genteel tradition, it seems to me that Marx is completely turned around. Surely the genteel Bostonians would have applauded the moral sentiment of antislavery and political freedom which the novel entertains. They would have welcomed the quest rather than the escape. Yet if Marx is wrong, what is there to say about the ending?

To begin with, the ending is, to use Huck's term, uncomfortable. The problem is to define the source of this discomfort. Without question, there is a change when Tom Sawyer reappears. The narrative movement changes from one of adventure to burlesque—a burlesque which, in place of Huck's sincere but helpless involvement in freeing a real slave, puts Tom Sawyer's relatively cruel yet successful lark of freeing a slave already free. It is not Mark Twain's failure to distinguish between the two actions which jeopardizes his book; rather, it is his ironic exposure of Tom's action which threatens the humor of the book and produces the inharmonious burlesque De Voto regrets. Tom appears in such an unfortunate light in the closing pages that many readers of *Huckleberry Finn* can never again read *Tom Sawyer* without in one way or another holding Tom

---

2. The perfect integration between this drift and the river's motion is in part responsible for the beautiful economy with which Mark Twain treats the river. Far from needing to provide extensive descriptions and facts about the river as he did in *Life on the Mississippi*, he was able to render the river enormously real with economy of means. The reason: the fugitive boy and the river are made one through Huck's language.

responsible for motives he had not had in the earlier book.

Tom's play seems unpardonable because he already knows that Jim is free. Yet this knowledge—which Tom withholds from Huck —finally clears up for Huck the mystery of Tom's behavior toward him. Upon at last discovering the knowledge Tom has withheld from him, Huck, who has been troubled by Tom's "badness," at last understands why his respectable companion has been able to commit such a crime. His only remaining problem is to find out why Tom spent so much effort "setting a free nigger free." This, too, is cleared up when Tom explains to the long-suffering Aunt Sally that he made his elaborate and vexing arrangements purely for "adventure."

Tom's adventures are a unique cruelty in a book which depicts so much cruelty. All the other cruelties are committed for some "reason"—for honor, money, or power. But Tom's cruelty has a purity all its own—it is done solely for the sake of adventure. After facing Tom's long play, it is possible to see Huck's famous remark about the King and the Duke in a larger perspective. "Human beings can be awful cruel to each other," Huck had said upon seeing the scoundrels ridden out of town on a rail. This statement not only points backward to the episodes with the King and the Duke, but serves as a gateway leading from the King and the Duke's departure to Tom Sawyer's performance. For Tom's pure play runs directly counter to a wish the journey has generated. That is the frustration of the ending—the inversion. Having felt Huck's slow discovery of Jim's humanity, the reader perforce deplores Tom's casual ignorance and unawareness.

Yet the judgment which the last ten chapters render upon Tom is surely the judgment rendered upon the moral sentiment on which the book has ridden. If the reader sees in Tom's performance a rather shabby and safe bit of play, he is seeing no more than the exposure of the approval with which he watched Huck operate. For if Tom is rather contemptibly setting a free slave free, what after all is the reader doing, who begins the book after the *fact* of the Civil War? This is the "joke" of the book—the moment when, in outrageous burlesque, it attacks the sentiment which its style has at once evoked and exploited. To see that Tom is doing at the ending what we have been doing throughout the book is essential to understanding what the book has meant to us. For when Tom proclaims to the assembled throng who have witnessed his performance that Jim "is as free as any cretur that walks this earth," he is an exposed embodiment of the complacent moral sentiment on which the reader has relied throughout the book. And to the extent the reader has indulged the complacency he will be disturbed by the ending.

To be frustrated by the ending is to begin to discover the meaning of this journey, which evokes so much indulgence and moral approval that the censor is put to sleep. Beneath the sleeping censor, the real rebellion of *Huckleberry Finn* is enacted. For there must be a real rebellion—a rebellion which cannot so easily be afforded—else Mark Twain is guilty of a failure far greater than the ending. If the "incorrect" vernacular of *Huckleberry Finn* is to be more than décor, it must enact an equally "incorrect" vision. Otherwise, the style becomes merely a way of saying rather than a way of being. It is not simply the "poetry" or "beauty" or "rhythm" of Huck's vernacular which makes his language work, but the presence of a commensurate vernacular vision. The reason that imitators of *Huckleberry Finn* fail—the reason that Mark Twain himself later failed—is that they lack the vision to match their style, and thus their language is merely décor. One has but to read Edgar Lee Masters' *Mitch Miller*—which is a "modern" attempt to show what the childhood of Huck and Tom was really like—to know how sentimental such language can be unless it is sustained by a genuinely radical vision. Even Sherwood Anderson's "I Want to Know Why," in many ways the finest example of vernacular vision directly derivative from *Huckleberry Finn*, falls far short of Mark Twain, because its end, though finely climactic, is unfortunately sentimental. The young boy's anguished appeal upon discovering the Jockey with the whore is, after all, just the same old truth we knew all the time.

What then *is* the rebellion of *Huckleberry Finn?* What is it but an attack upon the conscience? The conscience, after all is said and done, is the real tyrant in the book. It is the relentless force which pursues Huckleberry Finn; it is the tyrant from which he seeks freedom. And it is not only the social conscience which threatens Huck, but *any* conscience. The social conscience, represented in the book by the slaveholding society of the Old South, is easily seen and exposed. It is the false conscience. But what of the true conscience which the reader wishes to project upon Huck and which Huck himself is at last on the threshold of accepting? It, too, is finally false. Although the book plays upon the notion that all conscience is finally social, it does not stand on that line; for the action is not defining the conscience so much as rejecting it. Whether the conscience is "lower" social conscience or the "higher" inner conscience, it remains the tyrant which drives its victims into the absurd corners from which they cannot escape. Thus on the one hand, there is the "law" or "right" of slavery from which Jim is trying to escape and against which Huck finds himself in helpless rebellion. But there are then the "inner" codes which appear as equally absurd distortions. There is Pap's belief in freedom; there is the code of the feud which the Grangerfords and Shepherdsons hold to; there is the "honor" of Colonel Sherburn; and finally there is the "principle" of Tom Sawyer who rises proudly to the defense of Jim because he "is as free as any cretur that walks this earth." In every case the conscience, whether it comes from society or from some apparent inner realm, is an agent of aggression—aggression against the self or against another. Either the means or the excuse by which pain is inflicted, the conscience is both law and duty, erasing the possibility of choice and thereby constraining its victims to a necessary and irrevocable course of action.

From the "Southern" conscience, Huck first attempts to flee. But even in flight from it, borne southward on the great river, his "Northern" conscience begins to awaken. This is the apparently internal conscience—the Civil War he finds himself engaged in on the raft as it glides deeper and deeper into the territory of slavery, not of freedom. Our moral sentiment approves his flight from his Southern conscience, but with the approval comes the hope that he will discover his Northern conscience. But it is just here that Huck will not accept the invitation. For chapter after chapter he remains the fugitive—in flight from the old conscience and evading the development of a new one.

And the reason he evades it is clear—the conscience is *uncomfortable*. Indeed, comfort and satisfaction are the value terms in *Huckleberry Finn*. Freedom for Huck is not realized in terms of political liberty but in terms of pleasure. Thus his famous pronouncement about life on the raft: "Other places do seem so cramped and smothery, but a raft don't. You feel mighty free and easy and comfortable on a raft."[3] And later, when the King and the Duke threaten to break the peace, Huck determines not to take a stand against them, observing, "What you want above all things, on a raft, is for everybody to be satisfied, and feel right and kind toward the others."[4] In almost every instance Huck projects the good life in terms of ease, satisfaction, comfort. A satirist would see it in terms of justice; a moralist would have it as a place of righteousness. But a humorist envisions it as a place of good feeling, where no pain or discomfort can enter. This is why Huck does not see clothes, which figure so prominently as the garments of civilization, as veils to hide the body, or as the false dress whereby a fiction of status is maintained. This would be the satiric vision. As far as Huck is concerned, clothes and civilization itself are undesirable because they are essentially *uncomfortable*. "But I reckon I got to light out for the territory," he says as he departs, "because Aunt Sally she's going to adopt me and sivilize me, and I can't stand it."[5] When Huck says he "can't stand it," he is literally referring to

3. *The Writings of Mark Twain* (New York, 1922–25), XIII, 162. The conscience, on the other hand, is the source of discomfort. As Huck says, ". . . it don't make no difference whether you do right or wrong, a person's conscience ain't got no sense, and just goes for him anyway. If I had a yeller dog that didn't know no more than a person's conscience does I would pison him" (*Writings*, XIII, 321).

4. *Ibid.*, p. 174.

5. *Ibid.*, p. 405.

the cramped discomfort of submitting to the clothes and quarters of civilization. To be sure, the phrase suggests a vastly wider range of significances, but significances that are inexorably rooted in a logic of feeling, comfort, and bodily satisfaction. The significances are *our* discoveries, which are at once made possible by and anchored to the concrete image of the raft, the boy, and the Negro. The good feeling, comfort, and ease dominating this journey which makes its way through a society of meanness, cowardice, and cruelty are perfectly embodied by the raft adrift upon the river.

This logic of pleasure at the heart of the book must also be at the heart of any "positive" value we may wish to ascribe to the experience of reading it. Most criticism of *Huckleberry Finn*, however, retreats from the pleasure principle toward the relative safety of "moral issues" and the imperatives of the Northern conscience. This flight is made because of the uncomfortable feeling relating to Huck's "evasion," his "escape," and finally his "rejection" of civilization. What Huck is rejecting is, of course, the conscience—which Mark Twain was later to rail at under the name of the "Moral Sense." The conscience, the trap of adult civilization which lies in wait for Huck throughout the novel, is what he is at such pains to evade. It is his successful evasion which we as readers cannot finally face. The reader who rejects the paradox usually does so on the grounds that the book is "just" a humorous book. The one who detects and is disturbed by it is more likely to follow William Van O'Connor's pronouncements about the "dangers" of innocence and the "failure" of moral vision. A weakness in Huck—pontificates O'Connor in his attempt to prove that the book is *not* a great American novel—is that he does not "acknowledge the virtues of civilization and live, as one must, inside it."[6] Huck does acknowledge the virtues, of course, and upbraids himself for being uncomfortable with them.

But far from relying upon such cozy affirmations as O'Connor longs for, the book moves *down* the river into the deeper repressions of slavery, enacting at every moment a conversion of morality into pleasure. Extending the range of humor through the ills, the agonies, and the cruelties of civilization, it shows how much the conscience—whether Northern or Southern—is the negative force leading to acts of violence upon the self or upon another. Huck's "escape" is of course an escape from violence, a rejection of cruelty —his instinct is neither to give nor to receive pain if he can avoid it.

The prime danger to his identity comes at the moment he chooses the developing inner or Northern conscience. This moment, when Huck says "All right, then, I'll *go* to hell," is characteristically

6. William Van O'Connor, "Why *Huckle-*   Novel," *College English*, XVII (October *berry Finn* Is Not the Great American   1955), p. 8.

the moment we fatally approve, and approve *morally*. But it is with equal fatality the moment at which Huck's identity is most precariously threatened. In the very act of choosing to go to hell he has surrendered to the notion of a *principle* of right and wrong. He has forsaken the world of pleasure to make a moral choice. Precisely here is where Huck is about to negate himself—where, with an act of positive virtue, he actually commits himself to play the role of Tom Sawyer which he *has* to assume in the closing section of the book. To commit oneself to the idea, the *morality* of freeing Jim, is to become Tom Sawyer. Here again is the irony of the book, and the ending, far from evading the consequences of Huck's act of rebellion, realizes those consequences.

Mark Twain's real problem—his real dilemma—was not at all his inability to "face" the issues of slavery; certainly it was not a fear of the society or a failure of moral and political courage which brought Mark Twain to the tight place where Huck had to decide forever and ever. Rather, it was the necessities of his humorous form. For in order to achieve expression of the deep wish which *Huckleberry Finn* embodies—the wish for freedom from any conscience—Mark Twain had to intensify the moral sentiment. The moment there is any real moral doubt about Huck's action, the wish will be threatened. Yet when Huck makes his moral affirmation, he fatally negates the wish for freedom from the conscience; for if his affirmation frees him from the Southern conscience, it binds him to his Northern conscience. No longer an outcast, he can be welcomed into the society to play the role of Tom Sawyer, which is precisely what happens. When he submits to Tom's role, we are the ones who become uncomfortable. The entire burlesque ending is a revenge upon the moral sentiment which, though it shielded the humor, ultimately threatened Huck's identity.

This is the larger reality of the ending—what we may call the necessity of the form. That it was a cost which the form exacted no one would deny. But to call it a failure, a piece of moral cowardice, is to miss the true rebellion of the book, for the disturbance of the ending is nothing less than our and Mark Twain's recognition of the full meaning of *Huckleberry Finn*. If the reader is pushed to the limits of his humor, Mark Twain had reached the limits of his —he had seen through to the end. The disillusion begins not when Tom returns to the stage, but when Huck says "All right, then, I'll go to hell"—when our applause and approval reach their zenith. At that moment, which anyone would agree is Mark Twain's highest achievement, Huck has internalized the image of Jim; and that image, whose reality he has enjoyed during the fatal drift downstream, becomes the scourge which shames him out of his evasion. The whole process is disclosed in the lyric utterance leading to his decision. Having written the note to Miss Watson telling where Jim is, Huck feels cleansed and at last able to pray:

> But I didn't do it straight off, but laid the paper down and set there thinking—thinking how good it was all this happened so, and how near I come to being lost and going to hell. And went on thinking. And got to thinking over our trip down the river; and I see Jim before me all the time: in the day and in the night-time, sometimes moonlight, sometimes storms, and we a-floating along, talking and singing and laughing. But somehow I couldn't seem to strike no places to harden me against him, but only the other kind. I'd see him standing my watch on top of his'n, 'stead of calling me, so I could go on sleeping; and see him how glad he was when I come back out of the fog; and when I come to him again in the swamp, up there where the feud was; and such-like times; and would always call me honey, and pet me, and do everything he could think of for me, and how good he always was; and at last I struck the time I saved him by telling the men we had smallpox aboard, and he was so grateful, and said I was the best friend old Jim ever had in the world, and the *only* one he's got now; and then I happened to look around and see that paper.
>
> It was a close place.[7]

This lyrical rehearsal of the journey is also the journey's end. And the decision which ends it is cast in the positive locution of Tom Sawyer, not in Huck's essentially negative vernacular.[8] When Huck says he will go to hell, in five minutes of reading time he is there. For in this novel, which constantly plays against superstitious here-afters, there is no fire-and-brimstone hell but only civilization— which is precisely where Huck finds himself as a consequence of his own determination.

This dilemma and disillusion are what Mark Twain would not shrink from, but carried through, though it cost him almost every-thing—which is saying it cost him his good humor. In the bur-lesque chapters, he understandably though precariously turned upon his invention, upon his reader, and upon himself. Yet even here he did not entirely abandon the pleasure principle, but left his "seri-ous" readers pleased with themselves instead of the book, their moral complacency ruffled by nothing more than comfortable indig-nation at the evasions of humor.

As for Mark Twain, he had seen through to the end, and it

7. *Writings*, XIII, 296–97. Although Huck's language constantly describes his feelings and thoughts, they are so di-rectly wedded to external action and de-pendent on it that he seems to have no independent "thought." This passage is the only extended narrative of such an inner life. Once the decision is made, he hardly reflects upon his past. If he re-members, he keeps it to himself.
8. Huck's most characteristic errors of grammar are, significantly enough, his constant use of the double negative and his persistent confusion of verb tense.

almost killed him. He never would have so good a humor again. His despair, having set in at the moment of Huckleberry Finn's affirmation, never really let up. The only way he could survive was to try to swallow the joke which became more and more sour the rest of his embattled way. Having seen the limits of his humor, he turned upon them and railed at the conscience and the need for self-approval, the twin human characteristics which seemed to make the human race utterly ridiculous and damned.

And what of Huck? As Nick Carraway said of Gatsby, he came out all right. He went to the territory because he was true to himself and to his creator. He didn't go there to lead civilization either, but to play outside it. Refusing to grow up and tell the lie of the conscience, he left behind him a novel for all time. It was truly a novel of reconstruction. First, it had brought into fiction not the Old South but an entirely new one which the Northern conscience could welcome back into the Union. And in the process of its humor, it reconstructed the psyche, following the pleasure principle as far as it would go to discover in the southern reaches of the Great River the tyranny of the conscience which keeps the adult in chains and makes his pleasure the enactment of greater and greater cruelty. He had not reached childhood's end, but had disclosed the lie of the adult world. In his last moment he said, "so there ain't nothing more to write about, and I am rotten glad of it, because if I'd 'a'knowed what a trouble it was to make a book I wouldn't 'a'tackled it, and ain't a-going to no more." We of course constantly lecture Mark Twain about having turned away from his true vein of ore. The fact is, however, that he could not turn away but kept trying to do just what we want of him. He kept trying to call Huck back to tell another story. But Huck, though he came docilely, could never tell the truth. He had told all the truth he had to tell in one glorious lie.

ROY HARVEY PEARCE

"The End. Yours Truly, Huck Finn": Postscript†

In the last chapter of *The Adventures of Huckleberry Finn*, Huck speaks twice of going to "the Territory." The first time he is reporting Tom's plans, now that the evasion has been managed successfully, "to slide out of here, one of these nights, and get an outfit, and go for howling adventures amongst the Injuns, over in the Territory. . . ." The second time he is speaking of his own

† From *Modern Language Quarterly*, XXIV, 3 (September 1963), 253–56. Reprinted by permission of the publisher. The American first edition of *Huckleberry Finn* ends with a drawing, by E. W. Kemble, of Huck taking a bow. The caption, "The End. Yours Truly, Huck Finn," is printed just below Huck's feet and thus forms the last words of the book.

plans: "I reckon I got to light out for the Territory ahead of the rest, because Aunt Sally she's going to adopt me and sivilize me and I can't stand it. I been there before."

I suppose that the obvious irony of the two passages has not been pointed out precisely because it is so obvious. The Territory is, of course, the Indian Territory, which was to become Oklahoma. From the 1820's on, it had been organized and developed as a region to which the Indians could be safely removed away from civilized society, since their lands were needed for higher purposes than those to which they could put them. The cruelty and deprivation of removal was generally taken to be a price which had inevitably to be paid as American society passed through its God-ordained stages of development. One part of this price was said to be the yielding of a certain amount of freedom or, to put it as an article of faith in Manifest Destiny, the surrendering of a "lower" for a "higher" freedom.[1] It seems fairly evident that the man who was to write "To a Person Sitting in Darkness" and other such stories would be fully aware of the removal episode, with its justifications and consequences, and that he meant his readers to be aware of it too. Read in this light, what for Tom is yet another willful adolescent fantasy becomes for Huck a compelling actuality. Tom's willfulness effects a parody which points up some of the grotesqueness of the historically authentic pioneering, civilizing spirit. Huck's compulsion effects a satire which simply denies that that spirit is authentic despite its historical actuality. Huck will seek the freedom of the Territory just because it is an uncivilized freedom. (A better word, perhaps, is noncivilized freedom.) It is, indeed, the only true freedom for the authentic human being which Huck eventually comes to be—in spite of himself.

Yet there is more to the passages, particularly the second, than this. Huck speaks of lighting out for the Territory "ahead of the rest." These last four words comprise a crux which, so far as I know, no commentator has yet recognized. I suggest that here, at the end, Mark Twain introduces his own point of view, which, of necessity, is more encompassing than that of his character, Huck; and as a result Huck is given more to say than he could of himself possibly know.[2] From Huck's simple point of view, the allusion is to Tom's vague plans to go to the Territory; for Twain, it is to the boomer movement which was a prime factor in the taking over of Indian

1. See my *Savages of America* (Baltimore, 1953), particularly pp. 56–61.
2. Henry Nash Smith (*Mark Twain: The Development of a Writer* [Cambridge, 1962], pp. 134–37) points out that the Colonel Sherburn episode derives from Mark Twain's point of view and thus is intrusive, a "flaw" in the structure of *Huckleberry Finn*. I should think, however, that one could argue for Huck as a "reporter" in this and in other episodes (particularly the long "evasion") where he is in no position to participate in, much less dominate, the action and so render it in terms congruent with his sensibility and understanding. The question is: how much irony are we to allow Mark Twain? An incidental burden is that, in the end, we must allow him a good deal and demand only of *Huckleberry Finn* that it "contain" the elements of the irony.

lands, "civilizing" the Territory, and creating another American state. The effect is that Huck, all unknowing, is given a kind of prescience which his adventures at this point surely justify. No matter where he goes, he will be one step ahead not only of the Tom Sawyers of this world, but of the sort of people into whom the Tom Sawyers grow.

After the Civil War, there was constant agitation in Kansas and Missouri to open up the unsettled parts of the Indian Territory to whites. To this end, bills were repeatedly, if on the whole unsuccessfully, introduced in Congress. Pressures were put on the so-called Five Civilized Nations (Cherokees, Creeks, and Choctaws principally) to cede part of their lands in the Territory to be used as reservations for other Indians and, for due payment, to make them available for settlement by whites. In the late 1870's and into the 1880's, white incursions into the Territory were numerous enough to call for the use of troops to defend Indian rights. Moreover, in 1879, a court decision found that even those lands in the Territory which had been ceded to the government by Indians could not be settled by whites, since such lands had been ceded conditionally for future settlement by other Indians.

Inevitably, however, white incursions—by groups who came to be known as boomers—increased in tempo and number. Invaders were not jailed but fined. When they could not pay the fines, they were simply escorted to the territorial border by soldiers. The economics of the situation was complex: railroads encouraged and propagandized boomers; cattlemen, wanting to use the lands for grazing, opposed the boomers, who were farmers, and defended Indian rights—which included the right to rent their lands for grazing. The story (one of confusion, broken promises, and violence—all in the name of "civilization") moved toward its resolution in 1889, when the government bought certain lands from Indians and opened them to settlement as the Territory of Oklahoma.[3]

Boomerism, then, was the most recent expression of the westering American spirit. In the words of an 1885 petition to Congress, drawn up by B. L. Brush and John W. Marshall in Howard, Kansas, on behalf of boomerism:

> Resolved, That we are opposed to the policy of the Government in using the army to drive out or interfere with actual settlers upon any of the public domain, as being foreign to the genius of our institutions. . . .
> Resolved, As this selfsame, bold spirit, that is now advancing

3. The story is best outlined in Roy Gittinger, *Formation of the State of Oklahoma, 1803–1906* (Norman, 1939), pp. 68–157. On the boomers, see Carl Coke Rister, *Land Hunger: David L. Payne and the Oklahoma Boomers* (Norman, 1942).

to the front, has ever existed since the Pilgrim Fathers set their feet on Plymouth Rock, and will ever exist so long as we remain citizens of this grand Republic, that we, the citizens of Howard and vicinity, pledge ourselves to firmly support this grand element—the vanguard of civilization. . . .

Resolved, That we are opposed to the settlement of any more bands of wild Indians on the Indian Territory.[4]

Although I know of no direct allusion in Mark Twain's writings to the troubles in the Indian Territory, I think it most likely that he was well aware of them, for they were widely publicized and debated and of great interest to Congress. A considerable amount of boomer ferment developed in Twain's—and Huck's—Missouri, although Kansas was a more important center. The summer of 1883, when Twain was writing the last part of *Huckleberry Finn*,[5] David Payne and his boomers were particularly active in promoting their cause. One historian of Oklahoma reports that the general whose responsiblity it was to turn boomers back declared that in 1883 "the whole affair had become simply a series of processions to and from the Kansas line."[6]

Thus it would seem that in 1883, Mark Twain, now finally committed to a conception of a Huck Finn whose fate it must always be to seek a freedom beyond the limits of any civilization, ended his novel by contrasting Tom's and Huck's sense of the Territory. Note that Huck is willing to go along with Tom, if he can get the money to outfit himself for those "howling adventures amongst the Injuns. . . ." Jim tells Huck that, now that his father is dead, he does have the money. But he will, however, have to claim it himself. The matter of the money and the "howling adventures" is then dropped. Since Tom is "most well" now, Huck says, there "ain't nothing more to write about." He will "light out for the Territory ahead of the rest." In one sense, perhaps, he simply means ahead of Tom and Jim; in a larger sense (so I think we must conclude) he means ahead of all those people whose civilizing mission boomerism actualized in fact. The realities of the case are, as ever, contrasted with Tom's fantasies.

The Huck who seems willing to go along with Tom is, of course, not the Huck who, against the dictates of his conscience, has helped Jim in his quest for freedom. It is altogether necessary that this latter Huck must, alone, "light out for the Territory ahead of the rest." With the curious prescience which Mark Twain gives him, he knows that in antebellum days (as Mark Twain surely knew that summer of 1883), even in the Territory, he will be only

4. Quoted in Gittinger, pp. 272–73.
5. Walter Blair, "When Was Huckleberry Finn Written?" *American Litera-*
ture, XX (1958), 1–25.
6. Gittinger, p. 131.

one step ahead of the rest: boomers, dukes and dauphins, Aunt Sallies, Colonel Sherburns, and Wilkses—civilizers all. Certainly we are not to assume that Huck self-consciously knows the full meaning (even the full moral meaning) of what he says here. Yet we cannot conclude that this allusion is simply a matter of Mark Twain speaking out in his own person. Huck's view and Mark Twain's, in a culminating irony, here become one. Huck's prescience is, within the limits of the narrative, a matter of intuition, forced into expression by his hard-headed sense that he has almost always been one step "ahead of the rest." He can say his final "Yours Truly" and yet must be willing to go to hell for saying it.

Huck, Jim, and Tom

HENRY NASH SMITH

A Sound Heart and a Deformed Conscience†

Mark Twain worked on *Adventures of Huckleberry Finn* at intervals over a period of seven years, from 1876 to 1883. During this time he wrote two considerable books (*A Tramp Abroad* and *The Prince and the Pauper*), expanded "Old Times on the Mississippi" into *Life on the Mississippi*, and gathered various shorter pieces into three other volumes. But this is all essentially minor work. The main line of his development lies in the long preoccupation with the Matter of Hannibal and the Matter of the River that is recorded in "Old Times" and *The Adventures of Tom Sawyer* and reaches a climax in his book about "Tom Sawyer's Comrade. Scene: The Mississippi Valley. Time: Forty to Fifty Years Ago."

In writing *Huckleberry Finn* Mark Twain found a way to organize into a larger structure the insights that earlier humorists had recorded in their brief anecdotes. This technical accomplishment was of course inseparable from the process of discovering new meanings in his material. His development as a writer was a dialectic interplay in which the reach of his imagination imposed a constant strain on his technical resources, and innovations of method in turn opened up new vistas before his imagination.

The dialectic process is particularly striking in the gestation of *Huckleberry Finn*. The use of Huck as a narrative persona, with the consequent elimination of the author as an intruding presence in the story, resolved the difficulties about point of view and style that had been so conspicuous in the earlier books. But turning the story over to Huck brought into view previously unsuspected literary potentialities in the vernacular perspective, particularly the possibility of using vernacular speech for serious purposes and of transforming the vernacular narrator from a mere persona into a character with human depth. Mark Twain's response to the challenge made *Huckleberry Finn* the greatest of his books and one of the two or

† From *Mark Twain: The Development of a Writer*, by Henry Nash Smith. Cambridge, Mass.: The Belknap Press of Harvard University Press, © 1962 by the President and Fellows of Harvard College. Pp. 113–37. Reprinted by permission of the publishers.

three acknowledged masterpieces of American literature. Yet this triumph created a new technical problem to which there was no solution; for what had begun as a comic story developed incipiently tragic implications contradicting the premises of comedy.

Huckleberry Finn thus contains three main elements. The most conspicuous is the story of Huck's and Jim's adventures in their flight toward freedom. Jim is running away from actual slavery, Huck from the cruelty of his father, from the well-intentioned "sivilizing" efforts of Miss Watson and the Widow Douglas, from respectability and routine in general. The second element in the novel is social satire of the towns along the river. The satire is often transcendently funny, especially in episodes involving the rascally Duke and King, but it can also deal in appalling violence, as in the Grangerford-Shepherdson feud or Colonel Sherburn's murder of the helpless Boggs. The third major element in the book is the developing characterization of Huck.

All three elements must have been present to Mark Twain's mind in some sense from the beginning, for much of the book's greatness lies in its basic coherence, the complex interrelation of its parts. Nevertheless, the intensive study devoted to it in recent years, particularly Walter Blair's establishment of the chronology of its composition, has demonstrated that Mark Twain's search for a structure capable of doing justice to his conceptions of theme and character passed through several stages. He did not see clearly where he was going when he began to write, and we can observe him in the act of making discoveries both in meaning and in method as he goes along.

The narrative tends to increase in depth as it moves from the adventure story of the early chapters into the social satire of the long middle section, and thence to the ultimate psychological penetration of Huck's character in the moral crisis of Chapter 31. Since the crisis is brought on by the shock of the definitive failure of Huck's effort to help Jim, it marks the real end of the quest for freedom. The perplexing final sequence on the Phelps planatation is best regarded as a maneuver by which Mark Twain beats his way back from incipient tragedy to the comic resolution called for by the original conception of the story.

2

Huck's and Jim's flight from St. Petersburg obviously translates into action the theme of vernacular protest. The fact that they have no means of fighting back against the forces that threaten them but can only run away is accounted for in part by the conventions of backwoods humor, in which the inferior social status of the vernacular character placed him in an ostensibly weak position. But it also reflects Mark Twain's awareness of his own lack of firm ground to stand on in challenging the established system of values.

Huck's and Jim's defenselessness foreshadows the outcome of their efforts to escape. They cannot finally succeed. To be sure, in a superficial sense they do succeed; at the end of the book Jim is technically free and Huck still has the power to light out for the Territory. But Jim's freedom has been brought about by such an implausible device that we do not believe in it. Who can imagine the scene in which Miss Watson decides to liberate him? What were her motives? Mark Twain finesses the problem by placing this crucial event far offstage and telling us nothing about it beyond the bare fact he needs to resolve his plot. And the notion that a fourteen-year-old boy could make good his escape beyond the frontier is equally unconvincing. The writer himself did not take it seriously. In an unpublished sequel to *Huckleberry Finn* called "Huck Finn and Tom Sawyer among the Indians," which he began soon after he finished the novel, Aunt Sally takes the boys and Jim back to Hannibal and then to western Missouri for a visit "with some of her relations on a hemp farm out there." Here Tom revives the plan mentioned near the end of *Huckleberry Finn*: he "was dead set on having us run off, some night, and cut for the Injun country and go for adventures." Huck says, however, that he and Jim "kind of hung fire. Plenty to eat and nothing to do. We was very well satisfied." Only after an extended debate can Tom persuade them to set out with him. Their expedition falls into the stereotyped pattern of Wild West stories of travel out the Oregon Trail, makes a few gibes at Cooper's romanticized Indians, and breaks off.

The difficulty of imagining a successful outcome for Huck's and Jim's quest had troubled Mark Twain almost from the beginning of his work on the book. After writing the first section in 1876 he laid aside his manuscript near the end of Chapter 16. The narrative plan with which he had impulsively begun had run into difficulties. When Huck and Jim shove off from Jackson's Island on their section of a lumber raft (at the end of Chapter 11) they do so in haste, to escape the immediate danger of the slave hunters Huck has learned about from Mrs. Loftus. No long-range plan is mentioned until the beginning of Chapter 15, when Huck says that at Cairo they intended to "sell the raft and get on a steamboat and go way up the Ohio amongst the free states, and then be out of trouble." But they drift past Cairo in the fog, and a substitute plan of making their way back up to the mouth of the Ohio in their canoe is frustrated when the canoe disappears while they are sleeping: "we talked about what we better do, and found there warn't no way but just to go along down with the raft till we got a chance to buy a canoe to go back in." Drifting downstream with the current, however, could not be reconciled with the plan to free Jim by transporting him up the Ohio; hence the temporary abandonment of the story.

3

When Mark Twain took up his manuscript again in 1879, after an interval of three years, he had decided upon a different plan for the narrative. Instead of concentrating on the story of Huck's and Jim's escape, he now launched into a satiric description of the society of the prewar South. Huck was essential to this purpose, for Mark Twain meant to view his subject ironically through Huck's eyes. But Jim was more or less superfluous. During Chapters 17 and 18, devoted to the Grangerford household and the feud, Jim has disappeared from the story. Mark Twain had apparently not yet found a way to combine social satire with the narrative scheme of Huck's and Jim's journey on the raft.

While he was writing his chapter about the feud, however, he thought of a plausible device to keep Huck and Jim floating southward while he continued his panoramic survey of the towns along the river. The device was the introduction of the Duke and the King. In Chapter 19 they come aboard the raft, take charge at once, and hold Huck and Jim in virtual captivity. In this fashion the narrative can preserve the overall form of a journey down the river while providing ample opportunity for satire when Huck accompanies the two rascals on their forays ashore. But only the outward form of the journey is retained. Its meaning has changed, for Huck's and Jim's quest for freedom has in effect come to an end. Jim is physically present but he assumes an entirely passive role, and is hidden with the raft for considerable periods. Huck is also essentially passive; his function now is that of an observer. Mark Twain postpones acknowledging that the quest for freedom has failed, but the issue will have to be faced eventually.

The satire of the towns along the banks insists again and again that the dominant culture is decadent and perverted. Traditional values have gone to seed. The inhabitants can hardly be said to live a conscious life of their own; their actions, their thoughts, even their emotions are controlled by an outworn and debased Calvinism, and by a residue of the eighteenth-century cult of sensibility. With few exceptions they are mere bundles of tropisms, at the mercy of scoundrels like the Duke and the King who know how to exploit their prejudices and delusions.

The falseness of the prevalent values finds expression in an almost universal tendency of the townspeople to make spurious claims to status through self-dramatization. Mark Twain has been concerned with this topic from the beginning of the book. Chapter 1 deals with Tom Sawyer's plan to start a band of robbers which Huck will be allowed to join only if he will "go back to the widow and be respectable"; and we also hear about Miss Watson's mercenary conception of prayer. In Chapter 2 Jim interprets Tom's prank of hanging his hat on the limb of a tree while he is asleep as evidence that he has been bewitched. He "was most ruined for a servant, because he got stuck up on account of having seen the devil and been rode by witches." Presently we witness the ritual by which Pap Finn is to be redeemed from drunkenness. When his benefactor gives him a lecture on temperance, it will be recalled,

> the old man cried, and said he'd been a fool, and fooled away his life; but now he was a-going to turn over a new leaf and be a man nobody wouldn't be ashamed of, and he hoped the judge would help him and not look down on him. The judge said he could hug him for them words; so *he* cried, and his wife she cried again; pap said he'd been a man that had always been misunderstood before, and the judge said he believed it. The old man said that what a man wanted that was down was sympathy, and the judge said it was so; so they cried again.

As comic relief for the feud that provides a way of life for the male Grangerfords Mark Twain dwells lovingly on Emmeline Grangerford's pretensions to culture—her paintings with the fetching titles and the ambitious "Ode to Stephen Dowling Bots, Dec'd.," its pathos hopelessly flawed by the crudities showing through like the chalk beneath the enameled surface of the artificial fruit in the parlor: "His spirit was gone for to sport aloft/In the realms of the good and great."

The Duke and the King personify the theme of fraudulent role-taking. These rogues are not even given names apart from the wildly improbable identities they assume in order to dominate Huck and Jim. The Duke's poses have a literary cast, perhaps because of the scraps of bombast he remembers from his experience as an actor. The illiterate King has "done considerable in the doctoring way," but when we see him at work it is mainly at preaching, "workin' camp-meetin's, and missionaryin' around." Pretended or misguided piety and other perversions of Christianity obviously head the list of counts in Mark Twain's indictment of the prewar South. And properly: for it is of course religion that stands at the center of the system of values in the society of this fictive world and by implication in all societies. His revulsion, expressed through Huck, reaches its highest pitch in the scene where the King delivers his masterpiece of "soul-butter and hogwash" for the benefit of the late Peter Wilks's fellow townsmen.

By and by the king he gets up and comes forward a little, and works himself up and slobbers out a speech, all full of tears and flapdoodle, about its being a sore trial for him and his poor brother to lose the diseased, and to miss seeing diseased alive after the long journey of four thousand mile, but it's a trial that's sweetened and sanctified to us by this dear sympathy and these holy tears, and so he thanks them out of his heart and out of his brother's heart, because out of their mouths they can't, words being too weak and cold, and all that kind of rot and slush, till it was just sickening; and then he blubbers out a pious goody-goody Amen, and turns himself loose and goes to crying fit to bust.

4

Huck is revolted by the King's hypocrisy: "I never see anything so disgusting." He has had a similar reaction to the brutality of the feud: "It made me so sick I most fell out of the tree." In describing such scenes he speaks as moral man viewing an immoral society, an observer who is himself free of the vices and even the weaknesses he describes. Mark Twain's satiric method requires that Huck be a mask for the writer, not a fully developed character. The method has great ironic force, and is in itself a technical landmark in the history of American fiction, but it prevents Mark Twain from doing full justice to Huck as a person in his own right, capable of mistakes in perception and judgment, troubled by doubts and conflicting impulses.

Even in the chapters written during the original burst of composition in 1876 the character of Huck is shown to have depths and complexities not relevant to the immediate context. Huck's and Jim's journey down the river begins simply as a flight from physical danger; and the first episodes of the voyage have little bearing on the novelistic possibilities in the strange comradeship between outcast boy and escaped slave. But in Chapter 15, when Huck plays a prank on Jim by persuading him that the separation in the fog was only a dream, Jim's dignified and moving rebuke suddenly opens up a new dimension in the relation. Huck's humble apology is striking evidence of growth in moral insight. It leads naturally to the next chapter in which Mark Twain causes Huck to face up for the first time to the fact that he is helping a slave to escape. It is as if the writer himself were discovering unsuspected meanings in what he had thought of as a story of picaresque adventure. The incipient contradiction between narrative plan and increasing depth in Huck's character must have been as disconcerting to Mark Twain as the difficulty of finding a way to account for Huck's and Jim's continuing southward past the mouth of the Ohio. It was doubtless the convergence of the two problems that led him to put aside the manuscript near the end of Chapter 16.

The introduction of the Duke and the King not only took care of the awkwardness in the plot but also allowed Mark Twain to postpone the exploration of Huck's moral dilemma. If Huck is not a free agent he is not responsible for what happens and is spared the agonies of choice. Throughout the long middle section, while he is primarily an observer, he is free of inner conflict because he is endowed by implication with Mark Twain's own unambiguous attitude toward the fraud and folly he witnesses.

In Chapter 31, however, Huck escapes from his captors and faces once again the responsibility for deciding on a course of action. His situation is much more desperate than it had been at the time of his first struggle with his conscience. The raft has borne Jim hundreds of miles downstream from the pathway of escape and the King has turned him over to Silas Phelps as a runaway slave. The quest for freedom has "all come to nothing, everything all busted up and ruined." Huck thinks of notifying Miss Watson where Jim is, since if he must be a slave he would be better off "at home where his family was." But then Huck realizes that Miss Watson would probably sell Jim down the river as a punishment for running away. Furthermore, Huck himself would be denounced by everyone for his part in the affair. In this fashion his mind comes back once again to the unparalleled wickedness of acting as accomplice in a slave's escape.

The account of Huck's mental struggle in the next two or three pages is the emotional climax of the story. It draws together the theme of flight from bondage and the social satire of the middle section, for Huck is trying to work himself clear of the perverted value system of St. Petersburg. Both adventure story and satire, however, are now subordinate to an exploration of Huck's psyche which is the ultimate achievement of the book. The issue is identical with that of the first moral crisis, but the later passage is much more intense and richer in implication. The differences appear clearly if the two crises are compared in detail.

In Chapter 16 Huck is startled into a realization of his predicament when he hears Jim, on the lookout for Cairo at the mouth of the Ohio, declare that "he'd be a free man the minute he seen it, but if he missed it he'd be in a slave country again and no more show for freedom." Huck says: "I begun to get it through my head that he *was* most free—and who was to blame for it? Why, *me*. I couldn't get that out of my conscience, no how nor no way." He dramatizes his inner debate by quoting the words in which his conscience denounces him: "What had poor Miss Watson done to you that you could see her nigger go off right under your eyes and never say one single word? What did that poor old woman do to you that you. could treat her so mean? Why, she tried to learn you your book, she tried to learn you your manners, she tried to be good to you every way she knowed how. *That's* what she done." The counterargument is provided by Jim, who seems to guess what is passing through Huck's mind and does what he can to invoke the force of friendship and gratitude: "Pooty soon I'll be a-shout'n' for joy, en I'll say, it's all on accounts o' Huck; I's a free man, en I couldn't ever ben free ef it hadn' ben for Huck; Huck done it. Jim won't ever forgit you, Huck; you's de bes' fren' Jim's ever had; en you's de *only* fren' ole Jim's got now." Huck nevertheless sets out for the shore in the canoe "all in a sweat to tell on" Jim, but when he is intercepted by the two slave hunters in a skiff he suddenly contrives a cunning device to ward them off. We are given no details about how his inner conflict was resolved.

In the later crisis Huck provides a much more circumstantial account of what passes through his mind. He is now quite alone; the outcome of the debate is not affected by any stimulus from the outside. It is the memory of Jim's kindness and goodness rather than Jim's actual voice that impels Huck to defy his conscience: "I see Jim before me all the time: in the day and in the night-time, sometimes moonlight, sometimes storms, and we a-floating along, talking and singing and laughing." The most striking feature of this later crisis is the fact that Huck's conscience, which formerly had employed only secular arguments, now deals heavily in religious cant:

> At last, when it hit me all of a sudden that here was the plain hand of Providence slapping me in the face and letting me know my wickedness was being watched all the time from up there in heaven, whilst I was stealing a poor old woman's nigger that hadn't ever done me no harm, and now was showing me there's One that's always on the lookout, and ain't a-going to allow no such miserable doings to go only just so fur and no further, I most dropped in my tracks I was so scared.

In the earlier debate the voice of Huck's conscience is quoted directly, but the bulk of the later exhortation is reported in indirect discourse. This apparently simple change in method has remarkable consequences. According to the conventions of first-person narrative, the narrator functions as a neutral medium in reporting dialogue. He remembers the speeches of other characters but they pass through his mind without affecting him. When Huck's conscience speaks within quotation marks it is in effect a character in the story, and he is not responsible for what it says. But when he paraphrases the admonitions of his conscience they are incorporated into his own discourse. Thus although Huck is obviously remembering the bits of theological jargon from sermons justifying slavery, they have become a part of his vocabulary.

The device of having Huck paraphrase rather than quote the voice of conscience may have been suggested to Mark Twain by a discovery he made in revising Huck's report of the King's address to the mourners in the Wilks parlor (Chapter 25). The manuscript version of the passage shows that the King's remarks were composed as a direct quotation, but in the published text they have been put, with a minimum of verbal change, into indirect discourse. The removal of the barrier of quotation marks brings Huck into much more intimate contact with the King's "rot and slush" despite the fact that the paraphrase quivers with disapproval. The voice of conscience speaks in the precise accents of the King but Huck is now completely uncritical. He does not question its moral authority; it is morality personified. The greater subtlety of the later passage illustrates the difference between the necessarily shallow characterization of Huck while he was being used merely as a narrative persona, and the profound insight which Mark Twain eventually brought to bear on his protagonist.

The recognition of complexity in Huck's character enabled Mark Twain to do full justice to the conflict between vernacular values and the dominant culture. By situating in a single consciousness both the perverted moral code of a society built on slavery and the vernacular commitment to freedom and spontaneity, he was able to represent the opposed perspectives as alternative modes of experience for the same character. In this way he gets rid of the confusions surrounding the pronoun "I" in the earlier books, where it sometimes designates the author speaking in his own person, sometimes an entirely distinct fictional character. Furthermore, the insight that enabled him to recognize the conflict between accepted values and vernacular protest as a struggle within a single mind does justice to its moral depth, whereas the device he had used earlier— in *The Innocents Abroad*, for example—of identifying the two perspectives with separate characters had flattened the issue out into melodrama. The satire of a decadent slaveholding society gains immensely in force when Mark Twain demonstrates that even the outcast Huck has been in part perverted by it. Huck's conscience is simply the attitudes he has taken over from his environment. What is still sound in him is an impulse from the deepest level of his personality that struggles against the overlay of prejudice and false valuation imposed on all members of the society in the name of religion, morality, law, and refinement.

Finally, it should be pointed out that the conflict in Huck between generous impulse and false belief is depicted by means of a contrast between colloquial and exalted styles. In moments of crisis his conscience addresses him in the language of the dominant culture, a tawdry and faded effort at a high style that is the rhetorical equivalent of the ornaments in the Grangerford parlor. Yet speaking in dialect does not in itself imply moral authority. By every external criterion the King is as much a vernacular character as Huck. The conflict in which Huck is involved is not that of a lower against an upper class or of an alienated fringe of outcasts against a cultivated elite. It is not the issue of frontier West versus genteel East, or of backwoods versus metropolis, but of fidelity to the uncoerced self versus the blurring of attitudes caused by social conformity, by the effort to achieve status or power through exhibiting the approved forms of sensibility.

The exploration of Huck's personality carried Mark Twain beyond satire and even beyond his statement of a vernacular protest against the dominant culture into essentially novelistic modes of writing. Some of the passages he composed when he got out beyond his polemic framework challenge comparison with the greatest achievements in the world's fiction.

The most obvious of Mark Twain's discoveries on the deeper levels of Huck's psyche is the boy's capacity for love. The quality of the emotion is defined in action by his decision to sacrifice himself for Jim, just as Jim attains an impressive dignity when he refuses to escape at the cost of deserting the wounded Tom. Projected into the natural setting, the love of the protagonists for each other becomes the unforgettable beauty of the river when they are allowed to be alone together. It is always summer, and the forces of nature cherish them. From the refuge of the cave on Jackson's Island the thunderstorm is an exhilarating spectacle; Huck's description of it is only less poetic than his description of the dawn which he and Jim witness as they sit half-submerged on the sandy bottom.

Yet if Mark Twain had allowed these passages to stand without qualification as a symbolic account of Huck's emotions he would have undercut the complexity of characterization implied in his recognition of Huck's inner conflict of loyalties. Instead, he uses the natural setting to render a wide range of feelings and motives. The fog that separates the boy from Jim for a time is an externalization of his impulse to deceive Jim by a Tom Sawyerish practical joke. Similarly Jim's snake bite, the only injury suffered by either of the companions from a natural source, is the result of another prank played by Huck before he has learned what friends owe one another.

Still darker aspects of Huck's inner life are projected into the natural setting in the form of ghosts, omens, portents of disaster—the body of superstition that is so conspicuous in Huck's and Jim's world. At the end of Chapter 1 Huck is sitting alone at night by his open window in the Widow Douglas' house:

I felt so lonesome I most wished I was dead. The stars was shining, and the leaves rustled in the woods ever so mournful; and I heard an owl, away off, who-whooing about somebody that was dead, and a whippowill and a dog crying about somebody that was going to die; and the wind was trying to whisper something to me, and I couldn't make out what it was, and so it made the cold shivers run over me. Then away out in the woods I heard that kind of a sound that a ghost makes when it wants to tell about something that's on its mind and can't make itself understood, and so can't rest easy in its grave, and has to go about that way every night grieving. I got so downhearted and scared I did wish I had some company.

The whimpering ghost with something incommunicable on its mind and Huck's cold shivers suggest a burden of guilt and anxiety that is perhaps the punishment he inflicts on himself for defying the mores of St. Petersburg. Whatever the source of these sinister images, they develop the characterization of Huck beyond the needs of the plot. The narrator whose stream of consciousness is recorded here is much more than the innocent protagonist of the pastoral idyl of the raft, more than an ignorant boy who resists being civilized. The vernacular persona is an essentially comic figure; the character we glimpse in Huck's meditation is potentially tragic. Mark Twain's discoveries in the buried strata of Huck's mind point in the same direction as does his intuitive recognition that Huck's and Jim's quest for freedom must end in failure.

A melancholy if not exactly tragic strain in Huck is revealed also by the fictitious autobiographies with which he so often gets himself out of tight places. Like the protocols of a thematic apperception test, they are improvisations on the basis of minimal clues. Huck's inventions are necessary to account for his anomalous situation as a fourteen-year-old boy alone on the river with a Negro man, but they are often carried beyond the demands of utility for sheer love of fable-making. Their luxuriant detail, and the fact that Huck's hearers are usually (although not always) taken in, lend a comic coloring to these inventions, which are authentically in the tradition of the tall tale. But their total effect is somber. When Huck plans his escape from Pap in Chapter 7, he does so by imagining his own death and planting clues which convince everyone in St. Petersburg, including Tom Sawyer, that he has been murdered. In the crisis of Chapter 16 his heightened emotion leads him to produce for the benefit of the slave hunters a harrowing tale to the effect that his father and mother and sister are suffering smallpox on a raft adrift in mid-river, and he is unable to tow the raft ashore. The slave hunters are so touched by the story that they give him forty dollars and careful instructions about how to seek help—farther downstream. Huck tells the Grangerfords "how pap and me and all the family was living on a little farm down at the bottom of Arkansaw, and my sister Mary Ann run off and got married and never was heard of no more, and Bill went to hunt them and he warn't heard of no more, and Tom and Mort died, and then there warn't nobody but just me and pap left, and he was just trimmed down to nothing, on account of his troubles; so when he died I took what there was left, because the farm didn't belong to us, and started up the river, deck passage, and fell overboard."

5

A number of characters besides Huck are presented in greater depth than is necessary either for purposes of satire or for telling the story of his and Jim's quest for freedom. Perhaps the most striking of these is Pap Finn. Like most of the book, Pap comes straight out of Mark Twain's boyhood memories. We have had a glimpse of him as the drunkard sleeping in the shade of a pile of skids on the levee in the opening scene of "Old Times on the Mississippi." His function in the plot, although definite, is limited. He helps to characterize Huck by making vivid the conditions of Huck's childhood. He has transmitted to his son a casual attitude toward chickens and watermelons, a fund of superstitions, a picaresque ability to look out for himself, and even the gift of language. Pap takes Huck away from the comfort and elegance of the Widow's house to the squalor of the deserted cabin across the river, and then by his sadistic beatings forces the boy to escape to Jackson's Island, where the main action of the flight with Jim begins. After the three chapters which Pap dominates (5–7) we do not see him again except as a corpse in the house floating down the river, but Huck refers to him several times later, invoking Pap's testimony to authenticate the aristocratic status of the Widow Douglas, and to support the family philosophy of "borrowing."

In the sociological scheme of the novel Pap provides a matchless specimen of the lowest stratum of whites who are fiercely jealous of their superiority to all Negroes. His monologue on the "govment" in Chapter 6, provoked by the spectacle of the well-dressed free Negro professor from Ohio, seizes in a few lines the essence of Southern race prejudice. Huck shrewdly calls attention to his father's economic code. When the flooded river brings down part of a log raft, he says: "Anybody but pap would 'a' waited and seen the day through, so as to catch more stuff; but that warn't pap's style. Nine logs was enough for one time; he must shove right over to town and sell," mainly in order to buy whiskey.

But these documentary data supply only a minor part of the image of Pap in *Huckleberry Finn*. He provides some of the most mordant comedy in the book. The fashion in which he gives himself away in the monologue on "govment" is worthy of Jonson or Molière:

> It was 'lection day, and I was just about to go and vote myself if I warn't too drunk to get there; but when they told me there was a state in this country where they'd let that nigger vote, I drawed out. I says I'll never vote ag'in. Them's the very words I said; they all heard me; and the country may rot for all me—I'll never vote ag'in as long as I live. And to see the cool way of that nigger —why, he wouldn't 'a' give me the road if I hadn't shoved him out o' the way.

Even when the comedy verges on slapstick it retains its function as characterization. Pap is so completely absorbed in his diatribe that he barks his shins on the pork barrel:

> He hopped around the cabin considerable, first on one leg and then on the other, holding first one shin and then the other one, and at last he let out with his left foot all of a sudden and fetched the tub a rattling kick. But it warn't good judgment, because that was the boot that had a couple of his toes leaking out of the front end of it; so now he raised a howl that fairly made a body's hair raise, and down he went in the dirt, and rolled there, and held his toes; and the cussing he done then laid over anything he had ever done previous. He said so his own self afterwards. He had heard old Sowberry Hagan in his best days, and he said it laid over him, too; but I reckon that was sort of piling it on, maybe.

Pap's detached evaluation of his own accomplishment in swearing gives to his character an almost medieval flavor. In all his degradation he conceives of himself as enacting a role which is less a personal destiny than part of an integral natural-social reality—a reality so stable that he can contemplate it as if it were external to him. On election day he was drunk as a matter of course; it was an objective question, like an effort to predict the weather, whether he might be too drunk to get to the polls. When he settles down for a domestic evening in the cabin, he "took the jug, and said he had enough whiskey there for two drunks and one delirium tremens."

But when the delirium comes, it belies the coolness of his offhand calculation. Huck's description of the drunkard's agony is a nightmare of neurotic suffering that blots out the last vestige of comedy in Pap's image and relates itself in Huck's mind to the ominous sounds he had heard from his window in the Widow's house:

> [Pap] rolled over and over wonderful fast, kicking things every which way, and striking and grabbing at the air with his hands, and screaming and saying there was devils a-hold of him . . .

Then he laid stiller, and didn't make a sound. I could hear the owls and the wolves away off in the woods, and it seemed terrible still . . . By and by he raised up part way and listened, with his head to one side. He says, very low:

"Tramp—tramp—tramp; that's the dead; tramp—tramp—tramp; they're coming after me; but I won't go. Oh, they're here! don't touch me—don't! hands off—they're cold; let go. Oh, let a poor devil alone!"

Then he went down on all fours and crawled off, begging them to let him alone, and he rolled himself up in his blanket and wallowed in under the old pine table, still a-begging; and then he went to crying. I could hear him through the blanket.

Pap's hallucinations externalize inner suffering in images of ghosts and portents. Presently he sees in Huck the Angel of Death and chases him around the cabin with a knife "saying he would kill me, and then I couldn't come for him no more." In fact, the mystery of Pap's anguished psyche has had a supernatural aura all along. He is in a sense a ghost the first time we see him, for his faceless corpse has been found floating in the river; and immediately before his dramatic appearance in Huck's room Jim's hair-ball oracle has announced, "Dey's two angels hoverin' roun' 'bout him. One uv 'em is white en shiny, en t'other one is black. De white one gits him to go right a little while, den de black one sail in en bust it all up. A body can't tell yit which one gwyne to fetch him at de las'." Coming early in the story, at a time when Mark Twain had apparently not yet worked out the details of the plot, this sounds as if he had in mind the possibility of involving Pap more elaborately in the course of events. But aside from the relatively minor incidents that have been mentioned, what the angels might have led Pap to do is never revealed.

He does, however, have an important thematic function. He serves as a forceful reminder that to be a vernacular outcast does not necessarily bring one into contact with the benign forces of nature. Physical withdrawal from society may be plain loafing, without moral significance. Huck's life with Pap in the cabin foreshadows his life with Jim on the raft, but lacks the suggestion of harmony with the natural setting:

It was kind of lazy and jolly, laying off comfortable all day, smoking and fishing, and no books nor study. Two months or more run along, and my clothes got to be all rags and dirt, and I didn't see how I'd ever got to like it so well at the widow's, where you had to wash, and eat on a plate, and comb up, and go to bed and get up regular, and be forever bothering over a book, and have old Miss Watson pecking at you all the time. I didn't want to go back no more . . . It was pretty good times up in the woods there, take it all around.

More explicitly, Pap's denunciation of Huck for the civilized habits the Widow and Miss Watson have imposed on him is a grotesque version of vernacular hostility toward the conventions of refined society:

> Starchy clothes—very. You think you're a good deal of a big-bug, *don't* you? . . . You're educated, too, they say—can read and write. You think you're better'n your father, now, don't you, because he can't? . . . you drop that school, you hear? I'll learn people to bring up a boy to put on airs over his own father and let on to be better'n what *he* is . . . First you know you'll get religion, too. I never see such a son.

This adds another nuance to the book by suggesting that civilized values have something to be said for them after all.

The extent to which Mark Twain's imagination was released in *Huckleberry Finn* to explore multiple perspectives upon the Matter of Hannibal and the Matter of the River can be realized if one compares Pap with the sociologically similar backwoodsmen observed from the steamboat in "Old Times." These "jeans-clad, chills-racked, yellow-faced miserables" are merely comic animals. Pap is even more degraded than they are, lazier, more miserable, but he is not an object of scorn. The fullness with which his degradation and his misery are presented confers on him not so much a human dignity– although it is also that—as the impersonal dignity of art.

In relation to the whole of *Huckleberry Finn*, Pap serves to solidify the image of Huck's and Jim's vernacular paradise by demonstrating that Mark Twain is aware of the darker possibilities confronting them when they escape from the shore to the river. The mass of superstitions with which Pap is so vividly connected (we recall the cross of nails in his boot heel to ward off the devil), standing in contrast to the intimations of blissful harmony with nature in the passages devoted to Huck and Jim alone on the raft, keeps that lyrical vision from seeming mere pathetic fallacy. And the appalling glimpse of Pap's inner life beneath the stereotype of the town drunkard makes him into what might be called a note of tragic relief in a predominantly comic story.

6

It has become a commonplace of criticism that the drastic shift in tone in the last section of *Huckleberry Finn*, from Chapter 31 to the end, poses a problem of interpretation. The drifting raft has reached Arkansas, and the King and the Duke have delivered Jim back into captivity. They make their exit early in the sequence, tarred and feathered as punishment for one more effort to work the "Royal Nonesuch" trick. Tom Sawyer reappears by an implausible coincidence and takes charge of the action, which thereafter centers about his schemes to liberate Jim from confinement in a cabin on the plantation of Tom's Uncle Silas Phelps.

These events have for their prelude a vivid description of Huck's first approach to the Phelps place:

> When I got there it was all still and Sunday-like, and hot and sunshiny; the hands was gone to the fields; and there was them kind of faint dronings of bugs and flies in the air that makes it seem so lonesome and like everybody's dead and gone; and if a breeze fans along and quivers the leaves it makes you feel mournful, because you feel like it's spirits whispering—spirits that's been dead ever so many years—and you always think they're talking about *you*. As a general thing it makes a body wish *he* was dead, too, and done with it all.

And a few lines later:

> I went around and clumb over the back stile by the ash-hopper, and started for the kitchen. When I got a little ways I heard the dim hum of a spinning-wheel wailing along up and sinking along down again; and then I knowed for certain I wished I was dead —for that *is* the lonesomest sound in the whole world.

This passage has much in common with Huck's meditation before his open window in Chapter 1. They are the two most vivid expressions of his belief in ghosts, and in both cases the ghosts are associated in his mind with a deep depression not fully accounted for by the context of the story.

It would be reasonable to suppose that the cause of Huck's depression is the failure of his long effort to help Jim toward freedom. The reader knows that even if Huck could manage to rescue Jim from the Phelpses, they face insuperable difficulties in trying to make their way back up the Mississippi to free territory. Yet oddly enough, Huck does not share this estimate of the situation. He is confident he can find a way out of the impasse: "I went right along, not fixing up any particular plan, but just trusting to Providence to put the right words in my mouth when the time come; for I'd noticed that Providence always did put the right words in my mouth if I left it alone." Somewhat later, Huck points out to Tom that they can easily get Jim out of the log cabin by stealing the key, and "shove off down the river on the raft with Jim, hiding daytimes and running nights, the way me and Jim used to do before. Wouldn't that plan work?" Tom agrees: "Why, cert'nly it would work, like rats a-fighting. But it's too blame' simple; there ain't nothing *to* it. What's the good of a plan that ain't no more trouble than that?"

The tone as much as the substance of the references to the problem of rescuing Jim makes it plain that Huck's view of his predicament cannot account for his depression as he approaches the Phelps plantation. The emotion is the author's rather than Huck's, and it is derived from sources outside the story. In order to determine what these were we must consult Mark Twain's autobiographical reminiscences. The Phelps place as he describes it in the novel has powerful associations for him because it is patterned on the farm of his Uncle John A. Quarles where he spent summers as a boy. "I can see the farm yet, with perfect clearness," he wrote in his *Autobiography*.

> I can see all its belongings, all its details; the family room of the house, with a "trundle" bed in one corner and a spinning-wheel in another—a wheel whose rising and falling wail, heard from a distance, was the mournfulest of all sounds to me, and made me homesick and low spirited, and filled my atmosphere with the wandering spirits of the dead.

Additional associations with the Quarles farm are recorded in Mark Twain's "The Private History of a Campaign That Failed," written a few months after the publication of *Huckleberry Finn*. This bit of fictionalized autobiography describes his experiences as second lieutenant of the Marion Rangers, a rather informal volunteer militia unit organized in Hannibal in the early months of the Civil War. The Quarles farm is here assigned to a man named Mason:

> We stayed several days at Mason's; and after all these years the memory of the dullness, and stillness, and lifelessness of that slumberous farm-house still oppresses my spirit as with a sense of the presence of death and mourning. There was nothing to do, nothing to think about; there was no interest in life. The male part of the household were away in the fields all day, the women were busy and out of our sight; there was no sound but the plaintive wailing of a spinning-wheel, forever moaning out from some distant room—the most lonesome sound in nature, a sound steeped and sodden with homesickness and the emptiness of life.

The emotional overtones of the memories recorded in "The Private History" are made more explicit in a letter Mark Twain wrote in 1890:

> I was a *soldier* two weeks once in the beginning of the war, and was hunted like a rat the whole time . . . My splendid Kipling himself hasn't a more burnt-in, hard-baked and unforgettable familiarity with that death-on-the-pale-horse-with-hell-following-

after which is a raw soldier's first fortnight in the field—and which, without any doubt, is the most tremendous fortnight and the vividest he is ever going to see.

But while there are references to fear of the enemy in "The Private History," they are mainly comic, and the dullness and lifelessness that afflict the neophyte soldiers at the Mason farm do not suggest the feeling of being hunted like a rat. More significant, perhaps, is an incident Mark Twain places a few pages later in "The Private History." Albert B. Paine says it was invented; and it does have the air of fiction. But it reveals the emotional coloring of the author's recollections. He relates that he fired in the dark at a man approaching on horseback, who was killed. Although five other shots were fired at the same moment, and he did not at bottom believe his shot had struck its mark, still his "diseased imagination" convinced him he was guilty. "The thought shot through me that I was a murderer; that I had killed a man—a man who had never done me any harm. That was the coldest sensation that ever went through my marrow."

Huck also experiences a strong and not easily explicable feeling of guilt a few pages after his arrival at the Phelpses'. When he sees the Duke and the King ridden out of the nearby town on a rail, surrounded by a howling mob, he says:

> It was a dreadful thing to see. Human beings *can* be awful cruel to one another . . . So we poked along back home, and I warn't feeling so brash as I was before, but kind of ornery, and humble, and to blame, somehow—though *I* hadn't done nothing. But that's always the way; it don't make no difference whether you do right or wrong, a person's conscience ain't got no sense, and just goes for him *anyway*. If I had a yaller dog that didn't know no more than a person's conscience does I would pison him.

The close linkage of the Phelps and Mason farms with Mark Twain's memory of the Quarles place strongly suggests that Huck's depression is caused by a sense of guilt whose sources were buried in the writer's childhood. It is well known that Mark Twain was tormented all his life by such feelings. A fable written in 1876, "The Facts Concerning the Recent Carnival of Crime in Connecticut," makes comedy of his sufferings; but they were serious and chronic. In his twenties, because of an imaginary error in administering an opiate, he had insisted he was to blame for the death of his brother from injuries received in the explosion of a steamboat. Later he accused himself of murdering his son Langdon when he neglected to keep him covered during a carriage ride in cold weather, and the child died of diphtheria.

But why was Mark Twain's latent feeling of guilt drawn up into consciousness at a specific moment in the writing of *Huckleberry Finn?* The most probable explanation is that at this point he was obliged to admit finally to himself that Huck's and Jim's journey down the river could not be imagined as leading to freedom for either of them. Because of the symbolic meaning the journey had taken on for him, the recognition was more than a perception of difficulty in contriving a plausible ending for the book. He had found a solution to the technical problem that satisfied him, if one is to judge from his evident zest in the complicated pranks of Tom Sawyer that occupy the last ten chapters. But in order to write these chapters he had to abandon the compelling image of the happiness of Huck and Jim on the raft and thus to acknowledge that the vernacular values embodied in his story were mere figments of the imagination, not capable of being reconciled with social reality. To be sure, he had been half-aware from the beginning that the quest of his protagonists was doomed. Huck had repeatedly appeared in the role of a Tiresias[1] powerless to prevent the deceptions and brutalities he was compelled to witness. Yet Providence had always put the right words in his mouth when the time came, and by innocent guile he had extricated himself and Jim from danger after danger. Now the drifting had come to an end.

At an earlier impasse in the plot Mark Twain had shattered the raft under the paddle wheel of a steamboat. He now destroys it again, symbolically, by revealing that Huck's and Jim's journey, with all its anxieties, has been pointless. Tom Sawyer is bearer of the news that Jim has been freed in Miss Watson's will. Tom withholds the information, however, in order to trick Huck and Jim into the meaningless game of an Evasion that makes the word (borrowed from Dumas) into a devastating pun. Tom takes control and Huck becomes once again a subordinate carrying out orders. As if to signal the change of perspective and the shift in his own identification, Mark Twain gives Huck Tom's name through an improbable mistake on the part of Aunt Sally Phelps. We can hardly fail to perceive the weight of the author's feeling in Huck's statement on this occasion: "it was like being born again, I was so glad to find out who I was." Mark Twain has found out who he must be in order to end his book: he must be Tom.

In more abstract terms, he must withdraw from his imaginative participation in Huck's and Jim's quest for freedom. If the story was to be stripped of its tragic implications, Tom's perspective was the logical one to adopt because his intensely conventional sense of values made him impervious to the moral significance of the journey

---

1. In Greek mythology, Tiresias was blinded by the goddess Athena, who, in recompense, gave him the power to foretell the future but not to change it [*Editors*].

on the raft. Huck can hardly believe that Tom would collaborate in the crime of helping a runaway slave, and Huck is right. Tom merely devises charades involving a man who is already in a technical sense free. The consequences of the shift in point of view are strikingly evident in the treatment of Jim, who is subjected to farcical indignities. This is disturbing to the reader who has seen Jim take on moral and emotional stature, but it is necessary if everything is to be forced back into the framework of comedy. Mark Twain's portrayal of Huck and Jim as complex characters has carried him beyond the limits of his original plan: we must not forget that the literary ancestry of the book is to be found in backwoods humor. As Huck approaches the Phelps plantation the writer has on his hands a hybrid—a comic story in which the protagonists have acquired something like tragic depth.

In deciding to end the book with the description of Tom's unnecessary contrivances for rescuing Jim, Mark Twain was certain to produce an anticlimax. But he was a great comic writer, able to score local triumphs in the most unlikely circumstances. The last chapters have a number of brilliant touches—the slave who carries the witch pie to Jim, Aunt Sally's trouble in counting her spoons, Uncle Silas and the ratholes, the unforgettable Sister Hotchkiss. Even Tom's horseplay would be amusing if it were not spun out to such length and if we were not asked to accept it as the conclusion of *Huckleberry Finn*. Although Jim is reduced to the level of farce, Tom is a comic figure in the classical sense of being a victim of delusion. He is not aware of being cruel to Jim because he does not perceive him as a human being. For Tom, Jim is the hero of a historical romance, a peer of the Man in the Iron Mask or the Count of Monte Cristo. Mark Twain is consciously imitating *Don Quixote*, and there are moments not unworthy of the model, as when Tom admits that "we got to dig him out with the picks, and *let on* it's case-knives."

But Tom has no tragic dimension whatever. There is not even any force of common sense in him to struggle against his perverted imagination as Huck's innate loyalty and generosity struggle against his deformed conscience. Although Mark Twain is indulgent toward Tom, he adds him to the list of characters who employ the soul-butter style of false pathos. The inscriptions Tom composes for Jim to "scrabble onto the wall" of the cabin might have been composed by the Duke:

1. Here a captive heart busted.
2. Here a poor prisoner, forsook by the world and friends, fretted his sorrowful life.
3. Here a lonely heart broke, and a worn spirit went to its rest, after thirty-seven years of solitary captivity.

4. Here, homeless and friendless, after thirty-seven years of bitter captivity, perished a noble stranger, natural son of Louis XIV.

While he was reading these noble sentiments aloud, "Tom's voice trembled . . . and he most broke down."

7

Mark Twain's partial shift of identification from Huck to Tom in the final sequence was one response to his recognition that Huck's and Jim's quest for freedom was only a dream: he attempted to cover with a veil of parody and farce the harsh facts that condemned it to failure. The brief episode involving Colonel Sherburn embodies yet another response to his disillusionment. The extraordinary vividness of the scenes in which Sherburn figures—only a halfdozen pages all told—is emphasized by their air of being an intrusion into the story. Of course, in the episodic structure of *Huckleberry Finn* many characters appear for a moment and disappear. Even so, the Sherburn episode seems unusually isolated. None of the principal characters is involved in or affected by it: Jim, the Duke, and the King are offstage, and Huck is a spectator whom even the author hardly notices. We are told nothing about his reaction except that he did not want to stay around. He goes abruptly off to the circus and does not refer to Sherburn again.

Like Huck's depression as he nears the Phelps planatation, the Sherburn episode is linked with Mark Twain's own experience. The shooting of Boggs follows closely the murder of "Uncle Sam" Smarr by a merchant named Owsley in Hannibal in 1845, when Sam Clemens was nine years old. Although it is not clear that he actually witnessed it, he mentioned the incident at least four times at intervals during his later life, including one retelling as late as 1898, when he said he had often dreamed about it. Mark Twain prepares for the shooting in *Huckleberry Finn* by careful attention to the brutality of the loafers in front of stores in Bricksville. "There couldn't anything wake them up all over, and make them happy all over, like a dog-fight—unless it might be putting turpentine on a stray dog and setting fire to him, or tying a tin pan to his tail and see him run himself to death." The prurient curiosity of the townspeople who shove and pull to catch a glimpse of Boggs as he lies dying in the drugstore with a heavy Bible on his chest, and their pleasure in the re-enactment of the shooting by the man in the big white fur stovepipe hat, also help to make Bricksville an appropriate setting for Sherburn's crime.

The shooting is in Chapter 21, and the scene in which Sherburn scatters the mob by his contemptuous speech is in the following chapter. There is evidence that Mark Twain put aside the manuscript for a time near the end of Chapter 21. If there was such an interruption in his work on the novel, it might account for a marked change in tone. In Chapter 21 Sherburn is an unsympathetic character. His killing of Boggs is motivated solely by arrogance, and the introduction of Boggs's daughter is an invitation to the reader to consider Sherburn an inhuman monster. In Chapter 22, on the other hand, the Colonel appears in an oddly favorable light. The townspeople have now become a mob; there are several touches that suggest Mark Twain was recalling the descriptions of mobs in Carlyle's *French Revolution* and other works of history and fiction. He considered mobs to be subhuman aggregates generating psychological pressures that destroyed individual freedom of choice. In a passage written for *Life on the Mississippi* but omitted from the book Mark Twain makes scathing generalizations about the cowardice of mobs, especially in the South but also in other regions, that closely parallel Sherburn's speech.

In other words, however hostile may be the depiction of Sherburn in Chapter 21, in Chapter 22 we have yet another instance of Mark Twain's identifying himself, at least partially, with a character in the novel other than Huck. The image of Sherburn standing on the roof of the porch in front of his house with the shotgun that is the only weapon in sight has an emblematic quality. He is a solitary figure, not identified with the townspeople, and because they are violently hostile to him, an outcast. But he is not weaker than they, he is stronger. He stands above the mob, looking down on it. He is "a heap the best dressed man in that town," and he is more intelligent than his neighbors. The scornful courage with which he defies the mob redeems him from the taint of cowardice implied in his shooting of an unarmed man who was trying to escape. Many members of the mob he faces are presumably armed; the shotgun he holds is not the source of his power but merely a symbol of the personal force with which he dominates the community.

The Colonel's repeated references to one Buck Harkness, the leader of the mob, whom he acknowledges to be "half-a-man," suggest that the scene represents a contest between two potential leaders in Bricksville. Harkness is the strongest man with whom the townspeople can identify themselves. In his pride Sherburn chooses isolation, but he demonstrates that he is stronger than Harkness, for the mob, including Harkness, obeys his command to "*leave*—and take your half-a-man· with you."

Sherburn belongs to the series of characters in Mark Twain's later work that have been called "transcendent figures." Other examples are Hank Morgan in *A Connecticut Yankee*; Pudd'nhead Wilson; and Satan in *The Mysterious Stranger*. They exhibit certain common traits, more fully developed with the passage of time. They are isolated by their intellectual superiority to the community; they are contemptuous of mankind in general; and they have more than ordinary power. Satan, the culmination of the series, is omnipotent. Significantly, he is without a moral sense—that is, a conscience, a sense of guilt. He is not torn by the kind of inner struggle that Huck experiences. But he is also without Huck's sound heart. The price of power is the surrender of all human warmth.

Colonel Sherburn's cold-blooded murder of Boggs, his failure to experience remorse after the act, and his withering scorn of the townspeople are disquieting portents for the future. Mark Twain, like Huck, was sickened by the brutality he had witnessed in the society along the river. But he had an adult aggressiveness foreign to Huck's character. At a certain point he could no longer endure the anguish of being a passive observer. His imagination sought refuge in the image of an alternative persona who was protected against suffering by being devoid of pity or guilt, yet could denounce the human race for its cowardice and cruelty, and perhaps even take action against it. The appearance of Sherburn in *Huckleberry Finn* is ominous because a writer who shares his attitude toward human beings is in danger of abandoning imaginative insight for moralistic invective. The slogan of "the damned human race" that later became Mark Twain's proverb spelled the sacrifice of art to ideology. Colonel Sherburn would prove to be Mark Twain's dark angel. His part in the novel, and that of Tom Sawyer, are flaws in a work that otherwise approaches perfection as an embodiment of American experience in a radically new and appropriate literary mode.

EDWIN H. CADY

Huckleberry Finn by Common Day†

In the light of common day, which was characteristically Clemens's light, his masterpiece appears more realistic than a reading of the bulk of critical discussion during the past two decades would give one warrant to believe. *Adventures of Huckleberry Finn* by common light looks different (older and perhaps fresher) and more securely a masterpiece than some schools of judgment allow. Perhaps one cannot say that the great book *is* realism or only realism. But it may be worthwhile to see how it looks in certain contexts of its school and moment.

† From *The Light of Common Day: Realism in American Fiction*, by Edwin H. Cady. Copyright © 1971 by Indiana University Press. Reprinted by permission of the publisher. Pp. 88–89 and 101–19.

Not to repeat what has been well said by Henry Nash Smith and Harold Kolb, *Huckleberry Finn* is a brilliant hybridization of the major sources of native realism—of "frontier humor" in the full flowering of its vernacular tradition, its war against pretentiousness, its skill in the reductive techniques of the "sell"; and of the American travel book in its maturely antiromantic phase, with its insights into the meaning and importance of cultural relativity. It is, however, upon the triumph of Twain's novel in wedding an ancient, even archetypal, genre to a brand new, contemporaneous genre that I wish to focus. In a number of central, fateful ways the novel is a picaresque (meaning, for purposes of this discussion, a work of fiction in the tradition of the literature of roguery). It is also a *boy-book* (a book written not so much for the entertainment of boys as for the purpose of exploring and defining the experience—and its significance—of the American boy).

* * *

III

The form of *Adventures of Huckleberry Finn* is analogous to the shape of what is called a "block-I." The work consists of a long central narration, picaresque in form and substance and framed on either end by boy-book narratives. There is not a plot in the book so much as a series of actions ("box-car" or "beads-on-a-string" construction), and the actions serve varying purposes—presentational, critical, or technical—in the novel as a whole. The "author" is, as the second sentence tells us, "Mr. Mark Twain." But "Mr. Twain" does not appear in the book except as the writer of the introductory "Notice"; and Samuel L. Clemens, the creator of Mark Twain, does not appear except perhaps as the author of the second prefatory note, "Explanatory," on the dialects. Since, as Clemens had planned for a decade, the narrative point of view is "autobiographical," with Huck Finn telling us everything in the language of dramatic report, summary, or revery, I find it hard to determine the answer to questions about "the implied author."

For pluralistic as well as esthetic reasons * * * realists were concerned first and last with character, sacrificing every fictional consideration to present their vision of personhood. Technically the choice of a first-person narrator presents the artist from the beginning with a crux. Shall the teller be primarily an "I-narrator" or an "eye-narrator"? Shall the stress fall primarily on what the narrator sees, on what his vision reveals to us? Or shall it fall on how the observer-narrator responds and changes in response to outward events? On the whole, I should suppose the method of Joyce's *Ulysses* to be mainly illustrative of the self-conscious "I-narrator." Twain, prompted by realism, by his age's concept of the static psyche, and by the traditions of the picaresque, chose to present Huck largely as a lens to furnish us a sharper vision of otherwise unknowable reality. To use Jamesean terms, Huck "registers" for us, and "reveals." Because he can take us "inside" his own mind and emotions, he can expose himself as a figure of emergent moral reality, though not a maturing or altered personality. What we see through his eyes are a fresh, immediate, wonder-laden boy's world of nature and boy-life side by side with a rogue-riddled world of social failure and decadence.

The first three chapters, connecting with the boy-life of *Tom Sawyer*, begin subtly to introduce two themes: negative realism and the problem of "civilization." The original cover and title page of the book gave its full title as *Adventures of Huckleberry Finn (Tom Sawyer's Comrade)*; and from the beginning Tom's "comrade" plays Sancho to Tom's Quixote without fail. The boys are, naturally and forgivably, God's romantic fools and God's picaros. A little older, they might become what Twain recalled of himself at twenty —chuckle-headed, "a callow fool, a self-sufficient ass." A little older yet, "one-horse" men. But what would be despicable in men is sympathetic in boys. They can be robbers, Robin Hoods, vicarious heroes of toweringly bloody, absurd romance: and they are so, even Huck, except that Huck is often too ignorant, a "sap-head," to know how to enjoy the immunities of romance and forever brings a lethally pragmatic intelligence to bear. No quixotism can help Huck see camels and elephants, a caravan laden with diamonds, in a primer class's Sunday School picnic. Without malice, with a Sancho's phlegm, he concludes "that all that stuff was only just one of Tom Sawyer's lies. I reckoned he believed in the A-rabs and the elephants, but as for me I think different. It had all the marks of a Sunday-school."

Tom's romanticism formed the easier half of the "civilization" which oppressed Huck, however. Life with the Widow Douglas and Miss Watson turned out so "dismal regular and decent" he ran away, and only Tom could get him to go back. Eventually, though, Huck began to like housekeeping ways and began to learn in school that "six times seven is thirty-five." But he was apprehensive. Pap was sure to come back. And with chapter four begins the first of five main actions contained within the boy-life frame of the novel. Throughout them things happen to a largely passive Huck. For the most part he does not plan and does not move until he has to. But things happen. And in the first episode, which spans chapters four through seven and might be called "Pap against Civilization," it is the return of Pap which snatches the novel away from mere boy-life and negative realism.

Early in the novel, especially, no admiration can be too extravagant in appreciation of its fictional "business" scenes, Twain's transitions. They are glorious: Huck turning to Miss Watson's Jim for a little conjuring and their solemn foisting off of Huck's counterfeit quarter on Jim's magic hairball; Huck's escape from Pap's cabin; Huck succeeding after all in conning essential intelligence from canny Judith Loftus. The studies, the ingenuities, the wealth of power lavished on vision, characterization, drama, speech, language, just to move the action alone—one can say only that such technique is the overflow of a gusher of genius.

Certain incautious speculations about the novel have supposed that Twain intended it to become a general indictment of civilization in favor either of primitivism or the frontier. They seem to have ignored Pap. If life at the Widow's had been itchy and dismal, even to his son Pap was horrible:

> His hair was long and tangled and greasy, and hung down, and you could see his eyes shining through like he was behind vines. . . . There warn't no color in his face, where his face showed; it was white; not like another man's white, but a white to make a body sick, a white to make a body's flesh crawl—a tree-toad white, a fish-belly white. As for his clothes—just rags, that was all.

Pap was a real rogue close to the end of his road. He was a thief and a drunk, illiterate, filthy, full of howling hate against blacks, schools, cleanliness, and respectability, a con artist, and a sadist who cowhided and licked Huck with his "hick'ry" until he "was all over welts" and feared for his life. Pap was a man with nothing to show for the frontier experience but the experience of cultural erosion.

On the one hand, back with his Pap Huck could find things "lazy and jolly" and "pretty good times up there in the woods"; on the other, he scarcely got away with his life. If the counter and opposite to "civilization" were taken to be Pap, there would be much to say for town, school, and the Widow. Easy boy-life evading the cramps of civilization was one thing; real life with a real picaro was something else. Huck opted out and skipped out on both, "murdering" himself and running and hiding to drop even below the town bum's level, clean out of sight and legal being. He became technically a nonperson for the duration of the long, central section of the novel.

Escaping to use Jackson's Island as a hideout. Huck could play lonesome, autonomous Robinson Crusoe, monarch of all he surveys, until he stumbled upon his man Friday—Miss Watson's Jim, who had become another legal nonperson, a fugitive slave. And here of course begins the second main action of the novel ("Jim against

Civilization"), and we are presented with a third major tension to interact with and complicate all the rest. It will not do, the novel will not warrant it, to suppose Jim a "Black Christ." The novel's actual point would have seemed far more significant to Clemens, anyway: Jim is a man, altogether human, a person entitled to the dignities and compassions pertaining to personhood. But even Jim, as Woolman and Jefferson had argued must inevitably be true of a slave, was a bit of a picaro. His mighty brag about his witch's ride and his hairball swindle suggest that he is, like the boys, a sympathetic rogue but no saint. He is a man of warmth, authenticity, and dignity which are amazing not for their superhuman dimensions but their power to survive slavery and for the force with which they confound the stupid contempt of a smug slave civilization.

What unites the comrade of Tom Sawyer in solidarity with the despised and technically criminal black man is their lost, defiant, underground condition, their unpersonhood in the eyes of established society and its standards. His at-one-ness with Jim remains to the end a source of trouble and guilt to Huck. How can the comrade of Tom Sawyer be living and chumming with a black man? The comrade's answer is, because he is really unworthy of Tom, being so ignorant, lowdown, and orney as he is, dragged up as the son of the town drunk and bum, a boy that never had no show. The conditions of Huck and Jim become polar to society and its civilized standards. The unspoken problem, the potential morality not moralized, the issue developing toward eventual revelation is the ever more strained and ironic tension between those poles: one condition or the other must be wrong, must at last be condemned as not only absurd but evil.

When Huck, moving "as hard as I could go," bursts into the cave exclaiming, "Git up and hump yourself, Jim! There ain't a minute to lose. They're after us!" his personal identification with Jim has been unpremeditatedly solidified to a degree which no subsequent event or meditation could dissolve. And the next group of chapters, perhaps just barely unified enough to be an episode ("Huck and Jim"), seems to me to have taken out of context by some criticism. Going down the river on a raft in chapters twelve through sixteen restores to Huck familiar pleasures of Crusoeness and boy-picarism. Huck does say, "we lived pretty high"; but he had liked it in the sugar hogshead and Pap's cabin. The actual proportion between pages devoted to feelings of security and natural idyll and pages devoted to other things in this section of the novel is two to thirty-nine. The other things are terror, wreck, lostness, natural menace, failure, and disaster. It wasn't likely than an author of Clemens's generation would take seriously the notion of idyllic nature, and he did not. After Darwin there were few reasons to suppose that nature might be a safe and pleasant haven or that, like Emerson's poet, one could retire to his own green hills alone where man in the bush with God might meet. It seemed more likely that one might meet competition, suffering, and extinction in the bush; and nothing in Clemens's experiences of nature on the river or in the West had given rise to romantic expectations. Like the pilot's cub in "Old Times on the Mississippi," Huck had to learn to read the river; and what he read was hard, disillusioning stuff.

The most significant dramas in this third section of the book are two which portray moments when Huck succumbs to boyishness and the lure of Tom Sawyerism, when he tries to play the Don to Jim's Sancho. Seeing by lightning flashes the carcass of a steamboat wrecked on a rock and likely to wash away at any moment, Huck fires up with the idea of boarding and looting her. He persuades reluctant, sensible Jim by asking, "Do you reckon Tom Sawyer would ever go by this thing? Not for pie, he wouldn't. He'd call it an adventure—that's what he'd call it. . . . And wouldn't he throw style into it?—wouldn't he spread himself, nor nothing?" But when it turns out to be a real, not a boy's adventure; when they discover real cutthroats, not boy picaros on board the *Sir Walter Scott*, the adventure turns out to be an experience of sickening terror, no fun at all. Reality on the river is no joke.

Something of the same thing is true of the next adventure, which the author paced beautifully into Huck's narrative. Inevitably, part of the loot from the *Sir Walter Scott* consists of romanticistic fiction which Huck reads aloud to Jim about "kings and dukes and earls and such, and how gaudy they dressed, and how much style they put on." Jim is fascinated but, playing Sancho, not much impressed with royalty. He sees mighty sensible reasons for being less than convinced by the majesty or wisdom of Solomon and proves to Huck that he can outdo him at logic. We are prepared for the eventual entry of the Duke and the Dauphin; but, more immediately, we are prepared for the scene in which Huck's intellectual acceptance of Jim becomes final. Separated in a fog, they fight all night to find each other in a terror of blind lostness. When Huck finally does find the raft he catches Jim asleep, exhausted by labor, vigil, and grief. A devil of Tom Sawyerism and perhaps some pique at losing his argument possesses Huck. He ignores Jim's joy at reunion, persuades him that the danger was all a dream, tempts him into a wild interpretation of the dream, then lets him see that it was a joke, a "sell," and that Jim has been tricked, made a fool of.

Jim's reaction is a revelation to Huck. Jim's emotions are real, and Jim offended has dignity. Jim is a real person. Huck's evidence that Jim has been fooled is a litter of "leaves and rubbish on the raft and smashed oar" from the wild night of crashing into invisible tow-heads. Huck trips Jim's too eager interpretation with them, and Jim answers "steady without ever smiling":

> "When I got all wore out wid work, en wid de callin' for you, en went to sleep, my heart wuz mos' broke bekase you wuz los', en I didn' k'yer no mo' what become er me an de raf'. En when I wake up en fine you back agin', all safe en soun', de tears come en I could a got down on my knees en kiss yo' foot I's so thankful. En all you wuz thinkin 'bout wuz how you could make a fool uv ole Jim wid a lie. Dat truck dah is *trash*; en trash is what people is dat puts dirt on de head er dey fren's en makes 'em ashamed."
>
> Then he got up slow, and walked to the wigwam, and went in there, without saying anything but that. But that was enough. It made me feel so mean I could almost kissed *his* foot to get him to take it back.
>
> It was fifteen minutes before I could work myself up to go and humble myself to a nigger—but I done it, and I warn't ever sorry for it afterwards, neither. I didn't do him no more mean tricks, and I wouldn't done that one if I'd 'a' knowed it would make him feel that way.

After that, though scraps of "conscience" from a slave-holding "civilization" scorch him, Huck employs his finest picaresque talents to lie and connive and save Jim from slave-catchers until the river gets them. A steamboat runs smashing over the raft, and Huck comes up from a deep dive to avoid the paddle-wheel and finds Jim and the raft apparently gone forever. He swims ashore to stumble into the most poignant and perhaps significant of his adventures, with the Grangerford-Shepherdson feud, constituting the fourth major action of the novel

As we look down the great valley with Huck in a year sometime near 1840, the finest representatives we meet of what purports to be its civilization are the Grangerfords. They are gentry; and there is much to be said for them. They are clean, slim, handsome, courageous, generous, disciplined and by their lights honorable and cultivated Christian ladies and gentlemen. The tragedy is that in certain essential respects their light is darkness. After the knightly code of honor had degenerated into the *code duello* among European gentry, the code was sure to degenerate a step lower to the noncodes of shooting on sight and bushwhacking on the frontier. And so the feud possessed these best of citizens like a disease. In them civilization had murderously turned into anticivilization. The same could be said for the fate of the ideas of Castiglione: the arts of the courtier had become the gorgeous absurdities of a genteel romanticism. Huck's innocent accounts of the art of Miss Emmeline, especially the obituary of Stephen Dowling Botts, provide the finest and funniest castigations of sentimentality and Byronic strut ever achieved by a negative realist. But by the end of the episode, in two wonderfully *realized* chapters, the Grangerford-Shepherdson feud has become a Missouri *Romeo and Juliet* illustrating not merely aristocratic pride and greed for eminence but the agonies of an obsolete, vicious Sir Walter Scottism. Decayed romanticism has turned the best people in the book, in the region, suicidally irrational. Huck covers up his slain comrade's face and cries "a little" and moves on. There is nothing else to do.

Back on the raft, which hidden-out Jim has of course refurbished, life seems lovely for "two or three days"—especially since Huck and Jim do not sweat about the fact that, Cairo and the free states long gone by, Jim is going nowhere. And then the major picaros arrive, one jump ahead of the dogs and a lynch mob, and Huck naturally takes them aboard the raft. Here, at chapter nineteen, begins the final major action of the central core of *Adventures of Huckleberry Finn*. What could be called "The Duke and the Dauphin" contains four subepisodes to illustrate their preposterous roguery.

"It didn't take me long," says Huck, "to make up my mind that these liars warn't no kings nor dukes, at all, but just low-down humbugs and frauds. But I never said nothing, never let on": he knew where he was. "If I never learnt nothing else out of Pap, I learnt that the best way to get along with his kind of people is to let them have their own way." As events turn out, Huck's shrewd judgment has the defects of a boy's lack of forecast. Letting the rapscallions have their way will put Huck's life in danger and get Jim sold back into bondage; but technically it lets the central action of the novel surge forward.

As the last spinal episode of *Adventures of Huckleberry Finn*, "The Duke and the Dauphin" constitutes a brilliant picaresque. Here it becomes clear that the loose, shaggy progressions of the ancient form and the ironies traditional to its equivocal tone and point of view perfectly match the author's needs. Introducing the rogues on the raft and recounting their sack of Pokeville, Clemens "plays it" upon us his readers with dismaying skill. Our vicarious release through identification with the scoundrel in action is joyful. But at Bricksville we are brought up sharply, sickeningly, by a glimpse through the veils of fun and safety into tragic evil.

It is, I think, essential to see that, in some small defiance of chapter divisions, the adventure of "Bricksville" is all one action from the introduction in chapter twenty-one of the rapscallions' wonderful Shakespearian travesty to the summing up by Huck toward the end of chapter twenty-three: "Sometimes I wish we could hear of a country that's out of kings," and (of the Duke and Dauphin) "you couldn't tell them from the real kind." The elements of the adventure are: the shooting of Boggs and its aftermath; the circus; and "The Royal Nonesuch."

Problems of tone and perspective throughout "Bricksville" are extraordinary complex—and rich. In spite of a great deal of modern day longing to the contrary, Huckleberry Finn never is John Woolman. As a boy and as our perspective upon the action, Huck is an innocent but no bleeding heart. He has not quite learned to read the river. His compassion for old man Boggs's daughter is exceeded by his concern for the "drunk" circus rider, and his enthusiasm for the king "cutting shines" almost matches his delight in the circus. It is never clear that Huck makes much more of a distinction among the three "circuses" than the village loafers. Morally, that is all right for a boy, especially Huck, the picaresque son of a picaro, an innocent, sympathetic picaro, son and associate of antipathetic, guilty scoundrels. His condition makes him an ideal, and in "Bricksville" a virtually transparent, lens. But all the opposites are true for the rogues and their marks, the men of Bricksville. Their condition is evident at a glance. They are totally devoid of the satisfactions of civilization. The loafers perish about the slimy street, scrounging chaw-tobacco, dying for excitement, any relief from their horror of ennui: a dog-fight, torturing a dog to death, a fight, a shooting, a lynching—anything! And the Duke and the Dauphin are just the boys to give it to them, for a price. The picaros know how to "work" Bricksville. They know all the moves in advance because they know what is the matter. Without civilized reality, Bricksville is sick of rotten romanticism.

The circus is fine for a boy—innocent fantasy for the innocent. But the circus provides a foil and a curiously complex objective correlative for the Bricksville tragedy, the shooting of Boggs, because it reveals that Bricksville has no sense of human reality. One circus is as good as another; at last the real shooting and abortive lynching become only modes of entertainment: there is no reality. Sherburn shoots Boggs and Boggs insists upon getting shot because both are victims of Sir Walter Scottism—a disease, obviously, of the region's middle classes as well as its aristocracy. And when the mob comes to lynch him, Colonel Sherburn tells them what they really are: cowards, dupes, and silly dreamers. "Now the thing for *you* to do is to droop your tails and go home and crawl in a hole," Sherburn advises the men of Bricksville; and they do it.

The smashing success of the rapscallions' "campaign" with three nights of "The Royal Nonesuch" and their clean getaway with the loot tells us why Sherburn is right and what the situation means. Unable to score with fake Shakespeare, the king and duke promise salacity. The biggest line on their poster says, "LADIES AND CHILDREN NOT ADMITTED"; and, as the duke remarks, "if that line don't fetch them, I don't know Arkansaw!' " But he does know, and foresees exactly their reactions to his "sell." How does he know? Because he understands the ancient rules of picarism, which are much like the ancient rules of the gypsy and other confidence men. There's a little larceny is every human heart and so, although you can't cheat an honest man, you can gull almost anybody somehow. And what those con men know about their society is that, perishing of boredom, sodden in Sir Walter Scottism, it will do almost anything for a sufficiently attractive fantasy, no matter how absurd or destructive.

After "Bricksville" we come back to human reality with Jim, an authentic adult, a man, grieving over real losses. Though Huck says he understands Jim, the words he speaks suggest that the degree of his empathy has sometimes been overestimated:

> I know what it was about. He was thinking about his wife and his children, away up yonder, and he was low and homesick; because he hadn't ever been away from home before in his life; and I do believe he cared just as much for his people as white folks does for their'n. It don't seem natural, but I reckon it's so.

Then Huck reports the heartbreaking story of Jim's discovery that his "little 'Lizabeth" was deaf and dumb. I cannot feel that one ought to suppose that Huck's distancing of himself from Jim here is consciously or strategically ironic on Huck's part. There is biting human irony here, but it is the novel's irony, the author's irony, of which Huck serves as an instrument and in part the boy-innocent butt.

The irony is in fact only visible (as in the work of a realist it should be) to the reader and his perspectives. The irony is that the false, empty, stupid and grotesquely illusioned caricature of a "civilization" represented by Bricksville should presume to hold in chattel bondage and contempt a real man like Jim. In Huck's next adventure that irony is multiplied by the silly vulnerability to the duke and king of the Wilks family and most of the citizens of their nameless village. What "fetches" them so thoroughly that the picaros almost pull off a major confidence game, which includes swindling orphans and selling slaves off down the river, is a travesty of romantic sentimentality. Huck's language, because this is one disease of adult and feminine emotional life to which a boy is immune, tells us everything, "sobbing and swabbing," "tears and flapdoodle," "rot and slush," "all that soul-butter and hogwash." The upshot is that, though the deadbeats go too far and see their game bust, the self-condemnation of the "civilization" is made complete when the Wilks women, honest, generous women, reveal their moral idiocy Clemens may not, even during this final caper of the Duke and the Dauphin, have yet decided upon the damnation of the human race.

But there remains no doubt as to his novel's conclusion about the proslavery South.

That conclusion, it seems to me, is the nail driven home by Huck's famous meditation after the picaros, desperate for whiskey, have "played it" on him too:

> I thought till I wore my head sore, but I couldn't see no way out of the trouble. After all this long journey, and after all we'd done for them scoundrels, here was it all come to nothing, everything all busted up and ruined, because they could have the heart to serve Jim such a trick as that, and make him a slave again all his life, and amongst strangers, too, for forty dirty dollars.

The stages of Huck's thought are worth tracing. He thinks that Jim would be better off home, "as long as he'd *got* to be a slave," and he'd better write home. But he gives up the notion because (a) Miss Watson would "sell him straight down the river again" and, even if she didn't, "everybody naturally despises an ungrateful nigger" and Jim would always "feel ornery and disgraced"; and (b) everybody would find out that "Huck Finn helped a nigger to get his freedom" and he'd be justly shamed. All at once, and in the precise language of the fundamentalist conversion-experience which dominated the regional religion, Huck enters a crisis of conscience. Not yet meaning to become "good," he makes a discovery: "You can't pray a lie." So, "full of trouble" and confounded, he decides in fact to repent, to turn Jim in. At once his burden rolls away, and he feels "light as a feather. . . . good and all washed clean of sin for the first time I had ever felt so in my life."

But then Huck reflects in terms neither social nor religious, only human, about Jim the person, the self-sacrificial friend, the man he protected from slave-catchers, and crisis returns. He picks up the letter to Miss Watson which had made his act of contrition and instrument of salvation, and he considers:

> It was a close place. I took it up, and held it in my hand. I was a trembling, because I'd got to decide, forever, betwixt two things, and I knowed it. I studied a minute, sort of holding my breath, and then says to myself:
> "All right, then, I'll *go* to hell"—and tore it up.
> It was awful thoughts and awful words, but they was said. And I let them stay said: and never thought no more about reforming. I shoved the whole thing out of my head; and said I would take up wickedness again, which was in my line, being brung up to it, and the other warn't. And for a starter, I would go to work and steal Jim out of slavery again; and if I could think up anything worse, I would do that, too; because as long as I was in, and in for good, I might as well go the whole hog.

Couched in the language of evangelical "testimony," Huck's was the problem, as old as Abraham and Antigone, of conflict between a "good" conscience and a "right" conscience. The novel's irony reaches its peak, as everybody knows, when Huck (an innocent with every reason to believe that he really has chosen sin, death, and eternal torment) chooses rightly, morally, humanely in defiance of the legally, officially, theologically sanctioned "civilization" around him. The book is calculated, through irony, to make us feel that in fact what Huck rejects is neither civil nor humane but perverse, absurd, and uncivilized, a vicious nonsense which every sound heart, clear mind, and conscience undeformed ought to spurn. The point should be lost on no reader that Huck achieves this moment of superficially confused but actually, and ironically, accurate moral vision because he is a boy not reconciled to civilization and a pica-ro's boy "brung up" to "wickedness."

The irony resolves, of course, exactly opposite to Huck's supposi-tion. This is his climax, but he is saved by it, not damned. "Civili-zation" is damned; in the context of the whole novel it is totally damned. The only saving, enduring ground of civilization is that pitying, loving human heart which takes poor human nature, as King Lear and the best work of Hawthorne and Melville had taken it, as Howells and Stephen Crane took it, to be ultimate in itself.

IV

Although as a character Huck appears in a sizable number of other works, *Adventures of Huckleberry Finn* is weighty and significant beyond comparison with any of the others. Its greatness stems not from the charm or importance of Huck as a character (though he has become the object of a rather complicated and romantic per-sonality cult). Its greatness stems from the intellectual dimensions of the book, and these are rooted in the critical irony which deep-ens from chapter five through chapter thirty-one, where Huck recants and chooses hell. Since the intellectual, the critical, the moral, perhaps the metaphysical (if such exist in this book) move-ments of the novel peak in chapter thirty-one, why did the author not stop there? Why did he go on through the final eleven chapters of Tom Sawyerish farce and bathos? Firmly rejecting even such apologists as Lionel Trilling and T. S. Eliot, the majority verdict of contemporary criticism has been that the final section of the novel is an esthetic disaster, or almost so.

Is there anything else to be said? From the present point of view, yes; there is something to say which explains why to at least one reader the ending of *Adventures of Huckleberry Finn* has never seemed ruinous and why it never seemed difficult to agree with

Eliot: "it is right that the mood of the end of the book should bring us back to that of the beginning. Or if this was not the right ending for the book, what ending would have been right?" It makes a great deal of difference what one takes the book to be, what expectations one is prepared to insist that the book fulfill.

Huckleberry Finn is a triumph of its genre and not some other. It is not an epic nor a tragedy. It is not *Paradise Lost* or *King Lear* or *Moby-Dick*, though it shares certain of their insights into the human condition. Because it is a great work of the literary imagination, it speaks to us and our condition; but it speaks neither from the romantic ground which the sensibility of our times prefers nor from the Alexandrian ground of "well-made" art preferred by our much-structured criticism.

When the author's imagination was done with its critical dissection of the Sir Walter Scottish, chuckleheaded and criminal Old Southwest, his principal remaining problem was to know what to do with Jim. As has often been observed, the revealing journey down the river had been a voyage to nowhere, in practical terms an absurdity, for Jim. To kill him off or even leave him a fugitive in darkest America would have turned the book toward *Uncle Tom's Cabin*, toward romance and sentimentality. In the formal traditions of picarism, however, it did not necessarily matter whether the novel ended or where. The picaresque tones of farce and absurdity made anything possible. And the boy-book did not formally climax. It couldn't because, sweet as boyhood might be, losing it had to be supposed natural, inevitable, and right—no tragedy, just a fade-out from boy-life to a succeeding stage. Finally, the view and sensibility of the realist led to the conclusion that good art only cuts into a moving stream of life and need not misrepresent it by climax or resolution.

Therefore, I suppose, *Adventures of Huckleberry Finn* legitimately returns upon itself to end as it began in boy-life. Not changed, not even much sobered (he has, after all, resolved upon a permanent life of crime), Huck is delighted to see Tom Sawyer and have his help in "stealing" Jim from the Phelps Farm. Since there can no longer be much point to taking "civilization" seriously, the author, narrator, and reader can laugh and play along with Tom Sawyerism while the book modulates away from tragic implications and returns to its proper tone.

The proper tone was bathos and the proper technique anticlimax. How else could Jim be imagined, as of 1840, to be got safely home, as the proprieties of a comic fiction require? Perhaps Clemens let himself be run away with by Tom Sawyer and there is too much farce—it becomes a somewhat narrow issue of taste at last. With all the farce and parody, all the antiromantic japes, has the integrity of

Huck's developed soul been broken? I cannot think so. He is what he was and, never imagined to grow up, must always be: "Yours truly, Huck Finn." Has Jim's authentic dignity been violated, a more serious charge? I do not think so because no man could have his dignity genuinely threatened by a comic phantasmagoria and because his last real action stands as one of the few bits of unmistakable heroism in the book, when he returns himself to bondage, possibly death, to help the doctor care for wounded, delirious Tom Sawyer.

At the end of the ends, I would read by the lights of boy-book and picaresque even Huck's too-famous final remark: "I reckon I got to light out for the Territory ahead of the rest, because Aunt Sally she's going to adopt me and sivilize me and I can't stand it. I been there before." It is a boy-remark in a boy-book context, not a commitment to destiny. At its most significant, perhaps it pointed the way to those further "adventures" on which the author would indeed send Huck. But his new adventures were to be minor just as an Aunt Sally sort of civilization is trivial. The critical work, the major ironic work, of *Adventures of Huckleberry Finn* once done neither could nor needed to be done again. The book remains to us to read, each by his own best light.

KENNETH S. LYNN

You Can't Go Home Again†

In *Huckleberry Finn*, * * * Twain proposed to develop for the first time on a major scale the conflict adumbrated in the story. The novel was to be told in the first person, and the action was to be essentially psychological: in his own words, the boy would tell of being caught in the crossfire between his environment-trained conscience and his "Voices," as Twain's Joan would say, and of his agonizing struggle to decide whether or not to become a liberator.

* * *

The liberation theme is announced in the title of the novel's very first chapter: "I Discover Moses and the Bulrushers." For although Huck soon loses all interest in the Moses story, "because I don't take no stock in dead people," the humorous introduction of the Biblical saga at the very start of the book effectively ushers in the majestic theme of slavery and freedom, and inextricably asso-

† Chapter IX, Sections 3, 7, and 8 of *Mark Twain and Southwestern Humor* by Kenneth S. Lynn, by permission of Little, Brown & Co. Copyright © 1959, by Kenneth S. Lynn. The author's footnote in Section 8 has been renumbered.

ciates Huck—a native of the river valley which its most famous citizen, Abraham Lincoln, called the "Egypt of the West"—with the little Jewish child who, abandoned in a great, continental river, grew up to lead an enslaved people to freedom. In the early chapters the liberation theme is developed *a verso* in terms of the idea of confinement, for these describe Huck's life at the Widow's which Twain had been tempted to include in *Tom Sawyer* and then had decided not to on the grounds that they were not a part of Tom's story. Once again the tribe is attempting to administer the ephebic rites to a free-spirited boy, with comic results. When Huck is sworn into Tom Sawyer's gang and introduced to Miss Watson's and the Widow Douglas's piety, he is in both cases being shown how a respectable St. Petersburg boy is expected to behave, and in both initiations he resists the mysteries. Sancho Panza to Tom's Quixote, Huck sees only turnips and Sunday school picnickers where Tom imagines "julery" and "rich A-rabs." For his down-to-earth honesty, Tom calls him a "numskull," a judgment which is echoed by Miss Watson when she discovers that he has called on God for fishhooks as a result of her having told him that he would receive whatever he prayed for. But revealing as these incidents are, the most telling indication of Huck's spiritual difference from the rest of the community, as well as a premonition of the stirring drama of liberation that lies ahead, is his refusal to help Tom Sawyer tie up Nigger Jim "for fun."

Restless in his confinement to respectability, Huck echoes the narrator of *Roughing It* in his confession that "All I wanted was to go somewheres; all I wanted was a change." Yet in these early chapters, his rebellion does not seem much more serious, finally, than Tom's had been. His occasional forays into the freedom of his cast-off rags and his hogsheads are short-lived; by the time that winter comes we find him admitting that whereas he still prefers his old ways, "I was getting so I liked the new ones, too, a little bit." When his outcast Pap reappears and takes him off to the woods, Huck at first thinks he has regained his lost freedom, only to find that freedom means being locked up in a lonely cabin for days on end— means being a captive audience for his Pap's tirades about "free niggers"; and that for all the delights of shoelessness and pipe-smoking, he has in fact exchanged the discomforts and restrictions of respectability for a disreputable prison.

In writing the episode of Huck and Pap in their cabin home, Twain in all likelihood was drawing on the memory of his relationship with his own father. Although Twain's mother was warm-hearted, the family atmosphere in the Clemens household was dominated by the personality of his father, John Marshall Clemens. Thanks to this strange, austere, loveless man, the Clemenses were reserved and formal with one another to an almost unbelievable degree; at night, they shook hands before going to bed—a warmer gesture would have been unthinkable. Indeed, in later years Twain could remember only one time when a kiss was ever exchanged between members of the Clemens family. The story that Mrs. Clemens was disappointed in love and married her husband out of spite has never been satisfactorily verified, but there is no doubt as to the nature of the relationship between the father and his son Sam. As Twain recalled, "My father and I were always on the most distant terms when I was a boy—a sort of armed neutrality, so to speak." In such an atmosphere, Twain must have suffered almost daily from rejection, but the instance that seemed to him to epitomize all his experiences of parental neglect was the time when his family, moving from Florida, Missouri, to a new home in Hannibal, drove off without him. Writing an article in later years for the *North American Review*, Twain could still remember the "grisly deep silence" that fell upon the locked house after his family had gone, and the nameless terrors that gripped him as the afternoon waned into evening. The story is engrossing, but as Dixon Wecter has pointed out, untrue, for Twain was here describing as a personal experience something that in fact happened to his brother, Orion. So acute, apparently, was Twain's sense of rejection that in looking back on his early life he was convinced that it was surely he who had suffered the agony of being locked up and forgotten.

Huck's lonesome vigil in the locked-up cabin is the equivalent of the experience that Twain believed had happened to him. And Huck's outlaw Pap is a nightmare version of Twain's hardhearted father: "He was most fifty, and he looked it. His hair was long and tangled and greasy, and hung down, and you could see his eyes shining through like he was behind vines. . . . There warn't no color in his face, where his face showed; it was white to make a body's flesh crawl—a tree-toad white, a fish-belly white." Between this terrible father and his son armed neutrality is but the prelude to open war. The day after Pap tries to kill Huck with a claspknife, Huck manages to escape from the cabin by committing symbolic suicide and murder. So that his Pap will not pursue him, Huck simulates his own death by killing a wild pig and distributing its blood around the cabin; but this act has a double meaning, which emerges only when we recall Pap Finn's notorious habit of lying drunk amongst the hogs in the tanyard, as well as the drunkard's slobberingly self-pitying identification of himself with his sleeping companions: "There's the hand that was the hand of a hog." Huck's slaughter of the pig not only symbolizes his desire to end his own miserable life, but to slay his father and the sordid animality of his ways.

Bursting clear of the locked-up cabin, Huck is simply running away from his past, rather than toward any definable future. On the one hand, he is not prepared to go back and be "cramped up and sivilized" at the Widow's, while on the other—as his symbolic murder of his Pap makes clear—he has also rejected the life of a social outcast. He has neither embraced St. Petersburg nor turned his back on it. Slipping into the river, an officially dead Huck is "reborn." Yet he has no ideas about a new life and a new identity for himself. Irresolute and uncertain, Huck instinctively turns toward a familiar goal: Jackson's Island, Tom Sawyer's halfway-house of rebellion where all irrevocable decisions are magically held in abeyance.

The means by which Huck will find out who he now is is illustrated by a parable in Chapter XVI. The parable is a part of an episode which did not appear in the novel when it was finally completed, because Twain had already thrown it—the verb is his—into *Life on the Mississippi*. Unsure as to when, if ever, he would finish *Huckleberry Finn*, and wishing to flesh out his history of the river with a dramatization of "keelboat talk and manners" as they had existed in the 1840s, Twain improved a good book at the cost of looting his masterpiece of an episode of extraordinary richness, of great beauty and humor, which takes us to the heart of the novel.

The episode begins immediately after Huck and Jim's terrifying experience of getting lost in the fog. Drifting down an unfamiliar and "monstrous big river," the boy and the Negro decide that Huck should find out where they are by swimming over to a huge raft they have seen in the distance and gathering the information by eavesdropping. Under cover of darkness, Huck reaches the raft, climbs on board without being noticed, and settles down to listen to the talk of the raftsmen—to their colossal boasting, their roaring songs, and above all, to the fantastic tall tale about a man named Dick Allbright and the mysterious barrel that followed him on the river wherever he went rafting, bringing terror and death to his companions. Nothing, the teller of the tale assures his audience, could keep the barrel off Dick Allbright's trail, or mitigate its inexorable fatality, until finally a raft captain swam out to the barrel and hauled it aboard. Inside its wooden walls, the captain and his men found a stark naked baby—

". . . Dick Allbright's baby; he owned up and said so. 'Yes,' he says, a-leaning over it, 'yes, it is my own lamented darling, my poor lost Charles William Allbright deceased,' says he—for he could curl his tongue around the bulliest words in the language when he was a mind to. . . . Yes, he said he used to live up at the head of this bend, and one night he choked his child, which was crying, not intending to kill it—which was prob'ly a lie—and then he was scared, and buried it in a bar'l, before his wife got home, and off he went, and struck the northern trail and went to rafting; and this was the third year that the bar'l had chased him."

Crouched in the darkness, naked and afraid, Huck seems utterly apart from these coarse, rough men. Nevertheless, the fantasy of violence and terror which the raftsman has spun for the scoffing delight of his fellows vitally involves .the runaway boy, an involvement which Huck himself acknowledges. For when he is suddenly seized from his hiding-place and surrounded by strange men demanding to know his name, he jokingly replies, "Charles William Allbright, sir." Always in Twain the best jokes reveal the profoundest connections, and with the release of laughter triggered by this superbly timed response we are made aware that we have been eavesdropping on a parable about Huck Finn's life. The entire incident magnificently exemplifies how Mark Twain could exploit for the purposes of high art the tradition of Southwestern humor—and shows, too, what very different effects he achieved. The ignorant river waif who has replaced the Self-controlled Gentleman as auditor is deeply and personally involved in the story he hears, rather than amusedly aloof from it. Charles William Allbright afloat in his barrel mirrors the situation of Huck on the raft: having died, both boys have come alive again in the flowing waters of the great Mississippi. Charles William Allbright in his barrel also calls up once again the infant Moses hidden in the ark of bulrushes in the Nile, and in so doing associates the drama of liberating an enslaved people with the ideas of freedom and renewal of life that the river connotes. At the very heart of the parable there is an even more breathtaking illumination. Charles William Allbright, having lost his father, has taken to the river to go in search of him. In telling us that, the parable tells us things about Huck Finn that Huck himself cannot possibly communicate. Drifting down the river toward a goal he can neither define nor scarcely imagine, Huck is in fact looking for another father to replace the one he has lost. And this quest is also a quest for himself, because once Huck has found his new father he will know at last who he himself really is. Upon that recognition, in turn, rests the resolution of the struggle between Huck's conscience and the impulse of his generous heart as to what to do about Jim. The novel's grand theme, then, the Mosaic drama of liberation, depends ultimately upon the outcome of Huck's search for a father.

The parenthood problem is officially introduced in the fifth chapter of the novel, when Judge Thatcher and the Widow Douglas go to court to get permission to take Huck away from his Pap. Who should be his parents, the respectable aristocrats who are no blood relation to him, or his violent, drunken father? Nothing less than a human life is at stake; the decision would seem to call for the wisdom of Solomon. Echoing Huck's judgment of Moses, Nigger

Jim "doan' take no stock" in the wisdom of Solomon, yet in Chapter XIV—entitled "Was Solomon Wise?"—our laughter at Jim's stupidity carries with it the realization that the parenthood problem, like the liberation theme, has been given a deeper moral seriousness through a Biblical association. Jim regards it as utter foolishness that Solomon should have attempted to settle the parenthood dispute by offering to cut the child in two and give half to each mother —"De 'spute warn't 'bout half a chile, de 'spute was 'bout a whole chile; en de man dat think he kin settle a 'spute 'bout a whole chile wid a half a chile doan' know enough to come in out'n de rain." Twain himself was very fond of this chapter and delighted in reading it aloud in public lectures. But if it can be successfully taken out of context, the scene is also a vital element in the moral pattern of the novel. For Huck, like Solomon, is listening for the voice of truth and the accents of love as a means of identifying the true parent he seeks. Neither side in the legal contest so identifies itself, and therefore Huck retreats from both respectability and hoggishness to the way station of Jackson's Island. In doing so he is certainly not acting self-consciously: he is simply drifting with the tide— quite literally—and not even wondering what will happen to him next. All that this ignorant and inexperienced child is able to tell us directly about himself is that it is awful to be so "dreadful lonesome." Encountering the outcast colored man in hiding on the island, Huck is at first merely amused and exasperated by the black man's stupidity, but part of the drama of their relationship is Huck's gathering awareness that Jim is "most always right" about things that really matter, about how certain movements of the birds mean a storm is coming, about the dangers of messing with snakes, and the meaning of dreams. But while Jim's relationship to Huck is fatherly in the sense that he constantly is correcting and admonishing the boy, forever telling him some new truth about the world, he is identified even more unmistakably as Huck's father by the love that he gives him. As Huck is searching for a father, so Jim is attempting to rejoin his family, and he lavishes on the love-starved boy all of his parental affection. Jim's ludicrous horror at Solomon's apparent willingness to split a child in two is seen in retrospect to be a humorous statement of his loving care for the integrity of his white child.

As it gradually dawns on Huck—and the gradualness of his realization is very delicately controlled by Twain—that Jim loves him, the psychological battle within Huck's mind intensifies accordingly. * * * In Chapter XVI of *Huckleberry Finn*, an environment-trained conscience punishes Huck for his subversive association with the runaway slave with an even greater ferocity:

"Jim said it made him all over trembly and feverish to be so close to freedom. Well, I can tell you it made me all over trembly and feverish, too, to hear him, because I begun to get it through my head that he *was* most free—and who was to blame for it? Why, *me*. I couldn't get that out of my conscience, no how nor no way. It got to troubling me so I couldn't rest; I couldn't stay still in one place. It hadn't ever come home to me before, what this thing was that I was doing. But now it did; and it stayed with me, and scorched me more and more. I tried to make out to myself that *I* warn't to blame, because *I* didn't run Jim off from his rightful owner; but it warn't no use, conscience up and says, every time, 'But you knowed he was running for his freedom, and you could a paddled ashore and told somebody.' That was so—I couldn't get around that noway. That was where it pinched. Conscience says to me, 'What had poor Miss Watson done to you that you could see her nigger go off right under your eyes and never say one single word? What did that poor woman do to you that you could treat her so mean? Why, she tried to learn you your book, she tried to learn you your manners, she tried to be good to you every way she knowed how. *That's* what she done.'

I got to feeling so mean and so miserable I most wished I was dead."

With these words, the first of the novel's really notable representations of moral doubt, Huck at last comes to understand the dilemma confronting him. The battle in his mind is at this point fully joined.

And at this point, Twain could go no further. Having brought a rich and various novel to a moment of psychological crisis; having managed all the complexities of the action with superb facility; Twain abandoned *Huckleberry Finn* at the end of Chapter XVI and threatened to burn the manuscript. The author did not, probably could not, analyze why he was unable to go on. To Twain—accustomed as he was to writing by fits and starts—the failure of his inspiration may not even have bothered him as much as his bitter letter to Will Bowen might suggest. At least, not at first. For Twain was also accustomed to having his "tank" fill up again in a reasonable period of time. In this case, seven long years would pass before he would find himself able to finish the novel. Renewed efforts to get the book moving again during this Biblical period of barrenness resulted in a few additional chapters, but nothing more. Clearly, Twain in August of 1876 had run into unprecedented difficulties which his usual remedy for a recalcitrant manuscript of pigeonholing it for a time could not overcome.

The question—the fascinating question—is: What was the nature of those difficulties? What was the problem that arose in Chapter XVI and that so stubbornly resisted solution? Some of Twain's most knowledgeable critics, including Bernard DeVoto and Henry Nash Smith, have pointed to the fact that in Chapter XVI Huck and Jim discover they have drifted past Cairo in the fog, and that therefore Jim's plan of taking a steamboat up the Ohio toward a free state could no longer be used by Twain as an excuse for moving Huck and Jim downstream on the Mississippi. Now, Twain obviously wanted to have the two runaways continue their voyage southward, if only because it was the Mississippi Valley, not the Ohio, that he knew so well from his piloting days; yet to have a slave seek for freedom by heading deeper and deeper into the heart of the slave country was quite incredible. Baffled as to how to resolve this problem—so Professor Smith has argued—Twain abandoned the novel at the end of Chapter XVI; picked it up in the winter of 1879–1880 long enough to add Chapters XVII and XVIII; but was unable really to get rolling again until he struck upon the idea of introducing the King and the Duke. For once the King and the Duke come aboard the raft in Chapter XIX, they master it, and the desire of Nigger Jim to head for a free state perforce gives way to the plan of the two confidence men to proceed downstream in search of sucker money. Thus did Twain logically account for the continued southward progress of Huck and Jim. Once he had done this, he was able to go on with the book.

The flaw in this argument is that the introduction of the King and the Duke emphatically did not enable Twain to proceed very far or very fast. Thanks to the ingenious detective work of Walter Blair, we know that Chapter XIX—in which the two con men first appear—was probably written in the summer of 1880, as in all likelihood was Chapter XX. But having written these chapters, Twain's inspiration once again failed him, for on the basis of the evidence he has assembled Professor Blair suspects that Chapter XXI was not written until the spring of 1883, almost three years later. Therefore, the invention of the King and the Duke can hardly be said to have released Twain's pent-up imagination, and in view of that fact it does not seem very likely that whatever was stymieing him had much to do with the question of how to account for Huck and Jim's continuing to move south. (When one recalls the unexplained illogicalities and improbabilities with which his books are replete, it seems even less likely that a little detail like the direction of a slave's escape route would have delayed as resourceful a writer as Mark Twain for very long.) Yet what other explanation is there? The text of Chapter XVI itself supplies the clue to an alternative theory.

The chapter, to repeat, shows Huck for the first time fully acknowledging his moral dilemma. Perhaps in some way the boy's dilemma was the author's as well; perhaps Mark Twain no more than Huck Finn could decide what Huck should do about Nigger Jim. To a de-Southernized Twain, it was of course unthinkable that the boy should return the Negro to slavery. On the other hand, once Huck committed the "sin" of helping Jim to freedom he would place himself forever beyond the pale of heavenly St. Petersburg; he would be carrying his irresolute rebellion against the Happy Valley to the point of no return; he would be electing to become an outcast and a renegade, like his vile Pap. As *The Adventures of Tom Sawyer* unforgettably shows, the vision of an unfallen American Eden meant an enormous amount to Twain. And that vision was validated and defined by the thought of innocent boys playing there, in a dreaming and eternal summertime. That Huck should be cast out of St. Petersburg was thus equally unthinkable to Twain. Tom Sawyer's rebellion against this magic place had been simply child's play, ending in reconciliation and acceptance. But Huck Finn's rebellion had turned into a far more drastic business. It was as if Joan of Arc had been called on to save France by flouting Heaven's decrees. Unlike the hero of "Carnival,"[1] Huck did not bear a vindictive grudge against respectable society; for antebellum Missouri, unlike post-Civil War Connecticut, was seen by Twain at long distance in both space and time, a perspective which reduced all motives for hatred, all social coercions, to delightful jokes. Without a single exception, the respectable inhabitants of the Happy Valley whom Huck encounters in the first sixteen chapters of the novel—the Widow Douglas, Judge Thatcher, Tom Sawyer, Miss Watson, Judith Loftus, the night watchman, even Mr. Parker, the slave-hunter—are fundamentally decent people. What, indeed, had they done to Huck that he should treat them so mean? Twain in 1876 could present Huck's dilemma—brilliantly present it, because it sprang directly out of a deep conflict in his own feelings—but he was completely unable to resolve it.

* * *

7

Chapter XXI of the novel, Professor Blair suspects, was written in the spring of 1883—exactly a year after Twain's visit to the river. It was the first sign that the long drought in his "tank" was over. Then the following summer, at Elmira, inspiration came like a flood. Soon Twain was writing to Howells that "I haven't piled up MS so in years as I have done since we came here to the farm three weeks and a half ago. Why, it's like old times, to step right into the study, damp from the breakfast table, and sail right in and sail right on, the whole day long, without thought of running short of stuff or words. I wrote 4000 words today and I touch 3000 and upwards pretty often, and don't fall below 2600 any working day." To Orion and his family Twain averred that "I am piling up manuscript in a really astonishing way. I believe I shall complete, in two months, a book which I have been fooling over for 7 years. This summer it is no more trouble to me to write than it

---

1. Clemens's comic self-portrait, "Facts Concerning the Recent Carnival of Crime in Connecticut," 1876 [*Editors*].

is to lie." Shortly thereafter, the book was done.

Twain's altered view of the Valley society is immediately established in two sets of interrelated and successive chapters, XXI–XXII and XXIII–XXIV, the first four chapters written subsequent to the 1882 trip.

In Chapter XXII, Huck goes to a circus, sees a drunken man weaving around the ring on horseback, and is terribly distressed—although the crowd roars with delight. But it is not Huck's charming naïveté in not recognizing that the drunkard is a clown that Twain condemns, it is the callousness of the crowd. For this circus scene depends upon the preceding Chapter XXI, which really does involve a drunk, the drunken Boggs, who weaves down the street on horseback, shouting insults at Colonel Sherburn. When Sherburn mortally wounds Boggs, a crowd gathers excitedly around the drunk-ard to watch him die. Everyone is tremendously pleased—except Huck, and the dying man's daughter. By this juxtaposition of epi-sodes, each of which contrasts the boy's sympathetic concern with the gleeful howling of the crowd, Twain lays bare the moral callous-ness of a society that views life romantically—that regards suffering as a circus.

The Arkansas town in which these two chapters take place is another version of Hannibal, but the place has nothing in common with the lovely, white-painted town that had sustained Twain's imagination for twenty-nine years. In contrast to the heavenly St. Petersburg he had summoned up in *Tom Sawyer*, Bricksville, Arkansas, is a squalid hole:

"The houses had little gardens around them, but they didn't seem to raise hardly anything in them but jimpson-weeds, and sun-flowers, and ash piles, and old curled-up boots and shoes, and pieces of bottles, and rags, and played-out tinware. . . . There was generly hogs in the garden, and people driving them out. . . . All the streets and lanes was just mud; they warn't nothing else *but* mud—mud as black as tar and nigh about a foot deep in some places, and two or three inches deep in *all* places. The hogs loafed and grunted around everywhere."

Images of whiteness have been replaced by images of blackness and filth; gardens no longer bloom in this fallen Eden; and every-where there are hogs, heretofore associated not with organized society but with violent and unscrupulous outlaws. Twain once observed that the Negroes he knew as a boy feared being sold "down the river" as the equivalent of being sent to Hell, and Nigger Jim has run away precisely because of this fear. In Bricksville, the Negro's nightmare becomes the novel's reality. The 1883 version of Hannibal is a veritable Hell, populated by a company of the damned. Huck and Jim's voyage southward from St. Petersburg has in fact become—like the course of the stars that were hove out of the nest—a downward fall.

As if he were worried that the contrast between the two drunks was too subtle a condemnation, Twain chose—for the first and only time in the novel—to violate Huck's point of view in Chapter XXII and speak to the reader through another mask, in order that he might ram home his moral judgment of the society in explicit and unmistakable terms. The mask he chose to assume for this brief moment was a familiar one in Southwestern humor: the mask of a Southern aristocrat. Not, to be sure, the cool and collected Gentleman of the Whig myth, for Colonel Sherburn is self-admittedly a killer. Nor is Sherburn concerned to instruct the mob in the virtues of the temperate life. His furiously contemptuous opinion of the townspeople carries with it no hope that they will ever improve:

"Do I know you? I know you clear through. I was born and raised in the South, and I've lived in the North; so I know the average all around. The average man's a coward. In the North he lets anybody walk over him that wants to. . . . In the South one man, all by himself, has robbed a stage full of men in the daytime, and robbed the lot. . . . Why don't your juries hang murderers? Because they're afraid the man's friends will shoot them in the back in the dark—and it's just what they *would* do. So they always acquit; and then a *man* goes in the night with a hundred masked cowards at his back, and lynches the rascal. Your mistake is, that you didn't bring a man with you; that's one mistake, and the other is that you didn't come in the dark and fetch your masks."

The speech, as Professor Blair was the first to point out, is very like the passage that Twain cut from *Life on the Mississippi* about the withering-away of independent thought and action in Southern life. Sherburn's condemnation has been broadened out somewhat to make a more inclusive judgment of Americans everywhere, but it centers none the less on the degradation of human character in the monolithic South.

The point of ironic connection between Chapters XXIII and XXIV occurs in their conclusions. The last paragraph of Chapter XXIII is perhaps the most poignant moment in the entire novel, for it is here that Jim relates to Huck how his daughter, after recovering from scarlet fever, became a mysteriously disobedient child. Even when Jim had slapped her and sent her sprawling, she refused to obey his orders, but just as he was going for her again, he realized what was wrong: "De Lord God Almighty fogive po' ole Jim, kaze he never gwyne to fogive hisself as long's he live! Oh, she was plumb deef en dumb, Huck, plumb deef en dumb—en I'd ben a-treat'n her so!" On the last page of Chapter XXIV, the King and the Duke arrive at the little Tennessee town where they expect to rob the Wilks girls of their inheritance by playing the parts, respectively, of a parson and a deaf mute. When viewed beside Jim's sorrow and compassion for his deaf-and-dumb daughter, the spectacle of the two frauds talking on their hands is sickening— "It was enough," says Huck, "to make a body ashamed of the human race."

The striking difference between Huck's account of the confidence game that the King and the Duke work on the Tennessee town and the King's swindle of the Pokeville camp meeting is that the gullible townspeople now seem as subhuman as the crooks who defraud them. As Henry Nash Smith has pointed out, when the townspeople move rapidly up the street to have a look at the newly-arrived "parson" and "deaf mute," Huck likens them to soldiers marching along, thereby calling attention to their regimented minds and lives. A moment later, he refers to them as a "gang" which is "trotting along," as if they reminded him of a herd of squealing pigs. The people of what was once the Happy Valley are now not only associated with, but have actually become, the dirty animals which are the novel's leading symbol of degradation and sordidness. Huck Finn—and Mark Twain—have come a long way from St. Petersburg.

Sickened by society, Huck finds refuge in the fatherly bosom of Nigger Jim, even as Little Eva had turned to Uncle Tom. To what extent Twain had *Uncle Tom's Cabin* in mind when he conceived of the relationship between Huck and Jim can never be known, for with neighborly good manners he did not make public comments about Mrs. Stowe's famous book. We know that George Washington Cable burst into tears when he read the novel as a child; we know that the character of Uncle Tom had such a profound effect on Joel Chandler Harris that he seriously considered the novel to be a defense of slavery—on the grounds that any system which could produce such a holy man must necessarily be good; we know, indeed, the reaction of a vast number of individual Americans to *Uncle Tom's Cabin*; but not Mark Twain's. Yet Uncle Tom and little Eva, talking rapturously about reunion in Heaven, clearly have something to do with Huck's decision to go to Hell rather than send Jim back to slavery: in both instances, the black man and the white child are morally united against the organized world. Little Eva and Uncle Tom are brought together by their unquestioning acceptance of the Will of God; Huck and Jim are also united by their common beliefs—in the comparative harmlessness of stealing an occasional chicken or watermelon; in the delights of going naked in the starlight, and of smoking a pipe after breakfast; in the undoubted existence of ghosts, and the significance of "signs." In both novels, the child-Negro relationship exists on a level of emotional ecstasy, the extraordinary intensity of which derived from an unappeased longing of the author's.

For just as the religious ecstasy of Uncle Tom and Little Eva illuminates the spiritual biography of the doubt-ridden daughter of Lyman Beecher, so the raft life of Huck and Jim tells us much about the emotional hunger of John Marshall Clemens's son. Seeking for release from the emotional austerity of the Clemens household, the young Mark Twain had turned almost inevitably to the warm, black underworld of the slaves. Many, many years later, Twain could still recall

"the look of Uncle Dan'l's kitchen as it was on the privileged nights, when I was a child, and I can see the white and black children grouped on the hearth, with the firelight playing on their faces and the shadows flickering upon the walls, clear back toward the cavernous gloom of the rear, and I can hear Uncle Dan'l telling the immortal tales which Uncle Remus Harris was to gather into his book and charm the world with, by and by; and I can feel again the creepy joy which quivered through me when the time for the ghost story was reached—and the sense of regret, too, which came over me, for it was always the last story of the evening and there was nothing between it and the unwelcome bed."

Uncle Dan'l, Twain said, was the prototype of Nigger Jim, but as the above passage implies, Twain's memory of him was mixed up in his mind with his response to yet another literary image of the Negro, Uncle Remus. With characteristic modesty, Joel Chandler Harris felt that the only talent he had as a writer lay in his ability to transcribe accurately the Negro tales he had been listening to—on street corners, at railroad stations, along country roads—ever since the days when, as an impoverished and illegitimate child, he had found solace in the companionship of slaves. But Mark Twain assured Harris that "in reality the stories are only alligator pears—one eats them merely for the sake of the dressing." To Twain, the most meaningful part of the Uncle Remus stories was the part that Harris had contributed—the "frame," which dramatized the relationship between Uncle Remus and the little boy who comes to listen to his stories. The comment says as much about Twain as it does about Harris. Seeking for a quality of experience they could not find in their white lives, both men sent their boy-heroes in search of the companionship and understanding of the black man. He was a mythical figure, this Negro of Twain's and Harris's, a figure out of a dream, passionate, loyal, immensely dignified—a Black Christ, in sum, but with a very human sense of humor that Mrs. Stowe's great prototype notably lacked. In Uncle Remus's cabin, or spinning down the big river at night with Nigger Jim, there were beauty, and mystery, and laughter.

"It needs no scientific investigation," Harris wrote in the preface of his first book, "to show why [the Negro] selects as his hero the weakest and most harmless of all animals, and brings him out victorious in contest with the bear, the wolf, and the fox." Nor is any scientific investigation necessary to understand why Twain's and Harris's boys were drawn so irresistibly toward the black storyteller. In a world of wolves and foxes—and hogs—he was a bulwark and a refuge. The cave in *Tom Sawyer*, that vast, subterranean realm of darkness, was a place of ambivalent meaning: a place of magical excitement, full of mysterious chambers with exotic names, a dream-world where one could find the love of a young girl and buried treasure; yet death was down there, too, in the lurking presence of an "underground man" whose skin was not white; all in all, it was safer for Tom Sawyer to return to the white-painted Heaven above. But by the summer of 1883, the "cavernous gloom" of Uncle Dan'l's cabin had come to figure in Mark Twain's mind as a lonely boy's only haven. When the moment comes for Huck to choose whether to live by the precepts of his society-trained conscience or in spite of them, a Valley of Bricksvilles can offer no comparable image of love and warmth to his vision of the black man: "I see Jim there before me all the time: in the day and in the night-time, sometimes moonlight, sometimes storm, and we a-floating along, talking and singing and laughing." Unlike Tom Sawyer, Huck does not flee the "underground man"; he joins him.

8

When Moses led the Israelites to freedom he also moved toward his prophesied appointment with death; *Huckleberry Finn* likewise moves simultaneously toward triumph and tragedy. For the libera-tion of Jim inexorably enforces the tragic separation of the boy and the Negro. Throughout the long, final sequence at the Phelps farm,[2] the information is withheld from the reader that a repentant Miss Watson has freed Jim on her deathbed. Yet it is perfectly clear from the moment that Tom Sawyer arrives that something is ter-ribly wrong. Although Huck works night and day to liberate Jim from the locked-up cabin, the two of them are never really "in touch" again. They have become strangers to one another. Evi-dently, Mark Twain was only capable of imagining Huck and Jim's relationship as existing in the condition of slavery and under the aspect of flight—as an "underground" affair—although he tried very hard to imagine it otherwise. Hating to bring the story of the

2. The Phelps farm is another version of John A. Quarles's farm at Florida, Missouri, but it is a "one-horse" affair by comparison with the Grangerford establishment. Nothing more clearly il-lustrates the effect of the 1882 trip on the images of Mark Twain's memory than the difference in size and attrac-tiveness between the "before" and "after" portraits of the Quarles farm. As Twain observed to Howells in 1887, "When a man goes back to look at the house of his childhood it has always *shrunk;* there is no instance of such a house being as big as the picture that memory and imagination call for. Shrunk how? Why, to its correct dimen-sions: the house hasn't altered; this is the first time it has been in focus." Although Twain did not visit the Quar-leses in 1882, the general effect of the trip was to deflate all his childhood memories.

two runaways to a close, striving vainly to recreate the intense emotion that had lifted the middle section of the novel into the most memorable idyll in American literature, Twain prolonged and prolonged the final sequence into by far the longest—and the least successful—in the book.

Even the humor is not up to par. In certain moments, as Huck (masquerading as Tom Sawyer) and Tom (masquerading as his half-brother Sid) go cavorting through Aunt Sally's house, it is possible to believe that we are back once again in the high-spirited, comic world of *The Adventures of Tom Sawyer*. But Aunt Sally is Aunt Polly with a difference—the difference created by Twain's 1882 trip:

" 'Good gracious! anybody hurt?'
" 'No'm. Killed a nigger.'
" 'Well, it's lucky; because people sometimes do get hurt.'

Huck and Tom are no longer playing in Heaven; a shadow has fallen across their boyish good fun, stilling the reader's laughter.

If the Phelps farm sequence fails as humor, perhaps it succeeds as anguish. For Huck is pathetically reluctant to see his beautiful dream of the raft and the river come to an end. In "Chapter the Last" he responds excitedly to Tom Sawyer's gorgeous schemes for running Jim "down the river on the raft, . . . plumb to the mouth," and for having "howling adventures amongst the Injuns over in the Territory, for a couple of weeks or two." Having turned his back on society by refusing to turn his back on Jim, Huck seeks to avoid the terrors of lonesomeness by sticking close to the colored man. Preparing to light out for the Territory at the end of the novel, he seems almost jaunty at the prospect of a reunion there with Jim and Tom Sawyer. We may well wonder, however, if his jauntiness is not simply boyish bravado—or a mask for the author's bewildered sense of loss, growing out of his awareness of the final and terrible truth about his book: which is that *Huckleberry Finn* proposes, in W. H. Auden's words, the incompatibility of love and freedom.

In *Tom Sawyer Abroad*, Twain would try to write *Huckleberry Finn* all over again, with Jim and Huck aloft with Tom Sawyer in a balloon, instead of floating downstream on a raft. And he just couldn't do it. Throughout the book's tiresome length, Huck and the colored freedman are never really together in any meaningful sense. Huck is wrapped up in Tom Sawyer's schemes, while the sorrowing, compassionate figure of the slave in *Huckleberry Finn* is barely recognizable in the minstrel-show darky of the later book. In one of the numerous sequels to *Huckleberry Finn* that Twain obsessively sketched out in his later years, Jim has somehow been caught again, and Huck fantastically plans to free him by changing places with him and blacking his face, as if by making Huck a Negro Twain hoped to bridge the gulf that now separated "son" from "father." But this desperate masquerade also proved to be imaginatively un-workable, and Huck and Jim remained forever separated. It is scarcely necessary to know that in still another contemplated sequel Twain envisioned Huck as a broken, helplessly insane old man in order to sense that at the conclusion of *Huckleberry Finn* Huck's voyage has become, for all his superficial jauntiness, as doomed to defeat as Captain Ahab's, and that in lighting out for the Territory without Jim beside him he flees with "all havens astern."

LESLIE FIEDLER

Come Back to the Raft Ag'in, Huck Honey!†

It is perhaps to be expected that the Negro and the homosexual should become stock literary themes in a period when the explora-tion of responsibility and failure has become again a primary con-cern of our literature. It is the discrepancy they represent that haunts us, that moral discrepancy before which we are helpless, having no resources (no tradition of courtesy, no honored mode of cynicism) for dealing with a conflict of principle and practice. It used once to be fashionable to think of puritanism as a force in our lives encouraging hypocrisy; quite the contrary, its emphasis upon the singleness of belief and action, its turning of the most prosaic areas of life into arenas where one's state of grace is tested, confuse the outer and the inner and make hypocrisy among us, perhaps more strikingly than ever elsewhere, *visible*, visibly detestable, the cardinal sin. It is not without significance that the shrug of the shoulders (the acceptance of circumstance as a sufficient excuse, the sign of self-pardon before the inevitable lapse) seems in America an unfamiliar, an alien gesture.

And yet before the continued existence of physical homosexual love (our crudest epithets notoriously evoke the mechanics of such affairs), before the blatant ghettos in which the Negro conspicu-ously creates the gaudiness and stench that offend him, the white American must make a choice between coming to terms with insti-tutionalized discrepancy or formulating radically new ideologies. There are, to be sure, stopgap devices, evasions of that final choice;

† Copyright © 1971 by Leslie Fiedler. From the book *The Collected Essays of Leslie Fiedler*, Vol. I, pp. 142–51. Re-printed by permission of Stein and Day, Publishers. This essay was first published in *Partisan Review*, June 1948.

not the least interesting is the special night club: the "queer" café, the black-and-tan joint, in which fairy or Negro exhibit their fairyness, their Negro-ness as if they were mere divertissements, gags thought up for the laughs and having no reality once the lights go out and the chairs are piled on the tables by the cleaning women. In the earlier minstrel show, a Negro performer was required to put on with grease paint and burnt cork the formalized mask of blackness; while the queer must exaggerate flounce and flutter into the convention of his condition.

The situations of the Negro and the homosexual in our society pose quite opposite problems, or at least problems suggesting quite opposite solutions. Our laws on homosexuality and the context of prejudice they objectify must apparently be changed to accord with a stubborn social fact; whereas it is the social fact, our overt behavior toward the Negro, that must be modified to accord with our laws and the, at least official, morality they objectify. It is not, of course, quite so simple. There is another sense in which the fact of homosexual passion contradicts a national myth of masculine love, just as our real relationship with the Negro contradicts a myth of that relationship; and those two myths with their betrayals are, as we shall see, one.

The existence of overt homosexuality threatens to compromise an essential aspect of American sentimental life: the camaraderie of the locker room and ball park, the good fellowship of the poker game and fishing trip, a kind of passionless passion, at once gross and delicate, homoerotic in the boy's sense, possessing an innocence above suspicion. To doubt for a moment this innocence, which can survive only as *assumed*, would destroy our stubborn belief in a relationship simple, utterly satisfying, yet immune to lust; physical as the handshake is physical, this side of copulation. The nineteenth-century myth of the Immaculate Young Girl has failed to survive in any *felt* way into our time. Rather, in the dirty jokes shared among men in the smoking car, the barracks, or the dormitory, there is a common male revenge against women for having flagrantly betrayed that myth; and under the revenge, the rather smug assumption of the chastity of the revenging group, in so far as it is a purely male society. From what other source could arise that unexpected air of good clean fun which overhangs such sessions? It is this self-congratulatory buddy-buddiness, its astonishing naïveté that breed at once endless opportunities for inversion and the terrible reluctance to admit its existence, to surrender the last believed-in stronghold of love without passion.

It is, after all, what we know from a hundred other sources that is here verified: the regressiveness, in a technical sense, of American life, its implacable nostalgia for the infantile, at once wrong-headed and somehow admirable. The mythic America is boyhood—and who would dare be startled to realize that the two most popular most *absorbed*, I am sure, of the handful of great books in our native heritage are customarily to be found, illustrated, on the shelves of the children's library. I am referring, of course, to *Moby Dick* and *Huckleberry Finn*, so different in technique and language, but alike children's books or, more precisely, *boys'* books.

There are the Leatherstocking Tales of Cooper, too, as well as Dana's *Two Years Before the Mast* and a good deal of Stephen Crane, books whose continuing favor depends more and more on the taste of boys; and one begins to foresee a similar improbable fate for Ernest Hemingway. Among the most distinguished novelists of the American past, only Henry James completely escapes classification as a writer of juvenile classics; even Hawthorne, who did write sometimes for children, must in his most adult novels endure, though not as Mark Twain and Melville submit to, the child's perusal. A child's version of *The Scarlet Letter* would seem a rather far-fetched joke if it were not a part of our common experience. Finding in the children's department of the local library what Hawthorne liked to call his "hell-fired book," and remembering that *Moby Dick* itself has as its secret motto "*Ego te baptizo in nomine diaboli,*" one can only bow in awed silence before the mysteries of public morality, the American idea of "innocence." Everything goes except the frank description of adult heterosexual love. After all, boys will be boys!

What, then, do all these books have in common? As boys' books we should expect them shyly, guiltlessly as it were, to proffer a chaste male love as the ultimate emotional experience—and this is spectacularly the case. In Dana, it is the narrator's melancholy love for the *kanaka*, Hope; in Cooper, the lifelong affection of Natty Bumppo and Chingachgook; in Melville, Ishmael's love for Queequeg; in Twain, Huck's feeling for Nigger Jim. At the focus of emotion, where we are accustomed to find in the world's great novels some heterosexual passion, be it "platonic" love or adultery, seduction, rape, or long-drawn-out flirtation, we come instead on the fugitive slave and the no-account boy lying side by side on a raft borne by the endless river toward an impossible escape, or the pariah sailor waking in the tattooed arms of the brown harpooner on the verge of their impossible quest. "*Aloha, aikane, aloha nui,*" Hope cries to the lover who prefers him to all his fellow-whites; and Ishmael in utter frankness tells us; "I found Queequeg's arm thrown over me in the most loving and affectionate manner. You had almost thought I had been his wife . . . he still hugged me tightly, as though naught but death should part us twain . . . Thus, then, in our heart's honeymoon, lay I and Queequeg—a cosy, loving pair . . .

he pressed his forehead against mine, clasped me around the waist, and said that henceforth we were married."

In Melville, the ambiguous relationship is most explicitly rendered; almost, indeed, openly explained. Not by a chance phrase or camouflaged symbol (the dressing of Jim in a woman's gown in *Huck Finn,* for instance, which can mean anything or nothing at all), but in a step-by-step exposition, the Pure Marriage of Ishmael and Queequeg is set before us: the initial going to bed together and the first shyness overcome, that great hot tomahawk-pipe accepted in a familiarity that dispels fear; next, the wedding ceremony itself (for in this marriage like so many others the ceremonial follows the deflowering), with the ritual touching of foreheads; then, the queasiness and guilt the morning after the *official* First Night, the suspicion that one has joined himself irrevocably to his own worst nightmare; finally, a symbolic portrayal of the continuing state of marriage through the image of the "monkey rope" which binds the lovers fast waist to waist (for the sake of this symbolism, Melville changes a *fact* of whaling practice—the only time in the book), a permanent alliance that provides mutual protection but also threatens mutual death.

Physical it all is, certainly, yet somehow ultimately innocent. There lies between the lovers no naked sword but a childlike ignorance, as if the possibility of a fall to the carnal had not yet been discovered. Even in the *Vita Nuova* of Dante, there is no vision of love less offensively, more unremittingly chaste; that it is not adult seems beside the point. Ishmael's sensations as he wakes under the pressure of Queequeg's arm, the tenderness of Huck's repeated loss and refinding of Jim, the role of almost Edenic helpmate played for Bumppo by the Indian—these shape us from childhood: we have no sense of first discovering them or of having been once without them.

Of the infantile, the homoerotic aspects of these stories we are, though vaguely, aware; but it is only with an effort that we can wake to a consciousness of how, among us who at the level of adulthood find a difference in color sufficient provocation for distrust and hatred, they celebrate, all of them, the mutual love of *a white man and a colored.* So buried at a level of acceptance which does not touch reason, so desperately repressed from overt recognition, so contrary to what is usually thought of as our ultimate level of taboo—the sense of that love can survive only in the obliquity of a symbol, persistent, obsessive, in short, an archetype: the boy's homoerotic crush, the love of the black fused at this level into a single thing.

I hope I have been using here a hopelessly abused word with some precision; by "archetype" I mean a coherent pattern of beliefs and feelings so widely shared at a level beneath consciousness that there exists no abstract vocabulary for representing it, and so "sacred" that unexamined, irrational restraints inhibit any explicit analysis. Such a complex finds a formula or pattern story, which serves both to embody it, and, at first at least, to conceal its full implications. Later, the secret may be revealed, the archetype "analyzed" or "allegorically" interpreted according to the language of the day.

I find the complex we have been examining genuinely mythic; certainly it has the invisible character of the true archetype, eluding the wary pounce of Howells or Mrs. Twain, who excised from *Huckleberry Finn* the cussing as unfit for children, but who left, unperceived, a conventionally abhorrent doctrine of ideal love. Even the writers in whom we find it attained it, in a sense, dreaming. The felt difference between *Huckleberry Finn* and Twain's other books must lie in part in the release from conscious restraint inherent in the author's assumption of the character of Huck; the passage in and out of darkness and river mist, the constant confusion of identities (Huck's ten or twelve names; the question of who is the real uncle, who the true Tom), the sudden intrusions into alien violences without past or future, give the whole work, for all its carefully observed detail, the texture of a dream. For *Moby Dick* such a point need scarcely be made. Even Cooper, despite his insufferable gentlemanliness, his tedium, cannot conceal from the kids who continue to read him the secret behind his overconscious prose: the childish, impossible dream. D. H. Lawrence saw in him clearly the boy's Utopia; the absolute wilderness in which the stuffiness of home yields to wigwam, and "My Wife" to Chingachgook.

I do not recall ever having seen in the commentaries of the social anthropologist or psychologist an awareness of the role of this profound child's dream of love in our relation to the Negro. (I say Negro, though the beloved in the books I have mentioned is variously Indian and Polynesian, because the Negro has become more and more exclusively for us *the* colored man, the colored man *par excellence*.) Trapped in what have by now become shackling clichés —the concept of the white man's sexual envy of the Negro male, the ambivalent horror of miscegenation—they do not sufficiently note the complementary factor of physical attraction, the archetypal love of white male and black. But either the horror or the attraction is meaningless alone; only together do they make sense. Just as the pure love of man and man is in general set off against the ignoble passion of man for woman, so more specifically (and more vividly) the dark desire which leads to miscegenation is contrasted with the ennobling love of a white man and a colored one. James Fenimore Cooper is our first poet of this ambivalence; indeed, miscegenation is the secret theme of the Leatherstocking novels, especially of *The Last of the Mohicans*. Natty Bumppo, the man who boasts always of having "no cross" in *his* blood, flees by nature from the defilement of all women, but never with so absolute a revulsion as he displays toward the *squaw* with whom at one point he seems at the point of being forced to cohabit; and the threat of the dark-skinned rapist sends pale woman after pale woman skittering through Cooper's imagined wilderness. Even poor Cora, who already has a fatal drop of alien blood that cuts her off from any marriage with a white man, in so far as she is white cannot be mated with Uncas, the noblest of redmen. Only in death can they be joined in an embrace as chaste as that of males. There's no good woman but a dead woman! Yet Chingachgook and the Deerslayer are permitted to sit night after night over their campfire in the purest domestic bliss. So long as there is no mingling of blood, soul may couple with soul in God's undefiled forest.

Nature undefiled—this is the inevitable setting of the Sacred Marriage of males. Ishmael and Queequeg, arm in arm, about to ship out, Huck and Jim swimming beside the raft in the peaceful flux of the Mississippi—here it is the motion of water which completes the syndrome, the American dream of isolation afloat. The notion of the Negro as the unblemished bride blends with the myth of running away to sea, of running the great river down to the sea. The immensity of water defines a loneliness that demands love; its strangeness symbolizes the disavowal of the conventional that makes possible all versions of love. In *Two Years Before the Mast*, in *Moby Dick*, in *Huckleberry Finn* the water is there, is the very texture of the novel; the Leatherstocking Tales propose another symbol for the same meaning: the virgin forest. Notice the adjectives—the virgin forest and the forever inviolable sea. It is well to remember, too, what surely must be more than a coincidence, that Copper, who could dream this myth, also invented for us the novel of the sea, wrote for the first time in history the sea story proper.

The rude pederasty of the forecastle and the captain's cabin, celebrated in a thousand jokes, is the profanation of a dream; yet Melville, who must have known such blasphemies, refers to them only once and indirectly, for it was *his* dream that they threatened. And still the dream survives; in a recent book by Gore Vidal, an incipient homosexual, not yet aware of the implications of his feelings, indulges in the reverie of running off to sea with his dearest friend. The buggery of sailors is taken for granted everywhere, yet is thought of usually as an inversion forced on men by their isolation from women; though the opposite case may well be true: the isolation sought more or less consciously as an occasion for male encounters. At any rate, there is a context in which the legend of the sea as escape and solace, the fixated sexuality of boys, the myth of the dark beloved, are one. In Melville and Twain at the center of our tradition, in the lesser writers at the periphery, the archetype is at once formalized and perpetuated. Nigger Jim and Queequeg make concrete for us what was without them a vague pressure on the threshold of our consciousness; the proper existence of the archetype is in the realized character, who waits, as it were, only to be asked his secret. Think of Oedipus biding in silence from Sophocles to Freud!

Unwittingly, we are possessed in childhood by these characters and their undiscriminated meaning, and it is difficult for us to dissociate them without a sense of disbelief. What—these household figures clues to our subtlest passions! The foreigner finds it easier to perceive the significances too deep within us to be brought into focus. D. H. Lawrence discovered in our classics a linked mythos of escape and immaculate male love; Lorca in *The Poet in New York* grasped instinctively (he could not even read English) the kinship of Harlem and Walt Whitman, the fairy as bard. But of course we do not have to be conscious of what possesses us; in every generation of our own writers the archetype reappears, refracted, half-understood, but *there*. In the gothic reverie of Capote's *Other Voices, Other Rooms*, both elements of the syndrome are presented though disjunctively: the boy moving between the love of a Negro maidservant and his inverted cousin. In Carson McCullers' *Member of the Wedding*, another variant is invented: a *female* homosexual romance between the boy-girl Frankie and a Negro cook. This time the Father-Slave-Beloved is converted into the figure of a Mother-Sweetheart-Servant, but remains still, of course, satisfactorily black. It is not strange, after all, to find this archetypal complex in latter-day writers of a frankly homosexual sensibility; but it recurs, too, in such resolutely masculine writers as Faulkner, who evokes the myth in the persons of the Negro and the boy of *Intruder in the Dust*.

In the myth, one notes finally, it is typically in the role of outcast, ragged woodsman, or despised sailor ("Call me Ishmael!"), or unregenerate boy (Huck before the prospect of being "sivilized" cries out, "I been there before!") that we turn to the love of a colored man. By how, we cannot help asking, does the vision of the white American as a pariah correspond with our long-held public status: the world's beloved, the success? It is perhaps only the artist's portrayal of *himself*, the notoriously alienated writer in America, at home with such images, child of the town drunk, the hapless survivor. But no, Ishmael is in all of us, our unconfessed universal fear objectified in the writer's status as in the outcast sailor's: that compelling anxiety, which every foreigner notes, that we may not be loved, that we are loved for our possessions and not our selves, that we are really—*alone*. It is that underlying terror which explains our incredulity in the face of adulation or favor, what is called (once more the happy adjective) our "boyish modesty."

Our dark-skinned beloved will take us in, we assure ourselves, when we have been cut off, or have cut ourselves off, from all others, without rancor or the insult of forgiveness. He will fold us in his arms saying, "Honey" or "Aikane"; he will comfort us, as if our offense against him were long ago remitted, were never truly *real*. And yet we cannot ever really forget our guilt; the stories that embody the myth dramatize as if compulsively the role of the colored man as the victim. Dana's Hope is shown dying of the white man's syphilis; Queequeg is portrayed as racked by fever, a pointless episode except in the light of this necessity; Crane's Negro is disfigured to the point of monstrosity; Cooper's Indian smolders to a hopeless old age conscious of the imminent disappearance of his race; Jim is shown loaded down with chains, weakened by the hundred torments dreamed up by Tom in the name of bulliness. The immense gulf of guilt must not be mitigated any more than the disparity of color. (Queequeg is not merely brown but monstrously tattooed; Chingachgook is horrid with paint; Jim is portrayed as the sick A-rab died blue), so that the final reconciliation may seem more unbelievable and tender. The archetype makes no attempt to deny our outrage as fact; it portrays it as meaningless in the face of love.

There would be something insufferable, I think, in that final vision of remission if it were not for the presence of a motivating anxiety, the sense always of a last chance. Behind the white American's nightmare that someday, no longer tourist, inheritor, or liberator, he will be rejected, refused, he dreams of his acceptance at the breast he has most utterly offended. It is a dream so sentimental, so outrageous, so desperate, that it redeems our concept of boyhood from nostalgia to tragedy.

In each generation we *play out* the impossible mythos, and we live to see our children play it: the white boy and the black we can discover wrestling affectionately on any American sidewalk, along which they will walk in adulthood, eyes averted from each other, unwilling to touch even by accident. The dream recedes; the immaculate passion and the astonishing reconciliation become a memory, and less, a regret, at last the unrecognized motifs of a child's book. "It's too good to be true, Honey," Jim says to Huck. "It's too good to be true."

RALPH ELLISON

Change the Joke and Slip the Yoke†

* * *

In the Anglo-Saxon branch of American folklore and in the entertainment industry (which thrives on the exploitation and debasement of all folk materials), the Negro is reduced to a negative sign that usually appears in a comedy of the grotesque and the unacceptable. As Constance Rourke[1] has made us aware, the action of the early minstrel show—with its Negro-derived choreography, its ringing of banjos and rattling of bones, its voices cackling jokes in pseudo-Negro dialect, with its nonsense songs, its bright costumes and sweating performers—constituted a ritual of exorcism. Other white cultures had their gollywogs and blackamoors but the fact of Negro slavery went to the moral heart of the American social drama and here the Negro was too real for easy fantasy, too serious to be dealt with in anything less than a national art. The mask was an inseparable part of the national iconography. Thus even when a Negro acted in an abstract role the national implications were unchanged. His costume made use of the "sacred" symbolism of the American flag—with red and white striped pants and coat and with stars set in a field of blue for a collar—but he could appear only with his hands gloved in white and his face blackened with burnt cork or greasepaint.

This mask, this willful stylization and modification of the natural face and hands, was imperative for the evocation of that atmosphere in which the fascination of blackness could be enjoyed, the comic catharsis achieved. The racial identity of the performer was unimportant, the mask was the thing (the "thing" in more ways than one) and its function was to veil the humanity of Negroes thus reduced to a sign, and to repress the white audience's awareness of its moral identification with its own acts and with the human ambiguities pushed behind the mask.

* * *

It is not at all odd that this black-faced figure of white fun is for Negroes a symbol of everything they rejected in the white man's thinking about race, in themselves and in their own group. When he appears, for example, in the guise of Nigger Jim, the Negro is made uncomfortable. Writing at a time when the blackfaced minstrel was still popular, and shortly after a war which left even the abolitionists weary of those problems associated with the Negro,

† From *Partisan Review*, XXV, 2 (Spring 1958), 212–22. Copyright © 1958 by Ralph Ellison. Reprinted by permission of William Morris Agency, Inc.

1. In Constance Rourke, *American Humor: A Study of the National Character* (New York: Harcourt, Brace, 1931) [*Editors*].

Twain fitted Jim into the outlines of the minstrel tradition, and it is from behind this stereotype mask that we see Jim's dignity and human capacity—and Twain's complexity—emerge. Yet it is his source in this same tradition which creates that ambivalence between his identification as an adult and parent and his "boyish" naivete, and which by contrast makes Huck, with his street-sparrow sophistication, seem more adult. Certainly it upsets a Negro reader, and it offers a less psychoanalytical explanation of the discomfort which lay behind Leslie Fiedler's thesis concerning the relation of Jim and Huck in his essay "Come Back to the Raft Ag'in, Huck Honey!"

A glance at a more recent fictional encounter between a Negro adult and a white boy, that of Lucas Beauchamp and Chick Mallison in Faulkner's *Intruder in The Dust*, will reinforce my point. For all the racial and caste differences between them, Lucas holds the ascendency in his mature dignity over the youthful Mallison and refuses to lower himself in the comic duel of status forced on him by the white boy whose life he has saved. Faulkner was free to reject the confusion between manhood and the Negro's caste status which is sanctioned by white southern tradition, but Twain, standing closer to the Reconstruction and to the oral tradition, was not so free of the white dictum that Negro males must be treated either as boys or "uncles"—never as men. Jim's friendship for Huck comes across as that of a boy for another boy rather than as the friendship of an adult for a junior; thus there is implicit in it not only a violation of the manners sanctioned by society for relations between Negroes and whites, there is a violation of our conception of adult maleness.

In Jim the extremes of the private and the public come to focus, and before our eyes an "archetypal" figure gives way before the realism implicit in the form of the novel. Here we have, I believe, an explanation in the novel's own terms of that ambiguity which bothered Fiedler. Fiedler was accused of mere sensationalism when he named the friendship homosexual, yet I believe him so profoundly disturbed by the manner in which the deep dichotomies symbolized by blackness and whiteness are resolved that, forgetting to look at the specific form of the novel, he leaped squarely into the middle of that tangle of symbolism which he is dedicated to unsnarling, and yelled out his most terrifying name for chaos. Other things being equal he might have called it "rape," "incest," "parricide," or— "miscegenation." It is ironic that what to a Negro appears to be a lost fall in Twain's otherwise successful wrestle with the ambiguous figure in blackface is viewed by a critic as a symbolic loss of sexual identity. Surely for literature there is some rare richness here.

* * *

DANIEL G. HOFFMAN

Black Magic—and White—in *Huckleberry Finn*†

1

The most universal book to have come out of the United States of America begins with this preamble:

NOTICE

Persons attempting to find a motive in this narrative will be prosecuted; persons attempting to find a moral in it will be banished; persons attempting to find a plot in it will be shot.

What a way to begin: "No Trespassing!" This, of course, is only the first of the innumerable jokes, pranks, disguises, tricks, deceptions, ruses, and verbal extravagances that make *Adventures of Huckleberry Finn* a book that has won the world's heart. At the start Mark Twain establishes its tone of frontier humor. His preamble is nailed to a stake, and it posts the limits of his claim, and of ours, on the golden lode of his own remembered boyhood on the Mississippi.

But why such caution behind his bumptious fooling?

What a way to begin a book. Think, for instance, of the "Author's Prologue" to *Gargantua*, exactly three and a half centuries earlier. Rabelais began by comparing his book to the Sileni of old, "little boxes . . . painted on the outside with wanton toyish figures . . . and other such counterfeited pictures, at pleasure, to excite people unto laughter." But within those caskets lay "many rich and fine drugs . . . balm, ambergreese, amonomon . . . and other things of great price." And he goes on to speak of Socrates, for whose outer appearance "you would not have given the peel of an onion . . . always laughing, tippling, and merry, carousing to everyone, with continual gibes and jeers, the better by those means to conceal his divine knowledge."

Divine knowledge, of course, is not a commodity much in demand in the world, and those who find it burdening their souls are often hard-pressed to put a good face on the matter. The faces of Silenus, god of mirth, are as good a disguise as any.

Even Rabelais, in his mock-monkery fashion, drives a stake against the scholiasts, just as Mark Twain would do. If you believe, he says, that "Homer, whilst he was couching his Iliads and

† Chapter 15 (pp. 317–42) of *Form and Fable in American Fiction* by Daniel G. Hoffman. © 1961 by Daniel G. Hoffman and reprinted by permission of Oxford University Press, Inc.

Odysseys, had any thought upon those allegories" which the critics have "squeezed out of him," you may as well take the gospel sacraments to be written by Ovid. Now Mark Twain could be just as bookish, as well as just as truly comic, as Rabelais, but in posting his "Notice" he intuitively chose the vernacular way of warning off the critics who would squeeze the juice of allegorical lemons from a work which he had freshened with the juices of life. To divine knowledge he makes no claims. Yet what can explain his cautious parrying of critical exegesis but that he well knew the motive, the moral, and the plot of his own book—he had recognized the divine knowledge that came to him when he finally plumbed the images of his deepest recollection—and this he did not want abstracted from the only form in which it could retain the fullness of its truth: *Adventures of Huckleberry Finn*.

Despite his "Notice," scholars, annotators, and critics have poached all over Mark's place. Indeed, in the past generation there has been an unparalleled exploration of motive, moral, and plot in *Huckleberry Finn*. As regards the plot, many readers have taken Mark Twain literally, or at least assumed that the book has no more intrinsic a plot than the picaresque pattern of a journey imposes. Certainly their contention was strengthened by Bernard DeVoto's publication in *Mark Twain at Work* of the author's plan for a concluding episode—mercifully never carried out—which involved Huck, Jim and Tom's encountering an escaped circus elephant in the Louisiana bayous. The ending that he actually did give the book— Tom Sawyer's burlesque liberation of the already-freed slave—has been much criticized as disastrously out of key with the fundamental themes of the rest of the story. Yet T. S. Eliot and Lionel Trilling have found this ending satisfactory; other recent critics have contended the contrary against them as well as against Mark Twain.

As for the first two clauses in the author's "Notice," both motive and moral have been scrutinized with Geiger-counter sensitivity by critics of a dozen different persuasions. Where some find the theme of the book to be the search for freedom, another proposes the "theme of appearance versus reality." J. M. Cox suggests initiation and rebirth as its besetting theme, while Philip Young discovers that "an excessive exposure to violence and death" have produced "an ideal symbol" for dying, namely, a "supremely effortless flight into a dark and silent unknown." Yet again "death and rebirth" and "Huck's journey in search of a father" are urged by K. S. Lynn as themes, while R. W. Frantz terms Huck "a creature of fear." As for motive, the ingenious Leslie Fiedler reads the book as a wish-fulfillment of homosexual miscegenation. On the other hand Mr. Trilling has made a definitive case for "Huck's intense and even complex moral quality."[1]

Mark Twain should have known better; in Academe, as in Missouri, a notice without a sheriff proves utterly unavailing. This chapter is itself yet another act of trespass. An assortment of critical readings such as those just enumerated suggests that if the disguises Mark Twain painted upon his Sileni have been baffling in their variety, there is yet indeed a divine knowledge concealed within them. Although each of these essays is helpful in noting valuable themes and structures of the book, a most important pattern has not been sufficiently explored. This is the pattern of relationships in *Huckleberry Finn* between the human and the divine.

Mr. Eliot and Mr. Trilling agree in their readings that the River is a god, presiding over the action, its divinity everywhere implied though nowhere stated outright. But there is a more explicit supernaturalism in this book. Or, more properly, there is an exemplification and a testing of three attitudes toward the imaginative fulfillment of life, and these are largely indicated in supernatural terms. Each typifies the moral nature of those who profess it. Two of these imaginary supernatural worlds prove morally inadequate; the third —which pays homage to the river god—gives dignity to human life.

These attitudes, so compellingly dramatized by Mark Twain, are the conventional piety of the villagers; the irrelevant escape of the romantic imagination (as played by Tom Sawyer and an assorted adult cast of rapscallions and Southern gentlemen), and the world of supernatural omens which Jim, the runaway slave, best understands. Huck Finn is the sorcerer's apprentice. The superstitious imagination recognizes evil as a dynamic force; it acknowledges death. It is truer to the moral demands of life than is either the smug piety of Christian conformity or the avoidance of choice by escaping to fantasy and romance.

Bernard DeVoto has made it impossible for us to miss Mark Twain's indebtedness to Negro superstitions. Yet their significance in *Huckleberry Finn* has not adequately been shown. Jim's and Huck's beliefs in witches, ghosts, and omens are not merely authen-

1. T. S. Eliot, "Introduction" to *Adventures of Huckleberry Finn* (London, 1950); Lionel Trilling, *"Huckleberry Finn," The Liberal Imagination* (New York, 1951), pp. 104–17; William Van O'Connor, "Why *Huckleberry Finn* Is Not the Great American Novel," *College English*, XVII (Oct. 1955), 6–10; Leo Marx, "Mr. Eliot, Mr. Trilling, and *Huckleberry Finn*," *American Scholar*, XXII (Autumn 1953), 423–40; Lauriat Lane, Jr., "Why *Huckleberry Finn* Is a Great World Novel." *College English*, XVII (Oct., 1955), 1–5; James M. Cox, "Remarks on the Sad Initiation of Huckleberry Finn," *Sewanee Review*, LXII (Summer 1954), 389–405; Philip Young, *Ernest Hemingway* (New York, 1952), chap. 6; Kenneth S. Lynn, "Huck and Jim," *Yale Review*, XLVII (Spring 1958), 421–31; Ray W. Frantz, "The Role of Folklore in *Huckleberry Finn*," *American Literature*, XXVIII (Nov. 1956), 314–27: Leslie Fiedler, "Come Back to the Raft Ag'in, Huck Honey!" *An End to Innocence* (Boston, 1955), pp. 142–57.

tic touches of local color; they are of signal importance in the thematic development of the book and in the growth toward maturity of its principal characters. When understood as a commentary upon and criticism of the two conventional traditions of white society in reconciling the moral sense with the realities of life on the Mississippi, this folklore of the supernatural becomes a structural element essential to the work of art.

In working out the conflicts between the three otherworlds and their human representatives in *Huckleberry Finn* I hope to do full justice to the character of Jim. Insufficient notice has been taken of the ways in which Jim, as well as Huck, grows to maturity and assumes a man's full obligations. Some of the most important evidence of his development is given us in his role as seer and shaman, interpreter of the dark secrets of nature which the white folks in the church deny, secrets which Tom Sawyer and all the other romanticists along the Mississippi cannot discover.

These three commitments of the imagination allow Mark Twain to explore the possibilities of establishing sympathetic relations between man and nature and between man and man. The local conditions of Huck Finn's world are those of the sleepy village of "St. Petersburg"—or, to be more accurate biographically, of Hannibal, Missouri, the riverfront town where young Sam Clemens grew up, played with the outcast boy Tom Blankenship (the original of Huck), and listened to the Negroes speak of ghosts and omens. His best two books of boyhood create this river hamlet for us; several of the themes of *Huckleberry Finn* have their beginnings in *The Adventures of Tom Sawyer*. We should consider both books in order to explore the three otherworlds of Hannibal.

* * *

4

The third imaginary realm is the world of superstition, a world we enter as soon as we meet Huckleberry Finn. As DeVoto observes, "On page 64 of *Tom Sawyer*, Huckleberry Finn wanders into immortality swinging a dead cat." Huck and his cat symbolize freedom to Tom, who meets them on a Monday morning between his bondage at church the day before and his approaching incarceration in the district school. That dead cat also represents the lure of an unknown and forbidden world of spirits, omens, and dark powers, a world which attracts Tom not only by its Gothicism and horror but because, unlike his romantic escapades, this imaginary realm succeeds in transcending reality by rendering life itself in mythic terms. The boys exchange cures for warts; yet try as he will, Tom can never really enter Huck's world. When he tries to recover by incantation all the marbles he ever lost Tom's charm is bound to fail, for the first allegiance of his imagination—as we have seen—lies elsewhere. Besides, he is after all a village boy, nephew of the respectable Aunt Polly, brother of the model prig Sid Sawyer; Tom shares their status, and to him Huck is a "romantic outcast." Therefore Tom will never share Huck's secret wisdom—or his freedom.

The association of these superstitions in Mark Twain's mind with freedom from restraint is reiterated in the first chapter of *Huckleberry Finn*. This time it is Huck who sweats through the lessons, about Moses and "the Bulrushers." At last the widow "let it out that Moses had been dead a considerable long time; so then I didn't care no more about him, because I don't take no stock in dead people." Huck is then lectured on going to Heaven by Miss Watson; this is so depressing that by nighttime "I felt so lonesome I most wished I was dead."

"The stars were shining, and the leaves rustled in the woods ever so mournful; and I heard an owl, away off, who-whooing about somebody that was dead, and a whippoorwill and a dog crying about somebody that was going to die; and the wind was trying to whisper something to me, and I couldn't make out what it was, and so it made the cold shivers run over me. Then away out in the woods I heard that kind of a sound that a ghost makes when it wants to tell about something that's on its mind and can't make itself understood, and so can't rest easy in its grave, and has to go about that way every night grieving. I got so downhearted and scared I did wish I had some company. Pretty soon a spider went crawling up my shoulder, and I flipped it off and it lit in the candle; and before I could budge it was all shriveled up. I didn't need anybody to tell me that that was an awful bad sign and would fetch me some bad luck, so I was scared and most shook the clothes off of me. I got up and turned around in my tracks three times and crossed my breast every time; and then I tied up a little lock of my hair to keep witches away. But I hadn't no confidence."

Freedom from the restraints of civilization, yes; but such freedom has its dangers too. For Huck, the omens are an acknowledgment of the fact of death. "I didn't take no stock in dead people" applies to the dead lessons in Bible or school, not to these immanent realities. These portents are an admission of evil as a positive force in the natural world. His exorcisms attempt to control the operation of malevolent powers. But while he knows far more about such things than Tom does, Huck is still a mere disciple. The magus is Nigger Jim.

But when we first meet him, Jim is a slave. His superstitions, like the hagiolatry of the ignorant peasants in *The Innocents Abroad*, are the manacles upon his soul. Mark Twain dramatizes his bondage by the quality of his beliefs. Far from controlling nature, Jim in slavery is helpless before the dark powers, a gullible prey to every chance or accident which befalls him. This is made humorously manifest in chapter 2, when Tom and Huck find Jim snoozing on the widow's kitchen steps. Tom hangs his hat on a branch and leaves a five-cent piece on the table. "Afterward Jim said the witches bewitched him and put him in a trance, and rode him all over the state, and then set him down under the trees again, and hung his hat on a limb to show who done it." Other slaves come from miles around to hear Jim's expanding account of this marvel. It gives him status! But he is more than ever enslaved to his fears; and a week later Miss Watson decides to sell him down the river to a more arduous bondage. That is a fear he cannot transform into personal distinction through the artistic control of a tall tale. Jim runs away to Jackson's Island.

On the island he lives in terror of capture. Huck, having escaped from Pap, is there before him. Still the fearful, haunt-ridden man-child, Jim takes Huck for a ghost and drops to his knees, imploring, "Doan' hurt me—don't! I hain't ever done no harm to a ghos'. I alwuz liked dead people, en done all I could for 'em. You go en git in de river ag'in, wah you b'longs." But once he learns in earnest that Huck is alive, Jim realizes that he himself is free. The mighty river rises and the two move camp to a womb-like cavern. Animals take refuge in the trees, and "they got so tame, on account of being hungry, that you could paddle right up and put your hand on them if you wanted to; but not the snakes and turtles." This is an uneasy Eden, menaced by the implacable flooding river.

Now that he is free in this ambiguous paradise the nature of Jim's superstitious belief undergoes a change. We hear no more of ghosts and witches. Instead, Jim instructs Huck in the lore of weather, in the omens of luck, in the talismans of death. "Jim knowed all kinds of signs." Seeing young birds skip along means rain; catching one brings death. You must tell the bees when their owner dies or they will weaken and perish. Death is never far from the superstitious imagination. Jim goes on—don't shake the table-cloth after sundown, or count the things you cook for dinner, or look at the moon over your left shoulder—these bring bad luck. "It looked to me like all the signs was about bad luck, and so I asked him if there warn't any good-luck signs. He says: 'Mighty few—an' *dey* ain't no use to a body. What you want to know when good luck's a-comin' for? Want to keep it off?'" Luck is the folk concept of what the Greeks called Fate, the Anglo-Saxons, Wyrd. There is a stoical wisdom in Jim's resignation before it which makes a manly contrast to the psalm-singing optimism of Miss Watson and the revivalists, and to Tom's romantic evasions of reality.

Soon after they see the young birds flying, sure enough, it rains: a huge, frightening storm that reasserts the dominance of nature over man. The river rises, and as was foretold in so many of their omens, the House of Death floats by. When Jim's omens come true he is no more a gullible supplicant to witches. He is a magus now, a magician in sympathetic converse with the spirits that govern—often by malice or caprice—the world of things and men.

As soon as Jim begins to feel his freedom, his attitude toward Huck develops. One of the grand ironies of this book is that while it seems to show Huck protecting Jim, Jim is also taking care of Huck all along. Jim's folk wisdom saved Huck from the storm; Jim builds the wigwam on the raft. "I'd see him standing my watch on top of his'n, 'stead of calling me, so I could go on sleeping." Just after the storm, when the House of Death floats by, it is Jim who goes aboard first, sees the corpse, and won't let Huck behold it. Huck boyishly salvages an old straw hat, a Barlow knife, "a ratty old bedquilt. . . . And so, take it all around, we made a good haul." These squalid remnants, we discover much later, constitute Huck's patrimony from Pap, the father whose savagery he fled. So terrible was the self-destructive anarchic energy of Pap that Huck had to simulate self-destruction to escape him. But now it is Jim who comprehends the degradation of Pap's death and protects Huck from that cruel knowledge. Jim is now free to take the place that Pap was never worthy to hold as Huck's spiritual father. When Jim and Huck shove off from the House of Death their odyssey begins. Jim can now act as Huck's father, and Huck's first act is to protect him, as a son might do.

Because of this filial relationship, Huck cannot play tricks on Jim as he could on Tom or Ben Rogers. This he discovers when he kills a rattler and coils it in Jim's bed. Jim had warned him, "it was the worst bad luck in the world to touch a snake-skin." The dead snake's mate coils round it and bites poor Jim. But Jim has a folk cure—eating the snake's head roasted, tying the rattles around his wrist, and drinking whiskey. Just as his omens come true, his cures cure. Again we see Jim as medicine man, free to control—within mortal limits—his universe.

Another aspect of Jim's shamanistic role is his power to interpret oracles and dreams. Here, too, when in slavery this attribute parodies itself because Jim then held pretensions without power. He had a hairball from the fourth stomach of an ox with which he "used to do magic." Huck consults him after seeing Pap's footprints in the snow, to learn what Pap would do. Accepting Huck's counterfeit quarter, Jim reels off a counterfeit prophecy, concluding, "You wants to keep 'way fum de water as much as you kin." But when Huck returns to his room, "there sat Pap—his own self!" and the only escape from Pap is to flee by water. Jim's next oracular occasion comes when he and Huck find each other after being separated by the fog. Huck, as a joke, convinces Jim that they had been together on the raft all the time; Jim must have dreamed their separation. So Jim "said he must start in and 'terpret it, for it was sent for a warning." Towheads and currents stand for men who will aid or hinder them; their cries were warnings of trouble ahead, but all would work out well in the end. Then Huck points to the leaves, the rubbish, the smashed oar. Jim ponders:

"What do they stan' for? I's gwyne tell you. When I got all wore out wid work, en wid de callin' for you, en went to sleep, my heart wuz mos' broke bekase you wuz los', en I didn' k'yer no mo' what become er me en de raf'. En when I wake up en find you back ag'in, all safe en soun', de tears come, en I could 'a' got down on my knees en kiss yo' foot, I's so thankful. En all you wuz thinkin' 'bout wuz how you could make a fool uv ole Jim wid a lie. Dat truck dah is *trash*; en trash is what people is dat puts dirt on de head er dey fren's en makes 'em ashamed."

This speech, so moving in its avowal of dignity, combines Jim's attempt at magical interpretation (which is in fact accurate) with the realism that underlies it, and with his staunch adherence to the code of simple decencies by which good men must live. It is indeed the first major turning-point of the romance. It reinforces the lesson of the snakeskin: Huck now realizes that he is bound to Jim by ties too strong for mischievous trifling, ties so strong that he must break the strongest mores of the society he was raised in to acknowledge them. "It was fifteen minutes before I could work myself up to go and humble myself to a nigger; but I done it, and I warn't ever sorry for it afterward, neither."

Now that Huck has learned how he and Jim are inseparable, circumstances at once thrust them apart. In the next chapter their raft is run over by a paddlewheeler; when Huck gets ashore and sings out for Jim he finds himself alone. This, he thinks, is what comes of handling that snakeskin. He is taken in by the Grangerfords and does not find Jim again until after the shooting. Then the Duke and Dauphin come aboard. From this point on Jim and Huck are never again alone together, and Jim does not act as magus again. His powers have their mysterious source in the river, partaking of its inscrutable might. For if the river is a god, Jim is its priest. The river god is indifferent to humanity; he runs on, uncontaminated by the evils along his shores, asserting now and then in storms and floods which sweep the House of Death downstream his dominance and power over "the damned human race." Only when Jim is alone with Huck on the river island or drifting on the current is he so free from the corruption of civilization that he can partake of the river god's dark power. Jim responds on a primitive level to that power, through which he can interpret the signs that are older than Christianity.

But now he is on the sidelines while Huck observes the Duke and King play out their grasping roles. After their failure to filch Mary Jane Wilkes' patrimony, the King sells Jim to Tom Sawyer's Uncle Silas. Huck sets out to find him. Suddenly aware of his guilt in having aided a runaway slave, Huck wrestles again with his conscience. In a memorable climax to his discovery of his own natural goodness, Huck dares to defy the codes of Miss Watson's church and of Tom Sawyer's village by stealing Jim out of slavery again: "All right, then, I'll go to hell."

There are witches again on Uncle Silas's farm, for this is slave territory. Silas's slave, Nat, wears wool in his hair to ward them away, thinks he is bewitched when Tom tells him he is, knows this is true when a pack of hounds leap into Jim's cell through the escape hole the boys had Jim dig beneath the bed. But Jim knows better. Although manacled while Nat has the run of the place, Jim is spiritually free. Now that he has experienced the freedom of life on the raft, life in accord with the rhythms of nature, mere chains will not reduce him to subjection again. As Tom knows, he is legally free anyway. But Jim does not know this; his fortitude during his imprisonment is one of the signs of his moral stature.

Jim's stature is made manifest at the end of the book when, having suffered such needless discomfitures at Tom's hands, he voluntarily gives himself up in the swamp to help the doctor nurse back to health the boy who had plagued him. Then, brought back to the farm as he knew he would be—in chains, suffering the abuse of an angry mob, in momentary danger of lynching—Jim refuses to recognize Huck in the crowd lest he involve this other, truer friend in his own misfortunes. Jim's loyalty is so great that he is willing to sacrifice his freedom for his young friends' sakes. His selflessness is truly noble, a far cry from the chuckle-headedness of the slave who was ridden all over the country by witches when Tom Sawyer lifted his hat.

5

During the decade when critical opinion at last recognized the inherent dignity of Jim, *Adventures of Huckleberry Finn*, in response to strong pressure from the N.A.A.C.P., was removed from the high school curriculum in our largest city.[2] The most eloquent statement of the objections of a Negro reader to Mark Twain's characterization of Jim is that of the novelist Ralph Ellison:

2. New York *Times*, Sept. 12, 1957, pp. 1–2.

"Writing at a time when the blackfaced minstrel was still popular, and shortly after a war which left even the abolitionists weary of those problems associated with the Negro, Twain fitted Jim into the outlines of the minstrel tradition, and it is from behind this stereotype mask that we see Jim's dignity and human capacity—and Twain's complexity—emerge. Yet it is his source in this same tradition which creates that ambivalence between his identification as an adult and parent and his 'boyish' naïveté, and which by contrast makes Huck, with his street-sparrow sophistication, seem more adult. . . . Jim's friendship for Huck comes across as that of a boy for another boy rather than as the friendship of an adult for a junior; thus there is implicit in it not only a violation of the manners sanctioned by society for relations between Negroes and whites, there is a violation of our conception of adult maleness."[3]

Speaking of the blackfaced minstrel, the "smart-man-playing-dumb," Mr. Ellison remarks that his role grows "out of the white American's manichean fascination with the symbolism of blackness and whiteness." This color symbolism is openly appropriated in *Huckleberry Finn;* it is used in full awareness of its ironies. We remember Pap's first appearance in the book—his face "was white . . . a white to make a body's flesh crawl—a treetoad white, a fish-belly white"; he it is who out of pride of color would secede from the government because it permits "a free nigger from Ohio—a mulatter, most as white as a white man," to vote. This early in the book the falsity of the manichean color symbolism is dramatized.

But there is no gainsaying Mr. Ellison that when Jim analyzes the stock market, or asks "Was Sollerman Wise?" or kowtows to the bogus royalty or endures his torturous liberation for Tom's amusement he is indeed akin to the Mr. Bones of minstrel fame. I hope to have shown, however, that this is what he begins as, what he emerges from. Jim plays his comic role in slavery, when he bears the status society or Tom imposes upon him; not when he lives in his intrinsic human dignity, alone on the raft with Huck.

If Jim emerges from the degradation of slavery to become as much a man as Mark Twain could make him be, we must remember that Jim's growth marks a progress in Twain's spiritual maturity too. "In my school days I had no aversion to slavery. I was not aware that there was anything wrong with it. No one arraigned it in my hearing . . . the local pulpit taught us that God approved it, that it was a holy thing."[4] In 1855 Sam Clemens wrote home to his mother that a nigger had a better chance than a white man of getting ahead in New York. Mark Twain began with all the stereo-

3. 'The Negro Writer in America: An Exchange,' *Partisan Review* XXV (Spring 1958), 215–16.

4. *Mark Twain's Autobiography*, ed. Albert Bigelow Paine (New York, 1924), p. 101.

types of racial character in his mind, the stereotypes that he as well as Jim outgrows.

It is clear that supernatural folklore plays an important part in Twain's handling of Jim. Since this lore is used to differentiate Jim from the white characters, there remains the question of Mark Twain's accuracy in assigning folk belief to the black man.[5] In the preface to *Tom Sawyer*, Mark Twain makes explicit his assumption about the provenience of folk beliefs: "The odd superstitions touched upon were all prevalent among children and slaves in the West at the period of its story—that is to say, thirty or forty years ago" (1835–45). In both books the only whites who are superstitious are either young boys or riffraff like Pap—the two categories of white folks who might have picked up the lore of slave quarter. The only "white" superstition in *Huckleberry Finn*, attributed to the villagers in general, is belief in the power of bread and quicksilver to discover a drowned corpse.[6] More typical of the attitude of white characters toward superstition is the derision of the raftsmen when their companion tells the ghost story of the murderer pursued by the corpse of his slain child floating in a barrel beside the raft.[7] Twain's usual assumption is that white persons of any status higher than trash like Pap have little knowledge of, and no belief in, superstition.[8]

Mark Twain's memory played him wrong. Every one of the beliefs in witch-lore and in omens he used in *Huckleberry Finn* proves to be of European rather than African origin and to have been held widely among the whites as well as among the Negroes of the region. The witch who is warded off by tying one's hair with threads and who rides her victims by night is an old familiar European folk figure:

> This is that very Mab
> That plaits the manes of horses in the night

whom Mercutio described in *Romeo and Juliet* (I, iv, 88–9). Jim's fear of snakeskins, his belief that one must tell the bees of their keeper's death, his conviction that counting the things you cook for

5. 'Regarding the feelings, emotions, and the spiritual life of the Negro the average white man knows little,' writes Newbell Niles Puckett in his magisterial *Folk Beliefs of the Southern Negro* (Chapel Hill, 1926), vii. 'Should some weird, archaic, Negro doctrine be brought to his attention he almost invariably considers it a "relic of African heathenism," though in four cases out of five it is a European dogma from which only centuries of patient education could wean even his own ancestors.'
6. The identical belief is reported by Harry Middleton Hyatt in *Folklore from Adams County Illinois* (New York, 1935), a region on the opposite shore of river above Hannibal; item no.10283.
7. I followed Bernard De Voto (*The Portable Mark Twain*) in considering this episode, usually printed as chapter 3 of *Life on the Mississippi*, an integral part of the book for which it was originally written.
8. Pap wears a cross of nails in the heel of his boot as a charm against the devil.

supper, or shaking the tablecloth after sundown, or speaking of the dead, or seeing the moon over your left shoulder all bring bad luck, and that a hairy chest means he's "gwine be rich"—all these were known among the white folk of the Mississippi valley.[9] Only his divination with a hairball from the stomach of an ox is a Negro belief of voodoo origin.

Why, then, does Mark Twain make such a point of having only Negroes, children, and riffraff as the bearers of folk superstitions in the re-created world of his childhood? *Huckleberry Finn* was written while Twain lived among the insurance magnates, the manufacturing millionaires, and the wealthy literati of the Nook Farm colony in Hartford, Connecticut. It had been many years since he had lived in a superstitious frontier community, and in his own not-too-reliable memory this folklore became associated with the slaves he had known in his boyhood. The original of Jim, he writes in his *Autobiography*, was " 'Uncle Dan'l,' a middle-aged slave" on the farm of Mrs. Clemens' brother John Quarles. "I can see the white and black children grouped around the hearth" of the slave's kitchen, "and I can hear Uncle Dan'l telling the immortal tales which Uncle Remus Harris was to gather into his book and charm the world with."[1] On such nights Dan'l's favorite encore was no animal fable but—as Twain wrote it down years later, in 1881, for Joel Chandler Harris's benefit—"De Woman wid de Gold'n Arm,"[2] a ghost story widely collected by folklorists since. In those days, "every old woman" was an herb doctor; in Hannibal and Florida the young Sam Clemens knew also old Aunt Hannah, so old she had talked with Moses, who tied threads in her hair against witches. A subtle emotional complex binds together *superstition: slaves: boyhood freedom* in Mark Twain's mind. These three aspects of his experience had occurred most vividly together, and he seems, in his greatest book, not to have thought of any one of them without invoking both of the others. There is, then, no invidious intention behind his characterizing Jim by the superstitions common to both races.

I hope in the foregoing pages to have cleared Mark Twain of the imputation that "the humor of those scenes of superstition . . . illustrate the ridiculous inadequacy and picturesque inventiveness of the fearful human responses to the powers of evil," for such an interpretation—it is that of Francis Brownell[3]—would put all of

9. I have traced in detail the European origins and white provenience of these beliefs in 'Jim's Magic: Black or White?' *American Literature*, XXXII (March 1960), 47–54.
1. *Autobiography*, pp. 100, 112.
2. *Mark Twain to Uncle Remus*, ed.

Thomas H. English (Atlanta, 1953), pp. 11–13. Mark Twain gives another version of the tale in 'How to Tell a Story.'
3. 'The Role of Jim in *Huckleberry Finn*,' *Boston Univ. Studies in English*, I (1955). 81.

Jim's folk beliefs in the service of the degrading minstrel characterization to which Mr. Ellison objects. The minstrel stereotype,
as we have seen, was the only possible starting-point for a white
author attempting to deal with Negro character a century ago.
How else could young Sam Clemens have known a Negro in the
Missouri of the 1840's except as the little white boy on familiar
terms with his uncle's household retainer? The measure of Mark
Twain's human understanding—Mr. Ellison calls it his complexity
—is evident when we compare Jim to the famous Negro character
in the writings of Mark Twain's friend, Joel Chandler Harris, remembering that Sam Clemens was in real life to "Uncle" Dan'l
as the little boy in Harris's books is to Uncle Remus. The Georgia
author's Negro fablist never ceases to be the minstrel in blackface.
The poetic irony in the Uncle Remus books is one of which Harris
was probably unaware: the Negro's human dignity survives the
minstrel mask not in Uncle Remus's character but in the satirical
stories he tells the white boy. That many of these were thinly veiled
avowals of the Negro's pride and dignity and refusal to submit his
spirit to the unjust yoke of custom would not seem to have occurred to Joel Chandler Harris, whose conscious literary strategy was
to palliate Northern antagonism of the South by idealizing antebellum plantation life.[4] But Mark Twain tries to make Jim stride
out of his scapegoat minstrel's role to stand before us in the dignity
of his own manhood. It is true that Mark Twain's triumph here is
incomplete: despite the skillful gradation of folk belief and other
indications of Jim's emergent stature, what does come through for
many readers is, as Mr. Ellison remarks, Jim's boy-to-boy relationship with Huck, "a violation of our conception of adult maleness."
We remember that Mark Twain himself admired Uncle Remus
extravagantly, and much as he means for us to admire Jim—much
as he admires Jim himself—the portrait, though drawn in deepest
sympathy, is yet seen from the outside. The closest that Mark
Twain gets to Jim's soul, and the furthest from the stereotyped
minstrel mask, is the ethical coherence with which the author's
manipulation of folk superstitions allows him to endow the slave.
In both his emergence toward manhood through the exercise of his
freedom and in his supernatural power as interpreter of the oracles
of nature, Jim comes to be the hero of his own magic. The test and
proof of natural goodness, which raises Jim and Huck above religious
hypocrisy and selfish romanticism, is its transforming power upon
him. The fear-ridden slave becomes in the end a source of moral

4. This is a point I have discussed in
some detail in a review of *Joel Chandler
Harris—Folklorist* by Stella Brewer
Brookes, in *Midwest Folklore*, I (Summer 1951), 133–8. See also John Staf-
ford, 'Patterns of Meaning in *Nights
with Uncle Remus*,' *American Literature*, XVIII (May 1946), 89–108.

energy. The shifting of Jim's shape is reversed at the end, as he sinks back from his heroism to become the bewildered freed darky of reconstruction days, grateful to the young white boss for that guilt-payment of forty dollars. (It did bring true his only good luck omen: a hairy breast and arms meant that he's "gwineter be rich . . . signs is signs!") For Jim has status now, a status imposed by society, not, as was his moral eminence, determined by his inner nature. And it is status of which Huck is now afraid; for at the end he is preparing to flee again, this time to "light out for the territory ahead of the rest. . . . Aunt Sally she's going to adopt and sivilize me, and I can't stand it. I been there before." For Huck, *"there"* means the stasis of being a part of society. His voyage, like Jim's, was a quest for freedom too; after their idyll and their ordeals, both find only the equivocal freedom of status at the end of their odyssey. The pattern of action in this double quest depended upon their freedom of movement—of both spatial movement and social mobility. Freedom to die in each identity, freedom to be reborn anew in another—this pattern of action is the theme of the next chapter.

WALTER BLAIR

Tom and Huck†

A year after finishing *Tom Sawyer*, while reading chapter proofs for that book, Mark Twain started, as a sequel, *Adventures of Huckleberry Finn*, subtitled "Tom Sawyer's Comrade." Because of juxtapositions in time and subject matter the two books were closely related. One result was that, just as other writings had rehearsed parts of *Tom Sawyer*, that book rehearsed parts of the later novel.

On Jackson's Island, in chapter xiii of the book bearing his name, Tom talks about the superiority of a pirate's life over a hermit's:

" 'You see,' said Tom, 'people don't go much on hermits, now-a-days . . . but a pirate's always respected. And a hermit's got to sleep on the hardest place he can find, and put sack-cloth and ashes on his head, and stand out in the rain, and—'

" 'What does he put sack-cloth and ashes on his head for?' inquired Huck.

" '*I* dono. But they've *got* to do it. Hermits always do. You'd have to do that if you was a hermit.'

" 'Dern'd if I would,' said Huck.

" 'Well what would you do?'

† Chapter 5 (pp. 71–76) of *Mark Twain and Huck Finn* by Walter Blair. University of California Press, 1960. By permission of the publisher.

" 'I dono. But I wouldn't do that.'

" 'Why Huck, you'd *have* to. How'd you get around it?'

" 'Why I just wouldn't stand it. I'd run away.'

" 'Run away! Well you *would* be a nice old slouch of a hermit. You'd be a disgrace.' "

Tom's skimpy knowledge and his pedantic acceptance of books as authorities as contrasted with Huck's ignorance, his respect for Tom's learning, and his common sense are ingredients of this passage. The same incongruities occur in chapters xxv, xxxiii, and xxxv, when Tom and Huck discuss robber gangs, and in chapter xxvi, when they consider Robin Hood.

At the start of *Huck*, the same pair have an almost identical talk about robbers, and in chapter iii Tom discourses on genies—"as tall as a tree and as big around as a church":

" 'Well,' I says, 's'pose we got some genies to help *us*—can't we lick the other crowd then?'

" 'How you going to get them?'

" 'I don't know. How do *they* get them?'

" 'Why, they rub an old tin lamp or an iron ring, and then the genies come tearing in . . . and everything they're told to do they up and do it. . . .'

" 'Who makes them tear around so?'

" 'Why, whoever rubs the lamp or the ring. They belong to whoever rubs the lamp or the ring, and they've got to do whatever he says. . . .'

" 'Well,' says I, 'I think they are a pack of flat-heads. . . . And what's more—if I was one of them I would see a man in Jericho before I would drop my business and come to him for the rubbing of an old tin lamp. . . .'

" 'Shucks, it ain't no use to talk to you. . . . You don't seem to know anything, somehow—perfect sap-head.' "

The humor is essentially the same. At the end of the new novel, Tom again lectures—this time on prisoners' escapes—through a series of chapters.

A prediction made by Huck in chapter xxv of the earlier novel about what would happen if he found a treasure is fulfilled in the sequel; indeed, it may have suggested an inciting force: "Pap would come back to thish-yer town some day and get his claws on it if I didn't hurry up [and get rid of it]." Pap does return and in an attempt to get hold of the treasure seizes his son. To avoid Pap's abuse and being "sivilized" by Widow Douglas, Huck escapes to Jackson's Island.

There, just as he and Tom and Joe Harper do in chapter xiv of

Tom Sawyer, Huck watches the ferryboat hunt for his drowned body:

"Well, I was dozing off again, when I thinks I hears a deep sound of 'boom!' away up the river. I rouses up and rests on my elbow and listens; pretty soon I hears it again. I hopped up, and went and looked out at a hole in the leaves, and I see a bunch of smoke laying on the water a long ways up—about abreast the ferry. And there was the ferry-boat full of people, floating along down. I knowed what was the matter now. 'Boom!' I see the white smoke squirt out of the ferry-boat's side. You see, they was firing cannon over the water, trying to make my carcass come to the top."

In chapter xxviii of *Tom Sawyer*, Huck plans to sleep in the Rogers' hayloft with the consent of the slave, Uncle Jake:

"I tote water for Uncle Jake whenever he wants me to, and any time I ask him he gives me a little something to eat if he can spare it. That's a mighty good nigger, Tom. He likes me, becuz I don't ever act as if I was above him. Sometimes I've set right down and eat *with* him. But you needn't tell that. A body's got to do things when he's awful hungry he wouldn't want to do as a steady thing."

This is a crude pencil sketch of the escaping slave Jim, who joins Huck on the island and later goes down the river with him. And the vein of satire dealing with moral anomalies in a slaveholding society here briefly exposed was to be brilliantly exploited.

During the journey downstream, Huck does some reading and for a time he is to uneducated but commonsensible Jim what Tom is to Huck in *Tom Sawyer*—an argumentative instructor. The two investigate such topics as King Solomon, the French language, and the ways of royalty and nobility.

These and other repetitions relate the two novels. Nevertheless, there would be tremendous differences between these books, close in time though they were.

Comparison of even brief excerpts indicates one great difference— in the styles. The descriptions of daybreak preceding this chapter are an instance. In *Tom*, two squirrels (one in apologetic quotation marks) "skurry along . . . to inspect and to chatter at the boys"; in *Huck*, "a couple of squirrels set on a limb and jabbered at me very friendly." In *Tom*, "All Nature [with a capital N] was awake and stirring, now"; in *Huck*, "I could see the sun out at one or two holes." In *Tom*, "long lances of sunlight pierced down through the dense foliage far and near"; in *Huck*, "it was big trees all about, and gloomy in there," and "there was freckled places on the ground where the light sifted down through the leaves." If the earlier passage misses the contrived "prettiness" and artiness of a Victorian description, it barely does so; but the later passage appears to have no more concern with prettiness or artiness than Huck does. If the earlier passage gets its effect, it does so despite the handicap of its all but trite style. If the latter passage gets its effect, it does so largely because it is in a style which handles the detail naturally and in phrases striking enough to be memorable.

The shift to Huck as narrator would liberate Mark Twain from many limitations which an overweening desire to haul off and be literary in the third person had imposed. Huck's character, of course, would have a great deal to do with this. A boy so sensitive and so shrewd was bound to record scenes and actions with insight; but since he was unabashedly uncouth, he was bound to do this naturally and unpretentiously. Since he was almost completely humorless, he was bound to be incongruously naïve and somber on many laugh-provoking occasions. The author's experience would help him climb into Huck's skin. He too was sensitive and perceptive, and he too had been informed of his lack of manners and culture. And for purposes of both written and oral humor he had often impersonated a similar character, using language homely to him which had given him a freedom that the literary language of the day could not afford.

And the ideas in the new book would be more vital to Twain— and to his readers—than those in the earlier novel. *Tom* is a light book suitable for children and for adults satisfied with a funny story; *Huck* is a funny book suitable for children, too; but grownups who read it find depths in its humor and in its meanings which as childish readers they completely missed.

In *Tom Sawyer*, Mark Twain pictures with amusement and sympathy youngsters who were currently labeled Bad Boys, and he concludes by showing such youngsters triumphant. In a sense, therefore, the book was rebellious. But its attack was a playful one. The boys can resist civilization blamelessly and comically— blamelessly because they are not responsible, comically because their innocent insurrections contrast incongruously with the tensions of responsible grownups. Tom and his companions—even Huck—do not question the standards, nor does Mark. In 1875, when he finished this novel, he could make his happy ending a boy's attainment of respectability.

But in the new book, while Tom's character would be greatly simplified, Huck's would be made far more complex, and this outcast would be the narrator and the protagonist. Pap Finn, not on the scene in *Tom Sawyer*, would figure prominently because Huck was to live with him and escape from him. Jim would be pictured at full length because Huck would spend days and nights with him out on Jackson's Island, on the raft drifting downstream or ashore away from everybody else. On his journey, this waif would meet and come to know many other characters who could not have invaded Tom's childhood world except as melodramatic figures. Most of them would be adults. The civilization which they represent would differ greatly from that of godly St. Petersburg. Twain's attitude toward this civilization, moreover, would be very different. Many of its standards he would not accept but would question and reject. Huck would struggle with his own problems not in a childish but in an adult fashion. And whereas the ending of *Tom* shows the boy initiated into society, the new book would show the much more mature Huck fleeing from society.

These changes would come about because of the life the author led, the books he read, his ponderings, and the conclusions he reached about humanity during the seven-year period of the book's composition.

JUDITH FETTERLEY

Disenchantment: Tom Sawyer in *Huckleberry Finn*†

That Mark Twain's attitude toward Tom Sawyer had changed by the end of *The Adventures of Tom Sawyer*, that he had become disenchanted with his boy hero, is evidenced in a letter he wrote to Howells upon completing the novel:

> I have finished the story & didn't take the chap beyond boyhood. I believe it would be fatal to do it in any shape but autobiographically—like Gil Blas. . . . If I went on, now, & took him into manhood, he would just be like all the one-horse men in literature & the reader would conceive a hearty contempt for him. . . . By & by I shall take a boy of twelve & run him on through life (in the first person) but not Tom Sawyer—he would not be a good character for it.[1]

That he, however, curtailed his impulse to express this disillusionment in *Tom Sawyer* is indicated by another letter he wrote to Howells a few months later:

> As to that last chapter. I think of just leaving it off & adding nothing in its place. Something told me that the book was done when I got to that point—& so the strong temptation to put

† Reprinted by permission of the Modern Language Association of America from *PMLA*, 87, 1 (January 1972), 69–74. Footnotes are the author's; the last two have been renumbered.

1. *Mark Twain-Howells Letters*, ed. William M. Gibson and Henry Nash Smith (Cambridge, Mass.: Harvard Univ. Press, 1960), I, 91–92.

Huck's life at the widow's into detail instead of generalizing it in a paragraph, was resisted.[2]

Thus, while the ending of *The Adventures of Tom Sawyer* is somewhat uneasy, it is still Tom Sawyer's and Huck accepts Tom's pressure and values, swearing to "stick to the widder till I rot" in order to be accepted into Tom Sawyer's gang.[3] Tom is still cast in the role of having pleasures to offer which justify the compromises Huck has to make and Mark Twain's disenchantment with Tom waits for its real expression until *Adventures of Huckleberry Finn*, which he began writing in the summer of 1876, a year after concluding *Tom Sawyer*, and whose first three chapters are, according to Walter Blair, the result of "rewriting and probably elaborating discarded material from *Tom Sawyer*."[4] In these chapters the character of Tom Sawyer is quite different from what it was in the earlier book.

The first major difference is defined in Tom's initial action, which reveals him as an almost compulsive practical joker. It is impossible for him to pass up the opportunity of playing a trick on Jim even though it might mean getting caught and having to give up the evening's fun. Such a subordination of larger areas of pleasure to the need to play a joke is new to Tom. New also is the fact that cruelty is the sole motivation behind Tom's joke. Thus he initially wants to tie Jim to the tree "for fun," and when Huck dissuades him from this he concludes by devising a joke which will play on Jim's ignorance and expose him as a fool. Indicative of this change in the implications of Tom's actions is the fact that it never occurs to Huck, who is a willing partner to all Tom's schemes in *Tom Sawyer*, to take part in this prank.

Tom's joke on Aunt Polly the day after his glorious appearance at his own funeral is similar in certain ways to his joke on Jim, but a close comparison of the two situations reveals crucial differences. While cruelty is an element in the joke on Aunt Polly, it does not provide the motivation for it. The emphasis is not on Tom's imagination of Aunt Polly's reaction but on his satisfaction with his own intelligence, his own cleverness in making entertainment capital of his stealthy trip home. Thus, when Aunt Polly confronts him with the results of his cleverness, he can honestly respond, "I didn't think," and when he *does* think he can honestly feel remorse.[5] Such a response is impossible for the Tom Sawyer of *Huckleberry*

2. *Twain-Howells Letters*, I, 112–13.
3. Samuel L. Clemens. *The Writings of Mark Twain*, definitive ed. (New York: Gabriel Wells, 1922–25), VIII, 291.
4. *Mark Twain & "Huck Finn"* (Berkeley: Univ. of California Press, 1960), p. 100.
5. Similarly, when Aunt Polly rebukes Tom for having given Peter, the cat, a spoonful of Painkiller, Twain shifts the focus away from Tom's cruelty onto Aunt Polly's cruelty in having inflicted the medicine on Tom in the first place. Thus the final result of this joke, as of the one on Aunt Polly, is to place Tom in a good light.

Finn whose interest in a joke lies precisely in his imagination of its consequences. There is nothing clever in tying Jim to a tree. The motivation behind such a plan lies in the pleasure Tom expects from imagining Jim's feelings and predicament when he wakes up. Tom's pleasure in *Huckleberry Finn* is deeply entwined with cruelty.

After Tom has played his joke on Jim, he and Huck take off to meet the rest of the boys who are to form "Tom Sawyer's Gang." When they reach the cave Tom begins: "Now, we'll start this band of robbers and call it Tom Sawyer's Gang. Everybody that wants to join has got to take an oath, and write his name in blood." The oath which follows has only one element in it: the appropriate mode of murder for each itemized crime against the gang. It is simply a blueprint for killing and it suggests that Tom's major interest in the gang is the aggressions he can imagine it committing. Certainly aggression is an element of Tom's character in *Tom Sawyer* and colors his imagination, resulting in the fantasies of the Black Avenger of the Spanish Main. But again in that book it is but one element among many, a single fiber in a complex fabric. Further, Tom's investment in aggression is by no means so extreme in the earlier book. A simple comparison of the oath in *Huckleberry Finn* with the oaths in *Tom Sawyer*—the one by which Tom and Huck swear each other to secrecy over the murder of Dr. Robinson, and the one which Tom presents to Huck at the end of the book as his gang's—makes this point. In *Huckleberry Finn*, however, aggression *is* Tom's character. When pushed to give a meaning for the word "ransom," the only thing he can think of is that it must mean "to kill"; when asked at the end of the book why he took so much trouble to set a free slave free, he replies indignantly, "I wanted the *adventure* of it; and I'd 'a' waded neck-deep in blood to [get it]." It is this kind of change in Tom that Walter Blair responds to when he remarks that in *Huckleberry Finn* Tom "has become a simpler character."[6]

The process of forming Tom Sawyer's gang reveals a further transformation of Tom's character. In *Tom Sawyer*, Tom is acquainted with books and insistent on playing according to the patterns he finds there, but once again this is a relatively minor part of his character, secondary to his larger role of exposing the rigidities and hypocrisies of the various sets of rules held by the adults of St. Petersburg. Indeed, in accordance with Tom's role as a principle of reality in his world, the rules he insists on following frequently turn out to be justified. This is most notably the case in the episodes surrounding his search for buried treasure. Tom's superstitions about the kind of day Friday is turn out to be true. Friday is indeed a bad day; if he and Huck had gone into the haunted house that day as planned they would have walked in on Injun Joe who would have happily dispatched them. Further, all Tom's presuppositions, derived from the romances he has read, on the matter of where treasure is buried turn out to be correct. Haunted houses do contain treasure which robbers have been unable to come back for or have forgotten. Thus the treasure Tom finds is a testament to the reality he represents and his interest in rules is subsumed in that role.

Not so in *Huckleberry Finn*, where Tom's obsession with rules becomes the index to his unreality and makes him the butt rather than the agent of exposure. Further, Tom's obsession changes him from a character whose genius lies in his capacity to create brilliant situations in response to the immediate circumstances—the white-washing triumph, the flight to Jackson's Island, the staging of his own funeral—to a character who is both rigid (he constantly iterates, "you'd *have* to") and derivative: "Everybody said it was a real beautiful oath, and asked Tom if he got it out of his own head. He said some of it, but the rest was out of pirate-books and robber-books."

There are, however, more ominous implications to Tom's obsession with books in *Huckleberry Finn*. These implications are developed in Chapter iii, "We Ambuscade the A-rabs." In *Tom Sawyer*, the boys' world of play is self-contained. When Tom goes off on a Saturday afternoon to play general and wage a war, the other general is Joe Harper and the opposing army is another group of boys. In *Huckleberry Finn*, however, Tom's play world is not self-contained; his make-believe no longer sustains itself as make-believe but constantly attempts to become real by impinging on worlds outside itself which have nothing to do with it. It is one thing for a group of boys to pretend that they are a caravan of "Spanish merchants and rich A-rabs" bearing "ingots," and "di'monds" and "julery" and to have another group of boys rob them. That is play, a self-contained structure which imitates reality and to whose rules and conventions all parties agree. Such is the texture of Tom's activities in *Tom Sawyer*. In *Huckleberry Finn*, however, we have the spectacle of Tom trying to convince his gang that turnips are jewelry and hogs are bars of gold and that a Sunday school picnic is a caravan of wealthy traders. As Robert Regan has noted, this is akin to madness: "Here Tom appears only a little less than insane; the boy who has so wildly misread Cervantes verges upon becoming identified with Cervantes' hero."[7] The character who was the reality principle

---

7. *Unpromising Heroes: Mark Twain and His Characters* (Berkeley: Univ. of California Press, 1966), p. 133.

in *Tom Sawyer* has become a creature of delusion. What is more significant, however, is the nature of Tom's delusion. It does not matter so much whether Tom actually believes the claims he makes to his gang. Most likely he does not. What does matter is that he has lost that which made him the true hero of his own book: the perception of the nature of play as a symbiotic relationship between willing and aware parties.

With this loss of perception comes a concomitant loss of control. "We played robber now and then about a month, and then I resigned. All the boys did. We hadn't robbed nobody, hadn't killed any people, but only just pretended." It is impossible to imagine Tom's losing his gang in *Tom Sawyer* because he "only just pretended." The boys in *Tom Sawyer* delight in and thrive on Tom's pretending. It is for this that they turn to Tom as leader—he always has the most exciting game for them to play and the most exciting roles for them to be. Thus Joe Harper's plan to run off and be a hermit naturally gives way to Tom's more gaudy and satisfactory scheme of beings pirates and hiding out on Jackson's Island. But in *Huckleberry Finn*, Tom cannot deliver because he has changed the groundwork of his promises.

Tom's image as a leader has changed in accordance with his change of tactics. In *Huckleberry Finn*, he appears as a kind of petty tyrant, a hard taskmaster who makes the boys labor at stupid and uninteresting jobs. "He never could go after even a turnip-cart but he must have the swords and guns all scoured up for it, though they was only lath and broomsticks, and you might scour at them till you rotted, and then they warn't worth a mouthful of ashes more than what they was before." Quite different is the scene in *Tom Sawyer* which describes the battle between Tom's army and Joe's: "These two great commanders did not condescend to fight in person—that being better suited to the still smaller fry—but sat together on an eminence and conducted the field operations by orders delivered through aides-de-camp." Other boys still do all the work in *Tom Sawyer*, but they do it because they enjoy it, because Tom has made it fun, and so, of course, it isn't really work. One of Tom's defining characteristics in *Tom Sawyer*, succinctly dramatized in the whitewashing episode, is his capacity to convert all work into play. In *Huckleberry Finn* the process is reversed: what should be play becomes work.

In *Tom Sawyer*, Tom easily controls the boys because he has something to offer. Huck and Joe are in mid-flight from Jackson's Island on their way back home when Tom springs his plan of appearing at their own funeral and "then they set up a war whoop of applause and said it was 'splendid!' and said if he had told them at first, they wouldn't have started away." Since, in *Huckleberry*

Finn, Tom no longer has anything of value to offer, he has to devise all sorts of devious tactics to keep control. "Little Tommy Barnes was asleep now, and when they waked him up he was scared, and cried, and said he wanted to go home to his ma, and didn't want to be a robber any more." Tom first tries to manipulate him by ridicule, calling him a crybaby and laughing at him. When that doesn't work he gives him a nickel to keep him quiet. This anticipates the conclusion of the book where Huck records that Tom gave Jim forty dollars "for being prisoner for us so patient." Money has replaced pleasure as the currency of Tom's control, and his relationship with the world is no longer the symbiotic one of entertainer and entertained but is rather the tyrannical, aristocratic one of the haves and the have-nots.

2

The ending of *Huckleberry Finn* is a more elaborate statement of the changes in Tom's character which the first three chapters have revealed. Certainly the ending is a tour de force of the cruelty which derives pleasure from other people's suffering. Tom forces Jim to work as hard as any slave in order to carry out his elaborate plans, which include turning spoons into pens and then carving a series of mottoes with these pens into a grindstone which Jim has had to roll to the cabin. Tom insists on filling Jim's room with snakes and spiders and rats, which Jim must not only endure but play music to and tame, in spite of Jim's protestation that he doesn't need or like these creatures, in spite of his cry, "but what kine er time is *Jim* having." But worse than the physical pain which Tom inflicts on Jim is the psychological pain of what can only seem to Jim a toying with his freedom. For while Tom's plan is elegant and has gobs of style, it effectively destroys Jim's chances for freedom. Thus Tom's indignation when told that Jim has not gotten away but is chained in the cabin is one of the bleakest moments of the book.

The entire final sequence of the novel, however, is studded with instances of the pleasure Tom takes in other people's discomfort, beginning with his arrival at the Phelps's farm in the guise of William Thompson of Hicksville, Ohio. This disguise is adopted simply for the opportunity it provides to place Aunt Sally in the uncomfortable position of being insulted by a guest whom she has warmly welcomed. Typical, too, is the conclusion of the joke whereby she has to beg Tom, who has revealed himself as Sid, to kiss her again. Tom continues this kind activity throughout the course of the "evasion," constantly reducing Aunt Sally to a state of near hysteria over the loss of sheets and candlesticks and shirts, and over spoons which mysteriously appear and disappear until, to preserve her sanity, she has to give up worrying about them. But the height of this pattern is reached through Tom's "nonnamus" letters which terrorize not simply Aunt Sally and Uncle Silas but the entire neighborhood. But this is just "nuts" for Tom Sawyer. It is the source of his pleasure, the index of his control over the world, and the assured sign that his exploit will be talked about and his achievement recognized.

The thirst for glory is certainly a major motivation behind Tom's plan, and in Tom's eyes glory, like pleasure, is a product of difficulties overcome. Thus Huck's proposal is rejected because, "What's the good of a plan that ain't no more trouble than that?" Such a plan wouldn't create any talk and talk is what Tom is after. The desire for glory, the desire to be recognized as inordinately clever, is nothing new to Tom. It is certainly basic to his activities in *The Adventures of Tom Sawyer*. But in *Tom Sawyer* there is some reason for according Tom the recognition he seeks. His activities are strokes of genius and the egotism that motivates them is justified because it results in pleasure for everyone. While Tom's appearance at his own funeral gains considerable attention for him, his flight to Jackson's Island and apparent death provide the opportunity for both the adults and the other children to get attention. The Saturday before the funeral, the children of St. Petersburg all vie for the honor of having been the last one to see the boys or talk to them or touch them and "when it was ultimately decided who *did* see the departed last, and exchanged the last words with them, the lucky parties took upon themselves a sort of sacred importance, and were gaped at and envied by all the rest." But the adults get their chance, too. Aunt Polly, Sid, and Mary, as they enter the church, are the subject of everyone's solicitude and gaze. While they do not revel in this attention, it is implied that they do enjoy it. The minister is far more open in his pleasure at the opportunity to demonstrate his powers of oratory which Tom has provided. In *Huckleberry Finn*, however, this symbiotic context is lacking and Tom's passion for recognition appears as unredeemed egotism.

There is, however, one motivation to Tom's actions at the end of *Huckleberry Finn* which is new to him in this book: his obsession with doing things the right way. The words "right" and "wrong" and "principle" and "duty" and "honor" stud both Tom's speech and Huck's remarks on him in this final section, and Tom is constantly revealed as acting out of adherence to a strict code of right and wrong. Thus he constantly insists that the evasion takes the shape it does because that is right. He acts constantly upon the compulsions of his code rather than upon the promptings of his genius.

But it is clear that Tom's compulsions affect him in deeper ways.

His absolute conviction about his rights and wrongs prevents him from having any perspective on himself. One of the factors which makes Tom a sympathetic character in *Tom Sawyer* is his conscience. Rather than being always convinced he is right, he often suffers the pangs of conscience and experiences both guilt and remorse. Equally, he has a very definite sense of self. He knows the limits of his actions; he understands the trajectory he is to define. After pushing against the limits of what his community will stand by appearing at his own funeral and threatening to make the congregation look ridiculous in front of each other, his next act is the ultimately approvable one of saving Becky from the public humiliation of a whipping. In *Tom Sawyer*, Tom senses always what is expected of him, and he acts accordingly. In *Huckleberry Finn*, both the conscience and the self-perspective are lacking. What appears instead is the self-righteousness of a character who knows exactly what is right and what is wrong, and who knows that he is right, and who is thus uncontrollable. As Huck ruefully remarks, "he never paid no attention to me; went right on. It was his way when he'd got his plans set."

There is a far more significant dimension to Tom's moralism, however, than any of those yet discussed. If Tom's pleasure is connected with cruelty, his cruelty, in turn, is connected with his moralism. Thus, every aggression of Tom's against Jim is done under the aegis of right. The hypocrisy of such a pattern is blatant, and hypocrisy is a final characteristic which Tom has picked up in his transition from *The Adventures of Tom Sawyer* to *Adventures of Huckleberry Finn*. Again, in *Tom Sawyer*, Tom's role is to expose the hypocrisy of his community and to offer them something real in its stead. On Examination Day, a *locus classicus* of the hypocrisies of St. Petersburg, when the first prize is awarded to the speech whose content bears least relation to its form, Tom's action is to participate in lowering a cat over the schoolmaster's head until it succeeds in clawing off his wig, to expose the bald reality underneath. In *Huckleberry Finn* the action of the novel works to expose the hypocrisy of Tom Sawyer who, under the aegis of right, enacts cruelty after cruelty; who claims to be freeing Jim and in effect enslaves him; who presents himself as bold, daring, and adventurous and is, in fact, doing the safest thing that can be imagined—"setting a free slave free."[8]

3

The indictment of the character of Tom Sawyer is carried on equally in the numerous analogues to him that are found through-

8. James M. Cox, *Mark Twain: The Fate of Humor* (Princeton, N.J.: Princeton Univ. Press, 1966), p. 175.

out the novel. The similarity between Tom and Miss Watson is suggested in Chapter 3, which begins with Huck's testing Miss Watson's code and ends with his testing Tom's. The characters are linked both through their possession of codes and through the fact that their codes, under the pressure of Huck's tests, are exposed as a useless bunch of lies. The most crucial connection, however, is made through Jim, who reveals to Huck that it is the very Miss Watson who told him that he "must help other people, and do everything I could for other people, and look out for them all the time, and never think about myself," who has been unable to resist an $800 price on Jim. We remember that Tom, too, thinks of Jim in terms of money and covers up the reality of his actions toward Jim with the language of right and wrong. The two characters are thus connected through their mutual possession of the syndrome of moralism, aggression, and hypocrisy.

As Richard Adams has noted, Miss Watson's plan to sell Jim also links her to two other characters in the novel, the King and the Duke.[9] The scene in which the Wilks's Negroes are sold, mother away from children, acts out the horror which Jim has fled. But clearly there are many connections between Tom Sawyer and the Duke and King as well. Daniel Hoffman, in *Form and Fable in American Fiction*, has noted many of these:

> It is curious how closely the King and Duke's stock-in-trade of shifty disguises parallels Tom's dreams of glory memorized from old romances. Tom was always concerning himself about captive or outcast nobles; they turn up as the dispossessed Duke of Bilgewater and the lamented Dauphin of France. Tom was forever acting parts, and, as Mr. Eliot reminds us, he always needed an audience; they are professional thespians—the great David Garrick of Drury Lane and Edmund Kean. Tom's favorite sop to self-pity in *Tom Sawyer* was to imagine himself a pirate; but the only pirate we see is the King at the camp meeting, acting again. We remember, too, that Tom had tried to ambuscade the A-rabs; now, when the Duke wants to keep Jim from being recognized by slave-hunters, "He dressed Jim up in King Lear's outfit . . . and painted Jim's face and hands and ears and neck all over a dead, dull, solid blue, like a man that's been drowned nine days. Blamed if he warn't the horriblest-looking outrage I ever see. Then the Duke took and wrote out a sign on a shingle so: *Sick Arab—but harmless when not out of his head.*"[1]

These parallels clearly suggest the pains which Mark Twain was at to associate Tom Sawyer with these characters and thus to deni-

9. "The Unity and Coherence of *Huckleberry Finn*," *Tulane Studies in English*, 6 (1956), 99.

1. New York, 1961; paperback rpt., New York: Oxford Univ. Press, 1965, pp. 328–29.

grate him. The most important connection between Tom and the King and Duke, however, is, as Hoffman goes on to suggest, their attitude toward Jim. The King and Duke, like Tom, see Jim as an object, a possession which can be bought and sold for money. Thus when Huck, whose posture as Jim's owner is, ironically, a disguise he adopts to keep Jim free, asks the Duke what he has done with his "nigger," "the only nigger I had in the world and the only property," the Duke replies, "Fact is, I reckon we'd come to consider him *our* nigger; yes, we did consider him so—goodness knows we had trouble enough for him." Compare this to the language of Tom's exuberance at the height of the evasion:

> Tom was in high spirits. He said it was the best fun he ever had in his life, and the most intellectual; and said if he only could see his way to it we would keep it up all the rest of our lives and leave Jim to our children to get out; for he believed Jim would come to like it better and better the more he got used to it.

There is, however, a basic difference between the Duke and King and Tom. The Duke and King at least are honest with themselves. They know very well what they are and what they are doing; they have no delusions. The roles they adopt are strategies to gull others, not postures which they themselves believe in. Further, they do not have the language of morality. They never claim that what they are doing is right. The only legitimization they even faintly suggest— and it is in some ways a fair one—is that it is people's stupidity and hypocrisy, their insatiable demand for sensation, which supports them. Thus, in a certain respect, they come off better than Tom, who believes in his postures as right, and we can share Huck's pity for them as they are ridden out of town on a rail.

These same reservations do not apply, however, when we compare Tom to another set of characters in the book, the Grangerfords. Again, Hoffman has made an important comparison:

> When we, with Huck, fall in among the Grangerfords, we cannot help but think how they and Tom would have liked one another. (They do have a son named Tom!) These Grangerfords bow to each other at breakfast and drink to the health of their parents; they apologize to little Huck for the indignity of searching his pockets, and they have more culture than Huck believed could exist under one roof. The Grangerfords make a morality of manners, but their chivalric rituals, we come to learn, are a thin veneer over their essential barbarism. Their sense of honor is worthy but limited; they do not understand what it is to which they give their loyalty.[2]

2. Hoffman, pp. 327–28.

There is, however, a major similarity which Hoffman has not articulated. The focus of Twain's attention to the Grangerford-Shepherdson feud is not so much on the viciousness of the action as it is on the hypocrisy of calling that viciousness "honor." Contrary to Hoffman, the Grangerfords' sense of honor is not worthy; it is the very thing which makes them worse than the Duke and the King. The code of the Grangerfords and the Shepherdsons is that of Southern chivalry and honor and what Mark Twain is exposing through them is the hypocrisy of the Southern way of life in which murder is legitimized as justice and in which black men are castrated and lynched in the name of the honor of white women by the very men who are themselves destroying that honor.

In *Adventures of Huckleberry Finn* Southern chivalry is exposed as sneaking up behind a couple of kids and shooting them in the back. But the exposure of that cruelty is not so important as the exposure of the connection between that cruelty and the language of honor. What Mark Twain is recording in *Huckleberry Finn*, through the Grangerfords, through Miss Watson, and through Tom Sawyer, is his sense of the inevitable connection between moralism, the language of right and wrong with its inevitable concomitant of self-righteousness, and the fact, the act, of aggression. Thus one of the central, defining scenes of the book is the death of Boggs. "He made about a dozen long gasps, his breast lifting the Bible up when he drawed in his breath, and letting it down again when he breathed it out—and after that he laid still; he was dead." The Bible, proclaimed as the giver of life, is in reality used to crush life out.

Selected Bibliography

Articles reprinted in this edition are not included in the bibliography.

MARK TWAIN: GENERAL

Andrews, Kenneth R. *Nook Farm: Mark Twain's Hartford Circle.* Cambridge, Mass.: Harvard University Press, 1950.

Asselineau, Roger. *The Literary Reputation of Mark Twain from 1910 to 1950.* Paris: M. Didier, 1954.

Baetzhold, Howard G. *Mark Twain and John Bull.* Bloomington: Indiana University Press, 1970.

Baldanza, Frank. *Mark Twain: An Introduction and Interpretation.* New York: Barnes and Noble, 1961.

Bellamy, Gladys C. *Mark Twain as a Literary Artist.* Norman: University of Oklahoma Press, 1950.

Blues, Thomas. *Mark Twain and the Community.* Lexington: University of Kentucky Press, 1970.

Branch, Edgar M. *The Literary Apprenticeship of Mark Twain.* Urbana: University of Illinois Press, 1950.

Brooks, Van Wyck. *The Ordeal of Mark Twain.* Revised Edition. New York: E. P. Dutton, 1933.

Budd, Louis J. *Mark Twain: Social Philosopher.* Bloomington: Indiana University Press, 1962.

Canby, Henry Seidel. *Turn West, Turn East.* Boston: Houghton Mifflin, 1951.

Covici, Pascal, Jr. *Mark Twain's Humor.* Dallas: Southern Methodist University Press, 1962.

Cox, James M. *Mark Twain: The Fate of Humor.* Princeton: Princeton University Press, 1966.

DeVoto, Bernard. *Mark Twain at Work.* Cambridge, Mass.: Harvard University Press, 1942.

Ferguson, DeLancey. *Mark Twain: Man and Legend.* Indianapolis: Bobbs, Merrill, 1943.

Gerber, John C. "Mark Twain's Use of the Comic Pose." *PMLA* LXXVII (June 1962), 297–304.

———. "The Relation between Point of View and Style in the Works of Mark Twain." In Harold C. Martin, ed., *Style in Prose Fiction.* New York: Columbia University Press, 1959.

Hill, Hamlin. *Mark Twain: God's Fool.* New York: Harper and Row, 1973.

Kaplan, Justin. *Mr. Clemens and Mark Twain.* New York: Simon and Schuster, 1966.

Long, E. Hudson. *Mark Twain Handbook.* New York: Hendricks House, 1958.

Lynn, Kenneth S. *Mark Twain and Southwestern Humor.* Boston: Little, Brown, 1960.

Paine, Albert Bigelow. *Mark Twain, A Biography.* New York: Harper, 1912.

Regan, Robert. *Unpromising Heroes: Mark Twain and His Characters.* Berkeley: University of California Press, 1966.

Rogers, Franklin. *Mark Twain's Burlesque Patterns as Seen in the Novels and Narratives, 1855–1875.* Dallas: Southern Methodist University Press, 1960.

Salomon, Roger B. *Twain and the Image of History.* New Haven: Yale University Press, 1961.

Smith, Henry Nash. *Mark Twain: The Development of a Writer.* Cambridge, Mass.: Belknap Press, 1962.

Spengeman, William C. *Mark Twain and the Backwoods Angel.* Kent, Ohio: Kent State University Press, 1966.

Stone, Albert E., Jr. *The Innocent Eye.* New Haven: Yale University Press, 1961.

Tanner, Tony. "The Lost America—The Despair of Henry Adams and Mark Twain." *Modern Age,* V (Summer 1961), 299–310.

Wecter, Dixon. *Sam Clemens of Hannibal.* Boston: Houghton Mifflin, 1952.

MARK TWAIN: *HUCKLEBERRY FINN*

Adams, Richard P. "The Unity and Coherence of *Huckleberry Finn.*" *Tulane Studies in English,* VI (1956), 87–103.

Alter, Robert. *Rogue's Progress: Studies in the Picaresque Novel.* Cambridge, Mass.: Harvard University Press, 1964. Pp. 117–21.

Auden, W. H. "Huck and Oliver." *Listener,* L (October 1953), 540–1.

Banta, Martha. "Rebirth or Revenge: The Endings of *Huckleberry Finn* and

The American." *Modern Fiction Studies*, XV (1969), 191–207.

Barchilon, José, and Joel S. Kovel. "*Huckleberry Finn*: A Psychoanalytic Study." *Journal of the American Psychoanalytic Assoc.*, XIV (1966), 775–814.

Barnes, Daniel R. "Twain's *The Adventures of Huckleberry Finn*, Chapter I." *Explicator*, XXIII (April 1965), item 62.

Berkove, Lawrence I. "Language and Literature: The 'Poor Players' of *Huckleberry Finn*." *Papers of the Michigan Academy of Science, Arts, and Letters*, LIII (1968), 291–310.

Bernadete, Jane J. "*Huckleberry Finn* and the Nature of Fiction." *Massachusetts Review*, IX (Spring 1968), 209–26.

Blair, Walter. *Mark Twain and Huck Finn*. Berkeley: University of California Press, 1960.

———. "When Was *Huckleberry Finn* Written?" *American Literature*, XXX (March 1958), 1–25.

Branch, Edgar M. "The Two Providences: Thematic Form in *Huckleberry Finn*." *College English*, XI (January 1950), 188–95.

Burns, Graham. "Time and Pastoral; *The Adventures of Huckleberry Finn*." *Critical Review*, XV (1972), 52–63.

Cox, James M. "Remarks on the Sad Initiation of Huckleberry Finn." *Sewanee Review*, LXII (Summer 1954), 389–405.

Ensor, Allison. "The Contributions of Charles Webster and Albert Bigelow Paine to *Huckleberry Finn*." *American Literature*, XL (May 1968), 222–7.

Fiedler, Leslie. *Love and Death in the American Novel*. New York: Criterion, 1960. Pp. 553–91.

Frantz, Ray W., Jr. "The Role of Folklore in *Huckleberry Finn*." *American Literature*, XXVIII (November 1956), 314–27.

Fraser, John. "In Defense of Culture: *Huckleberry Finn*." *Oxford Review*, VI (1967), 5–22.

Gullason, Thomas A. "The 'Fatal' Ending of *Huckleberry Finn*." *American Literature*, XXIX (March 1957), 86–91.

Hansen, Chadwick. "The Character of Jim and the Ending of *Huckleberry Finn*." *Massachusetts Review*, V (Autumn 1963), 45–66.

Krause, Sydney J. "Huck's First Moral Crisis." *Mississippi Quarterly*, XVIII (Spring 1965), 69–73.

Lane, Lauriat, Jr. "Why *Huckleberry Finn* Is a Great World Novel." *College English*, XVII (October 1955), 1–5.

Leary, Lewis. "Tom and Huck: Innocence on Trial." *Virginia Quarterly Review*, XXX (Summer 1954), 417–30.

Levy, Leo B. "Society and Conscience in *Huckleberry Finn*." *Nineteenth-Century Fiction*, XVIII (March 1964), 383–91.

Lynn, Kenneth S. "Huck and Jim." *Yale Review*, XLVII (Spring 1958), 421–31.

Manierre, William R. "On Keeping the Raftsmen's Passage in *Huckleberry Finn*." *English Language Notes*, VI (1968), 118–22.

Marx, Leo. "The Pilot and the Passenger: Landscape Conventions and the Style of *Huckleberry Finn*." *American Literature*, XXVIII (May 1956), 129–46.

Moses, W. R. "The Pattern of Evil in *Adventures of Huckleberry Finn*." *Georgia Review*, XIII (Summer 1959), 161–66.

O'Connor, William Van. "Why *Huckleberry Finn* Is Not the Great American Novel." *College English*, XVII (October 1955), 6–10.

Rubenstein, Gilbert M. "The Moral Structure of *Huckleberry Finn*." *College English*, XVIII (November 1956), 72–76.

Rubin, Louis D., Jr. "Mark Twain and the Language of Experience." *Sewanee Review*, LXXI (Autumn 1963), 664–73.

Schmitz, Neil. "The Paradox of Liberation in *Huckleberry Finn*." *Texas Studies in Literature and Language*, XIII (1971), 125–36.

———. "Twain, *Huckleberry Finn*, and the Reconstruction." *American Studies*, XII (Spring 1971). 59–67.

Trachtenberg, Alan. "The Form of Freedom in *Adventures of Huckleberry Finn*." *Southern Review* (Autumn 1970), 954–71.

Vales, Robert L. "Thief and Theft in *Huckleberry Finn*." *American Literature*, XXXVII (January 1966), 420–29.

Vogelback, Arthur L. "The Publication and Reception of *Huckleberry Finn* in America." *American Literature*, XI (November 1939), 260–72.

Yates, Norris W. "The 'Counter-Conversion' of Huckleberry Finn." *American Literature*, XXXII (March 1960), 1–10.

Young, Philip. "*Adventures of Huckleberry Finn*." In *Ernest Hemingway*. New York: Rinehart, 1952. Pp. 181–212.